Praise for J. R. Ward's Black Dagger Brotherhood series

'Now here's a band of brothers who know how to show a girl a good time'
New York Times bestselling author, Lisa Gardner

'It's not easy to find a new twist on the vampire myth, but Ward
succeeds beautifully. This dark and compelling world is filled with
enticing romance as well as perilous adventure'
Romantic Times

'These vampires are *hot,* and the series only gets hotter . . . so hot it gave
me shivers'
Vampire Genre

'Ward wields a commanding voice perfect for the genre . . . Intriguing,
adrenaline-pumping . . . Fans of L.A. Banks, Laurell K. Hamilton and
Sherrilyn Kenyon will add Ward to their must-read list'
Booklist

'These erotic paranormals are well worth it, and frighteningly addictive . . .
It all works to great, page-turning effect . . . [and has] earned Ward an
Anne Rice-style following, deservedly so'
Publishers Weekly

'[A] midnight whirlwind of dangerous characters and mesmerizing
erotic romance. The Black Dagger Brotherhood owns me now. Dark
fantasy lovers, you just got served'
Lynn Viehl, *USA Today* bestselling author of *Evermore*

J.R. Ward lives in the South with her incredibly supportive husband and her beloved golden retriever. After graduating from law school, she began working in health care in Boston and spent many years as chief of staff for one of the premier academic medical centres in the nation.

Visit J.R. Ward online:

www.jrward.com
www.facebook.com/JRWardBooks
www.twitter.com/jrward1

By J.R. Ward

The Black Dagger Brotherhood series:

Dark Lover
Lover Eternal
Lover Revealed
Lover Awakened
Lover Unbound
Lover Enshrined
Lover Avenged
Lover Mine
Lover Unleashed
Lover Reborn
Lover at Last

The Black Dagger Brotherhood: An Insider's Guide

Fallen Angels series:

Covet
Crave
Envy
Rapture

LOVER
AT LAST

J. R. WARD

piatkus

PIATKUS

First published in the United States in 2013 by New American Library,
A Division of Penguin Group (USA) Inc., New York
First published in Great Britain in 2013 by Piatkus
Reprinted 2013 (four times)

A CIP catalogue record for this book
is available from the British Library.

Hardback ISBN 978-0-7499-5916-6
Trade paperback ISBN 978-0-7499-5580-9

Printed and bound in Great Britain by
Clays Ltd, St Ives plc

Papers used by Piatkus are from well-managed forests
and other responsible sources.

MIX
Paper from
responsible sources
FSC® C104740

Piatkus
An imprint of
Little, Brown Book Group
100 Victoria Embankment
London EC4Y 0DY

An Hachette UK Company
www.hachette.co.uk

www.piatkus.co.uk

DEDICATED TO:
YOU BOTH—
AT THE RISK OF INAPPROPRIATE LEVITY,
IT'S ABOUT TIME—
AND NO ONE DESERVES IT MORE THAN THE TWO OF YOU.

ACKNOWLEDGMENTS

With immense gratitude to the readers of the Black Dagger Brotherhood and a shout-out to the Cellies!

Thank you so very much for all the support and guidance: Steven Axelrod, Kara Welsh, Claire Zion, and Leslie Gelbman. Thank you also to everyone at New American Library—these books are truly a team effort.

Thank you to all our Mods for everything you do out of the goodness of your hearts!

With love to Team Waud—you know who you are. This simply could not happen without you.

None of this would be possible without: my loving husband, who is my adviser and caretaker and visionary; my wonderful mother, who has given me so much love I couldn't possibly ever repay her; my family (both those of blood and those by adoption); and my dearest friends.

Oh, and the better half of WriterDog, of course.

GLOSSARY OF TERMS AND PROPER NOUNS

ahstrux nohtrum (n.) Private guard with license to kill who is granted his or her position by the king.

ahvenge (v.) Act of mortal retribution, carried out typically by a male loved one.

Black Dagger Brotherhood (pr. n.) Highly trained vampire warriors who protect their species against the Lessening Society. As a result of selective breeding within the race, Brothers possess immense physical and mental strength, as well as rapid healing capabilities. They are not siblings for the most part, and are inducted into the Brotherhood upon nomination by the Brothers. Aggressive, self-reliant, and secretive by nature, they exist apart from civilians, having little contact with members of the other classes except when they need to feed. They are the subjects of legend and objects of reverence within the vampire world. They may be killed only by the most serious of wounds, e.g., a gunshot or stab to the heart, etc.

blood slave (n.) Male or female vampire who has been subjugated to serve the blood needs of another. The practice of keeping blood slaves has recently been outlawed.

the Chosen (n.) Female vampires who have been bred to serve the Scribe Virgin. They are considered members of the aristocracy, though they are spiritually rather than temporally focused. They have little or no interaction with males, but can be mated to Brothers at the Scribe Virgin's direction to propagate their class. Some have the ability to prognosticate. In the past, they were used to meet the blood needs of unmated members of the Brotherhood, and that practice has been reinstated by the Brothers.

chrih (n.) Symbol of honorable death in the Old Language.

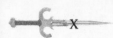

cohntehst (n.) Conflict between two males competing for the right to be a female's mate.

Dhunhd (pr. n.) Hell.

doggen (n.) Member of the servant class within the vampire world. *Doggen* have old, conservative traditions about service to their superiors, following a formal code of dress and behavior. They are able to go out during the day, but they age relatively quickly. Life expectancy is approximately five hundred years.

ehros (pr. n.) A Chosen trained in the matter of sexual arts.

exhile dhoble (pr. n.) The evil or cursed twin, the one born second.

the Fade (pr. n.) Nontemporal realm where the dead reunite with their loved ones and pass eternity.

First Family (pr. n.) The king and queen of the vampires, and any children they may have.

ghardian (n.) Custodian of an individual. There are varying degrees of *ghardians*, with the most powerful being that of a *sehcluded* female.

glymera (n.) The social core of the aristocracy, roughly equivalent to Regency England's *ton*.

hellren (n.) Male vampire who has been mated to a female. Males may take more than one female as mate.

hyslop (n or v): A term referring to a lapse in judgment, typically resulting in the compromise of the mechanical operations or rightful possession of a vehicle or other motorized conveyance of some kind. For example, leaving one's keys in one's car as it is parked outside the family home overnight, said oversight resulting in felonious joyrides by unknown third parties, is a *hyslop*.

leahdyre (n.) A person of power and influence.

leelan (adj.) A term of endearment loosely translated as "dearest one."

Lessening Society (pr. n.) Order of slayers convened by the Omega for the purpose of eradicating the vampire species.

lesser (n.) De-souled human who targets vampires for extermination as a member of the Lessening Society. *Lessers* must be stabbed through the chest in order to be killed; otherwise they are ageless. They do not eat or drink and are impotent. Over time, their hair, skin, and irises lose pigmentation until they are blond, blushless, and pale eyed. They smell like baby powder. Inducted into the society by the Omega, they retain a ceramic jar thereafter into which their heart was placed after it was removed.

lewlhen (n.) Gift.

lheage (n.) A term of respect used by a sexual submissive to refer to her dominant.

Lhenihan (n.) A mythic beast renowned for its sexual prowess. In modern slang, refers to a male of preternatural size and sexual stamina.

lys (n.) Torture tool used to remove the eyes.

mahmen (n.) Mother. Used both as an identifier and a term of affection.

mhis (n.) The masking of a given physical environment; the creation of a field of illusion.

nalla (n., f.) or *nallum* (n., m.) Beloved.

needing period (n.) Female vampire's time of fertility, generally lasting for two days and accompanied by intense sexual cravings. Occurs approximately five years after a female's transition and then once a decade thereafter. All males respond to some degree if they are around a female in her need. It can be a dangerous time, with conflicts and fights breaking out between competing males, particularly if the female is not mated.

newling (n.) A virgin.

the Omega (pr. n.) Malevolent, mystical figure who has targeted the vampires for extinction out of resentment directed toward the Scribe Virgin. Exists in a nontemporal realm and has extensive powers, though not the power of creation.

phearsom (adj.) Term referring to the potency of a male's sexual organs. Literal translation something close to "worthy of entering a female."

princeps (n.) Highest level of the vampire aristocracy, second only to members of the First Family or the Scribe Virgin's Chosen. Must be born to the title; it may not be conferred.

pyrocant (n.) Refers to a critical weakness in an individual. The weakness can be internal, such as an addiction, or external, such as a lover.

rahlman (n.) Savior.

rythe (n.) Ritual manner of assuaging honor granted by one who has offended another. If accepted, the offended chooses a weapon and strikes the offender, who presents him- or herself without defenses.

the Scribe Virgin (pr. n.) Mystical force who is counselor to the king

as well as the keeper of vampire archives and the dispenser of privileges. Exists in a nontemporal realm and has extensive powers. Capable of a single act of creation, which she expended to bring the vampires into existence.

sehclusion (n.) Status conferred by the king upon a female of the aristocracy as a result of a petition by the female's family. Places the female under the sole direction of her *ghardian*, typically the eldest male in her household. Her *ghardian* then has the legal right to determine all aspects of her life, restricting at will any and all interactions she has with the world.

shellan (n.) Female vampire who has been mated to a male. Females generally do not take more than one mate due to the highly territorial nature of bonded males.

symphath (n.) Subspecies within the vampire race characterized by the ability and desire to manipulate emotions in others (for the purposes of an energy exchange), among other traits. Historically, they have been discriminated against and, during certain eras, hunted by vampires. They are near extinction.

the Tomb (pr. n.) Sacred vault of the Black Dagger Brotherhood. Used as a ceremonial site as well as a storage facility for the jars of *lessers*. Ceremonies performed there include inductions, funerals, and disciplinary actions against Brothers. No one may enter except for members of the Brotherhood, the Scribe Virgin, or candidates for induction.

trahyner (n.) Word used between males of mutual respect and affection. Translated loosely as "beloved friend."

transition (n.) Critical moment in a vampire's life when he or she transforms into an adult. Thereafter, he or she must drink the blood of the opposite sex to survive and is unable to withstand sunlight. Occurs generally in the mid-twenties. Some vampires do not survive their transitions, males in particular. Prior to their transitions, vampires are physically weak, sexually unaware and unresponsive, and unable to dematerialize.

vampire (n.) Member of a species separate from that of Homo sapiens. Vampires must drink the blood of the opposite sex to survive. Human blood will keep them alive, though the strength it gives does not last long. Following their transitions, which occur in their mid-twenties, they are unable to go out into sunlight and must feed from the vein regularly. Vampires cannot "convert" humans through a bite or transfer of blood, though they are in rare cases able to breed with the other species. Vampires can dematerialize at will, though they must be able to calm themselves and concentrate to do so and may not carry anything heavy with them. They are able to strip the memories of humans, provided such memories are short-term. Some vampires are able to read minds. Life expectancy is upward of a thousand years, or in some cases even longer.

wahlker (n.) An individual who has died and returned to the living from the Fade. They are accorded great respect and are revered for their travails.

whard (n.) Equivalent of a godfather or godmother to an individual.

LOVER AT LAST

PRELUDE

Quinn, son of Lohstrong, entered his family's home through its grand front door. The instant he stepped over the threshold, the smell of the place curled up into his nose. Lemon polish. Beeswax candles. Fresh flowers from the garden that the *doggen* brought in daily. Perfume—his mother's. Cologne—his father's and his brother's. Cinnamon gum—his sister's.

If the Glade company ever did an air freshener like this, it would be called something like Meadow of Old Money. Or Sunrise over a Fat Bank Account.

Or maybe the ever-popular We're Just Better Than Everyone Else.

Distant voices drifted over from the dining room, the vowels round as brilliant-cut diamonds, the consonants drawled out smooth and long as satin ribbons.

"Oh, Lillie, this is lovely, thank you," his mother said to the server. "But that's too much for me. And do not give Solange so all that. She's getting heavy."

Ah, yes, his mother's perma-diet inflicted on the next generation: *Glymera* females were supposed to disappear from sight when they

turned sideways, each jutting collarbone, sunken cheek, and bony upper arm some kind of fucked-up badge of honor.

As if resembling like a fire poker would make you a better person.

And Scribe Virgin forefend if your daughter looked like she was healthy.

"Ah, yes, thank you, Lilith," his father said evenly. "More for me, please."

Qhuinn closed his eyes and tried to convince his body to step forward. One foot after another. It was not that tough.

His brandy-new Ed Hardy kicks middle-fingered that suggestion. Then again, in so many ways, walking into that dining room was belly-of-the-beast time.

He let his duffel fall to the floor. The couple of days at his best friend Blay's house had done him good, a break from the complete lack of air in this house. Unfortunately, the burn on reentry was so bad, the cost-benefit of leaving was nearly equal.

Okay, this was ridiculous. He couldn't keep standing here like an inanimate object.

Turning to the side wall, he leaned into the full-length antique mirror that was placed right by the door. So thoughtful. So in keeping with the aristocracy's need to look good. This way, visitors could check their hair and clothes as the butler accepted coats and hats.

The young pretrans face that stared back at him was all even features, good jawline, and a mouth that, he had to admit, looked like it could do some serious damage to naked skin when he got older. Or maybe that was just wishful thinking. Hair was Vlad the Impaler, spikes standing up straight from his head. Neck was strung with a bike chain—and not one bought at Urban Outfitters, but the link that had previously motivated his twelve-speed.

All things being equal, he looked like a thief who had broken in and was prepared to trash the place on the hunt for sterling silver, jewelry, and portable electronics.

The irony was that the Goth bullcrap wasn't actually the most offensive part of his appearance to his fam. In fact, he could have stripped down, hung a light fixture off his ass, and run around the first floor playing Jose Canseco with the art and antiques and not come close to how much the real problem pissed off his parents.

It was his eyes.

One blue. One green.

Oopsy. His bad.

The *glymera* didn't like defects. Not in their porcelain or their rose gardens. Not in their wallpaper or their carpets or their countertops. Not in the silk of their underwear or the wool of their blazers or the chiffon of their gowns.

And certainly not *ever* in their children.

Sister was okay—well, except for the "little weight problem" that didn't actually exist, and a lisp that her transition hadn't cured —oh, and the fact that she had the personality of their mother. And there was no fixing that shit. Brother, on the other hand, was the real fucking star, a physically perfect, firstborn son prepared to carry forth the family bloodline by reproducing in a very genteel, non-moaning, no-sweat situation with a female chosen for him by the family.

Hell, his sperm recipient had already been lined up. He was going to mate her as soon as he went through his transition—

"How are you feeling, my son?" his father asked with hesitation.

"Tired, sir," a deep voice answered. "But this is going to help."

A chill frog-marched up Qhuinn's spine. That didn't sound like his brother. Way too much bass. Far too masculine. Too . . .

Holy shit, the guy had gone through his transition.

Now Qhuinn's Ed Hardys got with the program, taking him forward until he could see into the dining room. Father was in his seat at the head of the table. Check. Mother was in her seat at the foot of the table opposite the kitchen's flap door. Check. Sister was facing out of the room, all but licking the gold rim off her plate from hunger. Check.

The male whose back was to Qhuinn was not part of the SOP.

Luchas was twice the size he'd been when Qhuinn had been approached by a *doggen* and told to get his things and go to Blay's.

Well, that explained the vacay. He'd assumed his father had finally relented and given in to the request Qhuinn had filed weeks before. But nope, the guy had just wanted Qhuinn out of the house because the change had come to the gene pool's golden child.

Had his brother laid the chick? Who had they used for blood—

His father, never the demonstrative type, reached out a hand and gave Luchas an awkward pat on the forearm. "We're so proud of you. You look . . . perfect."

"You do," Qhuinn's mother piped up. "Just perfect. Doesn't your brother look perfect, Solange?"

"Yes, he does. Perfect."

"And I have something for you," Lohstrong said.

The male reached into the inside pocket of his sport coat and took out a black velvet box the size of a baseball.

Qhuinn's mother started to tear up and dabbed under her eyes.

"This is for you, my precious son."

The box was slid across the white damask tablecloth, and his brother's now-big hands shook as he took the thing and popped the lid.

Qhuinn caught the flash of gold all the way out in the foyer.

As everyone at the table went silent, his brother stared at the signet ring, clearly overwhelmed, as their mother kept up with the dab-dab, and even their father grew misty. And his sister sneaked a roll from the bread basket.

"Thank you, sir," Luchas said as he put the heavy gold ring on his forefinger.

"It fits, does it not?" Lohstrong asked.

"Yes, sir. Perfectly."

"We wear the same size, then."

Of course they did.

At that moment, their father glanced away, like he was hoping the movement of his eyeballs would take care of the sheen of tears that had come over his vision.

He caught Qhuinn lurking outside the dining room.

There was a brief flash of recognition. Not the hi-how're-ya kind, or the oh-good-my-other-son's-home. More like when you were walking through the grass and noticed a pile of dog shit too late to stop your foot from landing in it.

The male went back to staring at his family, locking Qhuinn out.

Clearly, the last thing Lohstrong wanted was such a historic moment to be ruined—and that was probably why he didn't do the hand signals that warded off the evil eye. Usually everyone in the household performed the ritual when they saw Qhuinn. Not tonight. Daddio didn't want the others to know.

Qhuinn went over to his duffel. Slinging the weight onto his shoulder, he took the front stairs to his room. Usually his mother preferred him to use the servants' set, but that would mean he'd have to cut through all the love in there.

His room was as far away from the others' as you could get, all the way over to the right. He'd often wondered why they didn't take the

leap completely and put him in with the *doggen*—but then the staff would probably quit.

Closing himself in, he dumped his duds on the bare floor and sat on his bed. Staring at his only piece of luggage, he figured he had better do that laundry soon, as there was a wet bathing suit in there.

The maids refused to touch his clothes—like the evil in him lingered in the fibers of his jeans and his T-shirts. The upside was, he was never welcome at formal events, so his wardrobe was just wash-'n'-wear, baby—

He discovered he was crying when he looked down at his Ed Hardys and realized that there were a couple of drops of water right in the middle of the laces.

Qhuinn was never getting a ring.

Ah, hell . . . this hurt.

He was scrubbing his face with his palms when his phone rang. Taking the thing out of his biker jacket, he had to blink a couple of times to focus.

He hit *send* to accept the call, but he didn't answer.

"I just heard," Blay said across the connection. "How are you doing?"

Qhuinn opened his mouth to reply, his brain coughing up all kinds of responses: "Peachy fucking jim-dandy." "At least I'm not 'fat' like my sister." "No, I don't know if my brother got laid."

Instead, he said, "They got me out of the house. They didn't want me to curse the transition. Guess it worked, because the guy looks like he came through it okay."

Blay swore softly.

"Oh, and he got his ring just now. My father gave him . . . his ring."

The signet ring with the family crest on it, the symbol that all males of good bloodlines wore to attest to the value of their lineage.

"I watched Luchas put it on his finger," Qhuinn said, feeling as if he were taking a sharp knife and drawing it up the insides of his arms. "Fit perfectly. Looked great. You know, though . . . like, how could it not—"

He began weeping at that point.

Just fucking lost it.

The awful truth was that under his counterculture fuck-you, he wanted his family to love him. As prissy as his sister was, as scholar-geek as his brother was, as reserved as his parents were, he saw the love among

the four of them. He *felt* the love among them. It was the tie that bound those individuals together, the invisible string from one heart to the another, the commitment of caring about everything from the mundane shit to any true, mortal drama. And the only thing more powerful than that connection . . . was what it was like to get shut out from it.

Every fucking day of your life.

Blay's voice cut in through the heaving. "I'm here for you. And I'm so damned sorry. . . . I'm here for you. . . . Just don't do anything stupid, okay? Let me come over—"

Leave it to Blay to know that he was thinking about things that involved ropes and showerheads.

In fact, his free hand had already gone down to the makeshift belt he'd fashioned out of a nice, strong weave of nylon—because his parents didn't give him much money for clothes, and the proper one he'd owned had broken years ago.

Pulling the length free, he glanced across to the closed door of his bath. All he needed to do was tie the thing to the fixture in his shower— God knew those water pipes had been run in the good old days, when things were strong enough to hold some weight. He even had a chair he could stand up on and then kick out from underneath him.

"I gotta go—"

"Qhuinn? Don't you hang up on me—don't you dare hang up on me—"

"Listen, man, I gotta go—"

"I'm coming over right now." Lot of flapping in the background, like Blay was getting his clothes on. "Qhuinn! Do not hang up the phone—*Qhuinn . . . !*"

ONE

"Now, *that* a muthafuckn' whip rite chur."

Jonsey looked over at the idiot who was hunkered down next to him in the bus stop. The pair of them had been parked in the Plexiglas gerbil cage for three hours. At least. Although comments like that had made it seem a matter of days.

And were going to make shit justifiable homicide.

"You a white boy, you know that?" Jonsey pointed out.

"Say whaaaaat?"

Okay, make that three years of waiting. "Caucasian, dude. As in you need fuckin' sunblock in the summer. As in not like m'self—"

"Whatever, man, check out that ride—"

"As in why you gotta talk like you from the 'hood? You act a fool, yo."

At this point, he just wanted to get the night over. It was cold, it was snowing, and he had to wonder who he'd pissed off to get stuck with Vanilla Ice over here.

Matter of fact, he was thinking about pulling out of this bullshit altogether. He was making good paper dealing in Caldwell; he was two months out of prison for those murders he'd done as a juvie; the last

thing he was interested in was hanging with some white bitch determined to get street cred through vocabulary.

Oh, and then there was the Richie Rich neighborhood they were in. For all he knew, there was an ordinance out here that you weren't allowed on the streets after ten p.m.

Why the *hell* had he agreed to this?

"Will. You. Please. Look. At. That. Fine. Automobile."

Just to shut the guy up, Jonsey turned his head and leaned out of the shelter. As blowing snow got into his eyes, he cursed. Fucking upstate New York in the winter. Cold enough to ice-cube your balls—

Well . . . hello, there.

Across a shallow parking lot, sitting right in front of a sparkling-clean, no-graffiti'd, twenty-four-hour CVS, there was, in fact, a sweet-ass fucking whip. The Hummer was totally blacked out, no chrome anywhere—not on the wheels, not around the windows, not even on the grille. And it was the big-body—and, going by all that trim, no doubt had the big engine in it.

The ride was the kind of thing you'd see on the streets where he was from, the vehicle of a major dealer. Except they were far from the inner city out here, so it was just some cracker trying to look like he had a dick.

Vanilla-man hiked up his backpack, one-strapping it. "I'ma check it out."

"Bus is coming soon." Jonsey checked his watch, and did some wishful thinking. "Five, maybe ten minutes."

"Come on—"

"Bye, asshole."

"You scared or some shit?" The SOB lifted his hands and started going *Paranormal Activity*. "Oh, scurrrrrry—"

Jonsey outted his gun and punched the muzzle right into that dumb-ass face. "I got no problem killin' you right here. I done it before. I do it again. Now back the fuck off and do y'self a favor. Shut the fuck up."

As Jonsey met the guy's eyes, he didn't particularly care what the outcome was. Shoot the bitch. Don't shoot him. Whatever.

"Okay, okay, okay." Mr. Chatty backed away and left the bus stop. Thank. Fuck.

Jonsey put his gat away, crossed his arms, and stared in the direction the bus was going to come out of—like that might help.

Stupid fucking idiot.

He looked at his watch again. Man, enough with this shit. If a bus heading back into downtown got here first, he was just going to get on and fuck it all.

Shifting the backpack he'd been told to get, he felt the hard contour of the jar inside. The pack he understood. If he was going to transport product from the sticks into the 'hood, then yeah. But the jar? What the hell you need that for?

Unless it was loose powder?

The fact that he'd been chosen by C-Rider, the man himself, for this had been pretty fucking cool. Until he'd met White Boy—and then the idea he was special lost some juice. The boss man's instructions had been clear: Hook up with the dude at the Fourth Street stop. Take the last bus out to the 'burbs and wait. Transfer to the rural line when service resumed near dawn. Get off at the Warren County stop. Hoof it one mile to a farm property.

C-Rider would meet them and a bunch of other dudes out there for the business. And after that? Jonsey would be part of a new crew set to dominate the scene in Caldie.

He liked that shit. And full respect to C-Rider—that motherfucker was tight: high up in the 'hood; strung.

But if the rest of them were like Vanilla—

The roar of an engine made him assume something, anything from the Caldwell Transit Authority had finally shown, and he got to his feet—

"No fuckin' way," he breathed.

The blacked-out Hummer had pulled up right in front of the bus stop, and as the window went down, White Boy was full-on insane-in-the-membrane behind the wheel—and not just because Cypress Hill was, in fact, blaring.

"Get in! Come on! Get in!"

"What the fuck you do, yo?" Jonsey stuttered, even as he shot around behind the SUV and jumped into the passenger seat.

Holy motherfucking *shit*—bitch ass was not a total fool, not pulling off something like this.

The guy floored the accelerator, the engine roared, and the teeth of the tires grabbed onto the snowpack and shot them forward at fifty miles an hour.

Jonsey held on to whatever he found as they went gunning through

a red-light intersection and then rode up over the curb and across the parking lot of a Hannaford. As they shot out on the far side, the music buried the beeping sound that was going off because no one had put their seat belts on.

Jonsey started grinning. "Fuckin' yes, motherfucker! You crazy bitch, you fucking crazy ass snowflake . . . !"

"I think that's Justin Bieber."

Standing in front of a lineup of Lay's potato chips, Qhuinn looked overhead to the speaker inset into the ceiling tiles. "Yup. I'm right, and I hate that I know that."

Next to him, John Matthew signed, *How do you know?*

"The little shit is everywhere." To prove the point, he motioned to a greeting card display featuring Short, Cocky, and Fifteen-Minutes-Are-Up. "I swear, that kid is proof the Antichrist is coming."

Maybe it's already here.

"Would explain Miley Cyrus."

Good point.

As John went back to contemplating his finger food of choice, Qhuinn double-checked the store. Four a.m. and the CVS was fully stocked and completely empty—except for the two of them and the guy up at the front counter, who was reading a *National Enquirer* and eating a Snickers bar.

No *lessers*. No Band of Bastards.

Nothing to shoot.

Unless that Bieber display counted.

What are you going to have? John signed.

Qhuinn shrugged and kept looking around. As John's *ahstrux nohtrum*, he was responsible for making sure the guy came back to the Brotherhood's mansion every night in one piece, and after well over a year, so far, so good. . . .

God, he missed Blay.

Shaking his head, he randomly reached forward. When his arm came back at him, he'd snagged some sour cream and onion.

Looking at the Lay's logo, and the close-up of a single chip, all he could think of was the way he and John and Blay used to hang out at Blay's parents' house, playing Xbox, drinking beers, dreaming of bigger and better posttrans lives.

Unfortunately, bigger and better had turned out to be only the size and strength of their bodies. Although maybe that was just his POV. John was, after all, happily mated. And Blay was with . . .

Shit, he couldn't even say his cousin's name in his head.

"You good, J-man?" he asked roughly.

John Matthew snagged a Doritos old-school original and nodded. *Let's get drinks.*

As they headed deeper into the store, Qhuinn wished they were downtown, fighting in the alleys, going up against either of their two enemies. Too much downtime on these suburban details, and that meant too much dwelling on—

He cut himself off again.

Whatever. Besides, he hated having any contact with the *glymera*— and that shit was mutual. Unfortunately, members of the aristocracy were gradually moving back to Caldwell, and that meant Wrath had gotten inundated with calls about so-called slayer sightings.

Like the Omega's undead didn't have better things to do than stalk around barren fruit trees and frozen swimming pools.

Still, the king wasn't in a position to tell the dandies to go F themselves. Not since Xcor and his Band of Bastards had put a bullet in that royal throat.

Traitors. Fuckers. With any luck, Vishous was going to prove without a shadow of a doubt where that rifle shot had come from, and then the bunch of them could gut those soldiers, put their heads on stakes, and light the corpses on fire.

As well as find out exactly who on the Council was colluding with the new enemy.

Yup, user-friendly was the name of the game now—so one night a week, each of the teams ended up here in the neighborhood he'd grown up in, knocking on doors and looking under beds.

In museum-like houses that gave him the creeps more than any dark underpass downtown.

A tap on his forearm brought his head around. "Yeah?"

I was going to ask you the same thing.

"Huh?"

You stopped here. And have just been staring at . . . well, you know.

Qhuinn frowned and glanced at the product display. Then lost all train of thought—as well as most of the blood from his head. "Oh, yeah . . . ah . . ." Shit, had someone turned up the heat? "Um."

Baby bottles. Baby formula. Baby bibs and wet naps and Q-tips. Pacifiers. Bottles. Some kind of contraption—

Oh, God, a breast pump.

Qhuinn did a one-eighty so fast, he got faced by a six-foot-high stack of Pampers, bounced back into the land of NUKs, and finally ricocheted out of infant airspace thanks to an A+D rebound. What ever the hell that shit was.

Baby. Baby. Baby—

Oh, good. He'd made it up to the checkout counter.

Shoving a hand into his biker jacket, Qhuinn pulled his wallet free and reached behind for John's finger food. "Gimme your stuff."

As the guy started to argue, mouthing the words because his hands were full, Qhuinn snagged the Mountain Dew and Doritos that were clogging up communication.

"There ya go. While he's ringing us up, you can yell at me properly."

And what do you know, John's hands flew through the positions of ASL in various I-got-this combinations.

"Is he deaf?" the guy behind the cash register asked in a stage whisper. As if someone using American Sign Language was some kind of freak.

"No. Blind."

"Oh."

As the man kept staring, Qhuinn wanted to pop him. "You going to help us out here or what?"

"Oh . . . yeah. Hey, you got a tattoo on your face." Mr. Observant moved slowly, like the bar codes on those bags were creating some kind of wind resistance under his laser reader. "Did you know that?"

Really. "I wouldn't know."

"Are you blind, too?"

No filter on this guy. None. "Yeah, I am."

"Oh, so that's why your eyes are all weird."

"Yeah. That's right."

Qhuinn took out a twenty and didn't wait for change—murder was just a liiiiiittle too tempting. Nodding to John, who was also measuring the dear boy for a shroud, Qhuinn went to walk off.

"What about your change?" the man called out.

"I'm deaf, too. I can't hear you."

The guy yelled more loudly, "I'll just keep it then, yeah?"

"Sounds good," Qhuinn shouted over his shoulder.

Idiot was stage-five stupid. Straight up.

Stepping through the security bar, Qhuinn thought it was a miracle that humans like that got through the day and night at all. And the motherfucker had managed to get his pants on right and operate a cash register.

Would miracles never cease.

As he pushed his way outside, the cold slapped him around, the wind blowing at his hair, snowflakes getting in his nose—

Qhuinn stopped.

Looked left. Looked right.

"What the . . . where's my Hummer?"

In his peripheral vision, John's hands started flying around like he was wondering the same thing. And then the guy pointed down to the freshly fallen snow . . . and the deep treads of four monster tires that made a fat circle and headed out of the parking lot.

"Goddamn motherfucking *shit*!" Qhuinn gritted.

And he thought Mr. Observant was the stupid one?

TWO

ack at the Brotherhood's mansion, Blaylock sat on the edge of his bed, his naked body flushed, a sheen of sweat across his chest and shoulders. Between his legs his cock was spent, and his hips were loose from all kinds of bump and grind. At the other end of the spectrum, his breath was squeezed, his flesh requiring just a little more oxygen than his lungs could provide.

So naturally he reached for the pack of Dunhill Reds he kept on his side table.

The sounds of his lover showering in the bath across the way, along with the spicy scent of hand-milled soap, were achingly familiar.

Had it been almost a year now?

Taking out one of the cigarettes, he picked up the vintage Van Cleef & Arpels lighter Sax had given him for his birthday. The thing was made of gold and marked with the firm's trademark Mystery Set rubies, a 1940s lovely that never failed to please the eye—or do the job.

As the flame jumped up, the shower turned off.

Blay leaned into the lick of fire, inhaled, and flicked the top back down. As always, the slightest hint of lighter fluid lingered, the sweetness mingling with the smoke that he exhaled—

Qhuinn hated smoking.

Had never approved of it.

Which, considering the number of outrageous things the guy made a regular habit out of, seemed downright offensive.

Sex with countless strangers in club bathrooms? Threesomes with males and females? Piercings? Tattoos in various places?

And this guy didn't "approve" of smoking. Like it was a vile habit no one in his right mind would bother with.

In the bathroom, the hair dryer he and Sax shared went on, and Blay could imagine that blond hair he had just grabbed onto and pulled back hard flowing in the artificial breeze, catching the light, shining with highlights that were natural.

Saxton was beautiful, all smooth skin and sinewy body and perfect taste.

God, the clothes in that wardrobe of his. Amazing. Like the Great Gatsby had jumped out of the pages of the novel, gone down to Fifth Avenue, and bought out whole blocks of haute couture.

Qhuinn was never like that. He wore Hanes T-shirts and fatigues or leathers, and still sported the same biker jacket he'd had from just after his transition. No Ferragamos or Ballys for him; New Rocks with soles the size of truck tires. Hair? Brushed if it was lucky. Cologne? Gunpowder and orgasms.

Hell, in all the years Blay had known the guy—and it had been since birth practically—he'd never seen Qhuinn in a suit.

One had to wonder if the guy knew that tuxedos could be owned, not just rented.

If Saxton was the picture-perfect aristocrat, Qhuinn was a straight-up thug—

"Here. Tap your ashes in this."

Blay jerked his head up. Saxton was naked, perfectly coiffed and scented with Cool Water—and holding out the heavy Baccarat ashtray he'd bought as a summer solstice gift. It was also from the forties, and weighed as much as a bowling ball.

Blay complied, taking the thing and balancing it in the palm of his hand. "Are you off to work?"

Like that wasn't obvious?

"Indeed."

Saxton turned away and flashed a spectacular ass as he went to the closet. Technically, the guy was supposed to be living next door in one

of the vacant guest rooms, but over time his clothes had migrated in here.

He didn't mind the smoking. Even shared every once in a while after a particularly energetic . . . exchange, as it were.

"How's it going?" Blay said on an exhale. "Your secret assignment, that is."

"Rather well. I'm almost finished."

"Does that mean you can finally tell me what it's all been about?"

"You shall find out soon enough."

As the flapping of a shirt emanated from the walk-in, Blay turned his cigarette around and stared at the glowing tip. Saxton had been working on something top-secret for the king since the fall, and there had been no pillow talk about it—which was probably only one of the many reasons Wrath had made the male his private lawyer. Saxton had all the discretion of a bank vault.

Qhuinn, on the other hand, had never been able to keep a secret. From surprise parties to gossip to embarassing personal details like whether you'd gotten laid together by a cheap whore at—

"Blay?"

"I'm sorry, what?"

Saxton emerged, fully dressed in a tweed Ralph Lauren three-piecer. "I said, I'll see you at Last Meal."

"Oh. Is it that late?"

"Yes. It is."

Guess they'd screwed their way through the first place setting of the day—which was how they'd rolled ever since . . .

God. He couldn't even think about what had happened a mere week ago. Couldn't even put into mental words how he felt about the one thing he'd never worried about coming to pass—right in front of his own eyes.

And he'd thought being rejected by Qhuinn was bad?

Watching the guy have a young with a female—

Shoot, he needed to respond to his lover, didn't he. "Yes, absolutely. I'll see you then."

There was a hesitation, and then Saxton came over and pressed a kiss to Blay's lips. "You're off rotation tonight?"

Blay nodded, holding the cigarette out of the way so the male's beautiful clothes didn't get burned. "I was going to read the *New Yorker* and maybe start *From the Terrace.*"

Saxton smiled, clearly appreciating the appeal of both. "How I envy you. After I'm finished, I'm going to take a few nights off and just relax."

"Maybe we could go somewhere."

"Maybe we could."

The tight expression on that lovely face was quick and sad. Because Saxton knew that they weren't going anywhere.

And not just because a Sandals all-inclusive was so not in their future.

"Be well," Saxton said, brushing his knuckle down Blay's cheek.

Blay nuzzled that hand. "You, too."

A moment later the door opened and shut . . . and he was alone. Sitting on the messy bed, in the silence that seemed to crush him from all sides, he smoked his cigarette down to the filter, screwed it out in the ashtray, lit another.

Closing his eyes, he tried to remember the sound of Saxton moaning or the sight of the male's back arching or the feel of skin on skin.

He could not.

And that was the root of the problem, wasn't it.

"Let me get this straight," V drawled over the cell phone connection. "You lost your Hummer."

Qhuinn wanted to put his head through a plate-glass window. "Yeah. I did. So could you please—"

"How do you lose eight thousand pounds of vehicle?"

"That's not important—"

"Well, actually, it is if you want me to access the GPS and tell you where to find the damn thing—which is why you're calling, true? Or do you just think confession without detail is good for the soul or some shit."

Qhuinn gripped his phone hard. "Ileftthekeysinit."

"I'm sorry? I didn't catch that."

Bullshit. "I left the keys in it."

"That was a dumb-ass move, son."

No. Fucking. Kidding. "So can you help me—"

"Just e-mailed you the link. One thing—when you recover the vehicle?"

"Yeah?"

"Check to see if the jackers took a moment to put the seat forward—you know, get comfortable and shit. Because they probably weren't in a rush, what with having the keys." The sound of Vishous's yukking it up was like getting paddled in the nuts with a car fender. "Listen, I gotta go. I need both hands to hold my gut as I laugh my ass off attcha. Later."

As the call went dead, Qhuinn took a moment to rein in the desire to throw the phone.

Yeah, 'cuz losing that, too, was going to really help the situation.

Going into his Hotmail account, and wondering just how long it was going to take to live this one down, he got a bead on his frickin' car.

"It's heading west." He tilted the phone so John could see. "Let's do this."

Dematerializing, Qhuinn was dimly aware that the level of his rage was disproportionate to the problem: As his molecules scattered, he was a lit fuse waiting to connect with some dynamite—and it wasn't just about him being a dumb-ass, or the missing car, or the fact that he was looking like an idiot to one of the males he respected most in the Brotherhood.

There was so much other shit.

Taking form on a rural road, he checked his phone again and waited for John to show up. When the fighter did, he recalibrated and they went farther west, closing in, cross-referencing the direction . . . until Qhuinn ghosted onto the precise strip of ice-covered asphalt his fucking Hummer was on.

About a hundred yards ahead of the vehicle.

Whatever SOB was behind the wheel was going sixty miles an hour in the snow, heading for a curve. What a . . .

Well, calling them stupid was exactly the kind of kettle-black thing the night had devolved into.

Let me shoot the wheels, John signed, like he knew a gun in Qhuinn's hand was not the best idea.

Before the guy could up-and-out his forty, though, Qhuinn dematerialized . . . right onto the hood of the SUV.

He landed face-first into the windshield, his ass getting hit with the kind of breeze that turned him into a bug on all that glass. And then it was a case of oh-heeey-gurl-heeeey: Thanks to the glow from the dashboard, he caught the OMG! on the faces of the pair of guys in the front seat . . . and then his bright idea turned into goat fuck number two of the evening.

Instead of hitting the brakes, the driver wrenched the wheel, like he could maybe avoid what had already landed on the Hummer's hood. The torque threw Qhuinn free, his body going weightless as he wrenched around in space to keep his eyes on his ride.

Turned out he was the lucky one.

As Hummers were designed and built for things other than aerodynamics and braking facility, the laws of physics grabbed onto all that top-heavy metal and rolled the shit. In the process, and in spite of the snow cover, metal met asphalt, and the high-pitched scream soprano'd out into night—

The thunderous impact of the SUV nailing some kind of solid object the size of a house cut off all that caterwauling. Qhuinn didn't pay much attention to the crash, however, because he landed as well, the paved road smacking him on the shoulder and hip, his body doing its own version of greased pig down the snow-packed pavement—

CRACK!

His momentum was stopped short as well, something hard catching him in the head—

Cue a spectacular light show, like someone had lit off a firecracker right in front of his face. Then it was Tweety Bird time, little stars going around his vision as pain in various places started to check in.

Pushing against whatever was closest to him—he wasn't sure whether it was the ground or a tree or that red-suited fatty, Santa Claus, he eased himself over onto his back. As he flopped flat, the cold went to his head and helped to dull things.

He intended to get up. Check the Hummer. Beat the shit out of whoever had taken advantage of his blond moment. But that was just his brain playing with itself. His body had taken over the wheel and accelerator, and it had no intention of going anywhere the fuck.

Laying as still as he could, and breathing out uneven clouds of frost, time slowed down and then began to morph. For a second, he became confused as to what had put him in this at-the-side-of-the-road condition. The accident he'd caused?

Or . . . that Honor Guard from before the raids?

Was this back-flat on the asphalt thing a memory of his past or something that was actually happening?

The good news was that sorting out reality gave his brain something to do other than continue to hammer away at the get-moving stuff. The bad news was that the memories from the night his family had disavowed him were more painful than anything he currently felt in his body.

God, it was all so clear, the *doggen* bringing him the official papers and demanding some blood for a cleansing ritual. Him throwing that duffel bag over his shoulder and walking out of that house for the last time. The road stretching in front of him, empty and dark—

This road, he realized. This actual road was the one he'd gone down on. Or . . . was down on . . . whatever. When he'd left his parents' house, he'd intended to head out west, where he'd heard there was a clan of rogue assholes just like him. Instead, four males had shown up in hooded robes and beaten him to death—literally. He had gone to the door of the Fade, and on it, he had seen a future that he hadn't believed . . . until it happened. Was happening—right now. With Layla . . .

Oh, look, John was talking to him.

Right in front of his eyes, the guy's hands were going through the motions, so to speak, and Qhuinn intended reply with some kind of update—

"Is this real?" he mumbled.

John looked momentarily confuzzled.

It had to be real, Qhuinn thought. Because the Honor Guard had come to him in the summer, and the air he was inhaling was cold.

Are you okay? John mouthed as he signed.

Shoving his hand into the snowy ground, Qhuinn pushed as hard as he could. When he didn't budge more than an inch or two, he let that speak for itself . . . and passed the fuck out.

THREE

The sound of coke getting sniffed up a deviated septum made the man outside the door tighten his grip on his knife.

Fucker. What a fucker.

The first rule of any successful dealer was that you didn't use. Addicts who funded your business used. Associates you needed to leverage used. Bitches you needed out on the streets used.

Management did not use. Ever.

The logic was so sound, it was fundamental, and nothing different than, say, going to a casino that had a six-million-square-foot facility, enough catered food for a small country, and goddamned gold leaf everywhere—and being surprised that you lost all your money. If taking drugs was such a hot frickin' idea, why did people regularly die from the shit, destroy lives over it, get thrown in prison thanks to it?

Dumb-ass.

The man turned the knob and pushed. Of course the door was unlocked, and as he walked into the squalid room, the stench of baby powder would have overwhelmed him—if he hadn't gotten used to the smell on himself.

That nasty nose-pincher was the only thing he hadn't liked about

the change. Everything else—the strength, the longevity, the freedom—he'd been into. But damn, the smell.

No matter how much cologne he used, he couldn't get rid of it.

And yeah, he missed being able to have sex.

Other than that, the Lessening Society was his ticket to domination.

The sniffing stopped and the *Fore-lesser* looked up from the *People* magazine he'd made the lines on. Beneath the residue, some dude named Channing Tatum was staring at the camera, all hot as fuck. "Hey. What're you doing here?"

As those beady, strung out eyes struggled to focus, the "Boss" looked like he'd given a blow job to a powered doughnut.

"I got something for you."

"More? Oh, my God, how did you know? I only got two ounces left and I—"

Connors, a.k.a. C-Rider, moved fast, taking three steps forward, throwing his arm out wide, and swinging the knife in a fat circle—that terminated in the side of the *Fore-lesser's* head. The steel blade went in deep, slicing through the softer bone of the temple, piercing the buzzed-up gray matter.

The *Fore-lesser* went into a seizure—maybe because of the injury . . . more likely because his adrenal glands had just pumped a million cc's of holy-shit into his bloodstream and the stuff wasn't mixing well with the cocaine. As the little shit flopped off his chair and shimmied his way down to the floor, the knife stayed with Connors, disengaging from the side of the skull, its blade marked with black blood.

Connors met the shocked stare of his now-former superior and felt really good about this promotion he had going on. The Omega himself had come to him and offered him the job, no doubt recognizing, as they all did, that a sk8tr punk was not who you wanted in charge of any organization bigger than a poker game. Yeah, sure, the guy had been useful in growing the ranks. But quantity was not quality, and it didn't take the Army, Navy, Air Force or Marines to see that the Lessening Society was being overrun by lawless, ADHD juvies.

Hard to promote any kind of agenda with that kind of rank and file—unless you had a real professional running shit.

Which was why the Omega had put all this in motion.

"Wh-wh-wh—"

"You been fired, motherfucker."

The final part of the forced retirement came with another stabbing motion, this one taking that blade and driving it right into the center of the chest. With a *pop!* and a show of smoke, the regime change was complete.

And Connors was the head of everything.

Supremacy made him smile for a moment—until his eyes went around the room. For some reason, he thought of that Febreze commercial, the one where they'd shit up some place, spray like madmen, and drag "real people, not actors" into the scene to sniff around.

Man, except for the food remnants—which were a no-show, because slayers didn't require eats—everything fit: the mold on the ceiling, the ratty furniture, the dripping over at the sink . . . and especially the crap that went along with a multi-chemical addiction, like syringes, spoons, even the two-liter Sprite-bottle meth lab over in the corner.

This was not a seat of power. This was a common crack house.

Connors went over and snagged the little shit's cell phone. The screen was cracked and there was some kind of sticky patch on the back. The thing was not password-protected, and when he went into the messages section, all kinds of kiss-asses had blown up the phone, the texts blah-blah-blahing congrats about the induction ceremony that was going on tonight.

But the *Fore-lesser* hadn't known about it. Wasn't his gig.

Connors wasn't going to retaliate, however. Those brown-nosing douches were just trying to stay alive and would suck anyone's dick to keep breathing: He fully expected the same list to be hitting him up, and he wanted them to. Spies had their purpose in the grand scheme of things.

And, man, there was work to be done.

From what he had figured out during his own blessedly short period of ass-kissing, the Lessening Society had few assets left in terms of weapons or ammo or property. No cash, because what did come in from petty robberies had gone up the little shit's nose or into his arm. No master list of inductees, no troop organization, no training.

Lot of rebuilding needed to happen fast—

A cold draft shot into the room, and Connors turned around. The Omega had arrived from out of nowhere, the Evil's white robes shining brightly, the black shadow underneath looking like an optical illusion.

The repulsion that went through Connors was something he knew he was also going to have to get used to. The Omega always enjoyed a

special relationship with his *Fore-lesser*—and maybe that was why word had it they rarely lasted very long.

Then again, given who he picked . . .

"I took care of him," Connors said, nodding to the scorch mark on the floor.

"I know," the Omega replied, that voice warping through the fetid, chilly air.

Outside, a gust of wind blew snow against the windows, the gap on one sill letting some snowflakes in. As they entered the space, they fell to the floor in a shimmer, the temperature cold enough to sustain them, thanks to the master's presence.

"He is back home now." The Omega came forward like a draft, with no evidence that any kind of legs were moving him. "And I am very pleased."

Conners told his feet to stay put. There was nowhere to run to, nothing to escape—he just had to get through what was going to happen next.

At least he had prepared for this.

"I got some new recruits for you."

The Omega stopped. "Indeed?"

"A tribute, as it were." Or more like a defined endpoint to this shit: He had to head out soon, and he'd carefully planned these two events close together. The Omega, after all, was into his playthings, but liked his Society and its purpose of eliminating vampires even more.

"You please me to no end," the Omega whispered as he closed in. "I do believe we are going to get along just fine . . . Mr. C."

FOUR

The Chosen Layla had existed in her own body without any physical compromise for the entirety of her existence. Born in the Scribe Virgin's Sanctuary, and trained in the rarefied, preternatural peacefulness there, she had never known hunger, or fever, or pain of any note. Not heat nor cold, nor contusion, concussion, or contraction. Her body had been, as with all things in the mother of the race's most sacred space, always the placid same, a perfect specimen functioning at the highest level—

"Oh, God," she gulped as she shot out of bed and lurched into the bathroom.

Her bare feet skidded on the marble as she threw herself to her knees, popped the toilet seat, and leaned over to go face-to-face with the bowl's epiglottal hole.

"Just . . . do it. . . ." she gasped as the rolling nausea polluted her body until even her toes curled under and grabbed at the floor. "Please . . . for the Scribe Virgin's sake . . ."

If she could just empty the contents of her stomach, surely the torture would relent—

Taking her fore- and middle fingers into her throat, she shoved

them in so hard she choked. But that was the extent of it. There was no coordination of her diaphragm, no release of the greasy spoiled meat in her stomach . . . not that she'd actually eaten that—or anything else—for . . . how long had it been? Days.

Mayhap that was the problem.

Snaking her arm around her hips, she put her sweaty forehead on the hard, cool lip of the toilet and tried to breathe shallowly—because the sensation of air moving up and down the back of her throat made the impotent urge to throw up worse.

Mere days ago, when she had been in her needing, her body had taken control, the urge to mate strong enough to wipe out all thought and emotion. That supremacy had quickly passed, however, and likewise had the aches and pains from the relentless mating, her skin and bones once again resuming their backseat to her brain.

The balance was tipping back once more.

Giving up, she carefully repositioned herself, placing her shoulders against the blessedly chilly marble wall.

Considering how sickly she felt, her only extrapolation was that she was losing the pregnancy. She'd never seen anyone in the Sanctuary go through this—was this illness what was normal here on earth?

Closing her eyes, she wished she could talk to someone about it all. But very few knew her condition—and for the time being, she needed to keep things that way: Most were completely unaware that she had gone through her needing or been serviced. Autumn's fertile period had hit first, and in response, the Brotherhood had scattered far and wide as there was no taking chances with exposure to those hormones—for good reason, as she had learned firsthand. By the time people had returned to their normal rooms in the mansion? Her own had passed, and any residual hormonal fluxes in the air had been chalked up by all and sundry to Autumn's fading time.

The privacy in these two rooms of hers was not going to last if the pregnancy continued, however. For one, her status would be sensed by the others, especially males, who were particularly attuned to that sort of thing.

And two, after a while, she would begin to show.

Except if she felt this bad, how ever could the young survive?

As a vague sensation of tightness settled into her lower belly, like her pelvis was being compressed by an invisible vise, she tried to train her mind on something, anything other than her physical sensations.

Eyes the color of the night sky came to her.

Penetrating eyes, eyes that stared up from a face that was bloodied and distorted . . . and beautiful even in its ugliness.

Okay. This was *not* an improvement.

Xcor, leader of the Band of Bastards. A traitor against the king, a hunted male who was enemy to the Brotherhood and lawful vampires everywhere. The fierce warrior who had been born of a noble mother who did not want him because of his visage, and an unknown father who had never claimed parentage. An unwanted burden shuffled from home to orphanage until he'd entered the Bloodletter's training camp back in the Old Country. A remorseless fighter trained therein to great effect; then, in his maturity, a master of death who toured the land with a band of elite fighters first aligned to the Bloodletter himself, and thereafter, to Xcor—and no one else.

The information trail at the Sanctuary's library ended there because none of the Chosen were updating anything anymore. The rest, however, she could fill in herself: The Brotherhood believed the attempt on Wrath's life back in the fall had been made by Xcor, and she had further heard there were insurrectionists within the *glymera* working with the fighter.

Xcor. A traitorous, brutal male with no conscience, no loyalty, no principle save to serve himself.

Yet when she had looked into his eyes, when she had been in his presence, when she had unknowingly fed this new enemy . . . she had felt like a full female for the first time in her life.

Because he had looked upon her not with aggression, but with—

"Arrest that," she said aloud. "Stop that *right* now."

As if she were a young getting into a cupboard or some such thing.

Forcing herself to her feet, she drew her robe around her and resolved to leave her room and make her way down to the kitchen. A change of scenery was needed, and so was food—if only to give her churning stomach something to expel.

On her way out, she did not check her hair or her face in the mirror. Did not fuss over the way her robe fell. Didn't waste even a moment worrying which of her identical sandals to wear.

So much time she had wasted in the past over the minute details of her appearance.

She would have been much better served studying or training herself for a vocation. But that had not been permitted within the allowed prescription of activity for a Chosen.

As she stepped into the corridor, she took a deep breath, steadied herself, and started to walk in the direction of the king's study—

Up ahead, Blaylock, son of Rocke, burst out into the hall of statues, his brows down tight, his body clad in leather from the tops of his shoulders to the soles of his tremendous boots. As he strode forward, he was checking his weapons one by one, taking them out of holsters, replacing them, buckling them in.

Layla stopped dead.

And when the male finally looked upon her, he did the same, his eyes growing remote.

Deep red of hair, and lovely sapphire blue of eye, the fully blooded aristocrat was a fighter for the Brotherhood, but he was not a brute. No matter how he spent his nights out in the field, he remained at the compound a mannered, intelligent gentlemale of fine comportment and schooling.

So it was not a surprise that even in his rush, he bent slightly at the waist in formal greeting before resuming his hurry to the grand staircase.

In his descent down to the foyer, Qhuinn's voice came to her.

I'm in love with someone. . . .

Layla exercised her new habit of cursing under her breath. Such a sad state of affairs between those two fighters, and this pregnancy was not of aid.

But the die had been cast.

And they were all going to live with the consequences.

As Blay hit the staircase, he felt like he was being chased, and that was nuts. Nobody who was any threat was behind him. There was no masher in a Jason mask, or sick bastard in a bad Christmas sweater with knives for fingers, or killer clown . . .

Just a probably-pregnant Chosen who happened to have spent a good twelve hours fucking his former best friend.

No prob.

At least, there shouldn't have been any problem. The trouble was, every time he saw that female, he felt like he got punched in the gut. Which was another case of crazy. She had done nothing wrong. Neither had Qhuinn.

Although, God, if she was pregnant . . .

Blay booted all those happy thoughts to the background as he crossed through the foyer at a jog. No time to psycho-babble, even if it was just to himself: When Vishous called you on your night off and told you to be out front in your gear in five minutes, it was not because things were going well.

No details had been given during the phone call; none had been asked for. Blay had taken only a moment to text Saxton, and then he'd thrown on the leather and the steel, ready for anything.

In a way, this was good. Spending the night reading in his room had turned out to be torturous, and though he didn't want anyone in trouble, at least this pulled him into some activity. Bursting out through the vestibule, he—

Came face-to-face with the Brotherhood's flatbed truck.

The thing was kitted out to look authentically human, deliberately painted with red AAA logos and the made-up name of Murphy's Towing. Fake telephone number. Fake tagline of: "We're Always There for You."

Bullshit. Unless, of course, the "you" was one of the Brotherhood.

Blay hopped up into the passenger seat and found Tohr, not V, behind the wheel. "Is Vishous coming?"

"It's you and me, kid—he's still working on the ballistics testing of that bullet."

The Brother hit the gas, the diesel engine roaring like a beast, the headlights swinging in a fat circle around the courtyard's fountain and across the lineup of cars parked wheelbase-to-wheelbase.

Just as Blay checked out the vehicles and did the math about the one that was missing, Tohr said, "It's Qhuinn and John."

Blay's lids dropped shut for a split second. "What happened."

"I don't know much. John called V for an emergency assist." The Brother looked over. "And you and I are the only ones free."

Blay reached for the door handle, ready to pop the thing and dematerialize the fuck out of there. "Where are they—"

"Calm down, son. You know the rules. None of us can be out alone, so I need your ass in that seat or I'm violating my own goddamn protocol."

Blay slammed his fist into the door, punching hard enough that the sting in his hand cleared his head a little. Fucking Band of Bastards, cramping them all—and the fact that the rule made sense just pissed him off even more. Xcor and his boys had proven to be cagey, aggres-

sive, and completely without morals—not exactly the kind of enemy you wanted to meet up with all by your little lonesome.

But come on.

Blay grabbed his phone, intending to text John—but he stopped because he didn't want the guys distracted by his trying to get details. "Is there anyone who can get to them quick?"

"V called the others. Fighting's heavy downtown and nobody can break out of it."

"Goddamn it."

"I'll drive as fast as I can, son."

Blay nodded, just so he didn't come across as rude. "Where are they and how far?"

"Fifteen to twenty minutes. And out past the 'burbs."

Shit.

Staring out the window and watching the snow streak by, he told himself that if John was texting, they were alive, and for godsakes, the guy had asked for a tow truck, not an ambulance. For all he knew, they had a flat tire or a broken windshield, and getting hysterical was not going to shorten the distance, decrease the drama, if there was any, or change the outcome.

"Sorry if I'm being an ass," Blay muttered, as the Brother shot onto the highway.

"You do not need to apologize for being worried about your boys."

Man, Tohr was cool like that.

As it was late, late at night, the Northway didn't have any cars, just a semi or two, the wired drivers of which were going like bats out of hell. The tow truck didn't stay on the four-laner for long. About eight miles later, they got off at an exit well north of downtown Caldwell, in a suburban area that was known for mansions, not ranches, Mercedes, not Mazdas.

"What the hell are they doing out here?" Blay asked.

"Researching those reports."

"About *lessers*?"

"Yeah."

Blay shook his head as they went by stone walls as tall and thick as linebackers, and gates of fine, wrought-iron filigree which were closed to outsiders.

Abruptly, he took a deep breath and relaxed. The aristocrats who were moving back into town were spooked and seeing evidence of *lesser* activity in everything around them—which did not mean that slayers were in fact jumping out from behind garden statuary or hiding in their basements.

This was not a mortal event. It was a mechanical one.

Blay rubbed his face and slapped the shit out of his inner panic button.

At least until they came out on the other side of the zip code and found the accident.

As they rounded a bend in the road, there were a pair of taillights glowing red at the side—far off the shoulder, and upside down.

The fuck this was just a mechanical problem.

Blay jumped out before Tohr even started to pull over, dematerializing directly to the Hummer.

"Oh, Christ, no," he moaned as he saw two sunburst patterns in the front windshield—the kind of thing that could only be made by a pair of heads slamming into the glass.

Tripping through the snow, he went for the driver's-side door, the sweet sting of gas knifing into his nose, the smoke from the engine making him blink—

A high-pitched whistle cut through the night from over on the left. Whipping around, Blay searched the snow-covered landscape . . . and found two hulking shapes about twenty feet away, clustered at the base of a tree nearly the size of the one the Hummer had gotten hung up on.

Scrambling through the drifts, Blay rushed over and landed on his knees. Qhuinn was sprawled on the ground, his long, heavy legs stretched out, his upper body in John's lap.

The male just stared at him with those mismatched eyes, unmoving, unspeaking.

"Is he paralyzed?" Blay demanded, looking over at John.

"Not that I'm aware of," Qhuinn replied dryly.

I think he's got a concussion, John signed.

"I do not—"

He went flying off the hood of his car and hit this tree—

"I mostly missed the tree—"

And I've had to hold him down ever since.

"Which is pissing me off—"

"How we doing, boys?" Tohr said as he crunched over to them, his boots crushing the ice pack. "Anyone injured?"

Qhuinn shoved himself free of John and leaped up to the vertical. "No—we're all just—"

At that point, the guy's balance went wonky, his body listing so hard that Tohr had to catch him.

"You go wait in the truck," the Brother said grimly.

"Fuck that—"

Tohr jerked the guy forward so they were face-to-face. "Excuse me, son. What did you say? 'Cuz I know you didn't just f-bomb me, did you."

Okay. Right. Blay knew firsthand that there were few things in life Qhuinn backed down from; that being said, a Brother the guy respected, who was more than ready to finish the job that a pine tree had started, was definitely one of them.

Qhuinn looked over to his ruined SUV. "Sorry. Bad night. And I just got light-headed for a split second. I'm fine."

In typical Qhuinn fashion, the bastard broke free and walked off, heading toward the steaming pile of previously drivable metal like he'd thrown off his injuries by force of will.

Leaving everyone else in his dust.

Blay got to his feet and forced himself to focus on John. "What happened?"

Thank God for sign language; it gave him something to look at, and fortunately, John took his time filling in the details. When the narration was over, Blay could only stare at his friend. But come on, it wasn't as if anybody would make that shit up.

Not about someone they liked, at any rate.

Tohrment started to laugh. "He pulled a *hyslop*, is what you're saying."

"Not sure I know what that is?" Blay cut in.

Tohr shrugged and followed Qhuinn's trail through the snow, motioning with his arm toward the wreck. "Right here. This is the definition of a *hyslop*—precipitated by your boy leaving his keys in the ignition."

He's not my boy, Blay said to himself. Never has been. Never will be.

And the fact that that hurt worse than any kind of concussion was something, like so much, he kept quiet about.

Off to the side and out of the glow of the headlights, Blay hung back and watched as Qhuinn crouched down by the driver's door and cursed softly. "Messy. Very messy."

Tohr did the duty on the passenger seat. "Oh, look, a matched set."

"I think they're dead."

"Really. What gave that away. The fact they aren't moving or that this guy over here has no facial features left?"

Qhuinn straightened up and looked across the undercarriage. "We need to roll it and tow it."

"And here I thought we were going to toast marshmallows," Tohr said. "John? Blay? Get over here."

The four of them lined up shoulder-to-shoulder between the sets of tires and dug in with their boots, locking their positions in the snow. Four sets of hands palmed the panels; four bodies leaned into the ready; four pairs of shoulders tightened up.

A single voice, Tohr's, counted it out. "On three. One. Two. *Three*—"

The Hummer had already had a bad night, and this right-the-wrong thing made it groan so loudly that an owl was flushed across the road and a pair of deer took flight on bounding hooves through the trees.

Then again, the SUV wasn't the only one cursing. Everybody was going George Carlin under the deadweight as they worked to pry free gravity's hold on all that steel. The laws of physics were possessive, however, and as Blay's body strained, all his muscles tightening against his bones, he turned his head and shifted his grip—

He was standing next to Qhuinn. Right beside the guy.

Qhuinn's eyes were focused straight ahead, his lips peeled back from his fangs, his fierce expression the result of total anatomical effort. . . .

It was close to what he looked like when he came.

Holy inappropriateness, Batman. And too bad that fact did nothing to change his thought pattern.

The trouble was, Blay knew from firsthand experience what an orgasm did to the guy—although not because he was one of the cast of thousands who'd been a recipient. Oh, no. Never that. God for-fucking-bid the guy who'd stick his dick in anything that breathed—and maybe some inanimate objects—would ever do Blay.

Yeah, because that discerning sexual palate, which had led to Qhuinn balling everything in Caldwell between the ages of twenty and twenty-eight, had filtered Blay out of the fuck pool.

"She's . . . starting to move . . ." Tohr gritted. "Get under her!"

Blay and Qhuinn snapped into action, releasing their holds,

crouching down, shoving their shoulders under the lip of the roof. Facing each other, their eyes met as breath exploded out of their mouths, their thighs going into action, their bodies pitted in a war against all that cold, hard weight—that happened be slippery thanks to the snow.

Their added power was the turning point—literally. An axis formed on the opposite tires, and the Hummer's four-ton burden started shifted on them, getting lighter and lighter—

Why the hell was Qhuinn looking at him like that?

Those eyes, that pair of blue and green, were locked on Blay's—and they were not moving.

Maybe it was just concentration—like, he was actually focused only on the two inches in front of his face and Blay just happened to be on the far side of that.

Had to be . . .

"Easy, boys!" Tohr called out. "Or we'll flip the damn thing all the way over again!"

Blay let up on the graft, and there was a moment of suspension, a split second where the impossible happened, where an eight-thousand-pound SUV balanced perfectly on the edge of two tires, where what had been excruciating became . . . exhilarating.

And still Qhuinn stared at him.

As the Hummer landed with a bounce on all fours, Blay frowned and turned away. When he glanced back . . . Qhuinn's eyes were exactly where they had been.

Blay leaned in and hissed, "What?"

Before there was any kind of answer, Tohr went over and opened the SUV's side door. The smell of fresh blood floated over on the breeze. "Man, even if this isn't totaled, I'm not sure you're going to want it back. Cleanup in here is going to be a bitch."

Qhuinn didn't respond, seeming to have forgotten all about the Allstate Mayhem commercial his SUV was living out. He just stood there, staring at Blay.

Maybe the SOB had stroked out standing up?

"What's your problem?" Blay repeated.

"I'll bring the flatbed over," Tohr said as he started for the other vehicle. "Let's leave the bodies right where they are—you can dispose of them on the way home."

Meanwhile, Blay could feel John pausing and looking across at the pair of them—something Qhuinn didn't seem to care about, naturally.

With a curse, Blay solved the problem by jogging over to the tow truck and walking alongside as Tohr backed the thing up toward the Hummer's collapsed hood. Going for the winch, Blay unclipped the claw and started to free the cable.

He had a feeling he knew what was on Qhuinn's mind, and if he was right, the guy had better stay quiet and stay the fuck back.

He did *not* want to hear it.

FIVE

As Qhuinn stood in the stiff wind and watched Blay hook up the Hummer, loose snow blew up over his boots, the quiet, soft weight gradually obscuring the steel-toed tops. Glancing down, he had the vague thought that if he stayed where he was long enough, he would be completely covered by it, from head to toe.

Weird goddamn thing to come into his brain.

The roaring of the flatbed's engine brought his head back up, his eyes shifting over as the winch began to drag his ruined ride off the snowpack.

Blay was the one working the pull, the male standing to the side, carefully monitoring and controlling the speed of the draw so that no undue stress was put on the various mechanical components of this automotive Good Samaritan production.

So careful. So controlled.

In order to seem casual, Qhuinn went over by Tohr and pretended that he, like the Brother, was just monitoring the progress of the lift. Not. It was all about Blay, of course.

It had always been about Blay.

Trying to add to all the nonchalance, he crossed his arms over his chest—but had to drop them down again as his bruised shoulder hollered. "Lesson learned," he said to make conversation.

Tohr murmured something back, but damned if he heard it. And damned if he could see anything but Blay. Not for a blink. For a breath. For a beat of the heart.

Staring across the swirling snow, he marveled at how someone you knew everything about, who lived down the hall, who ate with you and worked with you and slept at the same time you did . . . could become a stranger.

Then again, and as usual, that was about the emotional distance, not the same job, under-the-same-roof shit.

The thing was, Qhuinn felt like he wanted to explain things. Unfortunately, and unlike his slut cousin, Saxton the Cocksucker, he had no gift with words, and the complicated stuff in the center of his chest was making that mute tendency worse.

After a final grind, the Hummer was up off the ground on the bed, and Blay started running chain in and out of the undercarriage.

"Okay, you three take this piece of junk back," Tohr said as flurries started to fall again.

Blay froze and looked at the Brother. "We go in pairs. So I need to leave with you."

Like he was beyond ready to bounce.

"Have you looked at what we got here? An incapacitated hunk of junk with two dead humans in it. You think this is a play-it-loose situation?"

"They can handle it," Blay said under his breath. "The two of them are tight."

"And with you they're even stronger. I'm just going to dematerialize home."

In the stretch of silence that followed, the straight line that ran from Blay's ass up to the base of his skull was the equivalent of a middle finger. Not to the Brother, though.

Qhuinn knew exactly who it was for.

Things moved fast from then on, the SUV getting secured, Tohr departing, and John hopping behind the wheel of the flatbed. Meanwhile, Qhuinn went around to the truck's passenger-side door, cranked it open, and stood to the side, waiting.

Like a gentlemale might, he supposed.

Blay came over, stalking through the snow. His face was like the landscape: cold, shut down, inhospitable.

"After you," the guy muttered, taking out a pack of cigarettes and an elegant gold lighter.

Qhuinn ducked his head briefly in a nod, then shuffled inside, sliding over the bench seat until his shoulder brushed John's.

Blay got in last, slammed the door, and cracked the window, putting the lit end of his coffin nail right at the opening to keep the smell down.

The flatbed did all of the talking for a good five miles or so.

Sitting in between what used to be his two best friends, Qhuinn stared out the windshield and counted the seconds between the intermittent swipes of the wipers . . . three, two . . . one . . . up-and-down. And . . . three, two . . . one . . . up-and-down.

There was barely enough snow loose in the air to require the effort—

"I'm sorry," he blurted.

Silence. Except for the growl of the engine in front of them and the occasional clang of a chain in back when they hit a bump.

Qhuinn glanced over, and what do you know, Blay looked like he was chewing on metal.

"Are you talking to me?" the guy said gruffly.

"Yeah. I am."

"You have nothing to apologize for." Blay stabbed the cigarette out in the dashboard's ashtray. And lit another. "Will you *please* stop staring at me."

"I just . . ." Qhuinn put a hand through his hair and gave the shit a yank. "I don't . . . I . . . I don't know what to say about Layla—"

Blay's head snapped around. "What you do with your life has nothing to do with me—"

"That's not true," Qhuinn said quietly. "I—"

"Not true?"

"Blay, listen, Layla and I—"

"What makes you think I want to hear one word about you and her?"

"I just thought that you might need some . . . I don't know, context or something."

Blay simply stared at him for a moment. "And why exactly do you think I'd want 'context.'"

"Because . . . I thought you might find it . . . like, upsetting. Or something."

"And why would that be?"

Qhuinn couldn't believe the guy wanted him to say it out loud. Much less in front of someone else, even John. "Well, because of, you know."

Blay leaned in, his upper lip peeling back from his fangs. "Just so we're clear, your cousin is giving me what I need. All day long. Every day. You and me?" He motioned back and forth between them with the cigarette. "We work together. That's it. So I want you to do us both a favor before you think I 'need' to know something. Ask yourself, 'If I were flipping burgers at McDonald's, would I be telling the fucking fry guy this?' If the answer is no, then shut the hell up."

Qhuinn refocused on the windshield. And considered putting his face through it. "John, pull over."

The fighter glanced across. Then started shaking his head.

"John, pull the fuck over. Or I'll do it for you."

Qhuinn was vaguely aware that his chest was pumping up and down and that his hands had become fists.

"Pull the fuck over!" he roared as he punched the dashboard hard enough to send one of the vents flying.

The flatbed shot to the side of the road and the brakes squealed as their velocity slowed. But Qhuinn was already out of there. Dematerializing, he escaped through that crack in the window, along with Blay's frustrated exhale.

Almost immediately, he re-formed at the side of the road, unable to keep himself in his molecular state because his emotions were running way too high for that. Putting one shitkicker in front of the other, he trudged through the snow, his need to ambulate drowning out everything, including the ringing pain in both sets of knuckles.

In the back of his head, something about the stretch of road registered, but there was too much noise in his skull for specifics to break through.

No idea where he was going.

Man, it was cold.

Sitting in the flatbed, Blay focused on the lit end of his cigarette, the little orange glow going back and forth like a guitar string.

Guess his hand was shaking.

The whistle that went off next to him was John's way of trying to get his attention, but he ignored it. Which got him slapped in the arm.

This is a really bad stretch for him, John signed.

"You're kidding me, right?" Blay muttered. "You're absolutely fucking kidding me. He's always wanted a conventional mating, and he's knocked up a Chosen—I'd say this is a great—"

No, here, right here. John pointed out to the asphalt. *Here.*

Blay shifted his eyes to the windshield only because he was too tired to argue. Out in front of the flatbed, the headlights illuminated everything, the snow-covered landscape blindingly white, the figure walking at the side of the road like a shadow thrown.

Red drops of blood marked the path of the footprints.

Qhuinn's hands were bleeding from when he'd bashed up the dash—

Abruptly, Blay frowned. Sat up a little higher.

Like puzzle pieces sinking into their proper slots, the random details about where they were, from the bend in the road, to the trees, to the stone wall beside them, came together and completed a picture.

"Oh, shit." Blay banged his head back against the rest. Closing his eyes briefly, he wanted to find another solution to this, anything other than him going out there.

He came up with a big, fat *nada.*

As he pushed open the door, the cold rushed into the warm interior of the truck cab. He didn't say anything to John. No reason to. Things like going out into a snowfall after someone were self-explanatory.

Taking a deep drag, he clomped through the accumulation. The road had been plowed earlier, but that was a much-earlier kind of thing.

Which meant he probably had to act fast.

Here in this rich part of town, where the tax base was as broad as the rolling lawns, you'd better believe that another one of those house-size yellow muni plows was going to come by right before dawn.

No need to play this out in front of humans. Especially with the pair of leaking, dead-and-gones in the Hummer.

"Qhuinn," he said roughly. "Qhuinn, stop."

He didn't yell. Didn't have the energy. This . . . thing, whatever it was between them, had gotten exhausting long ago—and this current side-of-the-road showdown was just one more episode he didn't have the strength for.

"Qhuinn. Seriously."

At least the guy slowed down a little. And with any luck he was so pissed off, he wouldn't put all the clues to their location together.

Jesus Christ, what were the chances, Blay thought as he glanced around. It was right about in this next half mile or so where that Honor Guard had done their business—and Qhuinn had nearly died from the beating.

God, Blay remembered tooling up that night, a different set of headlights picking out a dark figure, this time bleeding on the ground.

Shaking himself, he gave the name game one more shot. "Qhuinn."

The guy stopped, his shitkickers planting in the snow and going no farther. He didn't turn around, however.

Blay motioned for John to kill the headlights, and a second later all he had to deal with was the subtle orange glow of the truck's parking lights.

Qhuinn put his hands on his hips and looked up to the sky, his head tilting back, his breath escaping upward in a cloud of condensation.

"Come back and get in the flatbed." Blay took another drag and released the smoke. "We need to keep moving—"

"I know how much Saxton means to you," Qhuinn said gruffly. "I get that. I really do."

Blay forced himself to say, "Good."

"I guess . . . hearing it out loud is still a shock."

Blay frowned in the dim light. "I don't understand."

"I know you don't. And that's my fault. All of this . . . is my fault." Qhuinn glanced over his shoulder, his strong, hard face set grimly. "I just don't want you to think I'm in love with her. That's all."

Blay went to take a hit off his Dunhill, but didn't have enough draw in his lungs. "I'm . . . sorry—I don't get . . . why . . ."

Well, that was an awesome reply.

"I'm not in love with her. She's not in love with me. We are not sleeping together."

Blay laughed harshly. "Bullshit."

"Dead serious. I serviced her in her needing because I want a young, and so does she, and it began and ended there."

Blay closed his eyes as the wound in his chest got ripped open all over again. "Qhuinn, come on. You've been with her this whole last year. I've seen you—everyone's seen you two—"

"I took her virginity four nights ago. No one had been with her before that, including myself."

Oh, there was a picture he needed in his head.

"I am not in love with her. She is not in love with me. We are not sleeping together."

Blay couldn't hold still any longer, so he paced around, the snow packing under his boots. And then from out of nowhere, the voice of the Church Lady from *SNL* came into his head: *Well, isn't that speeeeeeeeeecial.*

"I'm not with anybody," Qhuinn said.

Blay laughed again with an edge. "As in a relationship? Of course not. But do not expect me to believe that you're spending your off time crocheting doilies and alphabetizing a spice rack with that female."

"I haven't had sex in almost a year."

That stopped him cold.

God, where the fuck was all the air in this part of the universe?

"Bullshit," Blay countered in a cracked voice. "You were with Layla—four nights ago. As you said."

In the silence that followed, the horrible truth raised its ugly-ass head again, the pain making it impossible for him to hide what he had so diligently been burying for the last few days.

"You were really with her," he said. "I watched the library chandelier going back and forth under your room."

Now Qhuinn was the one closing his eyes like he wanted to forget. "It was for a purpose."

"Listen . . ." Blay shook his head. "I'm really not clear on why you're telling me all this. I meant what I said—I don't need any explanation about what you do with your life. You and I . . . we grew up together, and that's it. Yeah, we shared a lot of stuff back then, and we were there for each other when it mattered. But neither one of us can fit into the clothes we used to wear, and this relationship between us is just the same. It doesn't fit in our lives any longer. We don't . . . fit anymore. And listen, I didn't mean to get pissy in the truck, but I think you need to be clear on this. You and I? We have a past. That's it. That's . . . all we'll ever have."

Qhuinn looked away, his face once again in the shadows.

Blay forced himself to keep talking. "I know this . . . Layla thing . . . is a big deal to you. Or I'm guessing it is—how could it not be, if she's pregnant. For me? I honestly wish you both well. But you don't owe me any explanations—and what's more, I don't require them. I've moved on from childish crushes—and that's what I had for you. Back then, it was just an infatuation, Qhuinn. So please take care of your female, and don't worry that I'm slitting my wrists because you've found someone to love. As I have."

"I told you. I'm not in love with her."

Wait for it, Blay thought to himself. Because it's coming.

This was classic Qhuinn, right here.

The male was incredible in the field. And loyal to the point of psychosis. And smart. And sexual to distraction. And a hundred thousand other things that Blay had to admit nobody else came close to. But he had one serious defect, and it wasn't his eye color.

He couldn't handle emotion.

At all.

Qhuinn had always run from anything deep—even if he didn't move. He could sit right in front of you and nod and talk, but when the emotions got strong for him, he would leave the inside of his skin. Just check right out. And if you tried to force him to confront them?

Well, that wasn't possible. No one forced Qhuinn to do anything.

And yeah, sure, there were a lot of good reasons for the way he was. His family treating him like a curse. The *glymera* looking down on him. Him having been rootless all his life. But whatever the stressors, at the end of the day, the male was going to run from anything that was too complicated, or required something from him.

Probably the only thing that could change that was a young.

So no matter what he said now, there was no doubt he was in love with Layla, but having been through the needing with her, and now waiting for the results, he was losing his mind from worry and pulling away from her.

And therefore standing here at the side of the road, blabbering about things that made no damned sense.

"I wish you both the very best," Blay said, his heart hammering in his chest. "I honestly do. I really hope this works out well for both of you."

In the tense quiet, Blay pulled himself out of the hole he'd once again fallen into, clawing his way back to the surface, away from the painful, burning agony at the center of his soul.

"Now, can we get in the truck and finish our job?" he said evenly.

Qhuinn's hands lifted briefly to his face. Then he ducked his head, shoved those bleeding knuckles into the pockets of his leathers, and started back for the flatbed.

"Yeah. Let's do that."

SIX

"Oh, my God, I'm going to come—I'm going to come—"

Farther south, in downtown Caldwell, in the parking lot behind the Iron Mask, Trez Latimer was happy to hear the newsflash—and not surprised. But nobody else in the tricounty area needed the update.

As he worked himself in and out of the very willing participant underneath his body, he shut her up by kissing her hard, his tongue entering that hot mouth, all that unnecessary commentary getting cut off.

The car they were in was cramped and smelled like the woman's perfume: sweet and spicy and cheap—shit, next time he was going to pick a volunteer with an SUV or, better yet, a Mercedes S550 with some proper space in the back.

Clearly, this Nissan product had not been built to house two seventy-five fucking the brains out of a half-naked dental assistant. Or had she been a paralegal?

He couldn't remember.

And he had more immediate issues to worry about. With an abrupt shift, he broke off the liplock because the closer he got to his own release, the farther his fangs extended from his upper jaw—and he didn't want to nick her by mistake: The taste of fresh blood would pitch him right over another more dangerous kind of edge, and he wasn't sure that feeding from her was a good idea—

Scratch that.

It was a bad idea. And not because she was just a human.

Someone was watching them.

Lifting his head, he looked out of the backseat window. As a Shadow, his eyes were three to four times more perceptive than those of a normal vampire, and he was easily able to penetrate the darkness.

Yup, someone was popcorn-and-Milk-Dudding it from over on the left by the staff entrance.

Time to wrap this up.

Immediately he took control, reaching in between their bodies, finding the woman's sex, and teasing her up as he continued to penetrate her, making her come so hard she jacked her head back and slammed it into the door.

No orgasm for him.

But whatever. Somebody loitering around took this fun-and-games quickie into different territory, and that meant he had to cut the crap. Even if he didn't get off.

He had a number of enemies thanks to his various associations.

And then there were . . . complications . . . that were all his own.

"Oh, my fucking *God*—"

Going by the explosive exhale, all that torquing, and those pulses that gripped Trez's thick cock, the dental assistant–paralegal–vet tech was having a rocking good time. He, however, had already pulled out of this nonsense mentally and might as well have been stalking out of the car, gunning for that—

It was a female. Yeah, whoever it was was definitely of feminine derivation—

Trez frowned as he realized who it was.

Shit.

Then again, at least it wasn't a *lesser*. A *symphath*. A drug dealer he needed to take care of. A rival pimp with an opinion. A vampire who was out of line. iAm, his brother—

But nah. Just a harmless woman, and too bad there was no going back to his slice of bliss. Mood was ruined.

The dental assistant/paralegal/vet tech/hairdresser was panting like

she'd tried to put a fireman hold on a piano. "That was . . . amazing . . .
that . . . was . . . ."

Trez pulled out and tucked his cock back behind his fly. Chances
were good he was going to have a case of neon balls in a half hour, but
he'd deal with that when it came.

"You're incredible. You're the most incredible—"

Trez let the barrage of silly words fall over him. "You, too, baby
girl."

He kissed her to make it seem like he cared—and he did, in a way.
These human women he used mattered in the sense that they were living beings, worthy of respect and kindness by the simple virtue of their
beating hearts. For a small while they let him use their bodies, and
sometimes their veins, and he appreciated these gifts, which were always given willingly, and sometimes more than once.

And the latter was the problem that was standing over there.

Zipping up, Trez carefully maneuvered his big body around so he
didn't crush his ten-minute partner or give himself a craniotomy on
the roof of the car.

Baby girl didn't seem to want to move, however. She just lay there
like a throw pillow against the seats, her legs still spread, her sex still
ready, her breasts still out and about and defying gravity like two can-
taloupes glued onto her rib cage.

Must be under the muscle, he thought.

"Let's get you dressed," he suggested, pulling the halves of her lace-
up bustier together.

"You were so fantastic. . . ."

She was like jelly—well, except for the hard-as-a-rock fake
boobs—all malleable and agreeable, but utterly unhelpful as he put her
back together, sat her up, and smoothed her extensions.

"This was fun, baby girl," he murmured, and he meant it.

"Can I see you again?"

"Maybe." He smiled at her tightly so that his fangs didn't show.
"I'm around."

She purred like a cat at that, and then proceeded to recite her
number, which he didn't bother to memorize.

The sad truth about women like her was that they were a dime a
dozen: In this city of several million, there had to be a couple hundred
thousand twenty-somethings with tight asses and loose legs who were

looking for a good time. In fact, they were all just variations of the same person, which was why he needed to keep them fresh.

With so much in common, a revolving door of new supply was required to keep him interested.

Trez was out of the car a minute and a half later, and he didn't bother scrubbing her memories. As a Shadow, he had many mind tricks he could call upon, but he'd stopped bothering with that years ago. Not worth the effort—and occasionally he did like a repeat.

Quick check of the watch.

Damn it, he was already going to be late getting over to iAm's—but he clearly had to deal with the problem by the back door before he closed up shop.

As he went over and stopped in front of the woman, she tilted her chin up and put one hand on her hip. This particular version of ready-and-willing had blond hair extensions and liked hot pants as opposed to skirts—so she looked ridiculous in the cold, with her fluffy pink Patagonia parka and her bare-ass legs in the breeze.

Kind of like a Sno Ball on two toothpicks.

"Getting busy?" she demanded. She was obviously trying to keep cool, but given the way her stiletto was tapping, she was hot and bothered—and not in a good way.

"Hey, baby girl." He called them all that. "You having a good night?"

"No."

"Well, that's too bad. Listen, I'll see you around—"

The woman made the colossal mistake of grabbing his arm as he went by her, her nails sinking into his silk shirt and clamping onto his skin.

Trez's head snapped around, his eyes flaring. But at least he managed to catch himself before he bared his fangs.

"What the *hell* do you think you're doing?" she said, leaning into him.

"Trez!" someone barked.

Abruptly, his head of security's voice cut into his brain. And good thing. Shadows were a peaceable species by nature—provided they were not aggressed upon.

As Xhex rushed over, like she knew murder was not one hundred percent out of the realm of possibility, he ripped his arm free of that

hold, feeling five blazes of pain from the woman's nails. Locking down his fury, he stared into the woman's face. "Go on home now."

"You owe me an explanation—"

He shook his head. "I'm not your boyfriend, baby girl."

"Damn straight, he know how to treat a woman!"

"So go on home to him," Trez said grimly.

"What do you do, fuck a different girl every night of the week?"

"Yeah. And sometimes twice on Sundays." Shit, he should have scrubbed this one. When had he been with her? Two nights ago? Three? Too late now. "Go on home to your man."

"You make me sick! You fucking cocksucking motherfucker—"

As Xhex stepped in between them and started speaking in a low voice to the hysteric, Trez was more than happy to have the backup . . . because what do you know, the chick in the Nissan picked that exact moment to K-turn in the parking lot and drive right on over.

Putting her window down, she smiled like she was into being the other woman. "I'll see you soon, lover."

Cue the crying: Baby girl with the pink parka, the boyfriend and the attachment disorder burst into a weeping jag worthy of a grave site.

Annnnnnnnd naturally that was when iAm showed up.

As his brother's presence registered, Trez closed his eyes.

Great. Just fucking wonderful.

SEVEN

About ten blocks away from Trez's bad-to-worse night, Xcor was wiping the blade of his scythe off with a chamois cloth that was soft as a lamb's ear.

Across the alley, Throe was on his phone, talking in a low voice. He had been thus e'er since the third of the three *lessers* they'd found in this quadrant of the city had been discharged back to the Omega.

Xcor was not interested in any delay, cellular or otherwise. The rest of his Band of Bastards were elsewhere downtown, seeking out either or both of their two enemies—and he would prefer to be engaged thusly.

But biological needs must. Goddamn it.

Throe ended his call and looked over, his handsome face drawn in serious lines. "She is willing."

"How kind of her." Xcor sheathed his scythe and put his cleaning cloth away. "I am, however, less interested in her acquiescence than in the issue of whether she is able."

"She is."

"And how do we know this?"

Throe cleared his throat and glanced away. "I went to her last night and availed myself."

Xcor smiled coldly. So that explained his soldier's absence—and the reason for the departure was a relief. He had feared that the other male had . . .

"And how ever was she."

"She was viable."

"Did you sample all her charms?"

The gentlemale, who had once been a highbrow member of the *glymera*, but was now useful, cleared his throat. "I, ah . . . yes."

"And how were they." When there was no answer, Xcor tracked through the black-stained snow, closing in on his second in command. "How was she, Throe? Wet and willing?"

The male's flush grew deeper on his perfectly handsome face. "She was adequate."

"How many times did you have her?"

"Several."

"And in varying positions, I hope?" When there was only a stiff nod, Xcor relented. "Well, you have then faithfully discharged your duty to your fellow soldiers. I'm quite certain that the others shall want to partake of both vein and sex as well."

In the awkward beat of silence that followed, Xcor would never have admitted it to anyone, but he'd pressed for details not to deliberately goad his subordinate . . . but because he was glad Throe had lain with the female. He wanted distance between the male and what had happened back in the fall. He wanted calendars full of years, and countless females, and rivers of other females' blood. . . .

"There is but one stipulation," Throe said.

Xcor thinned his mouth. As the female in question had not seen him yet, it couldn't be more cash—besides, he did not need to feed as of now. Thanks to . . . "And that is."

"It must be done at her abode. At first night tomorrow."

"Ah." Xcor smiled coldly. " 'Tis a trap then."

"The Brotherhood does not know who made the inquiry."

"You identified six males, did you not."

"I used not our names."

"No matter." Xcor glanced around the alley, his senses reaching out, searching for *lesser* or Brother. "I do not underestimate the king's reach. Nor should you."

Indeed, his own ambitions had pitted them all against a foe of worth. The assassination attempt on Wrath's life back in the autumn had been his open declaration of war, and as expected, there had been a predictable fallout: The Brotherhood had found his Band of Bastards' lair, infiltrated it, and left with the rifle pack that contained the weapon that had been used to put a bullet into the Blind King's throat.

Undoubtedly, they were going for proof.

The question was, of what? He did not know as of yet whether the king lived or had died, and neither did the Council, from what he understood. In fact, the *glymera* knew not that the attempt had even occurred.

Had Wrath survived? Or had he been killed and the Brotherhood was at the moment busy trying to fill the vacancy? The Old Law was very clear about the rules of succession—provided the king had off-spring, which he did not. So it would be his next nearest kin—assuming there were any.

Xcor wanted to know, but he made no inquiries. All he could do was wait until word presented itself—and in the meantime, he and his soldiers kept killing *lessers*, and he continued to shore up his power base within the *glymera*. At least both of those endeavors were going well. Every night, they stabbed slayers back to the Omega. And his limp-wristed contact on the Council, the not-particularly-venerable Elan, son of Larex, was proving quite naive and malleable—two characteristics very useful in a disposable tool.

Xcor was, however, growing tired of the information void. And indeed, this business with that female Throe had found was necessary but fraught with danger. A female capable of selling her veins and her sex to multiple users was certainly able to trade information for cash—and though Throe had kept their identities quiet, the number of them had been given. The Brotherhood must have appropriately guessed that none of the Band of Bastards were mated, and that sooner or later, in this new land, they would require what they had had a sufficiency of in the Old Country.

Mayhap this female was put up by the king and his private guard.

Well, they would find out on the morrow. Ambushes were easily set, and there was nary a more vulnerable moment than when a hungry male was at the throat and between the legs of a female. Yet it was time. His soldiers were willing to fight, but their faces were drawn, their eyes sunken, their skin stretched too tightly across their cheeks. Human

blood, that weak substitute, was not providing enough strength, and his bastards had been living off of it for too long. Back in the Old Country, there had been enough females to be of service when needs must. But e'er since they had come to the New World, they had had to make do.

If this was a trap, he was willing to fight the Brothers. Then again, he had been properly serviced—

Dearest Virgin Scribe, he could not think of that.

Xcor cleared his throat as pain in his chest made it hard to swallow. "Tell the female, first darkness is too early. We shall come instead at midnight unto her. And arrange for human feedings as soon as the night falls. If the Brothers are there, we shall engage with them from a position of relative strength."

Throe's eyebrows rose as if he were impressed with Xcor's thinking. "Aye. I shall do just that."

Xcor nodded and looked away.

In the silence, the events of the autumn crowded in between them, cooling the frigid December air even further.

That sacred Chosen was always with them both.

"The daylight is coming fast upon us," Throe said in his perfect accent. "It is time to depart."

Xcor glanced over to the east. The predawn glow had yet to arrive, but his second in command was correct. Soon . . . very soon . . . the deadly light of the sun would rain down, and no matter that it was at its weakest, with the winter solstice so recently passed.

"Call the soldiers off the field," Xcor said. "And meet them at base."

Throe typed in some combination of letters into a message that Xcor would not have been able to read. And then the soldier put his phone away with a frown.

"Are you not coming back?" Throe asked.

"Go."

There was a long pause. And then the other soldier said softly, "Wither thou goest?"

In that moment, Xcor thought of each of his fighters. Zypher, the sexual conqueror. Balthazar, the thief. Syphon, the assassin. And the other one who had no name, and too many sins to count. So he was referred to as Syn.

Then he considered fair, loyal Throe, his second in command.

Perfectly reared, impeccably blooded Throe.

Handsome, comely Throe.

"Go now," he told the male.

"And what of you?"

"Go."

Throe hesitated, and in the pause, that night when Xcor had nearly died came back to them both. How could it not have?

"As you wish."

His soldier dematerialized, leaving Xcor to stand against the wind alone. When he was sure he had been left, he sent his molecules likewise unto the cold gusts, venturing forth to the north, to a meadow that was covered in snow. Taking form, he stood at the base of its gentle hill, staring up at the beautiful tree standing proud and lovely at the apex.

He thought of the soft rise of a female's breast, of her elegant collarbones, of the most sublime column of a pale neck—

As the wind buffeted his back, he closed his eyes and stepped forward, drawn to return to the spot where he had met his *pyrocant*.

Where was his Chosen?

Did she still live? Had the Brotherhood taken her life for her kind, generous, unknown gift to the enemy of her king?

Xcor knew he would have died without her blood. Gravely injured during the attempt on Wrath's life, he had been on the verge of expiration when Throe had take him out to this field and summoned the Chosen and the deed had been done.

Throe had engineered it all. And, in the process, embedded a curse within Xcor's dark heart.

His ambitions remained as they had been: He intended to wrestle the throne from the Blind King and reign o'er the vampires. There was, however, a critical weakness that dogged him.

That female.

She had been wrongly drawn into the conflict among daggerhanded males, an innocent who had been manipulated and then used.

He sorely worried over her welfare.

Indeed, he had but one regret in his lifetime of evil deeds. If he had not sent Throe into the arms of the Brotherhood, his second in command would not have crossed her path and fed from her himself. And except for that intersection, Throe would not have then later called upon her service, and she would not have come unto them in

that field . . . and Xcor would never have looked into those compassionate eyes.

And lost a part of himself.

He was but a filthy, malformed, sireless cur, a traitor of the order and protection she rightfully lived under. He had not deserved her gift.

And neither had Throe—and not because he had fallen from his previous high station within the *glymera*.

No mortal male was deserving.

Coming to a stop under the tree, Xcor stared at the spot where he had lain sprawled before her . . . where she had knelt over him and scored her wrist, and he had opened his mouth to receive the power that only she could give him.

There had been a moment when their eyes had met and time had stopped . . . and then she had slowly lowered her wrist to his mouth.

Oh, that too-brief contact.

He had been convinced she was but an apparition of his errant mind, but as Throe had driven him back to the lair, it had come upon his consciousness that she was real. Very real.

Weeks had passed. And then one evening, out in the city, he had sensed her, and followed the echo of her blood in his veins to see her.

In those intervening minutes and hours, she had found out the truth about him: She had looked into the darkness, directly at him, and her distress had been evident.

Thereafter, his lair had been infiltrated. Likely because of her direction.

With a gust of wind, snow started to fall again, the snowflakes thickening in the air, swirling around, getting into his eyes.

Where was she now?

What had they done with her?

Off to the east, the glow of the sunrise began to gather in spite of the cloud cover, and his eyes burned—so he was careful to keep them trained on the peach harbinger of daylight, just for the pain.

He had never before been pulled asunder by his emotions like this. All his life he had been solely trained in survival—first through his years in the war camp, and then during his aeons under the Bloodletter, and now in this current era as head of his band of fighters.

But she had cleaved him, creating a vital fissure.

Sure as she had given him his life, she had taken a part of it, and he knew not what to do.

Mayhap he would just stand here and allow himself to be inciner-ated. It seemed an easier plight than what he was living under the now. . . .

What fate had befallen her?

He had to know.

It was as critical as his quest for the throne.

EIGHT

"So where did you dump the bodies?" V demanded as he strode out of the training center's rear exit.

As Qhuinn waited for John and Blay to get out of the flatbed, he let one of them answer V's question. He was too done to bother—matter of fact, as he glanced out the windshield and took a gander at the facility's underground parking lot, he considered just stretching out across the truck's front seat and going to sleep.

Too fucking tired to bother with anything else.

In the end, though, he followed John's lead and shifted his sorry ass out the driver's side door. He had to go check on Layla, and that wasn't going to happen from here.

Roadside confron notwithstanding, at least he and John and Blay had worked well together on the way home. About ten miles before the cutoff to the Brotherhood compound, they had pulled off onto a lumbering road, stripped the two dead men, and launched the bodies into a natural sinkhole that had no bottom that anyone could see. Then it was a case of backtrack, K-turn out on the road, and ghost away, allowing the snow, which had started to fall in earnest once again, to cover their tracks, as well as the various leaks that had left a trail of bright red blood. By noontime, assuming the accumulation estimates were correct, it would be as if nothing had happened at all.

A perfect snow job. Har-har.

He supposed he should feel bad for the dead dudes' families—no one was ever going to find those remains. But anecdotal evidence suggested the two guys had lived on the fringes, and not because they were hippies: guns, knives, a switchblade, weed, and some X had been found in their various pockets. And God only knew what was in those backpacks.

Violent lives tended to come to violent ends.

"—son of a bitch," V was saying as he walked around the Hummer on its flatbed pedestal. "What the fuck did they run into? A cement barricade?"

John signed something, and V looked over sharply at Qhuinn. "What the hell were you thinking? You could have been killed."

Qhuinn thumped his own chest. "Still beating."

"Dumb-ass." But the Brother smiled, flashing sharp fangs. "Meh, I would have done the same thing."

Out of the corner of his eye, Qhuinn noted that Blay was quietly and unobtrusively drifting toward the door that opened into the facility. He was going to disappear in another second and a half, finished with the drama that had once again been dropped at his feet.

Qhuinn felt a sudden, striking urge to follow the fighter into the hall and away from prying eyes. But like he needed to take another go at—

Your cousin is giving me what I need. All day. Every day.

Oh, Jesus, he was going to throw up.

"So any more personal effects?"

Qhuinn snapped out of the bullshit and got his useful on. "I'll get 'em."

Hopping up onto the flatbed, he forced open the crumpled rear door of the Hummer and squeezed through a twelve-inch gap to the backseat. It felt good to jam his body into places it didn't belong and didn't fit—gave his mind something to do, and the little ouchies from his injuries were another fantastic diversion.

The two backpacks had been bounced around pretty damn good. He found the one they'd seen first in the wheel well behind the passenger's seat, and the other was up in front on top of the brake and the accelerator. Weird luggage for those two as far as he could tell; the pedestrian vibe didn't go with all the other kinds of urban tuff guy that the stiffs had been sporting.

Way more middle school than middleman in the drug trade.

Unless they needed a place to put their meth lab merit badges or some shit.

As Qhuinn crabbed his way back into the rear seat, he made an abrupt decision not to go out the way he came in. Twisting himself around, he lay out on the ruined leather and brought his knees to his chest. With a sharp inhale, he punched his shitkickers into the other side door and blew it open, the metal hinges ripping free with a scream, the panel bouncing with a crash on the concrete.

Satisfying.

While the sounds echoed through the parking garage, V lit one of his hand-rolleds and leaned into the hole Qhuinn had just made. "You know they have door handles for that, true?"

Qhuinn sat up—and realized he'd just kicked open the only side that hadn't been wrecked.

Well, if that wasn't a metaphor for his whole fucking life at this point.

Throwing the pair of packs out, he launched himself free, landing hard as John caught the payload and started to unzip.

Crap. Blay had left. The door into the training center was just closing.

Cursing under his breath, he muttered, "Any cell phones still gotta be somewhere inside—even though the windows are shattered, the glass is still intact, so there should have been no fly-out."

"Well, well, well . . ." the Brother said on the exhale.

Qhuinn frowned and looked over at what John had found. What the . . . hell . . . "Are you kidding me?"

His best friend had just pulled out a ceramic jar—a cheapo one, like what you'd get from the housewares department at Target. And what do you know. The other guy had packed one, too.

What were the chances . . . ?

"We need to find those phones," Qhuinn muttered, jumping up onto the flatbed again. "Anyone got a flashlight?"

Vishous took off his lead-lined leather glove and held up his glowing hand. "Right 'chere."

As the Brother hopped up on the thin edge of the bed, Qhuinn went into a tuck and got back in the Hummer's rear compartment. "Don't hit me with that thing, will ya, V?"

"It'd be a spanking you'd never forget, I promise you."

Man, that hand was handy. As V put it inside, the whole interior was lit up bright as day, all the carnage inside throwing sharp, dark shadows. Crawling around, Qhuinn reached under seats, patting with his palms, stretching into corners. The smell was god-awful, a nasty combination of gas, burned plastic, and fresh blood—and every time he put a hand down, it fluffed up the residue from the air bags' powder.

But it was worth all the pseudo yoga positions.

He emerged with a pair of iPhones.

"I hate these things," V muttered as he put his glove back on and took the matched set.

Returning to the relatively fresh air, Qhuinn caught his breath and cracked his neck, then jumped down again. There was some kind of conversating at that point, and he nodded a couple of times like he knew what the fuck was being said.

"Listen, you mind if I take a T.O. and check in for a sec," he interjected.

V's diamond eyes narrowed. "With who?"

Right on cue, John jumped in, asking about the Hummer and its rehab plan—like somebody waving a torch in front of a T. rex to redirect it. As V started talking about the SUV's future as lawn sculpture, Qhuinn nearly blew a kiss at his buddy.

No one knew about Layla except for John and Blay—and things needed to stay that way during this early period.

As Qhuinn was John's *ahstrux nohtrum*, he couldn't go far—and he didn't. He eased on over to the door Blay had put to good use and got out his phone. As he dialed one of the house extensions and waited through the rings, he stared at his ruined vehicle.

He could remember the night he got the damn thing. Although his parents had had money, they hadn't felt a great burning need to provide for him as they had for his brother and sister. Before his transition, he'd gotten by selling red smoke on the sly, but he hadn't done a huge amount of traffic—just enough to close the gap of his paltry allowance, and keep from mooching off Blay all the time.

The cash crunch had ended as soon as he'd been promoted to John's personal guard. His new job had come with a serious salary— seventy-five grand a year. And considering he didn't pay taxes to the bullshit human government, and his room and board were paid for, he had a lot of green leftover.

The Hummer had been his first big purchase. He'd done his research on the Internet, but the truth was, he'd already known what he wanted. Fritz had gone out and done the negotiating and the official purchasing . . . and that first time Qhuinn had gotten behind the wheel, cranked the key, and felt the rumble under the hood, he'd nearly teared up like a pussy.

Now it was ruined: He was hardly a mechanic, but the structural damage was so severe, it just made no sense to save it—

"Hello?"

The sound of Layla's voice snapped him back to attention. "Hey. I'm just back. How you feeling?"

The precise enunciation that came back at him reminded him of his parents, every word perfectly pronounced and chosen with care. "I am well, thank you very much. I have rested and watched television, as you suggested. They had a *Million Dollar Listing* marathon."

"What the hell is that?"

"A show where they sell houses in Los Angeles—I thought for a little bit that it was fiction, but it turns out it's a reality show? I thought they made it all up. Madison has great hair—and I like Josh Flagg. He's rather shrewd and very kind to his grandmother."

He asked her a couple more questions, like what had she eaten and had she taken a nap, just to keep her talking—because in between the syllables, he was looking for clues of discomfort or worry.

"So you're okay," he said.

"Yes, and before you ask, I have already requested that Fritz bring me up Last Meal. And yes, I will eat all my roast beef."

He frowned, not wanting her to feel caged. "Listen, it's not just for the young's sake. It's also for yours. I want you to be well, you know?"

Her voice dropped a little. "You have always been thus. Even before we . . . yes, you have only ever wanted the best for me."

Focusing on the car door he'd busted, he thought of how good it had felt to kick the shit out of something. "Well, my plan is to hit the gym for a while. I'll check on you again before I crash, 'kay?"

"All right. Be well."

"You, too."

As he hung up, he realized V had stopped talking and was looking over at him like maybe something was way off—hair on fire, pants around the ankles, eyebrows shaved.

"You got yourself a female there, Qhuinn?" the Brother drawled.

Qhuinn looked around for a life raft, and got a whole lot of nothing. "Ah . . ."

V exhaled over his shoulder and came across. "Whatever. I'm going to go work on these phones. And you need to buy yourself another vehicle—anything as long as it's not a Prius. Later."

When John and he were alone, it was pretty clear the guy was warming up to say something about the showdown at the side of the road.

"I don't want to hear it, John. I just don't have the strength right now."

Shit, John signed.

"That about covers it, my man. You heading up to the house?"

Under the strict interpretation of the *ahstrux nohtrum* job, Qhuinn needed to be with John twenty-four/seven. But the king had given them a dispensation if they were within the confines of the compound. Otherwise Qhuinn would have been learning way too much about his buddy and Xhex.

And John would have had to witness him and Layla . . . um, yeah.

When John nodded, Qhuinn opened the door and held it wide. "After you."

He refused to look his friend in the face as the fighter passed, just couldn't do it. Because he knew exactly what was on the guy's mind—and he had no interest in talking about what had happened on that stretch of road he'd walked down before. Not the crap from tonight. Not the crap from . . . all those nights ago thanks to the Honor Guard.

He was finished with chatting it up.

Shit never helped anyone over nuthin'.

Saxton, son of Tyhm, closed the final Book of Oral History and could only stare at the fine-grain leather cover with its gold-embossed detailing.

The last one.

He couldn't believe it. How long had this research been going on? Three months? Four months? How could it be over?

A quick visual survey of the Brotherhood's library, with its hundreds and hundreds of volumes of law, discourse, and royal decrees . . . and he thought, yes, indeed, it had taken months and months to go through them all. And now, with the digging complete, the notations

made, and the legal path for what the king wanted to accomplish carved out, there should have been a sense of accomplishment.

Instead, he felt dread.

In his training and practice as a lawyer, he had tackled sticky problems before—especially after he had come here to this vast house and begun to function as the Blind King's personal solicitor: The Old Laws were very convoluted, archaic not just in their wording, but in their very content—and the ruler of the vampire race was not at all like that. Wrath's thinking was both straightforward and revolutionary, and when it came to his rule, the past and the future did not often coexist without a good deal of reframing—of the Old Laws, that was.

This was on a whole different level, however.

Wrath, as sovereign, could do fairly much what he wanted—provided the appropriate precedents were identified, recast, and recorded. After all, the king was the living, breathing law, a physical manifestation of the order necessary for a civilized society. The problem was, tradition didn't happen by accident; it was the result of generations upon generations living and making choices based on a certain set of rules that was accepted by the public. Progressive thinkers trying to lead entrenched, conservative societies in new directions tended to run into problems.

And this . . . further alteration of the way things were done? In the current political environment, where Wrath's leadership was already being challenged—

"You're deep in thought."

At the sound of Blay's voice, Saxton jumped and nearly lost his Montblanc over his shoulder.

Immediately, Blay reached forward as if to calm what had been ruffled. "Oh, I'm sorry—"

"No, it's all right, I—" Saxton frowned as he regarded the soldier's wet and bloodied clothing. "Dearest Virgin Scribe . . . what happened tonight?"

Evidently in lieu of answering, Blay headed over for the bar on the antique bombé chest in the corner. As he took his time choosing between the sherry and a Dubonnet, it was rather clear he was preparing a sequence of words in his head.

Which meant it had to do with Qhuinn.

In fact, Blay cared for neither sherry nor Dubonnet. And sure enough, he helped himself to a port.

Saxton eased back in his chair and looked upward at the chandelier that hung so far above the floor. The fixture was a stunning specimen from Baccarat, made in the middle nineteenth century, with all of the leaded-glass crystals and careful workmanship one would expect.

He recalled it swinging from side to side subtly, the rainbow refractions of light twinkling all around the room.

How many nights ago had that been? How long since Qhuinn had serviced that Chosen directly above this room?

Nothing had been the same since.

"A broken-down car." Blay took a long swallow. "Just mechanical issues."

Is that why your leathers are wet, and there is blood down the front of your shirt? Saxton wondered.

And yet he kept the demand to himself.

He had become used to keeping things to himself.

Silence.

Blay finished his port and poured another with the kind of alacrity typically reserved for drunkards. Which he was not. "And . . . you?" the male said. "How's your work?"

"I'm finished. Well, nearly so."

Blay's blue eyes shot over. "Really? I thought you were going to be at this forever."

Saxton traced that face he knew so well. That stare he'd looked into for what seemed like a lifetime. Those lips he had spent hours locked onto.

The crushing sense of sadness he felt was as undeniable as the attraction that had brought him to this house, his job, his new life.

"So did I," he said after a moment. "I, too . . . thought it would last far longer than it did."

Blay stared down into his glass. "It's been how long since you started?"

"I don't . . . I can't remember." Saxton put a hand up and rubbed the bridge of his nose. "It does not matter."

More silence. In which Saxton was willing to bet the very breath in his lungs that Blaylock's mind had retreated to the other male, the one he loved like nobody else, his other half.

"So what was it?" Blay asked.

"I'm sorry?"

"Your project. All of this work." Blay motioned his glass around

elegantly. "These books you've been poring over. If you're finished, you can tell me what it was all about now, right?"

Saxton briefly considered telling the truth . . . that there had been other, equally pressing and important things that he had been quiet on. Things that he had thought he could live with, but which, over time, had proven too heavy a burden to carry.

"You shall find out soon enough."

Blay nodded, but it was with that vital distraction that he had had since the very beginning. Except then he said, "I'm glad you're here."

Saxton's brows rose. "Indeed . . . ?"

"Wrath should have a really good lawyer at his side."

Ah.

Saxton pushed his chair back and got to his feet. "Yes. How true."

It was with a strange feeling of fragility that he gathered his reams of papers. It certainly seemed, in this tense, sad moment, as though they were all that sustained him, these flimsy, yet powerful sheets with their countless words, each handwritten and crafted with care, contained neatly in their lines of text.

He did not know what he would do without them on a night like this.

He cleared his throat. "What plans have you for what little remains of the eve?"

As he waited for the reply, his heart pounded within his rib cage, because he, and he alone, seemed to realize that the assignment from the king wasn't the only thing that was ending tonight. Indeed, the baseless optimism that had sustained him in the initial stages of this love affair had decayed into a kind of desperation that had had him grasping at straws in an uncharacteristic way . . . but now, even that was gone.

It was ironic, really. Sex was but a transient physical connection—and there were many times in his life when that had been all he'd been looking for. Even with Blaylock, in the beginning, such had been the case. Over time, however, the heart had gotten involved, and that had left him where he was tonight.

At the end of the road.

". . . work out."

Saxton shook himself. "I'm sorry?"

"I'm going to work out for a while."

After you've had a decanter of port? Saxton thought.

For a moment, he was tempted to push for precise details on the night, the minute whos and whats and wheres—as if they might unlock some sort of relief. But he knew better. Blay was a compassionate, kind soul, and torture was something he did only as part of his job when it was necessary.

There would be no relief coming, not from any combination of sex, conversing, or silence.

Feeling as though he were bracing himself, Saxton buttoned his double-breasted blazer up and checked that his cravat was in place. A passby of his pectoral revealed his pocket square was precisely arranged, but the French cuffs of his shirt need a sharp tug, and he took care of that promptly.

"I must needs take a break before I prepare to speak with the king. My shoulders are killing me from having been at that desk all night."

"Have a bath. It might loosen things up?"

"Yes. A bath."

"I'll see you later, then," Blay said as he poured himself another and came over.

Their mouths met in a brief kiss, after which Blay turned and strode out into the foyer, disappearing up the stairs to go change.

Saxton watched him depart. Even moved forward a couple of steps so that he could see those shitkickers, as the Brothers called them, ascend the grand staircase one step at a time.

Part of him was screaming to follow the male up into their bedroom and help him out of those clothes. Emotions aside, the physical sizzle between the two of them had always been strong, and he felt like he wanted to exploit that now.

Except even that Band-Aid was fraying.

Going over and pouring himself a sherry, he sipped it and went to sit before the fire. Fritz had refreshed the wood not long ago, and the flames were bright and active over the stack of logs.

This was going to hurt, Saxton thought. But it wasn't going to break him.

He would eventually get over this. Heal. Move on.

Hearts were broken all the time. . . .

Wasn't there a song about that?

The question was, of course, when did he talk to Blaylock about it.

NINE

The sound of cross-country skis traveling over snow was a rhythmic rush, repeated at a quick clip.

The storm that had drifted down from the north had cleared after dawn, and the rising sun that shone beneath the lip of the departing cloud cover sliced through the forest to the sparkling ground.

To Sola Morte, the shafts of gold looked like blades.

Up ahead, her target presented itself like a Fabergé egg sitting on a stand: The house on the Hudson River was an architectural showpiece, a cage of seemingly fragile girders holding stack upon stack of countless panels of glass. On all sides, reflections of the water and the nascent sun were like photographs captured by a true artist, the images frozen in the very construction of the home itself.

You couldn't pay me to live like that, Sola thought.

Unless it was all bulletproof? But who had the money for that.

According to the Caldwell public records department, the land had been purchased by a Vincent DiPietro two years before, and developed by the man's real estate company. No expense had been spared on the construction—at least, given the valuation on the tax rolls, which was north of eight million dollars. Just after building was completed, the property changed hands, but not to a person: to a real estate trust—with only a lawyer in London listed as trustee.

She knew who lived here, however.

He was the reason she'd come.

He was also the reason she had armed herself so thoroughly. Sola had lots of weapons in easy-to-reach places: a knife in a holster at the small of her back, a gun on her right hip, a switch hidden in the collar of her white-on-white camo parka.

Men like her target did not appreciate being spied on—even though she came only in search of information, and not to kill him, she had no doubt that if she were found on the property, things would get tense. Quick.

As she took her binocs out of an inside pocket, she kept still and listened hard. No sounds of anything approaching from the back or the sides, and in front, she had a clear visual shot at the rear of the house.

Ordinarily, when she was hired for one of these kinds of assignments, she operated at night. Not with this target.

Masters of the drug trade conducted their business from nine to five, but that would be p.m. to a.m., not the other way around. Daytime was when they slept and fucked, so that was when you wanted to case their houses, learn their habits, get a read on their staff and how they protected themselves during their downtime.

Bringing the house into close focus, she made her assessment. Garage doors. Back door. Half windows that she guessed looked out of the kitchen. And then the full floor-to-ceiling glass sliders started up, running down the rear flank and around the corner that turned to the river's shoreline.

Three stories up.

Nothing moving inside that she could see.

Man, that was a lot of glass. And depending on the angle of the light, she could actually see into some of the rooms, especially the big open space that appeared to take up at least half of the first floor. Furniture was sparse and modern, as if the owner didn't welcome people loitering.

Bet the view was unbelievable. Especially now, with the partial cloud cover and the sun.

Training the binocs on the eaves under the roofline, she looked for security cameras, expecting one every twenty feet.

Yup.

Okay, that made sense. From what she'd been told, the home-

owner was cagey as hell—and that kind of relentless mistrust tended to be accessorized with a good dose of security-conscious behavior, including but not limited to personal guards, bulletproof cars, and most certainly, constant monitoring of any environment the individual spent any amount of time in.

The man who'd hired her had all those and more, for example.

"What the . . ." she whispered, refocusing the binoculars.

She stopped breathing to make sure nothing shifted.

This was . . . all wrong. There was a wave pattern to what was inside the house: What furniture she could see was subtly undulating.

Dropping the high-powered lenses, she looked around, wondering if maybe her eyes were the problem.

Nope. All the pine trees in the forest were behaving appropriately, standing still, their branches unmoving in the cold air. And when she put the magnifiers up again, she traced the rooftop of the house and the contours of the stone chimneys.

All were utterly inanimate.

Back to the glass.

Inhaling deep, she held the oxygen in her lungs and balanced against the nearest birch trunk to give her body extra stability.

Something continued to be off. The frames of those sliding glass doors and the lines of the porches and everything about the house? Static and solid. The interiors, however, seemed . . . pixilated somehow, like a composite image had been created to make things appear as if there were furniture . . . and that image had been superimposed on something like a curtain . . . that happened to be subjected to a soft current of air.

This was going to be a more interesting project than she'd assumed. Reporting on the activities of this business associate of a "friend" of hers had not exactly lit a fire under her ass. She much preferred greater challenges.

But maybe there was more to this than first appeared.

After all, camouflage meant you were hiding something—and she'd made a career out of taking things from people that they wanted to keep: Secrets. Items of value. Information. Documents.

The vocabulary used to define the nouns was irrelevant to her. The act of penetrating a locked house or car or safe or briefcase and extracting what she was after was what mattered.

She was a hunter.

And the man in that house, whoever he was, was her prey.

TEN

Blay had no business getting near a hand weight, much less the kind of iron that was down in the training center's gym. Hammering back that port on an empty stomach had made him fuzzy and uncoordinated. But he had to have some kind of a direction . . . a plan, a destination to drag his sorry ass to. Anything other than going up to his room, sitting on that bed again, and starting the day in the same way he'd started the night—smoking and staring off into space.

Probably with a lot more port added in.

Stepping out of the underground tunnel, he walked through the office and pushed the glass door open.

As he went along, still drinking from a half-full glass, his mind was circling itself, wondering when all this bullcrap between him and Qhuinn was going to end. On his deathbed? God, he didn't think he could last that long, assuming he had a normal life span ahead of him.

Maybe he needed to move out of the mansion. Before Wellsie had been killed, she and Tohr had been able to live in a house of their own. Hell, if he did that, he wouldn't have to see Qhuinn except during

meetings—and with so many people in and around the Brotherhood, it was easy to get out of eyeshot.

He'd been doing that for a while now, actually.

In fact, under that construct, the pair of them wouldn't have to cross paths at all—John was always partnered with the guy because of the whole *ahstrux nohtrum* thing, and between the rotation schedule, and the way territory was divided up, he and Qhuinn never fought together except in an emergency.

Saxton could go back and forth to work—

Blay stopped dead at the entrance to the weight room. Through the glass window he saw a set of weights going up and down on the reclining squat machine, and he knew by the Nikes who it was.

Goddamn it, he couldn't get a break.

Leaning in, he hit his head once. Twice. Three—

"You're supposed to do reps on the machines—not on the door."

Manny Manello's voice was as welcome as a steel-toed kick in the ass.

Blay straightened up, and the world went wheeeeee a little—to the point that he had to surreptitiously put his free hand on the jamb just so that the balance issue didn't show. He also tucked his nearly done drink out of sight

The doc probably wouldn't think working out while under the influence was a good thing.

"How are you?" Blay asked, even though he didn't really care—and that wasn't a commentary on Payne's *hellren*. He didn't give a crap about much at the moment.

Manello's mouth started to move and Blay passed the time watching the man's lips form and release syllables. A moment later, a good-bye of some sort was exchanged, and then Blay was alone with the door again.

It seemed like a planker move to just stand there, and he'd told the good doctor he was going in. And besides, there were, what, twenty-five machines in the room? Plus barbells and free weights. Treadmills. StairMasters, ellipticals . . . plenty to go around.

I'm not in love with Layla.

With a curse, Blay pushed his way in and braced himself for an awkward oh-hey-it's-you. Except Qhuinn didn't even notice the arrival. Instead of going with the overhead music, the guy was wearing headphones that went all around his ears, and he'd moved over to the chin-up bar so he was facing away, into the concrete wall.

Blay stayed as far back as possible, hopping on a random machine—pecs. Whatever.

After putting down his glass and adjusting the pin on the stack of weights, he settled onto the padded seat, gripped the double handles, and started pushing out from his chest.

All he had to look at was Qhuinn.

Or maybe that was more because his eyes refused to go anywhere else.

The male was wearing a black wifebeater that put those tremendous shoulders of his on full display . . . and the muscles along them flexed up hard as he reached the apex of the pull, the ridges and contours those of a fighter . . . not a lawyer—

Blay stopped himself right there.

It was unfair to the point of nausea to make any comparison like that, ever. After the past year or so, he knew Saxton's body nearly as well as his own, and the male was beautifully built, so lean and elegant—

Qhuinn ground out another lift, the weight of his heavy lower body straining the strength in those arms and that torso. And, thanks to his exertions, sweat had broken out all over his skin, making him glow under the lights.

The tattoo on the back of his neck shifted as he released and descended to hang from his grip, and then it was up again. And down. And up.

Blay thought about the way the male had looked as they'd turned over the Hummer: powerful, masculine . . . erotic.

This was not happening.

He was not, in fact, sitting here, eyeing Qhuinn like this—

Images filtered in from years past, turning his brain into a television screen. He saw Qhuinn bending over a human woman who had been laid out ass up on the edge of a flat table, his hips pumping as he fucked her, his hands locked onto her hips to hold her in place. He hadn't had a shirt on at the time, and his shoulders had been tight, as they were now.

Hard body being used well.

There were so many pictures like that, with Qhuinn in different positions with different people, male and female. In the beginning, right after their transitions, there had been such a feeling of excitement as the two of them had gone on the hunt together—or rather, Qhuinn had gone trolling and Blay had taken whatever had been brought back.

So much sex with so many people—although at that point, Blay had stuck only with the females.

Maybe because he'd known they were safe, that they didn't "count" in so many ways.

So uncomplicated in the beginning. But sometime along the way, things had started to shift—and he'd begun to realize that as he watched Qhuinn with the randoms, he was picturing himself under that body, receiving what the guy was so good at giving. After a time, it hadn't been some stranger's mouth on Qhuinn's cock; it was his own. And when those orgasms came, and they always did, he was the one taking them in. It was his hands on Qhuinn's body, and his lips locked hard, and his legs that were spread.

And that had fucked everything up.

Shit, he could remember staying awake during the day and staring at his ceiling, telling himself that when they were yet again at the club, in those bathrooms, or wherever it went down, he wouldn't do that anymore. But each time they went out, it was like an addict being offered the precise flavor of pill he needed.

Then there had been those two kisses—the first one down the hall from here, in the clinic's examination room. And he'd had to beg for it. And then their second up in his bedroom, just before he'd gone out with Saxton for the first time.

He'd had to beg for that, too.

Abruptly, Blay gave up pretending that he was actually pumping iron and put his hands down on his thighs.

He told himself to leave. Just get the fuck off the seat and walk out before Qhuinn moved to the next thing and his cover was blown.

Instead, he found his eyes back on those shoulders and that spine, on the tight waist and tighter ass, on those muscular legs.

Maybe it was the alcohol. The afterburn of that argument in the flatbed. The whole sex-with-Layla thing . . .

But at the moment, he was sexed up. Hard as stone. Ready for it.

Blay looked down his chest to the front of his loose shorts—and felt like shooting himself in the head.

Oh, Jesus, he needed to get out of here right now.

As Qhuinn continued set after set of pull-ups, his hands were numb, and he felt like his biceps were being peeled from his bones with dull knives—and that was just mindless chatter in comparison to his shoulders. They were the real problem. Someone clearly had come up from behind, put varnish stripper across them, and then buffed them with an industrial sander.

No idea how many reps he'd done. No clue how many miles he'd run. No count of the sit-ups, squats, or lunges.

He just knew he was going to keep going.

Goal: total exhaustion. He wanted to pass out the moment he went upstairs and got horizontal on his bed.

Dropping from the bar, he put his hands on his hips, lowered his head, and breathed heavily. His right shoulder immediately seized up, but that was his dominant side, so he expected it. To loosen the knot of muscles, he swept his arm around in a big circle as he turned—

Qhuinn froze.

On the other side of the blue mats, Blay was on the machine closest to the door, sitting as still as the weights he was not lifting.

The expression on his face was volcanic. But he wasn't mad.

No, he wasn't.

He had a hard-on big enough to see from across the room. Maybe across the state.

Qhuinn opened his mouth. Shut it. Opened it again.

In the end, he decided this was a prime example of how life never failed to surprise. Of all the situations he thought they would ever be in? This was not it. Not after . . . well, everything.

He pulled his earphones off and let them hang from his neck, the pounding beat downshifting from concert-roar to impotent little hiss.

Is that for me? he wanted to ask.

For a split second, he thought it might be, but then how arrogant was that? The guy had just finished giving a speech about how the two of them were nothing but hourly wagers working side by side on vats of trans fat. Then Blay shows up with an arousal the size of a crowbar—and the first thing to come to his mind was it could, possibly, maybe, sort of, kind of . . . be for him?

What a prick he was.

And PS, what the hell would he do if he suddenly found himself in a parallel universe, with Blay pulling a hey-how-'bouta in that department?

Of course he wanted the guy.

For fuck's sake, he'd always wanted him—to the point where he had to wonder how much of that pushing-away thing that he'd done "for Blay's benefit" hadn't really been for his own.

Pondering that one, he noticed the glass down by the guy's feet. Ah, alcohol was involved—he sincerely doubted the dark inch in that squat glass was Coca-Cola.

Shit, for all he knew, Saxton had just texted him a crotch shot and a half, and that was the cause of all that erection.

And wasn't that a deflator.

Your cousin is giving me what I need all day long, every day.

"You got something else to say to me?" Qhuinn asked harshly.

Blay shook his head back and forth once.

Qhuinn frowned. Blay was not a hothead—never had been, and that was part of the reason that, for the longest time, they'd been so tight. Balance and all that crap. At the moment, however, the guy seemed like he was a thin inch from losing it.

Trouble in paradise between the happy couple?

Nah, they were too good together.

"Okay." Man, the idea of hanging around here while Blay amped up for another session with Saxton the Magnificent was untenable. "I'll see you later."

As he walked by, he felt Blay's eyes on him—but they weren't on the level of his face. At least, it didn't seem like it.

What the *fuck* was going on here?

Pushing out into the hall, he paused to double-check that the concrete walls weren't melting and that he didn't suddenly have fish for hands or something. Neither were true, but a trippy sense of unreality dogged him as he went down to the locker room. A shower was mandatory; he was covered in sweat, and as much as the *doggen* loved a good mess, he wasn't about to give them more work just because he'd tried to kill himself in the gym—

Hard. Aroused. Ready for sex.

As that image of Blay battered around the inside of his skull, he closed his eyes, and then hit the door into the land of tile and water fixtures. He intended to go over to the showers directly, but ended up stalling out in the front half of the room, where the lockers were stacked in orderly rows and the benches ran down the middle of the aisles.

Parking it, he unlaced his Nikes, kicked them off, and peeled his socks free.

Totally fucking aroused.

Blay had been out of his mind for it.

For some reason, Qhuinn's last two sexual encounters popped into his head. There had been that redheaded guy at the Iron Mask—the one he'd seduced and fucked in the bathroom. He'd picked the random out of the crowd for that one defining physical characteristic, and naturally the sesh had done nothing extraordinary for him. Then again, it had been like wanting Herradura, and putting ginger ale down your throat.

And then there had been the stuff with Layla—which had been nothing but a physically demanding job, like digging a trench or building a wall. . . .

God, he felt like a louse for thinking like that—and he meant no disrespect to the Chosen. But at least it was fairly clear she was of a similar mind.

That was it for the last year. Just those two.

Nearly twelve months of nothing, and he hadn't been jerking off, either. He just wasn't interested in anything, like his balls had gone into hibernation.

Funny, right after his transition he'd banged anything with two legs and a beating heart, and as he struggled to remember some of those many faces—God knew he hadn't bothered to get names a lot of the time—an uncomfortable feeling tightened his gut.

All that anonymous, nameless, faceless fucking . . . in front of Blay. Always with the guy, come to think of it. At the time, it had felt like a buddy/buddy kind of situation, but now he wondered.

Yeah, screw that. He *knew* what it had been about.

He was such a pussy, wasn't he.

Getting to his feet, he stripped naked and let his wifebeater and his b-ball shorts flop onto the bench in a wet mess. Walking to the shower room, he picked one of the showerheads at random, cranked the thing on, and stepped under the spray. The water was nut-shrinking cold, but he didn't care. He faced the onslaught, shutting his lids and opening his mouth.

That redhead in the club almost a year ago? When he'd been seducing the guy into the loo, it had been Blay in his mind the whole time.

It was Blay who'd he'd pushed back against the sink and kissed hard. Blay's cock he'd sucked off, and Blay's body he'd taken from behind and—

"For the love . . ." he groaned.

From out of nowhere, the image of his old friend sitting on the machine just now, his knees wide, his cock straining against the oh-so-thin material of those shorts entered his mind and shot down his spine, going straight between his legs. With a curse, he sagged and had to put a hand out on the slick tile.

"Oh . . . fuck . . ."

Leaning in, he rested his forehead on his arm and tried to concentrate on the feel of the water hitting the nape of his neck.

Not even close.

All he was aware of was the heartbeat in his cock.

Well, that and a ringing fantasy of him dropping to his knees and pressing in between Blay's open thighs, licking his way into that mouth . . . while burrowing under the waistband of those shorts and starting to give the guy a hand job he would never fucking forget.

Among so many other things.

Turning around to face away from the spray, Qhuinn pushed his hands into his hair, sluicing it back, arching his spine.

He could feel his cock sticking straight out from his hips, begging for attention.

But he wasn't going to do anything about it. Blay deserved better than that somehow—yeah, it didn't make sense, but it just felt nasty to be jerking off in the shower over the guy's arousal about someone else.

Hell, the guy's *partner*.

Qhuinn's own *cousin*, for chrissakes.

As his erection just hung out there, unfazed by that logic, he knew it was going to be a long frickin' day.

ELEVEN

Blay dropped his head with a curse as the weight room door eased shut. And of course, from that vantage point, all he could see was his cock.

Which did not help.

Shifting his eyes back up, he stared across at the chin-up bar, and knew he had to do something. Sitting here half-drunk with a party in his pants was hardly a position he wanted to get caught in. If a Brother like Rhage walked in on this? Blay would be hearing about it for the rest of his natural life. Besides, he was in his workout gear, surrounded by equipment, so he might as well get busy, pump some iron, and hope that Mr. Happy sank into a depression from lack of attention.

Good plan.

Really.

Yup.

When he glanced at the clock sometime later, he realized fifteen minutes had passed and he was no closer to constructive, repetitive motion, unless you counted breathing.

His erection had a suggestion for that kind of goal.

And his palm was immediately on board, going between his legs, finding that hard—

Blay burst up from the seat and went for the door. Enough with the bullshit—he was going to hit the loo in the locker room in the hope of cycling some of the alcohol out of his system. Then he was going to get on a treadmill and sweat the rest of the booze out.

After which it was time to head to bed—where, if he needed an outlet of the erotic variety, he was going to find it in the appropriate place.

The first sign that his new plan might have taken him only farther into the weeds came as he pushed his way into locker-landia: the sound of running water meant someone was doing the soap-and-shampoo thing. He was so focused on kicking himself in the butt, however, he didn't bother with any extrapolations.

Which would have made him stop, turn around, and find another toilet ASAP.

Instead, he went past the lockers and did his business. It wasn't until he was washing his hands that the math started to add up.

Of its own volition, his head cranked around in the direction of the showers.

You need to leave, he told himself.

As he turned off the faucet, the subtle squeak seemed loud as a scream, and he refused to look at himself in the mirrors. He didn't want to see what was in his eyes.

Go back to the door. Just go back to the door. Just—

The failure of his body to follow that simple command was not merely an exercise of physical rebellion. It was, tragically, his pattern.

And he would regret it later.

At the moment, however, when he made the choice to walk over, and duck around the tiled wall of the shower room, when he kept himself mostly hidden, when he spied on a male he shouldn't have . . . the mad rush of emotion was so achingly familiar, it was a suit of clothes tailor-fitted to his madness.

Qhuinn was facing into the showerhead he was standing under, one hand braced against the slick wall, his dark head bowed under the spray. Water ran over his shoulders and down the acres of supple skin that covered his powerful back . . . and then flowed onto his magnificent ass . . . and went ever farther, past those long, strong legs.

In the last year, the fighter had filled out quite a bit. Qhuinn had

been big after his transition, and had gotten even larger during those first few months of intense eating. But it had been a while since Blay had seen the male without his clothes on . . . and man, the punishing gym routines he'd been putting himself through showed in all that hard-cut muscle—

Abruptly Qhuinn shifted his position, pivoting around, tilting his head back, sluicing the water through his dark hair, that incredible body arching.

He'd kept his PA.

And holy shit, he was aroused—

An orgasm immediately threatened the head of Blay's cock, his balls getting tight as fists.

Wheeling around, he left the locker room like he was shot out of a cannon, punching through the door, jumping out into the corridor.

"Oh, shit . . . fucking . . . goddamn . . . fuck . . ."

Walking as fast as he could, he tried to get that image out of his head, reminding himself that he had a lover, that he'd moved on from all this, that you could self-destruct over the same thing only so many times and then you were done.

When none of that worked, he replayed the speech he'd given to Qhuinn in the tow truck—

Where the hell was the office?

Stopping short, he looked around. Oh, fantastic. He'd gone in the opposite direction from what he'd intended, and was now down past the clinic and into the classroom part of the training center.

Miles from the entrance to the tunnel.

". . . laceration that deep. But he wouldn't have it."

Manny Manello's deep voice preceded the man walking out into the corridor from the main examination room. A second later, Doc Jane made an appearance right behind him, an open chart in her hand, her fingertip tracing down a page.

Blay ducked through the first door he came to—

And ran right into a wall of blackness. Patting around for a light switch, because he was too scattered to turn any bulbs on mentally, he found one, flipped it, and blinded himself.

"Ow!"

The sharp shooter that rocketed from his shin to his brain told him he'd walked into something large.

Ah, a desk.

He was in one of the mini-offices that satellited the classrooms, and that was good news. With the training program still suspended because of the raids, there was no one down here, and no one likely to think of a reason to be in this empty little room.

He could have some privacy for a while—and that was a blessing. God knew he wasn't going to try to make it to the mansion now. With his luck he'd run into Qhuinn, and the last thing he needed was to be anywhere near the guy.

Going behind the desk, he sat down in the cushy office chair and brought his legs up, stretching them across the flat top that should have had a computer, a plant, and a holder full of pens on it. Instead, it was barren, although not dust-covered. Fritz would never stand for that even in an unused space.

Rubbing at the sore spot on the front of his calf, it was clear that he was going to have one hell of a black-and-blue mark. But at least the pain distracted him from what had driven him down here.

That didn't last, though.

As he tilted the chair back and closed his eyes, his brain returned to the locker room.

Was the torture never going to end, he thought.

And, God, his cock was pounding.

Considering his choices, he willed the lights off, closed his eyes, and ordered his brain to shut up and go to sleep. If he could just catch a few down here for an hour or two, he'd wake up sober, flaccid, and ready to face people again.

Now, *this* was a good plan, and it was also the perfect environment. Dark, a little cool, super-quiet in the way only facilities underground were.

Shimmying his body even deeper into the chair, he crossed his arms over his chest and got ready for the REM train to pull into his station.

When that didn't work, he started to imagine all kinds of "off" situations, like vacuums unplugged from the wall, and fires extinguished with water, and TV screens going black. . . .

Qhuinn had looked so eminently fuckable like that, his slick, smooth body carved with muscle, his sex so thick and proud. All that water would have made him both slippery and hot . . . and, dearest Virgin Scribe, Blay would have given almost anything to walk over the tile, get down on his knees, and take that sex into his mouth, feeling that blunt head with its piercing stroke over his tongue as he went up and down—

The disgusted noise he made echoed around, sounding louder than it probably had been.

Opening his eyes, he tried to clear any fantasies that involved sucking out of his mind. But all the pitch-black didn't help; it just formed the perfect screen to keep projecting on.

Cursing, he gave that yoga thing a shot, where you relaxed the tension in each and every part of the body, starting with the perma-twist between his eyebrows, then the rigid ropes that ran from his shoulders up to the base of his skull. His chest was tight, too, his pecs contracted for no good reason, his biceps digging into his upper arms.

Next, he was supposed to focus on his abs and then his butt and his thighs, his knees and calves . . . his this-little-piggy-went-homes.

He didn't make it that far.

Then again, trying to talk his arousal into any kind of malleability would have required powers of persuasion that his half-drunk brain didn't possess.

Unfortunately, there was only one sure-fire way of getting rid of Mr. Happy. And in the dark, by himself, with the umbrella of no-one-will-ever-know protecting the moment, why shouldn't he just work the damn thing, drain the burn, and pass out? It was no different from waking up at the fall of night with an erection—because God knew there was no emotional anything involved. And he was under the influence, right? So that was another pass.

He wasn't cheating on Saxton, he told himself. He wasn't *with* Qhuinn—and Saxton *was* the one he wanted. . . .

For a while, he continued to argue the pros and cons, but eventually his hand made the decision for him. Before he knew it, his palm was burrowing under his loose waistband and—

The hiss he let out when he gripped himself was like a gunshot in the silence, and so was the groan of the chair as the thrust of his hips pushed his shoulders into the leather padding. Hot and hard, thick and long, his cock was begging for attention—but the angle was all wrong, and there was no room for stroking in the damn shorts.

For some reason, the idea of stripping from the waist down made him feel dirty, but his sense of propriety went into the shitter pretty fast when all he could do was squeeze. Lifting his ass, he swept the

shorts off . . . and then realized he was going to need something to clean up the mess with.

The shirt came off next.

Naked in the dark, sprawled out long from the chair and to the desktop, he gave himself over, spreading his thighs, pumping up and down. The friction made his eyes roll back in his head, made him bite his lower lip—God, the sensations were so strong, flowing through his body—

Fuck.

Qhuinn was in his mind, Qhuinn was in his mouth . . . Qhuinn was inside of him, the two of them moving together—

This was wrong.

He froze. Just stopped dead. "Shit."

Blay released his cock, even though the mere process of letting the betrayal go made him grit his molars.

Opening his eyes, he stared into the darkness. The sound of his breath punching in and out of his chest made him curse again. So did his pounding need for an orgasm—which he refused to give in to.

He was *not* going to take this any further—

From out of nowhere, that image of Qhuinn arched under the falling spray slammed into his brain, taking over everything. Against his higher reasoning, and his loyalty, and his sense of fairness . . . his body went into instant overload, the orgasm shooting out of his cock before he could stop it, before he could tell it no, that wasn't right . . . before he could say, Not again. Never again.

Oh, God. The sweet, stabbing sensation repeated over and over until he wondered if it was ever going to end—even though he didn't help things along.

This physical reaction might be outside of his control. His response to it was not.

When he finally stilled, his breath was harsh and the coolness across the bare skin of his chest suggested he'd broken out in a sweat . . . and as his body recovered from the rush, his awareness returned—and his deflating erection was like a barometer of his mood.

Reaching forward, he patted over the desk until he found his shirt; then he wadded it up and pressed the thing into the juncture of his thighs.

The rest of the mess he was in was not going to be so easy to clean up.

*   *   *

Across town, on the eighteenth floor of the Commodore, Trez sat in a sleek steel-and-leather chair that faced a wall of windows overlooking the Hudson River. The noonday sun was shining down from a crystal clear, chrome-like sky, everything ten times brighter because of the fresh snow that had fallen overnight on the shores.

"I know you're there," he said dryly, taking a sip from his coffee mug.

When there was no reply, he spun his chair around on its swival base. Sure enough, iAm had come in from his bedroom and was sitting on the couch, iPad on his lap, forefinger striping across the screen. He would be reading the *New York Times* online edition, of course; he did that every morning when they got up.

"Well," Trez bit out. "Go on."

The only response he got was one of iAm's brows lifting. For, like, a split second.

The smug bastard wouldn't even look over. "Must be a fascinating article. What's it about? Recalcitrant brothers?"

Trez passed some time nursing his hot coffee. "iAm. Seriously. This is bullshit."

After a moment, his brother's dark stare lifted. The eyes that met his were, as always, completely uncluttered of emotion and doubt and all the messy stuff that mere mortals struggled with. iAm was preternaturally sensible . . . rather in the way of a cobra: watchful, intelligent, ready to strike, but unwilling to waste the power until it was needed.

"What," Trez ground out.

"It's redundant to tell you what you already know."

"Humor me." He took another draw off the rim of the mug, and wondered why the hell he was volunteering for this. "Go on."

iAm's lips pursed the way they did when he was considering his response. Then he flopped the red cover of the iPad down, each of the four sections landing like footsteps across the screen. He then put the thing aside, uncrossed his leg, and leaned forward to balance his elbows on his knees. The guy's biceps were so thick, the sleeves of his shirt looked like they were going to split wide.

"Your sex life is out of control." As Trez rolled his eyes, his brother kept on talking. "You are fucking three or four women a night, some-

times more. It's not about feeding, so don't waste either of our time by excusing it in that fashion. You are compromising the professional standards of—"

"I run liquor and prostitutes. Don't you think that's a little high-brow—"

iAm picked up the iPad and waved it back and forth. "Should I go back to reading?"

"I'm just saying—"

"You asked me to speak. If this is a problem, the solution is not to get defensive because you don't like what you hear. The answer is to not invite me to talk."

Trez ground his teeth. See, this was the issue with his fucking brother. Too goddamn reasonable.

Bursting up, he stalked across the open living room. The kitchen was like everything else in the condo: modern, airy, and uncluttered. Which meant that as he poured himself some more caffeine, he could see his brother in his peripheral vision.

Man, sometimes he hated this place: Unless he was in his bed-room with the door shut, he couldn't get a break from those damn eyeballs.

"Am I reading or talking?" iAm said calmly, like he didn't care either way.

Man, Trez desperately wanted to tell the guy to shove his nose back into the *Times*, but that was like a defeat.

"G'head." Trez went back to his chair and settled in for more ass kicking.

"You're not behaving in a professional manner."

"You eat your own food at Sal's."

"My linguine with clam sauce doesn't require a restraining order when I decide the next night I want the *Fra Diavolo*."

Good point. And somehow, that made him feel nearly violent.

"I know what you're doing," iAm said steadily. "And why."

"You're not a virgin, of course you do—"

"I know what they sent you."

Trez froze. "How."

"When you didn't respond, I received a phone call."

Trez pushed the rug with his foot and turned himself around to face the river. Shit. He figured he'd clear the air with this, you know, give his brother a little bitch session so that the two of them could go back to being normal—usually they were close as skin to bone, and the relationship was as fundamental as that to him.

He could handle just about anything except friction with his brother.

Unfortunately, the problems that had gotten alluded to over there were about the only thing in that "just about anything."

"Ignoring it will not make it go away, Trez."

This was said with a certain gentleness of tone—like the guy felt bad for him.

As Trez looked out over the river, he imagined that he was at his club, with humans all around and cash trading hands and the women who worked there doing their thing in the back. Nice. Normal. In control and comfortable.

"You have responsibilities."

Trez tightened his grip on his mug. "I didn't volunteer for them."

"It doesn't matter."

He spun around so fast, hot coffee went flying and landed on his thigh. He ignored the sting. "It should. It fucking *should*. I'm not some inanimate object that can be given to somebody. That whole thing is bullshit."

"Some would find it an honor."

"Well, I don't. I'm not getting mated to that female. I don't care who she is or who set it up or how 'important' it is to the s'Hisbe."

Trez braced himself for a barrage of oh-yeah-you-do. Instead, his brother looked sad, as if he wouldn't have wanted the curse, either.

"I'll say it again, Trez. This is not just magically going to disappear. And trying to fuck your way out of it? That's not only futile, it's potentially dangerous."

Trez rubbed his face. "The women are just humans. They don't matter." He turned back to the river again. "And frankly, if I don't do something, I'm going to go insane. A couple of orgasms has to be better than that, right?"

As silence resumed, he knew his brother disagreed with him. But proof positive that his life was in the shitter was the fact that the conversation dried up at that point.

iAm apparently wasn't into kicking a guy when he was down.

Whatever. He didn't care what was expected of him—he was *not* going back and being condemned to a life of service.

He didn't care if it was to the queen's daughter.

TWELVE

It was late in the afternoon when Wrath hit the wall. He was at his desk, ass on his father's throne, fingers running over a report written in Braille, when all of a sudden he couldn't take one more damn word of text.

Shoving the papers aside, he cursed and ripped his wraparounds off his face. Just as he was about to throw them at a wall, a muzzle kicked his elbow.

Putting an arm around his golden retriever, he tightened his hand on the soft fur that grew along the dog's flanks. "You always know, don't you."

George burrowed in deep, pressing his chest into Wrath's leg—which was the cue that someone wanted to be up and over.

Wrath leaned down and gathered all ninety pounds up in his arms. As he settled the four paws, lion's mane, and flowing tail so that everything fit, he supposed it was a good thing he was so fucking tall. Big thighs offered a bigger lap.

And the act of stroking all that fur calmed him, even though it didn't ease his mind.

His father had been a great king, capable of withstanding count-

less hours of ceremony, endless nights filled with the drafting of proclamations and summonses, whole months and years of protocol and
tradition. And that was before you layered on the perennial stream of
bitching that came at you from every corner: letters, phone calls,
e-mails—although of course the latters hadn't been an issue in his
pop's era.

Wrath had been a fighter once. A damn good one.

Putting his hand up, he felt along the side of his neck, to the place
where that bullet had entered him—

The knock on the door was sharp and to the point, a demand
more than a respectful request for entrance.

"Come in, V," he called out.

The astringent witch-hazel scent that preceded the Brother was a
clear tip-off that somebody was feeling pissy. And sure enough, that
deep voice had a nasty edge.

"I finally finished the ballistic testing. Damn fragments always
take forever."

"And?" Wrath prompted.

"It's a one hundred percent match." As Vishous sat down in the
chair across the desk, the thing creaked under the weight. "We got 'em."

Wrath exhaled, some of the impotent buzz draining from his
brain.

"Good." He ran his palm from the top of George's boxy head
down to his ribs. "This is our ammunition, then."

"Yup. What was going to happen anyway is now nice and legal."

The Brotherhood had known all along who had been on the trigger of the shot that had nearly killed him back in the fall—and the
duty of picking off the Band of Bastards one by one was something
they were looking at as so much more than a sacred duty to the race.

"Listen, I gotta be honest, true?"

"When are you not?" Wrath drawled.

"Why the hell are you tying our hands?"

"Didn't know I was."

"With Tohr."

Wrath repositioned George so that the blood supply to his left leg
wasn't completely cut off by the dog's weight. "He asked for the proclamation."

"We all have a right to take out Xcor. That asshole is the prize we
all want. It shouldn't be restricted to just him."

"He asked."

"It makes it more difficult to kill the bastard. What if one of us finds him out there and Tohr isn't with us?"

"Then you bring him in." There was a long, tense silence. "Do you hear me, V. You bring that piece of shit in, and let Tohr do his duty."

"The goal is to eliminate the Band of Bastards."

"And how's that keeping you from the job?" When there was no reply, Wrath shook his head. "Tohr was in that van with me, my brother. He saved my life. Without him . . ."

As the sentence drifted, V cursed softly—like he was running the math on that memory, and coming to the conclusion that the Brother who had had to cut a plastic tube free of his CamelBak and performed a tracheotomy on his king in a moving vehicle miles away from any medical help might have sliiiiiiightly more right to kill the perp.

Wrath smiled a little. "Tell you what—just because I'm nice guy, I'll promise you all a crack at him before Tohr kills the motherfucker with his bare hands. Deal?"

V laughed. "That does take the sting off of it."

The knock that interrupted them was quiet and respectful—a couple of soft taps that seemed to suggest whoever it was would be happy to be blown off, content to wait, and hoping for an immediate audience all at the same time.

"Yeah," Wrath called out.

Expensive cologne announced his solicitor's arrival: Saxton always smelled good, and that fit his persona. From what Wrath remembered, in addition to the guy's great education and the quality of his thinking, he dressed in the fashion of a well-bred son of the *glymera*. I.e., perfectly.

Not that Wrath had seen it recently.

He put his wraparounds on in a quick surge. It was one thing to be exposed in front of V; not going to happen in front of the young, efficient male who was coming through the door—no matter how much Sax was trusted and consulted.

"What have you got for me?" Wrath said as George's tail brushed back and forth in greeting.

There was a long pause. "Mayhap I should come back?"

"You can say anything in front of my brother."

Another long pause, during which V was probably eyeing the attorney like he wanted to take a chunk out of his fancy, pretty-boy ass for suggesting there was an information divide that needed to be respected.

"Even if it's about the Brotherhood?" Saxton said levelly.

Wrath could practically feel V's icy eyes swing around. And sure enough, the brother bit out, "What about *us.*"

When Saxton remained silent, Wrath clued into what it was. "Can you give us a minute, V?"

"Are you fucking me?"

Wrath picked up George and put him down on the floor. "I just need five minutes."

"Fine. Have fun with it, my lord," V spat as he got to his feet. "Fuckin' A."

A moment later, the door slammed shut.

Saxton cleared his throat. "I could have come back."

"If I'd wanted that, I would have told you to. Talk to me."

A deep breath was taken and let out, as if the civilian was staring at that exit and wondering if V's pissed-off departure might just cause him to wake up dead later on in the day. "Ah . . . the audit of the Old Laws is complete, and I can provide you with a comprehensive listing of all sections that require amendment, along with proposed rewording, and a timeline on which the changes could be made if—"

"Yes or no. That's all I care about."

Going by the whisper-soft sound of loafers treading an Aubusson, Wrath extrapolated that his lawyer was going for a little walkabout. From memory, he pictured the study, with its pale blue walls and its curlicue molding and all the flimsy, antique French furniture.

Saxton made more sense in this room than Wrath did with his leathers and his muscle shirt.

But the law prescribed who was to be king.

"You need to start flapping your gums, Saxton. I will guarantee you that you won't be fired if you tell me how it is straight up. Try editing the truth or softballing it? And you're out on your ass, I don't care who you're sleeping with."

There was another throat clearing. And then that cultured voice came at him from head-on across the desk. "Yes, you can do as you wish. I have concerns about the timing, however."

"Why? 'Cuz it's going to take you two years to make the amendments?"

"You're making a fundamental change to a section of society that

protects the species—and it could further destabilize your rule. I am not unaware of the pressures you're under, and it would be remiss of me not to point out the obvious. If you alter the prescription of who may enter the Black Dagger Brotherhood, it could well give even further opening for dissent—this is unlike anything you've attempted during your reign, and it's coming in an era of extreme social upset."

Wrath inhaled long and slow through his nose—and caught a whole lot of no bad juju: there was no evidence to suggest the guy was being duplicitous or not wanting to do the work.

And he had a point.

"I appreciate the insight," Wrath said. "But I'm not going to bow to the past. I refuse to. And if I had doubts about the male in question, I wouldn't be doing this."

"How do the other Brothers feel?"

"That's none of your business." In fact, he hadn't broached this idea with them yet. After all, why bother if there was no possibility of moving forward. Tohr and Beth were the only ones who knew exactly how far he was prepared to take this. "How long will it take you to make it legal?"

"I can have everything drawn up by dawn tomorrow—nightfall at the latest."

"Do it." Wrath made a fist and banged it onto the arm of the throne. "Do it now."

"As you wish, my lord."

There was a rustle of fine clothing, as if the male were bowing, and then more padding feet before one half of the double doors opened and shut.

Wrath stared off into the nothingness he was provided by his blind eyes.

Dangerous times was right. And frankly, the smart thing to do was add more Brothers, not think of reasons not to—although the counterargument to that was, if those three boys were willing to fight alongside them without being inducted, why bother?

But fuck that. It was old-school to want to honor someone who had put his life on the line so your own could continue.

The real issue, even apart from the laws, however . . . was, What would the others think?

That was more likely to put the kibosh on this than any legal snafu.

*   *   *

As night fell hours later, Qhuinn lay naked in tangled sheets, neither his body nor his mind at rest, even as he slept.

In his dream, he was back at the side of the road, walking off from his family's house. He had a duffel over one shoulder, a proclamation of disinheritance shoved into his waistband, and a wallet that was eleven dollars away from being empty.

Everything was crystal clear—nothing denatured due to memory's faulty playback: from the humid summer night to the sound of his New Rocks on the pebbles at the shoulder . . . to the fact that he was aware he had nothing in his future.

He had nowhere to go. No home to return to.

No prospects. Not even a past anymore.

When the car pulled in behind him, he knew it was John and Blay—

Except, no. It was not his friends. It was death in the form of four males in black robes who streamed out of four doors and swarmed around him.

An Honor Guard. Sent by his father to beat him for dishonoring the family's name.

How ironic. One would assume that knifing a sociopath who'd been trying to rape your buddy would be considered a good thing. But not when the assailant was your perfect first cousin.

In slow motion, Qhuinn sank down into his fighting stance, prepared to meet the attack. There were no eyes to look directly into, no faces to note—and there was a reason for that: The fact that the robes obscured their identities was supposed to make the person who'd transgressed feel as though all of society was disapproving of the actions he had taken.

Circling, circling, closing in . . . eventually they were going to take him down, but he was going to hurt them in the process.

And he did.

But he was also right: After what seemed like hours of defense, he ended up on his back, and that was when the beating really happened. Lying on the asphalt, he covered his head and his nut sac as best he could, the blows raining down on him, black robes flying like the wings of crows as he was struck again and again.

After a little while, he felt no pain.

He was going to die here at the side of the road—

"Stop! We're not supposed to kill him!"

His brother's voice cut through it all, sinking in in a way that the pummeling no longer did—

Qhuinn woke up with a shout, throwing his arms over his face, his thighs thrusting up to protect that groin of his—

No fists or clubs were coming at him.

And he was not at the side of the road.

Willing on some lights, he looked around the bedroom that he'd been staying in since he'd been kicked out of his family's home. It didn't suit him in the slightest, the silk wallpaper and the antiques something his mother would have picked out—and yet at the moment, the sight of all that old crap someone else had chosen, bought, hung, and kept after made him calm down.

Even as the memory lingered.

God, the sound of his brother's voice.

His own brother had been part of the Honor Guard that had been sent for him. Then again, that sent a more powerful message to the *glymera* about how seriously the family was taking things—and it wasn't as if the guy hadn't been trained. He'd been taught the martial arts, although naturally he'd never been allowed to fight. Hell, he'd barely been permitted to spar.

Too valuable to the bloodline. If he got hurt? The one who was going to walk in Daddio's footsteps and eventually become a *leahdyre* of the Council could be compromised.

Small risk of a catastrophic injury to the family.

Qhuinn, on the other hand? Before he'd been disavowed, he'd been put into the training program, maybe in hopes that he'd sustain a mortal injury in the field and have the good grace to die honorably for everyone.

Stop! We're not supposed to kill him!

That had been the last time he'd heard his brother's voice. Shortly after Qhuinn had been thrown out of the house, the Lessening Society had gone on a raid and slaughtered them all, Father, Mother, sister—and Luchas.

All gone. And even though a part of him had hated them for all they'd done to him, he wouldn't wish that kind of death on anyone.

Qhuinn rubbed his face.

Shower time. That was all he knew.

Getting up on his feet, he stretched until his back cracked, and checked his phone. A group text to everyone announced there was a meeting in Wrath's study—and a quick glance at the clock told him he was out of time.

Which was not a bad thing. As he flipped into high gear and hustled into the bath, it was a relief to focus on real stuff instead of the bullshit past.

Nothing he could do about the latter except curse it. And shit knew he'd done enough of that for twelve lifetimes.

Wakey-wakey, he thought.

Time to go to work.

THIRTEEN

round the same time Qhuinn was cleaning himself up at the main house, Blay came awake in the chair in that little underground office. The headache that served as his alarm clock was not from the port—it was from the fact that he'd skipped Last Meal. But man, he wished the booze had been behind the pounding in his skull. He could have used the out that he'd been a total, sloppy, lost-his-mind mess when he'd come down here.

Cursing, he withdrew his legs from the desktop and sat up. His body was stiff as a board, aches blooming in all kinds of places as he willed on the overhead light.

Crap. He was still naked.

But come on, like the modesty elves would have snuck in and clothed him in his sleep? Just so he wasn't reminded of what he'd done?

Putting his shorts on, he shoved his feet into his trainers and then reached for his shirt—before remembering what he'd used it for.

As he stared at the crumpled folds of cotton and felt the stiff places in the soft cloth, he realized that no amount of rationalization was going to change the fact that he'd cheated on Saxton. Physical contact with someone else was only one way of measuring infidelity—and yeah, that was the biggest divide. But what he'd done last night had been a violation of the relationship, even though the orgasm had been caused by his brain, not his hand.

Getting to his feet, he was half-dead as he went to the door and opened it a crack. If there was anyone around, he was going to duck back inside and wait for a clear shot into the corridor: He so completely did not want to get caught coming out of this empty office, half-clothed and looking like hell. The upside to living at the compound was that you were surrounded by people who cared about you; the downside was that everybody had eyes and ears, and no one's business was just their own.

When he didn't hear voices or footsteps, he exploded out into the hall and started walking briskly, like he'd been somewhere for a good reason and was heading to his room for an equally important purpose. He had a feeling he'd gotten away with it when he hit the tunnel. Sure, he didn't usually go shirtless, but a lot of the Brothers or males did when they were coming from the gym—nothing unusual.

And he really felt like he'd won the lottery when he stepped out from under the mansion's grand staircase and got another good dose of empty-bowling-alley. The only problem was that, going by the sounds of china being cleared in the dining room, it must be later than he'd thought. He'd obviously missed First Meal—bad news for his head, but at least he had some protein bars in his room.

His luck ran out as he took the stairs up to the second floor. Standing in front of the closed doors to Wrath's study, Qhuinn and John were dressed for fighting, their weapons strapped on, their bodies covered in black leather.

No way in hell was he looking at Qhuinn. Just having the guy in his peripheral vision was bad enough.

"What's going on?" Blay asked.

We've got a meeting now, John signed. *Or at least, we're supposed to. Didn't you get the text?*

Shit, he had no idea where his phone was. His room? Hopefully.

"I'll hit the shower and be right back."

You might not have to rush. The Brothers have been sequestered for the last half hour. I don't have any idea what's going on.

Next to the guy, Qhuinn was rocking back and forth in his shit-kickers, his weight shifting like he was on a walk even as he went nowhere.

"Five minutes," Blay muttered. "That's all I need."

He hoped the Brotherhood would open those doors by then—the last thing he wanted was to get stuck passing time anywhere near Qhuinn.

Cursing as he went, Blay jogged down to his room. Usually he took his time getting ready, especially if Sax was in the mood, but this was going to be a wham-bam, thank you, ma—

As he opened his door, he froze.

What the . . . hell?

Duffels. On the bed. So many of them he couldn't see more than an inch and a half of the king-size duvet—and he knew whose they were. Matching Guccis, in white with the navy blue logo and the navy blue and red cloth strapping—because according to Saxton, the traditional brown-on-brown with the red and green was "too obvious."

Blay shut the door quietly. His first thought was, Holy shit, Saxton knew. Somehow, the guy knew what had happened in the training center.

The male in question came out of the bathroom with an armful of shampoo, conditioner, and product. He stopped dead.

"Hi," Blay said. "Taking a vacation?"

After a tense moment, Saxton calmly came over, put his load down in a travel bag, and turned back around. As always, his beautiful blond hair was swept off his forehead in thick waves. And he was dressed perfectly, in another tweed suit with matching waistcoat, a red cravat and red pocket square adding just the right accent of color.

"I think you know what I'm going to say." Saxton smiled sadly. "Because you're far from stupid—just as I am."

Blay went to sit down on the bed, but had to recalibrate because there was nowhere to put himself. He ended up on the chaise lounge, and, with a discreet lean to one side, he tucked the wadded shirt under the skirting. Out of sight. It was the least he could do.

God, was this really happening?

"I don't want you to go," Blay heard himself say roughly.

"I believe that."

Blay looked across all those duffels. "Why now?"

He thought of the pair of them just the day before, under the sheets, having hard sex. They had been so close—although if he were brutally honest, maybe that had just been physically.

Take out the *maybe*.

"I've been fooling myself." Saxton shook his head. "I thought I could keep going with you like this—but I can't. It's killing me."

Blay closed his eyes. "I know I've been out a lot in the field—"

"That's not what I'm talking about."

As Qhuinn took up all the space between them, Blay wanted to scream. But what good would that do: it appeared that he and Saxton had gotten to the same difficult corner at the same sorrowful moment.

His lover looked over the luggage. "I've just finished that assignment for Wrath. It's a good time to make a break, move out and find another job—"

"Wait, so you're leaving the king as well?" Blay frowned. "However things stand between us, you need to keep working for him. That is bigger than our relationship."

Saxton's eyes dipped down. "I suspect that is far easier for you to say."

"Not true," Blay countered grimly. "God, I'm so . . . sorry."

"You've done nothing wrong—you need to know that I'm not angry at you, or bitter. You've always been honest, and I've always known that things were going to end like this. I just didn't know the timeline—I didn't know . . . until I reached the end. Which is now."

Oh, fuck.

Even though he knew Saxton was right, Blay felt a compulsive need to fight for them. "Listen, I've been really distracted for the last week, and I'm sorry. But things have a way of regulating, and you and I will get back to normal—"

"I'm in love with you."

Blay shut his mouth with a clap.

"So you see," Saxton continued hoarsely, "it's not that you have changed. It's that *I* have—and I'm afraid my silly emotions have put us at quite a distance from each other."

Blay surged to his feet and strode across the fine-napped carpet to the other male.

When he got to his destination, he was relieved to the point of tearing up that Saxton accepted his embrace. And as he held his first true lover against him, feeling that familiar difference in their heights and smelling that wonderful cologne, part of him wanted to debate this break up until they both gave in and kept trying.

But that wasn't fair.

Like Saxton, he'd had the vague notion that things were going to end at some point. And like his lover, he was also surprised it was now.

That didn't change the outcome, however.

Saxton stepped back. "I never meant to get emotionally involved."

"I'm so sorry, I'm . . . I'm so sorry. . . ." Shit, that was all that was coming out of his mouth. "I would give anything to be different. I wish I could . . . be different."

"I know." Saxton reached up and brushed a hand down the side of his face. "I forgive you—and you need to forgive yourself."

Whatever, he wasn't sure he could do that—especially as, at this moment, and as fucking usual, an emotional attachment he didn't want and couldn't change was yet again robbing him of something he wanted.

Qhuinn was a fucking curse to him, the guy really was.

About fifteen miles south of the Brotherhood's mountaintop compound, Assail woke up on his circular bed in the grand master suite of his mansion on the Hudson. Above him, in the mirrored panels mounted on the ceiling, his naked body was gleaming in the soft glow of the lights installed around the base of the mattress. The octagonal room beyond was dark, the interior shutters still down, the fallen night hidden.

As he considered all the glass in the house, he knew so many vampires would have found these accommodations unacceptable. Most would have avoided the manse altogether.

Too much risk during daylight hours.

Assail, however, had never been bound by convention, and the dangers inherent in living in a building with so much access to light were something to be managed, not bound by.

Getting up, he went over to the desk, signed into his computer, and accessed the security system that monitored not just the house, but the grounds. Alerts had sounded several times during the earlier hours of the day, notifications not of an impending attack, but of some kind of activity that had been flagged by the security system's filtering program.

In truth, he lacked the energy to be overly concerned, an unwelcome sign that he needed to feed—

Assail frowned as he reviewed the report.

Well, wasn't this instructive.

And indeed, this was why he'd installed all his checks and balances.

On the images feed from the rear cameras, he watched as a figure dressed in snowfield camouflage traveled on cross-country skis through the forest, closing in on his house from the north. Whoever it was stayed hidden in and among the pines for the most part, and surveyed the property from various vantage points for approximately nineteen minutes . . . before traversing the westerly border of trees, crossing into the neighbor's property, and going down onto the ice. Two hundred yards later the man stopped, got out the binoculars again, and stared at Assail's home. Then he circled around the peninsula that jutted out into the river, reentered the forest, and disappeared.

Bending in closer to the screen, Assail replayed the approach, zooming in to identify facial features, if possible—and it was not. The head was covered with a knit mask, with cutouts only for the eyes, nose, and mouth. With the parka and ski pants on as well, the man was covered in his entirety.

Sitting back, Assail smiled to himself, his fangs tingling in territorial response.

There were but two parties who might be interested in his business, and going by the daylight that had reigned during this recon, it was clear the curiosity was not generated by the Brotherhood: Wrath would never use humans as anything other than a last-resort food source, and no vampire could withstand that amount of sunshine without turning into a torch.

Which left someone in the human world—and there was only a single man with the interest and the resources to try to track him and his whereabouts.

"Enter," he said, just before a knock sounded on his door.

As the pair of males came in, he didn't bother to look away from the computer screen. "How did you sleep?"

A familiar, deep voice answered, "Like the dead."

"How fortunate for you. Jet lag can be a bore, or so I've heard. We had a visitor this morning, by the way."

Assail leaned to one side so his two associates could review the footage.

It was odd to have housemates, but he was going to have to get used to their presence. When he had come to the New World, it had been a solo trip, and he had intended to keep things that way for nu-

merous reasons. Success in his chosen field, however, had mandated that he pull in some backup—and the only people you could even partially trust were your family.

And the pair of them offered a unique benefit.

His two cousins were a rarity in the vampire species: a set of identical twins. When fully clothed, the only way anyone could tell them apart was by a single mole behind the earlobe; other than that, from their voices and their dark, suspicious eyes to their heavily muscled bodies, they were a mirror reflection of each other.

"I'm going out," Assail announced to them. "If our visitor comes again, be hospitable, will you?"

Ehric, the older one by a matter of minutes, glanced over, his face highlighted by the glow around the bed base. Such evil in that handsome combination of features—to the point that one nearly felt pity for the interloper. " 'Twill be a pleasure, I assure you."

"Keep him alive."

"But of course."

"That is a finer line than you two have at times appreciated."

"Trust me."

"It's not you whom I am worried about." Assail looked at the other one. "Do you understand me?"

Ehric's twin remained silent, although the male did nod once.

That grudging reaction was precisely why Assail would have preferred to keep his new life simple. But it was impossible to be in more than one place at a time—and this violation of privacy was proof that he couldn't do everything by himself.

"You know how to locate me," he said, before dismissing them from his room.

Twenty minutes later, he left the house showered, dressed, and behind the wheel of his bulletproof Range Rover.

Downtown Caldwell at night was beautiful at a distance, especially as he came over the inbound bridge. It was not until he penetrated the grid system of streets that the city's sludge became evident: the alleyways with their filthy snowdrifts and their oozing Dumpsters and their discarded, half-frozen homeless humans told the true story of the municipality's underbelly.

His worksite, as it were.

When he got to the Benloise Art Gallery, he parked in the back, in one of two spaces that were parallel to the building behind the facility. As he stepped free of the SUV, the cold wind swept into his camel-hair coat and he had to hold the two halves together as he crossed the pavement, approaching an industrial-size door.

He didn't have to knock. Ricardo Benloise had plenty of people working for him, and not all of them were of the art-dealer-associate type: A human male the size of an amusement park opened the way and stood to the side.

"He expecting you?"

"No, he is not."

Disneyland nodded. "You wanna wait in the gallery?"

"That would be fine."

"You need a drink?"

"No, thank you."

As they walked through the office area and into the exhibition space, the deference Assail was now accorded was a new thing—earned through both the huge product orders he'd been putting in as well as the spilled blood of countless humans: Thanks to him, suicides among disenfranchised males age eighteen to twenty-nine with criminal drug records had struck an all-time high in the city, making even the national news.

Imagine that.

As newscasters and reporters tried to make sense of the tragedies, he merely continued growing his business by any means necessary. Human minds were awfully suggestible; it required hardly any effort at all to get middlemen drug dealers to train their own guns on their temples and pull those triggers. And in the same way nature abhorred a vacuum, so too did the demands of chemical supplementation.

Assail had the drugs. The addicts had the cash.

The economic system more than survived the forced reorganization.

"I'll head up," the man said at a hidden door. "And let him know you're here."

"Do take your time."

Left to his own devices, Assail strolled around the high-ceilinged, open space, linking his hands and putting them at the small of his back. From time to time, he paused to look at the "art" that was hung on the walls and partitions—and was reminded why humans should be eradicated, preferably by slow and painful means.

Used paper plates tacked to cheap particleboard and covered with

handwritten quotes from TV commercials? A self-portrait done in dentifrice? And equally offensive were the aggrandizing plaques mounted next to the messes declaring this nonsense to be the new wave of American Expressionism.

Such a commentary on the culture in so many ways.

"He's ready now."

Assail smiled to himself and turned around. "How accommodating."

As he entered through that sneaky door and ascended to the third level, Assail did not fault his supplier for being suspicious and wanting more information on his single largest customer. After all, in the shortest of time, the drug trade in the city had been rerouted, redefined, and captured by a complete unknown.

One could respect the man's position.

But the digging was going to end here.

At the top of the set of industrial stairs, two other big men stood in front of another door, sure and solid as load-bearing walls. As with the guard on the first floor, they opened things up fast, and nodded at him with respect.

On the far side, Benloise was sitting at the end of a long, narrow room that had windows down one side, and only three pieces of furniture: his raised desk, which was nothing but a thick slab of teak with a modernist lamp and an ashtray on it; his chair, of some modern derivation; and a second seat across from him for a single visitor.

The man himself was like his environment: neat, officious, and uncluttered in his thinking. In fact, he proved that however illicit the drug trade was, the management principles and interpersonal skill sets of a CEO went a long way if you wanted to make millions in it—and keep your money.

"Assail. How are you?" The diminutive gentleman rose and put out his hand. "This is an unexpected pleasure."

Assail went across, shook what was extended and did not wait for an invitation to sit down.

"What may I do for you?" Benloise said as he himself resettled on his chair.

Assail took a Cuban cigar from out of his inside pocket. Snipping the end off, he leaned forward and put the snubbed piece right on the desk.

As Benloise frowned like someone had defecated on his bed, Assail smiled just short of flashing his fangs. "It's what I may do for you."

"Oh."

"I have always been a private man, living a private life by choice." He put away his clipper and took out his gold lighter. Popping the flame, he leaned in and puffed to get the cigar into a sustainable burn. "But above and beyond that, I am a businessman engaging in a dangerous manner of trade. Accordingly, I take any trespass of my property or intrusion upon my anonymity as a direct act of aggression."

Benloise smiled smoothly and eased back in his throne-like chair. "I can respect that, of course, and yet I am confounded as to why you feel the need to point this out to me."

"You and I have entered into a mutually beneficial relationship, and it is very much my desire to continue this association." Assail puffed on the cigar, releasing a cloud of French-blue smoke. "Therefore, I want to pay you the respect you are due, and make clear before I take action that if I discover any person upon my premises whom I have not invited thereupon, I shall not only eradicate them, I shall find the source of inquiry"—he puffed again—"and do what I must to defend my privacy. Am I being clear enough?"

Benloise's brows dropped down low, his dark eyes growing shrewd.

"Am I?" Assail murmured.

There was, of course, only one answer. Assuming the human wanted to live much past the following weekend.

"You know, you remind me of your predecessor," Benloise said in his accented English. "Did you meet the Reverend?"

"We ran in some of the same circles, yes."

"He was killed rather violently. About a year ago now? His club was blown up."

"Accidents happen."

"Usually in the home, so I've heard."

"Something you might keep in mind."

As Assail met those eyes straight on, Benloise dropped his stare first. Clearing his throat, the Eastern seaboard's biggest drug importer and wholesaler swept his palm over his glossy desk, as if he were feeling the grains that ran through the teak.

"Our business," Benloise said, "has a delicate ecosystem that, for all its financial robustness, must be carefully maintained. Stability is rare and highly desirable for men like you and me."

"Agreed. And to that end, I plan to return at the conclusion of the evening with my interim payment, as scheduled. As I always have, I

come to you in good faith, and give you no reason to doubt me or my intentions."

Benloise offered another smooth smile. "You make it sound as if I am behind," he moved his hand around, waving it dismissively through the air, "whatever has upset you."

Leaning in, Assail dipped his chin and glared. "I am not upset. Yet."

One of Benloise's hands surreptitiously dipped out of sight. A split second later, Assail heard the door down at the other end of the room open.

Keeping his voice low, Assail said, "This was a courtesy to you. The next time I find anyone on my property, whether you sent them or not, I shall not be even half so polite."

With that, he got to his feet and ground the lit cigar out upon the desk.

"I bid you a fond good evening," he said, before walking away.

FOURTEEN

Talk about a late start.

As Qhuinn dematerialized away from the mansion, he couldn't believe that it was ten o'clock at night and they were just getting started. Then again, the Brotherhood had stayed holed up in Wrath's study forever, and when he and John had finally been let in, V's announcement that the proof against the Band of Bastards was ironclad had led to a good half hour of trash-talking Xcor and his buddies.

Lot of creative uses of the word *fuck*, as well as some crackerjack suggestions for places to put inanimate objects.

He'd never thought of doing that with a garden rake, for example. Fun. Fun.

And Blay had missed it all.

Reassuming his form in a woodland area south and west of the compound, Qhuinn steeled himself against making any inferences about what had detained the guy—although the fact of the matter was, the fighter had gone up to his room and hadn't come back. And whereas most accidents happened in the home, it was a good guess that he hadn't had a slip-and-fall.

Unless Saxton had been playing throw rug on the marble in their bathroom.

Feeling like he wanted to slap himself, he surveyed the snow-covered landscape while John, Rhage, and Z appeared next to him. The coordinates for the location had been found in the phones of those car thieves from the night before, the seemingly abandoned property about ten or fifteen miles past where he'd caught up with his stolen Hummer.

"What the hell is that?"

As someone spoke up, he glanced over his shoulder. What-the-hell was right: Looming behind them was a boxy building tall as a church steeple and as unadorned as a recycling bin.

"Airplane hangar," Zsadist announced as he started walking in that direction. "Has to be."

Qhuinn followed, bringing up the rear in case anyone decided to pull a hi-how're-ya—

From out of thin air, Blay made his appearance, the male suited up in leather, and as heavily armed as the rest of them. In response, Qhuinn's feet slowed, then stopped in the snow, mostly because he didn't want to lose his footing and look like an asshole.

God, that was one grim motherfucker, he thought as Blay started walking forward. Was there some trouble in paradise?

Even though there was no eye contact between them, Qhuinn felt compelled to say something. "What's . . ."

He didn't finish the "doing" part of the sentence. Why bother? The guy stalked past him like he wasn't there.

"I'm great," Qhuinn muttered as he resumed trudging through the ice pack. "Doin' awesome, thanks for asking—oh, you having probs with Saxton? Really? How'd you like to go out and get a drink and talk about it? Yeah? Perfect. I'll be your after-dinner mint—"

He cut off the fantasy monologue as the breeze shifted and his nose got a whiff of sweet and nasty.

Everyone got their weapons out and focused on the airplane hangar.

"We're upwind," Rhage said quietly. "So there's got to be a big-ass mess in there."

The five of them approached the facility cautiously, fanning out, searching the ambient blue glow of reflected moonlight for anything that moved.

The hangar had two entryways, one that was bifurcated and big enough to fit a wingspan through, and the other that was supposed to be for people, and looked Barbie size in comparison. And Rhage was right: In spite of the fact that the icy winter gusts were hitting them in the back, the smell was enough to tingle the insides of the nose, and not in good way.

Man, cold usually dimmed the stink, too.

Communicating via hand signals, they split into two groups, with him and John taking one side of the mammoth double doors, and Rhage, Blay, and Z zeroing in on the smaller entrance.

Rhage went for the requisite handle while everyone braced for engagement. If there was a football team's worth of *lessers* in there, it made sense to send the Brother in first, because he had the kind of backup nobody else did: His beast loved slayers, and not in a relationship sense.

Talk about your thin mints.

Hollywood put his hand over his head. Three . . . two . . . one . . .

The Brother penetrated in total silence, pushing the door open and slipping inside. Z was next—and Blay went in with them.

Qhuinn felt a heartbeat of pure terror as the male jumped into the unknown with nothing but a pair of forties to protect him. God, the idea that Blay could die tonight, right in front of him, on this run-of-the-mill assignment, made him want to stop all this defending the race bullshit and turn the fighter into a librarian. A hand model. Hairdresser—

The shrill whistle that came no more than sixty seconds later was a godsend. And Z's all-clear was the signal for him and John to change positions, shuffling laterally to the now open door, and going through the—

Okay. Wow.

Talk about your oil slick. And holy fuckin' A from the stench.

The three who'd gone in first had busted out their flashlights, and the beams light-sabered around the cavernous space, cutting through the darkness, illuminating what at first looked like nothing but a sheet of black ice. Except it wasn't black and the shit wasn't frozen. It was congealed human blood—about three hundred gallons' worth. Mixed with a whole lot of Omega.

The hangar was the site of a massive induction, the scale of which made that thing out at that farmhouse a while back look like nothing more than a play date.

"Guess those boys who took your whip were heading to one hell of a party," Rhage said.

"Word," Z muttered.

As the beams of the flashlights highlighted an old, decrepit airplane in the back—and absolutely nothing else—Z shook his head.

"Let's search the outer area. There's nada in here."

Given that the cabin was nothing much from the exterior, just your typical hunting/fishing shack out in the woods, Mr. C was tempted to bypass the damn thing. Thoroughness had its virtues, however, and the cabin's location, about a mile or two into the tract of land, suggested it might have been used as a headquarters at some point.

All things considered, it would have been smarter to check out the property before he'd used that airplane hangar for the largest induction in the Lessening Society's history. But priorities were what they were: First, he had to put himself in control; second, he had to justify the promotion; and third, he had to deal with all those new *lessers*.

And that meant he needed resources. Fast.

Following the Omega's messy, grand ceremony, and the nauseous period that had lasted a number of hours thereafter, Mr. C had ordered the new recruits onto a school bus that he'd stolen from a used-truck dealership a week ago. Between exhaustion and the physical discomfort they were in, they had been such good little boys, filing on and sitting two by two like they were on some kind of fucked-up Noah's Ark.

From there, he'd driven them himself—because you didn't trust assets like that to anybody else—to the Brownswick School for Girls. The defunct prep school was in the suburbs on thirty-five acres of ignored, overgrown, dilapidated grounds, rumors of its being haunted keeping the normal folks out.

For now, the Lessening Society were squatters, but the For Sale sign on the corner near the road meant he could fix that. As soon as he pulled some cash together.

With his boys finishing up their recovery back at the school, and the current slayers downtown trolling for the Brotherhood, he was out on his own, cataloging the few assets left in the Society—including this stretch of mostly empty forest north of the city.

Although he was beginning to believe he was wasting his time.

Stepping up on the cabin's shallow porch, he shone a flashlight in through the nearest window. Potbellied stove. Rough wood table with two chairs. Three bunks that had no mattresses or sheets on them. Galley kitchen.

Heading around back, he found an electric generator that was out of gas, and a rusted-out oil tank, which suggested the place had had some kind of heating in it at some point.

Returning to the front, he toggled the door latch and found it locked.

Whatever. Not much in there.

Taking the map out of the inside of his bomber jacket, he unfolded the thing and located where he was. Checking off the little square, he got out his compass, adjusted his heading, and started walking in a northwesterly direction.

According to this map—which he'd found at the former *Forelesser's* crack house, this tract of property totaled some five hundred acres and had these cabins sprinkled around at random intervals. He gathered that the place had once been a camping area owned by multiple people, a kind of modern-day hunting preserve that had been lost to the New York State tax burden, and purchased by the Society back in the eighties.

At least, that was what the handwritten notations in the corner said, although God only knew if the Society was still the owner of record. Considering the financial state of the organization, the good ol' NYS might well have a gorilla-size tax lien on the acreage now, or have reseized the shit.

He paused and checked the compass again. Man, being a city boy, he hated rooting around out in the woods at night, clomping through the snow, checking shit off like some kind of forest ranger. But he had to see with his own eyes what he had to work with, and that was happening only one way.

At least he had a revenue stream lined up.

In another twenty-four hours, when those boys of his were finally on their feet again, he was going to start refilling the coffers. That was the first step to reclamation.

Step two?

World domination.

FIFTEEN

She was bleeding.

As Layla looked down at the toilet paper in her hand, the red stain on all that white was the visual equivalent of a scream.

Reaching behind herself, she flushed, and had to use the wall to steady her balance as she got to her feet. With one hand on her lower belly and the other thrown out at the sink counter and then the door-jamb, she stumbled into the bedroom and went right for the phone.

Her first instinct was to call Doc Jane, but she decided against that. Assuming she was in the process of miscarrying, there was a possibility of sparing Qhuinn the wrath of the Primale—provided she kept this under wraps. And using the Brotherhood's personal physician probably wasn't the best way to ensure privacy.

After all, there was only one reason a female bled—and questions about her needing and how she'd handled it would inevitably follow.

At the table by the bedside, she opened the drawer and drew out a small black book. Locating the number for the race's clinic, she dialed with a shaking hand.

When she hung up a little later, she had an appointment in thirty minutes.

Except how was she going to get out there? She couldn't dematerialize—too anxious, and anyway, pregnant females were discouraged from that. And she didn't feel as though she could drive herself. Qhuinn's lessons had been comprehensive, but she couldn't imagine, in her condition, getting on a highway and trying to keep up with the flow of human traffic.

Fritz Perlmutter was the only answer.

Going to the closet, she retrieved a soft chemise, twisted it into a thick rope, and secured it between her legs with the help of several pairs of underwear. The solution to her bleeding issue was incredibly bulky and made it hard to walk, but that was the least of her problems.

A phone call to the kitchen secured the butler to drive her.

Now she just had to get down the stairs, out the vestibule, and into that long saloon car in one piece—and without running into any of the males of the household.

Just as she was about to leave her room, she caught her reflection in the mirrors upon the wall. Her white robe and her formal hairstyle announced her rank of Chosen as nothing else could: Nobody beside the Scribe Virgin's sacred females in the species dressed like this.

Even if she appeared under the assumed name she had provided to the receptionist, all would guess her other-worldly affiliation.

Throwing off her robing, she attempted to draw on a pair of yoga pants, but the wadding she had applied to herself made that an impossibility. And the jeans she and Qhuinn had bought together wouldn't work, either.

Withdrawing the chemise, she used paper towels from the bath to deal with her problem and managed to get the denim on. A heavy sweater provided bulk and warmth, and a quick brush out and tieback of her hair made her look . . . almost normal.

Leaving her room, she held hard to the cellular device that Qhuinn had given her. She thought only briefly about calling him, but in truth, what was there to say? He had no more control over this process than she did—

Oh, dearest Virgin Scribe, she was losing their young.

The thought occurred to her just as she came to the apex of the

grand staircase: She was *losing* their young. At this very moment. Here outside of the king's study.

All at once the ceiling crashed down on her head and the walls of the grand, spacious foyer squeezed in so tight she could not draw a breath.

"Your grace?"

Shaking herself, she looked down the red carpet runner. Fritz was standing at the foot of the stairs, dressed in his standard livery, his old, lovely face clothed in concern.

"Your grace, shall we go now?" he said.

As she nodded and cautiously started downward, she couldn't believe it had all been for naught, all those hours of straining with Qhuinn . . . the frozen aftermath where she hadn't dared to move . . . the wondering and the worrying and the quiet, treacherous hope.

The fact that she had given the gift of her virginity away for naught.

Qhuinn was going to be in such pain, and the failure she was bringing upon him added immeasurably to her own suffering. He had sacrificed his own body in the course of her needing, his desire for a young of blood tie prompting him to do something he would not otherwise have chosen to.

That biology had its own agenda did not ease her.

The loss . . . still felt like her fault.

Hair of the dog that bit you.

Saxton believed that was the crude and yet rather apt saying.

Standing naked in front of the mirror in his bath, he put the hair dryer down and drew his fingers through things up top. The waves settled into their normal pattern, the blond strands finding a perfect arrangement to complement his square, even face.

The image he regarded was exactly as it had appeared the night before and the night before that, and yet as familiar as his reflection was, he felt like it was of a different, separate person.

His insides had changed so much, it seemed only reasonable to assume the transformation would be echoed in his appearance. Alas, it was not.

Turning away and walking out to his closet, he supposed he should not be surprised, either by his inner upset, or his outer, false composure.

After he and Blay had spoken, it had taken him an hour to move everything from the bedroom he had stayed in with his former lover back to this suite down the hall. He'd been given these accommodations when he'd initially come to stay within the household, but as things had progressed with Blay, his belongings had gradually made their way into that other room.

The process of migration had been incremental, just as his love had been: a case of one shirt here and a pair of shoes there, a hairbrush one night, and socks the next . . . a conversation of shared values followed by a seven-hour sexual marathon chased with a tub of Breyers coffee ice cream and only one spoon.

He had been unaware of the distance traveled by his heart, similar to the way a hiker became lost in the wilderness. A half mile out and you could still see where you had started, could easily find the way back home. But ten miles and a number of forks in your trail later and there was no going back. At that point, you had no choice but to marshal the resources to build yourself a shelter and put down fresh roots.

He had assumed he would be constructing this new personal place with Blay.

Yes, he had. After all, how long could unrequited love truly survive? As fire required oxygen to kindle, so too did emotion.

Not when it came to Qhuinn, apparently. Not for Blay.

Saxton was resolved about not leaving the royal household, however. Blay had been right about that—Wrath, the king, did need him, and moreover, he enjoyed his work here. It was fast-paced, challenging . . . and the egoist in him wanted to be the lawyer who reformed the law the proper way.

Assuming the throne didn't get overturned and he didn't lose his head under a new regime.

But you couldn't live your life worried about things like that.

Withdrawing a houndstooth wool suit from the closet, he picked a button-down and a vest out, and laid everything on the bed.

It was a sad, rather unattractive cliché to go looking for something nubile and pneumatic to self-medicate emotional pain with, but he much preferred having an orgasm over getting sloppy drunk. Also, the pretend-until-you-find-purpose-again maxim did hold water.

And was especially true as he looked at himself all dressed up in the bathroom's full-length mirror. He certainly appeared to have it together, and that helped.

Before he left, he double-checked his phone. The Old Laws had been recast per Wrath's orders, and now he was on standby—awaiting his next assignment.

He would find out what it was soon enough, he imagined.

Wrath was notoriously demanding, but never unreasonable.

In the meantime, he was going to drown his sorrow in the only kind of six-pack that appealed—something twentyish, six-foot-ish, athletic. . . .

And preferably dark haired. Or blond.

SIXTEEN

"Someone's already been by here."

As Rhage spoke, Qhuinn got out his penlight and shone the discreet beam down onto the ground. Sure enough, the prints through the snow were fresh, not airbrushed with loose flakes . . . and they went directly out into the clearing in the forest. Clicking the light off, he focused on the hunting cabin up ahead that seemed to be abandoned to the cold weather: no stream of smoke curling out of its stone chimney, no glow of illumination—and most important, no scents of anything.

The five of them closed in, circling the clearing and sidling up with a wide-angle approach. When there was no defensive reaction from anything, they all mounted the shallow porch and scoped out the interior through the single-paned windows.

"Nada," Rhage muttered as he went to the door.

A quick test of the handle—and it was locked.

With a thrust, the Brother slammed his massive shoulder into the panels and set the thing flying, fragments of the locking mechanism falling in a scatter along with splinters of wood.

"Hi, honey, I'm home," Hollywood shouted as he marched inside.

Qhuinn and John followed protocol and stayed on the porch as Blay and Z filed in and searched.

The woods were quiet around them, but his keen eyes traced those footprints . . . which, after a sojourn to the cabin, headed off in a northwesterly direction.

Damn well suggested someone was out here with them, searching the property at the same time.

Human? *Lesser?*

He was thinking the latter, given all the shit in that hangar—and the fact that this whole property was remote, and relatively secure because of that.

Although they were gonna want to bring Stanley Steemer into that building for a cleanup first.

Blay's voice drifted out the open door. "I got something."

It took all of Qhuinn's training not to break covenant with surveying the landscape and turn to look inside—and not because he particularly cared about whatever had been found. Throughout their searching, he'd been constantly checking on Blay, measuring to see if that mood had changed.

If anything, it had only gotten worse.

Soft voices went back and forth in the cabin, and then the three of them emerged.

"We found a lockbox," Rhage announced as he unzipped his jacket and slid the long, thin metal container in against his chest. "We'll open it later. Let's find the owner of those boots, boys."

Dematerializing at fifty- to sixty-foot clips, they fanned out through the trees, tracking the prints in the snow, following silently.

They came across the *lesser* about a half mile later.

The lone slayer was marching through the snow-covered forest at a clip that only a human with Olympic training could have sustained for more than a couple hundred yards. Clothes were dark, a pack was on the back, and the fact that he was navigating by sight alone was another clue that it was the enemy: Most Homo sapiens would not have been able to move that fast in such little light without battery-powered illumination.

Using hand signals, Rhage orientated the group into a reverse triangle formation that cupped around the *lesser's* trail. Continuing to advance along with him, they observed for about a football field's length and then, all at once, they closed in, surrounded the slayer, and blocked him at contrasting compass points with gun muzzles.

The *lesser* stopped moving.

He was a newer recruit, his dark hair and olive coloring suggesting that he was of Mexican or perhaps Italian descent, and he got points for showing no fear. Even though he was looking at a hurting, he merely calmly glanced over his shoulder, as if to confirm that he had in fact been ambushed.

"How you doing?" Rhage drawled.

The *lesser* didn't bother to answer, which was in contrast to what they had been seeing lately. Unlike the others, this was no young punk to talk smack and flash his gat. Calm, calculating . . . controlled, he was the kind of enemy that improved your job performance.

Not exactly a bad thing . . .

And sure enough, his hand disappeared into his coat.

"Don't be stupid, my man," Qhuinn barked, prepared to put a bullet in the bastard at a moment's notice.

The *lesser* didn't stop moving.

Fine.

He pulled his fucking trigger and dropped the bitch.

The instant the *lesser* hit the snow, Blay froze with his guns in place. The others did the same.

In the silent seconds that passed, they kept eyes locked on the downed slayer. No movement. No response from the periphery. Qhuinn had incapacitated the thing, and it appeared to have been working alone.

Funny, even if Blay hadn't heard the shot in his left ear, he'd have known Qhuinn was the shooter—everyone else would have given the enemy another chance to think things over.

As Rhage whistled in a short burst, that was the cue to close in. The five of them moved like a pack of wolves over downed prey, swift and sure, crossing the snow with guns up. The slayer remained utterly still—but there hadn't been a death in the family, so to speak. You needed a steel dagger through the chest for that.

But this was the desirable state. You wanted them to be able to talk.

Or at least, in a condition to be forced to talk—

Later, when he replayed what happened next . . . when his mind churned and burned over the facts obsessively . . . when he stayed up days trying to piece together how it all rolled out in hopes of divining a change in procedure that would ensure something like it never, ever went down again . . . Blay would dwell on the twitch.

That little twitch in the arm. Just an autonomic jerk seemingly unconnected with any conscious thought or will. Nothing dangerous. No signal of what was to come.

Just a twitch.

Except then, with a move that was blinking fast, the slayer outted a gun from somewhere. It was unprecedented—one second he was deadweight on the ground; the next, he was shooting in a controlled manner in a fat circle.

And even before the popping sounds faded, Blay caught the horrific image of Zsadist taking a slug right in the heart, the impact strong enough to stop the Brother's forward momentum, his torso throwing back, his arms ripping out to the side as he flipped off his feet.

Instantly, the dynamic changed. No one was looking to interrogate the bastard anymore.

Four daggers flashed high. Four bodies jumped in. Four arms slashed down with cold, sharp blades. Four impacts struck, one right after another.

They were too late, however.

The slayer disappeared right out from under them, their weapons stabbing the black-stained snow beneath where the enemy had landed, instead of an empty chest cavity.

Whatever—there would be time to question the unprecedented disappearance afterward. At the moment, they had a fighter down.

Rhage all but launched himself on top of the Brother, putting his body in the way of anything and everything. "Z? Z? Oh, mother of the race—"

Blay got out his phone and dialed. When Manny Manello answered, there was no time to be wasted. "We have a Brother down. Gunshot to the chest—"

"Wait!"

Z's voice was a surprise. And so was the Brother's arm shooting up and shoving Rhage to the side. "Will you get off me!"

"But I'm giving you CPR—"

"I will die before kissing you, Hollywood." Z tried to sit up, his breathing heavy. "Don't even think about it."

"Hello?" Manello's voice came through the phone. "Blay?"

"Hold on—"

Qhuinn dropped to his knees next to Zsadist, and in spite of the fact that the Brother didn't like to be touched, took hold under one armpit and helped the male get his torso off the snow.

"I have the clinic on the line," Blay said. "What's your status?"

In reply, Z reached up and unhinged his dagger holster. Then he dragged down the zipper of his leather jacket and ripped his white T-shirt in half.

To reveal the most beautiful bulletproof vest Blay had ever seen.

Rhage sagged in relief—to the point that Qhuinn had to catch him with his free hand and keep the guy off the ground, too.

"Kevlar," Blay mumbled to Manello. "Oh, thank God, he's wearing Kevlar."

"That's great—but listen, I need you to take the vest off and check to see if it held the bullet, 'kay?"

"Roger that." He glanced over at John and was glad to find the guy up on his feet, two guns out straight, eyes scanning the environs while the rest of them assessed the situation. "I'll take care of it."

Blay shuffled over and crouched down in front of the Brother. Qhuinn might have had the balls to make contact with Zsadist, but he wasn't going to do that without express permission.

"Dr. Manello wants to know if you can remove the vest so we can see if there was any injury?"

Z jerked his arms, and then frowned. Appeared to give things another try. After a third attempt, the Brother's hands managed to lift as high as the Velcro straps, but they couldn't seem to do much.

Blay swallowed hard. "May I take care of it? I promise not to touch you as much as possible."

Great grammar there. But he was serious.

Z's eyes lifted to his. They were black from pain, not yellow. "Do what you have to, son. I'll keep it tight."

The Brother looked away, his face screwed down hard into a grimace, the scar that made an S-curve from the bridge of his nose to the corner of his mouth standing out in harsh relief.

With a stern lecture, Blay ordered his hands to be steady and sure, and the message was somehow carried out: He tore apart the

fastening strips at the shoulders, the rips louder than the screaming in his head, and then peeled off the vest, terrified of what he was going to find.

There was a big round patch directly in the center of Z's broad, muscled chest. Right where the heart was.

But it was a bruise. Not a hole.

It was just a bruise.

"Surface wound only." Blay dug his finger into the dense webbing of the vest and found the slug. "I can feel the bullet in the vest—"

"Then why can't I move my—"

The smell of the Brother's fresh blood seemed to hit everyone's noses at the same time. Someone cursed, and Blay leaned in.

"You've been hit under the arm, too."

"Bad?" Z asked.

Over the phone, Manello said, "Get in there and look around if you can."

Blay lifted that heavy limb and flashed his penlight in at the underside. Apparently a bullet had entered the torso through the vest's small, unprotected pocket under the pit—a one-in-a-million shot that if you'd tried to re-create, you couldn't possibly pull off.

Fuck. "I don't see an exit wound. It's right on the side of his ribs, way up high."

"He's breathing steadily?" Manello asked.

"Labored but steady."

"Was CPR administered?"

"He threatened to castrate Hollywood if there was any kind of liplock."

"Look, let me just dematerialize." Z coughed a little. "Gimme some room—"

Everyone offered a variety of opinions at that point, but Zsadist would have none of it. Shoving people away, the Brother closed his eyes and . . .

Blay knew they had a real problem when nothing happened. Yes, Zsadist hadn't been killed, and he was a hell of a lot better off than he would have been without the vest. But he was not able to move himself—and they were in the middle of nowhere, so deep in the woods that even if they called for backup, nobody was going to be able to get an SUV within miles of them.

And worse? Blay had the sense that the slayer that had been taken down had been something considerably more than your run-of-the-mill *lesser*.

No telling when reinforcements would be coming in.

The sound of a text hitting somebody's phone sounded, and Rhage looked down. "Shit. The others are backed up downtown. We've got to handle this on our own."

"Goddamn it," Zsadist muttered under his breath.

Yup. That about covered it.

SEVENTEEN

Xcor had not expected this.

As he and his soldiers materialized to the communal feeding's prearranged location, he had anticipated a property that was run-down or mayhap on the verge of condemnation, a place in such financial state that a female would be forced into selling her veins and her sex to stay afloat.

No such thing.

The environs of the estate were appointed to a *glymera* standard, the sprawling manor house up on the hill glowing with warm light, the grounds manicured to within an inch of their lives, the smaller retainer cottage just inside the gates in perfect condition despite its obvious age.

Mayhap she was a lesser cousin of some great lineage?

"Who is this female?" he asked Throe.

His second in command shrugged. "I know not of her family personally. But I did verify her affiliation with a bloodline of worth."

All around, his fighters were antsy, their combat boots packing the snow beneath their feet as they paced in place, their breath leaving their nostrils as if they were racehorses at the gate.

"One wonders if she knows what she volunteered for," Xcor murmured, not particularly caring whether the female did or did not.

"Shall I?" Throe asked.

"Yes, afore the others burst free of their wills and break into that fair cottage of hers."

Throe dematerialized over to a quaint front door, its arched top and little lantern something one would expect to find outfitting a dollhouse. His right-hand male was not persuaded by the charm, however. The overhead illumination was abruptly cut off, surely because Throe willed it so, and the soldier's knock was hard and quick, a demand, not an inquiry.

Moments later, the portal opened. Firelight spilled out into the night, the golden yellow beams so intense they appeared at least nominally capable of melting the snow cover—and right in the middle of that lovely illumination, the figure of a female cut a dark, curvy silhouette.

She was naked. And the scent that drifted over on the icy breeze indicated that she was very ready.

Zypher growled softly.

"Keep your wits about you," Xcor commanded. "Lest your hunger be used as a weapon against us."

Throe spoke to her and then reached into his inner pocket to take out the cash. The female accepted what was given and then stretched one arm up high upon the jamb, angling her body so that one luscious breast was bathed in that soft light.

Throe glanced over his shoulder and nodded.

The others didn't wait for further invitation. Xcor's fighters converged upon the doorway, their male bodies so large, and in such number, that the female was instantly rendered invisible.

With a curse, he closed in on foot as well.

Zypher naturally went in first, taking her lips and cupping her breasts, but he wasn't alone. The three cousins fought for position, one going behind and arching his hips, as if he were rubbing his cock against her ass, the other two reaching for her nipples and her sex, their hands worming in as she was swarmed.

Throe spoke above the rising moans. "I shall stay outside on guard."

Xcor opened his mouth to command otherwise, and then realized it would make him look like he was avoiding the scene, and that was hardly a masculine thing to do.

"Aye, you do that," he muttered. "I shall guard the interior."

His males picked up the female, their dagger hands finding hold on her arms, her thighs, her waist, and en masse they carried her backward into the cozy confines. Xcor was the one who shut the door and made sure there was no locking device to pen them in. He was also the one to scope out the inside of the cottage. As his bastards carried their meal toward the fire, where a large fur rug had been laid flat upon the floor, he leaned into the closest window, lifted the drapery, and checked the panes of glass. Old and leaded, with wooden struts, not steel.

Not secure. Good.

"Someone get inside of me," the female moaned in a deep voice.

Xcor didn't bother to ascertain whether she was accommodated or not—although her rippling groan suggested she was. Instead, he looked around for any other doors or places from which an ambush could be staged. There appeared to be none. The cottage didn't have a second floor, the skeleton of its roof arching up above his head, and there was only a shallow bathroom, the door of which was open, a light left on revealing a claw-footed tub and an old-fashioned sink. The open kitchen was but a stretch of countertop and a few modest appliances.

Xcor glanced over at the action. The female was lying on her back, her arms T'd out from her torso, her neck exposed, her legs spread wide. Zypher had mounted her and was rhythmically thrusting into her, her head moving back and forth on the white fur as she absorbed the pounding. Two of the cousins had latched onto her wrists, and the other had taken out his cock and was fucking her mouth with it. Indeed, there was little of her that was not covered with male vampire, and her ecstasy at being used was obvious not only to the eye, but to the ear: Around the erection that was going in and out of her plump lips, her heavy breathing and erotic moans escaped into the balmy, sex-scented air.

Xcor walked over to the kitchen sink. There was nothing in the deep belly of it, no lingering remnants of a meal, no half-filled, abandoned glasses. There were dishes in the cupboards, however, and when he opened the European-size refrigerator, bottles of white wine were lined up horizontally on the shelves.

A male curse brought his eyes back to the fun and games. Zypher was just orgasming, his body bowing forward while his head kicked back—and in the midst of his release, one of the cousins was shoving him out of the way, taking his place, lifting the hips of the female and digging his arousal into her wet, pink sex. At least Zypher seemed entirely content to trade places; he beared his fangs, ducked his head under the now-heaving chest of his comrade, and nipped the breast of the female so he could feed close to her nipple.

The one at her mouth orgasmed as well, and she swallowed his release, sucking the head of the fighter's cock in desperate pulls, then letting go and licking at her slick mouth as if she were still hungry. Somebody else soon obliged, yet another arousal plunging in between her lips, the counterthrusting rhythm of what was going on at her head as well as between her legs bouncing her back and forth in a way she seemed to get off on.

Xcor went over and double-checked the bathroom, but his first assessment had been correct: There was nowhere to hide in its tight confines.

Having secured the interior, he had naught to do but lean back against the corner that offered the greatest visual access and witness the feeding. As things intensified, his fighters lost what semblance of civility they had, taking swipes at one another as lions would over a fresh kill, their fangs flashing, their eyes wild with aggression as they jockeyed for access. They did not completely lose their heads, however. And they took care of the female.

Soon enough, someone scored his vein and put it to her lips.

Xcor dropped his eyes to his boots and allowed his peripheral vision to monitor the environs.

There was a time when he would have become aroused at the sight—not because he was particularly interested in the sex, but more in the same manner that when he saw food, his stomach would grumble. And accordingly, in the past, when he had had the need to take a female, he had done just that. Usually in the dark, of course, so the dear girl wouldn't be offended or afeared.

He could well imagine the strained expressions males sported when they were in their erotic throes did little to improve his looks.

Now, though? He felt curiously unplugged from it all, as if he were watching a team of males move some heavy furniture or perhaps rake a lawn.

It was his Chosen, of course.

Having had his lips against her pure skin, having looked into her luminous green eyes, having smelled her delicate scent, he was ut-

terly uninterested in the well-used charms of that female in front of
the fire.

Oh, his Chosen . . . he had never known such grace existed, and
moreover, he could not have e'er surmised that he would be touched
so completely by that which was antithetical to him. She was his opposite, kind and giving when he was brutal and unforgiving, beautiful
to his ugliness, ethereal to his filth.

And she had marked him. Sure as if she had struck him and left a
scar deep within his flesh, he was wounded and weakened by her.

There was naught to be done.

Lo, even the memory of the moments he had shared with her,
when she had been fully clothed, and he had been so gravely injured,
were enough to stir him at his hips, his sorry sex stiffening for no good
reason a'tall: Even if they had not been on different sides of the war for
the throne, she would never have let him come to her as a male does
when he is enthralled with a female of worth. That breezy autumn
night when they had met under that tree, she had been performing a
valid service in her own mind. It had naught to do with him in particular.

But oh, he wanted her nonetheless. . . .

Abruptly, the female before the fire arched under the shifting, orgasming weights atop her, and he refocused on her. As if she sensed his
sexual arousal, her blissed-out, fuzzy stare drifted over in his direction,
and brief surprise flickered across her face—or what little he could see
of it around the thick forearm offering her nourishment.

Shock widened her eyes. She evidently had failed to notice his
presence—but now that she had, fear, not passion, clearly flared
within her.

Unwilling to disrupt the action, he shook his head and flashed her
his palm in a stop motion to reassure her that she was not going to
have to bear his bite—or worse, his sex.

The messaging apparently worked, because the dread left her expression, and as one of his soldiers presented his cock for attention, she
reached out and began stroking it over her head.

Xcor smiled to himself in a nasty way. This whore wouldn't have
him, and yet his body, in all its biological stupidity, insisted on re-
sponding to that Chosen as if the sacred female would e'er look twice
at him.

So silly.

Checking his watch, he was surprised to find that the feeding had been going on for an hour already. So be it. Provided his males complied with his two basic rules, he was content to let this continue: They had to remain substantially clothed, and their weapons had to be holstered with the safeties off.

That way, if the tenor changed, they could defend themselves quickly.

He was more than willing to give them the time.

After this interlude? The lot of them were going to be at their full strength—and with the way things were going with the Brotherhood . . . they were going to need to be.

EIGHTEEN

"No. Fucking no way."

Qhuinn had to agree with Z's read on Rhage's bright idea.

The bunch of them had struggled through the woods, with Rhage bearing most of Z's weight while everyone else circled the pair, ready to pick off anything or anyone who threatened from the fringes. They were now back at the airplane hangar, and Hollywood's solution to their mobility problem seemed like a complication with mortal implications, not anything that was actually going to help.

"How hard can it be to fly a plane?" As everyone, including Z, just looked at him, Rhage shrugged. "What. Humans do it all the time."

Z rubbed his chest and slowly sank to the ground. After gathering his short breath, he shook his head. "First of all, you don't know if . . . the damn thing . . . can even get airborne. It probably has no gas . . . and you've never flown before."

"You wanna tell me what our other option is? We're still miles from any plausible pickup location, you're not improving, and we could get ambushed. Let me at least get in there and see if I can get the engine to turn over."

"This is a bad call."

In the quiet that followed, Qhuinn did the math himself, and glanced over at the hangar. After a moment, he said, "I'll cover you. Let's do this."

Bottom line, Rhage was right. This foot-race of an evac was taking too long, and that *lesser* had disappeared before they'd stabbed him, not the other way around.

Had the Omega given his boys some special powers?

Whatever—a smart fighter never underestimated the enemy—especially when one of his own was down. They needed to get Z to safety, and if that meant an airlift, so the fuck be it.

He and Rhage filed into the hangar and flicked on their flashlights. The airplane was right where they'd left it in the back corner, looking like it was the ugly stepchild of some much prettier mode of transportation that had long since fled the scene. Closing in, Qhuinn saw that the propeller appeared to be sound, and, although the wings were dusty, he could hang his weight off of them.

The fact that the door hatch squeaked like a bitch when Rhage opened the way in was less than good news.

"Whew," Rhage muttered as he recoiled. "Smells like something died in there."

Man, must have been one hell of a stinky if the Brother could differentiate it from the rest of the smell inside the hangar.

Maybe this wasn't such a hot idea.

Before Qhuinn could offer a second read on the stench, Rhage turned himself into a pretzel and squeezed through the oval hole. "Holy shit—keys. There are keys—can you believe it?"

"How about gas?" Qhuinn muttered, as he swept his flashlight beam around in a wide circle. Nothing but that dirty-ass floor.

"You might want to step back there, son," Rhage hollered out of the cockpit. "I'ma try and fire this old lady up."

Qhuinn eased away, but come on. If the thing was going to go up in flames, like fifteen feet was going to make much of a difference—

The explosion was loud, the smoke was thick, and the engine sounded like it was suffering from a mechanical strain of whooping cough. But shit evened out. The longer they let it run, the more even the rhythm became.

"We gotta get out of here before we asphyxiate," Qhuinn yelled into the plane.

Right on cue, Rhage must have put the thing in drive or something, because the airplane eased forward with a groan like every nut and bolt in its body hurt.

And this thing was going to get airborne?

Qhuinn jogged in front and hit the double bay's seam. Gripping one side, he threw all the power in his body into the pull and ripped the thing apart, various latches and locks popping free and going flying.

He hoped the airplane didn't take inspiration from those fragments.

In the moonlight, the expressions on John's and Blay's faces were pretty fucking priceless as they got a good look at the escape plan—and he knew where they were coming from.

Rhage hit the brakes and squeezed out again. "Let's load him up."

Silence. Well, except for the wheezing plane behind them.

"You're not taking it up," Qhuinn said, almost to himself.

Rhage frowned in his direction. "Excuse me."

"You're too valuable. If that thing goes down, we can't lose two Brothers. Not going to happen. I'm expendable, you are not."

Rhage opened his mouth like he was going to argue. But then he shut it, a strange expression settling onto his beautiful face.

"He's right," Z said grimly. "I can't put you in jeopardy, Hollywood."

"Fuck that, I can dematerialize out of the cockpit if—"

"And you think you're going to be able to do that when we're in a spiral? Bullshit—"

A smattering of gunshots came from the tree line, piffing into the snow, whizzing by the ear.

Everyone snapped into action. Qhuinn dived into the plane, pulled himself into the pilot's seat, and tried to make sense of all the . . . fucking hell, there were a lot of dials. The only saving grace he had was that he'd—

Rat-tat-tat-tat!

—watched enough movies to know that the lever with the grip was the gas and the bow tie–shaped wheel was the thing you pulled up to go up, and pushed down to go down.

"*Fuck,*" he muttered as he stayed in a tuck position as much as he could.

Given the popping sounds that followed, John and Blay were

shooting back, so Qhuinn sat up a little higher and glanced at the rows of instruments. He figured the one with the little gas tank was what he was looking for.

Quarter of the tanks left. And the shit in there was probably half condensation.

This was a really bad idea.

"Get him in here!" Qhuinn yelled, sizing up the empty, flat field to the left.

Rhage was on it, throwing Zsadist into the airplane with all the gentleness of a longshoreman. The Brother landed in a crumpled pile, but at least he was cursing—which meant he was with it enough to feel pain.

Qhuinn didn't wait for any door-shutting bullcrap. He released the foot brake, hit the accelerator, and prayed they didn't skid out in the snow—

Half the glass windshield shattered in front of him, the bullet that did the damage ricocheting around the cockpit, the *whiff!* from the seat next to him suggesting the headrest had caught the slug. Which was better than his arm. Or skull.

The only good news was that the plane seemed ready to get the hell out of there, too, that rusty-ass engine spinning the prop at a dead run like the POS knew getting off the ground was the sole way to safety. Out the side windows, the landscape started striping by, and he oriented the middle of the "runway" by keeping the two sets of trees equidistant.

"Hold on," he yelled over the din.

Wind was ripping into the cockpit like there was an industrial fan filling up the space where the pane of glass had been, but it wasn't like he was planning on going high enough to require pressurization.

At this point, he just wanted to clear the forest up ahead.

"Come on, baby, you can do it . . . come on. . . ."

He had the throttle down flat, and he had to tell his arm to ease off—there was no more juice to be had, but breaking the goddamn thing was guaranteed to fuck them even harder.

The din got louder and louder.

Trees moved faster and faster.

The bumps became more and more violent, until his teeth were clapping together, and he became convinced one or both of the wings were going to unhinge and fall by the wayside.

Figuring there was no time to waste, Qhuinn pulled back as hard as he could on the steering wheel, gripping the thing tightly, as if that could somehow be translated to the body of the plane and keep it all together—

Something fell from the ceiling and fluttered back in Z's direction.

Map? Owner's manual? Who the fuck knew.

Man, those trees at the far end were getting close.

Qhuinn pulled even more, in spite of the fact that the wheel was as far toward him as it could go—which was a crying shame, because they were out of runway and still not off the ground—

Scraping sounds raked down the belly of the plane, as if underbrush were reaching up and trying to grab onto the steel plating.

And still those trees were even closer.

His first thought as he stared death in the face was that he was never going to meet his daughter. At least not on this side of the Fade.

His second and final was that he couldn't believe he'd never told Blay he loved him. In all the minutes and hours and nights of his life, in all the words he'd spoken to the male over the years they'd known each other, he'd only ever pushed him away.

And now it was too late.

Dumb-ass. What a fucking dumb-ass he was.

'Cuz it sure as hell appeared that his library card was getting stamped tonight.

Straightening up so the full force of that cold blast hit him square in the face, Qhuinn glared into the rush, picturing those pines ahead that he couldn't see because his eyes were watering from the wind. Opening his mouth, he screamed bloody murder, adding his voice to the maelstrom.

Goddamn it, he wasn't going down like a pussy. No ducking, no pathetic oh-please-God-no-saaaaaave-me. Fuck that. He was going to meet death with his fangs bared and his body braced and his heart pounding not from fear, but from a whole boatload of . . .

"Blow me, Grim Reaper!"

As Qhuinn was trying to get airborne, Blay had his gun muzzle pointed into the tree line and was pumping off rounds like he had an endless supply of lead—which he didn't.

This was a total goat fuck. He and John and Rhage were without any cover; there was no way of knowing how many slayers were in those woods; and for the love of God, all that ancient airplane was doing was leaving a toxic cloud of smoke in its wake as it rattled off like it was on a Sunday stroll.

Oh, and that POS was far from fucking bulletproof, but evidently had gas in its tank.

Qhuinn and Z were not going to make it. They were going to slam into that forest at the end of the field—assuming they didn't get blown up first.

In that moment, when he knew that one way or another a fireball was imminent, he split in half. The physical part of him remained plugged into fending off the attack, his arms sticking straight out, his forefingers squeezing out bullets, his eyes and ears tracking the sounds and sights of muzzle flashes and the movements of his enemy.

The other part of him was in that airplane.

It was as if he were watching his own death. He could imagine so very clearly the violent vibrating of the plane, and the out-of-control bumps over the ground, and the sight of that solid line of trees coming at him—sure as if he were staring out of Qhuinn's eyes and not his own.

That foolhardy son of a *bitch*.

There had been so many times when Blay had thought, He's going to kill himself.

So many times on and off the field.

But now this was the one that was going to stick—

The bullet struck him in the thigh, and the pain that raced from his leg to his heart suggested that his full attention needed to shift back to the fight: If he wanted to live, he had to completely focus.

Yet even as the conviction hit him, there was a split second when he thought, Just end this all now. Just be done with all the bullshit and the punishment of life, the almost-theres, the if-onlys, the relentless chronic agony he'd been in . . . he was so tired of it all—

He had no idea what made him hit the snow.

One moment he was staring toward the plane waiting for the burst of flames. The next he was chest-down on the ground, his elbows digging into the frozen, intractable earth, his injured leg throbbing.

Pop! Pop! Pop—

The roar that interrupted the sound of bullets was so loud he ducked his head, like that would help him avoid the chronic airplane's fireball.

Except there was no light and no heat. And the sound was over-head. . . .

Soaring. That bucket of bolts was actually in the air. Above them.

Blay spared a second to look up, just in case he'd gotten shot in the head and his perception of reality was fucked. But no—that piece-of-shit crop duster was up in the sky, making a fat turn and taking off in the direction that, if it could stay aloft, would eventually lead Qhuinn and Z to the Brotherhood's compound.

If they were lucky.

Man, that flight path wasn't pretty—it was not an eagle going straight and true through the night sky. More like a barn swallow fresh out of the nest—with a broken wing.

Back and forth. Back and forth, tipping from side to side.

To the point where it looked more like they had pulled off the impossible and gotten in the air . . . only to quickly crash and burn over the forest . . .

From out of nowhere, something caught him in the side of the face, smacking him so hard he flopped over onto his back and nearly lost hold of his forties. A hand—it had been a hand that had palmed his puss like a basketball.

And then a massive weight jumped on his chest, flattening him into the snowpack, making him exhale so hard, he wondered if he didn't need to look around for his liver.

"Will you get your fucking head down?" Rhage hissed in his ear. "You're going to get shot—again."

As the lull in shooting stetched from seconds to a full minute, *less-ers* emerged from the tree line up ahead, the quartet of slayers walking through the snow with their weapons drawn and poised.

"Don't move," Rhage whispered. "Two can play at this game."

Blay did his best not to breathe as heavily as the burn in his lungs was telling him he needed to. Also tried not to sneeze as loose flakes tickled his nose on every inhale.

Waiting.

Waiting.

Waiting.

John was about three feet away, and lying in a contorted position that made Blay's heart flicker—

The guy subtly flashed a thumbs-up, like he was reading Blay's mind.

Thank. Fuck.

Blay shifted his eyes around without changing the awkward angle of his head, and then discreetly exchanged a gun for one of his daggers.

As an unhinged hum started to vibrate in his head, he calibrated the *lessers'* movements, their trajectories, their weapons. He was nearly out of bullets, and there wasn't time to reload from his ammo belt—and he knew that John and Rhage were in a similar situation.

The knives that V had hand-made for them all were their only recourse.

Closer . . . closer . . .

When the four slayers were finally in range, his timing was perfect. And so were the others'.

With a coordinated shift and surge, he leaped up and started stabbing at the two closest to him. John and Rhage attacked the others—

Almost immediately, more slayers came from the woods, but for some reason, probably because the Lessening Society wasn't arming inductees all that well, there were no bullets. The second round rushed across the snow with the kind of weapons you'd expect to find in an alley fight—baseball bats, crowbars, tire irons, chains.

Fine with him.

He was so juiced and pissed off, he could use the hand-to-hand.

NINETEEN

Sitting on the examination table, with a frail paper gown covering her, and her bare feet hanging off the padded lip, Layla felt as though she were surrounded by instruments of torture. And she supposed she was. All manner of stainless-steel implements were laid out upon the countertop by the sink, their clear plastic wrappings indicating they were sterile and prepared for use.

She had been at Havers's clinic for an absolute eternity. Or at least, it seemed that way.

In contrast to the rushing ride across the river, when the butler had driven like he knew time was of all essence, ever since she had arrived herein there had been delay after delay. From the paperwork, to the waiting for a room, to the waiting for the nurse, to the waiting for Havers to present the blood test results to her.

It was enough to make one mad in the head.

Across from where she sat, a print framed in glass hung upon the wall, and she had long memorized the image's brushstrokes and colors, the bouquet of flowers depicted in vibrant blues and yellow. The name underneath it read: *van Gogh*.

At this point, she never wanted to see irises again.

Shifting her weight about, she grimaced. The nurse had given her a proper pad for her bleeding, and she was horrified to realize that she was going to need another soon—

The door opened on a knock, and her first instinct was to run—which was ridiculous. This was where she needed to be.

Except it was merely the nurse who had settled her here, taken that blood sample and her vitals, and made notations on a computer. "I'm so sorry—there's been another emergency. I just want to reassure you that you are next in line."

"Thank you," Layla heard herself say.

The female came over and put a hand on Layla's shoulder. "How are you doing?"

The kindness made her blink quickly. "I fear I shall need another . . ." She pointed down at her hips.

The nurse nodded and squeezed gently before going over to the cupboards and extracting a peach-wrapped square. "I've got more here. Would you like me to take you back down to the bathroom?"

"Yes, please—"

"Wait, don't get on your feet yet. Let me get you a better cover."

Layla looked down at her hands, her tangled, knotted hands that could not be still. "Thank you."

"Here you go." Something soft was draped around her. "Okay, let's get you standing."

Sliding off the table, she wobbled a little, and the nurse was right there, taking hold of her elbow, steadying her.

"We're going to go slowly."

And they did. Out in the hall, there were nurses rushing from room to room, and people coming and going for appointments, and other staff going at a dead run . . . and Layla couldn't believe she had ever been as fast as them. To keep out of the crush, she and her kindly escort stayed close to the wall to avoid getting mowed over, but the others were really quite nice. As if all knew that she suffered in some grave manner.

"I'm going to come in with you," the nurse said when they got to the facilities. "Your blood pressure is very low and I'm concerned you're a fall risk, okay?"

As Layla nodded, they went in and the lock was turned. The nurse relieved her of the blanket, and she awkwardly shuffled the paper out of the way.

Sitting down, she—

"Oh, dearest Virgin Scribe."

"Shh, it's okay, it's all right." The nurse bent down and gave her the fresh pad. "Let's take care of this. You're all right . . . here, no, you'll want to give that to me. We have to send it to the lab. There's a chance it can be used to determine why this is happening, and you're going to want that information if you try again."

Try again. As if the loss was already done.

The nurse snapped on gloves and got a plastic bag from out of a console. Things were taken care of discreetly and with alacrity, and Layla watched as the name she'd given was written on the outside of the bag in black marker.

"Oh, honey, it's okay."

The nurse took off her gloves, snapped out a paper towel from the holder on the wall, and knelt down. Taking Layla's chin in her gentle hand, she carefully dried cheeks that had become wet with tears.

"I know what you're going through. I lost one, too." The nurse's face became beautiful with compassion. "Are you sure we can't call your *hellren*?"

Layla just shook her head.

"Well, let me know if you change your mind. I know it's hard to see them upset and worried, but don't you think he'll want to be with you?"

Oh, however was she going to tell Qhuinn? He had seemed so sure of everything, as if he had already looked into the future and stared into the eyes of their young. This was going to be a shock.

"Will I know if I ever was pregnant?" Layla mumbled.

The nurse hesitated. "The blood test may tell, but it depends on how far along you are with what's happening."

Layla stared at her hands again. Her knuckles were white. "I need to know whether I'm losing a young or this is just the normal bleeding that occurs when one does not conceive. That's important."

"It's not for me to say, I'm afraid."

"You know, though. Don't you." Layla looked up and met the female's eyes. "Don't you."

"Again, it's not my place, but . . . with this much blood?"

"I was pregnant."

The nurse made a hedging motion with her hands, her lips pursing. "Don't tell Havers I said this . . . but probably. And you must know, there is nothing you can do to stop the process. It's not your fault, and you've done nothing wrong. It's just, sometimes, these things simply happen."

Layla hung her head. "Thank you for being honest with me. And . . . in truth, that is what I believe to be occurring."

"A female knows. Now, let's take you back."

"Yes, thank you very much."

Except Layla struggled with getting her panties in place as she stood up. When it became clear she couldn't get her hands coordinated, the nurse stepped in and helped with enviable ease, and it was all so embarrassing and frightening. To be so weak and at the mercy of another for such a simple thing.

"You have the most gorgeous accent," the nurse said as they rejoined the traffic in the hall, sticking once again to their slow lane. "It's so Old Country—my *granmahmen* would approve. She hates how English has become our dominant language here. Thinks it's going to be the downfall of the species."

The conversation about nothing in particular helped, giving Layla something to focus on other than how long she was going to be able to go until she needed to make this trip again . . . and whether things were getting worse with the miscarriage . . . and what it was going to be like when she was forced to look Qhuinn in the eye and tell him she had failed. . . .

Somehow they made it back to the exam room.

"It shouldn't be much longer. I promise."

"Thank you."

The nurse paused by the door, and as she went still, shadows crossed the depths of her eyes, as if she were reliving parts of her own past. And in the silence between them, a moment of communion was struck—and though it was unusual to have something in common with an earthbound female, the connection was a relief.

She had felt so alone in all this.

"We have people you can talk to," the female said. "Sometimes talking afterward can really help."

"Thank you."

"Use that white handset if you need help or feel dizzy, okay? I'm not far."

"Yes. I shall."

As the door shut, tears watered up her vision, and yet even as she

ached in her chest, the crushing sense of loss seemed disproportionate to the reality. The pregnancy was only in the very beginning stages—logically, there was not much to lose.

And yet to her, this was her young.

This was the death of her young—

There was a soft knock at the door, and then a male voice. "May I come in?"

Layla squeezed her eyes shut and swallowed hard. "Please."

The race's physician was tall and distinguished, with tortoiseshell glasses and a bow tie at his throat. With a stethoscope around his neck and that long white coat, he looked like the perfect healer, calm and competent.

He closed the door and smiled at her briefly. "How are you feeling?"

"Fine, thank you."

He regarded her from across the room, as if assessing her medically even though he did not touch her or use instruments. "May I speak frankly?"

"Yes. Please."

He nodded and pulled over a rolling stool. Sitting down, he balanced a file on his lap and stared into her eyes. "I see that you haven't listed your *hellren's* name—nor your father's."

"Must I?"

The physician hesitated. "Have you no next of kin, my dear?" When she shook her head, his eyes registered true sadness. "I'm so sorry for your losses. So there is no one here for you? No?"

When she just sat there, saying nothing, he took a deep breath. "All right—"

"But I can pay," she blurted in a rush. She wasn't sure where she could get the money, but—

"Oh, my dear, do not worry about that. I need not be renumerated if you are not able." He opened the file and moved a page out of the way. "Now, I understand that you have gone through your needing."

Layla just nodded, as it was all she could do to keep from screaming, "*What is the test result?!*"

"Well, I have looked at your blood results and they have shown some . . . things I didn't expect. If you so consent, I would like to take another sample and send it to my lab for a few more tests. Hopefully, I'll be able to make sense of it all—and I'd like to do an ultrasound, if

you don't mind. It's a standard exam that will give me an idea how things are progressing."

"As in, how much longer I have to miscarry until it is complete?" she said grimly.

The race's physician reached out and took her hand. "Let's just see how you are, shall we?"

Layla took a deep breath and nodded again. "Yes."

Havers went to the door and called for the nurse. When the female entered the room, she rolled in with her what appeared to be a desktop computer mounted on a cart: there was a keyboard, a monitor, and some wands mounted on the sides of the contraption.

"I shall allow my nurse to do the draw—her hands are far more competent than mine in that regard." He smiled in a gentle way. "And in the meantime, I'm going to check on another patient. I shall return imminently."

The second needle stick was far better than the first, as she knew what to expect, and she was briefly left by herself when the nurse departed to deliver the goods to the lab—wherever, whatever that was. Both of them returned shortly.

"Are we ready?" Havers asked.

When Layla nodded, he and his nurse conversed, and the equipment was arranged close to where she was sitting. The physician then rolled back over on his stool and pulled out two arm-like extensions from the sides of the examination table. Flipping what looked like a pair of stirrups free, he nodded to the nurse, who dimmed the lights and came around to put her hand on Layla's shoulder.

"Will you lie back?" Havers said. "And move down so that you're at the end of the table. You're going to put your feet here after you remove your undergarments."

As he indicated both of the footrests, Layla's eyes peeled wide. She'd had no idea that the examination was going to be—

"Have you never had an internal exam before?" Havers said with hesitation. As she began to shake her head, he nodded. "Well, that's not uncommon, especially if this was your first needing."

"But I can't take off—" She stopped. "I'm bleeding."

"We'll take care of that." The physician seemed utterly sure. "Shall we get started?"

Layla closed her eyes and leaned back so she was lying flat, the thin paper that covered the padded surface crinkling under her weight.

With a lift of the hips and a quick shuffle, she did away with what covered her.

"I'll take care of that for you," the nurse said quietly.

Layla's knees locked together as she patted around with her feet for those forsaken stirrups.

"That's it." That rolling stool squeaked as the doctor closed in. "But move down farther."

For a split second, she thought, *I can't do this*.

Curling her arms around her lower belly, she squeezed them in, as if she could somehow hold the baby inside of her at the same time she kept herself from flying apart. But there was nothing she could do, no conversations she could have with her body to calm it down and keep what had implanted, no loving pep talk she could impart to her young so it would keep trying to survive, no strain of words to calm her total panic.

For a split second, she longed for the cloistered life she had once found so stifling. Up in the Scribe Virgin's Sanctuary, the placid nature of her existence had been something she had taken for granted. Indeed, ever since she had come down to earth and tried to find purpose here, she had been rocked by trauma after trauma.

It made her respect the males and females whom she had been told were beneath her.

Down here, everyone seemed to be at the mercy of forces outside of their control.

"Are you ready?" the doctor asked.

As tears rolled out of the corners of her eyes, she focused on the ceiling above her, and gripped the edge of the table. "Yes. Do it now."

TWENTY

Holy shit, Qhuinn was completely out of control.

Almost no visibility. Plane wobbling back and forth like it had the DTs. Engine cutting in and out.

And he couldn't even check on Z. Too much wind to yell over, and he wasn't taking his eyes off wherever they were headed—or more like wherever they were going to crash-land—even though he couldn't see a damn thing—

What in a million years had made him think this was a good idea?

The one thing that appeared to be working was the compass, so at least he could orientate himself to where home base was: The Brotherhood compound was due north and a little east, on the top of a mountain surrounded by the invisible, defensive boundary of V's *mhis*. So directionally, he was right on, assuming that N-S-E-W dial was in fact more operational than, oh, say, everything else in the tin-can shit box.

As he looked to his right, the unrelenting wind coming through the half-shattered windshield slammed into his ear canal. Out the side window, he could see . . . a whole lot of dark. Which he took to mean they had passed through the suburbs and were out over the farmland.

Maybe they'd already hit the rolling hills that eventually turned into the mountain—

A sound like a car backfiring got his attention in a bad way—but what was worse?

The sudden silence that followed.

No engine clatter. Just the wind whistling into the cockpit.

Okay, now they were really in trouble.

For a split second, he thought about dematerializing out. He was strong enough, aware enough—but he wasn't leaving Z—

A strong hand landed on his shoulder, scaring the balls off him.

Z had dragged himself forward, and going by the expression on his face, he was having trouble staying on his feet—and not just because of the bucking and weaving.

The Brother spoke up, his deep voice cutting through the din. "Time for you to go."

"Fuck that," Qhuinn hollered back. Reaching forward, he went to try the ignition. Couldn't hurt, right?

"Don't make me throw you out."

"Try it."

"Qhuinn—"

The engine kicked back on, and the din reintensified. All good news. The trouble was, if the bastard'd gone out once, it was going to go out again.

Qhuinn shoved his hand into his jacket. As he snagged his cell phone, he thought of everyone they were both leaving behind—and he passed the thing to the Brother.

If there was a hierarchy in the reach-out-and-touch order, Z was at the top of the list. He had a *shellan* and a daughter—and if anyone was going to make a call, it was him.

"What's this for?" Zsadist said darkly.

"You can figure it out."

"And you can leave—"

"Not leaving—gotta fly this deathtrap until we hit something."

There was some further arguing at that point, but he wasn't moving from the driver's seat, and as strong as the Brother was under normal circumstances, Z wasn't in any condition to muscle around so much as a loaf of bread. And the convo didn't last long. After the talk dried up, Z disappeared, no doubt ducking back into the rear so he could make that last contact with those he loved.

Smart move.

Left to his own devices, Qhuinn closed his eyes and threw a prayer up to anyone who might hear the thing. And then he pictured Blay's face—

"Here."

He flipped open his lids. His cell phone was right in front of his face, held in place by Z's sturdy grip. And the GPS map was up and rolling, the little blinking arrow showing him exactly where they were.

"Another three miles," the Brother yelled over the roaring noise. "That's all we need—"

There was a boom and a fizzle—and then another round of that god-awful quiet. Cursing, Qhuinn focused hard on the little screen all the while hoping things would restart on their own. More north, obviously—but farther east. A lot farther. His guesstimate had been good, but hardly spot-on.

Without the phone? They'd be fucked.

Well, that and the whole no-engine thing.

Checking the precise location, he made some calculations in his head, and steered them to the right, trying to get that pointed indicator on the map heading exactly to their mountain. Then it was time to try to jump-start the engine again.

They were losing altitude. Not in that movie-spiral way, where there was a close-up on the altimeter and the thing was spinning fast as you wished the propeller was. But slowly, inexorably they were drifting down . . . and if they lost enough forward momentum, which was what that unreliable sewing machine under the hood was supposed to provide, they were going to drop out of the sky like a stone.

Working the ignition over and over again, he muttered, "Come on, come on, come *on*. . . ."

It was hard to keep the nose up with only one hand—and just as he was going to have to devote all of his attention to fighting with the steering wheel, Z's arm shot forward, kicked his hand out of the way, and took over trying to restart the engine.

For a split second, Qhuinn had an absurdly clear snapshot of the slave band peeking out from the cuff of the Brother's leather jacket— and then it was all business.

God, his shoulders were on fire from pulling back on the wheel shaft.

And to think he was dying to hear that racket from the—

All at once, the engine coughed back to life, and the change in their altitude was immediate. The instant those spark plugs and pistons started roaring again, the numbers began going up.

Keeping the throttle fully engaged, he checked the fuel gauge. On E. Maybe they were just out of gas, and it wasn't a mechanical issue?

Talk about splitting hairs.

"Just a little farther, baby—just a little more, come on, baby girl, you can do it. . . ."

As an endless stream of murmured encouragement left his lips, the impotent words were drowned out by the only thing that mattered— but come on, like the Cessna spoke English . . . ?

Man, it seemed like it took forever, the hoping and praying, his brain bouncing back and forth between best- and worse-case scenarios as miles were crossed at a dead-goddamn-slow pace.

"Tell me you called your females," Qhuinn shouted.

"Tell me you can keep us up off the ground."

"Not without lying."

"Bank us harder east."

"What?"

"East! Go east!"

Z zoomed in on the map and started running his fingertip in one direction, east to west.

"You want to land this way—behind the mansion!"

Qhuinn supposed he should take it as a positive sign that the guy was making landing plans that didn't involve fireballs. And the suggestion was a good one. If they could orient themselves along the long side of that big-ass house, on the far side of the swimming pool, they might wipe out a line of fruit trees . . . but there would be roughly the same amount of field they'd used to take off from.

Better than slamming into the huge retaining wall that ran around the property—

The engine didn't pop this time. It just went dead, like it was tired of playing hard to get, and was going to take a permanent TO.

At least they were within landing range.

One shot. That was all they had.

A single attempt to land them on the ground that, assuming he could coast them into the vicinity of the property, penetrate the *mhis*, and manage not to hit the house, the Pit, the cars, the gates, or anything of real or other sorta property . . . would result in him delivering the proud father and loving *hellren* and superb fighter . . . back into the arms of his family.

But Z wasn't all he was thinking about.

The Primale would oversee Layla's health and safety. Blay had his loving parents and Sax. John had his Xhex.

They were all going to be okay.

Qhuinn wrenched around. "Get in a seat! Back there! Get into a seat and strap yourself in—"

The Brother opened his mouth, and Qhuinn did the unthinkable. He slapped his open hand over the male's lips. "Sit the fuck down and strap in! We've come this far—let's not be the reason this fucks up!"

He snatched the phone back. "Go! I got us!"

Z's black eyes locked on his, and for a split second, Qhuinn wondered if he wasn't going to get thrown out of the cockpit. But then the miraculous happened: An instant connection sprang up between them, a chain with links as thick as thighs locking in from one to the other.

Z lifted his forefinger and pointed directly into Qhuinn's face. After he nodded once, he disappeared into the rear.

Qhuinn refocused.

Their coasting was keeping them aloft, and thanks to Z's direction, that little extra pull to the right had set them up well. According to the GPS, they were closing in on the juncture of roads that split around the base of the mountain, inch by inch. Inch . . . by inch . . .

He was pretty sure they were over the property now.

As the plane sank farther, he braced himself, continuing to pull back hard on the steering staff until his shoulders bit into the seat behind him. There was no landing gear to put down—the shit had been locked in place all along—

A sudden whistling noise penetrated the cockpit, and that, along with an abrupt change in angle, announced that gravity had started to win the fight, claiming the fiberglass and metal construction along with its pair of living-and-breathing as its prize.

They weren't going to make it—it was too soon—

A wild vibration followed, and for a moment, he wondered if they hadn't hit the ground and not noticed—treetops, maybe? No. Something . . .

The *mhis*?

The sudden buffering seemed to extend upward, and what do you know, the plane reacted differently, the nose leveling out through no

effort of Qhuinn's or help from the deadweight of that engine. Even the side-to-side teeter-tottering stopped.

Apparently, V's invisible defense not only kept out humans and *lessers*, it could hold a Cessna in the air.

Except then he had another problem. That vital lift didn't seem to let up.

With the way shit was going, it was like he was going to float up here for frickin' ever, overshooting the only landing strip they had—

Abruptly, the rattling resumed, and he checked the altimeter. They'd sunk down about twenty-five feet, and he had to wonder if they'd penetrated the barrier.

Lights. Oh, sweet baby Jesus, *lights*.

Out the side window, down below, he could see the glow of the mansion, and the courtyard. It was too far away to make out the details, but it had to be—yup, the small offshoot had to be the Pit.

Instantly, his brain three-dimensionalized and reoriented everything.

Fuck. His angle was wrong. If he kept going like this, he was going to land front to back on the property rather than down that long side. And the bitch of it was, he didn't have enough lift to execute a nice fat circle to get them pointed in the right direction.

When you were out of options, you had no choice but to make it work.

His biggest problem remained missing the back lawn. There was only one clearing on the mountain. Everything else? Trees that were going to chew them up.

He needed to be lower, like now.

"Brace yourself!"

Even though it was counterintuitive, he shoved the drive shaft forward, and pointed them at the ground. There was an instant spike in speed, and he prayed that he could recover from it when he got into the strike zone. And shit, the intense shaking got even worse, to the point that it made him dizzy as hell, and his forearms stung from holding on to the wheel.

Faster. Closer. Faster. Louder. Closer.

And then it was time. The house and gardens were up ahead, and coming at them at a dead fucking run.

He pulled up hard, and the new velocity gave them a brief lift.

Over the house . . .

"*Get ready!*" he screamed at the top of his lungs.

As slow-mo took over, everything was magnified: the sounds, the seconds, the sting in his eyes as he stared straight ahead, the feel of his body thrusting back into the seat—

Fuck. He didn't have any kind of harness on.

He hadn't bothered with it. Too much else to think of.

Dumb-ass—

At that very instant, they made contact with something. Hard. The plane bounced up, hit something else, ricocheted off-kilter, bounced again. All the while, his head smacked into the panels above him, and his ass got spanked by the seat, and his—

Cue the paint mixer.

The next phase of the landing from hell was a shake-rattle-and-roll that nearly threw him out of the cockpit. This was the ground—had to be—and damn, they were going fast. Lights whipped by the side windows, everything going Studio 54 until he was practically blinded. And given which side the strobe lighting was on, he figured they were in the garden—but they were running out of space.

Wrenching the wheel, he sent them into a tailspin, hoping that the same laws of physics that applied to out-of-control cars could translate here: no brakes, limited field, and the only way to slow their momentum was drag coefficient.

Centrifugal force slammed him against the side of the cockpit, and snow pelted his face; then something sharp.

Shit, they weren't slowing down at all.

And that twenty-foot-tall, eighteen-inch-wide security wall was coming up fast.

Talk about your full stops. . . .

TWENTY-ONE

Blay dematerialized to the mansion the instant the last slayer in that clearing was sent back to the Omega. With Qhuinn up in the air with Z, there was no reason to waste time waiting for another squadron to make an appearance.

Although really, like there was anything anyone could do to help the pair of them?

Re-forming in the courtyard, he—

Directly above him, making no sound at all, that godforsaken airplane blocked out the moon.

Holy *shit*, they'd made it—and goddamn, they were so close, he felt like he could reach up and touch the undercarriage of the Cessna.

The stone silence was not a good sign, however. . . .

The first impact came from the tops of the arborvitae hedge that confined the garden. The plane bounced off the pointed stops, caught some air, and then went out of sight.

Blay dematerialized around to the back terrace just in time to see the Cessna slam into the snow, the crash like a fat man doing a belly flop in a pool, great waves of white kicking up all over the place. And then the aircraft turned into the biggest Weedwacker known to man, the combination of its steel body and too-fast velocity ripping through stands of fruit trees, and beds of flowers that had been secured for the winter, and shit, even the lineup of bird fountains.

But fuck all that. He didn't care if the whole place got regraded, as long as that plane stopped . . . before the retaining wall.

For a split second, he was of half a mind to materialize in front of the thing and put his hands out, but that was crazy. If the Cessna didn't seem even annoyed at the marble statuary it was now mowing down, it wasn't going to give two shits about a living, breathing male—

For no apparent reason, all that out-of-control began to spin, the wing facing Blay swinging around as if Qhuinn was trying to steer. The fishtail was the perfect move—it went without saying that there were no brakes, and assuming the corkscrew stayed tight, it would give them more area to lose forward momentum in.

Shit, they were getting really close to the retaining wall—

Sparks lit up the night, along with a metal-on-stone scream that announced that "really close to the wall" had been replaced with "right up against"—but thanks to the wrenching turn Qhuinn had pulled off, they had skidded into a parallel position, rather than a head-on one.

Blay started running in the direction of the light show, and as he did, others joined him, a whole cast of people falling in line. There was no stopping this, but they could damn well be on hand when things—

Crunch!

—ended.

The airplane finally met an inanimate object it couldn't get the best of: the shed that was used to keep some of the lawn equipment and gardening supplies in at the very rear of the garden.

Dead stop.

And it was way too quiet. All Blay heard was the *pffing* impact of his shitkickers traveling through the snow, and his breath punching out into the cold air, and the scramble of the others behind him.

He was the first to reach the aircraft, and he went for the door that by some miracle was facing outward and not into the concrete wall. Wrenching the thing open, and getting out his flashlight, he didn't know what to expect inside—smoke? Fumes? Blood and body parts?

Zsadist was sitting rigid in a backward-facing seat, his big body strapped in, both hands locked on the armrests. The Brother was staring straight ahead and not blinking.

"Have we stopped moving?" he said hoarsely.

Okay, apparently even a Brother could feel shock.

"Yes, you have." Blay didn't want to be rude, but now that he was sure one of them had made it, he had to see if Qhuinn—

The male stumbled out of the cockpit. In the light of Blay's beam, he looked like he'd been on a hard-core amusement ride, his hair slicked back from his windburned forehead, his blue and green eyes peeled wide in a face that was striped with fresh blood, every limb on him shaking.

"Are you all right!" he hollered, like maybe his ears were ringing in the aftermath of a lot of noise. "Z—say something—"

"I'm right here," the Brother answered, grimacing as he pried one of his clawed hands off the armrest and held it up. "I'm okay, son—I'm all right."

Qhuinn grabbed onto what was extended, and that was when his knees went out from under him. He just crumpled around their clasped palms, his voice cracking so much he could barely speak.

"I just . . . wanted you to be okay. . . . I just . . . wanted you . . . to be okay—oh, God . . . for your daughter . . . I just wanted you to be okay. . . ."

Zsadist, the Brother who never touched anyone, reached out and put his free hand on Qhuinn's bent head. Looking up, he said softly, "Don't let anyone in here. Give him a minute, 'kay?"

Blay nodded and turned away, blocking the doorway with his body. "They're all right—they're all right. . . ."

As he babbled at the crowd, the number of faces staring up at him was a good dozen, but Bella wasn't among them. Where was she—

"Zsadist! *Zsaaaaaaaaaaaaaaadist!*"

The scream carried all the way across the glowing blue lawn as, up at the terrace, a lone figure shot out into the snow at a dead run.

Lots of people shouted back at Bella, but he doubted she heard a thing.

"*Zsaaaaaaaaaaadist!*"

As she skidded into range, Blay immediately reached for her, concerned she was going to slam right into the side of the plane. And, oh, God, he was never going to forget the expression on her face—it was more horrific than any war atrocity he'd ever seen, as if she were being flayed alive, sure as her arms and legs were strapped down and pieces of her very flesh were being peeled from her body.

Qhuinn jumped out of the aircraft. "He's okay, he's all right, I promise you—he's just fine."

Bella froze, like that was the last thing she expected anyone to say.

"My *nalla*, come inside," Z said in that same quiet tone he'd used on Qhuinn. "Come in here."

The female actually looked at Blay like she needed a check-in that she was hearing correctly. In response, he simply took her elbow and helped her through the aircraft's little doorway.

Then he turned away and once again blocked the portal. As sounds of a female weeping openly in relief emanated, he saw Qhuinn draw his hands over his eyes like the male was clearing his own face of tears.

"Holy shit, son, I didn't know you could fly a plane," somebody said.

As Qhuinn looked up and appeared to glance across the landscape, Blay did the same. Talk about your post-apocalyptic scenes: There was a gully extending all along the flight path, like the finger of God had drawn a little line right through the garden.

"Actually . . . I can't," Qhuinn mumbled.

V put his hand-rolled between his lips and extended his palm. "You got my Brother home in one piece. Fuck the rest of that shit."

"Word—"

"Yeah, thanks be to God—"

"Hell, yeah—"

"Amen—"

One by one, the Brotherhood came forward, each putting his dagger hand out. The procession took time, but nobody seemed to worry about the cold.

Blay certainly couldn't feel it. To the point that he became paranoid. . . .

Reaching into the warmth of his leather jacket, he found his rib cage and pinched himself as hard as he could.

Ow.

Shutting his eyes, he sent up a silent prayer that this was reality . . . and not the horror that might have been.

All the attention was making Qhuinn jumpy.

And it wasn't like his little flight of fancy had been a Zen frickin' experience. The burn in his face from all that wind, the aches in his shoulders and his back, the wobbly legs—he felt like he was still up

there, still praying to nothing he believed existed, still and forever on the verge.

Of dying.

Plus he was so damn embarrassed—breaking down in front of Z like that? Come on. What a fucking pussy.

"Mind if I take a look?" Doc Jane said as she approached the crowd.

Yeah, good idea. The whole purpose of this was because Z had been injured badly enough not to be able to dematerialize.

"Qhuinn?" the female said.

"I'm sorry?" Oh, he was in the way. "Here, let me get out of the—"

"No, not Zsadist. You."

"Huh?"

"You're bleeding."

"Am I?"

The doctor turned his hands over. "See?" Sure enough, his palms were dripping red. "You just wiped your face. You have a deep cut on your head."

"Oh. Okay." Maybe that was why he felt so spacey? "What about Z—"

"Manny's already in there."

Huh. Guess he'd missed that part. "You want to look at me here?"

She laughed a little. "How about we get you back to the house—if you can walk."

"I'll take care of him—"

"Let me get him—"

"I'll take him—"

"Got him—"

The chorus of volunteers was a surprise, and so were all the helping arms that appeared from out of nowhere: He was literally enveloped by thick fighting arms, and all but carried away from the site like someone surfing the crowd at a concert.

He glanced back, hoping to see Blay, praying to meet the guy's eyes, just to connect, even though that was crazy—

But Blay was there.

That beautiful blue stare was right there, so steady and true as it met his own that he felt like breaking down all over again. And he drew strength from those eyes, just as he'd done back when they'd spent so much time together. The truth was that he wished it were Blay getting him back to the mansion, but no one said shit to the Brother-hood when they kicked in en masse like this. And besides, no doubt the guy would feel like that was too close.

Qhuinn refocused on the way ahead. Holy . . . shit . . .

The garden was utterly decimated, half of the ten-foot-high hedge next to the house cut down, all kinds of trees knocked over, bushes mowed through, the remnants of the crash landing scattered around like bomb shrapnel.

Man, there was a lot of debris that looked like aircraft parts.

Oh, check it, a steel panel.

"Hold on," he said, pulling himself free. Bending down, he picked the sharp-edged fragment out of where it had melted into the snow. He could have sworn the thing was still warm.

"I'm really sorry," he said to no one in particular.

The king's voice boomed from in front of him. "For keeping my Brother alive?"

Qhuinn looked up. Wrath had come out of the library with George on one side of him and his queen on the other. The male looked as big as the mansion behind him—and just as strong: Even blind, he seemed like a superhero in those wraparound shades.

"I fucking trashed your yard," Qhuinn muttered as he went up to the royal male. "I mean . . . landscaped it in a bad way."

"It'll give Fritz something to do in the spring. You know how much he loves to pull weeds."

"That's the least of your problems. I'm pretty sure you're in back-hoe territory."

Wrath came forward, meeting him halfway across the terrace. "This is the second time, son."

"That I've ruined something mechanical in the last twenty-four hours? I know, right—next thing you know, I'll be blowing up a battle-ship."

Those jet-black brows sank low. "That is not what I'm talking about."

Okay, this had to end right now. He *really* hated having the atten-tion on him.

Deliberately ignoring the king's statement, he said, "Well, the good news, my lord, is that I'm not looking for a three-peat. So I think we're safe from now on."

There was a lot of grumbling in agreement.

"Can I get him to the clinic now?" Doc Jane cut in.

Wrath smiled, his fangs flashing in the moonlight. "You do that."

Thank God . . . he was so done with tonight.

"Where is Layla?" the doctor asked as they stepped into the warmth of the library. "I think you need to feed."

Fuck.

As the mother hens in black leather behind him started clucking in support of that idea, Qhuinn's eyes rolled back in his head. One crisis tonight was more than enough. The last thing he was interested in was explaining exactly why the Chosen could not be used as a blood source.

"You look woozy," somebody said.

"I think he's going over—"

Annnnnnd that was the last thing he heard for a while.

TWENTY-TWO

cross the river, at Havers's clinic, Layla finally had to get off the examination table and wander around the little room. She had lost all track of time at this point. Indeed, it felt as though she had been staring at the four walls forever—and would be for the rest of her natural life upon the earth.

The only part of her that remained fresh and engaged was her mind. The unfortunate thing was that it relentlessly churned over what that nurse had said . . . that this was a miscarriage. That in all likelihood, she had conceived—

When the knock she'd been waiting for finally came, it was unexpected and made her jump.

"Come in?" she said.

The nurse who had been so kind entered . . . but appeared changed. She refused to meet Layla's eyes, and her face was frozen in a mask. Draped over her arm was a bolt of white cloth, and she thrust the fabric forward while looking away. And then she dropped to a curtsy.

"Your grace," she said in a shaky voice. "I . . . we . . . Havers . . . we had no idea."

Layla frowned. "What are you—"

The nurse shook the robing, as if trying to get Layla to accept it. "Please. Put this on."

"What is this about?"

"You have Chosen blood in you." The nurse's voice quavered. "Havers is . . . distraught."

Layla struggled to comprehend the words. So this was not . . . about her pregnancy? "What— I don't understand. Why is he . . . he's upset because I am a Chosen?"

The other female blanched. "We thought you were . . . fallen?"

Layla put her hands over her eyes. "I may soon be—depending on what happens." She did *not* have the energy for this. "Would someone just tell me what the test results are and what I need to do to take care of myself?"

The nurse fumbled with the draping, still trying to hand it over. "He can't come back in here—"

"What?"

"Not if you're . . . he cannot be in here with you. And he should never have—"

Layla jacked herself forward, her temper flaring. "Let me make myself perfectly clear—I want to talk to the doctor." At the demand, the nurse actually looked up at her face. "I have a right to know what he found out about my body—you tell him to get in here *now.*"

There was nothing shrill in her voice. No high-pitched hysteria— just a flat, powerful tone she'd never heard come out of her mouth before.

"Go. And get him," she commanded.

The nurse lifted the drapery up. "Please. Put this on. He's . . ."

Layla forced herself not to yell. "I'm just another patient—"

The nurse frowned and squared her shoulders. "Excuse me, but that is not accurate. And as far as he's concerned, he violated you during the exam."

"What?"

The nurse just stared at her. "He's a good male. A fine male who is very traditional in his ways—"

"What in the Scribe Virgin's name does that have to do with anything?"

"The Primale can kill him for what he did to you."

"During the exam? I consented—it was a medical procedure I needed!"

"It does not matter. He did something unlawful."

Layla closed her eyes. She should have just used the Brotherhood's clinic.

"You must realize where he's coming from," the nurse said. "You are of a hierarchy that we don't come in contact with—and moreover, should not."

"I have a beating heart and a body that requires help. That's all he—and anybody else—needs to know. The flesh is the same."

"The blood is not."

"He must come see me—"

"He will not."

Layla refocused on the female. And then put her hand upon her lower belly. For all of her life, up until now, she had lived on the side of the righteous, serving faithfully, discharging her duties, existing within the prescribed parameters that were dictated by others.

No more.

She narrowed her eyes. "You tell that doctor he either comes and tells me in person what is going on—or I will go to the Primale and recite word-for-word what happened in here."

She deliberately shifted her stare to the machine that had been used during her internal exam.

As the nurse blanched, Layla felt no joy at the leverage she used. But there was no regret, either.

The nurse bowed deeply and backed out of the room, leaving that ridiculous fabric on the shallow counter by the sink.

Layla had never considered her Chosen status as either burden or benefit. It simply was all she had known: her lot cast, the fate that she had been given made manifest through breath and consciousness. Others were clearly not so phlegmatic, however—especially down here.

And this was just the beginning.

Then again, she was losing the pregnancy, wasn't she. So this was the end.

Reaching out, she took the white fabric and wrapped it around herself. She didn't care about the physician's delicate sensibilities, but if she covered herself up as they'd asked, maybe he would focus on her instead of what she was.

Almost immediately there was a knock on the door, and when Layla answered, Havers entered, looking like there was a gun to his head. Keeping his eyes on the floor, he only partially closed them in

together before crossing his arms over his stethoscope. "If I had known your status, I would never have treated you."

"I came to you willingly, a patient in need."

He shook his head. "You are a holiness upon the earth. Who am I to intervene in such a sacred matter?"

"Please. Just put an end to my suffering, and tell me where I stand."

He removed his glasses and rubbed the bridge of his nose. "I cannot divulge that information to you."

Layla opened her mouth. Shut it. "Excuse me?"

"You are not my patient. Your young and the Primale are—so I will speak to him when I can—"

"No! You mustn't call him."

The look he gave her suggested a disdain she imagined he usually reserved for prostitutes. And then he spoke in a low, vaguely threatening voice. "You are not in a position to demand a thing."

Layla recoiled. "I have come here of my own volition, as an independent female—"

"You are a Chosen. Not only is it unlawful for me to harbor you, but I can be prosecuted for what I did to you earlier. A Chosen's body is—"

"Her own!"

"—the Primale's by law, as it should be. You are unimportant—naught but a receptacle for what you are given. How *dare* you come in here like this, pretending to be a simple female—you put my practice and my life at risk with such duplicity."

Layla felt a wild rage tremble along every nerve ending in her body. "Whose heart beats within this chest?" She pounded on herself. "Whose breath is drawn here!"

Havers shook his head. "I will speak with the Primale, and only him—"

"You cannot be serious! I alone live within this flesh. No one else does—"

The physician's face tightened in distaste. "As I said, you are but a vessel for the divine mystery in your womb—the very Primale is within your flesh. That is more important—and accordingly, I will hold you here until—"

"Against my will? I don't think so."

"You will stay here until the Primale comes to fetch you. I shall not be responsible for setting you loose upon the world."

The two of them glared at each other.

With a curse, Layla threw off the draping. "Well, that's a great plan as far as you're concerned. But I'm getting naked right now—and I will be walking out like that if I must. Stay and watch if you like—or you could try to touch me, but I believe that would be considered another violation of some sort or another for you, wouldn't it."

The physician left so quickly, he stumbled out into the hall.

Layla didn't waste a second, yanking on her clothes and rushing into the corridor. Although it was unlikely that there was only the one way in and out through the reception area—there had to be escape routes, in case of an attack—unfortunately, she had no clue about the layout of the facility.

So her only choice was to head up front. And she had to do it on foot—she was too pissed off to dematerialize.

Falling into a jog, Layla went in the direction she'd come from— and almost immediately, as if they had been instructed to do so, female nursing staff jumped in her way, choking the hall, making it impossible for her to pass.

"If anyone shall touch my person," she hollered in the Old Language, "I shall regard it as a violation of my sacred sanctity."

All of them froze.

Meeting each one in the eye, she came forward and forced them to part, a path forming among the still figures and then closing shut behind her. Out in the waiting area, she stopped in front of the reception desk and stared hard at the female who was sitting up in alarm.

"You have two choices." Layla nodded to the reinforced exit door. "Either you voluntarily open that for me, or I blow it apart with my will—exposing yourselves and your patients to the onslaught of sunlight that is coming in"—she checked the big-faced clock on the wall—"less than seven hours. I'm not sure you can fix that kind of damage in time—are you?"

The click of the lock being sprung sounded loudly in the resonant silence.

"Thank you," she murmured politely as she headed out. "Your acquiescence is *much* appreciated."

After all, far be it from her to forget her manners.

* * *

Sitting behind his desk, with his leather-clad ass cozied in the throne his father had had made centuries and centuries ago, Wrath, son of Wrath, was running his forefinger up and down the smooth silver blade of a dagger-shaped envelope opener. Beside him on the floor, a faint snoring rose from George's muzzle.

The dog slept only during rare moments of downtime.

If someone knocked or entered, or if Wrath himself moved in any way, that big head rose, and that heavy collar jingled. The instanta-lert also came if somebody walked by in the hall, or ran a vacuum cleaner anywhere, or opened the vestibule door down in the foyer. Or set a meal out. Or sneezed in the library.

After the head raise, there was a sliding scale of response from nothing (dining room activity, vacuum, sneeze) to a chuff (downstairs door opening, walk-by) to an at-attention sit-up (knock, entry). The dog never was aggressive, but rather served as a motion detector, leaving the decision about what to do to his owner.

Such a gentleman the guide dog was.

And yet, although a tame nature was as much a part of the animal as his soft, long fur and his big, rangy body, Wrath had seen glimmers from time to time of the beast inside the lovely disposition: When you were around a bunch of highly aggressive, heavy-nutted fighters like the Brotherhood, heads got hot from time to time—even toward the king. And the shit didn't bother Wrath—he'd been with the motherfuckers too long to get riled at a little chest pumping or sac grabbing.

George, however, didn't like that. If any of them got into meathead territory toward their king, the hackles on that gentle dog would rise and he would growl in warning as he pressed his body close to Wrath's leg—like he was prepared to show the Brothers just how long real fangs were in the event things got physical.

The only thing Wrath loved more in his life was his queen.

Reaching down, he stroked the dog's flank; then refocused on the feel of his finger on the letter opener.

Jesus Christ. Airplanes falling out of the sky . . . Brothers getting injured . . . Qhuinn saving the day again . . .

At least the night hadn't been all drama of the heart-attack variety. In fact, they'd started out on a good note with the proof that they needed to move on the Band of Bastards: V had done his ballistics testing, and gee-fucking-whiz, the bullet that had come out of Wrath's neck had started its journey in a rifle found at Xcor's lair.

Wrath smiled to himself, his fangs tingling at the tips.

Those traitors were now officially on the hit list, with the full backing of the law—and it was time do to a little flushing.

At that moment, George let out a chuff—and the insistent knock that followed suggested Wrath might have missed the first bang on his door. "Yeah."

He knew who it was before the Brotherhood even entered: V and the cop. Rhage. Tohr. Phury. And at last, Z. Who, going by the thump, seemed to be using a cane.

They shut the door.

When no one sat down or made small talk, he knew exactly why they had come to him. "What's the verdict, ladies," he drawled as he leaned back in the throne.

Tohr's voice answered him. "We've been thinking about Qhuinn."

He bet they had. After introducing the idea at the meeting earlier tonight, he hadn't pressed them for a yes or no. There was plenty of shit that, as king, he was more than willing to cram down people's throats. Who the Brothers were going to welcome into the club was not one. "And?"

Zsadist spoke up in the Old Language. *"I, Zsadist, son of Ahgony, inducted in the two hundred forty-second year of the reign of Wrath, son of Wrath, hereby nominate Qhuinn, an orphan in the world, for membership unto the Black Dagger Brotherhood."*

Hearing formal words out of the Brother's mouth was a shocker. Z, above all of them, thought the past was a bunch of bullshit. Not when it came to this, apparently.

Jesus, Wrath thought. They were going to run with it. And fast— he'd thought it would take longer than this. Days of mulling over. Weeks. Maybe a month—and then, maybe, a no-go for a variety of reasons.

But they were playing ball—and accordingly, so was Wrath.

"Upon what basis do you make this pledge of your, and your blood-line's, name?" Wrath asked.

Now Z dropped the formal, and went for the real. "He brought me home safe to my *shellan* and my little female tonight. At the risk of his own life."

"Fair enough."

Wrath scanned the males who were standing around his desk, even though he couldn't see them with his eyes. Sight didn't matter, though. He didn't need operational retinas to tell him where they all were or how they were feeling about shit; the scents of their emotions were clear.

They were, as a group, steadfast, resolved, and proud.

But formalities needs must.

Wrath started with the one all the way on the end. "V?"

"I was ready to get on board when he crawled all over Xcor."

There was a grumble of agreement.

"Butch?"

That Boston accent came across loud and clear. "I think he's a wicked strong fightah. And I like the guy. He's aging up good, dropping all that attitude, getting serious."

"Rhage?"

"You shoulda seen him tonight. He wouldn't let me take that plane up—said two Brothers were too much to lose."

More of that grumbling approval. "Tohr?"

"That night you were shot? I got you out of there thanks to him. He's the right stuff."

"Phury?"

"I like him. I really do. He's the first to run into any situation. He will literally do *any*thing for any one of us—it doesn't matter how dangerous."

Wrath rapped his desk with his knuckles. "It's settled, then. I'll tell Saxton to make the changes, and we'll do it."

Tohr cut in. "With all due respect, my lord, we need to resolve the *ahstrux nohtrum* designation. He can't be watching John's ass as his primary directive anymore."

"Agreed. We'll tell John to release him—and I can't believe the answer will be no. After that, I'll have Saxton draw up the papers, and then following Qhuinn's induction, V, you take care of the ink on his face. Like if John had died of natural causes or some shit?"

There was a rustling of clothes, as if some of the Brothers were making the symbol of "Dearest Virgin Scribe forbid" over their chests.

"Roger that," V said.

Wrath crossed his arms over his chest. This was a historic moment, and well he knew it. Butch's induction had been legal because of the blood tie the male had with royalty. Qhuinn was a different story. No royal blood. No Chosen or Brotherhood blood, although he technically was an aristocrat.

No family.

On the other hand, that kid had proven himself again and again on the field, living up to a standard that, as far as the Old Laws currently stated, was reserved only for those of specific lineages—and that was bullshit. It wasn't that Wrath didn't appreciate the Scribe Virgin's breeding plan. The prescribed matings between the strongest males and the smartest females had in fact produced extraordinary results when it came to fighters.

But it had also resulted in defects like his blindness. And it restricted merit-based promotions.

Bottom line, this recasting of the laws concerning who could and could not be in the Brotherhood was not only appropriate in terms of the kind of society he wanted to create—it was a matter of survival. The more fighters the better.

Plus, Qhuinn had truly earned the honor.

"So be it," Wrath murmured. "Eight's a good number. A lucky number."

That low growl of agreement rippled through the air once again, the sound one of complete and utter solidarity.

This was the future, Wrath thought as he smiled and bared his fangs. And it was right.

TWENTY-THREE

As Sola Morte stood in her "boss's" office, her body was poised for a fight. Then again, that was her SOP, and not anything specific to the environment—or the way the conversation was going.

The latter certainly didn't improve her mood, however.

"I'm sorry, what?" she demanded.

Ricardo Benloise smiled in his typical cool, calm way. "Your assignment is completed. Thank you for your time."

"I haven't even told you what I found out there."

The man eased back in his chair. "You may collect your fee from my brother."

"I don't get this." When he'd called her no more than forty-eight hours ago, it had been a priority. "You said—"

"Your services are no longer required for that particular purpose. Thank you."

Was he working with someone else? But who in Caldwell did the kinds of things she did?

"You don't even want to know what I found out."

"Your assignment has been terminated." The man smiled again in such a professional manner, you'd have sworn he was a lawyer or a judge. Not a lawbreaker on a global scale. "I'm looking forward to working with you again in the future."

One of the bodyguards in the back took a couple steps forward, as if he were getting ready to take the trash out.

"There's something going on in that house," she said as she turned away. "Whoever it is, is hiding—"

"I don't want you going back there."

Sola stopped and looked over her shoulder. Benloise's voice was as mild as ever, but his eyes were dead on.

Well, this was interesting.

And the only possible explanation that held any logic was that Mr. Mysterious in that big glass house had warned Benloise off. Had her little visit been discovered? Or was this the result of the kind of hard-ball that routinely went down in the drug trade?

"Getting sentimental on me?" she said softly. After all, she and Benloise went back quite a ways.

"You are a very useful commodity." His slow smile took the sting out of the words. "Now go and be safe, *niña*."

Oh, for fuck's sake . . . there was no reason to bicker with the man. And she was going to get paid—so what the hell did she care?

She gave him a wave, strode to the door, and proceeded down the stairwell. Out in the gallery space, she headed into the back of the house, where the legitimate employees worked during legitimate business hours. Bypassing the file cabinets and the desks, which looked Barbie-size thanks to the industrial ceiling fifty feet overhead, she went into a narrow corridor that was marked only with security cameras.

Knocking on the door was pointless, but she did it anyway, the stout fireproof panels absorbing the sound of her knuckles like they were hungry. To help Benloise's brother out—not that Eduardo needed it—she turned to the nearest lens so her full face showed.

The locks released a moment later. And as strong as she was, even she had to put her shoulder into opening the way in.

Talk about another world. Ricardo's office was minimalist to the extreme; Eduardo's was something even Donald Trump, with his gold fetish, would feel suffocated by.

Any more marble and lamé in here and you'd be in a whorehouse.

As Eduardo smiled, his fake teeth were the shape and color of pi-

ano keys, and his tan was so deep and uniform, it looked like it had been colored on him with Magic Marker. As always, he was dressed in a three-piece suit—a uniform, kind of like Mr. Roarke's from *Fantasy Island*, except black instead of white.

"And how are you tonight?" His eyes took a travel down her body. "You're looking *very* well."

"Ricardo said to come see you for my money."

Instantly, Eduardo went stone-cold serious—and she was reminded of why Ricardo kept him around: Blood ties and competence together were a powerful combination.

"Yes, he told me to expect you." Eduardo opened up a desk drawer and took out an envelope. "Here it is."

He extended his arm across his desk, and she took what he offered, opening it immediately.

"This is half." She looked up. "This is twenty-five hundred."

Eduardo smiled exactly like his brother did: facially, but not in the eyes. "The assignment was not completed."

"Your brother called it off. Not me."

Eduardo put his palms up. "That is what you will be paid. Or you can leave the money here."

Sola narrowed her stare.

Slowly closing the flap of the envelope, she turned the thing over in her hand, reached forward, and put it faceup on the desk. Keeping her forefinger on it, she nodded once. "As you wish."

Turning away, she went to the door and waited for the unlock.

"*Niña*, don't be like this," Eduardo said. When she didn't reply, the creak of his chair suggested he was getting up and coming around.

Sure enough, his cologne wafted right into her nose and his hands landed on her shoulders.

"Listen to me," he said. "You are very important to Ricardo and me. We do not take you for granted—*mucho* respect, yes?"

Sola looked over her shoulder. "Let me out."

"*Niña.*"

"Right now."

"Take the money."

"No."

Eduardo sighed. "You do not need to be this way."

Sola enjoyed the guilt that threaded through the man's voice—the reaction was, in fact, precisely what she was after. Like a lot of men from their culture, Eduardo and Ricardo Benloise had been reared by a traditional mother—and that meant feeling guilt was a reflex.

More effective than yelling at them or kneeing them in the balls.

"Out," she said. "Now."

Eduardo sighed again, deeper and longer this time, the sound a confirmation that her manipulation had once again truly found home.

He wouldn't give her the money she was owed, however. Over-the-top office decor and flashback to his childhood dynamic aside, he was tighter than a bank vault. That being said, she was confident that she'd effectively ruined his evening, so there was satisfaction in that . . . and she was going to take care of what Ricardo owed her.

He could do it aboveboard. Or, as he had chosen, he could force her hand.

That came with a surcharge, of course.

Yup, it would have been so much cheaper for him just to give her the contract price, but she was not responsible for the decisions of others.

"Ricardo will be upset," Eduardo said. "He hates being upset. Please just accept the money—this is not right."

The logical part of her brain suggested that she take the opportunity to point out the unfairness of being cheated out of what she was owed. But if she knew these brothers, silence . . . oh, the silence . . .

As nature abhorred a vacuum, so did the conscience of a well-raised, well-bred South American.

"Sola . . ."

She just crossed her arms over her chest and stared straight ahead. Cue the Spanish: Eduardo broke into his native tongue, as if his angst had stripped him of his English skills.

He finally gave up and let her out about ten minutes later.

There would be roses on her doorstep at nine a.m. She wasn't going to be home, however.

She had work to do.

"*What do you mean, they didn't show up?*" Assail demanded in the Old Language.

As he sat back in the seat of his Range Rover, he held his cell phone tight to his ear. The red traffic light up ahead was hindering his forward progress, and it was difficult not to see it as a cosmic parallel.

His cousin was factual, as always. *"The pickups did not arrive at the prescribed time."*

"How many of them?"

"Four."

"What?" But there was no need for the male to repeat it. *"And no explanations?"*

"Nothing on the street from the seven others, if that's what you mean."

"What did you do with the extra product?"

"I brought it home with me just now."

As green flashed overhead, Assail hit the gas. *"I'm making the interim payment to Benloise, and then I'll meet you."*

"As you wish."

Assail turned right and headed away from the river. Two blocks up, a left had him approaching the gallery again; another left and he was going behind it.

There was a car already parked in the back, a black Audi, and he eased in behind the sedan. Reaching into the foot of the passenger seat, he took the silver metal briefcase by its black handle and got out of the SUV.

At that moment, the rear door of the gallery opened and someone emerged.

A female human, going by the scent.

She was tall and had long legs. Dark, heavy hair pulled back. Chin was up, as if she were ready to fight—or had just been in one.

But none of that was material to him. It was her parka—a camouflage white-on-cream parka.

"Good evening," he said in a low voice as they met in the middle of the alley, he on his way in, she on her way out.

She stopped and frowned, her hand sneaking into the interior of that coat of hers. In a flash, he wondered what her breasts looked like.

"Have we met?" she said.

"We are right now." He put his hand out and deliberately enunciated his words. "How do you do?"

She stared at his palm, and then refocused on his face. "Anyone tell you that you sound like Dracula with that accent?"

He smiled tightly so his fangs didn't show. "There have been certain comparisons made from time to time. Are you not going to shake my hand?"

"No." She nodded to the gallery's back door. "You a friend of the Benloises?"

"Indeed. And you?"

"I don't know them at all. Nice briefcase, by the way."

With that, she turned on her heel and walked over to the Audi. After the blinkers flashed, she got in, the wind catching her hair and blowing it over her shoulder as she disappeared behind the wheel.

He stepped out of her way as she pulled forward and sped off.

Assail watched her go—and found himself thinking with disdain about his business associate Benloise.

What kind of man sent a female to do that kind of business?

As the brake lights flared briefly, and then rounded the corner, Assail sincerely hoped that the line that had been drawn earlier in the night was respected. It would be a shame to have to kill her.

Not that he would hesitate for an instant if it came down to that.

TWENTY-FOUR

As Zypher lay on hard concrete, his many years as a member of the Band of Bastards meant he was well familiar with the lack of accommodations he was currently enjoying: his ass was numb from the cold as well as the absence of a mattress beneath his heavy body. Likewise, his head was cushioned only by the rucksack he had used to bring his few belongings to their new HQ in this warehouse basement. Further, the thin, rough blanket that covered him was not long enough, leaving his socked feet exposed to the chilly, damp air.

But he was in heaven. Absolute heaven.

Coursing through his veins was the blood of that female, and oh, the sustenance. Having gone without a proper feeding source for almost a year, he had become inured to the fatigue and the restless muscles and the aches. But that was over now.

Indeed, it was as if he were inflating with strength, his skin filling out again to its proper dimensions, his height returning once more to its feet and inches, his mind both logy in the aftermath, and sharpening moment by moment.

Now, if he had had a bed, he would have enjoyed it, of course. Soft pillows, sweet-smelling sheets, clean clothes . . . warm air in winter, cool air in summer . . . food for an empty stomach, water for a dry throat . . . all of these were good if one could get them.

They were not necessary, however.

A clean gun, a sharp blade, a fighter of equal skill to his left and to his right. That was what he required.

And of course, during downtime, it was good to have a female willing and on her back. Or her stomach. Or her side with one knee up to her breasts and her sex exposed and ready for him.

He wasn't fussy like that.

Dearest Virgin Scribe, this was . . . bliss.

Not a word that he used very often—and he didn't want to sleep through this awakening. Even as the others lay sunk in the repose of the dead, each in the same spacey recovery that he, himself, was buffered in, he remained utterly aware of his glorious internal glow.

There was only one thing that was getting on his nerves.

The pacing.

He cracked an eyelid.

Just on the edge of the candlelight, Xcor was walking back and forth, his path restricted by two of the massive column supports that held up the floor above them.

Their leader was never at ease, but this restlessness was different. Going by the way he was holding his cellular device, he was waiting for a call—and that explained why he was where he was. The only place you could get a phone signal down below was standing beneath one of the two trapdoors: The panels of them were made of wood, and the steel mesh that had been tacked underneath had been the only alteration made when they had chased off the vagrant humans, sealed up the exterior floors, and moved in.

That way, vampires couldn't materialize down below.

And shit knew humans weren't strong enough to pry open those six-inch-thick wooden boards—

The tinkling noise that emanated from their leader's phone was far too civilized for the environs, the false bell sounding out cheerfully sure as a wind chime tickled by a spring breeze.

Xcor stopped and looked at the phone as he let it ring once more. Twice more.

Clearly, the male did not want to appear as if he had been waiting.

When he finally answered and put the phone to his ear, his chin lifted and his body calmed. He was back in control.

"Elan," he said smoothly. There was a pause. And then those always low brows went all the way down. "At what date and time?"

Zypher sat up.

"The king called it?" Silence. "No, not at all. Only the Council would be allowed, at any rate. We shall remain on the periphery—at your request."

The last part was spoken with no small amount of irony, although it was doubtful that the aristocrat on the other end of the conversation picked up on that. From what little Zypher had seen and heard from Elan, son of Larex, he was less than impressed. Then again, the weak were easily manipulated, and Xcor well knew this.

"There is something you should know, Elan. An attempt was made upon Wrath's life in the fall—and be not surprised if there is an implication against myself and my soldiers at this forthcoming meeting—what? It occured at Assail's, actually—but any other specifics are not relevant. So, indeed, one can surmise that Wrath is calling the gathering for the purpose of exposing me and mine—recall that I have warned you of such? Just remember that you have been utterly protected. The Brothers and the king do not know of our relationship—that is, unless one of your gentlemales has reported it in some manner to them. We, however, have remained tight-lipped. Further, know also that I am not afraid of being branded a traitor or becoming a target for the Brotherhood. I realize, however, that you are of a far more cultured and refined sensibility, and not only do I respect this, I shall do all in my power to insulate you from any brutality."

Uh-huh, right, Zypher thought with an eye roll.

"You must remember, Elan, you are protected."

As Xcor smiled more widely, it was with a full show of fangs, as if he were on the verge of latching onto the other male's throat and tearing out his windpipe.

Good-byes were said shortly thereafter, and then Xcor ended the call.

Zypher spoke up. "All is well?"

Their leader's head turned on the top of his spine, and as their eyes met, Zypher felt sorry for the idiot on the phone . . . and for Wrath and the Brotherhood.

The light in his leader's stare was pure evil. "Oh, aye. All is very well indeed."

TWENTY-FIVE

s the sound of unanswered ringing came through the landline, Blay held the receiver to his ear and sat down on the
edge of his bed. This was weird. His parents should have
been home this time of the night. It was so close to dawn—

"Hello?" his mother said, finally.

Blay exhaled long and slow, and shifted himself back against the
headboard. Folding the bottom of his robe over his legs, he cleared his
throat. "Hi, it's me."

The happiness that suffused the voice on the other end made him
feel warm in his chest. "Blay! How are you! Let me get your father so
he can hop on the other extension—"

"No, wait." He closed his eyes. "Let's just . . . talk. You and me."

"Are you okay?" He heard the sound of a chair streaking across a
bare floor—and knew right where she was: at the oak table in her precious kitchen. "What's going on. You haven't been hurt, have you?"

Not on the inside. "I'm . . . okay."

"What is it?"

Blay rubbed his face with his free hand. He and his parents had
always been close—ordinarily, there was nothing that he didn't talk to

them about, and this breakup with Saxton was exactly the kind of thing he'd usually bring up: He was upset, confused, disappointed, a little depressed . . . all the usual emotional stuff he and his mom processed in a two-way street of phone calls.

As he stayed silent, however, he was reminded that there was, in fact, one thing he had never broached with them. One very big thing . . .

"Blay? You're scaring me."

"I'm okay."

"No, you're not."

True enough.

He supposed he hadn't come out to them with respect to his sexual orientation because your love life was not something most people shared with their parents. And maybe there was also a part of him, however illogical it was, that worried about whether or not they would look at him differently.

Take out the maybe.

After all, the *glymera's* policy on homosexuality was pretty clear: provided you were never overt about it, and you mated someone of the opposite sex like you were supposed to, you wouldn't be expelled for your perversion.

Yeah, 'cuz getting hitched to someone you weren't attracted to or in love with, and lying to them about sustained infidelity, was so much more honorable than the truth.

But God help you if you were a male and had a boyfriend on the up-and-up—as he had had for the last twelve months or so.

"I . . . ah, I broke up with someone."

Annnnd now it was crickets on his mother's side. "Really?" she said after a moment, like she was shocked, but trying to keep from showing it.

You think that's a surprise, guess what's coming next, Mom, he thought.

Because, holy shit, he was going to . . .

Wait, was he really going to do this now, over the phone? Shouldn't it be in person?

What exactly was the protocol here?

"Yes, I, ah . . ." He swallowed hard. "I've been in a relationship for most of the past year, actually."

"Oh . . . my." The hurt in her tone stung him. "I—we—your father and I never knew."

"I wasn't sure how to tell you."

"Do we know her? Or her family?"

He closed his eyes, his chest compressing. "Ah . . . you know the family. Yes."

"Well, I'm very sorry it didn't work out. Are you okay . . . ? How did it end?"

"It just died, to be honest."

"Well, relationships are so very difficult. Oh, my love, my dearest heart—I can hear how sad you are. Would you like to come home and—"

"It was Saxton. Qhuinn's cousin."

There was a sharp inhale over the connection.

As his mother went utterly silent, Blay's arm started shaking so badly he could barely hold the phone.

"I . . . I, ah . . ." His mother swallowed hard. "I didn't know. That ah, you . . ."

He finished what she could not in his head: *I didn't know that you are one of* those *people.*

Like gays were social lepers.

Oh, hell. He shouldn't have said a thing. Not *one* fucking thing about this. Goddamn it, why did he have to blow his whole life up at the same time? Why couldn't his first real lover break up with him . . . and then he'd wait a couple of years, maybe a decade, before he came out to his parents and they shut him down? But noooooo, he had to—

"Is that why you've never talked about who you were with?" she asked. "Because . . ."

"Maybe. Yes . . ."

There was a sniffle. And then a hitched breath.

Her disappointment coming over the connection was too much to bear, the crushing weight settling on his chest and rendering it impossible to breathe.

"How could you—"

He rushed to cut her off, because he couldn't bear to have her sweet voice say the words. "*Mahmen,* I'm sorry. Look, I didn't mean it, okay? I don't know what I'm saying. I'm just—"

"What have I or we ever done—"

"*Mahmen*, stop. Stop." In the pause that followed, he thought about quoting her some Lady Gaga, and backing it up with a whole lot of it's-not-your-fault, you've-done-nothing-wrong-as-a-parent stuff. "*Mahmen*, I just—"

He broke down at that point, weeping as quietly as he could. The sense that in his mother's view, he had let down his family just by being who he was . . . was a failure of acceptance that he was never going to get over. He just wanted to live, honestly and out front, with no apology. Like everyone else. To love who he loved, be who he was . . . but society had a different standard, and as he had always feared, his parents were a part of that—

Dimly, he was aware of his mother speaking to him, and he struggled to pull it together and end the call—

". . . to make you think you couldn't come to us with this? That it's something that would change how we feel about you?"

Blay blinked as his brain translated what he'd just heard into some language that made any kind of sense. "I'm sorry . . . ? What?"

"Why have you . . . what did we do to make you feel that anything about you would make you somehow . . . diminished in our eyes?" She cleared her throat, as if she were gathering herself. "I love you. You are my heart beating outside of my chest. I don't care who you are mated to, or whether they have blond hair or black hair, blue or green eyes, male or female parts—as long as you are happy, that's all I worry about. I want for you what you want for yourself. I love you, Blaylock—I love you."

"What . . . are you saying . . ."

"*I love you.*"

"*Mahmen* . . ." he croaked, tears forming again.

"I just wish you hadn't told me over the phone," she muttered. "I'd like to hug you right now."

He laughed in an ugly, sloppy way. "I didn't mean to. I mean, I didn't plan this. It just came out."

Funny choice of words, he thought.

"And I'm sorry," she said, "that things didn't work out with Saxton. He's a very nice gentlemale. Are you sure it's over?"

Blay scrubbed his face as reality recalibrated itself, the love he'd always known clearly still with him. In spite of the truth. Or maybe . . . because of it.

In moments like this, he felt like the luckiest son of a bitch in the world.

"Blay?"

"Sorry. Yeah, sorry. About Saxton . . ." He thought about what he'd done in that office down in the training center when he'd been alone. "Yes, *Mahmen*, it's over. I'm very sure."

"Okay, so here's what you have to do. You take some time and do some healing. You'll know when you've done enough. Then you have to be open to meeting somebody new. You are such a catch, you know."

And here she was, telling him to go meet another guy.

"Blay? Did you hear me? I don't want you to spend your life alone."

He mopped his face again. "You are the best mother on the planet, you know that."

"So when are you coming home to see me. I want to cook for you."

Blay relaxed into the pillows, in spite of the fact that his head was starting to ache—likely because even though he was alone, he'd still tried to hold things together during his crying jag. Likely also because he still hated where he was with Qhuinn. And he still missed Saxton in a way—because it was hard to sleep alone.

But this was good. This . . . honesty went a long way for him—

"Wait, wait." He sat upright off the pillows. "Listen, I don't want you to say anything to Dad."

"Dearest Virgin Scribe, why not?"

"I don't know. I'm nervous."

"Honey, he's not going to feel any differently than I do."

Yeah, but as the only born son and the last of the bloodline . . . and with the whole father/son thing . . . "Please. Let me tell him face-to-face." Oh, like that didn't make him want to throw up. "I should have done that with you. I'll come as soon as I'm off rotation—I don't want to put you in the position of keeping something from him—"

"Don't worry about that. This is your information—you have the right to share it with people whenever and however you want. I would appreciate your doing it soon, though. Under normal circumstances, your father and I tell each other everything."

"I promise."

There was a lull in the conversation. "So tell me about work—how's it going?"

He shook his head. "*Mahmen*, you don't want to hear about that."

"Sure I do."

"I don't want you to think my job is dangerous."

"Blaylock, son of my beloved *hellren*, exactly what kind of an idiot do you think I am?"

Blay laughed and then got serious. "Qhuinn flew an airplane tonight."

"Really? I didn't know he could fly."

Wasn't that the theme song for the evening. "He can't." Blay eased back again and crossed his feet at the ankles. "Zsadist got injured and we had to get him out of this remote location. Qhuinn decided to . . . I mean, you know how he is, he'll try anything."

"Very adventurous, a little wild. But what a lovely young male. Such a crying shame what his family did to him."

Blay fiddled with the tie on his robe. "You always did like him, didn't you. It's funny, I'd think a lot of parents wouldn't approve of him—on so many levels."

"That's because they buy into that whole tough-guy exterior. To me, it's what's inside that counts." She made a clucking sound, and he could just picture her shaking her head sadly. "You know, I'll never forget the night you brought him over for the first time. He was this tiny scrap of a pretrans, with that obvious imperfection that I'm sure he'd been given a hard time about at every turn. And yet even with that, he walked right up to me, stuck out his hand, and introduced himself. He met me directly in the eye, not in any kind of confrontation, but as if he wanted me to take a good look at him and throw him out then and there if I needed to." His mother exhaled a soft curse. "I would have taken him in that very night, you know. In a heartbeat. To hell with the *glymera*."

"You really, truly, totally are the best mother on earth."

Now she laughed. "And to think you say that without my even putting food in front of you."

"Well, lasagna would make you the best mother in the universe."

"I'll start boiling the noodles now."

As he closed his eyes, the return of the easy back-and-forth that had been the hallmark of their relationship seemed extra special.

"So tell me more about Qhuinn's bravery. I love to hear you talk about him, you get so animated."

Man, Blay refused to think about any of the whys on that one. He just launched into the tale, with some judicious editing so he didn't divulge anything the Brothers wouldn't want on the airways—not that his mother would ever say a thing to anybody.

"Well, we were out scoping this area, and . . ."

"Do you need aught else, sire?"

Qhuinn shook his head and chewed as fast as he could to clear his mouth. "No, thanks, Fritz."

"Mayhap some more roast beef?"

"Nah, thanks—oh, okay." He backed out of the way as more of the perfectly cooked meat hit his plate. "But I don't need—"

More potatoes. More squash.

"And I'll bring you another glass of milk," the butler said with a smile.

As the old *doggen* turned away, Qhuinn took a bracing breath and tucked in to his round two. He had a feeling that all of this food was Fritz's way of saying thank you, and it was odd—the more he ate, the more he started to feel hungry.

Come to think of it . . . when was the last time he'd had a meal?

As the butler delivered more moo, Qhuinn drank up like a good little boy.

Damn, he hadn't meant to waste this time in the kitchen. His original intention, when he'd come up from the clinic, had been to go right to Layla's room. Fritz, on the other hand, had had other ideas, and the old guy hadn't taken no for an answer—which suggested that it had been an order from on high. Like from Tohr, as head of the Brotherhood. Or the king himself.

So Qhuinn had given up and given in . . . and ended up sitting at this granite counter, getting stuffed tight as a piñata.

At least surrender was delicious, he thought a little later as he put his fork down and wiped his mouth.

"Here, sire, something for your dessert."

"Oh, thanks, but—" Well, well, well, what do we have here: a bowl of coffee ice cream with hot fudge sauce all over it—no whipped cream or nuts. Just the way he liked it. "You really didn't have to."

"It is your favorite, no?"

"As a matter of fact, yeah." And look, here was the silver spoon.

You know, it would be rude to let the stuff melt.

As Qhuinn started in on dessert, the stitches that Doc Jane had put in over his eyebrow began to throb under their bandage—and the pain reminded him of what a crazy-ass night it had been.

It seemed surreal to consider that an hour ago he'd been on the verge of death, dancing through the dark sky in a rattletrap piece-of-crap airplane he had no idea how to fly. Now? It was a case of Breyers' best. With hot fudge.

And to think he was actually relieved there were no nuts or whipped cream to shave off lest his palate be ruined. Because, yeah, that was a serious-ass problem right there.

As his adrenaline glands burped and a shot of anxiety trembled along every nerve in his body, he knew damn well the aftershocks were going to come and go. Kinda like whiplash for his nervous system.

But dealing with a case of post-disaster heebs was helluva lot better than going up in flames. Or down, as the case would have been.

After part two of his meal was finished, he did his best to help clean up before he went to see Layla, but Fritz got into a flutter about him even trying to carry his bowl and spoon anywhere near the sink. Giving in yet again, he headed out through the dining room, and paused to look around at the long table, picturing everyone sitting in their usual chairs.

All that mattered was that Z was back safely in the arms of his *shellan*—and no one else had been injured—

"Excuse me, sire," Fritz said as he hustled by. "The door."

Up ahead in the foyer, the *doggen* went to the security check-in screen. A second later, he sprang the lock on the interior of the vestibule.

And in came Saxton.

Qhuinn hung back. The last thing he wanted to do was tangle with that male right now. He was going to check on Layla, and then crash out—

The scent that drifted over to him wasn't right.

Frowning, he went over to the archway. Up ahead, his cousin chatted with Fritz for a moment and then started to walk toward the grand staircase.

Qhuinn inhaled deep, his nostrils flaring. Yeah, okay, that was Saxton's fancy cologne . . . but there was another smell mingling with it. Another cologne was all over the male.

It was not Blay's. Or anything the fighter would wear.

And then there was also the unmistakable scent of sex. . . .

There was no conscious thought going on as Qhuinn marched out into the open and barked, "Where you been."

His cousin halted. Looked over his shoulder. "I beg your pardon?"

"You heard me." On closer goddamn inspection, it was really frickin' obvious what the guy had been up to. His lips were red and there was a flush on his cheeks that Qhuinn was willing to bet had jack shit to do with the cold weather. "Where the *fuck* you been."

"I don't believe that's any of your business, cousin."

Qhuinn stalked over the mosaic floor, not stopping until his shit-kickers were steel-toed to the guy's pretty loafers. "You fucking *slut*."

Saxton had the nerve to look bored. "No offense, dearest relation of mine, but I don't have time for this."

The guy pivoted around—

Qhuinn snapped a hand out and grabbed an arm. With a yank, he brought them nose-to-nose again. And shit, the stank on the guy made him sick to his fucking stomach.

"Blay is out risking his life in the war—and you're fucking some random behind his back? Real classy, cocksucker—"

"Qhuinn, this is not your concern—"

Saxton tried to shove him off. Not a good idea. Before Qhuinn knew what he was doing, he locked his palms around the male's throat.

"How fucking *dare* you," he said with his fangs fully bared.

Saxton slapped both his hands on Qhuinn's wrists and tried to get free, jerking, pulling, getting absolutely nowhere. "You're . . . chok-ing . . . me. . . ."

"I should kill you right here, right now," Qhuinn growled. "How the *fuck* could you do that to him? He's in love with you—"

"Qhuinn . . ." The strangled voice grew thinner and thinner. "Qh—"

The thought of everything his cousin had, and everything the guy wasn't taking care of, gave him super-strength, and he channeled it right into his hands. "What the hell else you need, asshole? You think some strange is gonna be better than what you've got in your bed?"

The force of his onslaught started to push Saxton backward, the guy's shoes squeaking on the smooth floor as Qhuinn's shitkickers drove both of them on. Things halted when Saxton's shoulders slammed into the staircase's huge bannister.

"You fucking slut—"

Someone shouted. So did someone else.

And then there was a shitload of fast footfalls coming from different directions, followed by a bunch of people pulling at his arms.

Whatever. He just kept his eyes and his hands locked, the fury in his gut turning him into a bulldog that would . . .

Not . . .

Let . . .

Go . . .

TWENTY-SIX

"**S**o do you think you guys will ever come back to Caldwell?" Blay asked his mother.

"I don't know. Your father goes in and out for work so easily every night, and we both like the quiet and the privacy here in the country. Do you think it's any safer in town now—"

From out of nowhere, shouts penetrated the closed door of his room. A lot of them.

Blay glanced across and frowned. "Hey, *Mahmen*, I'm sorry to cut you off, but there's something going on in the house—"

Her voice dropped, fear lacing her words. "You're not being raided, are you?"

For a moment, that night at their Caldwell home a year and a half ago came back to him in a fast series of stomach churners: his own mother fleeing in terror, his father taking up arms against the enemy, the house ruined.

Even though the shouting seemed to be getting worse, he couldn't get off without reassuring her. "No, no, no, *Mahmen*—this place is tight as a tick. Nobody can find us, and even if they could, they can't

get inside. It's just sometimes the Brothers get into arguments—honestly, it's fine."

At least, he hoped it was. Things really appeared to be ramping up.

"Oh, that's such a relief. I can't have anything happening to you. Go take care of things, and call me when you know you're coming for a visit. I'll get your room all set, and I'll make you that lasagna."

On command, his mouth started watering. And so did his eyes, a little. "I love you, *Mahmen*—and thank you. You know, for . . ."

"Thank *you* for trusting me. Now go find out what's happening, and be safe. I love you."

Hanging up, he shifted off the bed and hit the door. The second he was out into the hall of statues, it was clear there was a big-time fight going on in the main part of the house: there were a lot of male voices carrying on, all of which were at a volume that had "emergency" written all over it.

Breaking into a jog, he beelined for the second-story balcony—

When he got a gander at the foyer, he didn't immediately understand what he was seeing down below: There was a whole knot of people at the base of the staircase, all with their arms reaching forward like they were trying to break apart a fight.

Except it wasn't between two Brothers.

What the fuck? Were they really trying to peel Qhuinn off Saxton . . . ?

Jesus, the vicious bastard had his hands around his cousin's throat and was, going by the gray pallor of the other male's face, about to kill him.

"What the hell are you doing!" Blay screamed, as he took the stairs at a dead run.

When he got to the fray, there were too many Brothers in the way—and those were not the kind of males you just elbowed aside. Unfortunately, if anyone was going to get through to Qhuinn, it would be him. But how the hell was he going to get the dumb-ass's attention—

There you go, he thought.

Shooting across the foyer, he broke the glass of the old-fashioned manual fire alarm with his fist and then reached in and pulled the lever down.

Instantly, noise exploded through the space, the acoustics of the cathedral ceiling acting like a magnifier as the jet-engine-loud alarm went haywire.

It was like hitting a bunch of fighting dogs with a bucket of water. All the action stopped and heads popped out of the tangle, looking around.

The only one who didn't pay any mind was Qhuinn. He was still locked on and squeezing hard.

Blay took advantage of all the hey-what-is-that and was able to push his way through.

Focusing on Qhuinn, he shoved his face right into the guy's grille. "Let him go, *now*."

The moment his voice registered, an expression of shock replaced the cold violence that had marked Qhuinn's puss—like he'd never expected to have Blay check in. And that was all it took. One simple command from him and those hands released so quick, Saxton dropped to the floor like deadweight.

"Doc Jane! Manny!" someone called out. "Get a medic!"

Blay wanted to scream at Qhuinn right then and there, but he was too terrified about Saxton's condition to waste time on any what-the-fuck-is-wrong-with-yous: The lawyer wasn't moving at all. Grabbing the guy's beautiful suit, Blay rolled him out flat and went for the carotid with his fingertips, praying he found a heartbeat. When he didn't, he tilted Saxton's head back and bent down to begin administering CPR.

Except then Saxton let out a cough and dragged in a trunkload of air.

"Manny's coming," Blay said roughly, even though he didn't know that to be true. But come on, *someone* had to be on the way. "Stay with me. . . ."

More coughing. More breathing. And the color started to come back into that handsome, refined face.

With a shaking hand, Blay pushed back the soft, thick blond hair from the forehead he had touched so many times before. As he looked into the fuzzy eyes staring up at him, he wanted to feel something soul defining and life altering and . . .

He prayed for that kind of reaction.

Hell, in that moment, he would have traded both his past and present for it.

But it was simply not there. Regret, anger on the male's behalf, sadness, relief . . . he logged all of those. That was it, however.

"Here, let me check him out," Doc Jane said as she put her black doctor's bag down and knelt to the mosaic floor.

Blay shuffled back to give V's *shellan* some room, but he stayed

close, even though it wasn't like he could do anything. Hell, he'd always wanted to go to medical school—but not so he could resuscitate
ex-lovers because some cocksucking psycho had tried to strangle them
in the front goddamn hall.

He glared up at Qhuinn. The fighter was still being held back by
Rhage, like the Brother wasn't entirely sure the episode was over.

"Let's get you to your feet," Doc Jane said.

Blay was right on that, helping Saxton up, holding him steady,
heading him over to the stairs. The pair of them were silent as they
ascended, and when they got to the second floor, Blay took them down
into his room out of habit.

Shoot.

"No, it's fine," Saxton murmured. "Just let me sit down in here for
a minute, would you?"

Blay thought about the bed, but when Sax stiffened as he headed
in that direction, he settled for the chaise longue. Helping the male off
his feet, he awkwardly stepped back.

In the silence that followed, violent anger hit him from out of
nowhere.

Now his hands shook for a different reason.

"So," Saxton said hoarsely. "How was your night?"

"What the hell happened down there?"

Saxton loosened his tie. Unbuttoned his collar. Took yet another
deep breath. "Family tiff, as it were."

"Bullshit."

Saxton shifted exhausted eyes over. "Must we do this?"

"What happened—"

"I think you and he need to talk. And once you do, I won't have
to worry about being jumped like a felon again."

Blay frowned. "He and I have nothing to say to each other—"

"With all due respect, the ligature marks around my neck would
suggest otherwise."

"How we doin' there, big guy?"

As Rhage's voice registered in Qhuinn's ear, it was clear the Brother
was checking to see if the drama was well and truly over. Not necessary.
The instant Blay had told him to cut the crap, Qhuinn's body had
obeyed, sure as if the guy held the remote to his TV.

Other people were milling around, looking him over, obviously also waiting to see if he showed any inclination to race up after Saxton and resume the death-grip routine.

"You good?" Rhage prompted.

"Yeah. Yeah, I'm okay."

The iron bars across his chest loosened and gradually dropped. Then a big hand clapped him on the shoulder and gave him a squeeze. "Fritz hates dead bodies in the front hall."

"But there's not a lot of blood with strangulation," somebody pointed out. "Clean-up would have been easy."

"Just a floor polish afterward," another guy chimed in.

There was a heavy pause at that point.

"I'm gonna go upstairs." As the hairy eyeballs started again, Qhuinn shook his head. "Not for a repeat. I swear on my . . ."

Well, he didn't have a mother, a father, a brother, a sister . . . or a young—although hopefully, that last one was a "yet" kind of thing.

"I just won't, 'kay?"

He didn't wait for any further commentary. No offense, but a plane crash and a homicide attempt on one of his few remaining relations was enough for the night.

With a curse, he started for the second floor—and remembered he still needed to do a drive-by with Layla.

Hanging a right at the top of the stairs, he went down to the guest room the Chosen had moved into and knocked on the door softly. "Layla?"

In spite of the fact that they were going to have a young together, he didn't feel comfortable just barging in without an invitation.

Round two with the knuckles was a little louder. So was his voice. "Layla?"

She must be sleeping.

Backing off, he went for his own room, walking past Wrath's office with its closed doors, and then going down the hall of statues. As he went by Blay's door, he couldn't help but stop and stare at the damn thing.

Jesus Christ, he'd nearly killed Saxton.

Still felt like following through.

He'd always known his cousin was a slut—and he hated being right about that. What the fuck was Sax thinking? The guy had the ultimate in his bed every goddamn day, and yet somehow, some ran-

dom in a bar or a club or the frickin' Caldwell Municipal Library was better than that? Or even necessary?

Faithless son of a bitch.

As his hands cranked into fists and he entertained the idea of kicking his way into that room just to pound Saxton's face into soup, he nearly couldn't control the impulse.

Let him go, now.

From out of nowhere, Blay's voice reverberated through his head once again, and sure enough, the violence was unplugged. Literally, between one moment and the next, he went from wild bull to neutral.

Weird.

Shaking his head, he walked over to his bedroom, went in, and shut the door.

After willing on the lights, he just stood there, feet glued to the floor, arms hanging like limp ropes, head lolling on the top of his spine. All about the going nowhere.

For no apparent reason, he thought of one of Fritz's beloved Dysons, the thing rolled into a service closet, left in the dark until somebody took it out for use.

Great. He'd been reduced to the level of a vacuum cleaner.

Eventually he cursed, and ordered himself to carry on with getting undressed and going to bed. The night had been a ballbuster from the moment the sun had gone down, and the good news was that the sorry mess was finally over: Shutters were in place to keep out the sun. House was getting quiet.

Time for a REM-sleep reboot.

As he gingerly took his muscle shirt off and grunted at all the aches and pains, he realized he'd left his leather jacket and his weapons down in the clinic. Whatever. He had extras up here if he needed them during the day, and he could get his stuff brought up before First Meal.

Going for the fly of his leathers, he——

The door behind him exploded open with such force, it ricocheted off the wall——only to be caught on the rebound by the hard grip of one pissed-off motherfucker.

Blay was rip-shit as he stood in the jambs, his body trembling with such rage that even Qhuinn, who had faced off with a lot of things in his life, went *whoa*.

"What the *fuck* is wrong with you," the male barked.

Are you kidding me, Qhuinn thought. How could the guy not have recognized that foreign scent on his own lover?

"I think you need to put that to my cousin."

As Blay marched forward, Qhuinn moved around the guy to—

Blay snatched a grab and bared his fangs with a hiss. "Running?"

In a quiet voice, Qhuinn said, "No. I'm shutting the damn door so no one else hears this."

"I don't give a fuck!"

Qhuinn thought of Layla down at the other end of the hall, trying to sleep. "Well, I do."

Qhuinn disengaged and shut them in together. Then before he could turn around, he had to close his eyes and take a little TO.

"You disgust me," Blay said.

Qhuinn hung his head.

"You need to get the fuck out of my life." The bitterness in that familiar voice went straight into his heart. "You stay the *hell* out of my business!"

Qhuinn looked over his shoulder. "You don't even care that he was with someone else?"

Blay's mouth opened. Closed. Then those brows dropped low. "What?"

Oh. Great.

In the rush of everything, Blay had clearly not clued in to the whys.

"What did you say?" Blay repeated.

"You heard me."

When there was no reply, no cursing, nothing thrown in terms of punches or objects, Qhuinn turned around.

After a moment, Blay crossed his arms, not around his chest, but his middle, as if he were vaguely nauseated.

Qhuinn scrubbed his face and spoke in a broken voice. "I'm sorry. I'm so fucking sorry. . . . I don't want this for you."

Blay shook himself. "What . . ." Those blue eyes focused. "That's why you attacked him?"

Qhuinn took a step forward. "I'm sorry . . . I just . . . he came in through the door and I caught the scent, and I just lost it. I wasn't even thinking."

Blay blinked, like maybe he was getting confronted with a foreign concept.

"That's why you . . . why the hell would you do that?"

Qhuinn took another step forward, and then forced himself to stop—in spite of an almost overwhelming need to get close to the guy. And as Blay shook his head like he was having problems understanding all of it, Qhuinn didn't mean to speak.

But he did. "Do you remember down in the clinic, well over a year ago . . ." He pointed to the floor, like, in case the guy had forgotten where the training center was. "It was before you and Saxton first . . ." Right. No finishing that one, not if he wanted to keep down all that food he'd eaten. "Remember what I told you?"

As Blay seemed confused, he helped the guy out. "I told you that if anyone ever hurt you, I would hunt them down and leave them for the sun?" Even he heard the way his voice dropped to a menacing growl. "Saxton hurt you tonight, so I did what I said I was going to do."

Blay rubbed his face with his hand. "Jesus . . ."

"I told you what was going to happen. And if he does that again, I can't promise you I won't finish the job."

"Look, Qhuinn, you can't . . . you can't be doing that shit. You just can't."

"Don't you care? He was unfaithful. That's not okay."

Blay exhaled long and slow, like he was tired of carrying a weight. "Just . . . don't do that again."

Now Qhuinn was the one shaking his head. He didn't get it. If he were in a relationship with Blay, and Blay stepped out on him? He'd never get over it.

God, why hadn't he taken advantage of what he'd been offered? He shouldn't have run. He should have stayed put.

Unbidden, his feet took another step forward. "I'm sorry. . . ."

All of a sudden, he was saying those words over and over again, repeating them with each footfall that brought him closer to Blay.

"I'm sorry. . . . I'm sorry. . . . I'm . . . sorry. . . ." He didn't know what the fuck he was saying or doing; he just had an urgency to repent for all his sins.

There were so many when it came to this honorable male who was standing dead still before him.

Finally, there was only one step left before his bare chest hit Blay's.

Qhuinn's voice dropped to a whisper. "I'm sorry."

In the thick silence that followed, Blay's mouth parted . . . but not in surprise. More like he couldn't breathe.

Reminding himself not to be a world-revolves-around-me asshole, Qhuinn brought it back to what was happening between Blay and Saxton.

"I don't want that for you," he said, his eyes roaming around that face. "You've suffered enough, and I know you love him. I'm sorry. . . . I'm so sorry. . . ."

Blay just stood in front of him, his expression frozen, his eyes darting around as if they couldn't light on anything. But he didn't pull back, jerk away, storm off. He stayed . . . right where he was.

"I'm sorry."

Qhuinn watched from a vast distance as his own hand reached out and touched Blay's face, the fingertips running over the five o'clock shadow. "I'm sorry."

Oh, God, to touch him. To feel the warmth of his skin, to inhale his clean, masculine scent.

"I'm sorry."

What the fuck was he doing? Man . . . too late to answer that—he was reaching forward with his other hand and putting the palm on that heavy shoulder.

"I'm sorry."

Oh, God, he was drawing Blay in, pulling that body up against his own. "I'm sorry."

He moved one of his hands to the nape of Blay's neck and pushed it deep into the thick hair that curled under there. "I'm sorry."

Blay was stiff, that spine straight as an arrow, his arms remaining around his tight belly. But after a moment, almost as if he were confused by his own reaction, the male began to lean in, that weight shifting subtly at first, and then more so.

With a quick jerk, Qhuinn wrapped his arms around the single most important person in his life. It was not Layla, although he felt a pang at that denial. It was not John, or his king. It wasn't the Brothers. This male was his reason for everything.

And even though it killed him that Blay was in love with someone else, he'd fucking take this. It had been too long since he'd touched the guy . . . and never like this.

"I'm sorry."

Palming the back of Blay's head, he urged the male closer to him, tucking that face into his own neck. "I'm sorry."

As Blay went with it, Qhuinn shuddered, turning his own face in-

ward, breathing in fully, pulling all of the sensations deep into his brain so he could remember this forever. And while his palm rubbed up and down, soothing that muscled back, he did what he could to make amends for so much more than his cousin's infidelity. "I'm sorry—"

With a quick shift, Blay shook his head. Shook himself free. Pushed back.

Pushed away.

Qhuinn's shoulders dropped. "I'm sorry."

"Why do you keep saying that?"

"Because . . ."

In that moment, as their eyes met, Qhuinn knew it was time. He'd blown so much with Blay; there had been so many missteps and deliberate misunderstandings, so many years, so many denials—all on his part. He'd pussied out for so long, but that was over.

As he opened his mouth to speak the three words on his tongue, Blay's eyes grew hard. "I don't need your help, okay? I can take care of myself."

Pound. Pound. Pound.

His heart was thumping so loud, he wondered if it was going to explode.

"You're going to stay with him," Qhuinn said numbly. "You're going to—"

"You don't pull that shit with Saxton—not ever again. Swear to it."

Even though it killed him, Qhuinn was powerless to deny the guy anything. "Okay." He lifted his palms. "Hands off."

Blay nodded, the deal sealed.

"I just want to help you," Qhuinn said. "That's all."

"You can't," Blay countered.

God, even though they were once again at odds, he craved more contact—and abruptly, he saw the pathway to exactly that. Tricky proposition, but at least there was some internal logic to it.

His arms lifted, his hands seeking, finding, latching on. Blay's shoulders. Blay's neck.

Sex surged in him, hardening his cock, making him pant. "But I can help you."

"How?"

Qhuinn edged in close, bringing his mouth right to Blay's ear. Then he deliberately put his bare chest against Blay's. "Use me."

"What?"

"Teach him a lesson." Qhuinn tightened his hold and tilted Blay's head back. "Pay him back the right way. With me."

To make things crystal clear, Qhuinn extended his tongue and ran it up the side of Blay's throat.

The hiss in response was loud as a curse.

Blay punched into him, shoving him back. "Have you lost your *fucking* mind?"

Qhuinn cupped his heavy, hard sex. "I want you. And I'll take you any way I can—even if it's only to get back at my cousin."

Blay's expression played table tennis between utter disbelief and epic anger.

"You fucking asshole! You turn me down for years, and then all of a sudden do a one-eighty? What the *fuck* is wrong with you!"

With his free hand, Qhuinn played with one of his nipple rings—and focused on what was doing at Blay's hip level: Underneath that robe, the male became fully erect, that terry cloth no match for the likes of that kind of hard-on.

"Are you out of your goddamn mind! What the fuck!?"

Usually Blay didn't curse or raise his voice. It was a turn-on to see him lose it.

Locking his eyes on his friend's, Qhuinn slowly sank down onto his knees. "Let me take care of that—"

"*What*?"

He leaned forward and tugged at the bottom of the robe, pulling it toward him. "Come here. Let me show you how I do."

Blay grabbed the tie that kept the two halves together, and yanked it tighter. "What the *hell* are you doing?"

God, the fact that he was on his knees, begging, seemed only appropriate. "I want to be with you. I don't give a shit why—just let me be with you—"

"After all this time? What's changed?"

"Everything."

"You're with Layla—"

"*No.* I'll say it however many times you need to hear it—I'm *not* with her."

"She's pregnant."

"One time. I was with her once, and just like I told you, it was only because I want a family and so does she. One time, Blay, and never again."

Blay's head fell back, his eyes closing as if someone were driving spikes under his fingernails. "Don't do this to me, for God's sake, you can't do this—" As his voice gave out, the anguish was a sad insight into all the problems Qhuinn had caused. "Why now? Maybe it's *you* who wants to get back at Saxton—"

"Fuck my cousin, it's got nothing to do with him for me. If you were alone, I'd still be right on this carpet, on my knees, wanting to be with you. If you were mated to a female, if you were dating someone all casual and shit, if you were in a million different places in life . . . I'd still be right here. Begging you for something, anything—one time, if that's all you've got."

Qhuinn reached out again, going under the robe, stroking a strong, muscled leg—and when Blay stepped back again, he knew he was losing the battle.

Shit, he was going to lose this chance if he didn't—

"Look, Blay, I've done a lot of shitty things in my life, but I've always kept it real. I almost died tonight—and that sets a male straight. Up there in that airplane, looking over the dark night, I didn't think I was going to make it. Everything got clear for me. I want to be with you because of that."

Actually, he'd known a fuck of a lot sooner, waaaaaaaay before the Cessna situation, but he was hoping the explanation made sense to Blay.

Maybe it did. In response, the guy weaved on his feet, as if he were going to give in—or leave. There was no telling which one it was.

Qhuinn rushed to get more words out. "I'm sorry I've wasted so much time—and if you don't want to be with me, I get it. I'll back off—I'll live with the consequences. But for the love of God, if there's a chance—for whatever reason on your side—revenge, curiosity . . . hell, even if you'll let me fuck you just once and never, ever again, for the sole reason of driving a stake through my heart? I'll take it. I'll take you . . . any way I can get you."

He reached out a third time, snaking his hand around the back of Blay's leg. Stroking. Pleading. "I don't care what it costs me. . . ."

TWENTY-SEVEN

Looming over Qhuinn, Blay was preternaturally aware of everything around him: the feel of Qhuinn's hand on the back of his thigh, the way the hem of the robe brushed against his calf, the scent of sex thickening the air.

In so many ways, he had wanted this his whole life—or at least ever since he'd survived his transition and had any sexual impulse at all. This moment was the culmination of countless daydreams and innumerable fantasies, his secret desire made manifest.

And it was honest: Qhuinn's mismatched eyes were without shadows—or doubts. The male was not only speaking the God's honest as he knew it in his heart; he was at peace with laying himself vulnerable like this.

Blay closed his lids briefly. This submission was the opposite of everything that defined Qhuinn as a male. He never surrendered—not his principles, not his weapons, never, ever himself. Then again, the turnaround did make some kind of sense. Facing death did tend to be followed by a come-to-Jesus chaser. . . .

The trouble was, he had a feeling this wasn't going to last. This "eye-opener" was undoubtedly tied to that plane ride, but as with a

heart attack victim resuming his piss-poor diet soon afterward, the "revelation" probably didn't have a long shelf life. Yeah, Qhuinn meant what he was saying in this heady moment—there was no doubting that. It was hard to believe it was permanent, however.

Qhuinn was who he was. And soon enough, after the shock wore off—maybe at nightfall, maybe next week, maybe a month from now—he was going to go back to his closed-off, hands-off, distant self.

Decision made, Blay reopened his lids and bent down. As their faces got closer, Qhuinn's lips parted, the fuller, lower one pursing as if he were already trying out the taste of what he wanted—and liking it.

Fuck. The fighter was so magnificent, his powerful bare chest glowing in the lamplight, his skin carrying a sheen of arousal, his pierced nipples rising and falling to the driving beat of his heated blood.

Blay ran his hand down the corded muscles of the arm that linked them, from the heavy thickness of the shoulder to the bulge of the biceps and the cut curl of the triceps.

He removed the palm from his thigh.

And stepped away.

Qhuinn paled to the point of going gray.

In the silence, Blay didn't say a word. He couldn't—his voice was gone.

On sloppy, loose legs, he scrambled for the way out, his hand flapping around the doorknob until it gathered enough coordination to open up the exit. Walking out, he couldn't have said whether he slammed the door or shut it quietly.

He didn't make it far. Barely three feet toward his room, he collapsed back against the smooth, cool wall of the hallway.

Panting. He was panting.

And all that effort wasn't doing any good. The suffocation in his chest was getting worse, and abruptly his vision was replaced by black-and-white checkerboard squares.

Figuring he was about to pass out, he sank down onto his haunches and put his head between his knees. In the recesses of his mind, he prayed that the hall stayed empty. This was not the kind of thing he wanted to explain to anyone: outside of Qhuinn's room, hard-on obvious, body shaking like he had his own personal earthquake going on.

"Jesus Christ . . ."

I almost died tonight—that sets a male straight. Up there in that airplane, looking over the dark night, I didn't think I was going to make it. Everything got clear for me.

"No," Blay said out loud. *"No . . ."*

Putting his head in his hands, he tried to breathe calmly, think rationally, act reasonably. He couldn't afford to go any deeper in this—

Those heated, glossy, mismatched eyes had been the stuff of legend.

"*No*," he hissed.

As his voice resonated inside his own skull, he resolved to listen to himself. No further. This would go no further.

He'd long ago lost his heart to that male.

There was no reason to lose his soul, too.

An hour later, maybe two, maybe six, Qhuinn lay naked between cool sheets, staring up in the dark at a ceiling he could not see.

Was this horrible, aching pain what Blay had felt? Like, after that showdown in his parents' basement—when Qhuinn had been prepared to leave Caldwell, and made it clear that there were gonna be no ties between them anymore? Or maybe after that time they'd kissed in the clinic, and Qhuinn had refused to go any further? Or following that final collision when they had nearly come together, right before Blay's first date with Saxton?

So damn hollow.

Like this room, really: Without illumination, and essentially empty, just four walls and a ceiling. Or a bag of skin and a skeleton, as it were.

Shifting his hand up, he put it over his beating heart just to reassure himself he still had one.

Man, fate had a way of teaching you things you needed to know, even if you weren't aware the lesson was required until it had been served to you: He'd spent way too much time wrapped up in himself and his defect and his failure to his family and society. Such a tangled fucking mess he'd been for so long, and Blay, because he'd cared, had been sucked into the vortex.

But when had he ever supported his best friend? What had he ever really done for the guy?

Blay had been right to leave this room. Too little, too late, wasn't that the saying? And it wasn't like Qhuinn was offering any kind of

winner. Underneath the surface, he was no more stable, really. No more at peace.

Nope, he deserved this—

The slice of light was lemon yellow, and it cut through the black field of his vision as if the blindness were cloth and the beam a sharp knife.

A figure slipped into his room silently, and shut the door.

By the scent, he knew who it was.

Qhuinn's heart began to thunder as he shot upright off the pillows. "Blay . . . ?"

There was the softest of rustling, a robe being dropped from the shoulders of a tall male. And then, moments later, the mattress depressed as a great, vital weight got up upon it.

Qhuinn reached through the darkness with unerring accuracy, his hands finding the sides of Blay's neck sure as if they had been led by sight.

No talking. He was afraid that words would cheat him of this miracle.

Lifting his mouth, he pulled Blay down to his own, and when those velvet lips were in range, he kissed them with a desperation that was returned. All at once, the pent-up past was released in a fury, and as he tasted blood, he didn't know whose fangs had scored what.

Who the fuck cared.

On a hard yank, he laid Blay down and then he rolled over on top of the other male, spreading those thighs and pushing himself between them until his hard cock came up against Blay's. . . .

They both groaned.

Dizzy from all the naked skin, Qhuinn began pumping his hips up and back, the friction of their sexes and their hot flesh magnifying the wet heat of their mouths. Frenzy, everywhere, hurry, hurry, hurry— holy fucking shit, there was too much hunger to make any sense of where his hands were, or what he was rubbing against, or— for fuck's sake, there was too much skin to touch, too much hair to pull, too much . . .

Qhuinn came hard, his balls going tight, his erection kicking between them, his come going everywhere.

Didn't slow him down in the slightest.

With a quick jerk, he broke away from the mouth he could have spent the next hundred years working, and shoved himself down Blay's chest. The muscles he came across were nothing like the human guys' he'd fucked—this was a vampire, a fighter, a soldier who had trained heavily and worked his flesh into a condition that was not just useful, but downright deadly. And holy hell was that a turn-on—but more than that, though, this was Blay; it was finally, after all these years . . .

Blay.

Qhuinn dragged his fangs down abdominals that were rock tight, and the scent of himself on Blay's skin was a marking that he knew he'd done on purpose.

That dark spice was going other places, too.

He groaned when his hands found Blay's cock, and as he circled the hard column, the guy arched up sharply, a curse cutting through the room, much in the same way the light had just moments before.

Qhuinn licked his lips, stood Blay's sex up, and let the head of that thick, blunt cock part his mouth. Sucking down deep, he took it to its base, opening his throat wide, swallowing everything. In response, Blay's hips shot up, and rough hands bit into his hair, forcing his head even farther down until he couldn't get any breath to his lungs—and who the fuck needed oxygen, anyway?

Digging his hands under Blay's ass, he tilted that pelvis and started going up and down, his neck straining under the punishing rhythm, his shoulders bunching and releasing as he followed through on exactly what he'd been offering before Blay had left.

He wasn't stopping with this, though.

Nope.

This was just the beginning.

TWENTY-EIGHT

As Blay jacked back against the pillows on Qhuinn's bed, his head nearly snapped off his spine. Everything was out of control, but he wouldn't have slowed things down in the slightest: With his hips pumping up and down, his cock was pushing in and sucking out of Qhuinn's mouth—

Thank God the lights were off.

The sensations alone were too much to handle—adding a visual? He wouldn't be able to—

The orgasm rocketed out of him, his breath catching, his body going tight all over, his sex kicking hard. And as he came in great spasms, he was milked by that mouth—and man, that suction kept the release barreling through him, great waves of tingling pleasure sweeping from his brain to his balls, his body hitting a different plane of existence altogether—

Without warning, he was flipped over with a rough hand, his body handled like it didn't weigh a damned thing. Then an arm shot under his pelvis and popped him up onto his knees. There was a brief lull, during which all he heard was heavy breathing behind him, the panting getting faster, and harder—

He heard Qhuinn orgasm and knew exactly what that was for.

Even though his whole body went weak with anticipation, he knew he had to get good and braced as a heavy hand landed on his shoulder and—

The penetration was a branding iron, brutal and hot, going right to the core of him. And he cursed on an explosive exhale—not because it hurt, although it did in the best possible sense. Not even because this was something he had wanted forever, although he had.

No, it was because he had the strangest sense he was being marked—and for some reason, that made him—

A hiss sounded at his ear, and then a pair of fangs sank into his shoulder, Qhuinn's grip shifting to his hips, his torso locked in so many places now. And then the relentless hammering started, Blay's molars clapping together, his arms having to hold both their bodies up, his legs and torso straining under the onslaught.

He had a feeling the headboard was slamming against the wall—and for a split second, he remembered that chandelier in the library going back and forth as Layla had been subjected to this.

Blay cursed the image. He couldn't allow himself to go there; he just couldn't. God knew there was plenty of time to dwell on that stuff later.

Right now? This was too damn good to waste. . . .

As the pounding continued, his palms slid on the fine cotton sheets, and he had to reposition them, pushing down into the soft mattress to try to keep himself in place. God, the sounds that Qhuinn was making, the grunting that reverberated from between the fangs buried in his shoulder, the thumping—yeah, that was the headboard. Definitely.

With pressure building up again in his balls, he was tempted to palm himself—but no hope of that. He needed both arms on the job—

Like Qhuinn read his mind, the male reached around and gripped him.

No pumping needed. Blay came so hard his vision went twinkle-twinkle-little-star, and at that very instant, Qhuinn started orgasming, too, those hips spearing inside and freezing for a split second before withdrawing an inch and going deep for another kicking explosion. And yeah, wow, the combination of them both doing their thing was so erotic, it just primed everything all over again: There was no break

for recovery, no pause at all. Qhuinn just resumed driving—if anything, it was like the release had made his need stronger.

As the sex raged on—and in spite of all the strength he had in his upper body—Blay ended up getting fucked clean off the bed, one hand locking on the side table to keep him from hitting the wall—

Crash.

"Shit," he said roughly. "The lamp—"

Qhuinn wasn't interested in home furnishings, apparently. The male just yanked Blay's head around and started kissing him, that pierced tongue penetrating his mouth, licking and sucking . . . like he couldn't get enough.

Dizzy. He got downright dizzy from it all. In every fantasy he'd ever had, he'd always pictured Qhuinn as a ferocious lover, but this was . . . on another level.

So it was from a distance that he heard himself say in a guttural voice, "Bite me . . . again. . . ."

A great growl from above threaded into his ears, and then another hiss ripped through the darkness as Qhuinn shifted positions, his massive weight torquing so that those sharp fangs could sink in deep on the side of the throat.

Blay cursed and wiped clean the rest of whatever was on the table, his chest taking the place of the objects, his sweat-streaked skin squeaking on the varnish as he lay half on his side. Throwing a hand out, he caught the flat plane of the floor and shoved back, keeping them both stable as Qhuinn fed and fucked him so good. . . .

Too many times to count, until the pillows were on the floor, the sheets were torn, another lamp got knocked over—and he wasn't sure, but he thought they banged the picture over the bed off the wall.

When stillness finally replaced all the straining and effort, Blay breathed heavily, and still felt like he was underwater.

Qhuinn was doing the same.

The growing wet patch at Blay's throat suggested things had gotten so out of hand that there had been no sealing up the vein that had been taken. Whatever. He didn't care, couldn't think, wasn't going to worry. The blissed-out, floating aftermath was too glorious to spoil, his body at once hypersensitive and numb, hot and temperate, sore and satiated.

Man, the sheets were going to need to be cleaned. And Fritz was undoubtedly going to have to find some Super Glue for those lamps.

Where exactly was he?

Putting his hand out, he patted around and ran into carpet and a dust ruffle . . . and a blanket chest. Oh, right—hanging off the far end of the bed. Which would explain the head rush he was rocking.

When Qhuinn finally eased off of him, Blay wanted to follow, but his body was far too interested in being an inanimate object. Or more like a bolt of cloth, maybe . . .

Gentle hands lifted him up and carefully, gingerly, rolled him over onto his back. There was some other movement at that point, and then he felt himself get repositioned against pillows that had been returned to their rightful place. Finally, a lightweight blanket was settled half-way up his body, as if Qhuinn knew that he was just about too hot to have any more coverage, and yet already feeling the chill as the sweat that covered him started to dry.

His hair was brushed back from his forehead, and then his head was eased to the side. Lips like silk kissed down the column of his neck, and then long, slow lapping sealed the puncture wounds that he had asked for and been given.

When it was done, he allowed his head to be turned toward Qhuinn. Even though it was pitch dark, he knew exactly what the face staring into his own looked like—flush on the cheeks, half-mast lids, lips red—

The kiss that was pressed against his own mouth was reverent, the contact no heavier than the warm, still air in the room. It was the consummate lover's kiss, the kind of thing he had wanted even more than the hot sex they'd just had—

Panic struck in the center of his chest and resonated outward through him in the blink of an eye.

His hands shot out of their own volition, shoving Qhuinn away. "Don't touch me. Don't you touch me like that—ever."

He sprang up off the bed and landed God only knew where in the room. Fumbling around, he hit various pieces of furniture, but then was able to orientate himself by the thin line of light that shone under the way out.

Grabbing his robe from the floor, he did not look back as he left.

Couldn't bear to see the aftermath in any kind of light.

That made it all too real.

* * *

Eventually, Qhuinn had to will the lights in his bedroom on. He couldn't stand the darkness any longer.

As illumination flooded the space, he blinked hard and had to put his arms up to shield his eyes. After things recalibrated in retina-land, he looked around.

Chaos. Total chaos.

So all of that had actually happened, huh. And how ironic that the inside of his head made this goddamn mess look military-order in comparison.

Don't you touch me like that.

Ah, hell, he thought as he scrubbed his face. He couldn't blame the guy.

For one thing, he'd shown about as much finesse as a bulldozer. Wrecking ball. Armed tank. The problem was, it had all been too much to show any patience: Instinct, as pure as octane and just as flammable, had lit him up—the session had been a case of letting the shit out.

Oh, God, he'd marked the guy.

Fuck. Not exactly good form, considering Blay was already in love and in a relationship . . . and going back to his lover's bed.

Then again, when a male was with the one he wanted, especially if it was the first time, that was what happened. Hell broke loose. . . .

It went without saying that it had been the best sex of his life, the first right fit after a long history of not-even-closes. The thing was, at the end, he'd wanted Blay to know that, had been searching for words and relying on touch to pave the way to the confession.

But it was clear the male didn't want to get close like that.

Which brought up a second, even more profound regret.

Revenge sex was not about attraction; it was about utility. And Blay had used him, just like he'd asked to be used.

That hollow feeling came back tenfold. A hundredfold.

Unable to stand the emotion, he burst up to his feet, and had to curse: The notable tightness in his lower back had fuck-all to do with the airplane accident, and everything to do with the pneumatics he'd just spent the last hour . . . or longer . . . throwing around.

Shit.

Going into the bath, he left the lights off, but there was more than enough to go by from the bedroom as he turned on the shower. This time, he waited for the water to get warm—his body was not up for another shocker.

It was so pathetic, but the last thing he wanted was to wash Blay's scent off his skin, but he was being driven mad from it. God, this must be what the *hellrens* in the house felt like when they got all possessive: He was of half a mind to stalk down the hall, burst into Blay's room, and shove Saxton out of the way. Matter of fact, he would have loved for his cousin to watch, just so the guy knew that . . .

To cut off that really frickin' healthy train of thought, he stepped into the glass enclosure and went for the soap.

Blay was in a relationship, he pointed out to himself—again.

The sex they'd just had had *not* been about emotionally connecting.

So he was, in this moment of emptiness, getting shanked by his own history.

Looked like this was another case of fate giving him what he deserved.

As he washed himself, the soap wasn't half as soft as Blay's skin, and didn't smell a quarter as good. The water wasn't as hot as the fighter's blood had been, and the shampoo wasn't as soothing. Nothing came close.

Nothing ever would.

As Qhuinn turned his face to the spray and opened his mouth, he found himself praying Saxton wandered off the range again—even though that was a shitty thing to hope for.

Problem was, he had a horrible feeling that another case of the infidelities was the only way Blay would come to him again.

Closing his eyes, he went back to that moment when he'd kissed Blay at the end . . . really, truly kissed him, their mouths meeting gently in the quiet after the storm. As his mind rewrote the script, he wasn't pushed away to the far side of a boundary he himself had created. No, in his imagination, things ended as they should have, with him stroking Blay's face and willing the lights on so they could look at each other.

In his fantasy, he kissed his best friend again, pulled back, and . . .

"I love you," he said into the spray of the shower. "I . . . love you."

As he closed his eyes against the pain, it was hard to know how much of what ran down his cheeks was water, and how much was something else.

TWENTY-NINE

The following day, late in the afternoon, Assail's visitor came back.

As the sun set and the last of the dusky pink rays pierced through the forest, he watched on his monitor as a lone figure on cross-country skis stood among the trees, poles balanced against hips, binoculars up at the face.

Or *her* hips, and her face, as it were.

The good news was that his security cameras not only had fantastic zoom, but their focus and sight line were easily manipulated by the computer's joystick.

So he went in even tighter.

As the woman dropped the binoculars, he measured the individual lashes around her dark, calculating eyes, and the red tinge to her fine-pored cheeks, and the steady rhythm that beat in the artery running up to her jawline.

The warning he'd given to Benloise had been received. And yet here she was again.

It was clear she was connected in some way with that drug wholesaler—and the night before she had apparently been angered by

Benloise, given the way she had marched out of the back of that gallery looking like someone had insulted her.

And yet Assail had not seen her before, and that was odd. In the past year or so, he had familiarized himself with the each-and-everys of Benloise's operation, from the incalculable number of bodyguards, to the irrelevant gallery staff, to the canny importers, to the man's flesh-and-blood brother who oversaw the finances.

So he could only assume she was an independent contractor, hired for a specific purpose.

Except why was she still on his own property?

He checked the digital readout on the lower right-hand corner of the screen. Four thirty-seven. Ordinarily, hardly a time to rejoice, as it was still too early to go out. But daylight saving time had kicked in, and that human invention to manipulate the sun actually worked in his favor six months out of the year.

It was going to be a little hot out there, but he would deal with it.

Assail dressed quickly, pulling on a Gucci suit along with a white silk shirt, and grabbing his double-breasted camel-hair overcoat. His pair of Smith & Wesson forties were the perfect accessories, of course.

Gunmetal was forever the new black.

Grabbing his iPhone, he frowned as he touched the screen. A call had come in from Rehvenge, along with a message.

Striding out of his room, he summoned the *leahdyre* of the Council's voice mail and listened to it on the way downstairs.

The male's voice was all about the no-bullshit, and one had to respect that: "Assail, you know who this is. I'm calling a Council meeting, and I want not just a quorum, but perfect attendance—the king's going to be there, and so will the Brotherhood. As the eldest surviving male of your bloodline, you've been on the Council roster, but recorded as inactive because you stayed in the Old Country. Now that you're back, it's time to start going to these happy little get-togethers. Call me with your schedule, so I can work out a time and location for everyone."

Coming to a halt before the steel door that blocked off the bottom of the stairs, he put the phone in one of his inside pockets, unlatched the lock, and slid the way open.

The first floor was dark because of the filtering shades that blocked out all light, and the huge open space of the living room appeared like a cavern in the earth rather than a glass cage perched on the shores of a river.

From the direction of the kitchen, he heard sizzling and smelled bacon.

Walking in the opposite direction, he went into the burled walnut–paneled office he'd given his cousins to use and entered his twenty-square-foot walk-in humidor. Inside, the temperate air, which was kept at a precise seventy degrees, and a humidity of exactly sixty-nine percent, was perfumed with the tobacco from dozens and dozens of boxes of cigars. After due consideration of his lineup, he took three Cubans.

The Cubans were the best, after all.

And were another thing Benloise provided him with—for a price.

Sealing up his precious collection, he reemerged into the living room. The sizzling had stopped, the subtle sounds of silver on china replacing the hiss.

As he came around into the kitchen, his two cousins were sitting on bar stools at the granite counter, the pair of them eating in precisely the same rhythm, as if there was some drumbeat, unheard by others, that regulated their movements.

They both looked up at him with the same angle to their heads.

"I'm leaving for the evening. You know how to reach me," he said.

Ehric wiped his mouth. "I've tracked down three of those missing dealers—they're back in action, ready to move. I'm making a delivery at midnight."

"Good, good." Assail quickly ran a check of his guns. "Try to find out where they were, will you?"

"As you wish."

The pair of them bowed their heads in a joint bob, and then went back to their breakfasts.

No food for him. Over by the coffeepot, he picked up an amber-colored vial and unscrewed the top. The lid had a little silver spoon attached to it, and the thing made a tinkling noise as he filled its belly with coke. One hit per nostril.

Wakey-wakey.

He took the rest with him, putting it into the same pocket as his cigars. It had been a while since he'd fed and he was beginning to feel the effects, his body lagging, his mind prone to a fuzziness that was unfamiliar.

The downside to the New World? Harder to find females.

Fortunately, uncut cocaine was a good substitute, at least for the time being.

Slipping a pair of nearly opaque-lensed sunglasses on, he went through the mudroom and braced himself at the back door.

Throwing the thing open—

Assail recoiled and groaned at the onslaught, his weight weaving in his loafers: In spite of the fact that ninety-nine percent of his skin was covered by multiple layers of clothing, and even with the dark glasses, the fading light in the sky was enough to make him falter.

But there was no time to give in to biology.

Forcing himself to dematerialize into the woods behind his house, he set about tracking the woman in the near darkness. It was easy enough to locate her. She was on the retreat, moving with speed on those cross-country skis, winding her way through the fluffy pine boughs and the skeletal oaks and maples. Extrapolating from her trajectory, and applying the same internal logic she had demonstrated on the security tapes from the previous morning, he was soon out ahead of her, anticipating right where her . . .

Ah, yes. The black Audi from the gallery. Parked at the side of the plowed road about two miles from his property.

Assail was leaning against the driver's-side door and puffing on a Cuban as she came out of the line of trees.

She stopped dead in the dual tracks she'd made, her poles at wide angles.

He smiled at her as he blew out a cloud of smoke into the gloaming. "Fine evening for exercise. Enjoying the view—of my house?"

Her breath was quick from the exertion, but not from any fear that he could sense—which was a turn-on. "I don't know what you're talking about—"

He cut off the lie. "Well, I can tell you that at the moment, I'm enjoying my view."

As his eyes went deliberately down her long, athletic legs in their form-fitting ski pants, she glared at him. "I find it hard to believe you can see anything with those glasses."

"My eyes are very sensitive to light."

She frowned and looked around. "There's hardly any left in the sky."

"There's enough to see you." He took another puff. "Would you like to know what I told Benloise last night?"

"Who?"

Now she annoyed him, and he sharpened his voice. "A piece of

advice. Don't play games with me—that will get you killed faster than any trespassing."

Cold calculation narrowed her stare. "I wasn't aware that property offenses carried a capital punishment."

"With me, there's a whole list of things that have mortal repercussions."

She kicked up her chin. "Well. Aren't you dangerous."

As if he were a kitten pawing at a string and hissing.

Assail moved so fast, he knew damn well her eyes were incapable of tracking him—one moment he was yards away, the next he was standing on the tips of her skis, trapping her in place.

The woman shouted in alarm and tried to jump back, but, of course, her feet were stuck in their bindings. To keep her from falling over, he grabbed her arm with the hand that wasn't holding his cigar.

Now her blood ran with fear, and as he inhaled the scent, he hardened. Jerking her forward, he stared down at her, tracing her face.

"Be careful," he said in a low voice. "I take offense quite readily, and my temper is not easily assuaged."

Although he could think of at least one thing she could give him that would calm him.

Leaning in, he inhaled deeply. God, he loved that scent of hers.

But now was not the time to get distracted by all that. "I told Benloise to send people to my home at his own risk—and theirs. I'm surprised he didn't inform you of those, shall we say, very clear property boundaries. . . ."

From the corner of his eye, he caught a subtle bunching of her shoulder. She was going to go for a weapon with her right hand.

Assail put his cigar between his teeth and caught that slender wrist. Applying pressure, and stopping only when pain deepened her breath, he bowed her body back so that she was completely, utterly aware of the power he had—over himself, over her. Over everything.

And that was when the arousal happened for the woman.

It had been so long, perhaps too long, since Sola had wanted a man.

It was not that she didn't find them desirable as a rule, or that there had been no offers for horizontal encounters from members of the opposite sex. Nothing had seemed worth the aggravation. And maybe, after that one relationship that hadn't worked out, she had regressed back to her strict Brazilian upbringing—which would be ironic, considering what she did for a living.

This man, however, got her attention. In a big way.

The holds on her arm and her wrist were nothing polite, and more than that, there was no quarter given because she was a woman, his hands squeezing to such a degree that pain funneled into her heart, making it pound. Likewise, the angle he'd forced her back into was testing the limits of her spine's ability to bend, and her thighs were burning.

To be turned on was . . . a gross dereliction of self-preservation. In fact, staring up into those black glasses, she was acutely aware that he could kill her right here. Snap her neck. Break her arms just to see her scream before suffocating her in the snow. Or maybe knock her out and throw her in the river.

Her grandmother's heavily accented voice came into her mind: *Why can you not meet a nice boy? A Catholic boy from a family we know? Marisol, you break my heart with this.*

"I can only assume," that dark voice whispered with an accent and infliction she was unfamiliar with, "that the message was not passed on to you. Is that correct? Did Benloise simply fail to convey to you that information—and that is why, after I expressly indicated my intentions, you still showed up looking at my house? I think that's what happened—mayhap a voice mail that has yet to be received. Or a text message—an e-mail. Yes, I believe that Benloise's communication was lost, isn't that right?"

The pressure on her was tightened even further, suggesting that he had strength to spare—which was a daunting prospect, to say the least.

"Isn't that right," he growled.

"Yes," she bit out. "Yes, that's right."

"So I can expect not to find you on your skis around here anymore. Isn't that right."

He jerked her again, the pain making her eyes roll back a little. "Yes," she choked.

The man relented enough so that she could grab some breaths. Then he kept speaking, that voice strangely seductive. "Now, there is something I need before I let you go. You will tell me what you know about me—all of it."

Sola frowned, thinking that was silly. No doubt a man like this would be well aware of any information a third party could garner about him.

So it was a test.

Given that she very much wanted to see her grandmother again, Sola said, "I don't know your name, but I can guess what you do, and also what you've done."

"And what's that?"

"I think you are the one who has been shooting all those penny-ante dealers in town to secure territory and control."

"The papers and the news reports have labeled the deaths suicides."

She just continued on—there was, after all, no reason to argue. "I know that you live alone, as far as I can tell—and that your house is outfitted with some very strange window treatments. Camouflage designed to appear as the interior of the home, but . . . they are something else above and beyond that. I just don't know what."

That face above her own remained utterly impassive. Calm. At peace. As if he wasn't muscling her in place—or threatening bodily harm. The control was . . . erotic.

"And?" he prompted.

"That's it."

He inhaled on the cigar in his mouth, the fat orange circle on the end glowing more brightly. "I'm only going to let you go once. Do you understand that?"

"Yes."

He moved so quickly she had to swing her arms out to regain her balance on her own, her poles digging into the snow. Wait, where did he—

The man appeared right behind her, his feet planted on either side of the tracks her skis had made, a physical barricade to the path she had traveled from his house. As her left biceps and her right wrist burned from blood returning to the areas it had been squeezed out of, a warning tickled across the nape of her neck.

Get out of here, Sola, she told herself. *Right now.*

Unwilling to run the risk of another capture, she shot forward into the plowed road, the waxed, scaled bottoms of her skis struggling to find purchase on the packed, iced-over snow.

As she went, he followed her, walking slowly, inexorably, like a great cat who was tracking prey that he was content only to play with—for now.

Her hands shook as she used the tips of her poles to spring the bindings, and she struggled to get her skis back in the rack on her car. The whole time, he stood in the middle of the road and watched her, that cigar smoke drifting over his shoulder in the cold drafts that funneled toward the river.

Getting inside her car, she locked the doors, started the engine, and looked in the rearview mirror. In the glow from her brake lights, he appeared downright evil, a tall, black-haired man with a face as handsome as a prince's, and as cruel as a blade.

Hitting the gas, she pulled off the shoulder and sped away, the car's all-wheel drive system kicking in and giving her the traction she needed.

She glanced into the rearview again. He was still there—

Sola's foot shifted onto the brake and nearly punched down.

He was gone.

Sure as if he had disappeared into thin air. One moment there in her sight . . . the next, invisible.

Shaking herself, she punched the gas again, and made the sign of the cross over her heavily beating heart.

With a crazy panic, she wondered, Just what the hell was he?

THIRTY

Just as the shutters were rising for the night, Layla heard the knock upon her door—and even before the scent drifted in through the panels, she knew who had come to see her.

Unconsciously, her hand went to her hair—and found that it was a mess, matted from her having tossed and turned all day long. Worse, she hadn't even bothered to change from the street clothes she'd put on to go to the clinic.

She couldn't deny him entrance, however.

"Come in," she called out, sitting up a little higher and straightening the covers that she'd pulled up to her breastbone.

Qhuinn was dressed in fighting clothes, which she took to mean he was on rotation for the night—but mayhap not. She was not privy to the schedule.

As their eyes met, she frowned. "You don't look well."

He brought a hand up to the bandage over his eyebrow. "Oh, this? It's just a scrape."

Except it wasn't the injury that had drawn her notice. It was his blank stare, and the grim hollows under his cheekbones.

He stopped. Sniffed the air. Blanched.

Immediately, she looked at her hands, her once again tangled hands. "Please shut the door," she said.

"What's happening?"

When the thing was closed as she requested, she took a deep breath. "I went to Havers's last night—"

"*What.*"

"I've been bleeding—"

"Bleeding!" He rushed forward, all but skidding onto the bed. "Why the *hell* didn't you tell me?"

Dearest Virgin Scribe, it was impossible for her not to cower in the face of his fury—in truth, she was out of strength at the moment, and unable to rally any self-preservation.

Instantly, Qhuinn dialed back on his anger, the male pulling away and walking around in a tight circle. When he faced her again, he said gruffly, "I'm sorry. I didn't mean to yell—I'm just . . . I'm worried about you."

"I'm sorry. And I should have told you . . . but you were out fighting, and I didn't want to bother you. I don't know . . . honestly, I probably wasn't thinking straight. I was frantic."

Qhuinn sat down beside her, his huge shoulders curling in as he linked his fingers and put his elbows on his knees. "So what's going on?"

All she could do was shrug. "Well, as you can sense . . . I am bleeding."

"How much?"

She thought about what the nurse had said. "Enough."

"For how long?"

"It started about twenty-four hours ago. I didn't want to go to Doc Jane, because I wasn't sure how private that would be—and also, she doesn't have a lot of experience with pregnancy in our species."

"What did Havers say?"

Now she was the one frowning. "He refused to tell me."

Qhuinn's head cranked around. "Excuse me?"

"Because of my Chosen status, he will speak only with the Primale."

"Are you fucking me."

She shook her head. "No. I couldn't believe it, either—and I'm

afraid I left there under less than optimal circumstances. He reduced me to an object, as if I am of no concern at all . . . naught but a repository—"

"You know that's not true." Qhuinn took her hand, his mismatched eyes burning. "Not to me. Never to me."

She reached out and touched his shoulder. "I know, but thank you for saying that." She shuddered. "I need to hear that right now. And as for what's happening with . . . me . . . the nurse said there's nothing anyone can do to stop this."

Qhuinn looked down at the carpet and stayed that way for the longest time. "I don't understand. It wasn't supposed to be like this."

Swallowing that horrible sense of failure, she sat up and stroked his back. "I know you wanted this as much as I did."

"You can't be losing it. It's just not possible."

"From what I understand, the statistics are not good. Not at the start . . . and not at the end."

"No, it's not right. I saw . . . her."

Layla cleared her throat. "Dreams don't always come true, Qhuinn."

It seemed like such a simplistic thing to say. So self-obvious as well. But it hurt to the core.

"It wasn't a dream," he said baldly. But then he shook himself, and looked at her again. "How are you feeling? Does it hurt?"

When she didn't immediately answer, because she didn't want to lie to him about the cramping, he got to his feet. "I'm going to get Doc Jane."

She snagged his hand, holding him in place. "Wait. Think about this. If I'm losing the . . . young . . ." She paused to gather some strength after she put that into words. "There's no reason to tell anyone anything. No one needs to know. We can just let nature—" Her voice cracked at that point, but she forced herself to go on. "—take its course."

"To hell with that. I'm not going to jeopardize your life just to avoid a confrontation."

"It won't stop the miscarriage, Qhuinn."

"The miscarriage isn't the only thing I'm worried about." He squeezed her hand. "You matter. So I'm going to get Doc Jane right now."

Yeah, fuck the keep-shit-quiet for real, Qhuinn thought as he headed for the door.

He'd heard stories about females hemorrhaging out during miscarriages—and though he wasn't about to share any of that stuff with Layla, he was going to act on it.

"Qhuinn. Stop," Layla called out. "Think about what you're doing."

"I am. And clearly." He didn't wait for any more arguing. "You stay there."

"Qhuinn—"

He could still hear her voice as he shut the door and took off at a run, going down the short hall and descending the stairs. With any luck, Doc Jane was still lingering over Last Meal with her *hellren*—the pair of them had been at the table when he'd gone up to check on Layla.

As he hit the foyer, his Nikes squeaked on the mosaic floor as he made for the archway into the dining room.

Seeing the physician right where she'd been was a stroke of luck, and his first instinct was to bark out her name. Except then he realized there were a number of Brothers at the table, eating dessert.

Shit. It was easy for him to say that he'd deal with the fallout if what they'd done got wide airtime. But Layla? As a sacred Chosen, she had a lot more to lose than he did. Phury was a pretty fair guy, so there was a good chance he would be cool with it. The rest of society?

He'd been there/done that when it came to being shut out, and he did not want that for her.

Qhuinn rushed around to where V and Jane were eased back and relaxed, the Brother smoking a hand-rolled, the ghostly physician smiling at her mate as he cracked a joke.

The instant the good doctor looked over at him, she sat forward.

Qhuinn dropped down and whispered into her ear.

Not even a second later, she was on her feet. "I gotta go, Vishous."

The Brother's diamond eyes lifted. Apparently, one look at Qhuinn's face was all it took: he didn't ask any questions, just nodded once.

Qhuinn and the physician hurried out together.

To Doc Jane's infinite credit, she didn't waste time with any how-did-this-pregnancy-happens. "How long has she been bleeding?"

"Twenty-four hours."

"How heavily?"

"I don't know."

"Any other symptoms? Fever? Nausea? Headaches?"

"I don't know."

She stopped him as they came to the grand staircase. "Go to the Pit. My bag's on the counter by the bowl of apples."

"Roger that."

Qhuinn never ran so fast in his life. Out of the vestibule. Across the courtyard in the snow. Punching in the code to the Pit. Racing into V and Butch's place.

Ordinarily, he would never have entered without knocking—hell, without a prearranged appointment time. Fuck that tonight, though—

Oh, good, that black bag was in fact by the Fujis.

Grabbing the thing, he raced out, shot back past the parked cars, and stamped his feet as he waited for Fritz to open the way into the mansion. He nearly plowed the *doggen* over.

As he got up to the second floor, he bolted past the open doors to Wrath's study and broke into the guest room Layla had been using. Closing the door, he panted on his way over to the bed, where the good doctor was sitting where he just had been.

God, Layla was white as a sheet. Then again, fear and blood loss would do that to a female.

Doc Jane was in midsentence as she took her bag from him. "I think I should start by taking your vitals—"

Boom!

As the thunderous noise rang throughout the room, Qhuinn's first thought was to throw himself on both the females as a shield.

But it wasn't a bomb. It was Phury throwing the door wide.

The Brother's yellow eyes were glowing, and not in a good way, as they went from Layla to Doc Jane to Qhuinn . . . and back again.

"What the hell is going on in here?" he demanded, nostrils flaring as he clearly caught the same scent Qhuinn had. "I see the doctor going up the stairs at a dead run. Then it's Qhuinn with her bag. And now . . . someone had better start talking. This goddamn minute."

But he knew. Because he was looking at Qhuinn.

Qhuinn faced the Brother. "I got her pregnant—"

He didn't get a chance to finish the sentence. Barely got through the p-word, as a matter of fact.

The Brother all but picked him up and threw him against the wall. As his back absorbed the impact, his jaw exploded in pain—which suggested the guy had also corked him a good one. Then rough hands pinned him in place with his feet dangling about six inches from the nice Oriental rug—just as people started to pool in the doorway.

Great. An audience.

Phury shoved his face into Qhuinn's and bared his fangs. "You did *what* to her?"

Qhuinn swallowed a mouthful of blood. "She went into her needing. I serviced her."

"You don't deserve her—"

"I know."

Phury slammed him again. "She's better than this—"

"I agree—"

Bang! Again with the wall. "Then why the fuck did you—"

The growl that permeated the room was loud enough to rattle the mirror on the wall next to Qhuinn's head—as well as the silver brush set on the bureau and the crystals on the sconces by the door. At first he was sure it was Phury . . . except then the Brother's brows came down hard and the male looked over his shoulder.

Layla was out of bed and closing in on the pair of them—and holy fucking shit, the look in her eyes was enough to melt paint off a car door: In spite of the fact that she was not well, her fangs were bared, and her fingers were curled into claws . . . and the icy draft that preceded her made the back of Qhuinn's neck prickle in warning.

That growl was nothing that should have come out of a male . . . much less a delicate female of Chosen status.

And if anything, her nasty tone of voice was worse: *"Let. Him. Go."*

She was looking up at Phury as if she were fully prepared to rip the Brother's arms out of their sockets and beat him with the stumps if he didn't do exactly what she said. Pronto.

And hey, what do you know—suddenly Qhuinn could breathe right, and now his Nikes were back on the floor. Just like magic.

Phury put his palms out in front of him. "Layla, I—"

"You do not touch him. Not about this—are we clear with each other?" Her weight was on the balls of her feet, as if she could lunge for the guy's throat at any second. "He was the father of my young, and he will be accorded all the rights and privileges of that station."

"Layla—"

"Do we understand each other?"

Phury nodded his multicolored head. "Yes. But—"

In the Old Language, she hissed, "*If any harm shall befall him, I will come after you, and find you where you sleep. I do not care where you lay your head or who with, my vengeance shall rain upon you until you drown.*"

That last word was drawn out, until its syllable was lost in more growling.

Dead silence.

Until Doc Jane said dryly, "Annnnd this is why they say the female of the species is more dangerous than the male."

"Word," someone muttered from out in the hall.

Phury threw his hands up in frustration. "I just want what's best for you, and not only as a concerned friend—this is my fucking job. You go through your needing without telling anyone, lay with him"—like Qhuinn was dog shit—"and then not tell anyone you're in medical trouble. And I'm supposed to be happy about this? What the fuck?"

There was some kind of conversation between the pair of them at that point, but Qhuinn didn't hear it: All of his consciousness had retreated deep into his brain. Man, the Brother's happy little commentary shouldn't have hurt like a bitch—it wasn't like he hadn't heard that stuff before, or hell, even thought it about himself. But for some reason, the words triggered a fault line that rumbled right down into the core of him.

Reminding himself that it was hardly a tragedy to have the obvious pointed out, he pulled free of the shame spiral and glanced around. Yup, everyone had shown up at the open door—and once again, things he would have preferred remain private were happening in front of a cast of thousands.

At least Layla didn't care. Hell, she didn't even seem to notice.

And it was kind of funny to see all these professional fighters unwilling to get within a mile of the female. Then again, if you wanted to survive doing the work they did, accurate risk assessment was something you developed early—and even Qhuinn, who was the object of the protective instinct the Chosen was rocking, wouldn't have dared touch her.

"*I hereby renounce my Chosen status, and all the rights and privileges thereto. I am Layla, fallen from this heartbeat onward—*"

Phury tried to cut her off. "Listen, you don't have to do this—"

"*. . . and evermore. I am ruined in the eyes of both tradition and*

practicality, virgin no more, conceived of a young, even though I am los-ing it."

Qhuinn banged the back of his head into the wall. Goddamn it.

Phury dragged a hand through his thick hair. "Fuck."

When Layla wobbled on her feet, everyone went for her, but she pushed all hands away and walked under her own steam back to the bed. Lowering her body gingerly, as if everything hurt, she hung her head.

"My die is cast, and I am prepared to live with the consequences, be as they may. That is all."

There were a number of brows going up at her dismissal of the whole crowd, but nobody said boo: After a moment, the peanut gallery shuffled off, although Phury stayed put. So did Qhuinn and the doc-tor.

The door was shut.

"Okay, especially after all that, I really need to check your vitals," Doc Jane said, easing the female back against the pillows and helping to resettle the covers that had been thrown off.

Qhuinn didn't move as a blood-pressure cuff was slid up a slender arm and a series of *puff-puff-puffs* sounded.

Phury, on the other hand, paced around—at least until he frowned and took out his phone. "Is this why Havers called me last night?"

Layla nodded. "I went there looking for help."

"Why didn't you come to me?" the Brother muttered to himself.

"What did Havers say?"

"I don't know because I didn't listen to the voice mail. I thought I'd have no reason to."

"He indicated he would deal only with you."

At that, Phury looked over at Qhuinn, that yellow stare narrow-ing. "Are you going to mate her?"

"No."

Phury's expression grew icy again. "What the hell kind of male are you—"

"He's not in love with me," Layla cut in. "Nor I with him."

As the Primale's head whipped around, Layla continued, "We wanted a young." She sat forward as Doc Jane listened to her heart from behind. "It began and finished there."

Now the Brother cursed. "I don't get it."

"We are both orphans in many ways," the Chosen said. "We are—were . . . seeking a family of our own."

Phury exhaled, and wandered over to the desk in the corner, taking a load off in the dainty chair. "Well. Ah. I guess this changes things a little. I thought that—"

"It matters naught," Layla interjected. "It is what it is. Or . . . was, as the case may be."

Qhuinn found himself rubbing his eyes for no particular reason. Not like they were blurry or some shit. Nah. Not at all.

It was just so . . . damned sad. The whole fucking thing. From Layla's condition, to Phury's impotent exhaustion, to his own driving ache in the chest, it was just some seriously sad goddamned business.

THIRTY-ONE

"This is just what I'm looking for."

As Trez spoke, he walked around the vast, empty space of the warehouse, his boots making loud impacts that echoed. From behind him, he could easily sense the relief that wafted out of the real estate agent standing by the door.

Negotiating with humans? Like taking candy from a baby.

"You could transform this part of the city," the woman said. "It's a real opportunity."

"True enough." Although it wasn't like the kind of stores and restaurants that would follow him were highbrow: more like tattoo and piercing shops, cheap buffets, XXX theaters.

But he didn't have a problem with all that. Even pimps could take pride in their work—and frankly, he tended to trust tattoo artists waaaaaaaay more than many so-called "upstanding citizens."

Trez pivoted around. The space was tremendous, nearly as tall as it was wide, with rows upon rows of square windows, many of which had been broken and covered up with plywood. The roof was sound— or at least mostly so, the corrugated tin sheaths keeping the snow, although not the cold, out. The floor was concrete, but there was

obviously a lower level—at various points there were trapdoors set underfoot, although none of them were easily opened. Electricals looked okay; HVAC was nonexistent; plumbing was a joke.

In his mind, however, he didn't see the place as it was now—nope, he could picture it transformed, a club of Limelight proportions. Naturally, the project was going to require a huge capital infusion, and a number of months to get the work done; in the end, however, Caldwell was going to have a new hot spot—and he was going to have another venue to make money in.

Everybody wins.

"So would you like to make an offer?"

Trez looked over at the woman. She was Ms. Professional in her black wool coat, and her dark suit with the below-the-knee skirt—ninety percent of her flesh covered, and not just because it was December. And yet even all buttoned up with the sensible hair, she was pretty in the way that all women were to him: She had breasts and soft smooth skin, and a place for him to play in between her legs.

And she liked him.

He could tell by the way she dropped her eyes from his, and by the fact that she didn't seem to know what to do with her hands—they were in her coat pockets, then playing with her hair, then tucking her silk shirt in. . . .

He could think of some things to keep her busy.

Trez smiled as he walked across to her—and didn't stop until he was just inside her personal space. "Yes. I want it."

The double entendre hit home, her cheeks reddening not from the cold, but arousal. "Oh. Good."

"Where do you want to do it," he drawled.

"Make the offer, you mean?" She cleared her throat. "All you have to do is tell me what you . . . want and I'll . . . make it happen."

Aw, she wasn't used to casual sex. How sweet.

"Here."

"I'm sorry?" she said, finally looking up into his eyes.

He smiled slow and tight so his fangs didn't show. "The offer. Let's do that here?"

Her eyes widened. "Really?"

"Yeah. Really." He stepped in closer, but not so close that they were touching. He was happy to seduce her, but she had to be one hundred percent sure she was into the grind. "You ready?"

"To . . . make . . . the offer."

"Yeah."

"It's, ah, it's cold in here," she said. "Maybe at my office? That's where most of the . . . offers . . . get handled."

From out of nowhere, the image of his brother sitting on the sofa at home, staring at him like he was the frickin' problem, hit him hard—and as it stuck around, he realized that he'd had sex with almost every woman he'd come across in the last . . . shit, how long?

Well, obviously, if they weren't of mateable age he hadn't been with them.

Or fertile.

Which cut out what, like, a dozen or two? Great. What a hero.

What the *fuck* was he doing? He didn't want to go back to this woman's office—for one thing, there wasn't enough time, assuming he wanted to be at the Iron Mask for opening. So the only option was right here, standing up, her skirt around her waist, her legs around his hips. Quick, to the point; then go their separate ways.

After he'd told her how much cash he was willing to pay for this warehouse, of course.

But then what? It wasn't like he was going to bang her at the closing. He rarely did repeats, and only if he was seriously attracted or really itchy—which in this case he was not.

For chrissakes, what exactly was he getting out of this? It wasn't like he was going to see her naked. Or have much skin-on-skin contact.

Unless . . . that was the point.

When was the last time he'd really been with a female? Like, properly. As in . . . nice dinner, little music, some necking that led to a bedroom . . . then long, slow, patient shit where he had a couple of orgasms.

And no choking sense of panic when it was over.

"You were going to say something?" the woman prompted him.

iAm was right. He didn't need to be doing this crap. Hell, he wasn't even attracted to the Realtor. She was standing in front of him; she was available; and that wedding ring on her finger meant she was probably not going to cause a lot of trouble after it was over—because she had something to lose.

Trez took a step back. "Listen, I—" As his phone went off in his coat, he thought, Perfect timing—and checked it. It was iAm. "'Scuse me. I have to take this. Hey, what you doing, little brother?"

iAm's reply was soft, like he'd lowered his voice. "We got company."

Trez's body tensed. "What kind and where."

"I'm home."

Oh, shit. "Who is it."

"It's not your betrothed, relax. It's AnsLai."

The high priest. Fantastic. "Well, I'm busy."

"He's not here to see me."

"Then he'd better go back where he came from, because I'm otherwise engaged." When there was nothing but silence over the connection, all he had to do was dub in the ass-kicking. Unable to keep still, he stalked around. "Look, what do you want me to do?"

"Stop running and deal with this."

"There's nothing to deal with. I'll catch you later, 'kay?"

He waited for a response. Instead, the line went dead. Then again, when you expected your brother to clean up your crap, the guy wasn't likely to be in the mood for a protracted good-bye.

Trez hung up and glanced over at the Realtor. Smiling widely, he walked to her and looked down. Her lipstick was a little too coral for her complexion, but he didn't care.

The shit wasn't going to be on her mouth for much longer.

"Let me show you how warm I can make it in here," he said with a slow smile.

Back at the Brotherhood mansion, up in Layla's room, a kind of détente had been reached among the various interested parties.

Phury wasn't trying to turn Qhuinn into a wall hanging. Layla was getting assessed. And the door had been shut so that anything that went down was going to have no more than a quartet of firsthand witnesses.

Qhuinn was just waiting for Doc Jane to speak.

When she finally took her stethoscope off from around her neck, she sat back. And the expression on her face gave him no hope.

He didn't understand it. He had seen his daughter at the door to the Fade: When he'd been beaten and left for dead at the side of the road by the Honor Guard, he had gone up to God only knew where, had approached the white portal . . . and had seen in the panels a young female whose eyes had started out one color, and ended up blue and green like his own.

If he hadn't been witness to that, he probably wouldn't have lain with Layla in the first place. But he'd been so sure that destiny was spelled out that it had never dawned on him . . .

Shit, maybe that young was the result of another pairing—somewhere else down the line.

But like he was going to be with anyone else? Ever?

Not possible. Not now that he'd had Blay once.

Nope.

Even if he and his former friend never got between the sheets again, he was never going to be with anybody else. Who could compare? And celibacy was better than second-best—which again, was what would be offered by the rest of the planet.

Doc Jane cleared her throat and took Layla's hand. "Your blood pressure is a little low. Your pulse rate is sluggish. I think both of these can be improved with a feeding—"

Qhuinn all but jumped on the bed with his wrist outstretched. "I got it—right here. I got—"

Doc Jane put her hand on his arm and smiled at him. "But that's not what I'm worried about."

He froze—and out of the corner of his eye, he saw Phury do the same.

"Here's the problem." The doctor refocused on Layla, speaking gently and clearly. "I don't know a lot about vampire pregnancies—so as much as I hate to say this, you need to go back to Havers's." She put her hand up, as if she anticipated arguments from all corners. "This is about her and the young—we have to get them to somebody who can treat her appropriately, even if, under other circumstances, none of us would darken that guy's door. And, Phury"—she looked over at the Brother—"you have to go with her and Qhuinn. Your being there will make it easier on everybody."

Lot of tight lips after that.

"She's right," Qhuinn said finally. And then he turned to the Primale. "And you need to say you're the father. She'll get more respect that way. With me? He might well refuse to treat her—if she's fallen, and has gotten fucked by a defective? He could turn us away."

Phury opened his mouth. Shut it.

It wasn't like there was much else to say.

As Phury got out his phone and called the clinic to inform the staff they were coming in, his tone of voice suggested he was ready to light the place up if Havers and his crew screwed around.

With that getting sorted, Qhuinn went over to Layla.

In a low voice, he said, "It's going to be different this time. He's going to make things happen. Don't worry—you're going to get treated like a queen."

Layla's eyes were wide, but she kept it together. "Yes. All right."

Bottom line? The Brother wasn't the only one ready to throw down. If Havers turned any of that *glymera* distaste on Layla, Qhuinn was going to beat the ego out of that male. Layla didn't deserve that shit—not even for choosing a reject to mate with.

Fuck. Maybe it was better that she lose the pregnancy. Did he really want to condemn a child to his DNA?

"You're coming, too?" she asked him, like she wasn't really tracking.

"Yup. I'll be right there."

When Phury hung up, he looked back and forth between them, his yellow eyes narrowing. "Okay, so they'll take us the second we get there. I'll have Fritz get the Mercedes warmed up, but I'm driving."

"I'm sorry," Layla said as she stared up at the great male. "I know I've let the Chosen and you down—but you did tell us to come to this side and . . . live."

Phury put his hands on his hips and exhaled. As he shook his head, it was clear he wouldn't have picked any of this for her. "Yeah, I said that. That I did."

THIRTY-TWO

*O*h, great unleashed power, Xcor thought as he regarded his soldiers, each of them armed and ready for a night of fighting. After twenty-four hours of recovery following that group feeding, they were chomping at the bit to get out and find their enemies—and he was ready to let release them from the warehouse's underspace.

There was only one problem: Someone was walking the floor above.

As if on cue, footsteps traversed the wooden hatch over his head.

For the last half hour, they had tracked the progress of their uninvited visitors. One was heavy—a masculine form. The other was lighter—a feminine variety. There were no scents to catch, however; the underground level was hermetically sealed.

In all likelihood, it was just a pair of humans passing through—although why two non-vagrants would waste time wandering around such a decrepit structure on a cold night, he could not guess. Whoever they were, whatever the reason they came, however, he would have no problem defending his squatter's rights, such as they were.

But there was no harm in waiting. If he could avoid slaughtering some useless humans here? It meant he and his soldiers could continue to use the space undisturbed.

No one said a thing as the walking about continued.

Voices mingled. Low and higher. Then a phone went off.

Xcor tracked the ringing and the conversation that ensued, walking in silence over to the other hatch where the speaker chose to stop. Going still, he listened hard, and caught one half of a very uninteresting conversation that gave nothing away as to the identity of the parties.

Not long thereafter, the unmistakable sounds of sex filtered down.

As Zypher chuckled softly, Xcor glared in the bastard's direction to shut him up. Even though each of the trapdoors had been locked from below, one never knew what kind of trouble those rats without tails could bring to any situation.

He checked his watch. Waited for the moaning to stop. Motioned for his soldiers to stay put when it did.

Moving in silence, he proceeded over to the trapdoor in the far corner of the warehouse, the one that opened up into what must have been a supervisory office. Unlatching it, he palmed one of his guns, dematerialized out, and inhaled.

Not a human.

Well, there had been one here . . . but the other was something else.

Over in the corner, the outer door clapped shut and the lock was engaged.

Ghosting across the way, Xcor put his back against the warehouse's sturdy brick wall and looked out of one section of the cloudy glass windows.

A pair of headlights flared down in front, in the shallow parking lot.

Dematerializing up and out of a busted pane, he shot forward to the roof of the warehouse across the street.

Well, wasn't this interesting.

That was a Shadow down there, sitting behind the wheel of the BMW with the driver's-side window down, and a human female leaning into the SUV.

Second time he'd run into one in Caldwell.

They were dangerous.

Getting out his phone, he called Throe's number by finding the male's picture in his contacts, and ordered his soldiers to go and fight. He would deal with this departure alone.

Down below, the Shadow reached out, pulled the woman into him by the neck, and kissed her. Then he put the vehicle in reverse and drove off without looking back.

Xcor shifted his position to keep up with the male, going from rooftop to rooftop, as the Shadow headed toward the club district on the surface roads that ran parallel to the river—

At first, the sensation in his body suggested a change in wind direction, the chilly gusts seeming to come up from behind him, as opposed to hitting him face-first. But then he thought . . . no. It was purely internal. Whatever ripples he felt were under his skin—

His Chosen was nearby.

His Chosen.

Immediately abandoning the Shadow's trail, he peeled off and headed closer to the Hudson River. What was she doing down—

In a car. She was traveling in a car.

From what his instincts were telling him, she was going at a fast speed that was nonetheless trackable. So the only explanation was that she was on the Northway, going sixty or seventy miles an hour.

Proceeding back in the direction of the rows of warehouses, he focused on the signal he was picking up on. As it had been months since he'd fed from her, he was panicked to find that the connection created by her blood in his veins was fading—to the point that it was difficult to pinpoint the vehicle.

But then he locked in on a luxury sedan thanks to the fact that it slowed down and got off at the exit that funneled traffic onto the bridges. Dematerializing up onto the girders, he planted his combat boots on the pinnacle of one of the steel risers and waited for her to pass under him.

Shortly thereafter she did, and then continued onward, heading to the other half of the city on the opposite shore.

He stayed on her, maintaining a safe distance, although he wondered who he was fooling. If he could sense his female?

It would be the same for her.

But he would not abandon her trail.

*   *   *

As Qhuinn sat in the passenger seat of the Mercedes, his Heckler &
Koch forty-five was held discreetly on his thigh, and his eyes flipped
incessantly from the rearview mirror to the side window to the windshield. Next to him, Phury was behind the wheel, the Brother's hands
doing a ten-and-two so tightly it was like he was strangling somebody.

Man, there was too much goddamn shit unraveling right now.

Layla and the young. That whole Cessna incident. What Qhuinn
had done to his own cousin the night before. And then . . . well, there
was the Blay thing.

Oh, dear God in heaven . . . the Blay thing.

As Phury got off the exit that would take them onto the bridges,
Qhuinn's brain shifted from worrying about Layla to reviewing all
kinds of pictures and sounds and . . . tastes from the daylight hours.

Intellectually, he knew what had happened between them hadn't
been a dream—and his body sure as hell remembered everything, like
the sex had been a kind of branding on his flesh that changed the way
he looked forever. And yet, as he went about dealing with the newest
frickin' drama, the too-short session seemed prehistoric, not less than
a night old.

He feared it was a one-and-only.

Don't you touch me like that.

Groaning, he rubbed at his head.

"It's not about your eyes," Phury said.

"I'm sorry?"

Phury glanced into the backseat. "Hey, how we doing?" he asked the
females. When Layla and Doc Jane answered in some sort of affirmative,
he nodded. "Listen, I'm going to shut the partition for a sec, 'kay? All
good up here."

The Brother didn't give them a chance to answer one way or another, and Qhuinn stiffened in his seat as the opaque shield rose up,
cutting the sedan into two halves. He wasn't going to run from any
kind of confrontation, but that didn't mean he was looking forward to
round two of this one—and if Phury was cutting the pair in the back
off, it wasn't going to be pretty.

"Your eyes are not the problem," the Brother said.

"Excuse me?"

Phury looked over. "My being pissed off about this has got nothing to do with any defect. Layla's in love with you—"

"No, she's not."

"See, you're really pissing me off right now."

"Ask her."

"While she's miscarrying your young?" the Brother snapped. "Yeah, I'll do that."

As Qhuinn winced, Phury continued. "See, here's the thing with you. You like living on the edge and being all wild—frankly, I think it helps you come to terms with the bullshit your family put you through. If you iconoclast everything? Nothing can hurt you. And believe it or not, I don't have a problem with that. You do you, and get through your nights and your days any way you can. But as soon as you break the heart of an innocent—especially if she's under my care? That's when you and I have an issue."

Qhuinn looked out his window. First off, props to the big man over there. The idea that there was a judgment against Qhuinn based on his character instead of a genetic mutation he hadn't volunteered for was a refreshing change. And hey, it wasn't that he didn't agree with the guy—at least not until about a year ago. Back before then? Hell, yeah, he'd been out of control on a lot of levels. But things had changed. He had changed.

Evidently, Blay becoming unavailable was the kind of boot in the balls he'd needed to finally grow the fuck up.

"I'm not like that anymore," he said.

"So you are in fact prepared to mate her?" When he didn't reply, Phury shrugged. "And there you go. Bottom line—I'm responsible for her, legally and morally. I may not be behaving like the Primale in some respects, but the rest of the job description I take pretty god-damn seriously. The idea that you got her into this mess makes me sick to my stomach, and I find it very hard to believe that she didn't do this to please you—you said you both wanted a young? Are you sure that it wasn't just you, and she did it because she wanted to make you happy? That's very much her way."

This was all presented as a rhetorical. And it wasn't like Qhuinn could criticize the logic, even if it happened to be wrong. But as he dragged a hand through his hair, the fact that Layla was the one who had come to him was something he kept to himself. If Phury wanted to think it was all his fault, that was fine—he'd carry that load. Anything to take the pressure and attention off Layla.

Phury stared across the seats. "It wasn't right, Qhuinn. That's not what a real male does. And now look at the situation she's in. You did

this to her. You put her in the backseat of this car, and that's just wrong."

Qhuinn squeezed his eyes shut. Well, wasn't that going to be banging around the inside of his head for the next hundred years. Give or take.

As they started over the bridge and left the twinkling lights of downtown behind, he kept his godforsaken yap shut, and Phury fell silent as well.

Then again, the Brother had said it all, hadn't he.

THIRTY-THREE

Assail ended up further tracking his prey from behind the wheel of his Range Rover. Much cozier this way—and it wasn't as if the woman's location was an issue now: While he'd been waiting by the Audi for her to come off his property, he'd attached a tracking device to the underbelly of her side-view mirror.

His iPhone took care of the rest.

After she'd left his neighborhood in a rush—following his deliberate dematerialization from sight just to further destabilize her—she had crossed the river and headed around to the backside of the city, where the houses were small, packed in close to one another, and finished with aluminum siding.

As he trolled behind her, keeping at least two blocks between their vehicles, he regarded the brightly colored lights in the neighborhoods, the thousands of strands of twinklers strung among bushes and hanging from roof lips and boxing out windows and doorframes. But that wasn't the half of it. Manger scenes placed prominently on tiny front lawns were spotlit, and there were also fat white snowmen with red scarves and blue pants that glowed from within.

In contrast to the seasonal accoutrements, he was willing to bet the Virgin Mary statues were permanent.

When her vehicle stopped and stayed that way, he closed in, parking four houses down and killing his lights. She didn't get out of the car right away, and when she finally did, she wasn't wearing the parka and tight ski pants she'd had on whilst spying on him. Instead, she had changed into a thick red sweater and a pair of jeans.

She'd let her hair down.

And the heavy, brunette weight reached below her shoulders, curling at the ends.

He growled in the darkness.

With quick, easy strides, she surmounted the four shallow concrete steps leading up to the modest entrance of the home. Propping open the screen door with its curlicue metalwork, she buttressed the thing with her hip, let herself in with a key, and closed things back up.

As a light came on downstairs, he watched her shape walk through the front room, the thin privacy drapes giving him only a sense of her movement, not any kind of clear view.

He thought of his own screens. It had taken him a long time to perfect that invention, and the Hudson River house had been perfect for piloting them. The barriers worked even better than he'd anticipated.

But she was smart enough to have picked up on the anomalies, and he wondered what the giveaway had been.

On the second floor, a light came on, as if someone who had been resting had stirred at her arrival.

His fangs pulsed. The idea that some human man was awaiting her in their mated bedroom made him want to establish his dominance— even though that didn't make sense. After all, he was tracking her for his own self-protection, and nothing more.

Absolutely nothing more.

Just as his hand sought the car door handle, his phone rang. Good timing.

When he saw who it was, he frowned and put the cell up to his ear. "Two calls in such a short time. To what do I owe this honor?"

Rehvenge was not amused. "You didn't get back to me."

"Was I required to?"

"Watch yourself, boy."

Assail's eyes remained locked on the little house. He was curiously desperate to know what was going on inside. Was she heading up the stairs, undressing as she went?

Exactly who was she hiding her pursuits from? And she was in fact hiding them—otherwise, why change in the car prior to entering the house?

"Hello?"

"I appreciate the kind invitation," he heard himself say.

"It's not an invitation. You're a goddamn member of the Council now that you're in the New World."

"No."

"Excuse me?"

Assail thought back to the meeting at Elan's house in the early winter, the one Rehvenge had not known about, the one to which the Band of Bastards had shown up and flexed their muscle. He also thought of the attempt on Wrath, the Blind King's life—on Assail's own property, for godsakes.

Too much drama for his liking.

With practiced ease, he launched into the same speech he had given Xcor's faction. "I am a businessman by predilection and purpose. Although I respect both the current sovereignty and the Council's power base, I cannot divert energy or time away from my enterprise. Not now, nor in the future."

There was a stretch of silence. And then that deep, ever-so-evil voice came over the connection. "I've heard about your business."

"Have you."

"I was in it myself for a number of years."

"So I understand."

"I managed to do both."

Assail smiled into the darkness. "Mayhap I am not as talented as you."

"I'm going to make something perfectly clear. If you don't show up at that meeting, I'm going to assume you're playing on the wrong team."

"By that very statement, you acknowledge there are two and they are opposed."

"Take it as you will. But if you're not with me and the king, you are my enemy and his."

And that was precisely what Xcor had said. Then again, was there any other position in this growing war?

"The king was shot at your house, Assail."

"So I recollect," he muttered dryly.

"I'd think you'd want to put to rest any notion of your involvement."

"I already have. I told the Brothers that very night that I had nothing to do with it. I gave them the vehicle in which they escaped with the king. Why would I do any such thing if I were a traitor?"

"To save your own ass."

"I am quite accomplished at that without the benefit of conversation, I assure you."

"So what's your schedule like?"

The light on the second story was extinguished, and he had to wonder what the woman was doing in the darkness—and with whom.

Of their own volition, his fangs bared themselves.

"Assail. You are seriously boring me with this hard-to-get bullshit."

Assail put the Range Rover in gear. He was not going to sit upon the curb whilst whatever happened inside . . . happened. She was clearly home for the night, and staying there. Besides, his phone would alert him in the event that her car was once again set into motion.

As he rolled into the street and gathered speed, he spoke with clarity. "I am herewith resigning my position on the Council. My neutrality in this battle for the crown shall not be questioned by either side—"

"And you know who the players are, don't you."

"I shall make this as bald as I am able—I have no side here, Rehvenge. I do not know how to state this more plainly—and I will not be pulled into the war either by you and your king, or by any other. Do not attempt to push me, and know that the neutrality I present to you is exactly what I give to them."

On that note, he had made a vow to Elan and Xcor not to reveal their identities, and he was going to keep it—not because he believed the group would e'er return the favor to him, but rather for the simple fact that, depending upon who won this tussle, a confidant to either side would be viewed either as a whistle-blower to be eradicated or a hero to be lauded. The problem was, one wouldn't know which until the end, and he was uninterested in such a gamble.

"So you have been approached," Rehv stated.

"I received a copy of the letter they sent in the spring of this year, yes."

"Is that the only contact you've had?"

"Yes."

"You're lying to me."

Assail stopped at a traffic light. "There is naught you may say or do to pull me into this, dear *leahdyre*."

With menace in abundance, the male on the other end growled, "Don't count on that, Assail."

With that, Rehvenge hung up.

Cursing, Assail tossed his phone onto the passenger seat. Then he made two fists and banged them on the steering wheel.

If there was one thing he could not abide, it was being sucked into the vortex of other people's arguments. He didn't give a pence who sat on the throne, or who was in charge of the *glymera*. He just wanted to be left alone to make his money off the backs of rats without tails.

Was that so fucking hard to understand?

When the light turned green, he stomped on the accelerator, even though he had no real destination in mind. He just drove in a random direction . . . and about fifteen minutes later, he found himself going over the river on one of the bridges.

Ah, so his Range Rover had decided to take him home.

As he emerged onto the opposite shore, his phone let off a chiming sound, and he nearly ignored it. But the twins had gone out to move Benloise's newest shipment, and he wanted to know if those petty deal-ers had shown up for their quotas after all.

It was not a phone call or a text.

That black Audi was on the move again.

Assail stomped on the brake, cut in front of semi that blew its horn like the f-word, and plowed up and over the snow-covered median.

He positively flew back over the inbound bridge.

From his vantage point at a rather distant periphery, Xcor required his binoculars to properly sight his Chosen.

The car that she had been traveling in, that vast black sedan, had continued onward after the bridge, going about five or six miles before getting off on a rural road that took it north. After another number of miles, and with little warning, it had turned onto a dirt lane that was choked on either side with hardy all-season undergrowth. Finally, it came to rest before a low-slung concrete building that was lacking not just pretense of any kind, but windows and, seemingly, a door.

He tightened up the focus as two males got out from the front. He recognized one instantly—the hair was a dead giveaway: Phury, son of

Ahgony—who, according to the gossip, had been made Primale of the Chosen.

Xcor's black heart began beating hard.

Especially as he recognized the second figure: It was the fighter with the mismatched eyes whom he had battled at Assail's as the king was spirited away.

Both males took out guns and surveyed the landscape.

As Xcor was downwind, and there appeared to be no one else around, he figured there was a reasonable expectation, barring the revelation of his position by his Chosen, that the pair would proceed with whatever they had planned for his female.

In fact, it appeared as if she were being delivered unto a prison.

Over. His. Dead. Body.

She was an innocent in this war, one used for nefarious purposes through no fault of her own—but clearly she was going to be executed or locked within a cell here for the rest of her time upon the earth.

Or not.

He palmed one of his guns.

It was a good night to take care of this business. Indeed, now was his chance to have her as his own, to save her from whatever punishment had been doled out on account of her having unwittingly aided and abetted the enemy. And mayhap the circumstances around her unjust condemnation would make her favorably predisposed toward her enemy and savior.

His eyes closed briefly as he imagined her in and among his bedding.

When Xcor once again lifted his lids, Phury was opening the rear door of the sedan and reaching inside. When the Brother straightened, the Chosen was drawn out of the vehicle . . . and taken by both elbows, the fighters holding on to her on each side as she was led toward the building.

When Xcor prepared to close in. After so long, a lifetime, he finally had her once more in the vicinity of his person, and he was not going to waste the chance destiny was providing him, not now—not when her life so obviously hung in the balance. And he would prevail in this—the threat to her strengthened his body to unimaginable power, his mind sharpened such that it both raced with attack possibilities and remained utterly calm.

Indeed, there were merely those two males guarding her—and with them, a female who not only appeared weaponless, but did not regard her vicinity as if she were trained for or inclined to conflict.

He was more than mighty enough to take his female's captors.

Just as he prepared to lunge forth, his Chosen's scent reached him on the stiff, cold breeze, that tantalizing perfume unique to her causing him to weave in his combat boots—

Immediately, he recognized a change in it.

Blood.

She was bleeding. And there was something else. . . .

Without conscious thought, his body moved itself in close, his form reestablishing corporeal weight and heft at a distance of a mere ten feet, behind an outbuilding set off from the main facility.

She was not a prisoner, he realized, being led to a cell or execution.

His Chosen was having difficulty walking. And those warriors were supporting her with care; even with their weapons out and their eyes searching for signs of an attack, they were as gentle with her as they would have been with the most fragile of blooms.

She had not been ill treated. She was marked not with bruises and welts. And as the trio progressed, she looked up at one male and then the other and spoke as if trying to reassure them—for in truth, it was not aggression tightening the brows of those warriors.

In fact, it was the same terror he felt upon smelling her blood.

Xcor's heart pounded even harder behind his breast, his mind trying to make sense of it all.

And then he remembered something from his own past.

After his birth *mahmen* had shunned him, he had been dropped at an orphanage in the Old Country and left for whatever fate befell him. Therein, he had stayed among the rare unwanted, most of whom possessed physical deformities such as his own, for nearly a decade—long enough to form permanent memories of what transpired at the sad, lonely place.

Long enough for him to piece together what it meant when a lone female appeared at the gates, was let in, and then screamed for hours, sometimes days . . . before giving birth to, in most cases, a dead young. Or miscarrying one.

The scent of the blood back then had been very specific. And the scent upon the cold wind of this night was the same.

Pregnancy was what he had in his nose now.

For the first time in his life, he heard himself utter in absolute agony, "Dearest Virgin in the Fade . . ."

THIRTY-FOUR

The idea that members of the s'Hisbe were in the Caldwell zip code made Trez want to pack up everything he owned, grab his brother, and RV it out of town.

As he drove from the warehouse to the Iron Mask, his head was so fucked-up, he had to consciously think of the turns to take, and the stop signs to brake at, and where he was supposed to park once he got to the club. And then after he turned the X5's engine off, he just sat behind the wheel and stared at the brick wall of his building . . . for like, a year.

Helluva metaphor, all the going-nowhere in front of him.

It wasn't like he didn't know how much he was letting his people down. The issue? He didn't give a shit. He was *not* going back to the old ways. The life he led now was his own, and he refused to let the promise he'd been born into cage him as an adult.

Not going to happen.

Ever since Rehvenge had done his good deed for the century and saved his and his brother's asses, things had turned around for Trez. He and iAm had been ordered to align themselves with the *symphath* outside of the Territory in order to work off the debt, and that "forcible" repayment had been his ticket to ride, the way out he'd been searching for. And although he did regret sucking iAm into the drama, the end result was that his brother had had to come with him, and that was just another part of the perfect solution he was now living. Leaving the s'Hisbe and coming into the outside world had been a revelation, his first, delicious taste of freedom: There was no protocol. No rules. No one breathing down his neck.

The irony? It was supposed to have been a slap on the back of the hand for daring to go beyond the Territory and tangling with Un-Knowables. A punishment intended to bring him back in line.

Hah.

And since then, in the recesses of his mind, he'd kinda been hoping the extent of his dealings with the UKs over the past decade or so would have contaminated him in the eyes of the s'Hisbe, making him ineligible for the "honor" he'd been given at his birth. Soiling him into a permanent freedom, as it were.

Problem was, if they'd sent AnsLai, the high priest, clearly that goal hadn't been accomplished. Unless the visit had been to disavow him?

He'd have heard from iAm on that, though. Wouldn't he?

Trez checked his phone. No VMs. No texts. He was in the doghouse with his brother again—unless iAm had decided to fuck all the bullshit and gone home to the tribe.

Damn it—

The sharp knock on his window didn't just bring his head around. It brought his gun out.

Trez frowned. Standing outside his car was a human male the size of a house. The guy had a beer belly, but his thick shoulders suggested he did regular physical labor, and that heavy, rigid jawline revealed both his Cro-Magnon ancestry as well as the kind of arrogance most common to big, dumb animals.

With great, bull-like puffs of breath pouring from his flared nostrils, he leaned in and pounded on the window. With a fist as big as a football, natch.

Well, obviously he wanted some attention, and what do you know. Trez was more than willing to give it to him.

Without warning, he threw open the door, catching the guy right in the nuts. As the human staggered backward and grabbed for his crotch, Trez rose to his full height and tucked his gun into the small of his back, out of sight, but within easy reach.

When Mr. Aggressive had recovered enough to look up, waaaaay

up, he seemed to lose his enthusiasm for a moment. Then again, Trez had easily a foot and a half, and seventy-five, maybe a hundred pounds on the guy. In spite of that Dunlop he was sporting.

"Are you looking for me," Trez said. Read: Are you sure you want to do this, big guy?

"Yeah. I is."

Okay, so both grammar and risk assessment were a problem for him. Probably had the same issue with single-digit adding and subtracting.

"Am," Trez said.

"What?" Pronounced *whut*.

"I believe it is, 'Yeah, I am.' Not 'is.'"

"You can kiss my ass. How 'bout that." The guy came closer. "And stay away from her."

"Her?" That narrowed it down to what, a hundred thousand people?

"My girl. She don't want you, she don't need you, and she ain't gonna have you no more."

"Who exactly are we talking about? I'm going to need a name." And maybe even that wouldn't help.

In lieu of an answer, the guy took a swing. It was likely meant to be a sucker punch, but the windup was so slow and laborious, the goddamn thing could have come with subtitles.

Trez caught that fist with his hand, palming it like a basketball. And then with a quick twist he had the piece of beef turned around and held in place—proof positive that pressure points worked, and the wrist was one of 'em.

Trez spoke into the man's ear, just so the ground rules were clearly received. "You do that again, and I'm going to break every bone in your hand. At once." He punctuated that with a jerk that left the guy whimpering. "And then I'm going to work on your arm. Followed by your neck—which you will not walk away from. Now, what the fuck are you talking about."

"She were here last night."

"Lot of women were. Can you be more specific—"

"He means me."

Trez looked over. Oh . . . fucking wonderful.

It was the chick who'd gone apeshit, his happy little stalker.

"I tole you I got this!" her BF shouted.

Yeah, uh-huh, the guy really looked in control of things. So appar-

ently both of them were into delusion—and maybe that explained the relationship: He thought she was a supermodel, and she assumed he had a brain.

"Is this yours?" Trez asked the woman. "Because if it is, would you take it home with you, before you need a bucket loader to clean up the mess?"

"I tole you not to come here," the woman said. "What you doing here?"

Annnnd more evidence of why these two were a match made in heaven.

"How about I let the pair of you sort this out?" Trez suggested.

"I'm in love with him!"

For a split second, the response didn't compute. But then, trashy accent aside, the shit sank in: The floozy was talking about *him*.

As Trez gave the woman the hairy eyeball, he realized this particular casual fuck had gone into the weeds in a *big* way.

"You are not!"

Well, at least the boyfriend used the verb correctly this time.

"Yes, I am!"

And that was when everything FUBARed. The bull launched himself at the woman, breaking his own wrist to get free. Then the two of them went nose-to-nose, screaming obscenities, their bodies arching in.

Clearly, they'd had practice at this.

Trez looked around. There was no one in the parking lot, and nobody walking by on the sidewalk, but he didn't need a domestic dispute rolling out in the back of his club. Inevitably, someone would see it and do a 911—or worse, that hundred-pound chippie was going to push her big, dumb boyfriend just one inch too far, and get good and trampled.

If he only had a bucket of water or, like, a garden hose to get them to disengage.

"Listen, you guys need to take this—"

"I love you!" the woman said, turning on Trez and grabbing the front of her bustier. "Don't you get it? I love you!"

Given the sheen of sweat on her skin—in spite of the fact that it was thirty degrees—it was pretty clear she was on something. Coke or meth, if he had to guess. X was generally not associated with this kind of aggression.

Great. Another bene.

Trez shook his head. "Baby girl, you don't know me."

"I do!"

"No, you don't—"

"Don't you fucking talk to her!"

The guy went for Trez, but the female got in the way, putting herself in front of a speeding train.

Fuck, now it was time to get involved: No violence against women around him. *Ever*—even if it was collateral.

Trez moved so fast, it was close to turning back time. He shifted his "protector" out of the line of fire, and threw out a shot that caught the charging animal right in the jaw.

Made little or no impression. Like hitting a cow with a wad of paper.

Trez got a fist in the eye, a light show exploding in half of his vision, but it was a lucky hit more than anything coordinated. His payback, however, was all that and so much more: with quick coordination, he unleashed knuckles in rapid succesion, working that gut, turning the guy's cirrhotic liver into a living, breathing punching bag—until the BF was doubled over, and listing heavily to port.

Trez finished things off by kicking that moaning deadweight onto the ground.

Whereupon he outted his gun and shoved the muzzle right in tight to the guy's carotid.

"You have one shot at walking away from this," Trez said calmly. "And here's how it's going to go. You're going to get up and you're not going to look at her or talk to her. You're going to go out around to the front of the club and get the fuck into a cab and go the fuck home."

Unlike Trez, the man didn't have a well-developed and maintained cardio system—he was breathing like a freight train. And yet, given the way his bloodshot, watery eyes were staring upward in alarm, he'd managed to focus in spite of the hypoxia, and had gotten the goddamn message.

"If you aggress on her in any way, if she's got so much as a split end thanks to you, if any of her property is compromised by anyone?" Trez leaned in close. "I'm going to come at you from behind. You won't know I'm there, and you won't live through what I'm going to do to you. I *promise* you this."

Yup, Shadows had special ways of disposing of their enemies, and though he preferred low-fat meat like chicken or fish, he was willing to make exceptions.

The thing was, in both his personal and his professional lives, he'd seen how domestic violence escalated. In a lot of cases, something big had to intervene in order to break the cycle—and what do you know? He fit that bill.

"Nod if you understand the terms." When the nod came, he jabbed the weapon even harder into that fleshy neck. "Now look into my eyes and know I speak the truth."

As Trez stared down, he inserted a thought directly into that cerebral cortex, implanting it as surely as if it were a microchip he'd installed in and among the curling lobes. Its trigger would be any kind of bright idea about the woman; its effect would be the absolute conviction that the man's own death would be inevitable and quick if he followed through.

Best kind of cognitive behavioral therapy there was.

One hundred percent success rate.

Trez jumped off and gave the fatty a chance to be a good little boy. And yup, the SOB dragged himself off the pavement, and then shook like a dog with his legs planted far apart and his loose shirt flapping around.

When he left, it was with a limp.

And that was when the sniffling registered.

Trez turned around. The woman was shivering in the cold, her look-at-me clothes offering no barrier to the December night, her skin pale, her high apparently drained—as if his putting a forty to her boyfriend's throat had been a sobering influence.

Her mascara was running down her face as she watched Prince Chow Hound's departure.

Trez stared up at the sky and did the internal-argument thing.

In the end, he couldn't leave her out here in the parking lot by herself—especially looking as shaky as she was.

"Where do you live, baby girl?" Even he heard the exhaustion in his own voice. "Baby girl?"

The woman glanced his way, and instantly her expression changed. "I never had someone take up for me like that before."

Okay, now he wanted to put his head through a brick wall. And gee, there was one right next to him.

"Lemme drive you home. Where do you live?"

As she closed in, Trez had to tell his feet to stay where they were—
and sure enough, she burrowed in tight against his body. "I love you."

Trez squeezed his eyes shut.

"Come on," he said, disengaging her and leading her to his car.
"You're going to be all right."

THIRTY-FIVE

As Layla was led into the clinic, her heart was pounding and her legs were shaking. Fortunately, Phury and Qhuinn had no problem supporting her weight.

However, her experience was completely different this time through—thanks to the Primale's presence. When the facility's exterior entry panel slid aside, one of the nurses was there to meet them, and they were immediately rushed back to a different part of the clinic from where she had been the night before.

As they were let into an examination room, Layla glanced around and hesitated. What . . . was this? The walls were covered in pale silk, and paintings in gold frames hung at regular intervals. No clinical examination table, such as the one she had been on the night before—here, there was a bed that was covered with an elegant duvet and layered with stacks of fat pillows. And then, instead of a stainless-steel sink and plain white cabinets, a painted screen obscured one whole corner of the room—behind which, she had to assume, the clinical tools of Havers's trade were kept.

Unless their group had been sent to the physician's personal quarters?

"He'll be right with you," the nurse said, smiling up at Phury and bowing. "May I get you anything? Coffee or tea?"

"Just the doctor," the Primale answered.

"Right away, Your Excellency."

She bowed again and rushed off.

"Let's get you up on this, okay?" Phury said over by the bed.

Layla shook her head. "Are you sure we're in the right place?"

"Yup." The Primale came and helped her walk across the room. "This is one of their VIP suites."

Layla looked over her shoulder. Qhuinn had settled into the corner opposite the screen, his black-clad body like a shadow thrown by a menace. He stayed preternaturally still, his eyes focused on the floor, his breathing steady, his hands behind his back. Yet he was not at ease. No, he appeared ready and able to kill, and for a moment, a spear of fear went through her. She had never been frightened of him before, but then again, she'd never seen him in such a potentially aggressive state.

But at least the banked violence didn't seem directed toward her, or even the Primale. Certainly not at Doc Jane as the female sat down in a silk-covered chair.

"Come on," Phury said gently. "Up you go."

Layla tried to lift herself, but the mattress was too far off the floor and her upper body was as weak as her legs.

"I've got you." Phury carefully slipped his arms around her back and ran them under her knees; then he lifted with care. "Here we go."

Settling on the bed, she grunted, a sharp cramp gripping her pelvic area. As every eye in the room locked on her, she tried to cover her grimace up with a smile. No succeeding there: although the bleeding remained steady, the waves of pain were intensifying, the duration of their grip growing longer, the spaces between them getting shorter.

At this point, it was soon going to be one steady agony.

"I'm fine—"

The knock on the door cut her off. "May I come in?"

The mere sound of Havers's voice was enough to make her want to bolt. "Oh, dearest Virgin Scribe," she said as she gathered her strength.

"Yeah," Phury said darkly. "Enter—"

What happened next was so fast and furious, the only way of describing it was with a colloquialism she had learned from Qhuinn.

All hell broke loose.

Havers opened the door, stepped inside—and Qhuinn attacked the doctor, springing forward from that corner, leading with a dagger.

Layla shouted in alarm—but he didn't kill the male.

He did, however, close that door with the physician's body—or mayhap it was the male's face. And it was hard to know whether the clap that resounded was the portal meeting the jambs, or the impact of the healer getting thrown against the panels. Probably a combination of both.

The terrifyingly sharp blade was pressed against a pale throat. "Guess what you're going to do first, asshole?" Qhuinn growled. "You're going to apologize for treating her like a goddamn incubator."

Qhuinn yanked the male around. Havers's tortoiseshell glasses were shattered, one lens spiderwebbed with cracks, the earpiece on the other side sticking out at a wonky angle.

Layla shot a look at Phury. The Primale didn't seem particularly bothered: He just crossed his arms over his huge chest and leaned back against the wall beside her, evidently completely at ease with this playing out as it did. Over in the chair across the way, Doc Jane was the same, her forest green stare calm as she regarded the drama.

"Look her in the eye," Qhuinn spat, "and apologize."

When the fighter jangled the healer as if Havers were naught but a rag doll, some jumble of words came out of the doctor.

Shoot. Layla supposed she should be a lady and not enjoy this, but there was satisfaction to be had at the vengeance.

Sadness, too, however, because it should never have come to this.

"Do you accept his apology," Qhuinn demanded in an evil tone. "Or would you like him to grovel? I'm perfectly fucking happy to turn him into a rug at your feet."

"That was sufficient. Thank you."

"Now you're going to tell her"—Qhuinn pulled that shake move again, Havers's arms flopping in their sockets, his loose white coat waving like a flag—"and *only* her, what the fuck is going on with her body."

"I need . . . the chart—"

Qhuinn bared his fangs and put them right against Havers's ear—as if he were considering biting the thing off. "Bullshit. And if you are telling the truth? That lapse of memory is going to cause you to lose your life. Right now."

Havers was already pale, but that made him go completely white.

"Start talking, Doctor. And if the Primale, who you're so fucking impressed by, would be kind enough to tell me if you look away from her, that would be great."

"My pleasure," Phury said.

"I'm not hearing anything, Doc. And I'm really not a patient guy."

"You are . . ." From behind those broken glasses, the male's eyes met her own. "Your young is . . ."

She almost wished Qhuinn would stop forcing the contact. This was hard enough to hear without having to face the doctor who'd treated her so badly.

Then again, Havers was the one who had to look, not her.

Qhuinn's eyes were what she stared into as Havers said, "You're losing the pregnancy."

Things got wavy at that point, which she took to mean she had teared up. She couldn't feel anything, though. It was as if her soul had been flushed out of her body, everything that had animated her and connected her to the world gone as if it had never been.

Qhuinn showed no reaction at all. He didn't blink. Didn't alter his stance or his dagger hand.

"Is there anything that can be done medically?" Doc Jane asked.

Havers went to shake his head, but froze as the sharp point of the knife cut into the skin of his neck. As blood leaked out and ran into the starched collar of his formal shirt, the red matched his bow tie.

"Nothing of which I am aware," the physician said roughly. "Not on the earth, at any rate."

"Tell her it's not her fault," Qhuinn demanded. "Tell her she did nothing wrong."

Layla closed her eyes. "Assuming that's true—"

"In humans that's usually the case, provided there's no trauma," Doc Jane interjected.

"Tell her," Qhuinn snapped, his arm starting to vibrate ever so slightly, as if he were a heartbeat away from dispatching his own violence.

" 'Tis true," Havers croaked.

Layla looked at the doctor, searching out the stare behind the ruined glasses. "Nothing?"

Havers spoke quickly. "The incidence of spontaneous miscarriage is presented in approximately one in three pregnancies. I believe, as with humans, it is caused by a self-regulation system that ensures defects of various kinds are not carried to term."

"But I am definitely pregnant," she said in a hollow tone.

"Yes. Your blood tests proved that."

"Is there any risk to her health," Qhuinn asked, "as this continues?"

"Are you her *whard*?" Havers blurted.

Phury interjected. "He's the father of her child. So you treat him with the same respect you would me."

That had the physician's eyes bulging, those brows surfacing above the busted tortoiseshell frames. And it was funny; that was when Qhuinn showed a modicum of reaction—just a flicker in his face before the fierce features resettled into aggression.

"Answer me," Qhuinn snapped. "Is she in any danger?"

"I-I—" Havers swallowed hard. "There are no guarantees in medicine. Generally speaking, I would say no—she is healthy on all other accounts, and the miscarriage appears to be following the generic course. Further . . ."

As the doctor continued to speak, his educated, refined tone so much more uneven than it had been the night before, Layla checked out.

Everything receded, her hearing disappearing, along with any sense of the temperature in the room, the bed beneath her, the other bodies standing around. The only thing she saw was Qhuinn's mismatched eyes.

Her sole thought as he held that knife against the other male's throat?

Even though they were not in love, he was exactly what she would have wanted as a father for her young. Ever since she had made the decision to participate in the real world, she had learned how rough life was, how others could conspire against you—and how sometimes principled force was all that got you through the night.

Qhuinn had the latter in spades.

He was a great, fearsome protector, and that was precisely what a female needed when she was pregnant, nursing, or caring for a young.

That and his innate kindness made him noble to her.

No matter the color of his eyes.

Nearly fifty miles to the south from where Havers was piss-pants terrified in his own clinic, Assail was behind the wheel of his Range Rover, and shaking his head in disbelief.

Things just kept getting more interesting with this woman.

Thanks to GPS, he had tracked her Audi from afar as she had decisively passed out of her neighborhood and gotten on the North-way. At each suburban exit, he expected her to get off, but as they'd left Caldwell well in the dust, he'd begun to think she might be heading all the way down into Manhattan.

Not so.

West Point, home of the venerable human military school, was about halfway between New York City and Caldwell, and as she exited the highway at that point, he was relieved. A lot happened down in the land of zip codes that started with 100, and he didn't want to get too far from home base for two reasons: One, he still hadn't heard from the twins about whether those minor-league dealers had showed up, and two, dawn was coming at some point, and he didn't like the idea of abandoning his heavily modified and reinforced Range Rover at the side of the road somewhere because he needed to dematerialize back to safety.

Once off the highway, the woman proceeded at precisely forty-five miles an hour through the township's preamble of gas stations, tourist hotels, and fast-food joints. Then on the far side of all that quick, cheap, and easy, things started to get expensive. Grand houses, the kind that were set back on lawns that looked like carpets, began to crop up, their low, loose stone walls quaintly crumbling at the sides of the road. She bypassed all of the estates, however, finally pulling over into the parking lot of a little park that had a river view.

Just as she got out, he drove right by her, his head turning in her direction, measuring her.

A hundred yards later, out of sight from where she was, Assail stopped his car on the shoulder of the road, emerged into the biting wind, and did up the buttons on his double-breasted coat. His loafers were not ideal for tracking through the snow, but he didn't care. His feet would put up with the cold and the wet, and he had a dozen more pairs waiting for him in his closet at home.

As her vehicle, not her body, had the tracking device on it, he kept his eyes on her. Sure enough, she was putting those cross-countries on, and then, with a white ski mask over her head and the pale camos covering her lithe body, she all but disappeared into the blue-washed winter landscape.

He stayed right with her.

Flashing out ahead at clips of fifteen to twenty yards, he found pines to shield himself behind as she progressed back toward the mansions, her skis eating up the snow-covered ground.

She was going to go to one of those big houses, he thought as he kept pace with her, anticipating her direction and, for the most part, guessing correctly.

Every time she went by him without knowing he was there, his body wanted to jump out at her. Take her down. Bite her.

For some reason, this human made him hungry.

And cat and mouse was very erotic, especially if only the cat knew the game was afoot.

The property she eventually infiltrated was nearly a mile away, but in spite of the distance, her blistering pace on those skis didn't lag in the slightest. She entered at the front right corner of the lawn, stepping up on the perennial low wall, and then resuming her course.

This made no sense. If she were compromised, she was an extra distance away from her car. Surely the nearer edge would have made more sense? After all, and in either case, she was exposed now, no trees to offer cover, no possible defense against trespassing available to her if she were sighted.

Unless she knew the owner. In which case, why hide yourself and sneak up at night?

The seven- or eight-acre lawn gradually rose toward a fifteen- to twenty-thousand-square-foot stone house, modernist sculptures sitting like blind, shiny sentries on the approach, the gardens sprawling out in the back. The whole time, she stuck close to that wall, and watching her from seventy-five feet up ahead, he found himself feeling impressed by her. Against the snow, she moved as a breeze would, invisible and quick, her shadow thrown against the gray stone wall such that it seemed to disappear—

Ahhhhhhh.

She'd chosen the route specifically for that, hadn't she.

Yes, indeed, the angle of the moonlight placed her shadow exactly on the stones, effectively creating further camouflage.

An odd tingle went through him.

Smart.

Assail flashed forward, finding a hiding place in and among the plantings at the side of the house. Up close, he saw that the grand manse was not new, although not ancient, either—then again, in the New World, it was rare to run into anything constructed earlier than

the eighteenth century. Lots of lead-paned windows. And porches. And terraces.

All in all? Wealth and distinction.

That was no doubt protected by plenty of alarms.

It seemed unlikely she was simply going to spy on the property as she had on his own. For one, there was a ring of forested growth on the far side of that stone wall she'd traversed. She could have jettisoned the skis, negotiated that stretch of ten- to twenty-foot-high bramble, and gotten plenty of view shed to the house. For another? In that case, she wouldn't need whatever was in the backpack she'd slung onto her shoulders.

The thing was nearly big enough to carry a body in, and it was full.

As if on cue, she stopped, got out her binoculars and surveyed the property, staying stock-still, only her head subtly moving. And then she started across the lawn proper, moving even faster than she had before, to the point where she was literally racing toward the house.

Toward him.

Indeed, she headed directly for Assail, for this juncture between the bushes that marked the front of the mansion, and the tall hedge that ran around to the rear garden.

Clearly, she knew the property.

Clearly, he had chosen the perfect spot.

And upon her approach, he stepped back only a little . . . because he wouldn't have minded getting caught spying.

The woman skied right up to within five feet of where he was, getting so close he could catch her scent not only in his nose, but down the back of his throat.

He had to stop himself from purring.

After the effort of covering that stretch of lawn so quickly, she was breathing heavily, but her cardiovascular system recovered fast—a sign of her overall health and strength. And the speed with which she now moved was likewise erotic. Off with the skis. Off with the pack. Open the pack. Extract . . .

She was going onto the roof, he thought, as she assembled what appeared to be a speargun, aimed the thing high, and pulled the trigger on a grappling hook. A moment later, there was a distant metal clang from above.

Glancing upward, he realized that she had picked one of the few stretches of stone that had no windows in it . . . and it was shielded by the very long wall of tall shrubs that he himself was obstructed by.

She was going inside.

At that point, Assail frowned . . . and disappeared from where he'd been watching her.

Re-forming around the back of the house at ground level, he peered into a number of windows, cupping his hands on the cold glass and leaning in. The interior was mostly dark, but not completely so: Here and there, lamps had been left on, the bulbs casting a glow on furnishings that were a combination of old antiques and modern art. Fancy, fancy: In its peaceful slumber, the place looked like a museum, or something that had been photographed for a magazine, everything arranged with such precision that one wondered if rulers hadn't been used to arrange the furniture and the objets d'art.

No clutter anywhere, no casually thrown newspapers, bills, letters, receipts. No coats cast over the back of a chair or pair of shoes kicked off by a sofa.

Each and every ashtray was clean as a whistle.

One and only one person came to his mind.

"Benloise," he whispered to himself.

THIRTY-SIX

Based on the regular vibrations that came from his breast pocket, Xcor knew his presence was being sought by his fighters.

He did not respond.

Standing outside the facility that his Chosen had been taken into, he was powerless to leave even as a regular flow of others of his kind drove up or materialized before the portal she had been taken through. Indeed, as so many came and went, there was no doubt this was a health clinic.

At least none appeared to notice him, too preoccupied were they with whate'er ailed them—in spite of the fact that he was standing all but out in the open.

Fates, the very thought of what had brought his Chosen here made him nauseated to the point of clearing his throat—

Dragging icy air into his lungs helped fight the gag reflex.

When had her needing come? It must have been fairly recently. He had last seen her . . .

Who was the sire? he thought for the hundredth time. Who had taken what was his—

"Not yours," he told himself. "*Not* yours."

Except that was his mind talking, not his instincts. At the core of him, in the most male part of his marrow, she *was* his female.

And ironically, that was what kept him from attacking the facility—with all of his soldiers, if necessary. As she was receiving care, the last thing he wanted to do was interrupt the process.

Whilst time passed, and the information void tortured him to the point of madness, he realized that he hadn't even known about this clinic. If she had been his? He wouldn't have known where to take her for help—certainly he would have sent Throe to find someplace, somehow, to ensure her care, but in the event of a medical emergency? An hour or two spent hunting for a healer could mean the difference between life and death.

The Brotherhood, on the other hand, had known exactly where to deliver her. And when she was released from the facility, they would undoubtedly return her to a warm, safe home, where there would be food aplenty, and a soft bed, and a stout force of at least six full-blooded warriors to protect her as she slept.

Ironic that he found ease in that vision. But then again, the Lessening Society was a very serious adversary—and say what one would about the Brotherhood, they had proven over the aeons to be capable defenders.

Abruptly, his thoughts shifted to the warehouse where he and his soldiers stayed. Those cold, damp, inhospitable environs were, in fact, a step up from some of the other places they had all made camp. If she were with him, wherever would he keep her? No males could e'er see her in his presence, especially if she were to change clothes or bathe—

A growl percolated up his throat.

No. No male would cast his eye upon her flesh or he would flay him alive—

Oh, God, she had mated with another. Had opened herself up and accepted another male within her sacred flesh.

Xcor put his face in his palms, the pain in his chest making him weave in his combat boots.

It must have been the Primale. Yes, of course she had lain with Phury, son of Ahgony. That was the way the Chosen propagated, if memory and rumor served.

Instantly, his mind was clouded by the image of her perfect face and her slender frame. To think that another had disrobed her and covered her with his body—

Stop it, he told himself. *Stop it.*

Dragging his mind away from that insanity, he challenged himself to define any appropriate living quarters he could have provided her. In any circumstance.

The only thought that came to him was going back and killing that female his soldiers had fed from. That cottage had been quaint and lovely. . . .

But where would his Chosen go during the day?

And besides, he would never shame her by allowing her to so much as walk upon that rug where all that sex had gone down.

"Pardon us."

Xcor went for the gun inside his jacket as he wheeled around. Except there was no need for force—it was simply a diminutive female with her young. Apparently, they had gotten out of a station wagon parked about ten feet away from him.

As the young cowered behind its mother, the female's eyes flared in fear.

Then again, when a monster was stumbled upon, its presence was not often greeted with joy.

Xcor bowed deeply, in large measure because the sight of his face surely could not be helping the situation. "But of course."

At that, he backed away from them both and then pivoted, returning to the original spot he'd occupied. Indeed, he had not realized how exposed he'd become.

And he did not want to fight. Not with the Brotherhood. Not with his Chosen as she was. Not . . . here.

Closing his eyes, he wished he could go back to that night when Zypher had taken him out to the meadow and Throe, under the guise of saving him, had condemned him to a kind of walking death.

A bonded male who was not with his mate?

Dead though animated—

Without warning, the portal pulled back and his Chosen appeared. Instantly, Xcor's instincts screamed for action, in spite of all the reasons to leave her be.

Take her! Now!

But he did not: The grim expressions of those who shepherded her with such care froze him where he stood—bad news had been imparted during their tenure inside.

As before, she was all but carried to the vehicle.

And even still, there was the scent of her blood upon the air.

His Chosen was resettled in the back of that sedan, with the female at her side. Then Phury, son of Ahgony, and the warrior with the mismatched eyes got into the front. The vehicle was turned about slowly, as if out of concern for the precious cargo in its rear compartment.

Xcor followed in their wake, materializing apace to the steady speed that was gained first upon the rural road at the end of the lane, and then upon the highway. When the car approached the suspension bridge, he once again spotted it from atop the highest girder, and then after his female passed beneath him, he jumped from rooftop to rooftop as the sedan circumvented downtown.

He tracked the vehicle north until it exited the highway and entered the farmland area.

He stayed with her the whole time.

And that was how he found the location of the Brotherhood.

THIRTY-SEVEN

As Blay twisted his family's signet ring around on his forefinger, his lit cigarette smoldered gently in his other hand, and his ass grew numb . . . and no one came back in through the vestibule's doors.

Sitting on the bottom step of the mansion's grand staircase, he wasn't going to fulfill his promise to his mother and head home. Not tonight, at least. After the craziness of the evening before, what with the crash landing and the attendant drama, Wrath had ordered the Brotherhood and the fighters to take twenty-four off. So technically, he should have called the 'rents and told his mom to bust out the mozzarella and the meat sauce.

But there was no way he was leaving the house. Not after hearing yelling from Layla's room, and then seeing her all but carried down the grand staircase.

Naturally, Qhuinn had been with her.

John Matthew had not.

So whatever had gone down apparently trumped the *ahstrux nohtrum* thing, and that meant . . . she had to be losing the young. Only something that serious would get a pass.

As he continued to bump-on-a-log it, with nothing but worry to keep him company, naturally his mind decided to make things worse: Shit, had he really slept with Qhuinn last night?

Taking a hard drag off his Dunhill, he exhaled a curse.

Had it really happened?

God, that question had been banging around his skull from the moment he'd woken up out of a hot-as-hell dream, with an erection that seemed to think the other male was sleeping next to him.

Replaying the scenes, for the hundredth time, all he could think was . . . talk about a plan misfiring. After he'd turned Qhuinn down when the guy had been on his knees, he'd gone back to his room and paced around, a debate he wasn't interested in having with himself turning his brain to *foie gras*.

But he'd made the right decision in leaving. Really. He had.

The problem was, it hadn't stuck. As the daylight hours had worn on, all he'd thought about was the time he'd gotten caught by his father stealing a pack of cigarettes from one of the family's *doggen*. He'd been a young pretrans, and as a punishment, his dad had made him sit outside and smoke every one of those unfiltered Camels. He'd been horribly sick, and it had been a year or two before he'd been able to stomach even secondhand smoke.

So that had been the new plan.

He'd wanted Qhuinn so badly for so long, but it had all been a hypothetical, parceled out in fantasies in ways he could handle. Not all at once, not the full-bore, overload, wrecking-ball stuff—and he'd known damn well that in real life, Qhuinn wasn't going to hold back or be easy. The "plan" had been to have the actual experience, and learn that it was just rough sex. Or hell, find out that it wasn't even *good* sex.

You weren't supposed to smoke all the cigarettes in the pack . . . and only want more.

Jesus Christ almighty, it had been the first time reality had been better than a fantasy, the absolute best erotic experience of his life.

Afterward, however, the kindness that Qhuinn had shown had been unbearable.

In fact, as Blay recalled that tenderness, he burst up from where he'd been sitting and marched around the apple tree—as if he had somewhere to go.

At that moment doors opened. Not the vestibule ones, however.

The library.

As he glanced over his shoulder, Saxton stepped out from the room. He looked like hell, and not just because, as fast a healer as the male was, he still had some residual jaw swelling thanks to Qhuinn's attack.

Good one, Blay thought. Way to express disappointment in someone's behavior: Let them fuck the shit out of you after they tried to strangle your ex.

Soooo classy.

"How are you?" Blay asked, and not in a social way.

It was a relief as Saxton came over. Looked him in the eye. Smiled a little like he was determined to make an effort.

"I'm exhausted. I'm hungry. I'm restless."

"Would you like to eat with me?" Blay blurted. "I'm feeling exactly that way, too, and the only thing I can do anything about is the need for food."

Saxton nodded and put his hands in the pockets of his slacks. "That is a stellar idea."

The pair of them ended up in the kitchen at the battered oak table, sitting side by side, facing out into the room. With a happy smile, Fritz immediately flipped into provide-sustenance mode and what do you know. Ten minutes later, the butler provided each of them with a bowl of steaming beef stew, as well as a crusty baguette to share, a bottle of red wine, and a stick of sweet butter on a little plate.

"I shall be back, my lords," the butler said on a bow. And then he proceeded to shoo everyone else out of the place, from the *doggen* who were prepping vegetables to the ones who were polishing silver to the window cleaners in the alcove beyond.

As the flap door shut behind the last of the staff, Saxton said, "All we need is a candle and this would be a date." The male leaned forward and ate with perfect manners. "Well, I suppose we would need a few other things, wouldn't we."

Blay glanced over as he put his cigarette out. Even with bags under those eyes and that mostly faded bruise on his neck, the attorney was something to look at.

Why the hell couldn't he—

"Do not say you're sorry again." Saxton wiped his mouth and smiled. "It really isn't necessary or appropriate."

Sitting beside the guy, it seemed just as unlikely that they had

broken up as it was that he had been with Qhuinn. Had any of the last couple of nights happened?

Well, duh. What had gone down with Qhuinn wouldn't have if he and Sax were still together. That he was very clear on—it was one thing to jerk off in secret, and that was bad enough. The full bifta? NFW.

Shit, in spite of the fact that he and Saxton had split up, he still felt like he should confess the transgression . . . although if Qhuinn was right, Saxton had already moved on in one sense of the word.

As they ate in silence, Blay shook his head, even though he hadn't been asked a question and there was no conversation. He just didn't know what else to do. Sometimes the changes in life came at you so fast, and with such fury, there was no way to keep up with reality. It took time for things to sink in, the new equilibrium establishing itself only after some period of your brain sloshing back and forth against the walls of your head.

He was still in the slosh zone.

"Have you ever felt as though hours were more properly measured in years?" Saxton said.

"Or maybe decades. Yes. Absolutely." Blay glanced over again. "I was actually just thinking that very same thing."

"Such a morbid pair we are."

"Maybe we should wear black."

"Armbands?" Saxton prompted.

"Whole deal, head to toe."

"Whatever shall I do with my flare for color?" Saxton flicked at his orange Hermès kerchief. "Then again, one can accessorize anything."

"Certainly explains the theory behind dental grilles."

"Pink plastic flamingos."

"The Hello Kitty franchise."

All at once, they both burst into laughter. It wasn't even that funny, but the humor wasn't the point. Breaking the ice was. Getting back to a new kind of normal was. Learning to relate in a different way was.

As things settled into chuckles, Blay put his arm around the male's shoulders and gave him a quick hug. And it was nice that Saxton leaned in for a brief moment, accepting what was offered. It wasn't that Blay thought that just because they'd sat down together, shared a meal, and had a laugh, all of a sudden everything was going to be smooth

sailing. Not at all. It was awkward to think Saxton had been with someone else, and utterly incredible to know he'd done the same—especially given who it had been.

You didn't downshift from being lovers for nearly a year to doing the pally-pally thing in the matter of a day or two.

You could, however, start forging a new path.

And put one foot after the other on it.

Saxton was always going to have a place in his heart. The relationship they'd shared had been the first one he'd had—not just with a male, but with anyone. And there had been a lot of good times, things he would carry with him as memories that were worth the brain space.

"Have you seen the back gardens?" Saxton asked as he offered the bread.

Blay broke off a piece and then passed the butter plate over as Saxton took a section for himself.

"They're bad, aren't they."

"Remind me never to attempt to weed with a Cessna."

"You don't garden."

"Well, if I ever do, then." Saxton poured some wine in his glass. "Vino?"

"Please."

And that was how it went. All the way from the stew through to the peach cobbler that miraculously appeared before them thanks to Fritz's perfect timing. When the last bite had been taken and the final napkin swipe made, Blay leaned back against the built-in bench's cushions and took a deep breath.

Which was about so much more than just a filled stomach.

"Well," Saxton said, as he laid down his napkin beside his dessert plate, "I do believe I'm finally going to take that bath I talked about nights ago."

Blay opened his mouth to point out that the salts the male preferred were still in his bathroom. He'd seen them in the cupboard when he'd taken his backup shaving cream out at nightfall.

Except . . . he wasn't sure he should mention it. What if Saxton thought he was asking the male to come and bathe in his suite? Was it too much of a reminder of how things had changed—and why? What if—

"I have this new oil treatment I'm dying to try," Saxton said as he slid out his side of the bench. "It finally arrived from overseas in today's mail. I've been waiting for ages."

"Sounds awesome."

"I'm looking forward to it." Saxton resettled his jacket on his shoulders, pulled his cuffs into place, and then lifted his hand in a wave, striding out without any sign of complication or strain on his face.

Which was helpful, actually.

Folding his own napkin up, he placed it beside his plate, and as he scooted free of the table, he stretched his arms over his head and bent backward, his spine cracking in a good way.

The tension in him returned as soon as he stepped into the foyer again.

What the hell was going on with Layla?

Damn it, it wasn't like he could call Qhuinn. The drama wasn't his own, or anything he was connected to: When it came to that pregnancy, he was no different from the others in the house who had also seen and heard the show and were no doubt just as worried as he was—but had no right to emergent updates.

Too bad his now-full gut didn't buy that. The thought of Qhuinn losing the young was enough to make him studiously consider the locations of the bathrooms. Just in case an evac order was issued by the back of his throat.

In the end, he found himself upstairs in the second-floor sitting room pacing around. From that vantage point, it was no problem to hear the vestibule door, and yet it wasn't like he was waiting out in the open—

The double doors of Wrath's study were pushed wide, and John Matthew emerged—from the king's sanctum.

Immediately, Blay strode across the sitting room, ready to see if maybe the guy had heard anything—but he stopped as he got a gander at John's expression.

Deep in thought. Like he'd received personal news of the disturbing variety.

Blay hung back as his buddy went off in the opposite direction, going down the hall of statues, no doubt to disappear into his room.

Looked like things were afoot in other people's lives, too.

Great.

With a soft curse, Blay left his friend be and resumed his own useless walking . . . and waiting.

*   *   *

Far to the south, in the town of West Point, Sola was prepared to enter Ricardo Benloise's house on the second floor, through the window at the end of the main hallway. It had been months since she had been inside, but she was banking on the fact that the security contact she had carefully manipulated was still her friend.

There were two keys to successfully breaking into any house, building, hotel or facility: planning and speed.

She had both.

Hanging from the wire she'd thrown onto the roof, she reached into the inside pocket of her parka, pulled out a device, and held it to the right corner of the double-hung window. Initiating the signal, she waited, staring at the tiny red light that glowed on the screen facing her. If for some reason it didn't change, she was going to have to enter through one of the dormers that faced the side yard—which was going to be a pain in the ass—

The light went green without a sound, and she smiled as she got out more tools.

Taking a suction cup, she pushed it into the center of the pane immediately below the latch, and then made a little do-si-do around the thing with her glass cutter. A quick push inward, and the space to fit her arm was created.

After letting the glass circle fall gently to the Oriental runner inside, she snaked her hand up and around, freed the brass-on-brass contraption that kept the window locked, and slid the sash up.

Warm air rushed to greet her, as if the house were happy to have her back.

Before going in, she looked down. Glanced toward the drive. Leaned outward to see what she could of the back gardens.

It felt like somebody was watching her . . . not so much when she'd been driving into town, but as soon as she'd parked her car and gotten on her skis. There was no one around, however—not that she'd been able to see, at any rate—and whereas awareness was mission critical in this line of work, paranoia was a dangerous waste of time.

So she needed to cut this shit.

Getting back in the game, she reached up with her gloved hands and pulled her ass and legs over and through the window. At the same time, she loosened the tension on the wire so there was slack to let her body transition into the house. She landed without a sound, thanks

not only to the rug that ran down the long corridor, but to her soft-soled shoes.

Silence was another important criterion when it came to doing a job successfully.

She stopped where she was for a brief moment. No sounds in the house—but that didn't necessarily mean anything. She was fairly certain that Benloise's alarm was silent, and very clear that the signal didn't go to the local or even state police: He liked to handle things privately. And God knew, with the kind of muscle he employed, there was plenty of force to go around.

Fortunately, however, she was good at her job, and Benloise and his goons wouldn't be home until just before the sun came up—he lived the life of a vampire, after all.

For some reason, the v-word made her think of that man who'd shown up by her car and then disappeared like magic.

Craziness. And the only time in recent memory that someone had given her pause. In fact, after getting confronted like that, she was actually considering not going back to that glass house on the river—although there was a fucked-up rationale for that. It wasn't that she was worried that she'd get physically hurt. God knew she was perfectly competent at defending herself.

It was the attraction.

More dangerous than any gun, knife, or fist, as far as she was concerned.

With lithe strides, Sola jogged down the carpet, bouncing on the balls of her feet, heading for the master bedroom that looked out over the rear garden. The house smelled exactly as she remembered it, old wood and furniture polish, and she knew enough to stick to the left edge of the runner. No squeaking that way.

When she got to the master suite, the heavy wooden door was closed, and she took out her lock pick before even trying the handle. Benloise was pathological about two things: cleanliness and security. Her impression, though, was that the latter was more critical at the gallery in downtown Caldwell than here at his home. After all, Benloise didn't keep anything under this roof other than art that was insured to the penny, and himself during the day—when he had plenty of bodyguards and guns with him.

In fact, that was probably why he was a night owl downtown. It

meant the gallery was never unattended—he was present after-hours, and his legitimate business staff was there during the day.

As a cat burglar, she certainly preferred to get into places that were empty.

On that note, she worked the locking mechanism on the door, sprang it free, and slipped inside. As she took a deep breath, the air was tinged with tobacco smoke and Benloise's spicy cologne.

The combination made her think of black-and-white Clark Gable movies for some reason.

With the drapes drawn and no lights on, it was pitch-black, but she'd taken photographs of the room's layout back when she'd come for that party, and Benloise was not the type of man to move things around. Hell, every time a new exhibit was installed at the gallery, she could practically feel the squirming under his skin.

Fear of change was a weakness, her grandmother always said.

Sure made things easier for her.

Slowing down now, she walked forward ten paces into what was the middle of the room. The bed would be on the left against the long wall, as would the archway into the bath and the doors to the walk-in closet. In front of her were the long windows that overlooked the gardens. Over to the right, there would be a bureau, a desk, some sitting chairs, and the fireplace that was never used because Benloise hated the smell of woodsmoke.

The security alarm panel was located between the entryway to the bath and the ornate headboard of the bed, beside a lamp that rose about three feet from a side table.

Sola pivoted in place. Walked forward four steps. Felt for the foot of the bed—found it.

Sidestep, one, two, three. Forward down the flank of the king-size mattress. Sidestep one to clear the table and the lamp.

Sola reached out her left hand. . . .

And there was the security panel, right where it needed to be.

Flipping the cover off, she used a penlight that she kept between her teeth to illuminate the circuitry. Taking out another device from her backpack, she hooked wires up to wires, intercepted the signals, and with the help of a miniature laptop and a program that a friend of hers had developed, created a closed loop within the alarm system such that, as long as the router was in place, the motion detectors she was about to set off wouldn't register.

As far as the motherboard was concerned, nothing was going to be amiss.

Leaving the laptop hanging by its connection, she walked out of the room, hit the hall, and took the stairwell down to the first floor.

The place was decorated to within an inch of its life, perpetually ready for a magazine shoot—although, of course, Benloise protected his privacy far too carefully to ever have his digs photographed for public consumption. On fleet feet, she passed through the front receiving hall, the parlor to the left, and went into his study.

Going around in the semi-darkness, she would have much preferred to strip off her white-on-white camo parka and snow pants— doing this in her black bodysuit was a cliché that was nonetheless practical. No time, though, and she was more worried about being sighted outside in the winter landscape than here in this empty house.

Benloise's private workspace was, like everything else under this roof, more stage set than anything functional. He didn't actually use the great desk, or sit on the mini-throne, or read any of the leather-bound books on the shelves.

He did, however, walk through the space. Once a day.

In a candid moment, he'd once told her that before he left each night, he strolled through his house looking at all his things, reminding himself of the beauty of his collections and his home.

As a result of that insight, and some other things, Sola had long extrapolated that the man had grown up poor. For one, when they spoke in Spanish or Portugese, his accent belied lower-class pronunciations ever so subtly. For another, rich people didn't appreciate their things like he did.

Nothing was rare to the rich, and that meant they took stuff for granted.

The safe was hidden behind the desk in a section of the bookcases that was released by a switch located in the lower drawer on the right.

She'd discovered this thanks to a tiny hidden camera she'd placed in the far corner during that party.

Following her triggering the release, a three-by-four-foot cutout in the shelving rolled forward and slid to the side. And there it was: a squat steel box, the maker of which she recognized.

Then again, when you'd broken into more than a hundred of the damn things, you got to know the manufacturers intimately. And

she approved of his choice. If she had to have a safe, this was the one she'd get—and yes, he'd bolted it to the floor.

The blowtorch she took out of her backpack was small, but powerful, and as she ignited the tip, the flame blew out with a sustained hiss and a white-and-blue glow.

This was going to take time.

The smoke from the burning metal irritated her eyes, nose, and throat, but she kept her hand steady as she made a square about a foot high and two feet across in the front panel. Some safes she was able to blow the doors off of, but the only way in with one of these was the old-fashioned way.

It took forever.

She got through, though.

Placing the heavy door section aside, she bit down on the end of her penlight again and leaned in. Open shelving held jewelry, stock certs, and some gleaming gold watches he'd left within easy reach. There was a handgun that she was willing to bet was loaded. No money.

Then again, with Benloise, there was so much cash everywhere, it made sense he wouldn't bother having the stuff take up safe space.

Damn it. There was nothing in there worth only five thousand dollars.

After all, on this job, she was merely after what she was fairly owed.

With a curse, she sat back on her heels. In fact, there wasn't one damn thing in the safe under twenty-five thousand. And it wasn't like she could break off half of a watchband—because how in the hell could she monetize that?

One minute passed.

A second one.

Screw this, she thought as she leaned the panel she'd cut out against the side of the safe and slid the shelving back into place. Rising to her feet, she looked around the room with the penlight. The books were all collectors' editions of first-run antique stuff. Art on the walls and the tables was not just super-expensive, but hard to turn into cash without going underground . . . to people Benloise was intimately connected to.

But she was not leaving without her money, goddamn it—

Abruptly, she smiled to herself, the solution becoming clear.

For many aeons in the course of human civilization, commerce had existed and thrived on the barter system. Which was to say one individual traded goods or services for those of like value.

For all the jobs she'd done, she'd never before considered adding up the aftermath ancillary costs to her targets: new safes, new security systems, more safety protocols. She could bet these were expensive—although not nearly as much as whatever she typically took. And she'd entered here taking for granted those additional costs were going to be borne by Benloise—kind of pecuniary damages for what he'd cheated her out of.

Now, though, they were the point.

On her way back to the stairs, she looked over the opportunities available to her . . . and in the end, she went over to a Degas sculpture of a little ballerina that had been placed off to the side in an alcove. The bronze depiction of the young girl was the kind of thing her grandmother would have loved, and maybe that was why, of all the art in the house, she zeroed in on it.

The light that had been mounted above the statue on the ceiling was off, but the masterpiece still managed to glow. Sola especially loved the skirting of the tutu, the delicate yet stiff explosion of tulle delineated by mesh metalwork that perfectly captured that which was supposed to be malleable.

Sola cozied up to the statue's base, wrapped her arms around it, and threw all of her strength into rotating its position by no more than two inches.

Then she raced up the stairs, unclipped her router and laptop from the alarm panel in the master bedroom, relocked that door, and headed out of the window she'd cut the hole in.

She was back in her skis and slicing through the snow no more than four minutes later.

In spite of the fact that there was nothing in her pockets, she was smiling as she left the property.

THIRTY-EIGHT

hen the Mercedes finally pulled up to the front entrance of the Brotherhood's mansion, Qhuinn got out first and went to Layla's door. As he opened it, her eyes lifted to meet his.

He knew he was never going to forget the way her face looked. Her skin was paper white and seemed just as thin, the beautiful bone structure straining against its covering of flesh. Eyes were sunken into her skull. Lips were flat and thin.

He had an idea in that moment of how she would look just as she died, however many decades or centuries that would happen in the future.

"I'm going to carry you," he said, bending down and picking her up.

The way she didn't argue told him exactly how little of her there was left.

As the vestibule doors were opened by Fritz, like the butler had been waiting for their arrival, Qhuinn regretted the whole thing: The dream that he'd briefly entertained during her needing. The hope he'd wasted. The physical pain she was in. The emotional anguish they were both going through.

You did this to her.

At the time, when he'd serviced her, he'd been solely focused on the positive outcome he'd been so sure of.

Now, on the far side, his shitkickers planted on the solid, foul-smelling earth of reality? Not worth it. Even the chance of a healthy young wasn't worth this.

The worst was watching her suffer.

As he brought her into the house, he prayed there wasn't a big audience. He just wanted to spare her something, anything, even if it was simply being paraded in front of a cast of sad, worried faces.

No one was around.

Qhuinn took the stairs two at a time, and as he came up to the second story, the wide-open double doors of Wrath's study made him curse.

Then again, the king was blind.

As George let out a chuff of greeting, Qhuinn just strode by, gunning for Layla's bedroom. Kicking open the door, he found that the *doggen* had been in and tidied up, the bed all made, the sheets undoubtedly changed, a fresh bouquet of flowers set on the bureau.

Looked like he wasn't the only one who wanted to help in whatever way he could.

"Do you want to change?" he asked as he kicked the door shut.

"I want a shower—"

"Let's get one started."

"—except I'm too afraid. I don't . . . want to see it, if you know what I mean."

He laid her down and sat on the bed beside her. Putting his hand on her leg, he rubbed her knee with his thumb, back and forth.

"I'm so sorry," she said roughly.

"Fuck—no, don't do that. You don't ever think that or say it, clear? This is *not* your fault."

"Who else's is it?"

"Not the point."

Shit, he couldn't believe the miscarrying thing was going to go on for another week or so. How was that possible—

The grimace that contorted Layla's face told him that a cramp had hit her again. Glancing behind, and expecting to find Doc Jane, he discovered they were alone.

Which told him more than anything else that there was nothing to be done.

Qhuinn hung his head and held her hand.

It had started with the pair of them.

It was ending with the pair of them.

"I think I'd like to go to sleep," Layla said as she squeezed his palm. "You look as if you need some, too."

He eyed the chaise lounge across the way.

"You don't have to stay with me," Layla murmured.

"Where else do you think I would be?"

A quick mental picture of Blay holding his arms wide flashed through his mind. What a fantasy, though.

Don't you touch me like that.

Qhuinn shook the thoughts out of his head. "I'll sleep over there."

"You can't stay in here for seven nights straight."

"I'll say it again. Where else would I be——"

"Qhuinn." Her voice got strident. "You have a job out there. And you heard Havers. This is just going to take as long as it does, and it's probably going to be a while. I'm not in any danger of bleeding out, and frankly, I feel as though I have to be strong in front of you, and I do not have the energy for that. Please come and check in, yes, do. But I will go mad if you camp out here until I stop with all this."

Quiet despair.

That was all Qhuinn had as he sat there on the edge of that bed, holding Layla's hand.

He got up to leave shortly thereafter. She was right, of course. She needed to rest as much as she could, and really, aside from staring at her and making her feel like a freak, there was nothing he could do.

"I'm never far."

"I know that." She brought his fist to her lips, and he was shocked by how cold they were. "You have been . . . more than I could have asked for."

"Nah. There's nothing that I've——"

"You have done what is right and proper. Always."

That was a matter of opinion. "Listen, I've got my phone with me. I'll be back in a couple of hours just to look in on you. If you're asleep, I won't disturb you."

"Thank you."

Qhuinn nodded and sidestepped over to the door. He had heard once that you were not supposed to show your back to a Chosen, and he figured the display of protocol couldn't hurt.

Closing the door behind him, he leaned back against it. The only person he wanted to see was the one guy in the house who had no interest in—

"What's going on?"

Blay's voice was such a shock that he figured he'd imagined it. Except then the male himself stepped into the doorway of the second-floor sitting room. As if he'd been waiting there all along.

Qhuinn rubbed his eyes and then started walking, his body seeking out the very thing he had been praying for.

"She's losing it," Qhuinn heard himself say in a dead voice.

Blay murmured something in return, but it didn't register.

Funny, the miscarriage hadn't seemed real until this moment. Not until he told Blay.

"I'm sorry?" Qhuinn said, aware that the guy seemed to be waiting for an answer.

"Is there anything I can do?"

So funny. Qhuinn had always felt as though he'd come out of his mother's womb an adult. Then again, there had never been any cootchie-coo crap for him, no darling-little-boy stuff, no hugs when he hurt himself, no coddling when he was frightened. As a result, whether it was character or the way he'd been brought up, he'd never regressed. Nothing to go back to there.

Yet it was in the voice of a child that he said, "Make it stop?"

As if Blay alone had the power to work a miracle.

And then . . . the male did.

Blay extended his arms wide, offering the only haven Qhuinn had ever known.

"Make it stop?"

Blay's body started to shake as Qhuinn uttered those words: After all these years, he'd seen the guy in a lot of moods and in a lot of circumstances. Never like this, though. Never . . . so completely and utterly ruined.

Never like a child, lost.

In spite of his need to keep really and truly far away from any emotional anything, his arms opened of their own accord.

As Qhuinn stepped in against him, the fighter's body seemed smaller and frailer than it actually was. And the arms that wound

around Blay's waist simply lay against him as if there were no strength in the muscles.

Blay held them both up.

And he expected Qhuinn to pull back quickly. Usually, the guy couldn't handle any kind of intense connection other than a sexual one for longer than a second and a half.

Qhuinn didn't. He seemed prepared to stand in the doorway to the sitting room forever.

"Come here," Blay said, drawing the male inside and shutting the door. "Over on the couch."

Qhuinn followed behind, shitkickers shuffling instead of marching.

When they got to the sofa, they sat down facing each other, their knees touching. As Blay looked over, the resonant sadness touched him so deeply, he couldn't stop his hand from reaching out and stroking that black hair—

Abruptly, Qhuinn curled in against him, just collapsed, that body folding in half and all but pouring into Blay's lap.

There was a part of Blay that recognized this was dangerous territory. Sex was one thing—and hard enough to handle, fuck him very much. This quiet space? Was potentially devastating.

Which was precisely why he'd gotten the hell out of that bedroom the day before.

The difference tonight, however, was that he was in control of this. Qhuinn was the one seeking comfort, and Blay could withdraw it or give it depending on how he felt: Being relied on was something altogether different from receiving—or needing.

Blay was good with being relied on. There was a kind of safety in it—a certainty, a control. It was not the same as falling into the abyss. And hell, if anyone would know that, it was him. God knew he'd spent years down there.

"I would do anything to change this," Blay said while stroking Qhuinn's back. "I hate that you're going through . . ."

Oh, words were so damned useless.

They stayed that way for the longest time, the quiet of the room forming a kind of cocoon. Periodically, the antique clock on the mantel chimed, and then after a long while, the shutters began to descend over the windows.

"I wish there was something I could do," Blay said as the steel panels locked into place with a *chunk*.

"You probably have to go."

Blay let that one stand. The truth was not something he wanted to share: Wild horses, loaded guns, crowbars, fire hoses, trampling elephants . . . even an order from the king himself could not have pulled him away.

And there was a part of him that got angry over that. Not at Qhuinn, but at his own heart. The trouble was, you couldn't argue with your nature—and he was learning that. In the breakup with Saxton. In coming out to his mom. In this moment here.

Qhuinn groaned as he lifted his torso up, and then scrubbed his face. When he dropped his hands, his cheeks were red and so were his eyes, but not because he was crying.

Undoubtedly his decade's allotment of tears had come out the night before as he'd wept in relief that he'd saved a father's life.

Had he known that Layla wasn't doing well then?

"You know what the hardest thing is?" Qhuinn asked, sounding more like himself.

"What?" God knew there was a lot to choose from.

"I've seen the young."

The fine hairs on the back of Blay's neck tingled. "What are you talking about."

"The night the Honor Guard came for me, and I almost died—remember?"

Blay coughed a little, the memory as raw and vivid as something that had happened an hour ago. And yet Qhuinn's voice was even and calm, like he was referencing an evening out at a club or something. "Ah, yeah. I remember."

I gave you CPR at the side of the goddamn road, he thought.

"I went up to the Fade—" Qhuinn frowned. "Are you okay?"

Oh, sure, doing great. "Sorry. Keep going."

"I went up there. I mean, it was like . . . what you hear about. The white." Qhuinn scrubbed his face again. "So white. Everywhere. There was a door, and I went up to it—I knew if I turned the knob I was going in, and I was never coming out. I reached for the thing . . . and that's when I saw her. In the door."

"Layla," Blay interjected, feeling like his chest had been stabbed.

"My daughter."

Blay's breath caught. "Your . . ."

Qhuinn looked over. "She was . . . blond. Like Layla. But her

eyes—" He touched next to his own. "—they were mine. I stopped reaching forward when I saw her—and then suddenly, I was back on the ground at the side of the road. Afterward, I had no clue what it was all about. But then, like, so much later, Layla goes into her needing and comes to me, and everything fell into place. I was like . . . this is *supposed* to happen. It felt like fate, you know. I never would have lain with Layla otherwise. I did it only because I *knew* we were going to have a little girl."

"Jesus."

"I was wrong, though." He rubbed his face a third time. "I was totally fucking wrong—and I really wish I hadn't gone down this path. Biggest regret of my life—well, second-biggest, actually."

Blay had to wonder what the hell could be worse than where the guy was at.

What can I do? Blay wondered to himself.

Qhuinn's eyes searched his face. "Do you really want me to answer that?"

Apparently he'd spoken out loud. "Yeah, I do."

Qhuinn's dagger hand reached out and cupped the side of Blay's jaw. "You sure?"

The vibe instantly shifted. The tragedy was still very much with them, but that powerful sexual undertow came back between one heartbeat and the next.

Qhuinn's stare started to burn, his lids dropping low. "I need . . . an anchor right now. I don't know how else to explain it."

Blay's body responded instantly, his blood spiking to the boiling point, his cock thickening, growing long.

"Let me kiss you." Qhuinn groaned as he leaned in. "I know I don't deserve it, but please . . . it's what you can do for me. Let me feel you. . . ."

Qhuinn's mouth brushed his own. Came back for more. Lingered.

"I'll beg for it." More with the caress of those devastating lips. "If that's what it takes. I don't give a fuck, I'll beg. . . ."

Somehow, that wasn't going to be necessary.

Blay allowed his head to get tilted so there was more room to maneuver, Qhuinn's hand on his face both gentle and in command. And then there was more of the mouth-on-mouth, slow, drugging, inexorable.

"Let me inside you again, Blay. . . ."

THIRTY-NINE

ssail got home about half an hour before dawn. Parking his Range Rover in the garage, he had to wait until the door went down to get out.

He had always considered himself an intellectual—and not in the *glymera* sense of the word, where one sat tall with self-importance and pontificated about literature, philosophy, or spiritual matters. It was more that there was little in life he could not apply his reasoning to and understand in its totality.

What in the hell had that woman done at Benloise's?

Clearly, she was a professional, with both the proper equipment and know-how, and a practiced approach to infiltration. He also suspected she'd either gotten plans to the house or had been in there previously. So efficient. So decisive. And he was qualified to judge: He'd followed her the whole time she'd been inside, ghosting through the window she'd opened, sticking to the shadows.

Tracking her from behind.

But this he did not understand: What kind of thief went to the trouble of breaking into a secured house, finding a safe, burning it open, and discovering plenty of portable wealth to lift . . . but didn't

take anything? Because he'd seen full well what she'd had access to; as soon as she'd left the study, he'd hung back, freed the shelving section as she had done, and used his own penlight to glance in the safe.

Just to find out what, if anything, she'd left behind.

When he'd come back out into the house proper, avoiding any pools of light, he'd watched as she'd stood for a moment in the front hall, hands on her hips, head rotating slowly, as if she were considering her options.

And then she'd gone over to what had to be a Degas . . . and pivoted the statue only an inch or so to the left.

It made no sense.

Now, it *was* possible that she'd gone into the safe looking for something specific that was not in fact there. A ring, a bauble, a necklace. A computer chip, a SanDisk, a document like a last will and testament or an insurance policy. But the delay in the hall had not been characteristic of her previous alacrity . . . and then she'd moved the statue?

The only explanation was that it had to be a deliberate violation of Benloise's property.

The problem was, when it came to vendettas against inanimate objects, it was hard to find much significance in her actions. Knock the statue over, then. Take the damn thing. Spray-paint it with obscenities. Beat it with a crowbar so it was ruined. But a minuscule turn that was barely noticeable?

The only conclusion he could draw was that it was a kind of message. And he didn't like that at all.

It suggested she might know Benloise personally.

Assail opened the driver's-side door—

"Oh, God," he hissed, recoiling.

"We were wondering how long you were going to stay in there."

As the dry voice drifted over, Assail got out and looked around the five-car garage in distaste. The stench was somewhere between three-day-old roadkill, spoiled mayonnaise, and denatured cheap perfume.

"Is that what I think it is?" he asked the cousins, who were standing in the doorway from the mudroom.

Thank the Scribe Virgin, they came forward and closed the way into the house—or that hideous smell was going to flood the interior.

"It's your drug dealers. Well, part of them, at any rate."

What. The. Hell.

Assail's long strides took him in the direction Ehric was pointing to—the far corner, where there were three dark green plastic bags thrown in a heap without care. Getting down on his haunches, he loosened the yellow tie of one, yanked apart the neck, and . . .

Met the sightless eyes of a human male he recognized.

The still-animated head had been severed cleanly from the spine about three inches below the jawline, and had oriented itself so that it could look out of its loosey-goosey coffin. The dark hair and ruddy skin were marked with black, glossy blood, and if the smell had been bad over by the car, up close and personal it made his eyes water and his throat tighten in protest.

Not that he cared.

He opened the other two bags and, using the Hefty plastic as a skin barrier, rolled the other heads into the same position.

Then he sat back and stared at the three of them, watching those mouths gape impotently for air.

"Tell me what happened," he said darkly.

"We showed up at the prearranged meeting place."

"Skating rink, waterfront park, or under the bridge."

"The bridge. We arrived"—Ehric motioned to his twin, who stood silent and watchful beside him—"on time with the product. About five minutes later, the three of them showed up."

"As *lessers*."

"They had the money. They were ready to make the transaction."

Assail whipped his head around. "They didn't come to attack you?"

"No, but we didn't figure that out until it was too late." Ehric shrugged. "They were slayers who came out of nowhere. We didn't know how many of them there were, and we were not taking any chances. It wasn't until we searched the bodies, and found the correct amount of money, that we realized they'd just come to do the deal."

Lessers in the trade? This was a new one. "Did you stab the bodies?"

"We took the heads and hid what was left. The money was in a backpack on that one on the left, and naturally, we brought the cash home."

"Phones?"

"Got them."

Assail started to slide a cigar out, but then didn't want to waste the taste. Reclosing the bags, he rose up from the carnage. "You are certain they were not aggressive?"

"They were ill-equipped to defend themselves."

"Being badly armed does not mean they weren't there to kill you."

"Why bring the money?"

"They could have been dealing elsewhere."

"As I said, it was in the correct amount and not one penny more."

Abruptly, Assail motioned for them all to proceed into the house, and oh, the relief that came with clean air. With the screens slowly descending over all the glass, and the coming dawn getting shut out, he went to the wine bar, retrieved a double magnum of Bouchard Père et Fils, Montrachet, 2006 and popped the cork.

"Care to join me?"

"But of course."

At the circular table in the kitchen, he sat down with three glasses and the bottle. Pouring the trio, he shared the chardonnay with his two associates.

He didn't offer the cousins any of his Cubans. Too valuable.

Fortunately, cigarettes made an appearance and then they all sat together, smoking and taking hits of bliss off the knife edge of his Baccarat.

"No aggression from those slayers," he murmured, leaning his head back and puffing upward, the blue smoke rising above his head.

"And the exact amount."

After a long moment, he returned his eyes to level. "Is it possible the Lessening Society is looking to get into my business?"

Xcor sat in candlelight, alone.

The warehouse was quiet, his soldiers yet to come home, no humans or Shadows or anything walking above him. The air was cold; same with the concrete beneath him. Darkness was all around, except for the shallow pool of golden illumination he sat at the outer rim of.

Some thought in the back of his mind pointed out that it was getting dangerously close to dawn. There was something else, too, something he should have remembered.

But there was no chance of anything getting through his haze.

With his eyes focused on the single flame before him, he replayed the night over and over again.

To say that he had found the Brotherhood's location was mayhap a stretch of the truth—but not a total fallacy. He'd been following that Mercedes out into the countryside incremental mile by incremental mile, with no real plan of what he could or should do when it stopped . . . when from out of nowhere, the signal of his blood in his

Chosen's body had not just been lost, but wildly redirected—sure as a ball thrown against a wall sharply changed its trajectory.

Confused, he had scrambled about, dematerializing this way, that way, up and back—as all the while, a strange feeling of dread came over him, like his skin was an antenna for danger and it was warning of imminent harm. Backing off, he had found himself at the base of a mountain, the contours of which registered, even in the bright, clear moonlight, as fuzzy, indistinct, unclear.

This had to be where they stayed.

Mayhap up at the top. Mayhap down the far side.

There was no other explanation—after all, the Brotherhood lived with the king to protect him . . . so undoubtedly, they would take precautions the likes of which no one else would, and perhaps have at their disposal technologies as well as mystical provisions that were otherwise unavailable.

Frantic, he had circled the vicinity, going around the base of that mountain a number of times, sensing nothing but the refraction of her signal and that strange dread. His ultimate conclusion was that she had to be somewhere in that vast, thick acreage: He would have sensed her traveling beyond it, in any direction, if she had come out on another side, and it seemed reasonable to assume that if she had gone to her sacred temple, upon some alternate plane of existence, or—Fates forbid—died, the resonant echoing of himself would have disappeared.

His Chosen was there somewhere.

Returning to the warehouse, to the present, to where he was now, Xcor rubbed his palms back and forth slowly, the rasping of the calluses rising up into the quiet. Over on the left, on the edge of the candlelight, his weapons were laid out one by one, the daggers, the guns, and his beloved scythe carefully arranged next to the messy pile of outer clothing he'd removed as soon as he'd chosen this particular spot on the floor.

He focused upon his scythe and waited for her to talk to him: She often did that, her blood-thirsty ways in lockstep with the aggression that flowed in his veins and defined his thoughts and motivated his actions.

He waited for her to tell him to attack the Brotherhood where they lay. Where their females were. Where their young slept.

The silence was worrisome.

Indeed, his arrival in the New World had been predicated upon a desire to gain power, and the biggest, boldest expression of that drive was overthrowing the throne—so, naturally, that was the course he had

chosen. And he was making headway. The assassination attempt in the fall, which had without a doubt put death sentences upon his and his soldiers' heads, had been a tactical move that had very nearly finished the whole war before it had gotten started. And his ongoing efforts with Elan and the *glymera* were promoting his agenda and shoring up his support in and among the aristocracy.

But what he had learned this night . . .

Fates, nearly a year's worth of work and sacrifice and planning and fighting paled in comparison to what he had discovered this night.

If his hunch was correct—and how could it not be?—all he had to do was marshal his soldiers and begin a siege as soon as night fell. The battle would be epic, and the Brotherhood and First Family's home permanently compromised no matter the outcome.

It would be a conflict for the history books—after all, the last time the royal homestead had been hit had been when Wrath's sire and *mahmen* had been slaughtered before his transition.

History repeating itself.

And he and his soldiers had a serious advantage that those slayers back then had not possessed: The Brotherhood now had several bonded members. In fact, he believed they were all bonded—and that was going to split those males' attentions and loyalties as nothing else could. Although their primary directive as the personal guard of the king was to protect Wrath, their very cores would be torn, and even the strongest fighter with the best of weapons could be weakened if his priorities were in two places.

Moreover, if Xcor or one of his males could get hold of even one of those *shellans*, the Brotherhood would fold—because the other thing that was true of them was that the pain of their Brothers was agony of their own.

One female of any of theirs would be all that was required, the ultimate weapon.

He knew it in his soul.

Sitting in the candlelight, Xcor rubbed his dagger hand against his other palm, back and forth, back and forth.

One female.

That was all he needed.

And he would be able to claim not only his own mate . . . but the throne.

FORTY

Quinn knew he'd put Blay in a totally unfair position.

Talk about pity fucks. But oh, God . . . looking into those blue eyes, those goddamn bottomless blue eyes that were open to him in the way they'd once been . . . it was all he could think about. And yeah, technically it was sex in terms of where he wanted his various body parts—well, one specifically. There was so much more to it than that, though.

He couldn't put it into words; he just wasn't that good working with syllables. But his desire for the connection was why he'd gone in for the kiss. He'd wanted to show Blay what he meant, what he needed, why this was important: His whole world felt like it was crashing and burning, and the loss that was happening just one door down the hall was going to hurt for a very long time.

Yet being with Blay, feeling the heat, making that contact, was like a promise of healing. Even if it lasted only as long as they were in this room together, he would take it, and hold it dear . . . and relive the memory when he needed to.

"Please," he whispered.

Except he didn't give the guy a chance to reply. His tongue snaked out and licked at that mouth, slipping inside, taking over.

And Blay's answer was in the way he allowed himself to get pushed back into the cushions of the couch.

Qhuinn had two vague thoughts: One, the door was only closed, not locked—and he took care of that by willing the brass bolt into place. His second oh-hey-now was that they couldn't trash the place. Going H-bomb all over his bedroom was one thing. This sitting room was public property, and done up all nice, with silk throw pillows and fancy-dancy drapes, and a whole lot of stuff that looked easily rippable, crushable, and, God forbid, stainable.

Besides, he had already wrecked his Hummer, torn up the garden, and then blendered his bedroom. So his Destructor quota had been waaaaaay reached for this calendar year . . .

Naturally, the most reasonable solution to not giving Fritz more to worry about was a quick trip down the hall to his own place, but as Blay's talented hands shot around to the front of Qhuinn's hips and started working his fly, he tossed that bright idea right into the shitter.

"Oh, God, touch me," he groaned, thrusting his pelvis forward.

He was just going to have to be neat and tidy about this.

Assuming that was possible.

When Blay's palm shoved into his leathers, Qhuinn's body went into an arch, his torso bowing back as he started to get worked. The angle was kind of wrong, so there wasn't a lot of friction, and his balls were getting pinched to fuck in the crotch of his pants, but holy hell, he didn't care. The fact that it was Blay was enough for him.

Man, after how many years of blow jobs, hand jobs, and jerking off, this felt like the first time anyone had ever touched him.

He needed to return the favor.

Snapping into action, he threw his chest forward, bringing their faces close. Man, he loved the look in those blue eyes as Blay stared up at him, hot, wild, glowing.

Willing.

Qhuinn grabbed on hard and brought their mouths together, grinding against those lips, shooting his tongue out, taking like a crazy—

"Wait, wait." Blay yanked back. "We're going to break the couch."

"Wha . . . ?" The guy was apparently talking English, but damned if he could translate. "Couch?"

And then he realized that he'd pushed Blay so far back into the arm, the thing was starting to bend out. Which was what more than five hundred pounds of sex would do to a piece of furniture.

"Oh, shit, sorry."

He was starting to retreat when Blay took control—and Qhuinn abruptly found himself off the sofa and onto the floor on his back, his legs shoved together, his leathers being yanked down to his ankles.

Perfect. Fucking. Idea.

Thanks to the fact that he went commando, his cock was all about the airtime, thick and straining as it popped out and lay, aching and swollen, upon his belly. Reaching down, he gave it a couple of strokes as Blay ripped off the shitkickers that blocked the way and tossed them aside. Pants were the next good-bye, and as God was his witness, Qhuinn had never been so glad to see a pair of leathers flying over a shoulder in his life.

And then Blay got to work.

Qhuinn had to shut his eyes as he felt his thighs get parted and a pair of fighter's hands drag up the inside of his legs. He immediately let go of his erection—after all, why have his palm in the way when Blay's could—

It wasn't the guy's hands that gripped him.

It was the warm, wet mouth Qhuinn had just kissed the hell out of.

For a split second, as the suction grabbed onto his head and shaft, he had a ball-shrinking thought that Saxton had taught Blay how to do this—his fucking cousin had done this to the guy, and had this done to him—

Stop it, he told himself. Whatever the history or the lessons learned, his erection was the one getting the attention at the moment. So fuck that shit.

To make sure that was clear, he forced his lids open. Fucking . . . hell . . .

Blay's head was going up and down over his hips, his fist holding the base of Qhuinn's cock, his other hand working his balls. But then, like he'd been waiting for eye contact, the guy pulled up to the top, popped the head free, and licked his lips.

"Wouldn't want you making a mess in this nice room," Blay drawled.

And then he extended the tip of his tongue to flick Qhuinn's PA, the pink flesh teasing at the gunmetal gray hoop and ball—

"Fuck, I'm coming right now," Qhuinn barked, a tremendous release boiling up. "I'm—"

He was powerless to stop things, any more than someone who'd jumped off a cliff could decide, like ten yards into the free fall, to pull back.

Except he didn't want to put the brakes on.

And he didn't.

With a mighty roar—that most certainly was heard elsewhere—Qhuinn's spine jacked off the floor, his ass going tight, his balls exploding, his arousal kicking hard in Blay's mouth. And it wasn't just his sex that was affected. The release coursed throughout his whole body, shimmering energy surging through him as he dug his fingers into the rug he was on, and gritted his teeth . . . and came like a wild animal.

Fortunately, Blay was more than capable at cleanup—and didn't that just make him orgasm even more. Also gave him plenty to watch: For the rest of his days, Qhuinn was never going to forget the sight of the male's mouth wrapped around him, cheeks sucking in as he drew out the release and took it all. Over and over and over again.

Usually Qhuinn was ready to go immediately afterward, but when the rolling waves finally stopped crashing into him, he went utterly limp, arms falling flat to the floor, knees going lax, head lolling.

All things considered, that had probably been the best orgasm of his life. Second only to the ones he'd had earlier in the day with the guy.

"I can't move," he mumbled.

Blay's laugh was deep and sexy. "You look a little wrung-out."

"Can I return the favor?"

"Can you lift your head?"

"Is it still attached to my body?"

"From what I can see, yes."

As Blay chuckled again, Qhuinn knew what he wanted to do—and was kind of surprised at himself. In all his sexual exploits, he'd never allowed himself to get fucked. That just wasn't part of the way things went. He was the conqueror, the taker, the one who established control and retained that superiority.

Bottoming just wasn't anything he'd been interested in.

Now he wanted it.

The only problem was, he literally couldn't move. And, well, there was something else—how could he tell Blay that he was a virgin?

Because he wanted to. If they ever went there, he wanted Blay to know. For some reason that was important.

Abruptly, Blay's face came into his line of vision, and God, the fighter was beautiful, his cheeks flushed, his eyes gleaming, those big shoulders blocking out everything.

And, oh, yeah, that smile was sexy as hell, so self-satisfied and self-confident—as if the fact that Blay had given such pleasure to someone else was enough to make him not even need a release of his own.

But that wasn't fair, was it.

"I don't think you're moving anytime soon," Blay said.

"Maybe. But I can open my mouth," Qhuinn replied darkly. "Almost as wide as you can."

Right, okay, the idea that he'd given Qhuinn an orgasm like that was so goddamned affirming, Blay had forgotten all about his own body.

The thing was, after so many years of getting shut down, it was a total rush to feel powerful against the guy, to be the one who set the pace . . . to be the person who took Qhuinn to an erotic, vulnerable place that was so much more intense than any other he'd been to. And that was what had happened. He knew exactly what Qhuinn looked and sounded like when he came, and Blay could say, without any equivocation, that he'd never seen his buddy undone like that, sprawled out on a rug, neck muscles straining, abs seized up, hips pumping hard.

Qhuinn had literally come for about twenty minutes straight.

And now, in the aftermath, a strange revelation: Until just this moment, Blay had never recognized the cynicism that Qhuinn carried in his face at all times . . . the furrowed brow, the perpetual snarking turn on one side of that mouth, the jaw that never, ever loosened up.

It was as if all the nastiness his family had done to him had permanently warped the features.

But that wasn't true, was it. During that orgasm, and now, as things calmed down, none of the tension was anywhere to be found. Qhuinn's face was . . . wiped clean of all reserve, appearing so much younger, Blay had to wonder why he'd never noticed the age before.

"So will you give me something to suck on as I recover?" Qhuinn asked.

"Wha . . . ?"

"I said I'm thirsty. And I need something to suck on." At this, Qhuinn bit his lower lip, his bright white fangs sinking into the flesh. "Will you help me?"

Blay's eyes rolled back into his head. "Yeah . . . I can do that."

"Then let me see you take your pants off."

Blay's legs popped him up from the floor so fast, he had fresh insights into the laws of physics, and while he kicked off his loafers, his hands shook to get his trousers unbuttoned. Things went quickly from there. And the whole time he was stripping, he was preternaturally aware of everything in the room—especially Qhuinn. The male was getting hard again, his sex thickening in spite of everything it had just been through . . . those heavy thighs clenching and that pelvis rolling . . . the lower belly so lean that every minute shift of the torso was reflected under taut, tan skin.

"Oh, yeah . . ." Qhuinn hissed, his fangs extending from his upper jaw, his hand seeking out his sex and stroking long and slow. "There it is."

Blay's breath started to pump, his heart rate going through the roof as Qhuinn's mismatched eyes latched onto his sex.

"That's what I want," the male growled, letting go of himself and reaching up with both hands.

For a split second, Blay wasn't sure how the body parts were going to work. Qhuinn was in front of the sofa, running parallel to the thing, so there wasn't a lot of room—

A subtle pumping growl percolated through the air as Qhuinn flexed his fingers—like he couldn't wait to get hold of what he wanted.

Fuck the advance planning.

Blay's knees obeyed the call, hinging forward, bringing his weight down to the floor by Qhuinn's head.

Qhuinn took over from there. His palms snaked out and grabbed on, drawing Blay in so that before he knew it, he had one knee behind the guy's head and the other leg thrown out to the side, all the way down by Qhuinn's hip.

"Oh . . . fuck . . ." Blay groaned as he felt his sex go in between Qhuinn's lips.

His body listed forward until his torso ended up sprawled on the couch cushions—and that was when he unexpectedly found himself with a boatload of leverage. Bracing his arms on the sofa, he distributed his weight among his knees, his feet, and palms . . . and then proceded to fuck the ever-loving shit out of Qhuinn's mouth.

The guy took it all, even as Blay unhinged his hips and thrust with everything he had.

With Qhuinn's fingers biting into his ass, and that incredible suction, and . . . Christ, that tongue piercing, the ball of which dug into his shaft with every stroke . . . Blay started to gear up for exactly the kind of orgasm Qhuinn had just had.

And yet, in the back of his mind, he wondered whether he was hurting the guy. At this point, he was going to come into his friend's stomach, for godsakes—

Too late to worry about that.

His body took over, going rigid in a series of racking spasms that ran from the top of his spine down into his legs.

And just as the out of control sensations were beginning to ebb, the world went wonky on him, like his sense of balance had been blown along with his—

No, the world was fine. Qhuinn had just popped him up off the floor, gotten out from underneath, and was positioning himself behind. . . .

As Qhuinn pushed inside with a lightning-fast strike, Blay let out a moan that he was quite sure could have been heard in Canada—

The squeal that pierced through the room made him frown, even through the pressure and the pleasure.

Oh. They were moving the couch over the floor.

Whatever. He'd buy the house another one if they broke the damn thing; he was *not* stopping this.

The rhythm was every bit as punishing as his had been—and in this case, payback was not just what he deserved; it was exactly what he wanted. With every thrust, his face got pushed into the soft cushions; with every retreat he could take a breath; then it was back in tight, the cycle starting all over again.

Readjusting his legs so that Qhuinn could go even deeper, Blay had some vague thought that they had definitely banged the sofa into a different position, but who the hell cared as long as it wasn't out into the hall?

At the last moment, just before he came again, he had the presence of mind to grab for his pants. Shaking his boxers free, he—

Qhuinn's hand reached over, took the Calvins and did the deed, making sure there was something to catch his release. Then a moment later, his chest was hauled off the couch so he was upright on his knees. Qhuinn handled everything, gripping Blay's cock while covering the head—all the while pounding, pounding, pounding . . .

They came at the same time, a pair of shouts echoing around the room.

In the midst of the orgasm, Blay happened to glance up. In the big old-fashioned mirror that hung between the two windows across the way, he saw them both, knew they were joined . . . and it made him come all over again.

Eventually, the thrusting slowed. Heart rates went down. Breathing grew easier.

In the leaded glass of the mirror, he watched as Qhuinn shut his eyes and tucked his head downward. Against the side of his throat, Blay felt the softest of brushes.

Qhuinn's lips.

And then the male's free hand drifted upward, pausing to stroke across Blay's pecs—

Qhuinn froze. Jerked back. Removed his lips, his touch. "Sorry. Sorry, I . . . know you're not into that with me."

The change in the guy's face, that return to the cynical normal, was like being robbed.

And yet Blay couldn't tell him to come back in close. Qhuinn was right; the instant that tenderness appeared, he started to get panicky.

The withdrawal was quick, too quick, and Blay missed the feeling of fullness and possession. But it *was* time to end this.

Qhuinn cleared his throat. "Ah . . . do you want to . . ."

"I'll take care of it," Blay mumbled, replacing Qhuinn's hand over the crumpled boxers at his hips.

During the sex, the silence in the room had been about privacy. Now, it just amplified the sounds of Qhuinn pulling his leathers back on.

Shit.

They had gone down the rabbit hole again. And while it was happening, the sensations were so intense and overpowering, there was no thinking of anything other than the sex. In the aftermath, though, Blay's body felt too cold in the seventy-degree air, different places throbbing from use, his legs loose and wobbly, his brain fuzzy . . .

Nothing seemed secure or sure. In the slightest.

Forcing himself to get dressed, he piled the clothes on as fast as he could, right down to his loafers. Meanwhile, Qhuinn was the one who returned the sofa where it belonged, carefully putting the feet of the legs back in the divots they'd made in the carpet. He also rearranged the throw pillows. Straightened the Oriental.

It was like it had never happened. Except for the boxers that Blay crushed in his fist.

"Thank you," Qhuinn said quietly. "I, ah . . ."

"Yeah."

"So . . . I guess I'll go now."

"Yeah."

That was it.

Well, other than the door closing.

Left alone, Blay decided he needed a shower. More food. Sleep.

Instead, he stayed in the second-story sitting room, looking at that mirror, remembering what he had seen in it. In his mind, he had some vague thought that they couldn't keep doing that. It wasn't safe for him emotionally; in fact, it was the equivalent of holding your palm above a lit burner over and over again—except every time you put your hand back above the flame, you lowered the distance between your flesh and the heat. Sooner or later? Third-degree burns were the least of your problems, because your whole goddamn arm was on fire.

After a while, however, that self-preservation thing wasn't what he dwelled on.

It was what had started the whole thing.

Make it stop.

Blay drew a hand through his hair. Then he looked at the closed door and frowned, his mind churning, churning, churning . . .

A moment later, he left in a rush, walking quickly.

Before breaking into a jog.

And then falling into a flat-out run.

FORTY-ONE

It was around ten in the morning when Trez headed over to Sal's Restuarant. The trip from the apartment at the Commodore to his brother's fine-dining establishment wasn't long, only ten minutes, and there were plenty of free parking spots in the lot when he got there.

Then again, the place didn't open, even to the kitchen staff for prep, until one in the afternoon.

As he walked over to the entrance, his boots crunching in the snow, he half expected the code that unlocked things from the outside not to work: iAm hadn't come home at the end of the night, and assuming those cocksuckers at the s'Hisbe hadn't taken the guy for collateral, there was only one place his brother could be: After two pots of coffee and a lot of checking his watch, Trez knew that if he wanted to make peace, he had to head across town.

Cool. The combination hadn't been changed.

Yet.

Inside, the place was old-school Rat Pack done right, a modern interpretation of the era that had spawned the likes of Peter Lawford and the Chairman of the Board: An entryway with black-and-red flocked wallpaper took you to the receiving area, where the coat check, retro hostess stand and cashier's desk were. To the left, and to the right, there were two main dining rooms, both done in black and red velvet and leather, but they weren't where the local made guys, politicians, and wealthy types hung out. The sweet spot was the bar up ahead, a wood-paneled room that had red leather banquettes set against the walls and, during regular hours, a tuxedoed bartender behind a thirty-foot oak stretch serving nothing but the best.

Striding into the bar's dim expanse, Trez headed around the far end of the five-tiered display of bottles and hit the flap door. As he pushed his way into the kitchen, the scent of basil and onion, oregano and red wine, told him just how stressed iAm was.

Sure enough, the guy was facing off at the sixteen-burner stove on the far wall, five huge pots simmering in front of him—and what do you want to bet there were things in the stoves, too. Meanwhile, wooden cutting boards were lined up on the stainless-steel counters, the dead heads of various kinds of peppers lolling around next to the very sharp knives that had been used.

Ten bucks to guess who the guy had been thinking of when he'd been chopping stuff.

"You going to talk to me at all?" Trez said to his brother's back.

iAm moved to the next pot, lifting its lid with a white dishcloth, a big slotted spoon going in and stirring slowly.

Trez leaned to the side and pulled over a stainless-steel stool. Taking a seat, he rubbed his thighs up and down.

"Hello?"

iAm went to the next pot. And then the next. Each had a separate spoon for flavor flagellation, and his brother was careful not to cross-contaminate.

"Look, I'm sorry I wasn't there when you came by the club tonight." Every evening, iAm headed over to the Iron Mask for a check-in after Sal's closed. "I had some business to take care of."

Shit, yeah, he did. Baby girl with the bouncer BF had taken forever to get out of his car when he'd gotten her to her house—eventually he'd walked her to the door, opened the way in, and all but toastered her through the jambs. Back at his Beamer, he'd hit the gas like he'd planted a bomb in the walk-up, and as he'd steamed over to the Iron Mask, all he'd heard in his head was iAm's voice.

You can't keep doing this.

iAm turned around at that point, crossing his arms over his chest and leaning back against the stove. His biceps were big to begin with, but cranked like that, they strained the bounds of the black T-shirt he was wearing.

His almond-shaped eyes were half-lidded. "You actually think I'm pissed off that you weren't around when I got to the club? Really. It's not because you left me to deal with AnsLai or some shit."

Annnnnnnnd they were off to the races.

"I can't see any of them face-to-face, you know that." Trez lifted his hands, all what-am-I-gonna-do? "They would try to force me to go back with them, and then what are my options? Fight? I'd end up killing the son of a bitch, and then where would I be?"

iAm rubbed his eyes like he had a headache. "Right now, it appears as if they're taking a diplomatic approach. At least with me."

"When are they coming back?"

"I don't know—and that's what makes me nervous."

Trez stiffened. The idea that his cool-as-a-cucumber brother was anxious made him feel like he had a knife to his throat.

Then again, he was well aware of exactly how dangerous his people could be. The s'Hisbe was largely a peaceable nation, content to stay out of the battles with the Lessening Society and away from pesky humans. Scholarly, highly intelligent, and spiritual, they were, on the whole, a pretty nice group of people. Provided you weren't on their shit list.

Trez looked at those pots and wondered what the meat in the sauces was. "I'm still working off the debt to Rehv," he pointed out. "So that obligation has to come first."

"Not to the s'Hisbe anymore. AnsLai said, and I'm quoting, 'It's time.'"

"I'm not going back there." He met his brother's eyes. "Not going to happen."

iAm turned back to the pots, stirring each one with its designated spoon. "I know. That's why I've been cooking. I'm trying to think of a way out of this."

God, he loved his brother. Even pissed off, the guy was trying to help. "I'm sorry I pulled a ghost and made you deal with this. I really am. That wasn't fair—I just . . . yeah, I really didn't think it was safe to be in the same room with the guy. I'm *very* sorry."

iAm's thick chest rose and fell. "I know you are."

"I could just disappear. That would solve the problem."

Although, man, it would kill him to leave iAm. The thing was, if he went on the lam from the s'Hisbe, he could never have any contact with the male again. Ever.

"Where would you go," iAm pointed out.

"Not a clue."

The good news was that the s'Hisbe didn't like to have any contact with UKs. No doubt even showing up at his and iAm's apartment had been traumatic, even if the high priest had just dematerialized onto the terrace. Dealing directly with humans? Being around them? AnsLai's head would explode.

"So what was your business?" iAm asked.

Great. Onto an equally happy subject.

"I went to see that warehouse property," he hedged. But come on, like he was going to voluntarily bring up the chick and her boy-friend?

"At one a.m.?"

"I made an offer."

"How much?"

"One four. The asking price is two and a half million, but there's no way they're going to get it. The place has been vacant for years, and it shows." Although . . . even as he said that, he had to admit he'd felt presences there. Then again, maybe that had just been his stress level talking. "My guess is that they'll come back at two, I'll throw out one six, and we'll come to terms at one seven."

"Are you sure you want to tackle that project right now? Unless you show up at the territory with your mating tackle ready to be used, the issue with the s'Hisbe is only going to escalate."

"If things come to a head, I'll deal with it then."

"When," iAm corrected. "That would be 'when.' And I know what happened in the back parking lot, Trez. With the guy and that woman."

Oooooof course he did. "You see the tapes or something?"

Goddamn security monitoring.

"Yes."

"I handled it."

"Just like you're handling the s'Hisbe. Perfect."

Temper flaring, Trez leaned in. "You want to be in my shoes, brother mine? I'd like to see how well you'd deal with this bullshit."

"I wouldn't be out fucking whores, I'll tell you that much. Which makes me wonder . . . isn't our real estate agent a female?"

"Fuck you, iAm. For real."

Trez shot off the stool and marched out of the kitchen. He had enough problems, FFS—he didn't need Mr. Superior with the Julia Child skills armchair-quarterbacking this whole thing with twelve kinds of potshot commentary—

"You can't keep putting this off," iAm called out from behind. "Or trying to bury it in between the legs of countless women."

Trez stopped, but kept his eyes on the exit.

"You just can't," his brother stated baldly.

Trez pivoted around. iAm was over by the bar, the flap door swinging next to him so that there was a strobe-light effect of bright, dark, bright, dark. Every time the illumination made an appearance, it looked like his brother had a halo around his whole body.

Trez cursed. "I just need them to leave me alone."

"I know." iAm rubbed his head. "And I honestly don't know what the fuck to do about it. I can't imagine living without you, and I don't want to go back there, either. I'm not coming up with any other options, though."

"Those women . . . you know, the ones I . . ." Trez hesitated. "Don't you think they'd get me off?"

"If they aren't," iAm said dryly, "I can't see why you're bothering with them."

Trez had to smile a little. "No, I mean with the s'Hisbe. I'm as far from a virgin as you can get at this point." Although at least he hadn't sunk to farm animal level. "And what's worse? They've all been UKs—mostly humans, too. That has to nasty them out. We're talking about the queen's daughter."

As iAm frowned like he hadn't fully considered the idea, Trez felt a ray of hope.

"I don't know," came the response. "Maybe that would work—but you've still cheated Her Majesty out of what she wants and needs. If they consider you compromised, they might just decide to kill you as a punishment."

Whatever. They'd have to bring him down first.

On a wave of aggression, Trez dipped his chin and glared out from beneath his brows. "If that's the case, they'll have to fight me. And I guarantee that won't go well for them."

*   *   *

Back at the Brotherhood mansion, Wrath knew that his queen was upset the moment she came through the doors of his study. Her luscious scent was tinged with a sharp, acidic overhang: anxiety.

"What is it, *leelan*?" he demanded, holding out his arms.

Even though he couldn't see, his memories provided him with a mental picture of her crossing the Aubusson rug, her long, athletic body moving with grace, her dark hair loose over her shoulders, her beautiful face marked with tension.

Naturally, the bonded male in him wanted to hunt down and kill whatever had upset her.

"Hi, George," she said to his dog. Going by the *thump-thump-thump* on the floor, the retriever got some love first.

And then it was the master's turn.

Beth climbed right up onto Wrath's lap, her weight next to nothing, her body warm and alive as he wrapped his arms around her and kissed her on either side of the neck and then on the mouth.

"Jesus," he growled, feeling the stiffness in her body, "you really are upset. What the fuck is going on?"

Goddamn it, she was shivering. His queen was actually trembling.

"Talk to me, *leelan*," he said as he rubbed her back. And prepared to get armed and head out into broad fucking daylight if he had to.

"Well, you know about Layla," she said in a rough voice.

Ahhhhh. "Yeah, I do. Phury told me."

As her head shifted onto his shoulder, he repositioned her, holding her cradled against his chest —and it was good. There were times—not often, but every once in a while—when he felt like less of a male because of his lack of sight: Once a fighter, he was now stuck behind this desk. Once free to roam wherever he wanted, he now relied on a canine for navigation. Once utterly self-sufficient, he now needed help.

Not exactly good for a male's ball sac.

But in a moment like this, when this amazing female was off-kilter and seeking him and only him for comfort and reassurance, he felt strong as a motherfucking mountain. After all, bonded males protected their mates with everything they had, and even with the burden of his birthright and this throne he was obligated to sit on, he remained at his core a *hellren* to this female.

She was his first priority, even above the king shit. His Beth was

the heart behind his ribs, the marrow in his bones, the soul in his physical body.

"It's just so sad," she said. "So damned sad."

"You've been to see her?"

"Just now. She's resting. I mean . . . on some level, I can't believe there's nothing that can be done."

"You talk to Doc Jane?"

"As soon as they all got back from the clinic."

As his *shellan* cried a little, the fresh-rain scent of his beloved's tears was like a knife in the chest—and he was not surprised at her reaction. He'd heard that females dealt with the loss of another's pregnancy badly—then again, how could they not relate? He sure as shit could put himself in Qhuinn's boots.

And oh, God . . . the idea of Beth suffering like that? Or worse, if she were to carry to term and—

Great. Now he had a case of the quakes.

Wrath put his face in his Beth's hair, breathing in, calming himself. The good news was that they were never going to have young, so he wouldn't have to worry about that.

"I'm sorry," he whispered.

"Me, too. I hate this for both of them."

Well, actually, he was apologizing for something else entirely.

It wasn't that he wanted anything shitty to happen to Qhuinn or Layla or their young. But maybe if Beth saw this sad reality, she'd be reminded of all the risks that presented themselves every step of the way when it came to pregnancy.

Fuck. That sounded horrible. That *was* horrible. For chrissakes, he honestly didn't want this for Qhuinn, and he really didn't want his *shellan* upset, either. Unfortunately, however, the sad truth was that he had absolutely no interest in placing his seed within her like that—*ever*.

And that kind of desperation made a guy think unforgivable things.

In a surge of paranoia, he mentally calculated the number of years since her transition—just over two. From what he understood, the average vampire female had her first needing about five years after the change, and then every ten years or so thereafter. So by all accounts, they had some time before they had to worry about all this. . . .

Then again, as a half-breed, there was no way to be sure in Beth's case. When humans and vampires mixed, anything could happen—

and he did have some reason to be conerned. She had, after all, mentioned kids once or twice before.

But surely that had to be in the hypothetical.

"So are you going to hold off on Qhuinn's induction?" she said.

"Yeah. Saxton is done updating the laws, but with Layla being where she's at? Not the right time to bring him into the Brotherhood."

"That's what I thought."

The two of them fell silent, and as Wrath took the moment to heart, he couldn't possibly imagine his life without her.

"Do you know something?" he said.

"What?" There was a smile in her voice, the kind that told him she had a clue about what he was going to say.

"I love you more than anything."

His queen laughed a little, and stroked his face. "I would never have guessed."

Hell, even he caught the surge of his bonding scent.

In response, Wrath cupped her face and leaned in, finding her lips and taking them in a soft kiss—that didn't stay that way. Man, it was always like this with her. Any contact at all and before he knew it, he was hard and ready.

God, he didn't know how human men handled it. From what he understood, they had to wonder whether their mates were fertile every single damn time they had sex—evidently, they couldn't pick up on the subtle changes of their females' scents.

He'd go fucking insane. At least when a female vampire was in her needing, everyone knew it.

Beth shifted in his lap, compressing his hard-on, making him groan. And usually, this was the cue for George to be led across to the double doors and temporarily banished. But not tonight. As much as Wrath wanted her, the pall in the house was putting a damper on even his libido.

And then there was Autumn's needing. Now Layla's.

He wasn't going to lie; the shit was making him tetchy. Hormones in the air had been known to have a ricochet effect in a house full of females, influencing one and then another and then a third into her needing, assuming she was fairly close to her time.

Wrath stroked Beth's hair and retucked his queen's head into his shoulder.

"You don't want to . . ."

As she let the sentence drift, he took her hand and lifted it up, feeling the heavy Saturnine Ruby that the queen of the race had always worn.

"I just want to hold you," he said. "It's enough for me right now."

Nestling in, she fit herself even more closely to him. "Well, this is nice, too."

Yeah. It was.

And curiously terrifying.

"Wrath?"

"Yeah?"

"Are you okay?"

It was a little while before he could answer, before he trusted his voice to be calm, and level, and no BFD. "Oh, yeah, I'm fine. Just fine."

As he smoothed her arm, running his hand up and down her biceps, he prayed that she believed it . . . and vowed that what was happening just one door down the hall would never, ever happen to them.

Nope. That crisis was not anything the pair of them were going to have to deal with.

Thanks be to the Scribe Virgin.

FORTY-TWO

ayla wasn't sleeping, of course.

When she'd told Qhuinn to go, she had meant the things she'd said about not wanting to keep up a front with him around. But the funny thing was, even with nobody in the room with her, she didn't get hysterical. No tears. No cursing.

She just lay on her side with her arms and legs curled up, her mind receding deep into her body, the constant monitoring of every ache and cramp a compulsion that was making her crazy. There was no changing that, however. It was as if some part of her was convinced that if she could only know what stage she was in, she could somehow have some control over the process.

Which was, of course, bullshit. As Qhuinn would say.

The image of him in the clinic, with his dagger at the healer's throat, was like something out of one of the books in the Sanctuary's library—a dramatic episode that was part of someone else's life.

Her vantage point on the bed, however, reminded her that that was not the case. . . .

The knock on her door was soft, which suggested it was a female.

Layla closed her eyes. As much as she appreciated whatever kind-

ness was awaiting a response, she would have so much preferred that whoever it was stayed out in the hall. The queen's brief visit had been taxing, even though she'd appreciated it.

"Yes." When her voice didn't carry farther than her own ears, she cleared her throat. "Yes?"

The door opened, and at first she didn't recognize who it was from the shadow that filled the space between the jambs. Tall. Strong. Not a male, though . . .

"Payne?" she said.

"May I come in?"

"Yes, of course."

As Layla went to sit up, the warrior female motioned her to lie down, and then shut them both in together. "No, no, please . . . be at ease."

One lamp had been left on over at the bureau, and in the gentle light, the blooded sister of the Black Dagger Brother Vishous was quite fearsome, her diamond eyes seeming to sparkle out of the strong angles of her face.

"How ever are you?" the female asked softly.

"I am very well, thank you. And yourself?"

The fighter came forward. "I'm very sorry about . . . your condition."

Oh, how Layla wished this was something Phury or the others had not shared with anyone. Then again, her exit from the house had been rather dramatic, the sort of thing that would be cause for concerned questioning. Still, her privacy would have had her avoid this unwelcome, though compassionate, intrusion.

"I thank you for your kind words," she whispered.

"May I sit down?"

"But of course."

She expected the female to rest upon one of the chairs that had been arranged with a sense of decorum. Payne did not. She came over to the bed and lowered her weight beside Layla.

Compelled to at least appear to be a good hostess of sorts, Layla pushed herself up, wincing as a set of cramps froze her halfway.

As Payne cursed softly, Layla had to lie back down. In a rough voice, she said, "Forgive me, but I cannot have visitors at this time— no matter how well intended you are. Thank you for your expression of sympathy—"

"Are you aware of who my mother is," Payne cut in.

Layla shook her head against her pillow. "Please just leave—"

"Do you know?" the female said roughly.

Abruptly, Layla wanted to cry. She just didn't have the energy for any conversation at this point—but most certainly not about *mahmens*. Not when she was losing her own young.

"Please."

"I am birthed of the Scribe Virgin."

Layla frowned, the words registering even through the pain, mental and physical. "I'm sorry?"

Payne took a deep breath, as if the revelation were not something she rejoiced in, but rather a kind of curse. "I am of the Scribe Virgin's very flesh, born of her long ago, and hidden from the records of the Chosen and the eyes of all third parties."

Layla blinked in shock. The female's appearance up above had been a mystery of sorts, but she had certainly asked no questions as it was not her place to. The one thing she was clear on was that there had never been any mention of the race's holiest mother having e'er birthed a child.

In fact, the entire structure of the belief system was predicated upon that *not* having occurred.

"How is this possible?" Layla breathed.

Payne's brilliant eyes were grave. "It was not what I would have wished. And it is not something I speak of."

In the tense moment that followed, Layla found it impossible not to see the truth in what the female spoke. Nor the strident anger, the cause of which one could guess at.

"You are a holy one," Layla said with awe.

"Not in the slightest, I assure you. But my lineage has provided me with a certain . . . how shall we say it? Ability."

Layla stiffened. "And that would be?"

Payne's diamond eyes never wavered. "I want to help you."

Layla's hand went to her lower belly. "If you mean get this over with sooner . . . no."

She had her young for such a precious short time within her. No matter how long the pain went on, she was not going to sacrifice one minute of what was no doubt her one and only pregnancy.

She would never put herself through this again. In the future, when her needing hit, she would be drugged, and that was it.

Once in a lifetime was too much for the loss she was sustaining now.

"And if you believe you can stop this," Layla tacked on, "it is not possible. There is naught that any may do."

"I'm not so sure about that." Payne's eyes were rapt. "I'd like to see if I can save the pregnancy. If you'll let me."

At the abandoned Brownswick School for Girls campus, Mr. C had taken up res in what had once been the headmistress's office.

The cracked sign outside in the hall told him so.

As there was no heat, the ambient air temperature was exactly that of the great outdoors, but thanks to the Omega's blood, cold was not a problem. And thank fuck for that: Across the overgrown, snow-covered lawn, in the main dormitory on the ridge, nearly fifty *lessers* were sleeping the sleep of the dead.

If those bastards had required BTUs or food, he'd have been shit out of luck.

But nah, all he had to do was provide them with shelter. Their inductions took care of the rest—and the fact that they needed to unplug from consciousness every twenty-four hours was a relief.

He needed time to think.

Jesus Christ, what a mess.

Compelled by an urge to pace, he went to push his chair back, and then remembered that he was sitting on an overturned drywall bucket.

"Goddamn it."

Looking around the decrepit room, he measured the plaster that was hanging in sheets from the ceiling rafters, the boarded-up windows, and the hole in the floorboards over in the corner. Place was just like the bank accounts he'd found.

No money anywhere. No ammo. Weapons that could be used for blunt-force trauma, and that was about it.

After his promotion, he'd been so fucking pumped, full of plans. Now he was staring at a whole lot of no cash, no resources, no nothing.

The Omega, on the other hand, was expecting all kinds of results. As had been made amply clear during their little "visit" late last night.

And that was another problem. He hated that shit.

At least he could do something about the rest of it.

Stretching his arms over his head and cracking his shoulders, he thanked God for two things: One, that the cell phones hadn't been cut off—so he could communicate with his men in the field, and had Internet access. And two, that all those years on the street had given him an iron fist when it came to controlling dumb-ass young idiots in the drug trade.

He had to bring in some paper. Stat.

He'd had a fucking plan for that, too, sending the Society's last nine thousand, three hundred dollars off with three of his boys at midnight last night. All those bastards had had to do was make the buy, get the dope, and bring it back here, where he'd cut the shit, then parcel it out to the new inductees for sale on the street.

Trouble was, he was still waiting for the fucking delivery.

And he was getting pretty goddamn impatient waiting to find out where either the drugs or his money had gone.

It was possible the cocksuckers had run off with one or the other, but if that was the case, he was going to hunt them down like dogs and show all of the others what happened when you—

As his phone rang, he picked the thing up, saw who it was, and hit *send.*

"It's about fucking time. Where the fuck are you and where is my shit."

There was a pause. And then the voice that came over the connection was not anything like that of the pimple-faced pusher he'd given the cell, the cash, and the last working gun the Society had to.

"I have something you want."

Mr. C frowned. Very deep voice. Laced with an edge he recognized from the streets, and an accent he couldn't place.

"It's not the piece-of-shit phone you're calling me on," Mr. C drawled. "I got plenty of those."

After all, when you didn't have anything in your hand, your holster or your wallet, bluffing was your only option.

"Well, good for you. Have you plenty of what you sent to me, too? Money? Manpower?"

"Who the fuck is this?"

"I'm your enemy."

"If you took my fucking cash, you bet your ass you are."

"Actually, 'tis a simplistic answer to what is a rather complex problem."

Mr. C burst to his feet, knocking over the bucket. "Where's my *fucking* money, and what did you do with my men?"

"I'm afraid they can't come to the phone anymore. That's why I'm calling."

"You have no idea who you're dealing with," Mr. C bit out.

"On the contrary, you are the one at that particular disadvantage—as well as so many others." When Mr. C was about to snap, the guy cut him off. "Here's what we're going to do. I'm going to call you at nightfall with a location. You, and you alone, are going to meet me there. If anyone comes with you, I will know, and you will never hear from me again."

Mr. C was used to feeling disdain for others—came with the job when all you dealt with were two-bit street thugs and strapped drug addicts. But this guy on the other end of the connection? Self-controlled. Calm.

A professional.

Mr. C dialed back his temper. "I don't need to play games—"

"Yes, you do. Because if you want drugs to sell, you need to come to me."

Mr. C got quiet. This was either a lunatic with delusions of grandeur, or . . . somebody with true power. Like, maybe the one who'd been killing off all the middlemen in the Caldwell drug trade over the last year.

"Where and when?" he said gruffly.

There was a dark laugh. "Answer your phone at nightfall, and you'll find out."

FORTY-THREE

Layla couldn't speak as Payne's words sank in.

"No," she said to the other female. "No, Havers told me . . . there is nothing that can be done."

"Medically, that may well be true. I may have another way, however. I don't know whether it will work, but if you'll allow me, I'd like to do what I can."

For a moment, Layla could only breathe.

"I don't . . ." She felt the flat plane of her stomach. "What will you do to me?"

"I'm not sure, to be honest." Payne shrugged. "In fact, it hadn't even dawned on me that it might help your situation. But I have been known to heal that which needs healing. Again, I'm not sure whether it applies here. We could try, though—and it won't hurt you. That I can promise."

Layla searched the fighter's face. "Why . . . would you do this for me?"

Payne frowned and focused elsewhere. "You do not need to know the whys."

"Yes, I do."

That profile grew positively cold. "You and I are sisters in my mother's tyranny—casualties of her grand plan for the way things must be. We were both jailed by her in different ways, you as a Chosen, myself as her blooded daughter. There is nothing I will not do to aid you."

Layla lay back. She had never before considered herself a casualty of the mother of the race. Except . . . as she considered her desperation for a family, her sense of rootlessness, her very lack of identity outside of her service as a Chosen . . . she had to wonder. Free will had led her here to this horrid spot, but at least she had picked the route and the means. As a member of the Scribe Virgin's special class of females, she had had no such choice, about anything in her life.

Anything at all, really.

She was losing the pregnancy; this was self-evident. And if Payne thought there was a chance of . . .

"Do what you will," she said roughly. "And I thank you no matter the outcome."

Payne nodded once. Then she brought up her hands, flexing them, the fingers flaring wide. "May I touch your stomach?"

Layla pushed down the covers. "Must I take off my shirt altogether?"

"No."

Just as well. Even the shift of the duvet heralded a further cramping, the minute change in weight cause for—

"You are in such pain," the other female murmured.

Layla didn't answer as she exposed the skin of her stomach. Clearly, her expression had already said enough.

"Just relax. This shouldn't cause you any distress—"

As contact was made, Layla jerked her head up. The fighter's hands were warm like bathwater as they landed ever so softly on her lower abdomen. Soothing like bathwater as well. Strangely soothing, as a matter of fact.

"Does this hurt you?" Payne asked.

"No. It feels . . ." As another cramping geared itself up, she gripped the sheets, bracing herself—

Except the crest of the pain didn't rise as it had previously, surely as if the sensation were a great, cragged mountain, the top of which had been sheared off.

It was the first relief she'd gotten since it had all started.

With a groan of submission, she let her head go lax, the pillows cushioning a sudden weariness that told her just how much discomfort had been in her body.

"And now we begin."

All at once, the lamp across the room flickered . . . and then went out.

Its illumination was soon replaced, however.

From Payne's gentle hands, a soft glow began to emanate, the warmth of her touch intensifying, that strange, wondrous easing seeming to penetrate beneath the skin, and the muscle, and any bone that was in the way . . . going directly into Layla's womb.

And then there was an explosion of sorts.

With a hiss, she gave herself up to the great surge of energy that abruptly burrowed into her, that heat never burning and yet boiling away the pain, lifting the agony up and out of her flesh surely as the steam from a pot rose and drifted away.

But it was not over. A great flush of euphoria sped throughout her body, its golden tendrils pulsating out of her pelvic area and flowing up through her torso to her mind and her very soul as her legs and arms tingled as well.

Oh, great, poignant relief . . .

Oh, incredible power . . .

Oh, sweet saving grace.

The healing was still not over, however.

In the midst of the maelstrom, Layla felt a . . . what was it? A shifting in her womb. A tightening, mayhap? But not a cramping, no, not that. More as if that which had been lagging found a bracing strength.

She became gradually aware that her teeth were chattering.

Looking down her body, she saw that everything was trembling, and that was not all.

Her physical form was glowing. Every inch of her skin was as a shade on a lamp, revealing the light beneath, her clothes acting as frail barriers to that which was streaming from her.

In the illumination, Payne's face was harsh, as if there were a great cost to her in transferring the wondrous healing to another. And Layla would have moved away, stopped this, if she could have—because the other female began to look positively haggard. There was no way to break the connection, however; she had no control of her limbs, no way of even speaking.

It seemed to last forever, the vital communion between them.

When Payne finally jerked back, breaking the link, she slumped off the bed, landing in a heap on the floor.

Layla opened her mouth to shout. Tried to reach for her savior. Strained against her body's still-glowing deadweight.

But there was naught she could do.

The last thing that registered before she lost consciousness was her concern for the other female. And then all went dark.

FORTY-FOUR

Quinn woke up with a hard-on.

He lay on his back, his hips moving on their own, the rolling motion stroking that erection against the weight of the duvet and the sheets. For a moment, as he lingered in that half-awake stage before true consciousness arrived, he imagined it was Blay creating the friction, the male's palms sliding up and down . . . in a preamble to some mouth action.

It was when he reached out to bury his fingers in that red hair that he realized he was alone: His hands found only sheets.

In a fit of hope-springs-eternal, he threw out an arm, patting the space next to him, ready to find that warm, male body.

Just more sheets. That were cold.

"Fuck," he breathed.

Opening his eyes, the reality of where he was hit hard and deflated his arousal. In spite of the hookups, those two amazing, pounding sessions, Blay was right now, at this very moment, waking up with Saxton.

Probably having sex with the guy.

Oh, God, he was going to throw the hell up.

The idea that Blay was touching another, riding another, licking and stroking another—his fucking cousin, as a matter of fact—was nearly as unbearable as the Layla shit. The fact of the matter was, courtesy of what had gone down, any attraction Qhuinn had for the guy had been magnified instead of diminished.

Great. Another round of good news.

It was with absolutely no enthusiasm whatsoever that Qhuinn dragged himself out of bed and into the bathroom. He didn't want to turn the light on, had no interest in seeing that he looked like dog shit, but shaving with nothing save touch to go by was not the brightest idea.

As he flicked the switch, he blinked hard, a headache starting to pound right behind both his eyes. No doubt he needed to eat again, but for fuck's sake, his body's relentless demands were getting him down.

Starting the water in the sink, he picked up his Edge shaving gel and filled his palm with a little swirl. As he rubbed his hands together to puff the stuff up, he thought about his cousin. He had a feeling, although he didn't know it for certain, that Saxton would use an old-fashioned brush to suds his jaw and cheeks up. And no Gillette razors for him. Probably had a barber's thing with a mother-of-pearl handle.

Qhuinn's father had had one of those. And his brother had been given one with initials on it after his transition.

Along with that signet ring.

Well, good for them. Besides, given that those two were both dead, it wasn't like they were shaving anymore.

When his face was covered with white, just like the landscape outside, he picked up his regular, pedestrian Mach 3 with its disposable head. . . .

For no apparent reason, he thought maybe he should put a new one on.

Yeah, like a fresh, super-sharp, clean one.

Qhuinn rolled his eyes at himself. Nothing like having your self-worth wrapped up in three little blades and a moisturizing strip. Real fucking logical, that one.

Self-administered ass slap aside, he started rummaging through the drawers under the counters, pulling them out, inventorying all manner of bath and beauty crap that he never used, never looked at.

Pulling out the last drawer, the one closest to the floor, he stopped. Frowned. Bent down.

There was a little black velvet box in there, the kind of thing you put jewelry in. Except he didn't own any, and certainly not from Reinhardt's, that highbrow place downtown. As no one else stayed in his room, he wondered if maybe it had been there since he'd moved in and he'd just never seen it?

Taking the box out, he flicked the lid and—

"Son of a bitch."

Inside, like they were worth something, were all his gunmetal gray earrings, as well as the hoop he'd always worn in his lower lip.

Fritz must have collected them when cleaning one night, and put them in the box. Only explanation—because Qhuinn certainly hadn't bothered with them after he'd taken them out one by one. He'd just tossed them in the back of one of the bathroom cabinets.

Qhuinn fingered the steel links, thinking back to when he'd bought them and put them in. His father had been mortified; his mother, too—to the point where she'd excused herself from Last Meal and taken to her private quarters for a full twenty-four hours after he'd waltzed into the dining room wearing them.

The piercing place had told him not to put the hoops in until the studs that had been used to make the holes had had a chance to heal up. But that advice was for humans. Within a couple of hours, everything was good to go and he'd done the swap.

In Blay's loo, as a matter of fact.

Qhuinn frowned, remembering the moment he'd stepped out into the guy's bedroom. Blay had been over on the bed, nursing a Corona, watching TV. His head had turned, his expression open and relaxed— until he'd taken a look at Qhuinn.

His face had tightened up ever so subtly. The kind of thing that, unless you knew a person really, really well, you wouldn't notice. But Qhuinn had.

At the time, he'd assumed it was because the obvi-Goth shit had been a little much for Mr. Conservative. But now, thinking back on it, he recalled something else. Blay had refocused on the plasma screen . . . and casually taken a pillow and put it on his lap.

He must have gotten hard.

As Qhuinn recast that whole scene in his head, his own sex thickened again.

Except that was a waste of time, wasn't it.

Staring at those goddamned earrings, he thought about his rebellions and his anger and his fucked-up idea of what he had to have to be happy in life.

A female. If he could find one who'd take him.

What . . . a lie . . . that would have been.

Funny, cowardice came in many forms, didn't it. You didn't have to be shrinking in a corner, shaking like a pussy and sniveling. Hell no. You could be a big, loud noise with a tough attitude and a face full of piercings and a snarl to show the world . . . and still be nothing but a cocksucking coward. After all, Saxton might wear three-piece suits and cravats and loafers, but the male knew who he was, and he wasn't afraid of having what he wanted.

And what do you know, Blay was waking up in the guy's bed.

Qhuinn closed the lid and put the piercings back where he'd found them. Then he glanced up into the mirror. What was he doing again? he thought as he looked at his face.

Oh, yeah. Shaving.

That was it.

About twenty minutes later, Qhuinn left his room. Walking down the hall of statues, he passed by the closed doors to Wrath's study and kept going.

As he continued onward, it was hard to stare into the second-story sitting room, hard to stay cool as that couch came into view.

Never going to look at that piece of furniture in the same way. Hell, maybe even all sofas were ruined for him, forever.

At Layla's door, he leaned in and put his ear to the panels. When he didn't hear anything, he wondered exactly what he thought he'd find out that way.

He knocked quietly. When there was no answer, he was gripped at the throat by an irrational fear, and without conscious thought, he threw open the door.

Light poured into the darkness.

His first thought was that she had died; that Havers, the son of a bitch, had lied, and the miscarriage had gotten out of hand and killed her: Layla was unmoving as she lay against the pillows, her mouth slightly open, her hands clasped over her chest as if she'd been arranged by a funeral director who had respect for the dead.

Except . . . something was different, and it took him a minute to figure out what it was.

There was no overwhelming scent of blood. In fact, only her delicate, cinnamon fragrance marked the air, freshening it in a way that brightened the whole room up.

Was the miscarriage finally over?

"Layla?" he said, even though he'd told her that if he found her asleep, he would let her stay that way.

It was a relief to see her brows twitch as her name registered to her brain, even under the veil of sleep.

He had the sense that if he were to say it again, she would wake.

Seemed cruel to force consciousness on her. What did she have to greet her when she woke up? The pain she'd been feeling? The sense of loss?

Fuck that.

Qhuinn quietly ducked out, shut the door and just stood there. He wasn't sure what to do with himself. Wrath had told him to stay home, even if John Matthew went out—he guessed it was a kind of compassionate leave from the *ahstrux nohtrum* thing. And he did appreciate it. There was so little he could do to help Layla—at least he could stick around in case she needed anything. Soft drink. Aspirin. Shoulder to cry on.

You did this to her.

Going by the chiming that floated out from that godforsaken sitting room, he figured he'd missed First Meal. Nine p.m. Yup, he'd slept through it, and just as well. If he'd had to sit at the table and spend forty-five minutes in the company of nearly two dozen people who were trying not to stare at him, he'd lose his fucking mind.

The sound of someone walking down below in the foyer brought his head up.

Without any particular thought or plan, he wandered over to the balustrade and looked down.

Payne, V's ass-kicking sister, was coming out of the dining room.

He didn't know the female all that well, but he respected the shit out of her. Impossible not to, given the way she handled herself in the field . . . tough, really tough. At the moment, however, Dr. Manello's *shellan* looked like she'd been beaten up in a bar fight: She was walking slowly, her feet shuffling across the mosaic floor, her body stooped, her grip on her mate's arm all that appeared to be keeping her upright.

Had she been injured in some hand to hand?

No scent of blood.

Dr. Manello said something to her that didn't carry, but then the guy nodded in the direction of the billiards room—like he was asking her if she wanted to go in there.

They headed that way at a snail's pace.

Given that he didn't appreciate people staring, Qhuinn backed off from the railing and waited until the coast was clear. Then he jogged down the grand staircase.

Food. Workout. Recheck on Layla.

That was going to be his night.

Heading for the kitchen, he found himself wondering where Blay was. What he was doing. Whether he was out fighting or in for the evening and . . .

Given that he didn't know where Saxton was, he stopped that line of inquiry right there.

If Qhuinn had been off rotation, and able to spend some P-time with the guy, he knew what he'd be doing.

And Saxton, his cocksucking cousin, was no fool.

FORTY-FIVE

Assail's lack of feeding finally caught up with him about five hours after night fell. He was putting on his shirt, a pale blue button-down with French cuffs, when his hands started to shake so badly, there was no fastening the damn thing closed over his chest. And then the exhaustion hit, so overwhelming that he swayed on his feet.

Cursing under his breath, he went over to his bureau. On the polished mahogany top, his vial and spoon were waiting, and he took care of business in two quick inhales, one for each nostril.

Nasty habit—and one he fell back into only when he really needed it.

At least the blow took care of the tiredness. But he was going to have to find a female. Soon. Indeed, it was a miracle he'd lasted this long: The last time he'd taken a vein had been months ago, and the experience had been less than enthralling, a fast-and-dirty with a female of the species well versed in providing sustenance to needful males. For a price.

What a nuisance.

After arming himself and retrieving a black cashmere overcoat, he

headed down the stairs and unlocked the steel sliding door. As he opened the way into the first floor, he was greeted by the sounds of guns being checked.

In the kitchen, the twins were running several forties through their paces.

"Have you made the call?" Assail asked Ehric.

"As you said."

"And?"

"He's going to be there and he's coming alone. Do you need weapons?"

"Have them." He picked up the keys to the Range Rover from a silver dish on the counter. "We're taking my vehicle. In the event someone is injured."

After all, only an idiot took the word of an enemy, and his SUV came with an undercarriage device that could be very helpful if there was a mass attack.

Boom.

Fifteen minutes later, the three of them were crossing the bridge into Caldwell, and as Assail drove along, he was reminded of why bringing the cousins here had been an inspired idea: Not only were they good backup, they were not inclined to waste breath on useless conversation.

The silence was a welcome fourth passenger in their transport.

Over on the downtown side of the Hudson, he got off at an exit that curled around and emptied out beneath the Northway. Proceeding parallel to the river, he entered the forest of thick pylons that held up the roads, the landscape bald, dark, and essentially empty.

"Park over here to the right about a hundred meters," Ehric said from the back.

Assail pulled to the side, popped the curb, and stopped on the shoulder.

The three of them emerged into the cold, their overcoats open, guns in hand, eyes scanning. As they walked forward, Ehric's twin brought up the rear, the three Hefty bags from the garage in one of his hands, the black plastic making a rustling noise as they all went along.

Above them, traffic growled by, the cars moving at a steady pace, an ambulance siren wailing in a high-pitched scream, a heavy truck rumbling over the girders. As Assail inhaled deeply, the air was icy in his sinuses, any smells of dirt or dead fish killed by the cold.

"Straight ahead," Ehric said.

They calmly and steadily crossed the asphalt and entered upon more of the hard, frozen ground. With the great concrete slabs of the road blocking out the sun, nothing grew here, but there was life—of a sort. Homeless humans in makeshift dwellings of cardboard and tarps were hunkered down against the winter, their bodies wrapped up so tight, you couldn't tell which way they were facing.

Considering their preoccupation with staying alive, he was not worried about interference from them. Besides, no doubt they were used to being peripherals in this sort of business, and knew not to intrude.

And if they did? He would not hesitate to put them out of their misery.

The first sign that their enemy had shown was a stench on the wind. Assail was not particularly well versed in the ways of the Lessening Society and its members, but his keen nose was not able to ascertain any nuances within the bad smell. So he took that to mean that instructions had been followed and this was not a case of thousands arriving at the scene—although it was possible that the Omega's denizens had only one bouquet.

They would soon find out.

Assail and his males stopped. And waited.

A moment later, a single *lesser* stepped out from behind a pylon.

Ah, interesting. This one had been a "client" before, coming with cash to accept measures of X or heroin. He'd been right on the edge of being eliminated, his volume of purchasing just under the cutoff of middleman qualification.

Which was the only reason he still breathed . . . and had therefore, at some point, been turned into a slayer. Come to think of it, the fellow hadn't been around lately, so one could surmise that he'd been adjusting to his new life. Or non-life, as the case may be.

"Jesus . . . Christ," the *lesser* said, clearly catching their scents.

"I meant it when I said I was your enemy," Assail drawled.

"Vampires . . . ?"

"Which puts you and me in a curious position, does it not." Assail nodded at the twins. "My associates came here in good faith last night. They were equally surprised with what they discovered when your men arrived. Certain . . . aggressive behaviors . . . on our part were exhibited before things were sorted. My apologies."

As Assail nodded, the three Hefty bags were tossed over.

Ehric's voice was dry. "We are prepared to tell you where the rest of them are."

"Pending the disposition of this transaction," Assail added.

The *lesser* glanced down, but otherwise showed no reaction. Which suggested he was a professional. "You brought the product?"

"You paid for it."

The slayer's eyes narrowed. "You're gonna do business with me."

"I can assure you I'm not here for the pleasure of your company." As Assail motioned with his hand, Ehric took out a wrapped package. "A few ground rules first. You will contact me directly. I will not accept calls from anyone else within your organization. You may delegate drop-off and pickup to whomever you wish, but you will provide me with the identity and number of the representatives you are sending. If there is any kind of ambush, or if there is any deviation from my two rules, I will cease to transact with you. Those are my only stipulations."

The *lesser* looked back and forth between Assail and the cousins. "What if I want to buy more than this?"

Assail had considered this probability. He hadn't spent the past twelve months getting middlemen to shoot themselves in the head for nothing—and he wasn't about to cede his hard-won power to anyone. This was a unique opportunity, however. If the Lessening Society wanted to make some money on the streets, he was fine with providing them the drugs to do so. It wasn't as if this foul-smelling son of a bitch was going to be able to get to Benloise because Assail was going to make sure that didn't happen. More to the point, Assail had a rate-limiting issue inherent in his business model—with just the three of them, he had more product than he had sellers.

So it was time to start outsourcing. His stranglehold on the city complete, the next phase was to handpick some third parties for contract work, so to speak.

"We're going to start slowly and see how it goes," Assail murmured. "You need me. I'm the source. So it's your choice how we proceed. I am certainly not . . . how do you say . . . disinclined to increase your orders. Over time."

"How do I know you're not working with the Brotherhood?"

"If I were, I would have them ambush you right now." He indicated the bags at the feet of the slayer. "Further, as a gesture of good faith, and in recognition of your losses, I have credited you three thousand dollars in this delivery. One grand for each of our, shall we say, misinterpretations from last night."

The slayer's brows popped.

In the silence that followed, the wind blew around them all, coats sweeping out, the *lesser's* jacket collar whistling.

Assail was content to wait for a reaction. There were one of two answers: Yes, in which case Ehric was going to throw over the package. No, at which time the three of them opened fire on the fucker, disabled him, and stabbed him back to the Omega.

Either was acceptable to him. But he was hoping for the former.

There was money to be made. For both sides.

Sola kept her distance from the quartet of men who had gathered under the bridge: lingering on the fringes, she used her binocs to focus on the meeting.

Mr. Mystery Man, a.k.a. the Great Roadside Houdini, was backed up by two huge bodyguards who were mirror images of each other. From all appearances, it seemed that he was running the meeting, and that was not a surprise—and she could guess at the agenda.

Sure enough, the twin on the left stepped forward and gave a package the size of a child's lunch box to the man who was on his own.

As she waited for the deal to wind down, she knew she was taking her life into her own hands on this one—and not because she was under the bridge after dark.

Considering the run-in she'd had with the man the night before, it was highly doubtful he was going to appreciate her getting on his tail, following him out here, and playing third-party witness to his illegal activities. But she had spent most of the last twenty-four hours thinking about him—and getting pissed off. It was a free fucking country, and if she wanted to be out here on public property, she was allowed.

He wanted privacy? Then he should take care of business somewhere other than out in the goddamn open.

As her temper resurged, she gritted her teeth . . . and knew that this was her worst character defect at work.

For her entire life, she had been the type to do whatever she was told not to. Of course, when that involved things like, No, you can't

have a cookie before dinner, or, No, you can't take the car out; you're grounded, or . . . No, you should not go see your father in prison . . . the implications were very different from what was going down in front of her.

No, you may not go back to that house.

No, you may not watch me anymore.

Yeah, whatever, big shots. *She* was going to decide when she'd had enough, thank you very much. And at the moment? She had *not* had enough.

Besides, there was another angle to her tenacity: she didn't like losing her nerve, and that was what had happened last night. As she'd pulled away from her confrontation with that man, it had been from a place of fear—and that was *not* going to be the way she ran her life. Ever since that tragedy, oh, so long ago, when things had changed forever, she had decided—vowed, was more like it—that she would never again be afraid of anything.

Not pain. Not death. Not the unknown.

And certainly not a man.

Sola tightened up the focus, closing in on his face. Thanks to the city's glow, there was enough for her to see it properly, and yup, it was just as she remembered. God, his hair was so damn black, almost as if he'd colored it. And his eyes—narrowed, aggressive. And his expression, so haughty and in control.

Frankly, he looked too classy to be what he was. Then again, maybe he was cut from the Benloise cloth of drug dealer.

Shortly thereafter, the two sides went their separate ways: the single man turned and walked in the direction he'd come from, a collection of barely filled trash bags slung over his shoulder; the other three recrossing the pavement, returning to the Range Rover.

Sola jogged back to her rental car, her dark bodysuit and ski mask helping her blend into the shadows. Getting behind the wheel of the Ford, she ducked down out of sight and used a mirror to monitor the one-way that ran underneath the bridge.

The road was the only exit available. Unless the man was willing to risk a pullover by the CPD for going against traffic.

Moments later, the Range Rover passed her by. After allowing it to get slightly ahead, she hit her own gas and slid into position about a block behind.

When Benloise had given her the assignment, he'd provided her with the make and model of the man's SUV, in addition to that address out on the Hudson. Not the name, though.

All she had was that real estate trust and its single trustee.

As she tracked the threesome, she memorized the license plate. One of her friends down at the police station might be able to help with that; although, given that the house was owned by a legal entity, she surmised he'd done the same with automobile.

Whatever. There was one thing she was sure of.

Wherever he was going next, she was going to be there.

FORTY-SIX

The shout blasted through the dim bedroom, loud, sharp, unexpected.

As it reverberated in her ears, Layla didn't immediately know who had woken her up with it. What had—

Glancing down, she knew she was sitting upright, the sheets crushed in her tight hands, her heart pounding, her rib cage pumping.

Looking around, she found that her mouth was wide open . . .

Closing her jaw, she knew she must have made the sound. There was no one else in the room. And the door was shut.

Lifting her hands, she twisted her wrists so they were palm up, then palm down. The illumination in the room, such as it was, was not coming from her flesh anymore. It was the bathroom light.

Jerking herself to the side, she peered over the edge of the bed.

Payne was no longer lying in a heap. The female must have left— or been carried out?

Her first thought was to go and find Vishous's sister, just jump up and start searching. Although she hadn't understood exactly what had transpired between them, there was no doubt that it had cost the fighter dearly.

But Layla stopped herself, as worry for her own well-being took over: Her awareness shifted from the external to the internal, her mind burrowing into her body, searching out and expecting to find the cramping, the warm welling between her legs, the strange lagging aches that rode her bones.

Nothing.

As a room could go silent when all who were within it went quiet, so too could the corporeal form when all its component parts had no complaints.

Shifting the covers from herself, she moved her legs over so that they dangled off the edge of the high mattress. Subconsciously, she braced herself for the god-awful sensation of blood leaving her womb. When there was nothing of the sort, she wondered if the miscarriage hadn't concluded itself. But hadn't Havers said that it would be another week?

It took courage to stand up. Even though she supposed that was ridiculous.

Still nothing.

Layla went into the bathroom slowly, expecting at any moment for the onslaught of symptoms to return and take her down to her knees. She waited for the pain to strike, for those rhythmic cramps to come back, for that process to once again establish dominance over her body and her mind.

I don't know whether it will work, but if you're willing, I'd like to do what I can.

Layla all but ripped off her clothing, shedding what covered her in a mad dash. And then she was on the toilet.

No bleeding.

No cramps.

Half of her went into a sorrow so deep, she feared there was no bottom to the emotion—in a strange way, during the process of the miscarriage, she'd felt as though she'd still had some kind of connection with her young. If it was over? Then the death was complete—even though logically she knew there was naught that had lived or was capable of survival; otherwise, the pregnancy wouldn't have terminated itself.

The other half of her was struck by a resonant hope.

What if . . .

She took a shower quickly, in spite of the fact that she didn't really know why she was rushing, or where she would go.

Looking down at her stomach, she ran her soapy hands over the smooth, flat stretch of skin.

"Please . . . anything you want, take anything you want . . . give me this life inside of me, and you can take anything else. . . ."

She was talking to the Scribe Virgin, of course—not that the race's mother was listening anymore.

"Give me my young . . . let me keep it . . . *please*. . . ."

The desperation she felt was nearly as bad as the physical stuff had been, and she stumbled out of the shower, drying herself roughly and throwing on clean something-or-others.

From what she'd watched of the television, human women had tests they could take themselves, sticks and whatnot apparently designed to inform them of their body's procreational mysteries. Vampires had nothing of the sort—at least, not of which she was aware.

But males knew. They always knew.

Bursting out of her room, she hurried in the direction of the hall of statues, praying that she ran into someone, anyone—

Except Qhuinn.

No, she didn't want him to be the one who figured out whether a miracle had happened . . . or nothing had changed. That was just too cruel.

The first door she came to was Blaylock's and she knocked on it after a hesitation. Blay had known about the situation all along. And at his core, he was a very good male, a strong, good male.

When there was no answer, she cursed and turned away. She hadn't checked the time, but given that the shutters were up and there was no scent of dinner being served down below, it was probably in the middle of the night. No doubt he had gone fighting—

"Layla?"

She wrenched around. Blay was leaning through the doorway of his room, his expression one of surprise.

"I'm so sorry—" As her voice cracked, she had to clear it. "I . . . I—"

"What's wrong? Are you—whoa, easy, there. Here, let's get you to sit down."

As something came up and caught her bottom, she became aware that he'd settled her on the gold-leafed bench just outside his room.

He knelt down in front of her and took her hands. "Can I get Qhuinn for you? I think he's—"

"Tell me if I'm still pregnant." As his eyes peeled wide, she squeezed his palms. "I need to know. Something . . ." She wasn't sure whether Payne wanted her to talk about what had gone on between them. "I just need to know whether it's over or not. Can you . . . please, I need to know. . . ."

As she started to babble, he put his hand on her upper arm and stroked it. "Calm down. Just take a deep breath—here, breathe with me. That's it . . . okay . . ."

She did her best to comply, focusing on the steady, even tone of his deep voice.

"I want to call Doc Jane, all right?" When she started to argue, he shook his head firmly. "You stay right here. Promise me that you won't go anywhere. I'm just going to grab my phone. You stay here."

For some reason, her teeth started to chatter. Odd, as it wasn't cold.

A second later, the soldier came back and knelt down again. He had his phone up to his ear, and he was talking.

"Okay, Jane's coming right now," he said as he put the thing away. "And I'm going to hang here with you."

"But you can tell, can't you? You can tell, you can scent it—"

"Shhh . . ."

"I'm sorry." She turned her face away, dropping it down low. "I don't mean to drag you into this. I just . . . I'm so sorry."

"It's okay. You don't worry about that. We're just going to wait for Doc Jane. Hey, Layla, look at me. *Look* at me."

When she finally glanced into his blue eyes, she was struck by his kindness. Especially as the male smiled gently.

"I'm glad you came to me," he said. "Whatever's wrong, we'll take care of it."

Staring into that strong, handsome face, feeling the reassurance he offered so generously, sensing the marrow-deep decency of the fighter, she thought of Qhuinn.

"Now I know why he's in love with you," she blurted.

Blay went positively white, all the color draining out of his cheeks. "What . . . did you say . . . ?"

"I'm here," Doc Jane called out from down by the head of the stairs. "I'm right here!"

As the doctor came running down to them, Layla closed her eyes.

Shit. What had just come out of her mouth.

*　　*　　*

Downtown, at the warehouse Xcor had spent the day in, the leader of the Band of Bastards finally emerged into the cold darkness of the night.

He had his weapons on his body, and his phone in his hands.

Sometime during the long daylight hours, the sense that he'd forgotten something had finally resolved itself, and he'd recalled that he'd told his soldiers to decamp from the location. Which explained why none of them came before dawn.

Their new lair was not downtown. And upon further reflection, it had been a miscalculation on his part to try to establish a headquarters in this part of town, even if things had appeared deserted: Too much risk of discovery, complication or compromising circumstances.

As they had learned the night before with that visit from the Shadow.

Closing his eyes briefly, he thought it was odd how events could cascade so far beyond one's original intentions. If it hadn't been for that Shadow's intrusion, he wondered whether he would ever have been able to track his Chosen. And if he hadn't followed her to that clinic, he wouldn't have learned that she was with young . . . or made his discovery about the Brotherhood.

Casting himself into the brisk wind, he materialized on the rooftop of the highest skyscraper in the city. The gusts were vicious at the high altitude, whipping his full-length coat out around his body, his scythe's holster all that kept it on his back. His hair, which had been getting longer and longer, tangled and obstructed his vision, obscuring the view of the city stretching out beneath his feet.

He turned in the direction of the King's mountain, the great rise distant on the horizon.

"We thought you were dead."

Xcor pivoted on his combat boots, the wind plastering his hair back from his face.

Throe and the others were standing in a semi-circle around him.

"Alas, as I live and breathe." Except, in truth, he only felt dead. "How fare the new accommodations?"

"Where were you?" Throe demanded.

"Elsewhere." As he blinked, he remembered searching that odd, foggy landscape, going around and around the base of that mountain. "The new accommodations—how are they?"

"Fine," Throe muttered. "May I have a word with you?"

Xcor cocked a brow. "Indeed, you appear anxious to do so."

The pair of them stepped to the side, leaving the others in the wind—and coincidentally, he happened to face the direction of the Brotherhood's compound.

"You cannot do that," Throe said over the loud, frosty gusts. "You cannot just disappear for the day again. Not in this political climate— we assumed you'd been killed, or worse, captured."

There was a time when Xcor would have countered the censure with a sharp rebuff or something far more physical. But his soldier was correct. Things were different between the bunch of them—ever since he'd sent Throe into the belly of the beast, he had started to feel a reciprocal connection with these males.

"I assure you, it was not my intention."

"So what happened? Where were you?"

In that moment, Xcor saw before himself a crossroads. One direction took him and his soldiers to the Brotherhood, into a bloody conflict that would change their lives forever for good or ill. The other?

He thought of his Chosen being held upright by those two fighters, as carefully handled as cut glass.

Which was it going to be.

"I was in the warehouse," he heard himself say after a moment. "I spent the day in the warehouse. I returned there distracted, and it was too late to take myself anywhere else. I passed the daylight hours beneath the floor, and my phone had no reception. I came here as soon as I left the building."

Throe frowned. "It's well past sundown."

"I lost track of time."

That was the extent of information he was willing to give. No more. And his soldier must have sensed that line of demarcation, for although Throe's brows remained tight, he followed up no more.

"I require only a short tally here and then we shall depart to find our enemies," Xcor declared.

As he took out his phone, he could not read the screen, but he knew how to check his voice mails. There were some hang-ups—Throe and the others, in all likelihood. And then there was a message from someone he'd been expecting to hear from.

"It is I," Elan, son of Larex, announced. There was a pause, as if in his head, he was piping in a trumpet fanfare. "The Council is meeting on the morrow at midnight. I thought you should know. The location is at an estate here in town, the owners of which having recently moved back from their safe house. Rehvenge was quite insistent with regard to the scheduling, so I can only guess that our fair *leahdyre* is carrying a message from the king. I shall keep you fully informed of what transpires, but I do *not* expect to see you. Be well, my ally."

As he hit *delete*, Xcor bared his fangs, and the resurgence of his aggression felt good—a return to normal.

How dare that effete little aristocrat tell him to do anything.

"The Council is meeting tomorrow night," he said as he put his phone away.

"Where? When?" Throe asked.

Xcor looked out over the city toward the mountain. Then he turned his back upon that compass point.

"The fine Elan has determined we shall not be there. What he fails to realize is that that will be my choice. Not his."

As if neglecting to impart an address would keep him away if he desired otherwise?

"Enough conversation." He strode over to the gathering of his soldiers. "Let us go down onto the streets and engage as warriors do."

Between his shoulder blades, his scythe started talking to him once again, her voice keen and clear in his mind, her blood-thirsty words like a lover's entreaty.

Her silence had been strangely unsettling.

It was with no small relief that he dematerialized from the lofty heights of the skyscraper, his iron will training his molecules toward the ground and into the field of engagement. In so many ways, the prior twenty-four hours had felt as though they had been lived by another.

He was back in his old skin now, however.

And ready to kill.

FORTY-SEVEN

huinn was eleven miles into a twenty-mile run on the tread-mill when the door to the training center's workout room opened.

The second he saw who it was, he hopped off onto the side rails and banged on the *stop* button: Blay was standing in the jambs, his eyes jumping around, his face all fucked-up—and not because someone had beaten him or something.

"What happened?" Qhuinn demanded.

Blay shoved a hand into his red hair. "Ah, Layla's down in the clinic—"

"*Shit.*" He jumped off and headed for the door. "What's wrong—"

"No, no, nothing. She's just in for a checkup. That's all." The guy stepped to the side, clearing the exit. "I figured you'd want to know."

Qhuinn frowned and stopped where he was. As he scrutinized the other male's expression, he came to a conclusion that made him anxious: Blay was fronting about something. Hard to pinpoint exactly how he knew that, but then again, after being friends with someone since childhood, you learned to read their minutiae.

"Are you okay?" he asked the guy.

Blay motioned in the direction of the clinic. "Yeah. Sure. She's in the exam room right now."

Right, clearly, the topic was closed. Whatever it was.

Snapping into action, Qhuinn jogged down the corridor, and nearly burst through the closed door. At the last minute, though, a sense of decorum pulled him up short. Some examinations of pregnant females involved very private places—and even though he and Layla had had sex, they certainly weren't intimate like that.

He knocked. "Layla? You in there?"

There was a pause and then Doc Jane opened up. "Hi, come on in. I'm glad Blay found you."

The physician's face gave nothing away—and that made him psychotic. Generally speaking, when doctors did that professionally pleasant thing, it was not good news.

Looking beyond V's female, he focused on Layla—but Blay was who he grabbed onto, snagging a hold on the guy's arm.

"Stay if you can?" Qhuinn said out of the corner of his mouth.

Blay seemed surprised, but he complied with the request, letting the door shut them all in together.

"What's going on?" Qhuinn demanded.

Checkup, his ass: Layla's eyes were wide and a little wild, her hands jittery as they played with her loose, tangled hair.

"There's been a change," Doc Jane said with hesitation.

Pause.

Qhuinn nearly screamed. "Okay, listen up, people—if someone doesn't tell me what the fuck is going on, I'm going to lose my goddamn mind all over this room—"

"I'm pregnant," Layla blurted.

And this is a change how? he wondered, his head starting to hum.

"As in the miscarriage appears to have stopped," Jane said. "And she's still pregnant."

Qhuinn blinked. Then he shook his head—and not as in back and forth, as in how someone would masturbate a snow globe.

"I don't get it."

Doc Jane sat on a rolling stool, and opened a chart on her lap. "I gave her the blood test myself. There's a sliding scale of pregnancy hormones—"

"I'm going to be sick," Layla cut in. "Right now—"

Everybody rushed at the poor female, but Blay was the smart one.

He brought a wastepaper basket with him, and that was what the Chosen used.

As she was heaving, Qhuinn held her hair back and felt a little dizzy.

"She's *not* okay," he told the doctor.

Jane met his eyes over Layla's head. "This is a normal part of being pregnant. For female vampires, too, apparently—"

"But she's bleeding—"

"Not anymore. And I did an ultrasound. I can see the gestational sac. She is still pregnant—"

"Oh, shit!" Blay yelled.

For a split second, Qhuinn couldn't figure out why the guy was cursing. And then he realized . . . huh, the ceiling had traded places with the wall.

No, wait.

He was passing out.

His last conscious thought was that it was really cool of Blay to catch him as he went over like a tree in the forest.

In the context of the English language, there were many more important words than "in." There were fancy words, historic words, words that meant life or death. There were multi-syllabic tongue-twisters that required a sort out before speaking, and mission-critical pivotals that started wars or ended wars . . . and even poetic nonsensicals that were like a symphony as they left the lips.

Generally speaking, "in" did not play with the big boys. In fact, it barely had much of a definition at all, and, in the course of its working life, was usually nothing but a bridge, a conduit for the heavy lifters in any given sentence.

There was, however, one context in which that humble little two-letter, one-syllable jobbie was a BFD.

Love.

The difference between someone "loving" somebody versus being "in love" was a curb to the Grand Canyon. The head of a pin to the entire Midwest. An exhale to a hurricane.

Now I know why he . . .

As Blay sat on the floor of the exam room with Qhuinn's loose-as-a-goose body in his lap, he couldn't for the life of him remember what Layla had said next. Had it been "loves you"? In which case, well, yeah,

he knew that the guy loved him as a friend and had for decades. And that didn't change a thing.

Or had it been with the addition of the "in."

In which case, he was kind of considering taking Qhuinn's lead and having a little TO on the tile.

"How's my other patient doing?" Doc Jane asked as Layla collapsed back on the exam table.

"Breathing," Blay replied.

"He'll come around."

One would hope, Blay thought as he focused on Qhuinn's face—like those familiar features, even though he was out of it, could somehow answer the question one way or the other.

The Chosen couldn't possibly have said "in love."

Couldn't have been it. He simply refused to let two bouts of great sex rewrite someone else's words.

"Are you sure this is okay?" he heard Layla say to Doc Jane.

"The throwing up? According to what Ehlena told me earlier, it can most certainly be part of the symptoms of a successful pregnancy. In fact, it can be a sign that things are progressing well. It's the hormones."

"I don't have to return to Havers's, do I?"

"Well, Ehlena's coming back from visiting her father tonight. So we need to find out how much she's comfortable treating—and then see where you're at. I won't lie . . . I think this is a miracle."

"I agree."

While the females spoke, Blay kept his eyes on Qhuinn's closed lids. It was a miracle, all right. Straight up—

As if on cue, the guy came around, those thick, dark eyelashes batting as if they were trying to decide how serious he was about staying conscious.

"Layla!" he shouted as he burst upright.

Blay pushed himself backward, letting the guy go. Feeling a little stupid.

Especially as Qhuinn shot to his feet and went to the female.

Blay stayed where he was, settling back against the closed cupboards under the sink, his knees up, his hands on his thighs. Even though it tore him to pieces, he couldn't help but watch the two of them together, Qhuinn's dagger hand impossibly gentle as he smoothed the blond hair away from Layla's face.

He was saying something to her, something soft and reassuring.

Before Blay knew it, he was out in the hall, walking somewhere, anywhere. As hard as it was to accept compassion from Qhuinn . . . it was downright impossible to witness it being imparted on someone else—even if they more than deserved it.

The idea that Layla had been given in her needing exactly what he'd had for the last two days made his chest ache—but what was worse? It appeared that with her, the pneumatics had served their biological purpose. She was pregnant—and thanks to Payne, he had a feeling she was going to stay that way.

Overall, he'd done the right thing in going to V's sister the day before. Assuming that that had been the cause of the amazing turnaround. But still, and even though it didn't make sense, he felt—

"Are you okay?"

He stopped immediately, Qhuinn's voice a shock. One would figure the guy would have stayed with the Chosen.

Bracing himself, he shoved his hands in his pockets and took a deep breath before turning around.

"Yeah, I'm fine. Just figured you two would want some privacy."

"Thanks for catching me." The male lifted his palms. "I don't know what happened in there."

"Relief."

"I guess."

There was an awkward moment. Then again, they had specialized in them, hadn't they.

"Listen, I'm going to go back to the house." Blay tacked on a smile and hoped the guy bought it. "It's good to have a night off."

"Oh, yeah. Saxton's probably waiting for you."

Blay opened his mouth, but then caught the "why" that was about to fly out from between his lips. "Yup, he is. Take care of your girl. I'll see you at Last Meal, maybe."

As he strode off and ducked into the office, he knew he was being a coward for hiding behind a nonexistent relationship. But when you had a bad cut, you needed a Band-Aid.

Christ, no wonder Saxton had broken up with him.

What a fucking romantic.

FORTY-EIGHT

As Assail drove through the grand gates of an estate in the wealthy part of Caldwell, he was annoyed. Exhausted. On edge. And not just because he'd been doing cocaine regularly and not eating.

The cottage was over to the left, and he parked the Range Rover grille-first beneath one of the cheerful little windows. He would have preferred to have dematerialized here—so much less complicated. But after he'd dropped the twins off by that Goth club, the Iron Mask, he'd had to face the reality that if he didn't feed, he was not going to be able to go on.

He hated this. It wasn't that he minded the money it cost. It was more that he wasn't particularly attracted to the female—and did not appreciate her attempts to change that.

Swinging his door wide, he got out, and the cold air hitting his face slapped some awareness into him, making him cognizant of just how logy he'd been.

At that very moment, a car went by out on the street beyond, some kind of domestic sedan.

And then the quaint portal of the cottage opened.

Assail's fangs tingled as the female in between the jambs registered to his senses. Dressed in something black and lingerie-esque, she was ready for him, the heady scent of her arousal marking the air, although that wasn't what got his lust going. It was her vein, nothing more, nothing less . . .

Assail frowned and looked beyond the cottage, into the forest that rimmed the estate.

Through the skeletal trees, the rear lights of the car that had just passed by flared red. Then whoever it was turned the vehicle around, the headlights swinging in a fat circle—and then extinguishing.

Immediately, Assail went for his gun. "You go inside. We're not alone."

The female promptly canned the come-on and disappeared into the cottage, shutting the door with a bang.

Dematerializing into the woods would have been the best move, but of course, he was too damned starved for that—

Abruptly, the wind shifted direction and came at him, and his nostrils flared.

Assail growled softly—and not in a warning. More like a greeting, of sorts.

As if he would e'er forget that particular combination of pheromones.

His little burglar had turned the tables on him, doing to him what he had done to her the night before. How long had she been on his trail? he wondered, a shaft of respect driving through his chest at the same time he grew frustrated.

He did not like the idea that she might have seen him under the bridge. Knowing her, though, he couldn't rule that out.

Drawing in a long, slow breath, he caught nothing else of significance. Which meant she was alone.

Information gathering? For whom?

Assail pivoted back around to the cottage and smiled darkly. No doubt once he was inside she would close in . . . and far be it from him not to give her a show.

He knocked once, and the female opened up again.

"Are we okay?" she asked.

His eyes went over her face, and then lingered on her hair. It was dark. Thick. Rather like his little burglar's.

"All clear. Just a human with car trouble."

"So there's nothing to worry about?"

"Not a thing."

As relief eased the tension out of her face, he shut them in together and threw the lock.

"I'm so glad you came back to me again," the female said, letting the lace-trimmed halves of her satin robe fall back apart.

Tonight she was wearing a black negligee that pushed her breasts high and made her waist look like he could span it with only one of his hands. She smelled overdone: too much hand cream, body lotion, shampoo, conditioner, and perfume marking her body.

He really wished she wouldn't go to the effort.

With a quick shift of the eyes, Assail checked the position of all the windows. Naturally, none of them had changed: There were two narrow ones on either side of the stone fireplace. A stretch of three panes of glass over the sink. And then that bowed-out section over to the left that was above the built-in seat with its cushions and needlepoint pillows.

His burglar would choose the window to the right of the fireplace. It was out of the glow from the lantern over the front door, and in the lee of the chimney.

"Are you ready for me?" the female purred.

Assail ducked his hand into the inside of his jacket. The thousand dollars in cash was folded once, the ten hundred-dollar bills forming a thin folio.

Moving sinuously, he put his back to the bay window and the fireplace. For some reason, he didn't want his burglar to see him make payment.

The rest of what was going to happen, however, he very much wanted her to witness.

"Here."

As the female took the money, he didn't want her to count it. And she didn't.

"Thank you." She stepped back and put the bills in a red pottery jar. "Shall we?"

"Yes. We shall."

Assail closed in and assumed control, taking the female's face between his hands, tilting her head back, and kissing her hard. In response, she moaned, as if the unexpected advance was something she not only welcomed, but hadn't dared expect.

He was glad she enjoyed it. But her pleasure was not what this was about.

Moving her around, he took her over to the sofa that ran down the little cottage's far wall, pushing her with his body, using his strength to lay her out with her head in the direction of the fireplace. As she reclined, she cast her arms out to the sides, rolling her breasts upward until they strained the satin cups that covered them.

Assail mounted her fully clothed and with his coat on, his knee going between hers, one of his hands reaching down and pulling up that floor-length negligee—

"No, no," he said as she went to wind her arms around his neck. "I want to see you."

Bullshit. He wanted her to be seen from the window.

Whilst she complied readily, he went back to kissing her and getting that long skirting out of the way—and the second it was, she split her legs wide.

"Fuck me," the female said, arching under him.

Well, that wasn't going to be possible. He wasn't hard.

But not everyone needed to know that.

In order to appear impassioned, he shrugged his overcoat free of his shoulders, and then with a quick slash of his fangs, he bit through the negligee's straps, exposing the female's breasts to the firelight, the nipples going instantly tight atop acres of pale flesh.

Assail paused, as if taken by what he saw. And then he extended his tongue and dropped his head.

At the last moment, just before he started to lick and suckle, he lifted his eyes, focusing on the blackened window on the right, meeting the stare of the woman who he knew was there in the shadows, watching him. . . .

A shot of pure, undiluted lust shot through his body, taking over, replacing higher reasoning as the driver of his actions. The female underneath him ceased to be one of his species that he had bought for a short time.

She became his burglar.

And it changed everything. With a sudden surge, he struck the column of the female's throat, taking the vein, drawing what he needed . . .

All the while imagining that the human woman was beneath him.

*   *   *

Sola gasped—

And ripped herself away from the cottage's window.

As her back hit the hard, bumpy side of the river-stone chimney, she closed her eyes, her heart pounding against her ribs, her lungs dragging in cold air.

On the backs of her lids, all she saw were the bare-naked breasts laid out before him, his dark head descending, his tongue flicking free of his mouth . . . and then his eyes lifting and meeting hers.

Oh, Jesus, how had he known she was there?

And shit, she was never going to forget the image of that woman splayed out beneath him, that coat of his cast aside, his body surging into the cradle of those slender hips. She could imagine the warmth of the fire beside them, and the even more powerful heat coming off of him—the feel of skin on skin, the promise of ecstasy.

Don't look again, she told herself. *He knows you're here—*

The keening cry of a woman orgasming vibrated out of the cottage, laying waste to the wholesome appearance of the place.

Sola leaned back into the window, peering through the glass again . . . even though she knew she shouldn't.

He was inside the woman, his lower body pumping, his face buried in her neck, his arms bowed out to support his heavy upper torso.

He wasn't looking up anymore. And he was going to be busy for a while longer.

Now was the time to retreat.

Besides, like she really needed to watch?

With a curse, Sola ghosted away from the site, beating feet through the scratchy underbrush, dodging the thin, leafless trees. When she got to her rental car, she jumped in, locked the doors, and started the engine.

Shutting her eyes once more, she replayed the entire scene: her closing in on the cottage, coming up to the window, staying in the shadows thrown by the chimney.

Him standing across the open room, the woman in front of him, her graceful body covered with black satin, her long, dark hair reaching down to the small of her back. He had put his hands to her face and kissed her hard, his shoulders curling as he'd bent down to make the contact with an utterly erotic expression . . .

And then he'd eased the woman over to the couch.

Even though it killed her to admit it, Sola had felt a stab of irrational jealousy. But that hadn't been the worst of it: her own body had responded, her sex blooming between her legs sure as if it had been her mouth he was working, her waist his hands were on, her breasts that were up against his chest. And that reaction had only intensified as he'd positioned the woman on that couch, his face marked with dark hunger, his eyes glittering as if what was beneath him was a meal to be eaten.

Watching was wrong. Watching was bad.

But even the threat to her personal safety—and, arguably, her mental heath—hadn't been enough to get her away from the glass. Especially as he'd reared up and dragged that heavy black overcoat off his shoulders. It had been impossible for her not to picture him naked, seeing his broad chest exposed to the firelight, imaging what his abs would look like curling up tight beneath his skin. . . . And then it had appeared that he'd bitten—*bitten*, for godsakes—through the spaghetti straps of the negligee's bodice.

Just as the woman's goddamn frickin' perfect breasts were exposed . . . he had looked at her.

With no warning whatsoever, those glittering, predatory eyes had risen and drilled right into her own, a sly smile lifting the corner of his mouth.

Like the show was just for her.

"Shit. *Shit.*"

One thing was clear: If he'd wanted to teach her a lesson about spying? Hard to think of a better way—short of making her eat the barrel of a forty.

Sola eased off the shoulder and got onto the road. As the Ford Taurus took ten miles to accelerate to the speed limit of forty-five, she wished she were in her Audi: With her blood still pumping through her veins, she needed some outward expression of the roar trapped in her body.

Some kind of outlet.

Like . . . sex, for example.

And not with herself.

FORTY-NINE

As Adirondack Great Camps went, Rehv's had everything: huge rustic main house sided in cedar shingles and covered with porches. A number of outer buildings, including guest cottages. Lake view. Lotta bedrooms.

After Trez and iAm took form in the side yard, they walked around through the snow to the back entrance into the kitchen. Even in winter, the place gave off a cozy vibe, with all that buttery glow coming through the diamond-paned glass. But not everything was Sugar Plum Fairy time: The wealthy Victorians who had built these compounds as a way to escape the heat and industrialization of the cities during the summers had most certainly not equipped them with laser-sighted motion detectors, state-of-the-art contacts on all windows and doors, and not one, but several, different motherboards controlling a fully integrated, multi-interface alarm system.

Boo-yah.

Trez's thumbprint on the discreetly mounted pad to the left of the door opened the way into the house's hub—an industrial-size kitchen that was kitted out with stainless-steel appliances on a level with Sal's.

Something was baking in the Viking oven. Bread, it smelled like.

"I'm hungry," Trez remarked as he shut the door. The locking mechanism bolted itself, but he checked anyway out of habit.

Off in the distance, someone was vacuuming—probably a Chosen. Ever since Phury had taken over as Primale, and essentially freed that cloistered group of females from the Far Side, Rehv had been letting them stay at the camp. Made sense. Lot of privacy, especially off-season, plus the remoteness from the city provided a soft transition from, if Trez understood things correctly, the placid sameness of the Sanctuary to the frenetic, sometimes traumatic nature of life on Earth.

It had been a long time since he'd been in the house—not since the Chosen had taken up res, as a matter of fact. Then again, when Rehv had blown up ZeroSum, and ended his role as a drug kingpin, that debt between them had lost some of its repayment traction.

Besides, now that the guy didn't have to make deliveries of rubies and sex to the princess anymore, there hadn't been much reason to come north.

Apparently that had changed, however.

"Yo, Rehv, where you at?" Trez hollered, his voice booming.

As much as his stomach protested, he and his brother walked out into the main hall. Victorian ephemera was everywhere, from the garnet-colored Orientals on the floor, to the tapestry-covered benches, to the taxidermied bison, deer, moose, and bobcat heads mounted around the rough stone fireplace.

"Rehv!" he called out again.

Man, that racoon lamp had always given him the creeps. So did the stuffed owl with the sunglasses.

"He'll be right down."

Trez turned around at the female voice.

And in that one moment, had the course of his life change forever.

The staircase down from the second floor was a straight shot, the shallow steps and their simple railing emerging from above without architectural artifice.

The female in the white robe standing at their base turned them into a stairway from heaven. She was tall and slender, but her curves were in all the right places, her loose dress unable to conceal her high, large breasts or the graceful swell of her hips. Her skin was smooth and the color of café au lait, her hair dark and coiled up high on her head. Eyes were pale and heavily fringed.

Lips were full and rosy.

He wanted to kiss them.

Especially as they moved, enunciating whatever she was saying with intoxicating precision—

iAm's sharp elbow in his rib cage made him jump. "Ow! What the fuck—frick, I mean. Shit—I mean, crap."

Way to be calm, cool, and collected, asshole.

"She asked if we wanted any food," iAm muttered. "I said, no, not for me. Now it's your turn."

Oh, he wanted to eat something, all right. He wanted to fall to his knees at her feet and get under that—

Trez closed his eyes and felt like a total flipping bastard. "Nah, I'm good."

"I thought you said you were hungry."

Trez popped his lids and glared at his brother. Was the guy trying to make him look like an idiot?

The knowing light in those black eyes suggested, yes, iAm was.

"No. I'm fine," he ground out. Subtext: Don't push it, douche.

"I was just going to check on my bread."

Trez's eyes shut again, the Chosen's voice lilting in his ears, the sound of it both raising his blood pressure and calming him down at the same time.

"You know," he heard himself say, "maybe I will see if I can scrounge up a meal."

She smiled at him. "Follow me. I'm sure we can find something to your liking."

As she headed around for the entryway they'd just come through, Trez blinked like the dumb-ass he was.

It had been a very, very long time since a female had spoken anything to him without a double entrendre . . . but as far as he could tell, those words, which could arguably be considered a come-on—at least given his lust filter—had held no promise of a blow job or some full-on sex. Or even attraction of any kind.

Naturally, this made him want her more.

His feet started in her direction, his body following rather as a dog would its master, with no thought of deviating from the path chosen by her for him—

iAm grabbed his arm and yanked him back. "Don't even fucking *think* about it."

Trez's first impulse was to rip himself free, even if he left his own limb behind in his brother's grip. "I don't know what you're talking about—"

"Do not make me grab your hard-on to prove my point," iAm hissed.

Numbly, Trez looked down at the front of himself. Well. What do you know. "I'm not going to . . ." *Fuck her* came to mind, but God, he couldn't use the f-word around that female, even in the hypothetical. "You know, do anything."

"You actually expect me to believe that."

Trez's eyes flipped over to the doorway she'd disappeared through. Shit. Talk about having no credibility on the subject of abstinence.

"She is not available to you, do you understand me," iAm gritted out. "That's not fair to someone like her—more to the point, if you tap that, Phury is going to come after you with a black dagger. That is *his*, not *yours*."

For a split second, Trez bristled at that—except not because his inner feminist was roaring about females being treated as property, although of course that was wrong. No, it was because . . .

Mine.

From somewhere deep inside of him, that word emanated outward, as if every cell in his body had suddenly found its voice and was speaking the only truth that mattered.

"Sorry to keep you waiting."

At the sound of Rehv's voice, Trez dragged his consciousness back from the cliff it had unexpectedly found itself flying off of.

The *symphath* king was coming down the same stairs the Chosen had used, the male's cane steadying him, his black mink coat keeping his medicated body warm.

As iAm said something and Rehv replied, Trez refocused on the doorway to the kitchen. What was she doing in there—oh, man. Probably bending down to look at that bread . . .

A subtle growl percolated up his throat.

"Excuse me?" Rehv demanded, purple eyes narrowing.

Another shot in the ribs brought Trez back to reality. "Sorry. Indigestion. How you been?"

Rehv cocked a brow, but then shrugged. "I need your help."

"Anything," Trez said, meaning it.

"There's a Council meeting tomorrow night. Wrath's going to be

there. The Brotherhood will provide protection, but I want you both to come on the QT."

Trez recoiled. The Council had met regularly prior to the raids of a couple of years ago, and Rehv had never needed backup. "What's doing?"

"Wrath got shot back in the fall."

What. The. Fuck.

Trez ground his molars. "Who?" After all, he liked the king.

"Band of Bastards. You don't know them, but you may meet them tomorrow night—if you agree to come."

"Of course we'll be there." As iAm nodded, Trez crossed his arms over his chest. "Where?"

"I'm having it at this estate in Caldwell at midnight. It's one of the few that wasn't infiltrated by the Lessening Society—the family was mostly wiped out nonetheless, however, because they were visiting another bloodline in town at the time the attack went down." Rehv went over and sat down on the tapestry-covered sofa, twirling his cane on the floor between his legs. "Let me tell you how we're going to roll. Wrath is now totally blind, but the *glymera* don't know this. I want him seated in the morning parlor when those aristocrats arrive so they don't see him relying on anyone to find his place. Then . . ."

As Rehv continued to lay out the plan, Trez took a seat in front of the fire and nodded in the right places.

In his mind, however, he was in that kitchen, with that female. . . .

What was her name? he wondered.

Just as important . . .

When could he see her again?

FIFTY

Downstairs in the clinic's examination room, Qhuinn felt like he was up in the air, flying high. And not in a soon-to-crash POS Cessna with a wounded Brother in the back.

"I'm sorry, could you say that again?"

Doc Jane smiled as she brought a rolling table over to the bedside. Dimly, the stuff on it registered, but he was more focused on what might or might not come out of the physician's mouth. "You guys are still pregnant. Her hormone levels are doubling exactly as they should, blood pressure's perfect, heart rate's great. And still no bleeding, right?"

As the physician looked over at Layla, the Chosen shook her head, her expression as poleaxed as he sure as shit felt like. "None at all."

Qhuinn took a little walk, his hand dragging through his hair, his brain cramping. "I don't understand this. . . . I'm mean, this is what I want—what we want—but I don't get why she had the . . ."

After having ridden the roller coaster down into hell, it was completely disarming to hit an unexpected rise back in the direction of earth.

Doc Jane shook her head. "This is probably not helpful, but Ehlena's never seen this before, either. So I get your confusion, and more to the point, I understand better than you know how treacher-

ous hope can be. It's hard to give yourself over to any optimism after where you both have been."

Man, V's *shellan* was so not an idiot.

Qhuinn focused on Layla. The Chosen was in a loose white robe, but not the kind she'd worn as a member of the Scribe Virgin's sacred sect of females. It was an everyday bathrobe, and underneath was a hospital johnny that had pink and red hearts on a white background. And on that rolling table? Turned out it was a box of saltine crackers and a six-pack of little Canada Dry ginger ales.

Talk about your over-the-counter medications.

Doc Jane opened the crackers. "I know that the last thing you're thinking of is food." She handed one of the flaky, salty squares over. "But if you eat this, and have a little of the soda? Might settle things down in there."

And what do you know, it did. Layla ended up working her way through half a sleeve, and two of the small green bottles.

"That really helps, huh?" Qhuinn murmured as the Chosen lay back and sighed in relief.

"You have *no* idea." Layla put her hand on her lower belly. "Whatever it takes, I will do it, eat it, drink it."

"The nausea's that bad, huh."

"It's not about me. I don't care if I throw up for the next eighteen months, as long as the young is all right. I'm just scared that with the heaving, I'll lose . . . well, you know."

Okay, anyone who thought females were the weaker sex had their head fucking wedged.

He looked at Doc Jane. "What do we do now?"

The doctor shrugged. "My advice? Trust in the symptoms and in the test results, otherwise, you're going to go crazy. Layla's body is, and has been, driving all this. If right now there are no indications of a miscarriage, but in fact every reason to believe that the pregnancy has resumed a positive course? Take a deep breath and go one night at a time. If you look forward too much, or get stuck dwelling over the past couple of days? You're not going to get through this in one piece."

Word, Qhuinn thought.

The good doctor's phone went off. "Hold on a sec—shoot. I have to check on that *doggen* who cut his hand last night. Layla, as far as I'm concerned, there's no medical reason to make you stay down here. I don't want you leaving the compound for the next couple of nights, though. Let's get some time under our belts, okay?"

"But of course."

Doc Jane left a moment later, and Qhuinn was at a loss. He wanted to help Layla back to the main house, but she wasn't crippled, for godsakes. Still, he felt like carrying her around—for like, the rest of the frickin' pregnancy.

He leaned back against the stainless-steel cabinets. "I find myself wanting to ask you how you are every two seconds."

Layla laughed a little. "That makes the both of us."

"You want to go to back to the house?"

"You know . . . I actually don't. I feel . . ." She looked around. "Safer down here, to be honest."

"Makes sense to me. You need anything?"

She nodded at her little tray full of anti-nausea stuff. "As long as I've got this, I'm good. And you should feel free to go out and fight."

Qhuinn frowned. "I thought I'd stay in. . . ."

"And do what? I'm not telling you to leave, by any means. But I have a feeling it's just going to be me sitting here and stewing. If something happens, I can call you and you can come right home."

Qhuinn thought about where the Brotherhood and the fighters in the house were heading at midnight: the Council meeting.

If it had been a normal evening of engaging in the field, he probably would have stayed put. But with Wrath actually in the world, meeting with those assholes in the *glymera*?

"Okay," he said slowly. "I'll keep my phone with me, and I'll make it clear to the others that if you call, I'm out of there."

Layla took a sip of her ginger ale, and then stared into the cup, like she was watching the bubbles rise around the ice.

He thought of where they'd been the night before at Havers's—out of control, terrified, in mourning.

Shit could still go back to that, he reminded himself. It was way too early to get attached again.

And yet he couldn't seem to help himself. Standing in the tiled room, with the scent of Lysol disinfectant in his nose, and the lip of the counter he was leaning against biting into his ass . . . he realized this was the moment he started to love his young.

Right here, right now.

As a male bonded with his female, so too did a father to his off-

spring—and accordingly, his heart just opened wide and let it all in: the commitment that came with choosing to try for a child, the terror of losing them that he bet never went away, the joy that there was something of you on the face of the earth after you were gone, the impatience to meet them in person, the desperate desire to hold them in your arms and look into their eyes and give them all the love you had to give.

"Is it okay . . . can I touch your stomach?" he asked in a small voice.

"Of course! You don't have to ask." Layla lay back with a smile. "What's in there is half yours, you know."

Qhuinn rubbed nervous hands together as he approached the table. He had certainly touched Layla during the needing, and then afterward in a solicitous manner when a situation called for it.

He had never thought of touching his baby.

Qhuinn watched from a vast distance as his dagger hand reached out. Jesus, the tips of the fingers were trembling like crazy.

But they stilled the instant he made the connection.

"I'm right here," he said. "Dad's right here. I'm going nowhere. Just gonna wait until you're ready to come out into the world, and then your mom and I are going to take care of you. So you hang tight, we clear? Do your thing, and we'll wait for however long it takes."

With his free hand, he took Layla's palm, and put it over his own.

"Your family is right here. Waiting for you . . . and we love you."

It was totally stupid to talk to what was, no doubt, nothing but a bundle of cells. But he couldn't help it. The words, the actions . . . they were at once totally his, and yet coming from a place that was foreign to him.

Felt right, though.

Felt . . . like what a father was supposed to do.

Left-hand forty. Check.

Right forty. Check.

Backup ammo on the waist belt. Check.

Daggers one and two in the chest holster. Check.

Leather jacket—

As a knock sounded on Blay's door, he leaned out of his closet. "Come in?"

When Saxton entered, he pulled his jacket onto his shoulders and pivoted. "Hey. How are you?"

Something was up.

The other male's eyes made a quick three-sixty on Blay's "working wardrobe," as they'd once called it. Unease drew Sax's pale eyebrows upward; then again, he'd never seemed entirely comfortable around the weapons.

"Heading out into the field, then," the male murmured.

"To a meeting of the Council, actually."

"I didn't realize that required so many guns as accessories."

"New era."

"Yes, indeed."

There was a long pause. "How are you?"

Saxton's eyes went around the room. "I wanted to be the one to tell you."

Oh, fuck. Now what.

Blay swallowed hard. "About?"

"I'm leaving the house for a little while—for a vacation, as it were." He put his hand out to stop any arguing. "No, it's not permanent. I've gotten everything in order for Wrath, and there's nothing he needs for the next couple of days. Naturally, if he does, I'll come right back. I'm going to be staying with an old friend. I truly need some rest and relaxation—and before you worry, I swear I am returning, and this is honestly not about us. I've been working for months straight and I just want to have no schedule, if that makes sense?"

Blay took a deep breath. "Yes, it does. Where are you . . ." He stopped himself with a reminder that that was none of his business anymore. "Let me know if you need anything?"

"I promise."

On impulse, Blay walked over and put his arms around his former lover, the platonic connection as unforced and natural as his previously amorous one had been. Holding onto the male, he turned his face in.

"Thank you," Blay said. "For coming and telling me—"

At that moment, someone passed by in the hall, the stride faltering.

It was Qhuinn; Blay knew by the scent even before the tall, powerful figure registered visually. And in the brief hesitation before the guy kept going, their eyes locked over Saxton's shoulder.

Qhuinn's face became a mask instantly, the features freezing, giving nothing away.

And then the fighter was gone, his long legs taking him out of the open door's frame.

Blay stepped away and forced himself to replug into the good-bye. "When will you be back?"

"A couple of days at the least, no longer than a week."

"Okay."

Saxton glanced around the room again, and as he did, it was clear he was remembering. "Be well, and be careful out there. Do not try to be a hero."

Blay's first thought was . . . well, since Qhuinn was usually the first in line for that, it was unlikely he was going to have to put any kind of Superman outfit on.

"I promise."

As Saxton left, Blay stared off into space. He didn't see what was in front of him, or remember what he and Saxton had shared in the room. Rather, his mind was next door with Qhuinn, and Qhuinn's things . . . and the memories he had of that session with Qhuinn.

Shit.

Glancing at the clock, he put his phone into the chest pocket of the jacket and headed out. As he jogged down to the staircase, voices from the foyer echoed through the hall, a sign that the Brotherhood had already gathered and was waiting for the departure signal.

Sure enough, they were all there. Z and Phury. V and Butch. Rhage, Tohr, and John Matthew.

As he descended, he found himself wishing that Qhuinn was going to come with them—but surely the male was staying home, given the Layla situation.

Where was Payne? he wondered as he went to stand next to John Matthew.

Tohr nodded a hello in Blay's direction. "Okay, we're waiting for one more, and then we'll start moving. First wave will go to the location. On the all-clear, I will dematerialize with Wrath to the house with backup by—"

Lassiter skidded in from the billiards room, the fallen angel glowing from his black-and-blond hair and white eyes, all the way down to his shitkickers. Then again, maybe the illumination wasn't his nature, but that gold he insisted on wearing.

He looked like a living, breathing jewelry tree.

"I'm here. Where's my chauffeur hat?"

"Here, use mine," Butch said, outing a B Sox cap and throwing it over. "It'll help that hair of yours."

The angel caught the thing on the fly and stared at the red S. "I'm sorry, I can't."

"Do not tell me you're a Yankees fan," V drawled. "I'll have to kill you, and frankly, tonight we need all the wingmen we've got."

Lassiter tossed the cap back. Whistled. Looked casual.

"Are you serious?" Butch said. Like the guy had maybe volunteered for a lobotomy. Or a limb amputation. Or a pedicure.

"No fucking way," V echoed. "When and where did you become a friend of the enemy—"

The angel held up his palms. "It's not my fault you guys suck—"

Tohr actually stepped in front of Lassiter, like he was worried that something a lot more than smack talk was going to start flying. And the sad thing was, he was right to be concerned. Apart from their *shellans*, V and Butch loved the Sox above almost everything else—including sanity.

"Okay, okay," Tohr said, "we have bigger things to worry about—"

"He has to sleep at some point," Butch muttered to his roommate.

"Yeah, watch yourself, angel," V sneered. "We don't like your kind."

Lassiter shrugged, like the Brothers were nothing more than yappy dogs circling his ankles. "Is someone talking to me? Or is that just the sound of losing—"

Lot of shouting at that point.

"Two words, bitches," Lassiter sneered. "Johnny. Damon. Oh, wait, Kevin. Youkilis. Or Wade. Boggs. Roger. Clemens. Is it that the food sucks in Boston? Or just the ball game?"

Butch lunged at that point, clearly prepared to light the guy up like a Christmas tree—

"What the *fuck* is going on down there!"

The bellowing voice from above shut off the Sox-versus-Yankees showdown.

As Tohr hauled the cop out of angel range, everyone looked over while the king was led downward by his queen. Wrath's presence tightened everyone up, the crew going professional. Even Lassiter.

Well, except for Butch. But then, he'd been "wicked hyped up," as he'd call it, for the last twenty-four hours—and he had good reason to be tetchy: His *shellan* was going to be at the Council meeting. Which, from the Brother's point of view, was like having two Wraths there. The

trouble was, Marissa was the oldest of her line, and that meant if Rehv wanted full attendance, she had to be present.

Poor bastard.

In the lull that followed, Blay's dagger hand started to tingle, and he had an almost irresistible urge to palm a weapon. All he could think about was that this was nearly identical to the prelude to Wrath's shooting back in the fall—on that night, they had all gathered here, and Wrath had come down with Beth . . . and a bullet had been shot out of a rifle and ended its trajectory in the king's throat.

Apparently, he wasn't the only one thinking like that. A number of hands went to holsters and stayed put.

"Oh, good, you're here," Tohr said.

Blay turned with a frown, and had to swallow his reaction. It wasn't Payne who joined them; it was Qhuinn. And man, the male looked more than ready to fuck some shit up, his eyes grim, his body taut as a bowstring in its black leather.

For a moment, a fissure of pure, sexual awareness shot through Blay.

To the point that a totally inappropriate fantasy occurred to him: namely, he and Qhuinn ducking into the pantry for a quick, clothes-stay-on fuck.

With a groan, he refocused on the king. Which was only appropriate. Wrath was what mattered here, not his frickin' love life. . . .

A feeling of unease replaced the lust.

Were he and Qhuinn ever going to be together again?

God, what a strange thought. It wasn't like the sex was a good idea emotionally. Arguably, it was an extremely bad one.

But he wanted more of it. God help him.

"All right, let's do this," Tohr spoke up. "Everyone know where we're going?"

It was a troubling relief to have the grave nature of the assignment in front of them clear his brain of everything but the commitment to save Wrath's life . . . even if it cost him his own.

That was better than worrying about the Qhuinn shit, though.

For certain.

FIFTY-ONE

Quhinn took form on a snow-covered terrace, and as everyone in the Brotherhood but Butch materialized alongside of him, he was not surprised by all the swank. The estate that the Council meeting was being held at was your standard *glymera* setup: lot of land that had been cleared and landscaped. Little cottage down by the entrance that looked like it belonged on a postcard of the Cotswalds. Big-ass mansion that, in this case, was made of brick and had dentil molding, shiny shutters, and slate roofing.

"Let's do this," V said, walking over to a side door.

The instant he pounded on it, the thing opened, as if that, along with so much, had been prearranged. But oh, man, if this was their hostess? The female who stood in the doorway was dressed in a long dark evening gown that was cut down to her navel, and she had a ring of diamonds around her throat the size of a Doberman's collar. Her perfume so heavy it was like a slap in the sinuses—in spite of the fact that he was still outdoors.

"I'm ready for you," she said in a low, husky voice.

Quhinn frowned, thinking that even in that designer whatever it was, the chick came off as a tart. Not his problem, though.

As he filed in with the others, the room they entered was some kind of conservatory, the oversize potted green things and grand piano suggesting many an evening with guests staring up at some opera singer yodeling in the corner.

Gag.

"This way," the female announced with a flourish of a hand that sparkled.

In her wake, that perfume—maybe it was more than sprays from a single source, like a layering of all kinds of crap?—nearly colored the air behind her, and her hips were doing double duty with every step, like she was hoping they were all looking at her ass and wanting a piece of it.

Nope. As with the others, he was searching every nook and cranny, ready to shoot and ask questions after the body dropped.

It wasn't until they came out to the front hall, with its oil paintings spotlit from the ceiling, and its dark red Oriental rugs, and the . . .

Shit, that mirror was exactly like the one that had hung in his parents' house. Same position, same floor-to-ceiling, same curlicue gold leafing.

Yeah, he had the creeps. Bad.

The whole house reminded him of the mansion he'd grown up in, everything in its place, the decor far, far, far from middle-class, yet not anything gaudy and Trumpilicious. Nah, this shit was that subtle blend of old wealth and classic sense of style that could only be bred, not taught.

His eyes searched out Blay.

The guy was doing his job, staying tight, checking the place out.

Blay's mom and pops hadn't been quite this rich. But his home had been so much nicer on so many levels. Warmer—and that hadn't been about the HVAC systems.

How were Blay's parents? he wondered abruptly. He'd spent almost more time under their roof than his own, and he missed them. The last time he'd seen them . . . God, long time. Maybe that night of the raids, when Blay's father had gone from Mr. Suit accountant to serious ass-kicker. After that, the pair of them had moved out to their safe house, and then he and Blay had completely fallen apart.

He hoped they were well—

The image of Blay and Saxton standing chest-to-chest, hip-to-hip, in Blay's bedroom sliced into his brain.

God . . . damn . . . that had hurt.

And man, karma was good at its job.

Replugging into reality, he followed that double-jointed pelvis and the Brotherhood into a huge dining room that had been set up to Tohr's specifications: All the drapery had been pulled across the bank of windows that overlooked the back gardens, and the flap door that he figured led into the kitchen had been barricaded by a weighty antique sideboard. Whatever table had sat in the center of the room had been removed, and twenty-five matching mahogany chairs with red silk seats had been lined up in rows facing a marble fireplace.

Wrath was going to stand in front of the mantel to make his address, and Qhuinn went over and checked that the steel flue was closed. It was.

On either side of the fireplace, there were two sets of paneled doors that opened into an old-fashioned receiving salon. He and John Matthew and Rhage did a walk-through of the room, closed the thing off, and then he took up res in front of the entrance on the left, and John Matthew did the same on the right.

"I trust all is to your liking?" the female said.

Rehv went over to the fireplace and turned to face all the empty chairs. "Where's your *hellren*?"

"Upstairs."

"Get him down here. Now. Otherwise, if he moves through the house, he's liable to get shot in the chest."

The female's eyes flared, and this time when she walked off, there was no exaggeration to her hips, no check-me-out toss of the hair over the shoulder. Clearly the we're-not-fucking-around message had been received, and she wanted whoever her mate was to live through the night.

In the wait that followed, Qhuinn kept his gun in his palm, his eyes on the room, his hearing fine-tuned for something, anything out of order.

Nothing.

Which suggested their host and hostess had followed orders—

A strange prickling unease tickled its way up his spine, causing him to frown and go from high alert to DEFCON I. On the far side of the fireplace, John seemed to catch the same gist, his gun lifting, his eyes narrowing.

And then a cold mist hit Qhuinn's ankles.

"I've asked a couple of special guests to join us," Rehv said dryly.

At that moment, two columns of haze pulled up from the floor, the disturbance of air molecules finding forms . . . that Qhuinn instantly recognized.

Thank fuck.

With Payne out of commission for whatever reason, he'd been feeling like they were a little light on coverage, even recognizing the skills in the Brotherhood. But as Trez and iAm appeared, he took a deep breath.

Now that was a pair of straight-up killers, the kind of thing you really didn't want against you in any kind of fight. The good news was that Rehvenge had long been aligned with the Shadows, and Rehv's connection with the Brotherhood and the king meant that the two brothers were obviously willing to come and play a little backup.

Qhuinn stepped up to say hello to the pair, greeting them as the others did with a palm join, a quick pull, and a clap on the back. "Hey, my man . . ."

"What's doing . . ."

"How you been . . ."

After the hi-how're-yas were done, Trez glanced around. "Okay, so we're just going to stay outta sight unless you need us. But rest assured, we're here."

After a course of thank-yous from the Brothers, Rehv said a couple of private words to the Shadows . . . and then the two were gone, misting out of their forms and seething around the floors, that cold draft now a reassurance.

Perfect timing. Less than a minute later, the hostess came back with a diminutive older male at her side. Given the way vampires aged, with a rapid acceleration of physical decline toward the end of the life span, Qhuinn guessed the guy had five years left. Ten at the very most.

Some introductions were made, but Qhuinn didn't care about that shit. He was more worried about whether the rest of the house was empty.

"Any *doggen* here?" Rehv demanded as the female settled her geezer into one of the dining chairs.

"As you have requested, they are all gone for this part of the evening."

V nodded to Phury and Z. "The three of us'll search the premises. See if that's right."

Even though Blay trusted himself, the Brotherhood, and John Matthew, and Qhuinn, he felt a lot better knowing the Shadows were around. Trez and iAm were not just awesome fighters, and inherently dangerous to anyone they declared an enemy; they had a striking advantage over the Brotherhood.

Invisibility.

He wasn't sure whether they could actually engage while in that state, but it didn't matter. Anyone who broke in here—like, say, the Band of fucking Bastards—would make an engagement assessment that included only the visible hard bodies in the room.

Not those two brothers.

So this was good.

At that moment, V returned with Phury and Z from their walk-around—and Butch was with them, suggesting the Brother had just arrived via car. "Clear."

There was a brief pause. And then, as prearranged, Tohr went to the front door and opened the way in for Wrath.

Showtime, Blay thought, his eyes flicking in Qhuinn's direction before he snapped himself back into focus.

Tohr and the king entered the dining room side by side, their heads together as if they were in deep conversation about something important, the Brother's hand on Wrath's forearm like the guy was trying to drive some point home.

It was all an act for the host and hostess.

Tohr was, in fact, leading Wrath by that hold on the arm, taking him over to the fireplace, positioning him right in the middle of the mantelpiece. And that conversation? It was about where the two aristocratic hosts were sitting, where the chairs were aligned, where the Brothers and the fighters were—and the two Shadows as well.

While Wrath nodded, the king deliberately moved his head around as if his keen eyes were taking the details of the room in. And then he acknowledged the host and hostess as they were brought forward to kiss his huge black diamond ring.

After that, the crème de la crème of the *glymera* began to arrive.

From his assigned spot at the back of the room by the wall of

windows, Blay got a good look at each one. Jesus, he could remember some of them from his life back before the raids, before he'd started living at the mansion and fighting with the Brothers. His parents had not been on a par with these males and females, but rather on the periphery—still, his family's bloodlines had been good ones, and they had been included in many festival celebrations at the big houses.

So these folks were not unknown to him.

But he sure as hell couldn't say he'd missed them.

In fact, he had to laugh to himself as a number of the females frowned and looked down to their delicately clad feet, Louboutins being lifted and shaken . . . as if the chill of the Shadows were registering.

When Havers arrived, the race's healer looked a little frazzled. No doubt he was nervous about seeing his sister again, and he had reason to be. From what Blay understood, Marissa had kicked his ass across the room at the last formal meeting of the Council.

Blay was sorry he'd missed that one.

Marissa arrived shortly after her brother, and Butch went over to her, greeting her with a lingering kiss before leading her, with a proud and protective arm, to a seat in the corner right next to where he was stationed. After the cop helped her into her chair, he stood beside her, big, broad, and mean-looking . . . especially as he locked eyes with Havers and smiled with fangs bared.

Blay found himself envying the couple a little. Not about the familial estrangement, for sure. But God . . . to be able to be seen with your mate in public, show your love for them, have your relationship respected by everyone else? Heterosexual couples took that for granted because they never knew anything different. Their unions were sanctioned by the *glymera*, even if the pairs were not in love, or were cheating on each other or were otherwise a fraud.

Two males?

Hah.

Just one more reason to resent the aristocracy, he supposed. Although in reality, he had the sense he wasn't going to have to worry about being discriminated against. The male he wanted was never going to stand beside him in public, and not because Qhuinn gave a shit about what people thought. One, the guy wasn't demonstrative like that. And two, sex did not a couple make.

Otherwise that bastard would be engaged to half of Caldwell, FFS.

Oh, what was he saying.

He was long over that Qhuinn pipe dream thing.

Really.

Totally—

"Shut it," he muttered to himself as the last of the Council arrived.

Rehv didn't waste any time. Every second that Wrath was in front of this group, the king was not only mortally exposed, but also running the chance that his blindness would somehow be ferreted out.

The *symphath* king addressed the Council, his purple gaze scanning the crowd, a sly smile on his face—like maybe he was enjoying the fact that this group of know-it-alls had no clue that a sin-eater was leading them. "I hereby call this meeting of the Council to order. The date and time are . . ."

As the preamble continued, Blay kept his eyes busy, checking out the backs of the males and females, where the arms and hands were, whether anyone was twitchy. Naturally, the group had turned out in black tie and velvet, with jewels on the females, and gold pocket watches on the males. Then again, it had been a long time since they'd been together formally, and that meant that their desire to compete with one another for the social upper hand had no doubt suffered from grossly insufficient airtime.

". . . our leader, Wrath, son of Wrath."

As polite applause sounded, and the crowd straightened in their chairs, Wrath took a single step forward.

Man, blind or not, he certainly appeared to be a force of nature: Even though he wasn't dressed in some kind of ermine-trimmed robe, the king was irrefutably in charge, his massive body and long dark hair and black wraparounds making him more menace than monarch.

And that was the idea.

Leadership, especially when it came to the *glymera*, was based in part upon perception—and no one could deny that Wrath looked like a living, breathing representation of power and authority.

And that deep, commanding voice didn't hurt, either.

"I recognize that it has been a long time since I've seen you. The raids of nearly two years ago decimated a lot of your families, and I share in your pain. I, too, lost my bloodline in a *lesser* raid, so I know exactly what you're going through as you try to get your lives back on track."

A male down in front shifted in his chair. . . .

But it was only a change in position, not the prelude to a weapon coming out.

Blay eased back on his stance, as did several others. Goddamn, he couldn't wait to get through this meeting and have Wrath back home safe.

"Many of you knew my father well, and remember his time in the Old Country. My sire was a wise and temperate leader, a gentlemale of logical thinking and regal bearing who occupied himself solely with the betterment of this race and its citizenry." Wrath paused, those wraparounds making a circle of the room. "I share a few of my father's characteristics . . . but not all. In fact, I am not temperate. I am not forgiving. I am a male of war, not of peace."

At this, Wrath unsheathed one of his black daggers, the dark blade flashing in the light of the crystal chandelier overhead. Out in front of the king, the crowd of highfliers reacted with a collective shiver.

"I am very comfortable with conflict, be it of the legal or mortal kind. My father was a mediator, a bridge maker. I am a grave maker. My father was a persuader. I am a taker. My father was a king who would willingly sit at your dinner tables and converse with you about minutiae. I am not that male."

Yeah, whoa. The Council had no doubt never been addressed like this. But Blay couldn't disagree with the approach. Weakness was not respected. Moreover, with this group, law alone probably wasn't going to keep Wrath's throne stable anymore.

Fear, on the other hand?

Much better chance.

"My father and I do have one thing in common, however." Wrath angled his head down, as if he were staring at the black blade. "My father caused the deaths of eight of your relations."

There was a collective gasp. But Wrath didn't let that slow him up.

"Over the course of my father's reign, there were eight attempts on his life, and no matter how long it took, whether it was days, weeks, or even months, he made it his business to find out who was behind each . . . and he hunted the individuals down personally, and killed them. You may not have heard the true stories, but you will know of the deaths—the perpetrators were beheaded with the tongues removed. Surely, as you cast your mind back, you can recall members of your bloodlines who were interred that way?"

Fidgeting. Lot of fidgeting. Which suggested memories had been jogged.

"You will further recall that those deaths were attributed to the

Lessening Society. I say unto you now, I know the names, and I know where the graves are, because my father made sure I memorized them. It was the first lesson in kingship he ever taught me. My citizenry is to be honored, protected, and served well. Traitors, on the other hand, are a disease to any lawful society and need to be eradicated." Wrath smiled in a purely evil way. "Say what you will about me, I studied well at the foot of my father. And let us be clear—my father, not the Brotherhood, was the one who attended those deaths. I know because he beheaded four of them in front of me. That was how important the lesson was."

Several of the females moved closer to whatever male happened to be seated beside them.

Wrath continued. "I will not hesitate to follow my father's lead in this. I recognize that you all have suffered. I respect your trials and I want to lead you. I will not, however, hesitate to treat *any* insurgency against me and mine as the act of a traitor."

The king lowered his chin, and appeared to glare out from behind the wraparounds, to the point that even Blay felt a frisson of adrenaline.

"And if you think what my father did was violent, you haven't seen a goddamn thing yet. I will make those deaths look merciful. I swear on my lineage."

FIFTY-TWO

On some level, Assail could not believe he was walking into a restaurant. For one, he didn't frequent human haunts as a rule, and two, he had no interest in eating in the dive: The air smelled like fried food and beer, and from what he saw on the trays of the waitresses, he was uncertain whether the entrées were graded safe for non-animal consumption.

Oh, look. Across the way, there was a stage that had a wall of chicken wire in front of it.

Classy.

"Well, hello, there," someone purred at him.

Assail cocked an eyebrow and glanced over his shoulder. The human woman was dressed in a tight shirt and a pair of blue jeans that had clearly been stitched onto her legs. Hair was blond and stick straight. Makeup was heavy, with the lipstick shiny enough to qualify as an exterior oil paint.

He'd rather spoon his own eyes out then engage in any fashion with the likes of her.

He willed her to forget she'd seen him and turned back around. There was a heavy crowd, with more people than there were tables and chairs, so he had good cover as he went over to a corner and scanned. . . .

And there she was.

His little burglar.

Cursing under his breath, he dimly recognized the waste of time this all was—especially given that the cousins were, at this very moment, making a deal with that *lesser* again. Unfortunately, however, as soon as he'd gotten an alert that that black Audi of hers had gone on the move, he'd been compelled to find the thing and follow it.

He had not been prepared for this.

Whatever was she doing here? And why was she dressed like that?

As she found one of the few empty tables and sat down alone, he found himself not approving of the way her hair was down around her shoulders, the dark weight curling about her face. Or the formfitting shirt that was revealed as she took off her coat. Or—she had makeup on, too, for godsakes. And not like that woman who had just oiled her way up to him. His burglar had kept things light, in a way that magnified her features. . . .

She was beautiful.

Too beautiful.

All the men in the restaurant were looking her over. And that made him want to kill each and every one of them by ripping their throats out with his teeth—

As if they were in agreement with that plan, his fangs tingled and began to descend into his mouth, his body tensing.

But not yet, he told himself. He needed to find out why she was here. After having followed her to Benloise's mansion, he had expected any number of destinations . . . although never this. What was she doing—

Her head turned, and for a moment, he thought she had somehow sensed him, even though she was not a vampire.

But then a very tall, very well-built human man approached her table.

His burglar looked up at the guy. Smiled at the guy. Got to her feet and wrapped her arms around the guy's big shoulders.

Assail's hand went into his coat and found his gun.

Indeed, he saw himself going over and putting a bullet between the man's eyes.

"Hey, you ever been here before?"

Assail's head cranked around. A rather large human male had approached him and was staring at him with a certain aggression.

"I asked you a question."

There were two responses, Assail decided. He could verbally reply, thus entering into some kind of dialogue that would consume his attention—arguably not a bad idea, given that his hand remained locked on his gun, and his impulses had not shifted from those of a homicidal inclination.

"I'm talking to you."

Or he could . . .

Assail bared his descended fangs and growled deep in his throat, redirecting his wrath away from the scene of his burglar with that human fool for whom she had dressed and made herself up.

The guy with the questions threw up his hands and took a step back. "Hey, it's cool, whatever. My bad. Whatever."

The man disappeared into the crowd, proving that in certain circumstances, rats without tails could dematerialize as well.

Assail's eyes returned to that table. The "gentleman" who had taken a seat across from his burglar was leaning in, his eyes locked on her face even while she examined the menu and glanced around.

Something was going to have to be done about this.

Sola closed the menu and laughed. "I never said that."

"You did." Mark Sanchez smiled. "You told me I had nice eyes."

Mark was exactly what she needed on a night like tonight. He was really easy to look at, super charming, and as long as he didn't make her drop and give him ten thousand, she had nothing to worry about: As a personal trainer? He was a demon. She should know.

"So is this a way to butter me up?" He eased back as the waitress brought them both beers. "Try to get me to go light on you in the gym?"

"I know better than that." Sola took a draw from the thick, ice-cold rim of her mug. "No quarter given. That's your policy."

"Well, to be fair, you've never asked for any special treatment." There was a pause. "Not that in your case, I wouldn't be willing to cut you some slack . . . in some areas."

Sola ducked the eye contact that was flashing her way. "So you don't date clients, huh."

"No. Not usually."

"Conflict of interest."

"It could get messy—but in certain cases, it's worth the risk."

Sola glanced around the pub. Lot of people. Lot of talk. Air that was hot and thick.

She frowned and stiffened. In the far corner, something . . . someone . . .

"You okay?"

She shook herself free of the paranoia. "Yes, sorry—oh, yes, we'd like to order," she said as the waitress returned. "I'll have a cheese-burger. Assuming my personal trainer doesn't throw an embolism from disapproval."

Mark laughed. "Make that two. But hold the fries. On both plates."

As the waitress took off, Sola tried not to look in the direction of that dark, back corner. "So . . ."

"I didn't think you'd ever take me up on this. I asked you out how long ago?"

As Mark smiled, she noticed that he had fantastic teeth, straight and really white. "It's been a while, I guess. I've been busy."

"So what do you do for a living?"

"This and that."

"In what field?"

Ordinarily, she got pissed quick when people became nosy. But his affect was calm and easy, so this was just date conversation.

"I guess you could call it criminal justice."

"Oh, you're into the law."

"I'm very familiar with it, yes."

"That's cool." Mark cleared his throat. "So . . . you look really good."

"Thanks. I think it's my trainer."

"Oh, somehow I think you'd be doing fine without me."

As they fell into an uncomplicated back-and-forth, she actually started to relax—and then their dinners arrived and they got another round of beer. It was so . . . normal being in the bar, doing the one-on-one thing, getting to know somebody else.

The exact opposite of what she'd played witness to the night be-fore.

Sola shivered as images came back to her . . . the candlelight, that black-haired man looming over the half-naked woman like he was go-

ing to devour her, the two of them unleashed and uninhibited. . . . Then those glittering eyes looking up and meeting her own through the glass as if he'd known all along that she was watching.

"You okay?"

Sola forced herself to focus. "Sorry, yes. You were saying?"

As Mark resumed talking about his training for the Iron Man, she found herself back in the cold outside of that cottage, watching that man and that woman.

Shoot. She'd engineered this date only because she'd wanted an outlet. It wasn't because she particularly cared about Mark, as nice as he was.

In fact, maybe she had done this because her personal trainer happened to be really tall, and really well built, with very dark hair and very pale eyes.

When guilt rang her bell, she thought, oh, for chrissakes. She was an adult. Mark was an adult. People had sex for all kinds of different reasons—just because she didn't want to marry the guy didn't mean she was breaking some cardinal rule . . . except, crap. Her grandmother's morality aside, and his shiny, pearly whites and big shoulders to the contrary, she wasn't actually attracted to Mark.

She was attracted to the man Mark reminded her of.

And that was what made this wrong.

FIFTY-THREE

Even though Qhuinn was hardly an arbiter of taste when it came to meetings of the Council, it was pretty damn clear to him that the assembled group had come to the house expecting one thing, only to get something else entirely.

Wrath didn't waste or mince words and, after laying the smackdown, wrapped things up within five or ten minutes.

This was a good thing, actually. The faster he finished, the quicker they could get him home.

"In closing," the king said in his bass voice, "I appreciate the opportunity to address this august group."

In this case, "august" clearly meant "a-hole-ish."

"I have other commitments at this time." Namely, staying alive. "So I will be departing. However, if you have any comments, please direct them to Tohrment, son of Hharm."

A blink of the eye later and the king left the building with V and Zsadist.

In the wake of the departure, all the fancy-pants in the dining room stayed sitting in their chairs, shock and now-what playing across their attractive features. Clearly, they had expected more . . . but also

less. Kind of like children who had pushed their parents too far and finally gotten a wooden spoon on the ass.

From Qhuinn's perspective, it was pretty fucking amusing, actually.

The party finally began to break up after the hostess rose to her feet and yammered on about what an honor it was to have had all the yada, yada, yada.

Qhuinn cared about one and only one thing.

And that was the text that came through on his phone about a minute later: Wrath was home safe.

Exhaling slowly, he put his cell back in the inside pocket of his leather jacket and thought about setting off a couple of rounds into the floorboards to get this bunch of stiffs to dance a little. He'd probably get in trouble for that, though.

Bummer.

The crowd started to file out shortly thereafter, to the clear dissatisfaction of the hostess, as if she had gotten dressed up and rearranged her house with the expectation of a long, socially prominent evening—only to find that all she got were two seconds of celebrity and a bucket of KFC for eats.

Sorry, lady.

Tohrment lorded over the exodus, standing in front of the fireplace, nodding his head, saying a few words. In this delegation, Wrath had made a wise choice. The Brother had the appearance of an ass-kicker, with all his weapons, but he'd always been willing and internally inclined to be a peacemaker, and that was no different tonight.

He was especially nice to Marissa when Butch's mate left, his face showing a flash of genuine affection as he hugged her and nodded as the cop escorted her out. That slice of real was immediately replaced by his professional mask, however.

Eventually, the hostess helped her ancient *hellren* to his feet, and made some noise about taking him upstairs.

And then there was only one.

Elan, son of Larex, lingered before the bank of draped windows.

Qhuinn had had an eye on the guy the whole time, counting exactly how many of the Council members came up to him, shook his hand, murmured in his ear.

Each and every one.

So it was not exactly a surprise that instead of leaving like a good little boy, he made his way up to the fireplace like he wanted an audience.

Great.

As Elan approached Tohr, the closer he got, the more he had to lift his chin to keep eye contact with the Brother.

"It was quite an honor to have an audience with your king," the gentlemale said gravely. "I hung on his every word."

Tohr murmured something in return.

"And I've been struggling with something," the aristocrat hedged. "I was hoping to speak with him directly about this, but . . ."

Yeah, don't hold your breath for that, buddy.

Tohr stepped in to fill the silence. "Anything you tell me will go straight to the king's ears, without filter or interpretation. And the fighters in this room are sworn to secrecy. They will die before they repeat a word."

Elan glanced over at Rehv, clearly expecting a similiar pledge from the male.

"The same goes for me," Rehvenge muttered as he leaned into his cane.

Abruptly, Elan's chest puffed up as if this kind of personalized attention was more what he'd been hoping for out of the meeting. "Well, this has lain heavily upon my heart."

Certainly not your pecs, Qhuinn thought. You're built like a ten-year-old boy.

"And that is," Tohr prompted.

Elan crossed his arms behind the small of his back and paced a bit—as if he were taking time with his words. Something told Qhuinn that they had been prepared beforehand, however—though he couldn't have said what it was.

"I expected your king to address a certain rumor that I have heard."

"Which is?" Tohr said in an even tone.

Elan stopped. Turned. Spoke clearly. "That he was shot back in the fall."

No one showed any reaction. Not Tohr or Rehv. Not the remaining Brothers in the room. Certainly not Qhuinn or his boys.

"What is your source for this?" Tohr asked.

"Well, in all honesty, I thought he would be here tonight."

"Really." Tohr glanced at the empty chairs and shrugged. "You want to tell me what you heard?"

"The male made reference to a visitation by the king. Similar to when Wrath came and saw me at my home over the summer." This was reported with self-importance, as if that was the highlight of Wrath's year, right there. "He said that the Band of Bastards shot at the king whilst on his property."

Again with the no reactions.

"But obviously, your king survived." The pause suggested Elan was expecting details to be filled in. "He's doing rather well, as a matter of fact."

There was a long silence, as if both sides of the conversation were expecting the other to put the quiet to good use.

Tohr cocked his brows. "With all due respect, you haven't told us much of anything, and gossip has been going on since the beginning of time."

"But here's the odd thing. He also talked to me about it before it occurred. I didn't believe him, however. Who would arrange for an assassination attempt? It seemed . . . simply the boasting of a male otherwise dissatisfied with the way things were being handled. Except then, a week later, he said that the Band of Bastards had followed through, that Wrath had been shot. I didn't know what to do. I had no way of getting in touch with the king personally, and no way to verify that the individual was speaking the truth. I let it all go—until this meeting was called. I wondered if maybe it was . . . well. It clearly wasn't, but then I wondered why he wasn't here."

Tohr stared down at the smaller male. "It would help if you gave us a proper noun."

Now, Elan frowned. "You mean you don't know who is on the Council?"

As Rehv rolled his eyes, Tohr shrugged. "We have better things to do than worry about Rehvenge's membership."

"In the Old World, the Brotherhood knew who we are."

"There's an ocean between us and the motherlands."

"More's the pity."

"That's your opinion."

Qhuinn took a step forward, with the intention of stepping in, in the event the Brother locked hands on the SOB's skinny neck: Someone should probably catch the head before it bounced all over their hosts' rugs. And the deadweight of the body.

Seemed only hospitable.

"So who are you talking about," Tohr pressed.

Elan looked around at the still, deadly males who were focused on him. "Assail. His name is Assail."

Deep in downtown Caldwell, where the darkened streets formed a rats' maze, and the sober humans were few and very far between, Xcor swung his scythe in a fat circle about five and a half feet up from the slushy, black-stained ground.

The *lesser* was caught in the neck, and the head, now freed from its spinal tether, flew chin over temple, chin over temple, through the cold, gusty wind. Black blood spiraled out from the severed arteries as the rudderless lower half of the body collapsed forward into a pratfall.

And that was that.

Rather disappointing, really.

Spinning around, he held his beloved over his shoulder so that she curled behind him protectively, watching his back as he braced himself for whatever was coming next. The alley he had entered to chase that now incapacitated slayer was open at the far end, and behind him, the three cousins were stationed shoulder-to-shoulder should more arrive from that direction—

Something was coming.

Something was . . . on a fast approach, the din of an engine growing louder and louder and—

The SUV skidded into the alley, its tires finding little or no purchase on the icy roadway. As a result of the lack of traction, the vehicle slammed into the wall, its high-beams blinding Xcor.

Whoever was behind the wheel didn't hit the brakes.

The engine roared.

Xcor faced off at the vehicle and closed his eyes. No reason to keep his lids peeled, as his vision had ceased to function. No real concern who was driving, whether it was slayer, vampire or human.

They were coming at him, and he was going to stop that. Even though it was probably easier to get out of the way.

He had never particularly cared for easy, however.

"Xcor!" someone yelled.

Grabbing a deep breath of that icy air, he let out a battle cry as he tracked the approach, his senses reaching out and positioning the SUV in space as it traveled forward. His scythe disappeared in a moment, and his guns, eager to participate, came out in both palms.

He waited another twenty feet.

And then he started pumping off rounds.

With his silencers on, the bullets made only impact sounds as they blew out the front windshield, pinged off the grille, took out a tire. . . .

At which point those blinding headlights swung away, the back end of the vehicle hinging around, the overall trajectory unchanged thanks to that tremendous acceleration—even as everything went haywire.

Just before the side panel took him out, Xcor leaped off the ground, his boots springing up, the roof just barely going under their treads as three thousand pounds plus of out-of-control streaked beneath his airborne body.

As Xcor's combats landed back on the ground, the end of the car's forward momentum came at the expense of a Dumpster, the trash receptacle stopping the vehicle better than any set of brakes could.

Xcor wasted no time in closing in, both guns up, triggers ready. Although he had discharged a number of rounds, he knew he had at least four left in each gun. And his soldiers had once again fallen in behind him.

Coming up to look inside, he didn't care what he found: one of his own kind, a man or a woman, a *lesser*, it mattered not to him.

The smell of spoiled meat and treacle informed him which of his many enemies he confronted, and indeed, as he leaned in through the blown-out front windshield, two new recruits, who still retained their dark hair color and ruddy skin tones, were lolling in the front seat.

Even with their seat belts engaged, they were in rough shape. Aside from being riddled with bullets, their visages carried the wear and tear of their having banged around in the sedan's cabin, slammed into the dashboard, and been pelted with shattered glass: Black blood greased up their busted noses and lacerated cheeks and chins, the shit dripping onto their chests as water from faucets in the bath.

No airbags. Mayhap a malfunction.

"I dinnae think ye were gonna make it," Balthazar muttered.

"Aye," someone else agreed.

Xcor threw off the concern as he holstered his guns, grabbed hold of the driver's side door, and yanked the thing clean off its mountings. As the squeal of metal torn asunder echoed in the alley, he tossed the panel aside, unsheathed his steel dagger, and leaned in.

As with all *lessers*, these denizens of the Omega still moved and blinked in spite of their catastrophic injuries—and would continue to do so in perpetuity if left in this state, even as their forms decayed over time.

There was one and only one way to kill them.

Xcor drew his right forearm across over his left shoulder and buried the blade of his dagger square in the chest of the one who had been behind the wheel. Turning his head aside and shutting his eyes so he wasn't blinded again, he waited for the pop and flash to fade before leaning over the seat and doing the same to the passenger.

Then he turned to go over and dispatch the beheaded, squirming corpse . . . that had tire tracks across its chest, thanks to the car's path through the alley.

Stalking through black-stained slush, he lifted his dagger hand again over his shoulder and buried the blade into the sternum with such power, the point of the weapon went into the asphalt.

When he rose to his feet once again, his breath left his nose in locomotive puffs. "Search the vehicle, and then we must needs depart."

He checked the time. The Caldwell police were disappointingly responsive, even in this part of town—and the constant threat of human involvement that he lived under was, as always, a bore. But with all luck, they would be gone as if they had never been in a matter of minutes.

Sheathing his blade, he glanced up to the sky, cracking his neck and loosening his shoulders.

It was impossible not to think of that Council meeting which had been scheduled; it had been on his mind all night long. Had Wrath shown? Or had it only been Rehvenge and representatives of the Brotherhood? If the king had in fact been in attendance, Xcor could well imagine the agenda: show of strength, warning, then a quick departure.

As mighty as the Brotherhood was, and as much as Wrath would want to flex his muscle before that group of faithless aristocratic sycophants, it was hard to imagine that a male who'd nearly been killed so recently was going to take any chances: If solely through self-interest,

the Brotherhood would want him alive, as that was their seat of power, too.

And that was why he'd chosen to stay away.

There was no harm in letting Wrath attempt to regain some of his lost stature, and much to lose in a direct confrontation with the Brotherhood in front of that particular audience: The potential for collateral damage was too great. The last thing he wanted was to spook the *glymera* into retreating from him . . . or kill them off altogether in the process of taking out the king.

But he had in fact discovered, thanks to Throe's contacts, exactly where and when the assembly was occurring. Which would be now . . . and at that female's estate, the one from whom his soldiers had fed in that little cottage.

Evidently, she was willing to allow others the use of not only her garden, but her halls as well.

And soon enough, he would have a transcript of what had transpired provided to him by the mouthpiece that was Elan—if for no other reason than that the male would want to enjoy the access that he'd had and show off a bit—

A whistle of appreciation by the back end of the ruined car brought his head around.

Zypher was standing by the open trunk door, his brows high as he bent in and brought out . . . a cellophane-covered brick of something white.

" 'Tis quite a bounty they have," he said, holding it high.

Xcor marched over. There were three more like it, just tossed into the back loose as if the pair of slayers had been more concerned with their physical safety than the disposition of the drugs.

At that moment, sirens began to sound from the east, mayhap related to the crash, mayhap not.

"We take the packages with us," Xcor ordered. "And depart the now."

FIFTY-FOUR

All in all, the date wasn't half-bad.

As Sola got up from her chair and started to put her coat on, Mark came in behind her and helped settle the wool on her shoulders.

The way his hands lingered suggested he was more than open to this being the end of dinner, but the beginning of the rest of the night. He wasn't pushy, though. He stepped back and smiled, indicating the way to the exit with a gallant hand.

Moving in front of him, it seemed like some kind of mental-health felony that he didn't make her blood boil . . . and yet that highly aggressive, dominating man from the night before did.

She was going to have to give her libido a pep talk. Or maybe a spanking . . .

Perhaps from that other guy, part of her suggested.

"No," she muttered.

"Sorry, what?"

Sola shook her head. "Just talking to myself."

After wending their way through the crowd, they got to the res-

taurant's door, and wow, what a sinus-clearer when they stepped out into the night.

"So . . ." Mark said, shoving his hands into the pockets of his jeans, his well-developed torso bunching up—and yet still not managing to get close to the size of—

Stop it.

"Thanks for dinner, you didn't have to pay."

"Well, this was a date. You said so." He smiled again. "And I'm a traditional kind of guy."

Do it, she said to herself. Ask him if you can go back to his house.

After all, there could be no hanky-panky going on at hers. Ever. Not with her grandmother upstairs—the woman's deafness was highly selective.

Just do it.

This is why you asked him. . . .

"I've got an early-morning meeting," she blurted. "So I have to head off. But thank you very much—and I'd like to do this again."

To give Mark credit, he covered any disappointment he might have felt with another of those winning grins.

"Sounds good. This was cool."

"I'm just parked back here." She thumbed over her shoulder. "So . . ."

"I'll walk you to your car."

"Thanks."

They were silent as their boots crackled through the salt that had been put down over the ice.

"Nice night."

"Yes," she said. "It is."

For some reason, her senses began to fire in warning, her eyes searching the darkness outside of the lit parking lot.

Maybe it was Benloise coming after her, she thought. He undoubtedly knew by now that someone had broken into his home and his safe, and had also probably noticed the shift in that statue's position. Hard to know whether he would retaliate, though. In spite of the business he was in, he had a certain code of conduct that he adhered to—and on some level, he must be aware that what he'd done in canceling that job and cutting her pay had been wrong.

He would most certainly understand the message.

Besides, she could have taken everything he'd locked up.

Approaching her Audi, she disengaged the alarm. Then she turned around and looked up.

"I'll call you?"

"Yes, please," Mark said.

There was a long pause. And then she reached a hand up, slid it behind his neck, and drew his mouth down to her own. Mark immediately went with the invitation, but not in a pushy, domineering way: As she tilted her head, he did the same, and their lips met, brushing lightly, then with a little more pressure. He didn't crush her to him, or trap her against the car . . . there was no sense of out-of-control.

No feeling of great passion, either.

She broke the contact. "I'll see you soon."

Mark exhaled hard, like he'd gotten turned on. "Ah, yeah. I hope so. And not only in the gym."

He lifted his hand, smiled one last time, and walked to his truck.

With a quiet curse, Sola got behind her wheel, shut the door, and let her head fall back against the rest. In the rearview mirror, she watched his taillights come on, and saw him make a fat turn and head out of the parking lot.

Closing her lids, she didn't see Mark's gleaming smile, or imagine his lips against hers, or feel his hands roaming her body.

She was back to being outside of that cottage looking in, playing witness to a pair of hot, slightly evil eyes looking up at her over the exposed breast of another woman.

"Oh, for the love of God . . ."

Shaking herself out of the memory, she feared that in this case, her craving for, oh, say, chocolate, was not going to be eased by a diet soda. Or a Snackwell's cookie. Or even one single Hershey's Kiss.

At this rate, she was going to have to melt down a case of Lindt truffles and run them through an IV directly into her vein.

Putting her foot on the brake, she hit the button on the dash and heard the engine flare to life. As the headlights lights came on—

Sola jerked back into her seat and let out a scream.

When Qhuinn returned to the mansion with the others, he broke rank as soon as he was through the vestibule and into the grand foyer. Moving at a quick jog, he mounted the staircase and headed directly to

Layla's room: According to her texts, she'd decided to leave the clinic after all, and he was anxious to find out how she was doing.

Knocking on the door, he started praying. Again.

Nothing like pregnancy to make an agnostic religious.

"Come in?"

At the sound of her voice, he braced himself and ducked inside. "How're you feeling?"

Layla looked up from the *Us Weekly* magazine she was reading on the bed. "Hi!"

Qhuinn recoiled at the cheerfulness. "Ah . . . hi?"

Glancing around, he saw *Vogue*, *People*, and *Vanity Fair* on the duvet around her, and across the way, the TV was nattering on, a commercial for underarm deodorant segueing into one for Colgate toothpaste. There were ginger ales and saltines on the side table next to her, and then, on the opposite stand, a cleaned-out carton of Häagen-Dazs and a couple of spoons on a silver tray.

"I'm feeling really nauseous," Layla said with a smile. Like that was good news.

He supposed it was. "Any . . . you know . . ."

"Not in the slightest. Not even a little. I'm not throwing up, either. I just have to make sure I eat a little all the time. Too much and I feel sick—same if I go too long without putting something in there."

Qhuinn eased back against the jambs, his legs literally wobbling from relief. "That's . . . awesome."

"Do you want to sit down?" As if he were looking as pale as he suddenly felt.

"No, I'm good. I'm just . . . I've been really worried about you."

"Well, as you can see"—she indicated her body—"I'm just doing my thing—and thank the Virgin Scribe for that."

As Layla smiled over at him, he really liked the way she looked— and not from any sexual sense of the word. It was just . . . she appeared calm and relaxed and happy, her hair down loose over her shoulders, her coloring perfect, her hands and her eyes steady. In fact, she seemed . . . really healthy all of a sudden, that sallow cast to her skin now noticeable for its absence.

"So I guess you've had some visitors," he commented, as he nodded to the mags and the dead soldier of ice cream.

"Oh, everyone's been by. Beth stayed the longest. She stretched out right next to me—we didn't talk about anything in particular. We just read and looked at pictures and watched a *Deadliest Catch* marathon. I love that show—it's where all these humans go out on boats into the sea? It's very exciting. Made me feel glad to be warm and on dry land."

Qhuinn rubbed his face, and prayed that his sense of balance began to return quick: Evidently, his adrenal glands were still struggling to catch up to reality, the idea that there was no drama, no emergency, no dire anything to react to curiously hard to handle.

"I'm glad people are dropping in," he mumbled, feeling like he had to say something.

"Oh, yes, there've been"—Layla looked away, a strange expression tightening her features—"quite a number of them."

Qhuinn frowned. "Nobody weird, though, right?"

He couldn't imagine that anyone in the house would be anything other than supportive, but he had to ask.

"No . . . not weird."

"What." As Layla just fingered the cover of the magazine in her lap, some brunette, bubble-headed, blank-eyed bimbo's face distorted and went back to normal, distorted and went back to normal. "Layla. Tell me."

So he could go lay down some motherfuckin' boundaries if he had to.

Layla pushed her hair back. "You're going to think I'm crazy . . . or, I don't know."

He went over and sat down next to her. "Okay, look. I don't know how to say this right so I'm just going to get the words out. You and I? We're going to be facing a lot of . . . you know, personal shit in connection with . . ." Oh, God, he really hoped she kept the pregnancy. "We might as well start being fully honest with each other now. Whatever it is? I won't judge. After all the crap I've done in my own life? I ain't judging no one over nothing."

Layla took a deep breath. "All right . . . well, Payne came and saw me last night."

He frowned again. "And."

"Well, she said she might be able to do something for the pregnancy. She wasn't sure whether it would work, but she didn't think it would hurt me."

Qhuinn's chest tightened up, a stab of fear making his heart pound. V and Payne had things about them that were not of this world. And that was cool. But not around his young—for fuck's sake, V's hand was a straight-up killer. . . .

"She took her hand and laid it on my belly, right where the young is. . . ."

A sensation like Qhuinn's inner toilet had flushed all the blood out of his head hit hard. "Oh, God—"

"No, no." She reached for him. "It wasn't bad. It felt . . . good, actually. I was . . . bathed in this light—it flowed through me, strengthening me. Healing me. It focused on my abdomen, but it went so much further than that. Afterward, I was so worried about her, though. She collapsed on the floor next to the bed. . . ." Layla motioned downward, to the floor. "But then I lost consciousness. I must have slept for a long time. When I finally woke up? That was when I felt . . . different. At first, I assumed it was because the miscarriage had stopped because it was . . . over. I ran out and found Blay, and he took me down to the clinic. That's when you came and Doc Jane told us that . . ." Layla's elegant hand touched her lower abdomen, and then lingered there. "That was when she told us that our young is still with us—"

Her voice broke at that point, and she blinked quickly. "So you see, I think she saved our pregnancy."

After a long moment of shock, Qhuinn whispered, "Oh . . . shit."

Back in the parking lot of the restaurant, Assail loomed over the hood of his burglar's Audi, standing fully in the glare of the headlights.

Much as he'd done the night before, he locked eyes with her by instinct rather than by sight.

And as he stood in the cold, he was hot from his temper, and so much else: As that sack of excrement on two legs had escorted her to her car, and had the insanity to kiss her, Assail had been confronted anew by two choices: Track the man into the night and follow through on all that throat tearing, or wait until the human left, and . . .

Something deep inside of him had made up his mind: He had been incapable of leaving her.

His burglar put down her window, and the scent of her arousal made him hard.

It also made him smile. It was the first time all night he'd caught a whiff of it—and that cooled his temper more than anything else could have.

Well, except perhaps skinning that man alive.

"What do you want," she snarled.

Oh, wasn't that the question.

He moved around to her side of the car. "Did you enjoy yourself?"

"Excuse me?"

"I believe you heard the question."

She threw open the driver's side door and jumped out. "How *dare* you expect *any* explanation from me about *anything*—"

He cranked his weight forward on his hips, leaning in toward her. "May I remind you that you invaded my privacy first—"

"I didn't jump in front of your car and—"

"Did you like what you saw last night?" That clammed her up. And as the silence persisted, he smiled a little. "So you admit you were watching."

"You goddamn *knew* I was," she spat.

"So, answer the question. Did you like what you saw," he said in a voice that was husky even to his own ears.

Oh, yes, he thought as he inhaled deeply. She did.

"Never mind," he purred. "You don't need to put it in words. I already know your answer—"

She slapped him so fast and so hard, his head actually kicked back on his spine.

His first instinct was to bare his fangs and bite her, to punish her, to tantalize himself—because there was no better spice to pleasure than a little pain. Or a lot of it.

He righted his head and lowered his lids. "That felt good. Do you want to do it again?"

As another bloom emanated from her, he laughed down deep in his chest, and thought, yes, indeed, this reaction from her had just ensured that that human man was going to keep living. Or at least die by the hands of another.

She wanted himself. And no other.

Assail eased even closer, until his lips were right next to her ear. "What did you do when you got home? Or couldn't you wait that long."

She took a deliberate step back. "You want to know? Fine. I changed the cat litter, made myself two scrambled eggs and a piece of cinnamon toast, and then I put myself to bed."

He took a deliberate step forward. "What did you do when you were in between the sheets?"

As that scent of hers flared once again, he put his mouth back

where it had been . . . close, oh, so close. "I think I know what you did. But I want you to tell me."

"Screw you—"

"Did you think of what you saw?" As a gust of wind blew some of her hair into her eyes, he tucked the strands back. "Did you imagine it was you I was fucking?"

Her breath began to pump in her chest, and—dearest Virgin in the Fade—that made him want to take her. "How long did you stay?" he breathed. "Until the female finished . . . or until I did?"

Her hands punched him away. "Fuck off."

In a quick shift, she shot around his body, jumped back into her car, and slammed the door.

He moved just as fast.

Surging in through the open window, he turned her head and kissed her hard, his mouth taking over, the drive to wipe clean any trace of that human male making his sex pound.

She kissed him back.

With equal strength.

As his shoulders were too big to fit through the window, he wanted to claw through the steel. He had to stay where he was, however, and that made him even more aggressive, his blood roaring in his veins, his body straining as his tongue entered her, his hand snaking behind her neck, burying into her hair.

She was slick and sweet and hot as hell.

To the point that he had to break off for a deep breath or run the risk of passing out.

As he separated them, he met her eyes. They were both heaving, and as her arousal thickened the air, he wanted to be inside of her.

To mark her . . .

The sound of his phone going off was exactly the wrong thing at the wrong time: The ringing from his coat seemed to snap her back to reality, her eyes flaring as they slid away, her hands locking on the steering wheel as if she were trying to ground herself.

She didn't look at him as she put the window up, engaged the engine, and drove off.

Leaving Assail panting in the cold.

FIFTY-FIVE

Quhinn left Layla's room shortly thereafter, his shitkickers carrying him fast across the narrow rug that ran down the corridor to the head of the stairs. As he kept going by Wrath's study, he was vaguely aware of someone calling his name, but he paid no attention.

At the far end of the hall of statues, past Z and Bella's suite, the room where Payne and Manny stayed had a closed door, but the sound of a television quietly murmured on the far side.

Qhuinn took a second to collect the pieces of his blown mind, and then knocked.

"Enter," came the response.

As he stepped inside, the room was awash in a blue glow, the TV providing the light. Payne was lying in the bed, her skin so pale it reflected the changing images projected onto it.

"Greetings," she said in a slurred voice.

"Jesus . . . Christ . . ."

"No, I am afraid not." She smiled. Or at least, half of her mouth did. "Pardon me if I do not get up to offer greetings."

He shut the door softly. "What happened?"

Even though he sort of knew.

"Is she well?" Payne asked. "Is your female pregnant still?"

"The tests seem to indicate so."

"Good. That pleases me."

"Are you dying?" he blurted out. And then wanted to knee himself in his own 'nads.

She laughed roughly. "I do not believe so. I'm very weak, however."

Qhuinn's feet carried him across the carpet. "So . . . what happened?"

Payne struggled to push herself higher on her pillows, but then gave up. "I think I'm losing my gift." She groaned as she moved her legs under the duvet. "When I first came here, I was able to lay hands and heal with little or no after effects. Every time I do it, however, the effort appears to drag me down further. And what I endeavored with your female and your young was . . ."

"You nearly killed yourself," he filled in.

She shrugged. "I woke up on the floor next to her bed. I dragged myself down here. Manny got me out of bed earlier, and I did have some energy. Now, it seems to have flagged once more."

"Is there anything I can do?"

"I think I must needs go to my mother's sanctuary." This was said with total derision. "For a recharge, as it were. It seems logical, as that may well have been the locus of my gift. I just need to get strong enough to make the trip, so to speak—well, that and gather the will to. I should much prefer to remain down here. The decision, however, appears to be making itself for me. One cannot negotiate with one's physical form, after a point."

Yeah, he knew how that was.

"I can't . . ." He dragged a hand through his hair. "I don't know how to thank you."

"When she gives birth, then you may thank me. There is much unknown ahead that is still to be crossed."

Not anymore, he thought. His vision, the one on the door to the Fade, was once again on track to coming true.

And this time it was going to stay that way.

Qhuinn withdrew one of the daggers from his chest and streaked the sharp blade across the inside of his palm. As blood welled and started to drip, he offered himself to the female.

"I hereby offer the oath of my—" He stopped short. He didn't have any bloodline to speak of, not with that disavowal in his background. *"I offer the oath of my honor to you and yours from now until the final beat of my heart and the last breath in my lungs. Anything you shall call upon me for shall be provided without question or hesitation."*

On one level, it seemed ridiculous to put himself out like that to the daughter of a motherfucking deity. Like Payne needed any help?

Payne's dagger hand met his and latched on tight. *"I would rather have your honor than any bloodline upon the earth."*

As their eyes met, he had a thought that it was not male-to-female, but fighter-to-fighter, in spite of their sexes.

"I will never be able to thank you enough," he said.

"Would that she makes it through. Both of them, that is."

"I have the sense they will now. Thanks to you."

It felt weird to want to bow to the female, but some things you just went with, and he did. Then he turned away, not wanting to keep her up if she was going to rest.

Just as his hand locked onto the doorknob, Payne murmured, "If you thank anyone, it should be Blaylock."

Qhuinn froze. Cranked back around. "What . . . did you say?"

Assail stayed put as that Audi skidded out of the parking lot and hit the road beyond like his burglar had planted a bomb in the restaurant and just hit the detonator.

His body told him to go after her, stop that car, and drag her into the backseat.

His mind, however, knew better.

As he felt the surging in his body, he knew that the extent to which he lost control around her was dangerous. He was a male who defined himself by his self-possession. With that female? Especially if that sex of hers was aroused?

He was consumed with the need to possess her.

So he needed to regather his own reins.

In point of fact, he had no business wasting time stalking some human woman, hanging out in the corner of a cheap dive, watching her with a man.

Also consumed with the urge to kill her cheeseburger dinner companion.

What in the name of the Scribe Virgin had happened to him?

The answer, when it came to him, was something he firmly rejected.

In a bid to refocus his energies, he took out his phone to ascertain who had called and broken the spell that had well needed rupturing.

Rehvenge.

On so many levels, he had no desire to speak with the male. The last thing he was interested in was a rehash of all the reasons he had to participate in the social and political standstill that was the Council.

But it was better than going after his burglar—

He didn't even know her name, he realized.

And it would be in his best interests to never find out, he told himself.

As he returned the call, he held the iPhone to his ear and put his free hand into the pocket of his wool coat to keep it warm. "Rehvenge," he said as the male picked up. "I'm talking to you more than I speak with my *mahmen.*"

"I thought your mother was dead."

"She is."

"You have a very low standard for communication."

"What may I do for you." 'Twas not a question. No reason to encourage a response.

"Actually, it's what I can do for you."

"With all due respect, I prefer to take care of business myself."

"A very good policy. And as much as I know you like your 'business,' that isn't why I called. I thought you might like to know that the Council met with Wrath tonight."

"I believe I resigned during our last conversation. So I fail to see what this has to do with me?"

"Your name came up at the end. After everyone had left."

Assail arched a brow. "In what capacity."

"A little birdie said you set Wrath up with the Band of Bastards at your home this past fall."

Assail's grip tightened on his phone. And during the brief pause that followed, he chose his words with extreme care. "Wrath knows that isn't true. I was the one who gave him the vehicle he got away in. As I told you before, I am not, and never have been, connected with any insurgency. In fact, I removed myself from the Council precisely because I do not wish to be embroiled in any drama."

"Relax. He did you a favor."

"In exactly what manner."

"The individual said it in front of me."

"And again, I inquire, how does that equate to a—"

"I knew he was lying."

Assail became quiet. It was, of course, a good thing that Rehvenge knew the statement to be untrue. But how?

"Before you ask," the male murmured darkly, "I'm not going to go into exactly why I'm so sure of it. What I will say, however, is that I'm prepared to reward your loyalty with a gift from the king."

"A gift?"

"Wrath is a male who's aptly named. He understands, for example, how an individual would feel if he were to be wrongly accused of treason. He knows that someone who would falsely implicate another with information not widely known is likely trying to shift blame for his own actions—particularly if the person talking had a . . . well, shall we say, an affect . . . that indicated not just deceit, but a certain level of scheming. As if he were paying you back for something he considered indicative of disloyalty or bad judgment."

"Who is it," Assail breathed. Even though he knew.

"Wrath is not asking you to do any kind of dirty work. In fact, if you choose not to take action, the individual will be dead within twenty-four hours. The king just feels, as I do, that your interests are not only aligned with ours, in this case, they supersede them."

Assail closed his eyes, vengeance boiling his blood in much the same manner in which the sexual instinct had just done. The end result, however, was going to be oh, so very different. "Say the name."

"Elan, son of Larex."

Assail popped his lids and bared his fangs. "You tell your king I shall take care of this with alacrity."

Rehvenge laughed darkly. "That I'll do. I promise it."

FIFTY-SIX

Blay was antsy as he paced around his room. Although he was fully dressed for fighting, he was going nowhere. None of them were.

After the Council meeting, Tohr had ordered the Brotherhood to stay in on a just-in-case. Rehv was reaching out to the Council members, connecting outside of the mansion, getting a sense of where the *glymera* were. As the guy couldn't very well show up with a six-pack of Brothers on his ass—at least, not if he wanted to preserve some pretense of civility—they had to chill. But given the political climate, it was important that backup was ready in case the Reverend needed it.

Not that he went by that name anymore . . .

The door to his room opened wide without a knock, a hello, a hey-are-you-decent.

Qhuinn stood in between the jambs, breathing hard, like he'd run down the hall of statues.

Damn, had Layla lost the pregnancy after all?

Those mismatched eyes searched around. "You by yourself?"

Why the hell would— Oh, Saxton. Right. "Yes—"

The male took three strides forward, reached up . . . and kissed the ever-loving shit out of Blay.

The kiss was the kind that you remembered all your life, the connection forged with such totality that everything from the feel of the body against your own, to the warm slide of another's lips on yours, to the power as well as the control, was etched into your mind.

Blay didn't ask any questions.

He just held on, slipping his arms around the other male, welcoming the tongue that entered him, kissing back even though he didn't understand what had motivated this.

He probably should care. Probably should pull away.

Shoulda, woulda, coulda.

Whatever.

He was vaguely aware that the door was open into the hall, but he didn't care—even though things were going to get pretty goddamn indiscreet pretty quick.

Except Qhuinn abruptly put the brakes on, ending the liplock and separating them. "Sorry. This isn't why I came."

The fighter was still panting, and that, as well as the burn in that incredible stare, was nearly enough for Blay to say something along the lines of, *That's fine, but can we finish what we started first.*

Qhuinn walked back and shut the door. Then he shoved his hands into the pockets of his leathers—like it was either that or he was worried they might latch on again.

Fuck the pockets, Blay thought as he tried to subtly rearrange his erection. "What is it?" he asked.

"I know you went to see Payne."

The words were spoken clearly and slowly—and they were the one thing that Blay couldn't really handle. Breaking eye contact, he wandered around his room.

"You saved the pregnancy," Qhuinn announced, the tone in his voice too close to awe for comfort.

"So she's still okay?"

"You saved the—"

"Payne did."

"V's sister said it never would have dawned on her to try—until you went and talked with her."

"Payne's got some serious talent—"

Qhuinn was suddenly right in his way, a solid wall of muscle that

there was no going through. Especially as the male reached up and brushed Blay's cheek. "You saved my daughter."

In the silence that followed, Blay knew he had something he was supposed to say. Yeah . . . it was right on his tongue. It was . . .

Shit. With Qhuinn looking at him like that, he couldn't remember his own name. Blaysox? Blacklock? Blabberfox? Who the fuck knew . . .

"You saved my daughter," Qhuinn whispered.

The words that came out of Blay's mouth were ones he would later regret—because it was especially important, in light of the sex that seemed to be happening from time to time, to keep a distance.

But linked as they were, stare-to-stare, he was powerless to stop the truth. "How could I not try . . . it was killing you. I couldn't not try something. Anything."

Qhuinn's lids closed briefly. And then he gathered Blay in an embrace that connected them from head to foot. "You're always there for me, aren't you."

Talk about bittersweet: The reality that the male was going to form a family with someone else, with a female, with Layla, bit into the center of Blay's chest.

It was his curse, in so many ways.

He released his arms from Qhuinn's back and stepped off. "Well, I hope it—"

Before he could finish, Qhuinn was in front of him yet again, and those blue and green eyes were burning.

"What," Blay said.

"I owe you . . . everything."

For some reason, that hurt. Maybe because after years of trying to give himself to the guy, the gratitude was finally earned by helping him have a kid with someone else.

"Whatever, you'd have done the same for me," he said roughly.

And yet even as he put that out there, he wasn't sure. If someone attacked him? Well, sure, of course Qhuinn would back him up. But then again, the tough-edged SOB loved to fight and was a natural hero—that wasn't anything about Blay.

Perhaps that was the point of this emptiness. Everything had always been on Qhuinn's terms. The friendship. The distance. Even the sex.

"Why are you looking at me like that?" Qhuinn asked.

"Like how."

"As if I'm a stranger."

Blay rubbed his face. "Sorry. Just been a long night."

There was a long, tense moment, during which all he could feel was Qhuinn's stare.

"I'll go," the fighter said after a pause. "I guess I just wanted . . . yeah. Anyhow."

The sounds of shitkickers headed for the exit had Blay cursing—

The knock on the door was a single one and very loud: a Brother.

Rhage's voice cut easily through the panels. "Blay? Tohr's called a meeting to go over tomorrow night's territory. You know where Qhuinn is?"

Blay looked across his room at the guy. "No, I don't."

Oh, for fuck's sake, Qhuinn thought at the interruption. Although in reality, the conversation was over, wasn't it.

The good news was that at least Rhage didn't come in. No doubt Blay would prefer the pair of them not got caught hanging in his room.

Hollywood wrapped things up with, "If you see him, let him know if he wants to attend we're convening in five. Totally understand if he'd rather stay with Layla."

"Roger that," Blay said in a dead voice.

As Rhage went next door and knocked on Z's door, Qhuinn rubbed his face. He had no idea what had gone through Blay's mind just now, but the way those blue eyes had stared at him had made him feel as if a ghost had passed over his grave.

Then again, what did he expect? He barged into the room that the guy shared with Saxton, pulled a major liplock, and then got all mushy over the Payne thing. . . . This was Saxton space. Not Qhuinn space.

He had a habit of taking things over, though, didn't he.

"I won't come in here again," Qhuinn said, trying to make some kind of amends. "I just wanted you to know that . . . I owe you so much."

Qhuinn went over to the door and leaned in, listening for Rhage's voice, closing his eyes, waiting for the hall of statues to be clear.

Jesus, he could be a selfish prick sometimes; he really could—

"Qhuinn."

His body turned on a dime, sure as if Blay's voice was a ripcord that yanked him around. "Yeah?"

The male walked forward. When they were eye-to-eye, Blay said, "I still want to fuck you."

Qhuinn's brows popped so high, they nearly landed on the carpet. And instantly, he went hard.

The only trouble was, Blay didn't seem happy about the reveal. But why would he be? He wasn't the kind of male who could two-time someone easily—although clearly Saxton's lack of monogamy had cured him of being faithful.

Kind of made Qhuinn want to strangle his cousin again. And the only thing that stopped him from going and finding the slut was that in this case, the situation worked for Qhuinn.

"I want to be with you, too," he said.

"I'll come to your room after dawn."

Qhuinn didn't want to ask. Had to. "What about Saxton?"

"He's gone on vacation."

Reaaaaaaaaaaaaaally. "For how long?"

"Just a couple of days."

Too bad. Any chance of an extension . . . for like a year or two? Maybe forever?

"Okay, it's a—" Qhuinn stopped himself before he finished that with *date*.

There was no sense kidding himself. Saxton was away. Blay wanted to get laid. And Qhuinn was more than willing to supply the male with what he wanted.

That construct was *not* a date. But fuck it.

"Come to me," he said in a growl. "I'll be waiting for you."

Blay nodded, like they'd made a pact, and then he was the one who left first, his body shifting with aggression as he walked by and went through the door.

Qhuinn watched the guy go. Stayed behind. Nearly shut himself in just so he could pull himself together.

Suddenly, he was fucked in the head, in spite of the promise that they'd be hooking up in a matter of hours: That expression on Blay's face haunted him, to the point where his chest started to ache. Shit, maybe this current series of hookups was just a further evolution of the bad spots they'd been in before, a new facet of their collective unhappiness.

It had never dawned on him that they weren't good for each other. That there wouldn't be, in the future, some kind of meeting of the minds now that he'd opened himself after all these years.

Curling up a fist, he slammed it into the doorjamb, the imprint of the molding biting back into the heel of his hand.

As pain flared and then thumped, for some reason, he thought of punching that flatbed's dashboard and screaming to get out. Felt like that had been a lifetime ago.

But he wasn't turning back. If sex was what he could have, he was going to take it. Besides, what Blay had done for Layla?

Surely that meant something. The guy had cared enough to change the course of Qhuinn's entire life.

Not that Blay hadn't done that long ago.

FIFTY-SEVEN

Assail took form beside a babbling brook that remained ice-free thanks to its constant movement.

The house before him was one he had been to only one prior time, a brick Victorian with the period's quintessential gingerbread motifs marking its porches and doorways. So quaint. So homey. Especially with those long four-paned windows made of leaded glass, and the curls of smoke lazying out of not one, but three of its four chimneys.

Which seemed to indicate its owner was back home for the night.

Fine timing, as it were: Dawn was coming soon, so it was logical to batten down one's personal hatches for the sun. Secure one's environment. Prepare for the hours that one needed to stay inside to protect oneself from harm.

Assail stalked across the pristine snow, leaving tracks with deep tread. No loafers for this job. No business suit, either.

No Range Rover for his burglar to follow.

Coming up the side lawn, he went over to the floor-to-ceiling windows of the very receiving room into which the master of the house had, not so very long ago, welcomed certain members of the Council . . . along with the Band of Bastards.

Assail had been numbered among the males at that meeting. At least until it had become clear that he had to remove himself or get drawn into precisely the kind of discourse and drama he was uninterested in.

At the glass, he looked inside.

Elan, son of Larex, was at his desk, a landline telephone up to his ear, a brandy snifter at his elbow, a cigarette smoldering in a cut-crystal ashtray beside him. As he leaned back in his leather club chair and crossed his legs at the knees, he appeared to be in a state of relaxation and self-satisfaction akin to that of postcoital bliss.

Assail made a fist, the black leather of his glove creaking ever so subtly.

And then he dematerialized into the very room, re-forming directly behind the male's chair.

On one level, he couldn't believe that Elan didn't fortify his abode with greater security—a fine steel mesh over the windows and within the walls, for example. Then again, the aristocrat clearly suffered from a lack of appropriate risk assessment—as well as an arrogance that would grant him a greater sense of safety than he actually possessed.

". . . and then Wrath shared a story about his father. I must confess, in person, the king is quite . . . ferocious. Although not enough to change my course, naturally."

No, Assail was going to take care of that.

Elan leaned forward and reached for the cigarette. The thing was screwed onto one of those old-fashioned holders, the kind that females tended to use, and as he brought the end to his lips to take a drag, the tip extended out past the edge of the chair.

Assail unsheathed a shiny steel blade that was as long as his forearm.

It had e're been his preferred weapon for this sort of thing.

His heart rate was as steady as his hand, his breathing even and regular whilst he loomed behind the chair. With deliberation, he stepped to one side, positioning himself so that his reflection appeared in the window opposite the desk.

"I am not aware whether it was the entire Brotherhood. How many of them are left? Seven or eight? This is part of the problem. We do not know who they are anymore." Elan tapped his cigarette, the

small stack of ash falling into the belly of the ashtray. "Now, whilst I was at the meeting, I instructed a colleague of mine to be in touch with you—I beg your pardon? Of course I gave him your number, and I resent the tone in your— Yes, he was here at the meeting at my home. He is going to— No, I shan't do it again. Shall you cease interrupting me? I think so, yes."

Elan took a drag and released the smoke in a rush, his annoyance manifested in his breath. "May we move on? Thank you. As I was saying, my colleague shall be in touch with regard to a certain legal provision which may help us. He has explained it to me, but as it is rather technical, I assumed you would wish to question him yourself."

There was a rather long pause. And when Elan spoke next, his tone was calmer, as if placating words had soothed the ruffled feathers of his ego. "Oh, and one last thing. I took care of our little problem with a certain 'business-minded' gentlemale—"

Assail deliberately curled up his fist.

As that leather once again let out its quiet sound of protest, Elan straightened in his seat, his crossed foot returning to the floor, his spine stretching upward such that his head appeared over the back of the chair. He looked left. Looked right.

"I must needs go—"

At that moment, Elan's eyes went to the window across from him, and he saw the reflection of his killer in the glass.

As Xcor stood in an insulated room with a proper heating system, he had to admit he preferred Throe's newest choice of living quarters over that warehouse dungeon they had been in previously. Mayhap he would thank the Shadow who had intruded, if their paths e'er crossed anew.

Then again, perhaps the sense of warmth in his body was his temper flaring, and not a function of good, operational ductwork: The aristocrat on the other end of his cellular phone was testing his last nerve.

He did *not* want to be contacted by anybody else on the Council. Managing one member of the *glymera* was quite enough.

Although he typically took a pacifying approach with Elan, his wrath licked out. "Do not give my number to anyone else."

Elan and he went back and forth a bit, the aristocrat's own ire rising.

Which was, of course, no good. One wanted a usable tool in one's hands. Not something with a prickly grip.

"My apologies," Xcor murmured after a bit. "It is just that I prefer to deal with decision makers only. That is why I contact you and you alone. I have no interest in the others. Only you."

As if Elan were a female and theirs was a romantic liaison.

Xcor rolled his eyes as the aristocrat fell for it, and resumed his discourse. ". . . and one last thing. I took care of our little problem with a certain 'business-minded' gentlemale—"

Instantly, Xcor's attention picked up. What in Fate's name had the idiot done now?

In truth, this could be monstrously inconvenient. Say what one would about Assail's failure to see the light around Wrath's dethroning, that particular "gentlemale" was not cut from Elan's fragile, rippable silk. And as much as Xcor detested dealing with the son of Larex, he had invested considerable time and resources in the relationship. 'Twould be a shame to lose the miscreant now, and have to establish yet another conduit within the Council.

"What did you say?" Xcor demanded.

Elan's tone changed, wariness creeping in. "I must needs go—"

The scream that blared through the phone was so loud and high-pitched, Xcor ripped the cell away from his ear and held it outward.

At the sound, his fighters, who were lounging around the room in various positions, turned their heads in his direction, playing witness, as he did, to Elan's murder.

The caterwauling went on for quite some time, but there was no begging for mercy—either because his assailant was working quickly, or because it was very clear, even to a dying male, that there would be none from the attacker.

"Messy," Zypher remarked as yet another crescendo vibrated out of the phone. "Very messy."

"Still has an airway," another pointed out.

"Not for long," another chimed in.

And they were right. No more than a moment later, something hit the floor hard and that was the end of the sounds.

"Assail," Xcor said sharply. "Pick up the fucking phone. *Assail.*"

There was a rustling, as if the receiver Elan had been speaking into had been retrieved from wherever it had fallen to. And then there was the sound of raking breath on the line.

Which suggested Elan might well be in pieces.

"I know this is you, Assail," Xcor said. "And I can only guess that Elan o'erstepped and the indiscretion got back to your ears. However, you have taken my partner from me, and that cannae go un*ahvenged.*"

It was a surprise when the male answered, his voice deep and strong. "Back in the Old Country, provisions were made for affronts against one's reputation. Surely you not only recall them, but you shall not deny me my right of retribution in the New World."

Xcor bared his fangs, though not because he was frustrated with the one he was speaking to. Fucking Elan. If the dumb bastard had just stuck to being an informant, he'd still be alive—and Xcor could have had the satisfaction of killing him at the end of all of this.

Assail continued. "He stated unto representatives of the king that I was responsible for your rifle shot, the one that was discharged upon my property without my knowledge or permission—and," he cut in before Xcor could speak, "you are well aware of exactly how little I had to do with that attack, are you not."

Back in the Bloodletter's time, this conversation would never have occurred. Assail would have been hunted down as an obstructionist and eliminated for both purpose and sport.

But Xcor had learned his lesson.

As his eyes went to Throe, standing so tall and elegant among the others, he thought, aye, he had learned that there was an appropriate place and time for certain . . . standards, he believed the word was.

"I meant what I said unto you, Xcor, son of the Bloodletter." As Xcor flinched at the reference, he was glad this conversation was occurring over the phone. "I have no interest in either your agenda or the king's. I am a businessman only—I am resigned from the Council, and I am unaligned with you. And Elan attempted to make a traitor out of me—something which, as you well know, comes with a price on one's head. I took Elan's life because he tried to take mine. It is entirely lawful."

Xcor cursed to himself. The male had a rather good point. And whereas Assail's rigid neutrality had at first seemed unbelievable, now Xcor was beginning to . . . well, *trust* was not a word he used with anyone other than his soldiers.

"Tell me something," Xcor drawled.

"Yes?"

"Is his piggish head still attached to that weak little body of his?"

Assail chuckled. "No."

"Do you know that is among my favorite ways of killing?"

"A warning for me, Xcor?"

Xcor glanced back at Throe, and thought again of the virtue of codes of behavior among even warring males.

"No," he declared. "Just something we have in common. Fare thee well, Assail, for what is left of this night."

"Yourself as well. And in the words of our mutual acquaintance, I must needs go. Afore I am forced to slaughter the *doggen* butler who is pounding, at this very instant, upon the door I have locked."

Xcor threw his head back and laughed as he ended the call.

"You know," he said to his fighters, "I rather like him."

FIFTY-EIGHT

The following evening, as the shutters rose and an alarm clock Blay didn't recognize started to chirp, he opened his eyes.

This was not his room. But he knew exactly where he was.

Next to him, against his back, Qhuinn stirred, the male's body stretching against his own, naked skin brushing against naked skin— and didn't that make his wake-up erection start to throb.

Qhuinn reached across Blay's head, his heavy arm extending over, his hand slapping the clock into silence.

Lest there be any question as to whether he'd welcome a quickie before the whole shower-dress–First Meal thing, Blay arched, pushing his ass into the seat of Qhuinn's pelvis. The groan that shot into his ear made him smile a little, but things got serious as Qhuinn's dagger hand snaked downward and found Blay's cock.

"Oh, fuck," Blay breathed as he moved his leg up and out of the way.

"I've got to be inside of you."

Funny, Blay was thinking the exact same thing.

As Qhuinn mounted him, Blay eased onto his stomach, crushing Qhuinn's palm into that hard ridge of arousal.

It didn't take long for the rhythm to get fast and furious, and as Blay's balls tightened with yet another release, he marveled that his desperation for the guy only seemed to grow—you'd think the number of times the pair of them had come together—literally—during the day would have taken this burn down to a rolling boil.

Not the case.

Giving himself over to the pleasure, Blay gritted his teeth as his release shot out at the same time Qhuinn's hips locked up tight and the male grunted.

There was no second round. Not that Blay didn't want it and Qhuinn wasn't able—the clock was the problem.

When Blay reopened his eyes, the digital readout told him that Qhuinn's alarm provided for only fifteen minutes of get-ready—time for a male's quick shower and arming, nothing extra. Kind of made him wish the fighter had been more of a mousse, double-shave, cologne, matching-outfit sort of guy.

With another of his trademark erotic groans, Qhuinn eased them onto their sides, keeping them joined. As the guy breathed deeply, Blay realized he could have stayed like this forever, just the two of them in a silent, dim room. In this moment of peace and quiet, there was no overhang of the past, or anything that needed to be said but wasn't, or third parties, real or fabricated, between them.

"At the end of the night," Qhuinn said in a gravelly voice, "will you come to me again."

"Yes, I will."

There was no other answer that occurred to him. In fact, he wondered how he was going to wait through the twelve hours of darkness and meals and work until he could slip away and come back here.

Qhuinn muttered something that sounded like, "Thank God." Then he moaned as he disengaged, withdrawing himself. In the aftermath, Blay stayed where he was for a brief moment, but ultimately he had no choice save to get up, go out the door, and return to where he belonged.

Thank God no one saw him.

He made it back to his own room without anyone playing witness to the walk of shame, and yup, within fifteen minutes he was showered, leathered, and armed. Stepping out of his door, he—

Qhuinn came out of his at exactly the same moment.

Both of them froze.

Ordinarily, walking down together would have been marginally awkward, the kind of thing that they would have made small talk during.

But now . . .

Qhuinn dropped his eyes. "You go first."

"Okay." Blay turned to walk away. "Thanks."

Blay cast his chest holster and his leather jacket over his shoulder and strode off. By the time he hit the stairwell, it felt like years had passed since they'd lain so close together. Had the day between them even fucking happened?

Jesus, he was starting to feel insane.

Entering the dining room below, he took a random empty chair and hung his stuff over the back as the others did—even though Fritz hated weapons around his food. Then he thanked the *doggen* who presented him with a fully loaded plate, and began to eat. He couldn't have told you what had been served to him, or who was talking around the table. But he knew exactly when Qhuinn came through the jambs: His core started to hum, and it was impossible not to glance over his shoulder.

There was an immediate physical impact as he took in that huge body clad in black, and dripping in weapons—like a car battery had been hooked up to his nervous system.

As Qhuinn didn't meet his eyes, he supposed that was a good thing. The others around the table knew them both too well, especially John, and things were complicated enough without the benevolent peanut gallery getting a chance to weigh in—not that anything would be said publicly. Privately, though? Pillow talk ran rampant through the household.

Something to envy.

Qhuinn started forward, then abruptly changed direction and walked allllll the way around to the other side of the table, to the only chair, other than the one next to Blay, that was empty.

For some reason, Blay thought of the conversation he'd had with his mother over the phone, the one where he had finally admitted to a member of his family who he really was.

Unease feathered across his nape. Qhuinn would never do something like come out, and not because his parents were dead, or because, when that pair had been alive, they had hated their son.

I see myself with a female long-term. I can't explain it. It's just the way it's going to be.

Blay pushed his plate away.

"Blay? Hello?"

Shaking himself, he glanced at Rhage. "I'm sorry?"

"I asked you if you were ready to play Nanook of the North."

Oh, that's right. They were going back to that stretch of forest where they'd found the cabins and the *lesser* with the special power for going ghost—as well as that airplane which was, at the moment, gathering snow in the backyard.

He, John, and Rhage were on deck for the assignment. And Qhuinn.

"I . . . yeah, absolutely."

The most beautiful member of the Brotherhood frowned, his Caribbean blue eyes narrowing. "You okay?"

"Yup. Just fine."

"When was the last time you fed?"

Blay opened his mouth. Shut it. Tried to do the math.

"Uh-huh. I thought so." Rhage leaned forward and spoke around Z's chest. "Yo, Phury? Do you think one of your Chosen can come here and fill in for Layla at dawn? We've got some blood needs."

Great. Just what he wanted to do at the end of the night.

About an hour later, Qhuinn took a sharp breath as he materialized in the cold. Flurries fluttered around his face, getting into his eyes and his nose. One by one, John, Rhage, and Blay assumed form with him.

As he faced off at the airplane hangar, the hollowed-out shell brought back memories of that *fakakta* Cessna, and the Hail Mary trip, and the crash landing.

Happy, happy, joy, joy.

"Good to go?" he said to Rhage.

"Let's do this."

The plan was to proceed at quarter-mile clips until they came to the first few cabins they'd already been to. After that, they would locate the other buildings on the property, using the map they'd found previously as a guide. Just your typical search/recon protocol.

He had no clue what they would find, but that was the point. You didn't know until you did the job.

As Qhuinn sent himself forward, he was acutely aware of where Blay was. Yet as he re-formed in front of the first cabin they came to, he didn't look over when Blay appeared about five feet away. Not a good idea. Even though they were on assignment, all he had to do was close his eyes and his mind was flooded with images of naked bodies intertwined in the dim light of his bedroom.

Further visual confirm that the guy was hot as fuck was not a help.

He was ashamed to admit it, but right now, the only thing keeping him together was the fact that Blay had promised to come to him at dawn. The aftermath-awkwardness at First Meal had made him crave the communion even more, to the point where he was shaken by the idea that someday, in the near future, Saxton would be back and Blay would stop walking over from next door—and then what the fuck was he going to do.

What a goddamn mess.

At least Layla was doing well: still nauseated and smiling constantly.

Still pregnant, thanks to Blay's intervention . . .

"East by northeast," Rhage said as he consulted the map.

"Roger that," Qhuinn replied.

And so they went on, going deeper into the territory, the forest fanning out all around them for hundreds and hundreds of yards . . . and then by a mile. And then by several miles.

The cabins were largely the same, roughly twenty by twenty, open-spaced in the center, no bathroom, no kitchen, just a roof and four walls to file down the worst of the weather's teeth. The farther in they went, the more dilapidated the structures became—and they were all empty. Logical. This was a long trek if you were on foot—and *lessers*, as strong as they were, couldn't dematerialize.

At least, most of them couldn't.

That had to have been the *Fore-lesser*, he thought. Only explanation for how that injured slayer had gone ghost like that.

The seventh cabin they came to was directly on a trail that had been used frequently enough at some point so that they could still see its path through the evergreens.

This one was missing a number of panes of glass, and its door had been blown open, a snowdrift barging in like a burglar. Qhuinn crunched grimly through the ice pack, his shitkickers making mince-meat of the pristine surface as he closed in on the porch. With a flashlight in his left hand and a forty-five in his right, he jumped up under the eaves and leaned in.

Same shit, different dead space.

As he swept the interior, there was a whole lot of absolutely frickin' nothing. No furniture. Some built-in shelving that was empty. Cobwebs that waved in the breeze coming through the busted window-panes.

"Clear," he called out.

Turning away, he thought this was bullshit. He wanted to be downtown kicking ass, not out here in the middle of nowhere, hunting and pecking and coming up with nada.

Rhage put a penlight between his teeth and unfolded the map once again. Making a mark with a pen, he tapped the heavy paper. "Last one is about a quarter mile to the west."

Thank. Fuck.

Assuming everything was as snore as it had been, they should be out of this and engaging the enemy in the alleys within fifteen, maybe twenty minutes.

Piece of cake.

FIFTY-NINE

"You look really happy."

Layla glanced over. On some level, it was unfathomable that the queen of the race was propped up next to her on the bed, reading *Us Weekly* and *People*, and watching television. Then again, except for the huge blood red Saturnine Ruby that winked on her finger, she was as normal as could be.

"I am." Layla put aside the article on the newest season of *The Bachelor* and laid her hand upon her belly. "I am ecstatic."

Especially given that Payne had stopped by earlier, and appeared to be back to feeling like herself. Although Layla's wish for the pregnancy to continue was nearly pathological, the idea that the blessing had come at a cost to the other female had not sat well.

"Do you wish to have young?" Layla blurted. And then had to add, "If it does not offend—"

Beth batted away the concern. "You can ask me anything. And, God, yes. I want some so badly. It's funny, back before my change? I had no interest in them—at all. They were a noisy, out-of-control complication that I honestly didn't know why people bothered to bring into their lives. Then I met Wrath." She pushed her dark hair back and laughed. "Needless to say, everything has changed."

"How many needings have you had?"

"I'm waiting. Praying. Counting down."

Layla frowned and made busywork opening a new sleeve of saltines. It was hard to remember much in specific of those crazy hours with Qhuinn—but it had been a trial of epic proportions.

Given the miracle that was still resting within her, it had all been worth it.

However, she couldn't say she ever wanted to go through her fertile time again. At least not unmedicated.

"Well, I wish your needing for you soon, then." Layla bit into yet another cracker, the square splintering and melting in her mouth. "And I can't believe I'm saying that."

"Is it as rough as . . . I mean, I didn't get to talk to Wellsie much about hers before she passed, and Bella's never said anything about her time." Beth looked down at the queen's ring, as if admiring the way its facets captured and reflected the light. "And I don't know Autumn all that well—she's lovely, but given everything she and Tohr have just been through, it doesn't seem an appropriate topic to bring up with her."

"It's mostly a blur, to be honest."

"Probably a blessing, huh."

Layla winced. "I wish I could tell you otherwise—but yes, I believe it is a blessing."

"It's got to be worth it, though."

"Without a doubt—I was just thinking that very thing, as a matter of fact." Layla smiled. "You know what they say about pregnant females, yes?"

"What?"

"If you spend time with them, they'll encourage your needing to come."

"Reeeeeeally." The queen grinned. "Then you could be the answer to my prayers."

"Well, I'm not sure whether it's true. On the Far Side, we're fertile all the time. It's only here on Earth that females are subjected to hormone fluctuations—but I have read about the effect in the library."

"Then let's do our own experiment, shall we?" Beth offered her palm for a shake. "Besides, I like being here. You're very inspirational."

Layla's brows peaked as she shook what was presented to her. "Inspir—oh, no. I cannot see that at all."

"Think of everything you've been through."

"The pregnancy has resolved itself, though—"

"Not just that. You're the survivor of a cult." As Layla gave her a blank look, the queen asked, "You've never heard of that?"

"I know the word's definition. But I'm not sure it applies to me."

The queen glanced away, as if she didn't want to create discord. "Hey, I could be wrong, and you would certainly know better than me—besides, you're happy now, and that's what matters."

Layla focused on the television across the way. From what she understood, a cult was not a good thing, and *survivor* was a term usually associated with people who had been through some kind of trauma.

The Sanctuary had been as placid and temperate as a spring day upon the earth, all the females in the sacred place calm and at peace with their important duties to the mother of the race.

No coercion. No strife.

For some reason, Payne's voice entered her mind.

You and I are sisters in my mother's tyranny—casualties of her grand plan for the way things must be. We were both jailed by her in different ways, you as a Chosen, myself as her blooded daughter.

"I'm sorry," the queen said, reaching out and touching Layla's arm. "I didn't mean to upset you. I honestly don't know what the hell I'm talking about."

Layla snapped herself back to attention. "Oh, please, do not concern yourself." She clasped the queen's hand. "I take no offense at all. But now, let us speak of happier things—such as your *hellren*. He must be impatient for your time to come as well."

Beth laughed tightly. "That is not exactly where he's at."

"Surely he must want an heir?"

"I think he'll give me one. But only because I want a child as badly as I do."

"Oh."

"'Oh' is right." Beth gave Layla's palm a squeeze. "He just worries too much. I'm strong and healthy, and ready for it. Now, if I could just get my body to get in gear—hopefully, it will take your cue."

Layla smiled and rubbed her flat belly. "Did you hear that, little one? You need to help your queen. It's important for the royal family to have a young."

"But it's not for the throne," Beth interjected. "Not on my part. I just want to be a mom, and I want to have my husband's kid. At the core, it's as simple as that."

Layla fell silent. She was so glad to have Qhuinn with her on this journey—but it would have been wonderful to have a proper mate to lie beside her and cradle her during the day, to love her and hold her and tell her that she was precious not solely for what her body could do, but for what she inspired in his heart.

An image of Xcor's harsh face flashed into her mind's eye.

Shaking her head, she thought, no, she mustn't dwell on that. She needed to keep herself calm and relaxed for the young as surely her stress was transmitted to that which her womb nurtured. Besides, she had already been blessed with much, and if this pregnancy went to term and she lived through the birth?

She had been granted a true and abiding miracle.

"I'm sure it will work out with the king," she announced. "Fate has a way of giving us what we need."

"Amen, sister. Amen."

Sola pulled her Audi directly into the driveway of the glass house on the river, and she parked right at the rear door of the damn thing.

Getting out, she planted her boots in the snow, put her hand inside her parka on the butt of her gun, and shut the door with her hip. As she marched up to that back entrance, she made eye contact with the roofline.

There had to be security cameras up there.

She didn't bother to ring the doorbell or knock on the door. He would know she was here. And he if he wasn't home? Well, then she'd think of a nice little calling card of some sort to leave him.

Maybe a security alarm that went off? An open window or cupboard?

Or something missing from inside . . .

The door opened and there he was, live and in person—exactly as he had been the night before, and yet, as ever, somehow taller, more dangerous, and sexier than she remembered.

"Isn't this a bit obvious for you?" he drawled.

He was dressed in a dark suit of some designer variety—and the thing had to have been hand-tailored as well, given the way it fit him so perfectly.

"I'm here to set something straight," she said.

"And you appear to want to dictate terms." As if this were a quaint idea. "Anything else? Did you happen to bring dinner? I'm hungry."

"Are you going to let me in, or do you want to do this in the cold?"

"Is your hand on a weapon, by any chance?"

"Of course it is."

"In that case, do come in."

As he stepped aside, she rolled her eyes. Why the fact that she could shoot him would encourage the man to let her into his house was a mystery—

Sola froze as she looked into a modern kitchen. Standing shoulder-to-shoulder were two men who were identical images of each other. They were also as big as the man she'd come for, just as dangerous—and they each had a gun in their hand.

They had to be the ones who'd been with him under the bridge.

The door clapped shut, and even though her adrenal glands let out a burst of warning, she kept the reaction to herself.

The one she had come to see smiled as he brushed past her. "These are my associates."

"I want to speak with you alone."

The man eased back against a granite counter, put a cigar between his teeth, and lit it with a gold lighter. As he clipped the top shut, he exhaled a puff of blue smoke and looked over at her. "Gentlemen, will you excuse us for a moment."

The twin Mr. Happys didn't look pleased with the dismissal. Then again, you could probably have tried to give them both a winning lottery ticket and they would have eaten your hand clean off your wrist. Just on principle.

They did walk off, however, moving in a synchronized way that was highly unsettling.

"Where'd you find that pair?" she asked dryly. "The Internet?"

"It's amazing what one can secure on eBay."

Abruptly, she cut the crap: "I want you to stop following me."

The man took a pull on that cigar, the fat end glowing bright orange. "Do you."

"You've got no reason to. I'm not going to come here again—in any capacity."

"Really."

"You have my word."

There was nothing Sola hated more than admitting defeat—and disengaging from the surveillance of this guy and his property was a kind of quitting. But that run-in last night, while she'd been on a date with an innocent bystander, for godsakes, had told her things were getting out of control. She was perfectly capable of playing cat and mouse—she did it all the time in her profession. With this man, however? There was no ultimate goal to be won; no payday awaiting her for information gathered; no intention for her to rob him.

And the stakes were escalating.

Especially if they ever kissed again—because she doubted she would stop it, and the definition of stupid was sleeping with someone like him.

"Your word?" he said. "And exactly how much is that worth."

"It's all I have to offer you."

His eyes, those laser beams, narrowed on her mouth. "I'm not so certain of that."

His accent and that deep, delicious voice turned the syllables into a caress—something that she could almost feel on her skin.

Which was precisely why she was doing this. "You've got no reason to follow me. Effective right now."

"Mayhap I like the view." As his eyes traveled down her body, another shock went through her, but not the anxious kind. "Yes, I find that I do. Tell me something, did you enjoy your evening out? Food to your liking? Companionship . . . to your liking?"

"I'm stopping this tonight. You're not going to see me again."

As that was all she had to say, she went to turn away.

"Do you honestly think it ends here between you and me?"

His dark, beautiful voice held an ominous threat in it.

Sola looked over her shoulder. "You asked me not to trespass or spy—I'm not going to."

"And I say to you once again, do you *honestly* think it ends like this."

"I'm giving you what you want."

"Not even close," he growled.

For a moment, that connection that had been forged in the cold, when their lips had locked in her car and their bodies had strained, sprang back to life.

"It's too late to retreat." He took another puff. "Your chance to get away has come . . . and gone."

She turned to face him. "Not to put too fine a point on it—but

bullshit. I'm not afraid of you, or anyone else—so come at me. But know that I will hurt you to defend myself—"

An abrupt sound vibrated through the air between them.

Purring? Was the man actually purr—

He took a step forward. Then another. And as a gentleman might, he held his cigar to the side, like he didn't want to burn her or get smoke in her face.

"Tell me your name," he said. Or commanded, more like it.

"I find it hard to believe you don't already know it."

"I do not." This was said with an arch of the brow, as if information seeking was beneath him. "Tell me your name, and I will let you leave here now."

God . . . his eyes . . . they were moonlight and shadow intertwined, an impossible color somewhere between silver and violet and pale blue.

"As our paths will not be crossing, it's not relevant—"

"Just so you know . . . you will give yourself to me—"

"Excuse me—"

"But you will beg me for it first."

Sola jutted forward, her temper blowing all her let's-be-reasonable right out of the water. "Over my dead body."

"Sorry, not to my taste." He dropped his chin and stared at her from beneath lowered lids. "I prefer you hot . . . and wet."

"Not going to happen." She pivoted away and headed for the door. "And we're done."

Just as she entered the anteroom, her eye caught something on the bench that ran down the squat space's far wall.

Her head whipped around, and her feet faltered. It was a knife, a very long knife, so long it was nearly a sword.

There was bright red blood on the blade.

"Rethinking your departure?" he said in that dark voice from directly behind her.

"No." She shot over to the door and yanked it open. "I'm right on target with it."

Slamming the thing behind her, she wanted to run to her car, but refused to give in to panic even as she expected him to come after her.

And yet the man stayed put, looming in the window of the door she had put to good use, watching her while she got in, started her engine and put the Audi into gear.

As she backed out of the drive, her heart was pounding—

Especially as a truly terrifying thought occurred to her.

Shoving her hand into her purse, she felt around for her phone, and when she found it, she went into her contact lists, selected one, and hit *send*. Frazzled by fear, she put the cell up to her ear even though she was Bluetooth enabled—and it was against the law in New York not to be hands-free.

Ring.

Ring.

Ring—

"Hi! I was hoping to hear from you."

Sola sagged in the driver's seat, her head falling back against the rest. "Hi, Mark."

God, the sound of the man's voice was a relief.

"Are you okay?" her trainer asked.

She thought of that bloody blade. "I am. Yes. Are you just getting off work?"

As they embarked on a pleasant enough conversation, she drove off, her foot heavy on the gas pedal, the landscape streaking by: White snow. Grungy, salted road. Skeletal trees. Little old-fashioned cabin with a light on inside. Flat, bald space over the river to the left.

Every time she blinked, she saw the shape in the windows of that door. Watching. Planning. Wanting . . .

Her.

And goddamn it, her body was desperate to be caught by him.

SIXTY

s Qhuinn rematerialized, his flashlight illuminated the final cabin. He didn't wait for the others this time, just marched forward, gunning for the door, which was intact and shut tight—

His first clue that something was off came when he grabbed the rough-hewn handle: a low-level electrical charge licked into his hand and traveled up his arm.

Retracting his palm, he shook things out, his instincts going on high alert.

"What is it?" Rhage asked as the Brother stalked up onto the shallow porch.

Qhuinn glanced around, noting that Blay and John were on the periphery. "I don't know."

Rhage went for the door—and had the same reaction, recoiling sharply. "What the fuck."

"I know, right," Qhuinn muttered as he stepped back and ran his light around the exterior.

The two windows on either side of the entrance had been boarded up, and as he walked over and looked down the structure's flank, the same was true of the ones on that side, as well.

"Fuck this," Rhage growled. The Brother took three steps back and then rushed at the door, his heavy shoulder angled like a battering ram.

And what do you know, the impact splintered the wooden panels—

All at once, a blinding light seared through the night, illuminating the forest like a bomb had gone off, turning Rhage getting thrown backward into a movie.

As Blay and John rushed across to do a damage assessment on the fighter, Qhuinn lunged forward, bracing himself as he went for the jambs, expecting to get nailed with a couple hundred volts' worth of God-only-knows-what.

Instead, he hit nothing but air, his forward momentum so great he had to tuck into a ball and roll to keep from landing on his face. A breath later, he punched up off the floor and landed in a crouch, gun in one hand, flashlight in another.

Something smelled bad.

"Behind you," Blay said, as a second beam of light joined his own.

The air inside the cabin was curiously warm, as if there were a heater plugged in somewhere—except that wasn't possible. No electricity and no gas tank. And no one had been here for a while, going by the undisturbed layer of dust on the floorboards and the delicate, vertical cobwebs that hung from the ceiling as motionless as heavy ropes.

"What's that," Blay demanded.

As Qhuinn brought his beam around, he frowned. There were a number of what appeared to be oil drums up against the far wall, the grouping clustered together, as if they'd been scared by something and had circled the wagons for self-protection.

Qhuinn walked over, all the while panning his flashlight in fat circles, and he frowned once more as he got a good look at the large-bore canisters. None of them had lids, and his light seemed to reflect off some sort of oil.

"What . . . the hell is this?"

Leaning over the closest one, he took a deep breath in through his nose, and got a sinus burn full of slayer stench. Going by the way his beam didn't penetrate the surface of the liquid, he knew it could be

only one thing, and you sure as shit couldn't use it to power a heater or a generator.

It was the blood of the Omega.

"Behind you," Rhage said, as the Brother entered.

A soft whistle announced that John had come in as well.

"Is that what I think it is?" Blay muttered as he stood beside Qhuinn.

Qhuinn put his flashlight between his teeth and reached forward with his bare hand. Just as he made contact with the viscous nasty, something surged within the drum—

"Fuck!" he shouted, jumping back.

As his flashlight landed on the floor and rolled to the side, Blay's beam illuminated what had moved.

An arm.

There was someone inside the drum.

"Jesus Christ," Blay breathed.

Behind them, Rhage's voice barked loudly, "V? We need backup out here. Stat."

Qhuinn bent down and snagged his light. Returning it to the oily liquid, he watched as that forearm moved again in slow motion just under the surface, the shift bringing the outside of the wrist and the back of the hand into view. . . .

Something flashed, the passing glint catching Qhuinn's eye. Re-angling his beam, he bent further over the drum.

The hand wasn't right, its joints deformed, all or part of each finger gone, as if put through a grinder. . . .

That glimmer broke through the cesspool of the Omega's blood once more.

It was . . . a ring?

"Wait, wait, Qhuinn—you need to pull back—"

Qhuinn ignored the commentary as he leaned in even farther, getting closer—closer. . . .

Closer . . .

At first, he couldn't believe what he was looking at. He simply couldn't be looking at a family crest ring.

But what else could it be? It was on the forefinger, the only digit that hadn't been hacked off. And it was gold—even through the black oil, the yellow glow was obvious. And the ring itself had a broad face into which was pressed a—

"Qhuinn," Rhage said sharply. "Get the fuck away——"

The arm moved again, the pale hand breaching the surface of the liquid, appearing as a specter's might from out of the grave, reaching out. . . .

The Omega's blood retracted from the surface of the ring, revealing . . .

"Qhuinn, I am not playing——"

Noise exploded in the cabin, filling the air.

He was completely unaware that it was a shout coming from his own mouth.

At first, Blay thought that whatever was in the drum had grabbed onto Qhuinn and pulled him in——and that was why Qhuinn screamed. On instinct, he jumped forward and grabbed onto Qhuinn's waist, throwing out his anchor and yanking back.

What came out of that drum would haunt Blay's nightmares for years . . . decades afterward.

In fact, what was inside hadn't latched onto Qhuinn; it was the other way around. And as Blay hauled back, a male form was extracted from the tight squeeze, the Omega's blood pouring out in rivers, splashing onto the cold wooden planks of the cabin's floor, hitting Blay's shitkickers and leathers, drenching Qhuinn.

Qhuinn had to scramble to keep his grip from slipping off, his gun and flashlight long forgotten, his gloved hands slapping and scratching to keep from losing contact. . . .

As they hoisted . . .

The oil drum fell over onto its side as the male sprawled out flat at their feet.

No one moved. It was as if they had all stepped in and assumed their positions in a tableau.

Blay recognized who it was immediately.

He couldn't believe it.

The dead had returned to the living . . . . in a manner of speaking.

Qhuinn squatted down and touched the male's shoulders. Then he spoke his brother's name roughly: "Luchas?"

The response was immediate. His brother's hands began to slowly pinwheel, his mangled legs shifting, his naked body trying to move. His skin was bruised all over, the harsh illumination from the flash-

lights showing every contusion and cut and black-and-blue, the stain of the Omega's blood gradually receding from the pale skin.

Dear God, what had they done to him? One of his eyes was swollen shut, and his mouth was lopsided, as if he'd been punched there. As he grimaced, it appeared that his teeth had all been spared, but that was about the only mercy he seemed to have been given.

"Luchas?" Qhuinn said again. "Can you talk to me?"

From off to the side, Rhage was on his phone again. "V? We've really got a situation. What's your ETA . . . what? No, abso no—I need you now. . . . No, you. And Payne." Hollywood glanced over and mouthed, *Do you guys know who he is?*

Blay had to clear his throat, his reply tripping and stumbling out. "It's his . . . brother."

Rhage blinked. Shook his head. Leaned in. "I'm sorry, what did you—"

"His brother," Blay repeated loudly and clearly.

"Jesus . . ." Rhage whispered. And then he snapped back into action. "Now, V. *Now.*"

"Luchas, can you hear me?" Qhuinn spoke.

Vishous burst into the cabin a split second later. The Brother was covered in *lesser* blood and bleeding red thanks to a gash across his face—he was also breathing like a freight train and had a dripping black dagger in his hand.

The instant he saw what they were all clustered around, he stopped. "What the fuck is that?"

Rhage quickly made slashing motions across his throat, shutting up any further commentary. Then he grabbed V's arm and dragged him out of earshot. When the pair came back, V was showing no emotion at all.

"Let me take a look at him," V said.

Qhuinn just kept talking at his brother, the words coming out in a steady stream that didn't make much sense. Then again, as far as anyone had known, the male had been killed in the raids, along with Qhuinn's mother, father, and sister. So, yeah, this was enough to make even Shakespeare sport a case of the babbles.

Except . . . this wasn't possible, Blay thought. There had been four bodies at the house—and Luchas had been among them.

Blay should know. He'd been the one to go in and do the identifying.

He put a hand on Qhuinn's shoulder. "Hey."

Qhuinn's words drifted off. Then he looked up into Blay's eyes. "He's not answering me."

"Can you let V take a quick look? We need a medic's opinion." And maybe a helluva lot more to answer what the hell was going on here. "Come on, stand over here with me."

Qhuinn straightened and pulled back, but he didn't go far, and his eyes never left his brother. "Have they turned him?" He crossed his arms and curled himself forward. "Do you think they turned him?"

Blay shook his head, and wished he could lie. "I don't know."

SIXTY-ONE

s Qhuinn stared down at the cabin floor, his brain was firing in a series of disconnected flashes, the concrete notion that his whole family had been wiped out colliding into what appeared to be a very different reality.

He kept coming back to a night long, long ago, when he'd walked through the front door of his parents' to find his family sitting together at that dining room table . . . and his brother getting that ring that was on his now mangled hand.

You'd think the sight of the guy tortured but alive would be all he'd concentrate on.

"What's going on, V?" he demanded. "How is he?"

"He's alive." The Brother shifted his black dagger around and wiped the blade off on his leather-clad thigh. "Son? Son, can you look at me?"

Luchas just kept staring up at Qhuinn, his perfectly matched pair of beautiful gray eyes bloodshot and crazy wide. His mouth was moving, but no sound was coming out.

"Son, I'm going to have to cut you, okay? Son?"

Qhuinn knew exactly what V was going for. "Do it."

Qhuinn's heart banged like a fist against his sternum as the Brother took that black blade and streaked the point down the outside of Luchas's arm. The guy didn't even flinch; then again, with what was going on for him? Drop in the bucket.

Please be red, please be red, please be—

Red blood welled and seeped out, a brilliant contrast to the staining black oil that he was covered with.

Everyone let out the breath they'd been holding.

"Okay, son, that's good, that's good. . . ."

They hadn't turned him.

V got up from the floor and tipped his head to the side, motioning for a private convo. As Qhuinn went over, he took Blay's arm and brought him along. It was just the most natural thing to do. This was serious shit, and he knew he wasn't tracking—and there was no one else he'd rather have with him.

"I don't have a blood pressure cuff or a stethoscope, but I'll tell you right now—his pulse is weak and erratic, and I'm pretty damn sure he's in shock. I don't know how long he's been in there or what they did to him, but he is alive in the conventional sense. The problem is, Payne's out of commission." V's eyes glowed. "And you two know why."

Ah, so he'd spoken with his sister.

"She's not going to be able to work her magic," the Brother continued, "and we're a million miles from everywhere."

"Bottom line," Qhuinn said grimly.

V stared him right in the eye. "He's going to die in the next couple of—"

"V!" Rhage barked. "Get over here!"

Down on the floor, Luchas's battered body was drawing up into itself, his broken hands curling into his palms, his knees cranking in tight, his spine curling toward the cabin's ceiling.

Qhuinn jacked over and fell to his knees by his brother's head. "Stay with me, Luchas. Come on, fight it—"

Those gray eyes relocked on Qhuinn's, and the agony in them was so shattering, Qhuinn was barely aware of V rushing over and taking the glove off of his glowing hand.

"Qhuinn!" the Brother shouted, like maybe he'd said Qhuinn's name a couple of times.

He didn't look away from his brother. "What?"

"This could kill him, but maybe it'll get his heart beating right. It's a bad shot—but it's the only one he's got."

In the split second before he replied, he felt an overwhelming need for his brother to come through this some way, somehow. Even though he barely knew the guy, and had resented him for years—and then been beaten by him when Luchas had joined that Honor Guard—he hadn't realized until they were gone how rudderless you were on the planet when there was no blood of yours walking the earth with you.

Then again, that void was exactly what had spurred him on during Layla's needing. And what had made him reach for Blay instinctively.

Love 'em or hate 'em, by blood or by heart, family was a kind of oxygen.

Necessary for the living.

"Do it," he said once more.

"Wait," Blay cut in, whipping his belt off and giving it to Qhuinn. "For his mouth."

Just one more reason to love the guy. Although it wasn't like he needed yet another.

Qhuinn angled the strap into his brother's open mouth and held it in place as he nodded to V. "Stay with me, Luchas. Come on, now— stay with . . ."

Out of the corner of his eye, he tracked that bright white light closing in on his brother's sternum. . . .

Luchas's chest jerked high, his whole body spasming off the floor-boards as a brilliant glow shot through him, funneling down his arms and his legs, radiating up to his head. The sound he made was inhuman, a guttural moan that went straight into Qhuinn's marrow.

When V yanked back his hand, that glowing palm raising high, Luchas dropped like the deadweight he was, his body bouncing, his limbs flapping.

He blinked rapidly, as if a stiff breeze were blowing into his face.

"Hit him again," Qhuinn demanded. When V didn't respond, he glared. "One more time."

"This is fucking nuts," Rhage muttered.

V measured the male for a moment. Then brought that deadly hand back into range. "Once more—that's all you get," he said to Luchas.

"Damn straight," Rhage cut in. "Any more and you could make a s'more out of the son of a bitch."

The second shot was just as bad—that battered body contorting wildly, Luchas making that god-awful sound before landing back down in a clatter of bones.

But he took a deep breath. A big, powerful, deep breath that expanded his rib cage.

Qhuinn felt like praying, and he guessed he did as he started chanting, "Come on, come on. . . ."

The mangled hand, the one with the ring, stretched out and grabbed onto Qhuinn's shirt. The hold was weak, but Qhuinn leaned in.

"What," he said. "Talk slow. . . ."

That hand skipped over his jacket.

"Talk to me."

His brother's hand locked on the grip of one of his daggers. "Kill . . . me. . . ."

Qhuinn's eyes peeled wide.

Luchas's voice was nothing like it had been, nothing but a hoarse whisper. "Kill . . . me . . . brother . . . mine. . . ."

SIXTY-TWO

"How you holding up?" Blay asked.

Standing on the porch of the cabin, Qhuinn breathed in and caught a hint of smoke on the air. Blay had lit up again, and much as Qhuinn hated the habit, he didn't blame the guy. Hell, if he were into that kind of thing, he'd have busted out the coffin nails, too.

He glanced over. Blay was staring at him patiently, clearly prepared to wait for a response to the question even if it took what was left of the night.

Qhuinn checked his watch. One a.m.

How long was it going to take the rest of Brotherhood to get here? And was this evac plan they were all rocking really going to work—

"I feel like I'm losing my fucking mind," he replied.

"I'm with you." Blay exhaled in the opposite direction. "I can't believe that he's . . ."

Qhuinn stared at the trees ahead of them. "I never asked you about that night."

"No. And frankly, I don't blame you."

Behind them, in the cabin, Rhage, V, and John were with Luchas.

Everyone had taken their jackets off and wrapped them around the male in hopes of keeping him warm.

Standing in his muscle shirt and his weapons, Qhuinn didn't feel the cold.

He cleared his throat. "Did you see him."

Blay had been the one to go back to the mansion after the raids. Qhuinn simply hadn't had the sac to ID the bodies.

"Yes, I did."

"Was he dead then?"

"As far as I knew, yes. He was . . . yeah, I didn't think there was any chance he was alive."

"You know, I never sold the house."

"So I'd heard."

Technically, as a disavowed member of the family, he had had no rights to the property. But there had been so many killed that no one made any claims to the estate, and it had, according to the Old Laws, reverted to the king's ownership—whereupon Wrath had promptly given it in fee simple to Qhuinn.

Whatever the hell that meant.

"I didn't know what to think when I was told they'd gotten slaughtered." Qhuinn looked up to the sky. The forecast was for more snow, so no stars were to be seen. "They hated me. I guess I hated them. And then they were gone."

Beside him, Blay went very still.

Qhuinn knew why and a sudden awkwardness had him shoving his hands into his pockets. Yes, he absolutely despised talking about emotions and crap, but there was no keeping the shit down. Not out here. In private. With Blay.

Clearing his throat, he kept going. "I was relieved more than anything, to be honest. I can't tell you what it was like growing up in that house. All those people looking at me like I was a walking, talking curse on them." He shook his head. "I used to avoid them as much as possible, using the servants' stairs, staying in that part of the house. But then the *doggen* threatened to quit. Actually, the biggest bene of my getting through the transition was that I could dematerialize out the window of my room. Then none of them had to deal with me."

Even when Blay cursed softly, Qhuinn still didn't feel like shutting up. "And you know what the real head fuck was? I saw that love was possible when my father looked at my brother. It would have been one

thing if the bastard had just hated all of us—but he didn't. And that just made me realize how locked out I was." Qhuinn glanced over. Shuffled his shitkickers. "Why are you looking at me like that."

"Sorry. Yeah, sorry. You just . . . you've never talked about them. Ever."

Qhuinn frowned and measured the sky again, picturing the twinkling lights of the stars even though he couldn't see them. "I wanted to. With you, that is. Not with anyone else."

"Why didn't you?" As if this was something the guy had wondered for a while.

In the silence that followed, Qhuinn sifted through memories he had never dwelled on, seeing himself. Seeing his family. Seeing . . . Blay. "I loved going to your house. I can't tell you what it meant to me—I remember the first time you invited me over. I was convinced your parents were going to kick me out. I was ready for it. Hell, I dealt with that shit at my own house all the time, so why wouldn't complete strangers do the same? But your mom . . ." Qhuinn cleared his throat again. "Your mom sat me down at your kitchen table and fed me."

"She was mortified that she made you sick. Right afterward, you ran into the bathroom and threw up for an hour."

"I wasn't throwing up in there."

Blay's head whipped around. "But you said—"

"I was crying."

As Blay recoiled, Qhuinn shrugged. "Come on, what was I going to say. That I pussied out and wept next to the sink on the floor? I ran the water so no one heard and flushed the toilet every once in a while."

"I never knew."

"That was the plan." Qhuinn glanced over. "That was always the plan. I didn't want you to know how bad it was at my house, because I didn't want you to feel sorry for me. I didn't want you or your parents to feel like you had to take me in. I wanted you to be my friend—and you were. You always have been."

Blay looked away fast. Then rubbed his face with the hand he didn't have the cigarette in.

"You guys were what got me through it," Qhuinn heard himself say. "I lived for the night, because I could go over to your house. It was the only thing that kept me going. You were the only thing, actually. It was . . . you."

As Blay's eyes returned to his own, he had the sense the guy was searching for words.

And God help them both, if it hadn't been for Saxton, Qhuinn would have dropped the l-word right then and there, even though the timing was stupid.

"You can, you know," Blay said finally. "Talk to me."

Qhuinn stamped his feet and bunched up his shoulders, stretching the muscles of his back. "Be careful. I might take you up on that."

"It would help." As Qhuinn glanced over again, Blay was the one shaking his head. "I don't know what I'm saying."

Bullshit, Qhuinn thought—

Without warning, V emerged from the cabin, lighting up a hand-rolled as he came out. As Qhuinn fell silent, he wasn't sure whether he was relieved the conversation had been forced to an end or not.

On the exhale, Vishous said, "I need to make sure you understand the consequences."

Qhuinn nodded. "I already know what you're going to say."

Those diamond eyes locked on his own. "Well, let's just open air it anyway, shall we? I don't sense any of the Omega in him, but if it comes out, or if I've missed something, I'm going to have to take care of him."

Kill me, brother mine. Kill me.

"You do what you have to."

"He can't go into the mansion."

"Agreed."

V put out his nonlethal hand. "Swear to it."

It felt strange to clasp the Brother's palm and bind his word on the contact—because that was what next of kin had to do in situations like this, and shit knew he hadn't been next to anything for anybody ever: Even before the disavowal by his family, he'd have been the last person to vouch for the bloodline.

Times had changed though, hadn't they.

"One other thing." V tapped the tip of the hand-rolled. "It's going to be a long, hard recovery for him. And I'm not just talking about the physical shit. You need to prepare yourself."

What, like they'd had a relationship before this or something? He

might share some DNA with the guy, but other than that, Luchas was a stranger. "I know."

"Okay. Fair enough."

In the distance, a pair of high-pitched whines cut through the darkness.

"Thank fuck," Qhuinn bit out as he went back into the cabin.

Over in the corner, next to the drum that had been overturned, his brother was nothing but a pile of jackets, his twisted body covered by the makeshift blankets.

Qhuinn stalked across the floorboards, nodding to John Matthew and Rhage.

Kneeling down next to his brother, he felt like he was in a dreamscape, not reality. "Luchas? Listen, here's what's going to happen. They're going to take you out on a sled. You're going to our clinic for treatment. Luchas? Can you hear me?"

As the pair of snowmobiles tore up to the cabin, Blay tracked their progress from the porch, watching their headlights get bigger and brighter, the pair of engines dimming into steady purrs as they reached their destination. Oh . . . this was good: Behind one of them, there was a covered sled, the kind of thing he'd seen on TV during the Olympics when some skier had crashed through the ropes and been evac'd down a mountain.

Perfect.

Manny and Butch dismounted and jogged over.

"They're right in there," Blay said, getting out of the doctor's way.

"Luchas? You with me?" he heard Qhuinn murmur.

Peering in, Blay wathced as Manny bent over Luchas's body. Man, what a fucking night. And he'd thought the air show from a couple of evenings ago had been full of drama?

It's always been you.

Turning back to face the forest, Blay rubbed his face again, like that was going to help. And he wanted to light up another Dunhill, but the longer this took, the more paranoid he became. The last thing this situation needed was a squadron of *lessers* showing up before they could get Luchas out to safety.

Better to have a forty than a cig in his hands.

It's always been you.

"You okay?" Butch asked.

In the spirit of honesty, because that seemed to be tonight's theme song, he shook his head. "Not in the slightest."

The cop clapped him on the shoulder. "So you knew him."

"I thought I did, yes." Oh, wait, the question was about Luchas. "I mean, yes, I did."

"It's gotta be wicked tough, this whole thing."

Blay glanced over his shoulder again and got another eyeful of Qhuinn crouching next to his brother. His old friend's face was ancient in the beams of those flashlights, to the point where Blay wondered if he had actually seen it relaxed after they'd been together—or whether he'd been mistaken.

You were the only thing . . . actually.

"It is tough," he muttered.

And strange, too.

Right after his transition, he had looked for some sign that the way he felt about his friend was reciprocated, some clue as to where Qhuinn was at. But there had been nothing that he had been able to see— nothing other than abiding loyalty, friendship, and kick-ass fighting skills: Through the hookups they'd had with other people, and the training, and then the nights out in the field . . . he had always been on the far side of the connection he'd wanted, staring into a wall he couldn't get around.

That short time on this porch?

It was the first time he'd ever gotten a glimpse of what he'd longed for even more greatly than the sex.

Shit, for a treacherous moment, he wondered if there had in fact been an "in" involved when Layla had spilled the beans outside of his bedroom.

"They're moving him." Butch snagged Blay's arm and got him out of the way of the door. "Come stand with me."

Luchas had been properly covered now, a silver Mylar blanket wrapped around him from head to foot, nothing but the barest hint of his face showing. They had put him onto a collapsible stretcher, with Qhuinn at one end and V on the other. Manny walked alongside, as if he were not sure whether he was going to need to resuscitate things at any given moment.

Over at the sled, they transferred Qhuinn's brother and strapped him down.

"I'm driving him out," Qhuinn announced as he mounted up and gunned the snowmobile's engine.

"Slow and steady," Manny warned. "He's a fucking mass of broken bones."

Qhuinn glanced over at Blay. "Ride with me?"

No reason to answer that. He marched over and got on behind the guy.

Typical of Qhuinn, he didn't bother waiting for the others. He just nailed the accelerator and took off. He did, however, listen to the good doctor: He made a broad turn and followed the tracks that had been made, keeping the speed fast enough to make some time, but not so much so that they blendered Luchas.

Blay kept two guns out.

As Manny and Butch rode up beside them, the other Brothers and John Matthew dematerialized at regular distances, appearing at the sides of the two parallel tracks.

It took a hundred years.

Blay literally thought they were never going to get out of there. It seemed as though the high-pitched, whining engines, and the blur of the dark forest, and the brilliant white patches of clearings were going to be the last things he saw.

He prayed the entire way.

When the big, boxy hangar structure finally came into view, parked right next to it was the single most beautiful thing Blay had ever seen.

V and Butch's Escalade.

Things moved lickety-split from there: Qhuinn pulling up alongside the SUV, Luchas transferred into the backseat, snowmobiles reloaded onto the trailer hitched to the back, Qhuinn going over to the passenger seat of the vehicle.

"I want Blay to drive," he said before getting in.

There was a heartbeat of a pause. Then Butch nodded and tossed the keys over. "Manny and I will be in the back back."

Blay got behind the wheel, moved the seat to accommodate his legs, and powered up the engine. As Qhuinn settled next to him, he looked over.

"Put on your seat belt."

The male did as he was told, stretching the nylon strap around his chest and clicking it into place. Then he immediately cranked himself around to focus on his brother.

A feeling of single-minded determination set Blay's shoulders and tightened his hands. He didn't care what he had to mow over, take down, or leave grille marks on; he was going to get Qhuinn and his brother to the training center and into the clinic.

Hitting the gas, he didn't look back.

SIXTY-THREE

Trez frowned at the adding machine he'd been punching numbers into. Reaching out for the white tongue of paper that hung over the side of his desk, he tried to see the column of numbers he'd been making.

He blinked.

Rubbed his eyes. Reopened them.

Nope. The shimmering circle in the upper right-hand quadrant of his vision was still there, and it was not a function of glare.

"Fuck . . . me."

Shoving the receipts he'd been totaling aside, he looked at his watch, then put his head in his hands. As he squeezed his eyes shut, the aura was still in place, the pattern of interlocking geometrics sparkling with all the colors of the rainbow.

He had about twenty-five minutes before all hell broke loose—and he was not going to be able to dematerialize.

Fumbling for his office phone, he hit the intercom. Two seconds later, Xhex's voice came out of the speaker, tinnier than usual. Which meant the sensitivity to sound was kicking in.

"Hey, what's up?" she said.

"I'm getting a migraine. I gotta bounce."

"Oh, man, that sucks. Didn't you get one just a week ago?"

Whatever. Not the point. "Can you take over?"

"You need a ride home?"

Yes. "No. I can make it." He began gathering his wallet, his cell, his keys. "Call me if you need me, 'kay?"

"You got it."

Trez took a deep breath as he cut the connection and got to his feet. He felt perfectly fine—for the moment. And the good news was, he was no more than fifteen minutes from his apartment—even assuming he hit all red lights. Which would leave him about ten minutes to get into sweats, line up a wastepaper basket and a towel beside his bed, and prepare for total digestive collapse.

Six, seven hours from now? He was going to feel better.

Unfortunately, the here-to-there was going to suck.

On his way to his office's closed door, he slung his jacket onto his shoulders and braced himself for the music on the far side.

When he stepped out, he walked right into the wall of iAm's considerable chest.

"Gimme your keys," was all his brother said.

"You don't have to—"

"Did I ask you for an opinion?"

"Goddamn Xhex—"

"Right behind your brother," the female cut in. "And I know you meant that as a compliment."

"I'm fine," Trez said, as he tried to angle his vision so that his head of security was out of his blind spot.

"You have how many minutes before the pain hits?" Xhex smiled, flashing her fangs. "Do you really want to be wasting any of them arguing with me?"

Trez bitched his way out of his club, and the instant the cold air hit his sinuses, his stomach seized up—like it was getting ready to go to town early.

Sliding into the passenger seat of his own BMW, he closed his eyes and leaned his head back. The aura was getting larger, the original line of shimmer splitting into two and fanning outward, moving slowly toward the edge of his vision.

During the trip home, he found himself feeling glad iAm wasn't a talker.

Although it wasn't as if he didn't know what the guy was thinking. Too much stress. Too many headaches.

He probably needed to feed as well—but that was not happening for a while.

As his brother drove with alacrity, Trez passed the time picturing where they were in the city; what traffic lights they were going through or stopping at; what turns they were making; where the Commodore was, its towering length looming higher and higher the closer they got.

A sudden decline told him that they were going into the parking garage—and that he'd fallen behind in his mental mapping: as far as he'd known, they were still a couple of blocks away.

Lot of left-hand turns came next as they spiraled down three floors and parked in one of the two spots they were allotted.

By the time they filed into the elevator and iAm punched the eighteenth button, the aura had wandered off the confines of his vision, disappearing as if it had never been.

Calm before the storm.

"Thanks for driving me home," he said. And meant it. He hated relying on anyone else, but it was pretty damn hard not to hit anything when you had a neon sign flashing in the back of both eyeballs.

"I figured it was better this way."

"Yeah."

He and his brother hadn't talked about the high priest's visit since it happened, but that hi-how're-ya from AnsLai was still very much between them—but at least iAm had put aside the pissed off long enough to get him back here.

Trez's first clue that the headache was gearing up was the way the subtle ding that announced its destination shot through his brain like a bullet.

He groaned as the doors slid open. "This is going to be bad."

"Didn't you have one last week?"

He wondered how many more people could ask him that.

iAm took care of the lock on the door, and Trez dumped his jacket three feet into the apartment. He shed his black cashmere sweater on the way down to his bedroom, and was unbuttoning his silk shirt as he walked into—

As he froze, the one and only thing that shot through his head was that scene from the movie *Trading Places*—when Eddie Murphy walks into his room at the fancy digs and a half-naked chick sits up in his bed and goes, "Hey, Billy Ray."

The difference in this situation was that his stalker, the one with the bouncer boyfriend and the trust issues, was blond, and not wearing early eighties Spandex pants. Matter of fact, she was fully, motherfucking, buck-ass naked.

The gun that appeared over his shoulder was steady and accessorized with a suppressor.

So iAm could have killed her, no problem.

"I thought you'd be glad to see me," the chippie said, looking back and forth between him and his brother's muzzle.

Like she wanted to make herself more appealing, she lifted one arm to fuss with her hair—but if she were hoping her breasts would sway enticingly, she was out of luck: Those rock-hard falsies of hers were as unmovable as something bolted to a wall.

"How did you get in here," Trez demanded.

"Aren't you glad to see me?" When no one answered her, and that gun stayed up, she pouted. "I got friendly with the security guard, okay. What. Oh, come on . . . fine, I blew him, okay."

Classy.

And that dumb-ass bastard rent-a-cop was going to be out of a job.

Trez walked over to the pile of clothes by the end of the bed. "Put these back on and get out."

God, he was tired.

"Oh, come on," she whined as her things fluttered all around her. "I just wanted to surprise you when you got home from work. I thought this would make you happy."

"Well, it doesn't. You need to get the fuck out—" As she opened her mouth like she was going to go psycho on him, he shook his head and cut her off. "Don't even think about it. I'm not in the mood, and my brother over here really doesn't care whether you walk out of here or get carried out in a bag. Get dressed. Get out."

The chippie looked back and forth again. "You were so nice to me the other night."

Trez winced as the pain stepped up to the plate and started swinging on the right side of his head. "Honey, I'm going to be real honest here. I don't even know your name. We banged twice—"

"Three times—"

"I don't care how many it was. What I do know is that you're going

to let this go tonight. If you come around me or my place again, I'm going to . . ." The Shadow in him wanted to go in a more blood-thirsty direction, but he forced himself to stay on human terms she'd understand. ". . . call the police. And you don't want that, because you're a drug addict who deals on the side, and if they search your shit, your car, your place, they're going to find more than just paraphernalia. They're going to bust you and that idiot meathead you're sleeping with for possession with intent to distribute, and you're going to fucking jail."

The chippie just blinked.

"Don't push me, sweetie," Trez said in an exhausted voice. "You won't like what happens."

Say what you would about the kid; she was quick when she was properly motivated. A matter of moments later, after some yoga poses to get that plastic rack squeezed into a "blouse" that was two sizes too small, she was on her way, cheapie purse slung over her shoulder, her skyscraper stillies dangling from the ankle straps.

Trez didn't say another word. Just followed in her wake to the door, opened the way out . . . and shut the thing in her face as she turned around to say something.

He threw the lock manually.

iAm put his weapon away. "We need to move. This location is compromised."

His brother was right. It wasn't like they'd kept where they lived a big-ass secret, but staying at the Commodore was predicated on the idea that a security guard wouldn't be stupid enough to let a woman into someone's place without the permission of the owners.

If that could happen once, it could happen again—

Abruptly, the pain intensified, like the volume on his cranial concert from hell had suddenly been cranked.

"I'm going to go throw up for a while," Trez mumbled as he wheeled away. "We'll start packing as soon as this migraine is over. . . ."

He had no idea what iAm replied, or even if the guy did.

Fuck.

SIXTY-FOUR

Standing outside the training center's examination room, Qhuinn had his hands in the pockets of his leathers, his teeth locked tight, and his brows drawn all the way together.

Waiting. Waiting . . .

Medical shit was a lot like fighting, he decided: long periods of nothing doing, interjected with bursts of life-or-death.

It was enough to stamp you certifiable.

He glanced over at the door. "How much longer do you think it will be?"

Across the way, Blay crossed and uncrossed his long legs. The guy had stretched out on the floor about a half hour ago, but that had been his only concession to the wormhole of time they'd been sucked into.

"It's got to be winding down now," he replied.

"Yeah. Only so many parts to a body, right."

After a moment, Qhuinn focused on the other male properly. There were dark circles under Blay's eyes, and his cheeks had hollowed out. He was also paler than usual, his face far too light.

Qhuinn went over, leaned against the wall, and let his shitkickers slide out until his ass hit the floor next to Blay's.

Blay glanced up and smiled a little, then resumed staring at the tips of his boots.

Qhuinn watched as his own hand reached out and brushed his friend's jaw. As Blay started and looked over, Qhuinn was surprised to find he wanted to do so much more—and not sexually. He wanted to draw the male across his lap and have Blay put his head down. He wanted to stroke those strong shoulders and pass his fingers through that short red hair. He wanted to get some passerby to find a blanket and bring it over, so he could wrap some warmth around the powerful body that seemed to have been weakened.

Qhuinn forced his eyes away and dropped his hand.

God, he felt so fucking . . . trapped. Even though there were no chains on him.

Glancing down, he double-checked his wrists. Ankles. Yup, totally free over here. Nothing holding him back.

Closing his lids, he tilted his head back against the wall. In his mind, he was touching Blay—and again, not sexually. Just feeling the vitality beneath the skin, the shift of the muscle, the solidity of the bone.

"I think you should go see Selena," he said to the guy.

Blay exhaled as if he had someone sitting on his chest. "Yeah. I know."

"We could go together," Qhuinn heard himself volunteer.

He opened his eyes in time to see Blay's head whip around.

"Or you could, you know, do it on your own." Qhuinn cracked his knuckles. "Whatever you feel comfortable with."

Shit. In light of the whole Saxton thing, that might go too far. Feeding, after all, could be seen as more intimate than sex—

"Yeah," Blay said softly. "I'll do that."

Qhuinn's heart started to beat hard. And again, it wasn't because he was all hopped to get it on with the guy. He just wanted to . . .

Share, he supposed was the right word.

No, wait. It went further than that. He wanted to take care of the male.

"You know, I don't think I ever thanked you," Qhuinn murmured. As Blay's baby blues shot over, he wanted to look away—the eye contact was almost too much. But then he thought of his brother in that hospital bed—and all the ways people got robbed of time.

Jesus, he'd held so much in for so many reasons—all of which had seemed perfectly valid. But how arrogant was that? That kind of reti-

cence assumed he'd have the time to talk about stuff when he wanted. That the person he had in the back of his mind would always be around. That he himself would be.

"For what?" Blay asked.

"For driving us home. Me and Luchas." He heaved a great breath in and let it out slowly. "And for sitting out here with me all night. For going to Payne and getting her to help. For backing me up on the field, and during training. Also, for all those beers and video games. The chips and the M&M's. The clothes I borrowed. The floor I slept on when I stayed over. Thanks for letting me hug your mom and talk with your dad. Thank you . . . for the ten thousand kind things you've done."

From out of nowhere, he thought once again of that night when he'd walked in and witnessed his father giving that gold signet ring to his brother.

"Thank you for calling that night," he said gruffly.

Blay's eyebrows shot up. "Which night?"

Qhuinn cleared his throat. "After Luchas went through his change, and my father gave him . . . you know, the ring." He shook his head. "I went up to my room and I was going to do something . . . yeah, something really stupid. You called me. You came over. Do you re-member?"

"I do."

"It wasn't the only time you did something like that."

As Blay looked away, Qhuinn knew exactly where the guy's mind had gone. Yup, that night hadn't been the only ledge he'd nearly jumped off of.

"I've said I was sorry," Qhuinn intoned. "But I don't think I've ever said thank you. So, yeah . . . thank you."

Before he knew what he was doing, he put his hand out, offering his palm. It seemed appropriate to mark this moment, right here, right now, outside of his busted-to-fuck brother's operating room, with some kind of solemn contact.

"Just . . . thank you."

Unbelievable.

After what had felt like lifetimes with Qhuinn, Blay had thought that the surprises were finally over. That the male couldn't pull any-thing else that would leave him speechless.

Wrong.

Jesus . . . of all the imaginary conversations he'd had in his head with the guy, talks when he'd pretended that Qhuinn opened up, or said something close to "the right thing," it had never been about gratitude. But this . . . was exactly what he needed to hear, even though he hadn't known that.

And that offered palm broke his damn heart.

Especially given that the male's brother was on death's door in the room across from them.

Blay didn't shake the hand that was offered.

He reached over, took a hold of the fighter's face, and drew Qhuinn in for a kiss.

It was supposed to be only a split-seconder—like their lips were the ones doing the handshake thing. When he went to pull back, though, Qhuinn captured him, and held him in place. Their mouths met again . . . and again . . . and once more, their heads tilting to the sides, the contact lingering.

"You're welcome," Blay said roughly. Then he smiled a little. "Can't say it was all a pleasure, though."

Qhuinn laughed. "Yeah, I can imagine pants were definitely not fun." The male got serious. "Why the hell did you stay around?"

Blay opened his mouth, the truth on the tip of his tongue—

"Oh. Shit. Ah . . . 'scuse me, boys, didn't mean to interrupt."

Qhuinn jerked back so fast, he literally ripped his face out of Blay's hold. Then he jumped up onto his feet and faced off with V, who'd come out of the OR. "No problem, nothing going on."

As V's expression registered a boatload of yeah-right, Qhuinn just looked at the Brother head-on, like he was daring Vishous to have a different opinion than his own.

In the silence between the two males, Blay got up more slowly, and found that he was light-headed, and not because he needed to feed.

No problem, nothing going on.

Sure as hell hadn't felt that way for him. Buuuut once again, Qhuinn had snapped out of any closeness, shied away, pulled back, unplugged.

Except come on. Bad time. Bad place. And V was the last person you wanted to go hearts-and-flowers in front of.

It was, however, a good reminder. Stressful situations had a way of making even the most rigid of personalities malleable—for a time.

Sadness, shock, intense anxiety . . . it could all make someone vunerable and liable to talk in ways they normally wouldn't simply because they had had all their defenses knocked to shit. The unusual behavior didn't signal a sea change, though. It was not indicative of some kind of religious conversion where, from that day onward, everything was forever different.

Qhuinn was reeling from what was doing with his brother. And any revelations, or heartfelt statements, that came out of his mouth were undoubtedly a product of the stress the guy was under.

Period.

No, "in" love going on here. Not really. Not permanently. And he needed to fucking remember that.

". . . bones are going to be set?" Qhuinn asked.

Blay shook himself to attention as V lit up a hand-rolled and exhaled away from the two of them. "He's got to be stabilized first. Selena's going to feed him again, and then we're going to open up his abdomen and do exploratory surgery to find out where the bleeding is. After we see how he's doing? We'll work on the bones."

"Do we have any idea what happened to him?"

"He's not real verbal at the moment."

"Yeah. Okay."

"So we need your consent. He's not capable of understanding the risks and benefits."

Qhuinn pushed his hand through his hair. "Yeah. Of course. Do what you have to."

V exhaled again, the scent of Turkish tobacco filling the air and reminding Blay exactly how many hours, minutes, and seconds it had been since he'd last lit up himself.

"You've got Jane, Manny, Ehlena, and myself in there. We're not going to let anything happen to him, 'kay?" He clapped Qhuinn on the shoulder. "He's going to pull through. Or the four of us are going to die trying."

Qhuinn murmured some thanks at that point.

And then V glanced at Blay. Looked at Qhuinn. Cleared his throat.

Yup, the Brother was doing all kinds of math in his head. Great.

"So you guys just keep hanging here. I'll come out and update you as soon as I know anything. So. Yeah."

The Brother's brows lifted high on his forehead, the tattoos at his

temple distorting as he tamped out his barely smoked hand-rolled on the sole of his shitkicker.

"Be with you in a few," he said as he ducked back inside.

In the wake of the Brother's departure, Qhuinn paced around, eyes on the concrete floor, hands on his lean hips, weapons that he'd neglected to take off catching the fluorescent light and glinting.

"I'm going to go have a smoke," Blay said. "I'll be right back."

"You can light up here," Qhuinn cut in. "There's a seal on the door."

"I need a little fresh air. I won't be long, though."

"Okay."

Blay strode off in a hurry, gunning for the door at the far end of the corridor that opened into the parking garage. When he got to the thing, he punched his way out and breathed in deep.

Fresh air, his ass. All he got was a noseful of dry, earthy, concrete-y stuff.

At least it was cooler, though.

Fuck.

He'd left his cigarettes in his goddamn jacket. On the floor. Outside of the OR.

As he cursed and stomped around, he was tempted to hit something—but a set of busted knuckles was just one more thing he'd have to explain to people.

And shit knew the eyeful V had just gotten was more than enough.

Pushing his hands into the pockets of his leathers, he frowned as the one on the right shoved into something.

Saxton's lighter. The one the male had given him on his birthday.

Taking the thing out, he turned it over and over in his palm, thinking about everything that had been said in that corridor.

There had been a time when he would have taken those words and put them on the mantelpiece of his head and his heart, giving them pride of place that ensured their preciousness stayed with him for the rest of his living days.

There had been so many years when those moments at that cabin and on that cold, hard floor just now would have been enough to clear away all the conflict, and the strife, and the pain, wiping everything clean such that he could relate as a virgin would to Qhuinn.

Fresh start.

All not just forgiven, but forgotten.

That was no longer the case.

God, he was probably too young to be this old, but life had a way of being about experience, rather than calendar days. And standing out here, alone, he was positively geriatric: He was absolutely, totally, completely fresh out of the optimistic, rose-colored naïveté that came with a younger person's outlook on life.

When one believed that miracles were not impossible . . . but merely unusual.

Thank fuck V had come out when he had.

Otherwise, three little words would have leaked from his mouth. And undoubtedly doomed him in ways he couldn't even guess at.

Bad time. Bad place.

For that kind of thing.

Forever.

SIXTY-FIVE

As iAm paced around the apartment, he kept his gun on him—even though it was highly unlikely that there would be a round two with some naked bimbo jacking her way into his and his brother's home-sweet-home.

Goddamn it, he wanted some red smoke. Just to take the edge off.

Because, right now? He was on the edge of violence.

The good news, he supposed, was that he didn't really have a target, and that was effectively keeping him in check: That migraine was beating the hell out of his brother. And that poor, used-up woman that had been frog-marched out of here? She was already being tortured on too many levels to count. Now, the security guard was an excellent candidate—but the motherfucker had gotten off an hour ago, and iAm wasn't going to leave Trez in a vulnerable state just so he could issue a correction to an imbecile—

Off in the distance, he heard a whispering through the plumbing pipes.

It was the toilet in Trez's bathroom being flushed. Again.

And then came the muttered cursing, and the creak of the bed frame as Trez resettled into his bed.

Poor. Bastard.

iAm went over to the huge windows that faced the river, and stopped to stare across the water at Caldwell's opposite side. Putting his hands on his hips, he ran through the places they could move to. Short list. Hell, one of the main benes of the Commodore had been its security; they hadn't even bothered with turning the alarm on.

Which had been a mistake.

They needed someplace safe. Secure. Impregnable.

Especially if his brother continued with the hit-it-and-quit-it shit, and AnsLai kept doing "diplomatic" drive-bys.

iAm resumed his pacing. It was impossible to ignore the fact that his brother was getting worse. The sexual stuff had been going on for years—and for the longest time, iAm had just chalked it up to a healthy male's drive for mating.

Something that he had often thought he lacked.

Then again, his brother had been fucking enough females for the both of them.

In recent months, however, it had become clear that there was an addiction process at work—and that had been even before the high priest had started showing up. Now that things seemed to be coming to a head with AnsLai? The s'Hisbe's machinations were just going to put more pressure on his brother, and that was going to make him act out even more.

Shit. iAm felt like he was standing in front of a train crossing, triangulating the speed of the locomotive's engine with the approach of an oncoming car . . . and seeing the carnage that was going to result. The metaphor was also apt when it came to the helplessness he felt because he couldn't put the brakes on either force: He wasn't behind the wheel or in the engineer's seat. All he could do was sit back and watch.

Or scream at the side of the road was more like it.

Where the *hell* could they go—

Frowning, he lifted his eyes up from the view, up past the molding, up to the ceiling.

After a moment, he took out his cell phone and made a call.

When he hung up, he went down to his brother's room. Opening the door a crack, he said into the dense, black silence, "I'm going out for a second. Won't be long."

Trez's moan could have meant anything from, "Cool," to, "Oh,

God, not so loud," to, "Have fun, I'm going to hang here and hurl some more."

iAm walked fast. Out of the apartment. To the elevator.

Inside of which, he hit the button marked "P" for "Penthouse."

When the doors slid open, there were two choices: One direction took him to the Brother Vishous's place. The other to his old friend's.

He strode down and rang Rehvenge's bell.

When the *symphath* opened up, Rehv appeared as he always was: mohawked, purple-eyed, mink clad. Dangerous. Little bit evil.

"Hey, my man, how you be," the male said as they embraced and clapped each other on the shoulder. "Come in."

As iAm entered the Reverend's private space for the first time in a good year or so, he found that nothing had changed, and for some reason, that was a relief.

Rehvenge went over to a leather sofa and sat down, propping his cane up next to him and crossing his legs at the knees. "What do you need?"

As iAm tried to put together the right words, Rehv swore a little. "Man, I knew this wasn't a social call—but I didn't expect your emotions to be a fucking mess."

Ah, yes, the sin-eater way meant that there was no hiding anything from the male.

Still, it was difficult to speak of it all. "I'm not sure you're aware of what's been going on with Trez?"

Rehv frowned, his dark brows narrowing that intense, violet stare. "I thought the Iron Mask was doing good business. You boys in trouble? I've got plenty of cash if you need—"

"Business is great. We've got more money than we can spend. The issue is my brother's extracurricular activities."

"He's not into drugs, is he," Rehv said darkly.

"Women."

Rehv laughed and brushed that off with the flick of a dagger hand. "Oh, if that's all it is—"

"He's completely out of control—and one of them magically appeared in his bed tonight. We got home and there she was."

Rehv went back to the frowning. "In your apartment? How the fuck did she get in?"

"The lowest common denominator with a security guard." iAm paced around the modern room, dimly noting that the view was, in fact, better from this height. "Trez has been fucking anything that moves for years, but lately he's been so reckless—not wiping memories, hitting 'em more than once, not worrying about consequences."

"What the *hell* is wrong with him?"

iAm turned and faced the half-breed who was the closest thing to family he had outside of his flesh and blood. Matter of fact, he trusted the guy more than ninety-nine percent of his own bloodline.

"Trez is mated."

Long silence. "Excuse me?"

iAm nodded. "He's mated."

Rehv got up off that couch. "Since when?"

"Birth."

"Ohhhhhh." Rehv whistled softly. "So it's a s'Hisbe thing."

"He was promised to the queen's first daughter."

Rehv was silent for a while. Then he shook his head. "That would make him the future king, would it not."

"That's right. And even though we are a matriarchal society, that is not an irrelevancy."

"Check us out," the male murmured. "He and I and Wrath. Quite the trifecta."

"Well, it's different for the s'Hisbe, of course. The queen is the one who dictates everything for us."

"So what's he still doing on the outside. With all us UnKnow-ables?"

"He doesn't want anything to do with the s'Hisbe."

"Has he got a choice?"

"No." iAm glanced over at the wet bar in the corner. "Mind if I have a drink?"

"Are you kidding me? I'd be getting hammered if I were you."

iAm wandered over, considered his options, and ended up picking a decanter that had a little necklace reading *Bourbon* around its throat. He went straight up, and as he took a pull off the rim of a cut-crystal glass, he savored the burn over his tongue. "Nice."

"Parker's Heritage Collection, Small Batch. The best."

"I didn't think you were a big drinker."

"That's no excuse for not knowing what you serve your guests."

"Ah."

"So what's the plan?"

iAm tilted his head back, emptied the glass into his mouth and

swallowed hard. "We need somewhere safe to stay. And not just because of the women thing. We had a visit by the high priest this past
week—and given we're on the outside, that means they're getting serious back home. They're looking for him—and if they find him? I'm
afraid he's going to kill the s'Hisbe's representative. Then we've really
got a problem."

"You think he'd take it that far?"

"Yes, I do." iAm poured a refill. "He's not going back there, and I
need time to figure out how to resolve the conflict before something
disastrous happens."

"You guys want to move into my house up north?"

iAm downed his second bourbon on a oner. "No." He leveled his
eyes. "I want us to move into the Brotherhood compound."

As Rehv cursed long and low, iAm poured himself a third. "It's the
safest place for us."

Xcor was covered in *lesser* blood and sweat as he returned to his new
lair. His fighters were still downtown, engaging with the enemy, but he
had had to pare off and seek shelter.

Damn cut on his arm.

The house that Throe had found them was located in a modest
neighborhood full of modest homes with two-car garages and swing
sets in their backyards. Among its advantages was that it was located at
the end of a cul-de-sac, and there was an empty building lot on one
side and a Caldwell Sewer Department processing unit on the other.
They had it for three months, with an option to buy.

As he dematerialized through the heavily draped windows of the
family room, he scoffed at the padded sofa that formed an L, its tufted
cushions like rolls of fat, its color akin to beef stew.

Although he appreciated working heat, the fact that the facility
had come "furnished" was annoying to him. He feared he was alone in
this, however: Over the past few days, he'd oft caught one or another
of his soldiers reclining on that godforsaken monster, their heads lying
back, their legs stretched out in comfort.

What was next? Throw blankets?

Stalking up the narrow staircase, he missed the doom and gloom
of the castle they still owned back in the Old Country. Longed for the
heft of the stone that had surrounded them, and the impregnable na-

ture of the layout, with its moat and high walls. Mourned, too, the fun they had had spooking the villagers, giving physical presence to the stuff of myth.

Good times, as they said here in the New World.

On the second floor, he refused to look into the bedrooms. The pink of the one in front burned his eyes, and the sea foam green of the other was another assault on the senses as well. And there was no relief to be had as he walked into the master bedroom. Flowered wallpaper, everywhere. Even on the bed, and across the windows, and all over that chair in the corner.

At least his combat boots crushed the thick carpet, leaving tread prints like bruises on his way to the bath.

For godsakes, he was not even sure what color to call the scheme in here.

Raspberry?

Shuddering, he wanted to keep the lights over the sink off, but with the rosebud curtains drawn, the illumination from the streetlamps below was drowned out completely, and he needed to see what he was doing—

Oh, dearest Fates.

He'd forgotten about the lace shades on the sconces.

Indeed, in any other environment, the twin red glows might have suggested something of a sexual nature. But not in this land of nicey-nicey. Here, they were a set of gumdrops glowing on the wall.

He nearly choked from the estrogen.

In a fit of self-preservation, he popped both of the offenders free of their lightbulbs and put them under the sink. The glare was offensive to his retinas, but it was the difference between cursing and hand-wringing: Always, he would choose the former.

Removing his scythe first, he placed her on the counter between the twin sinks. Next, he took off her halter, then stripped his coat, his daggers and his guns from his body. The undershirt he wore was stained from long nights of fighting, but it was cleaned regularly—and would be used again. Clothes, after all, were naught but the hides vampires had not been given at birth.

They were not for personal decoration—at least, not for him.

Turning to the mirror, he muttered at the sight of himself.

The slayer that he'd been fighting hand-to-hand had been viciously good with a knife, likely the result of its former life on the streets, and

what a rush to combat with one of fine skills. He had won, of course, but it had been a bracing battle.

Unfortunately, however, he'd taken home a lovely souvenir of the conflict: The gash ran up the front of his biceps and around to the side, terminating at the top of his shoulder. Quite nasty. But he'd had worse.

And accordingly, he knew how to treat himself. Lined up upon the counter were the various and sundry items that he and his fighters required from time to time: a bottle of CVS rubbing alcohol, a BIC lighter, several sewing needles, a spool of black nylon fishing line.

Xcor grimaced as he took off his shirt and the short sleeve that had been sliced through raked over the wound and split it wide. Gritting his teeth, he went still, the pain sharpening to the point that his stomach clenched up like a fist.

Breathing deep, he waited until the sensations passed, and then went for the alcohol. Twisting off the white cap, he leaned over the sink, braced himself and—

The sound that came out from his locked teeth was part growl, part groan. And as his vision checkerboarded, he closed his eyes and leaned his hip into the lip of the sink.

Inhaling hard, his sinuses stung from the smell, but there was no putting the cap back on yet: his fine motor skills were no doubt shot.

Taking a walk to clear his head, he went back into the bedroom and gave his body a chance to recalibrate. As the pain stayed with him, like he had a dog attached to his arm that was trying to eat him alive, he cursed many times.

And ended up downstairs. Where the liquor was.

Never one for imbibing, he investigated the canvas bag of bottles that Zypher had brought with them from the warehouse. The soldier enjoyed a drink from time to time, and although Xcor did not approve, he had long ago learned that one had to make certain allowances when it came to aggressive, restless fighters.

And on a night like tonight, he found himself grateful.

Whiskey? Gin? Vodka?

What did it matter.

He picked one randomly, split the seal on the cap, and tilted his head back. Opening his throat, he poured whatever it was down, swallowing in spite of the fact that his esophagus burned like it was afire.

Xcor continued to drink as he went back upstairs. Further drinking as he paced around some more and waited for the effects to kick in.

Even more drinking.

He wasn't sure how long it took, but eventually he was back in the bright light of the bathroom, drawing a two-foot length of black line through the head of a thin needle. Facing the broad, rectangular mirror over the sinks, he was grateful that the *lesser's* blade had found his left arm. It meant that, as a right-handed male, he could handle this on his own. Had it been the other side? He would have had to get help.

The booze helped greatly. He barely flinched as he pierced his own skin and made a neat knot with the help of his teeth.

Indeed, alcohol was a curious substance, he thought as he began to make a row of stitches. The numbness that had come upon him made him feel as though he had been submerged in warm water, his body loosening, the pain still making an appearance, but the volume on the agony turned way down.

Slow. Precise. Even.

When he got to the top of his shoulder, he made another knot; then he snipped the needle free, put everything back where he'd found it, and started the shower.

Stripping his leathers down his legs, he kicked off his combat boots and stepped beneath the spray.

This time, the groan was from relief: As the warm water blanketed his sore shoulders, stiff back, and tight thigh muscles, the sense of comfort was nearly as overwhelming as the agony had been.

And for once, he allowed himself to give in to it. Probably because he was drunk.

Easing against the tile wall, the water hit him right in the face, but in a gentle way, like rain, before it traveled down the front of his body, going over his chest and his hard belly, past his hips and his sex—

From out of nowhere, he saw his Chosen leaning over him, her eyes glowing green in the moonlight, the tree overhead seeming to shelter them both.

She was feeding him, her slender, pale wrist at his mouth, his throat swallowing rhythmically.

In the midst of his alcohol-induced haze, the sexual need came upon him, seeming to unfold in his pelvis like an open hand.

He became hard.

Opening his eyes—not that he'd been aware of shutting them— he stared down at himself. The brilliant light over the sinks had been dimmed by the opaque curtain that kept the water from getting

loose in the bathroom, but there was more than enough illumination to go by.

He wished it had been completely dark . . . for it brought him no joy to see the arousal, that length standing out so stupid and proud from his body.

He could not fathom what it was thinking: If the likes of whores had to be paid extra to accommodate his impulses, he was hard-pressed to imagine that lovely Chosen doing aught but run screaming in the opposite direction—

Abruptly, that struck him as depressing, especially as the throbbing between his legs grew stronger. In truth, his body was such a sad instrument, so pathetic in this desire—remaining unaware that it was unwanted by all.

In particular, by the one it desired.

Turning around, he tilted his head back and pushed his hands through his hair. Time to stop thinking and get clean. The soap in the dish that was mounted on the tile did its duty with alacrity upon his skin and his hair—

And he was still erect when it was time to get out.

The cold air would take care of that.

Stepping onto the bath mat, that was also done in that god-awful deep pinky red, he toweled himself off.

Still erect.

Glancing at his fighting clothes, he found himself loath to put them upon his skin. Rough. Scratchy. Dirty.

Mayhap the feminine environment was contaminating him.

Xcor ended up in the big bed, naked, upon his back.

Still erect.

A quick glance at the clock on the bedside table and he knew he didn't have long before the house was inundated with fighters.

This was going to have to be quick.

Funneling his hand under the sheets and down his body, he gripped himself. . . .

Xcor's eyes shut hard and he moaned, his torso twisting from the heat and need that curled up from his lower body. As the pillow came up to greet the side of his face—logically, it was the other way around, he supposed—he began to pump up and down.

Delicious. Especially at the top, where his blunt head ached for attention and got it on every upstroke. Faster. Tighter.

All the while seeing his Chosen.

In truth, the image of her did more for him than what he attended to down below. And as the sensations grew ever stronger, he realized for the first time why his soldiers did this so often. So good. So very, very good . . .

Oh, his female was beautiful. To the point where, in spite of the power of what he was doing to himself, he was not distracted from her visage. Instead, she became achingly clear to him, from her pale hair to her red lips to her slender neck—all the way down that long, elegant body that was both hidden and revealed by the pristine white robing she had worn.

What would it be like to be wanted by such a creature? To be held within her sacred body as a male of worth . . .

At that very moment, the reality of her pregnancy re-landed on him like a physical weight. But at least it was too late. Even as his heart chilled and his chest began to ache with the knowledge that she had accepted another, his body continued on its joyride, the conclusion as unstoppable as a—

The orgasm that swept through him made him cry out—and thank the Fates for the pillow that caught his capitulation: At that very moment, down below, he heard the first of his soldiers walk through the house, the drumbeat of combat boots an unmistakable thunder he would recognize anywhere.

The aftermath of his release was wretched on too many levels to count. He had turned upon his injured shoulder; he had come all over his hand and abdomen as well as the sheets; and the vision of loveliness was gone from his head, his hard reality all that remained.

The pain inside of him was raw as a fresh wound.

But at least none would otherwise know of it.

He was, after all, first and foremost, a soldier.

SIXTY-SIX

"Yes, absolutely you can go see him. He's groggy, but aware."

As Doc Jane smiled up at Qhuinn, he jacked his leathers higher on his hips and tucked in his muscle shirt. He drew the line at smoothing his hair down, however, forcing his arms to stay at his sides even though his palms were itching to pull a drag-through.

"And he's going to be okay?"

The doctor nodded as she began to untie the surgical mask that was hanging around the front of her neck. "We removed the vampire equivalent of the human spleen, and that took care of the internal bleeding. We also went through him with a fine-toothed comb. Near as we can figure, he was in some kind of stasis in that oil drum, the Omega's blood somehow preserving him in his current state in spite of the injuries. If he'd been left out, I'm very certain he would have died."

The curse that brought about a miracle, Qhuinn thought.

"And he's not contaminated?"

Jane shrugged. "He bleeds red, and no one can sense any of the Omega in him—it was just a case of on or around him."

"Okay. All right." Qhuinn glanced at the door. "Good."

Time to go in, he told himself. Come on. . . .

His eyes went to Blay's. During the course of the four-hour operation, the guy had gone back and forth down the hall, taking breaks out in the parking lot for cigs. He'd always returned, though.

God, he looked grim.

Had ever since V had come out and found them . . . yeah.

Christ, what timing had that been.

"I'll go in now," he said.

It wasn't until after Blay nodded that he actually entered the OR.

Pushing his way through the door, the first thing he was greeted with was that antiseptic smell that he associated with postfight contusions. Next was the subtle beeping by the gurney in the center of the room, and the sound of Ehlena typing at the computer.

"I'll give you some private time," she said in a kind voice, as she got to her feet.

"Thanks," he replied quietly.

As the door shut behind her, Qhuinn retucked his shirt even though it didn't need the help. "Luchas?"

Waiting for his brother to respond, he glanced around. The debris of the operation, the bloody gauze pads, the used instruments, the plastic tubing, was all gone—nothing but the still body under those white sheets, and a stuffed red biohazard bag to show for the hours that had passed.

"Luchas?"

Qhuinn went over and stared down. Man, he didn't typically have problems with his blood pressure, but when he got a gander at his brother's drawn face, things went for a spin, a surge of dizziness making him realize exactly how tall he was—and how far he had to fall.

Luchas's eyes fluttered open.

Gray. They had both been gray, and still were.

Qhuinn reached behind and rolled over a little stool. As he sat down, he didn't know what to do with his arms, his hands . . . his voice.

He had never expected to see a member of his family again. And that had been back before the raids, when he'd been kicked out.

"How you doing?" What a dumb-ass question that was.

"He kept . . . me . . ."

Qhuinn leaned in close, but damn, that weak, hoarse voice didn't carry far. "What?"

"He kept me . . . alive. . . ."

"Who?"

". . . because of you."

"Who are you talking about?" Hard to imagine the Omega had a vendetta against—

"Lash . . ."

At the sound of the name, Qhuinn's upper lip peeled off his fangs. That motherfucker cousin of theirs—who turned out not to be blood at all, but rather, the transplanted son of the Omega. As a kid, the SOB been an obnoxious show-off. As a pretrans in the training program, he'd made John Matthew's life a living hell. As a posttrans?

His true father had welcomed him back into the fold, and utter destruction had been the result. Lash was the one who had led the raids. After centuries of the Lessening Society having to hunt and peck for vampire enclaves, that bastard had known exactly where to send the slayers—and because he had been adopted into an aristocratic family, he had decimated the upper classes.

But apparently Daddio and the golden boy had had a falling-out.

Shit, the idea Lash had tortured his brother? Just made him want to kill him all over again.

As Luchas groaned and took a deep breath, Qhuinn raised a hand to . . . pat him on the shoulder or something. But he didn't follow through. "Listen, you don't need to talk."

Those bloodshot gray eyes locked on his. "He kept me alive . . . because of what I did . . . to you. . . ."

Down on the gurney, tears welled and started to fall, his brother's emotions spilling out on his cheeks, regret mingling with what was undoubtedly physical pain as well as the narcotics used to treat it.

Because Qhuinn was hard-pressed to think that the guy would be showing anything like this under normal circumstances. That hadn't been the way they'd all been raised. Etiquette over emotion.

Always.

"The Honor Guard. . . ." Luchas started to cry in earnest. "Qhuinn . . . I'm so sorry . . . sorry. . . ."

We're not supposed to kill him!

Qhuinn blinked and went back to that beating at the side of the road, those males in black robes surrounding him and whaling on him as he'd tried to protect his head and his balls. Then it was up to the door to the Fade, to meet his daughter.

So strange the way things came full circle. And how some tragedies actually led to good things.

Now, Qhuinn did touch his brother, resting his dagger hand on that thin shoulder. "Shh . . . it's cool. We're good, it's cool. . . ."

He wasn't sure whether that was true, but what else was he going to say while the guy cracked?

"He wanted . . . to turn me. . . ." Luchas took a deep breath. "He brought me . . . back around. Woke up in the woods—his males beat me . . . did things to me . . . put me in that . . . blood. I waited for them to come back—never did."

"You're safe here." That was all he could think of. "You don't worry about a damn thing—no one's getting anywhere near you."

"Where . . . am I . . ."

"The Brotherhood's training center."

Those eyes widened. "In truth?"

"Yeah."

"Indeed . . ." Luchas's expression shifted, those once handsome features tightening even further. "What of *Mahmen*. Papa. Solange?"

Qhuinn just shook his head back and forth.

And in response, a sudden strength came into that frail voice. "Are you sure they are dead? Are you certain?"

As if he didn't wish what he had suffered on any of them.

"Yeah, we're sure."

Luchas sighed and closed his eyes.

Shit. Qhuinn felt a little cheap about lying, but in spite of the fact that the machines by the bed suggested his brother was stable, if the guy tanked, he didn't want to send Luchas to the grave thinking that after what had been done with him, no one could be sure how many others had been taken—or when.

In the quiet, Qhuinn looked down at his brother's hand. That signet ring had been left on—maybe because the knuckle above it was so swollen, they would have had to cut it off.

The crest that had been carved into the gold face carried the sacred symbols that only the Founding Families could mark their lineage with. And yeah, wow, it was completely deranged—and grossly inappropriate—to covet the goddamn thing. After everything that had happened, you'd think he'd be disgusted.

Then again, maybe it was just a knee-jerk reaction, an echo from all those years of hoping against hope he'd get one of his own.

"Qhuinn?"

"Yes?"

"I'm sorry. . . ."

Qhuinn shook his head, even though Luchas's lids were closed. "You don't worry about anything. You're safe. You're back. It's all going to be okay."

As his brother's chest rose and fell again like he was relieved, Qhuinn rubbed his face and didn't feel good about any of it. Not his brother's condition—or his return.

It wasn't that he wanted the guy dead. Tortured. Frozen forever.

But he had closed the door on all that family-dynamic stuff. Relegated it to the back of his mental file cabinet. Put it away for good, never to be looked at again.

What could you do, though?

Life specialized in curveballs.

The unfortunate thing was that they somehow inevitably ended up catching him in the nuts.

When a soft whistle sounded next to Blay, he jumped. "Oh, hey, John."

John Matthew lifted his hand in a wave. *How're things?*

As Blay shrugged, he thought it might be a good idea to stand up off the floor again. His ass had gone numb, which meant it was time for another of his walkabouts.

Grunting as he got to his feet, he stretched his back. "I guess okay. Luchas was awake enough after surgery so Qhuinn's in there now."

Oh. Wow.

While Blay walked things off in a tight circle, John settled against the wall. He was dressed in sweats, and the guy's hair was still wet—and there was a bite mark on his neck.

Blay looked away. Opened his mouth to say something. Ran out of gas for conversation.

From the corner of his eye, he saw John sign, *So, how's Saxton?*

"Ah, good. He's good—on a little vacation."

He's been working really hard.

"Yeah, he has." As he hoped the topic ended there, it felt odd to keep something from John. Other than Qhuinn, the guy had been the closest friend he had—although they had drifted during the last year, too. "But he'll be back soon."

You must miss him. John glanced away, like he knew it was pushing it.

Made sense. Blay had always shut down any conversation about his relationship, diverting talk to other subjects.

"Yeah."

So how's Qhuinn holding up? I didn't want to intrude, but . . .

Blay could only shrug again. "He's been in there awhile. I'm taking that as good news."

And Luchas is going to make it?

"Time will tell, but at least they got him patched up." Blay took out his Dunhills and lit up, exhaling slowly. When there was nothing but an awkward silence, he said, "Listen, I'm sorry if I'm being weird."

The truth was, that bite mark was a reminder of what was going to have to happen for him, and he really didn't need that so front-and-center.

Qhuinn's voice barged into his head: *We could go together.*

What the hell had he agreed to?

You're stressed, John signed as he focused on the door. *We're all stressed. Everything is . . . stressful.*

Blay frowned as the guy's mood registered. "Hey, are you okay?"

After a moment, John signed, *The strangest thing happened the other night. Wrath called me into his office and told me that Qhuinn was no longer my* ahstrux nohtrum. *I mean, that's fine, that's cool—it's actually uncomplicated things a lot. But Qhuinn never said anything to me, and I don't know if I should say something to him? I also didn't know that was possible. I mean, when it started, it was like, "Your pink slip is a double-tap, and that's that," you know? Did he just quit? Is it because of the Layla thing? I thought they weren't getting mated.*

Blay exhaled a curse, the smoke curling up over his head. "I have no clue."

Shit, that mating thing probably should have occurred to him—and maybe that was why Qhuinn had jumped out of range when V had appeared.

Could Qhuinn and Layla be getting hitched now that the young was okay—

The door swung wide, and Qhuinn came out, looking like he'd been kicked in the head. "Oh, hey, John, whassup."

As the two clapped each other on the shoulder, Qhuinn glanced over, but then carried on with a back-and-forth with John.

And then he and Qhuinn were alone after John left a moment later.

"Are you okay?" Qhuinn said.

Clearly, the question of the hour, wasn't it.

"Actually, I'm going to ask you that. How's Luchas?" Blay pulled a V and stubbed his cigarette out on the tread of his shitkicker.

Before Qhuinn could answer, Selena came out of the office, as if she had been summoned from the main house. The Chosen walked toward them gracefully, but with purpose, her traditional white robing flowing around her legs.

"Greetings, sires," she said as she approached. "Dr. Jane indicated that I was required?"

As Blay exhaled, he felt like punching himself. This was the last thing he—

"Yeah, both of us," Qhuinn answered.

Blay closed his eyes as a sudden surge rocked him. The idea of watching Qhuinn feed was like a drug in his bloodstream, loosening him up and threatening to get him hard. But really, it wasn't—

"Down the hall would be great," Qhuinn murmured.

Well, it was better than a bedroom. Right? More professional, yes?

And he did need the feeding—and Qhuinn no doubt had to as well after all the drama.

Blay ditched his cigarette butt into a trash can and brought up the rear as Qhuinn led the way. Going along, he didn't track the Chosen's movements. Nope, not in the slightest. His eyes were glued to Qhuinn's, from those shoulders, to those hips . . . to that ass. . . .

Okay, this was going to stop. Right now.

He just needed to pull himself together, do the feeding, and make an excuse to get gone.

Maybe this plan would be one that actually worked?

In through a doorway. Conversation. Polite smiling, even though he didn't know what had been asked or answered of him.

Ah, one of the hospital rooms, he realized. This was really good—a clinical environment. Just take the vein and move along, with one biological function not necessarily leading to another—

"I'm sorry?" the Chosen said, looking at him with an open face.

Great. He'd been loose-lipping it, but there was no telling how much he'd shared.

"I'm sorry," he said smoothly. "I'm just hungry as all get-out."

"In that case, would you like to be first?" Selena asked.

"Yeah, he would," Qhuinn replied as he settled back against the door.

Well, there you go, Blay thought. Everything was settled. When Qhuinn started? He was going to leave.

Stepping forward, he wondered how this was going to work precisely, but Selena solved that one by drawing up a chair and sitting by the hospital bed. Roger that—Blay hopped up on the mattress, his weight displacing the pillow from the slightly raised head, the springs creaking. And then his mind shut down, which was a relief. As Selena stretched out her arm and drew her white sleeve back, his hunger came to the forefront, his fangs dropping down from his upper jaw, his breath deepening.

"Please partake as you wish," she said placidly.

"I thank you for the gift, Chosen," he answered in a low voice.

Leaning down, he struck deeply, but as gently as he could—and on the first swallow, he knew it had been too long. With a great howl, his stomach roared with need, his civility draining out of him, his instincts taking over: He drew hard, drinking faster and faster, the power landing in his gut and spreading out from there—

His eyes went to Qhuinn.

Dimly, he was aware that yet again, one of his plans was soon going to be out the window, gone and forgotten. In fact, this had been a very bad idea—assuming he didn't want to fuck the guy again: Logic was difficult enough when it was just a case of conflicting emotions. A full-on sexual urge, spurred by the drinking?

He was an asshat of the first order; he truly was.

And that was especially true as he watched Qhuinn's erection inflate behind the fly of the fighter's leathers.

Fuck.

Fuck.

Man, one of these days, he was going to be strong enough to walk away. He really was, honest.

Oh, FUCK.

SIXTY-SEVEN

As Qhuinn watched the show, his tongue parted his mouth and took a lick of his lips.

Across the shallow room, Blay was up on the hospital bed, that perfect torso angled forward so he could partake of the Chosen's vein, his hands, those capable, well-trained, strong hands, holding the fragile wrist to his mouth with care—as though, even in the throes of feeding, he was a gentlemale.

As he continued to drink, his torso curved around even tighter, his rib cage flexing and settling with every breath, his head subtly shifting with every swallow.

It was all Qhuinn could do to stay where he was. He so wanted up on that mattress as well, twisting that body around so he could come in from behind. He wanted to be at the male's throat as Blay took from the Chosen. He wanted to fuck the guy for twelve or fifteen hours straight when they were both done.

After all the drama with Luchas, this short, intense respite from the shock and pain was a glorious, guilty relief: it was just too damn good to focus on something like this—his tired mind and exhausted body ready to be refreshed so he could come back to reality fighting strong once again.

God, his brother . . .

Shaking his head, he deliberately gave his brain something erotic to play with: As Blay's hand sneaked between his legs and rearranged something at his fly, it was pretty damn clear he was fully aroused.

As if that delicious scent didn't make it obvious.

Just as Qhuinn was about to lose it, Blay lifted his head and let out a chuffing sound of satisfaction. Then the male licked at the puncture wounds he'd made.

You know what, Qhuinn thought. Fuck the feeding. All he needed was Blay. . . .

"And you, sire?" the Chosen asked.

Crap. He probably should do it.

Besides, Blay was clearly in a postfeeding logy state, his body slow, his eyes fuzzy—and Qhuinn took advantage of it, pushing himself between the fighter and the Chosen, his ass rubbing against the hard ridge of Blay's cock as he hopped up onto the bed.

While Blay let out a groan, Qhuinn leaned over and took the female's other wrist. Holding it with one hand, he used his other to yank out the bottom of his muscle shirt—and then shove Blay's palm down the front of his own pants.

Qhuinn kept his own groan to himself by taking a hard pull on the Chosen's vein, but Blay's hiss sounded out.

Maybe the Chosen would assume it—

Qhuinn's eyes rolled back in his head as Blay stroked him, the friction threatening to make him come right then and there—which was not something he wanted to do in front of Selena.

But, oh, fuck, that was—

He put his own hand down there, stilling that movement.

So Blay just gave his balls a good squeeze.

Qhuinn climaxed on his next swallow, the orgasm shooting out of him before he could think of any kind of boring and unattractive distraction, the pleasure cresting with such power, he sagged in his own skin.

Blay's chuckle was erotic as hell.

Whatever, payback was going to be a bitch, Qhuinn vowed to himself.

And as it turned out, he couldn't wait for it. He retracted his fangs and stopped drinking before he'd had his fill—because his hunger for something else had completely taken over, and it was beyond time to send Selena on her way.

Getting the Chosen out in a polite but expeditious manner was an autopilot maneuver—he had no clue what he was saying—but at least she was smiling and looking pleased, so he must have done the right thing.

He was very conscious of locking the door, however.

As he turned around, he found Blay stretched out and attending to himself, his hand stroking up and down between his legs. His fangs were still elongated from the feeding, and his eyes were glowing from under heavy lids, and holy fuck was he hot . . .

Qhuinn ditched his shitkickers. His leathers. His shirt.

Blay orgasmed before he even started for the bed, the male arching up and moaning as his head shot back on the thin pillow, and his hips jerked.

Like Qhuinn buck-ass naked was too much to handle.

Best. Compliment. Ever.

Qhuinn attacked the bed, pouncing on Blay, finding that velvet mouth and taking it over. Clothes were ripped—the buttons on the fly of Blay's leathers popping free and landing like coins tossed onto the linoleum, his shirt getting torn into pieces. And then they were skin-on-skin, nothing separating their flesh.

As they writhed against each other, Qhuinn knew what he wanted. And he was too desperate and hungry to ask nicely—or even talk about it.

All he could do was break off from that mouth, roll away from Blay . . . and reach behind, pulling the male onto him as he stretched one leg up.

What do you know, Blay took over from there. And knew exactly what to do.

Qhuinn felt himself get positioned with rough hands—before he knew it, he was up on his knees, his face in the mattress, his breath hammering out of his mouth. It was all so foreign, letting someone else take charge—and he felt vulnerable, too, even through the wanting—

"Oh *fuck!*" he bellowed as the possession was struck, the sensations of pain and pleasure, stretching and accommodation, mixing into a cocktail that made him come so hard he saw stars.

And then Blay started moving.

Qhuinn braced his arms and bore backward, holding his own as that whole virginity thing was done and dusted but good.

Oh, man, it was an incredible rush, and it only got better. As Blay's arm snaked around his chest and locked on, the angle changed, the penetrations going deeper and deeper, faster and faster, the bed begin-ning to rock back and forth against the wall, the panting in his ear growing harsher and harsher. . . .

The cusp was the single greatest burn he'd ever felt, the edge of not just his release, but Blay's, tightening him up all over, his thighs clench-ing, his pelvis tilting to receive, his great arms holding them both up off the bed—

When Blay came, the thrusts locked him in so hard Qhuinn's head banged into the wall—not that he noticed or cared. And then that cock started jerking wildly . . .

And Qhuinn felt well and truly owned for the first time in his life.

It was . . . nothing short of a miracle.

Naturally, it took a while for Blay to have had his fill. And, funnily enough, Qhuinn was so totally fine with that.

When things eventually reached a pause that lasted longer than a minute and a half, Qhuinn released the tension in his arms and sank down to the bed, turning onto his side. Blay was apparently exhausted as well, his body following the lead and stretching out behind him.

Blay's arm stayed in place.

And what mattered now, in spite of the whole experience, was the loose, heavy weight of that limb. Lying as it did, it made them not two males who'd had sex and happened to be side by side . . . but lovers.

In actuality, he'd never had a lover before—and not because he'd just bottomed for the first time in his life. He'd had plenty of sex. But there had never been someone he'd wanted to hold him afterward. Never someone he'd wanted to hold back.

Yeah . . . Blay was his first real lover.

And though he'd missed out on that honor when it came to the guy, it seemed apt that Blay be his. No one could ever take away your first—and he counted himself lucky. He'd heard through the grapevine that a lot of times it was either really painful—for females—or just such a mad scramble, nothing registered.

This, he would remember forever.

Behind him, Blay was still breathing deeply, the heat radiating from him, their bodies still joined.

And Qhuinn wanted to take advantage of this quiet space: Ever so slowly—like maybe if he didn't move too fast the guy wouldn't

notice—he covered Blay's forearm with his own . . . then put his hand over his friend's.

Closing his eyes, he prayed that this was okay. That they could stay like this for just a little bit.

Shit, the sudden fear he felt was nothing short of torture, and it made him think about the nature of courage.

Specifically how little he'd had of it when it had come to Blay.

From out of the blue, he remembered telling the guy that he only saw himself with a female, long-term. That that was the reason he couldn't take Blay up on what he was offering. At the time, he'd meant every word of it—but he hadn't looked very far into the conviction.

He'd been a coward back then, hadn't he.

"God, I feel raw," he whispered.

"What?" came a sleepy response.

"I feel . . ." Exposed.

Like if Blay pulled away right now? He would shatter into pieces that would never fit together right again.

Blay let out a snuffle and jerked his arm, pulling Qhuinn closer, not pushing him off. "You cold? You're shaking."

"Warm me?"

There was some shuffling, and then a blanket was thrown over them both. Then the lights went off.

As Blay took a deep breath and seemed content to settle in for the duration, Qhuinn closed his eyes . . . and dared to thread his fingers through his best friend's, forming a seal of their hands.

"You okay?" Blay asked in a muffled way. Like there was nothing but a pilot light left on in his brain—but he did care.

"Yeah. Just cold."

Qhuinn opened his lids against the darkness. The only thing he could see was the line of light that came under the door at floor level.

As Blay drifted off, that breathing becoming ever more slower and even, Qhuinn stared ahead, even though he couldn't see anything in front of him.

Courage.

He thought he'd had all he needed—that the way he'd grown up had made him tougher and stronger than anyone else. That the way he did his job, running into burning buildings or jumping into the captain's seats of busted-up aircraft, proved it. That how he lived his life, essentially apart, meant he was strong. Meant he was safe.

The true measure of courage was still waiting for him, however.

After way too many years, he'd finally told Blay he was sorry. And then after way too much drama, he'd finally told the guy he was grateful.

But coming forward and being real about the fact that he was in love? Even if Blay was with someone else?

That was the true divide.

And goddamn him, he was going to do it.

Not to break the pair of them up—no, that wasn't it. And not to burden Blay.

In this case, payback, as it turned out, was actually a pledge. Something that was made with no expectations and no reservations. It was the jump without a parachute, the leap without knowing, the trip and the fall without anything to catch you.

Blay had done that not once, but several times—and yeah, sure, Qhuinn wanted to go back to any of those moments of vunerability and beat his earlier incarnations so badly that his head cleared, and he recognized the opportunity he'd been given.

Unfortunately, shit didn't run that way.

It was time for him to repay the strength . . . and in all likelihood, bear the pain that was going to come when he was turned down in a far more kindly manner than he'd provided for.

Forcing his lids down, he brought Blay's knuckles to his mouth, brushing a kiss against them. Then he gave himself up to sleep, letting himself fall into unconsciousness, knowing that, at least for the next few hours, he was safe in the arms of his one and only.

SIXTY-EIGHT

The following evening, as night fell, Assail sat naked at his desk, his eyes tracing the computer screen in front of him. The monitor's imaging was split into four quadrants that were marked north, south, east, and west, and from time to time, he manipulated the cameras, changing their focus and direction. Or mayhap he moved to other lenses around the house. Or went back to the ones he had been watching.

Having taken a shower and shaved hours ago, he knew he had to get dressed and go out. That *lesser* with the hearty appetite for product was up in arms, claiming he'd been cheated of a supply of cocaine. Except the twins had completed that particular transaction according to the slayer's wishes —and they had it videotaped.

Just a little precaution Assail had initiated.

So he didn't know what it was all about, but he was certainly going to find out: He had sent the recording to the *lesser's* phone about an hour ago, and was awaiting a response.

Mayhap it was going to involve another face-to-face meeting.

And his disgruntled buyer was not the only thing hanging over him. It was getting to be that time of month when Benloise and he needed to do their own squaring up—a complicated transfer of funds that made everyone edgy, including Assail: Even though he did regular weekly payments, they totaled but a quarter of his actual purchases, and on the thirtieth, he was going to have settle the balance sheet up.

Lot of cash. And people could make very poor decisions when there was that much money in play.

There was also the issue that, for the first time, he was going to want the twins to accompany him. He didn't imagine Benloise was going to appreciate the added company, but it was appropriate for his two associates to be brought further into the fold—and this payment was going to be the largest he'd ever made.

A record sure to be broken if he and that *lesser* continued to do business together.

Assail shifted the mouse. Clicked on one of the quadrants. Panned the security camera around, searching the backwoods behind his house.

Nothing moved. No shadows darted. Not even the limbs of the pines shifted in any kind of wind.

No tracks of skis. No hidden figure peering out.

She could be watching him from another vantage point, he thought. Across the river. Across the road. Down the lane.

With distraction, he reached out for the vial of powder he kept beside the keyboard. He had used toward the late afternoon, when the waning light of day had necessitated switching to night vision for the cameras. He had also used a couple of times since then, just to keep himself awake.

He had not slept for two days at this point.

Or was it three?

As he moved the tiny silver spoon around, drawing it in a circle at the base of the vial, all he got was the clinking of metal on glass.

He looked inside.

Evidently he had finished the lot of it.

Irritated by simply everything in his existence, Assail threw the vial aside and leaned back in his chair. As his mind spun and the compulsion to go from image to image to image tightened like a noose around his freedom of choice, he was dimly aware his brain was buzzing in an unhealthy manner.

He was locked in, however. Going nowhere rather quickly.

Where was his beautiful burglar?

Surely she could not have meant what she said.

Assail rubbed his eyes, and hated the way his mind was racing, thoughts rocketing back and forth from one side of his skull to the other.

He simply could not believe she meant to stay away.

As his phone went off, he reached for it with reflexes that were too quick, too pent-up. And when he saw who it was, he ordered his brain to pull itself together.

"Did you get the video?" he demanded, in lieu of "hello."

His biggest client's voice was not pleased. "How do I know when it was taken?"

"You must be aware of what your men were wearing at the time."

"Then where is my product?"

"That is not for me to say. Once I make the deal with your representatives, my responsibility is discharged. I delivered the requested goods at the time and place of mutual agreement, and thus fulfilled my duty to you. What happens thereafter is not my concern."

"If I ever catch you fucking with me, I'm going to kill you."

Assail let out a bored breath. "My dear man, I wouldn't waste my time with the likes of that. How would you then get what you require? And to that end, may I remind you that there is no incentive for me to be dishonest with you or your organization. The profit you represent is what matters to me, and I shall do my level best to keep the funds flowing my way. It's business."

There was a long silence, but Assail knew better than to assume that it was because the slayer on the other side of the conversation was confused or lost.

"I need another supply," the *lesser* muttered after a moment.

"And I shall gladly provide it."

"I need a loan." Now Assail frowned—but the *lesser* continued before he could cut in. "You float me this next order, and I'll make sure you get paid."

"That is not how I do business."

"Here's what I know about you and yours. You have a small operation that controls a huge area. You need distributors—because you killed all the ones that were here before. Without me and my organization? No offense, you're fucked. You can't begin to service all of Caldwell—and your product is worth nothing if you can't get it into the hands of users." When Assail didn't immediately reply, the *lesser* laughed softly. "Or did you think you were unknown, my friend?"

Assail gripped his cell phone hard.

"So I'm thinkin' you're right," the slayer concluded. "You and me are homies. I don't need to deal with whoever the big wholesaler is. Especially not in my . . . current incarnation."

Yes, the smell alone would make Benloise shut the door in his face, Assail thought.

"I need you. You need me. And that is why you're gonna bring my order to me and give me forty-eight hours to pay for it. It's just like you said. We got shit without the other, brother."

Assail bared his fangs, the reflection of his face in the glass of the monitor fearsome indeed.

And yet he kept his voice even and calm. "Where would you like to meet."

As the *lesser* laughed again, like he was enjoying this, Assail focused on the snarling image of himself. It would be unwise for the slayer to get greedy, or take too many liberties.

The one thing that was always true about business? No one was irreplaceable.

As Trez came awake, he felt as though he were floating on a cloud—and for a split second, he wondered if he was. His body felt completely weightless, to the point where he wasn't sure whether he was on his back or his stomach.

A strange sound filtered in through his fog.

Shhhscht.

He lifted his head, and orientation came to him in a rush: The red glow of his alarm clock told him he was on his stomach and running diagonally down the bed.

That sound came again.

What was it? Metal on metal?

He could sense iAm moving around down the hall, his brother's presence as known to him as his own. So if it was anyone else in the apartment or a threat of any kind? iAm would handle that shit.

Pushing himself up, he got out of bed and—yeah, whoa, the room spun around. Then again, there was absolutely, positively nothing in his stomach. Matter of fact, it was possible he'd thrown up his liver, kidneys, and lungs during that migraine. The good news was that the pain was gone, and the spacey aftermath wasn't bad. Kind of like being drunk, with the hangover front-loaded.

When he walked into the loo, he knew better than to turn on the lights. Little early for that still.

The shower felt so good he nearly teared the fuck up. And he didn't bother shaving—there'd be time for that later, after he'd thrown some fuel into his gut. Robe was nice—toasty, especially as he curled the lapels in and covered his throat up.

Bare feet kind of sucked, especially as he stepped out of his bedroom and into the marble-floored hallway, but he needed to find out what the hell that—

Trez stopped as he came to the doorway of his brother's suite of rooms. iAm was in his closet, taking out shirts that were on hangers. As he pulled another armful together on the brass rod, that *shhhscht* sounded again.

Naturally, his brother didn't seem surprised that Trez had made an appearance. He just threw the load on his bed.

Fuck.

"Going somewhere?" Trez muttered, his voice too loud in his head.

"Yes."

Crap. "Listen, iAm, I didn't mean—"

"I'm packing you up, too."

Trez blinked a couple of times.

"Oh?" At least the guy wasn't pulling out solo. Unless he wanted the satisfaction of pitching Trez's gear off the balcony?

"I've found us somewhere more secure."

"Is it in Caldwell?"

"Yes."

Cue the *Jeopardy!* theme. "You wanna give me a zip code?"

"I would if I could."

Trez groaned and leaned against the jamb, rubbing his eyes. "You've got us somewhere to go—and you don't know where it is?"

"No, I do not."

Okay, maybe it hadn't been a migraine, but a stroke. "I'm sorry. I'm not following—"

"We have"—iAm looked at his watch—"three hours to get packed up. Clothes and personals only."

"So it's furnished," Trez said dryly.

"Yes. It is."

Trez wasted some time watching his brother be extra efficient with the packing. Shirts were stripped off the hangers, folded precisely, put in black LV Epi luggage. Pants, same. Guns and knives went into matching steel briefcases.

At this rate, the guy was going to be done with his shit in a half hour.

"You gotta tell me where we're going."

iAm looked over. "We're moving in with the Brotherhood."

Trez's brain got flushed, the fog clearing in an instant. "I'm sorry. What."

"We're moving in with them."

Trez's eyes bulged. "I'm . . . wait, I didn't hear that right."

"You did."

"By whose authority."

"Wrath, son of Wrath."

"Shiiiiiiiiit. How in the hell did you pull that off?"

iAm shrugged, like he'd done nothing more than make a reservation at a Motel 6. "I talked to Rehvenge."

"Didn't know the male had that kind of pull."

"He doesn't. But he went to Wrath—who appreciated our backing him up at that Council meeting. The king feels as though we'd be additive on the home front."

"He's worried about a raid," Trez said softly.

"Maybe he is. Maybe he isn't. But what I do know is that no one's going to find us there."

Trez exhaled. So that was the "why" of it all: His brother didn't want him to be dragged back to the s'Hisbe any more than he did.

"You are amazing," he said.

iAm just shrugged again, as was his way. "Can you start packing your stuff, or should I do the first shift on that?"

"Nah, I'm good." He knocked on the jamb and started to turn away. "I owe you, my brother."

"Trez."

He glanced over his shoulder. "Yeah?"

His brother's eyes were grim. "This is not a get-out-of-jail-free thing. You can't run from the queen. I'm just buying us some time, here."

Trez looked down at his bare feet—and wondered how far, in fact, he could go if they were covered by Nike.

Pretty fucking far.

His brother was the one tie he hadn't cut, the only thing he felt

like he didn't want to leave behind in order to save himself from a gilded life of sexual enslavement.

And in a moment like this, with the guy once again having stepped up to the plate in a big way . . . he wondered if it was possible that he couldn't walk away from iAm.

Maybe he was going to have to cave in to his destiny, after all.

Fucking queen. And her goddamn daughter.

The traditions made no sense. He'd never met the young princess. No one had. That was the way it worked—the next in line to the throne was as sacred as her mother, because she was the one who was going to lead them in the future. And like a rare rose, nobody was allowed to see her until she was properly mated.

Purity and all that.

Blah, blah, blah.

Once she was hitched, however, she was free to come out to society, free to live her life—within the s'Hisbe. The sad-sack motherfucker who married the bitch? He took her place inside the palace walls, doing whatever the hell she wanted, when she wanted—assuming he wasn't worshipping at her mother's feet at the moment.

Yeah, that was a party.

And they thought he should feel honored to strap that yoke on?

Really.

He'd turned his body into a garbage dump in the last decade, fucking all those humans—and what was truly whacked? He wished that all those pesky Homo Sapiens diseases were the kind of thing he could pick up. No-go on that one. He'd had as much unsafe sex as he could with the other species and he was still healthy as a horse.

Pity.

"Trez?" iAm straightened. "Trez? Talk to me. Where you at?"

Trez stared at his brother, memorizing that proud, intelligent face and those bottomless, penetrating eyes.

"I'm right here," he murmured. "See?"

He held out his hands and did a little circle in his bare feet, in his robe, in his spacey, fuzzy, post-migraine haze.

"What's going on in that mind of yours?" iAm demanded.

"Nothing. I think it's great what you did. I'ma go pack up and get ready. They sending a car or something?"

iAm narrowed his stare, but he did answer. "Yeah. A butler named Fred? Or was it Foster?"

"I'll be ready."

Trez walked off, the dregs of that headache draining from him as he looked into the future . . . and really worried about this one last tie of his.

But this move was a good thing. iAm was right: He had been fooling himself these last few years, aware that the princess was aging, and time was passing, and his day of reckoning was fast approaching.

There were things you could put off. This was not one of them.

Fucking hell, maybe he was going to have to disappear. Even if it killed him.

Besides, if his brother was with Rehv in the king's household? iAm was going to have the kind of support he was going to need if Trez up and got ghost.

And maybe, after the way shit was going?

The guy would be relieved to get rid of him.

SIXTY-NINE

Qhuinn's whole life took another corkscrew about fifteen hours after he lost his virginity. Later, he would decide that the comes-in-threes thing might be true. When the shit went down, though, all he wanted to do was live through it. . . .

Sometime during the hours of the day, he and Blay had woken up, split up, gone their separate ways.

Qhuinn would have preferred that they return to the main house together, but he'd had to stop by Luchas's room, and Blay had been anxious to get back to his place and shower. And in a way, it hadn't been all that bad, because Qhuinn had had a chance to check on Layla as well.

When it came to his brother, and the Chosen, all was quiet on both fronts: The pair of them had been asleep in their respective beds—Luchas's color was better, and for the first time, when Qhuinn had walked into Layla's bedroom? He had sensed the pregnancy: The hormone wave had hit him as soon as he'd entered, and he'd stopped dead, it was so strong.

Which had been really good.

What he hadn't been so happy about had been going by Blay's door, and wanting to knock and duck inside—and go back to sleep.

Instead, he'd ended up within his own four walls all by his lone-some.

In bed. In the dark. Drifting in and out of REM-landia for the two hours he had before First Meal was served.

So when his door was thrown wide and a lineup of tall males in hooded black robes came filing in, his past and his present collided, the two becoming interchangeable—such that the attack by the Honor Guard jumped up out of the graveyard of his memory and landed right in his room at the mansion.

Unsure whether he was dreaming or any of this was real, his first thought was that he was glad Blay wasn't with him. The guy had al-ready found him dead at the side of the road once. No one needed a replay on that.

His second was that he was going to take out as many as he could before they finally finished the job on him.

With a battle cry, Qhuinn exploded out of his bed, his naked body going on the attack with such power, he actually plowed over the first two males. Spinning with his legs, he kicked and punched at anything that came at him, and there was a brief satisfaction as his targets cursed and jumped out of range—

Something locked around his chest from behind, and swung him around with such force, his feet popped off the ground and flew in a crazy circle—

Helllllllllo, wall.

The impact was a three-point bulletin to his fight-back bright idea, his face, torso, and hips slamming into the plaster so hard, he no doubt left a cartoon-style 3-D rep of himself on the shit.

Instantly, he palmed the flat plane, prepared to shove his way off—

The grip that latched onto his nape and held him in place might as well have been steel. There was literally no give in the flesh and bone, even as he strained, his body refusing to be dominated—

"Chill, asswipe. Just fucking *chill* before I'm forced to hurt you."

The sound of Vishous's voice made no fucking sense.

And then abruptly, from out of the corner of his eye, he noticed that a ring had formed around him, all those black robes surrounding him, just like that grip on his neck.

But they were not attacking.

"Just relax," V said into his ear. "Breathe for me, come on, now—just breathe easy. No one's going to hurt you."

The talking helped, that cool, calm voice reaching through the fight-or-flight response and turning down the volume on his panic's roar.

In the aftermath, Qhuinn started to shake, his muscles processing the adrenaline. "Vishous?"

"Yup. It's me, buddy. You need to keep breathing."

"Who . . . else?"

"Rhage."

"Butch."

"Phury."

"Zsadist."

"Tohr."

The voices all matched the names, those deep, serious, no-bullshit tones sinking into his brain, helping to ground himself in a reality that didn't involve the past.

And then the last one was the final rung of the ladder that got him out of that mental tailspin and back to what was real. "Wrath."

Qhuinn went to jerk his head toward the king, but the impulse got him nowhere.

"I'm going to let you go, buddy, okay?" V said. "You gonna mind your manners?"

"Yeah."

"On three. One. Two. Three—"

Vishous leaped back and landed in a hand-to-hand combat pose: arms up, fists ready, stance stable. In spite of the fact that the Brother's face was covered by the hood, Qhuinn could just picture the expression: No doubt that if Qhuinn made any move, he'd be reintroduced to the wall—and that acquaintance had already been well and truly made, fuck him very much.

He felt about six inches flatter.

With a curse, Qhuinn turned around slowly, keeping his hands where the Brotherhood could see them. "Are you kicking me out of the house?"

He had no clue what the hell he'd done, but with his history of pissing people off—on purpose and by default? Could be anything.

"No, you idiot," V said with a laugh.

Facing the lineup of hooded, solemn figures, he searched where the faces were, making contact, reminding himself that these were the guys he had fought with side by side, that they'd always had his back, that they'd worked together.

So what the hell was going—

The third figure from the left lifted his arm, a long finger extending out and pointing to the dead center of Qhuinn's chest.

Instantly, Qhuinn was back in the carcass of the Cessna, the in-flight drama over, Zsadist alive and well, the goal reached . . . that male singling him out as he was now.

In the Old Language, Wrath said, *"You shall be asked a question. You shall be asked it only once. Your answer shall stand the test of time, extending out from this moment unto your bloodline forever more. Are you prepared to be asked."*

Qhuinn's heart began to thunder. Eyes bouncing around, he couldn't believe that this was . . .

Except . . . how was it possible? Based on his bloodlines and his defect, it wasn't legal for someone like him to—

From out of nowhere, the image of Saxton working in that library for all those nights hit him.

Holy . . . fuck.

So many questions: Why him? Why now? What about John Matthew, whose chest already, magically, bore the marking of the Brotherhood?

As his mind raced, he knew he had to answer, but shit, he couldn't—

With a sudden clarity, he thought of his daughter, picturing that image that he'd seen in the door to the Fade.

Qhuinn looked at each of the hoods again. How ironic, he thought. Nearly two years ago, an Honor Guard of black robes had been sent to him to make sure he knew his family didn't want him. And now, here these males were, come to draw him into a different kind of fold—that was every bit as strong as that of blood.

"Hell, yeah," he said. "Ask me."

Blay's first clue that something big was up was the sound of footfalls going by his room: He was in front of his mirror, shaving, when he heard them come down the hall of statues, heavy, repetitive—a lot of them.

Had to be the Brotherhood.

Then, as he bent over the sink to rinse the residual shaving cream off his cheeks, something hard dropped to the floor next door—or was thrown at a wall. In what sure as shit seemed like Qhuinn's room.

Cranking off the hot and cold mix, he snagged a towel and wrapped it around his hips as he jogged out of his suite and headed down to—

Blay skidded to a halt. Qhuinn's room was dark, but the light from the corridor shone in . . . on a circle of black robes that surrounded the guy. As he was held face-first against the wall.

Blay's only thought was that a second Honor Guard had come for the fighter—even though he knew damn well that it was the Brotherhood under all those robes. Had to be, right?

Vishous's voice solved that one, the male's words slow and even.

Then Qhuinn was released. As he turned around, he was white as a sheet, shaking as he stood naked in the center of that circle of hooded figures.

Wrath cut through the silence, the king's deep baritone filling the darkness. *"You shall be asked a question. You shall be asked it only once. Your answer shall stand for the test of time, extending out from this moment unto your bloodline forever more. Are you prepared to be asked."*

Blay put his dagger hand up to his mouth as the thing fell open. This couldn't be . . . could it? They were inducting him into the Black Dagger Brotherhood?

Instantly, he put it all together—Saxton working for all those months; Qhuinn's acts of heroism; John getting informed that the guy was no longer his *ahstrux nohtrum.*

Wrath must have changed the Old Laws.

Holy fucking *shit.*

"Hell, yeah. Ask me."

Blay had to smile as he ducked away and went back to his room. Leave it to Qhuinn to be blunt.

As he shut his door, he stayed against it, waiting. Moments later, those heavy footsteps came again, filing past his room, going down the hall, disappearing . . . changing history forever.

In all the aeons of the Brotherhood, there had never been anyone inducted who wasn't the son of a Brother and a female of Chosen blood. Qhuinn was technically an aristocrat —even with him forsaken by his family, and with his "defect," his lineage was what it was. But he didn't have the kind of DNA credentials—or the warrior name—that the others did.

And yet, assuming he lived through the ceremony, he would return to the mansion as a male among equals, forsaken no more.

It was good that Luchas was alive to see this. That was going to matter.

Blay got dressed, and when he checked his phone, he saw the group text that had gone out from Tohr, saying that no one was going out into the field tonight—and that they were getting a pair of new roommates: The Shadows were coming to stay at the mansion.

Cool. Given the disquiet with the aristocracy, and that attempt on Wrath's life? Nothing better than having those two killers under the roof. Coupled with Lassiter's antics, that meant the king had a trio of guys with extra skills protecting him.

With any luck, Trez and iAm would be permanent fixtures.

Leaving his room, he jogged down the stairs and was not surprised to find the *doggen* running around, setting up a feast.

How long was it going to take, he wondered.

And man, he wished he had something to occupy the time.

Wandering into the billiards room, because he knew better than to approach Fritz with an offer to help with the preparations, he picked up a cue and racked a set of balls. As he was chalking the tip, the bell at the vestibule's door went off.

"I've got it," he hollered out as he took his cue with him, striding over to the security check-in screen.

Saxton was on the stoop, the male looking rested and healthy.

Blay opened the way in. "Welcome back."

There was a moment of surprise on the other male's face, but he recovered fast with a smile. "Hello."

Blay wasn't sure whether they should embrace or not. Did they shake?

"We need to stop this awkwardness," Saxton announced. "Come here."

"I know, right?"

After a quick hug, Blay grabbed the male's matching Gucci bags, and the pair of them hit the grand staircase, ascending side by side.

"So how was the vacation?" Blay asked.

"Wonderful. I went to my aunt's—the one who still talks to me? She has a place down in Florida."

"Dangerous place for vampires. Not a lot of basements."

"Ah, but she lives in a stone castle." Saxton nodded around at the foyer. "Not unlike this one. The evenings were warm, the ocean was wonderful, and the nightlife was—"

As Saxton stopped short, Blay glanced over. "It's all right, you know. I'm glad you had a good time. Honest."

Saxton regarded him steadily, and then murmured, "You've been busy yourself, haven't you."

Damn redheaded coloring. Any blush had always shown—and right now, his face was on frickin' fire.

As they took a left in front of Wrath's study and headed down the hall of statues, Saxton laughed a little. "I'm happy for you—and I'm not going to ask any questions."

He knew the "who," Blay thought. "Yeah. So."

"How about you fill me in on the gossip," Saxton said as they went into the male's room. "I feel like I've been gone forever."

"Well . . . brace yourself."

Luchas. Trez and iAm. Qhuinn and the induction.

By the time Blay was finished downloading, Saxton was sitting on his bed with his mouth hanging open.

"But you knew about the Qhuinn thing, didn't you," Blay said as he finally stopped reporting.

"Yes, I did." Saxton straightened his bow tie, even though the tight knot was perfectly symmetrical. "And I have to say, even though I don't know as much as you do about how he is in the field, everything that I've heard suggests it is an honor well placed. I understand he played a big role in getting Wrath safe when the assassination was attempted?"

"He's brave, that's true."

Among many other things.

As Blay looked out into the hall and pictured those hooded figures clustered around his friend, all he could think of was . . . what the hell were they going to do to him?

SEVENTY

Quinn had no clue where he was.

Before they'd left his room, he'd been given a black robe and instructed to put the hood up, lock his eyes on the floor and keep his hands clasped behind his back. He was not to speak unless spoken to, and it was made clear that how he acted was part of what he'd be judged on.

No being an asshole or a pussy.

He could do that.

Next stop after getting led down the grand staircase had been V's Escalade; he knew by the tang of Turkish tobacco and the sound of the engine. Short drive, executed slowly. And then he was told to get out, cold air seeping under the hood of his robe as well as the hem.

His bare feet traversed an icy-cold, frozen stretch of earth, and then hit smooth, hard-packed dirt that had no snow on it. Going by the acoustics, it was clear they were heading through a corridor or maybe a cave . . . ? It wasn't long before he was jerked to a stop, heard some kind of gate was opened, and then found himself on a decline. A little later, he was yanked to a halt a second time, and then there was another whisper, as if one more barrier of some sort was being cleared.

Smooth marble under his bare feet now. And the shit was warm. There was also a mellow light source—candlelight.

God, his heartbeat was loud in his ears.

After a number of yards, he was again pulled to a stop, and then he heard shifting fabric everywhere around him. The Brothers disrobing.

He wanted to look up, see where they were at, find out what was doing, but he did not. As instructed, he kept his head down and his eyes on the—

A heavy hand landed on the nape of his neck, and Wrath's voice boomed in the Old Language. "*You are unworthy to enter herein as you stand now. Nod your head.*"

Qhuinn nodded.

"*Say that you are unworthy.*"

In the Old Language, he replied, "*I am unworthy.*"

From all around him, the Brothers let out an explosive shout in the Old Language, a disagreement that made him want to thank them for having his back.

"*Though you are unworthy,*" the king continued, "*you desire to become as such this night. Nod your head.*"

He nodded.

"*Say that you wish to become worthy.*"

"*I wish to become worthy.*"

This time the tremendous shout from the Brothers was one of approval and support.

Wrath continued. "*There is only one way to become worthy, and it is the right and proper way. Flesh of our flesh. Nod your head.*"

Qhuinn nodded.

"*Say that you wish to become flesh of our flesh.*"

"*I wish to become flesh of your flesh.*"

As soon as his voice faded, a chanting started up, the deep voices of the Brotherhood mingling until they formed a perfect chord and a perfect cadence. He did not join in, because he had not been told to do so—but as someone stepped in front of him, and somebody fell in line behind him, and then the whole group started weaving side by side, his body followed their lead.

Moving together, they became one unit, their powerful shoulders shifting back and forth to the rhythm of the chanting, their weight ticktocking on their hips—the lineup of them beginning to move forward.

Qhuinn started chanting. He didn't mean to; it just happened. His lips parted, his lungs filled, and his voice joined the others. . . .

The instant it did, he started to cry.

Thank fuck for the hood.

All of his life he had wanted to belong. Be accepted. Be one among a many that he respected. He had wanted it with such a need that the denial of any and all unity had nearly killed him—and he had survived only by revolting against authority, customs, norms.

He hadn't even been aware of giving up on ever finding this communion.

And yet now here he was, somewhere in the earth, surrounded by males who had . . . chosen him. The Brotherhood, the most respected fighters in the race, the most powerful soldiers, the elite of the elite . . . had *chosen* him.

No accident of birth, this.

To have been considered a curse, but be embraced here and now? Abruptly, he felt as if he were whole in a way that he had never been before—

All at once the acoustics changed, their collective chanting richocheting around, as if they had entered a tremendous space with a lot of loft.

A hand on his shoulder brought him to a halt.

And then the chanting and the movement stopped, the final strains of their voices drifting away.

Somebody grabbed onto his arm and drew him forward. "Stairs," Z's voice said.

He went up about six of them, and then there was a straightaway. When he was stopped, it was with his chest and his toes against what seemed to be a marble wall of the same sort of rock the floor was made of.

Zsadist walked off, leaving him where he was.

His heart banged against his sternum.

The king's voice was loud as thunder. "*Who proposes this male?*"

"*I do,*" Zsadist answered.

"*I do,*" Tohr echoed.

"*I do.*"

"*I do.*"

"*I do.*"

"*I do.*"

Qhuinn had to blink repeatedly as, one by one, every single Brother spoke up. Every single fucking one of the Brothers proposed him.

And then came the last.

The voice of the king resonated loud and clear: "*I do.*"

Fuck him, he needed to blink more.

Then Wrath continued, his aristocratic inflection of the Old Language backed up by a warrior's strength. "*On the basis of the testimony of the assembled members of the Black Dagger Brotherhood, and upon the proposals by Zsadist and Phury, sons of the Black Dagger warrior Ahgony; Tohrment, the son of the Black Dagger warrior Hharm; Butch O'Neal, blooded relation of mine own line; Rhage, the son of the Black Dagger warrior Tohrture; Vishous, son of the Black Dagger warrior known as the Bloodletter; and mine own as Wrath, son of Wrath, we find this male before us, Qhuinn, son of no one, an appropriate nomination unto the Black Dagger Brotherhood. As it is within my power and discretion to do so, and as it is suitable for the protection of the race, and further, as the laws have been reconstructed to provide that this is right and proper, I have waived all requirements of lineage. We may now begin. Turn him. Unveil him.*"

Before anyone came over to him, Qhuinn squared his shoulders, and managed a quick brush under his eyes—so he was a male once more as he was pivoted around and the robe was taken from him—

Qhuinn gasped. He was up on a dais, and the cave that was before him was lit with a hundred black candles, the flames creating a symphony of soft, golden light that flickered over the rough-hewn walls and reflected off the glossy floor.

But that was not what really got his attention: Right in front of him, between him and the tremendous, illuminated space, was an altar.

In the center of which was a large skull.

The thing was ancient, the bone not the white of the newly dead, but carrying the darkened, pitted patina of the aged, the sacred, the revered.

That was the first Brother. Had to be.

As his eyes shifted away from it, he was struck with awe: Down on the floor, looking up at him, were the living, breathing carriers of the great tradition. The Brotherhood stood shoulder-to-shoulder, the naked bodies of the fighters forming a tremendous wall of flesh and muscle, that candlelight playing across their strength and power.

Tohr took Wrath's arm and led the king up the stairs that Qhuinn himself had just surmounted.

"Back up against the wall, and grip the pegs," Wrath commanded in English as he was escorted to the altar.

Qhuinn obeyed without hesitation, feeling his shoulder blades and ass hit the stone as his hands brushed a pair of stout, dowel-like protrusions.

When the king brought up his arm, Qhuinn suddenly knew exactly how each of the Brothers had gotten that star-shaped scarring on their pectoral: An aged silver glove was locked onto Wrath's hand, barbs marking the knuckles of the thing—and within the fist, was the handle of a black dagger.

With a minimum of fuss, Tohr extended Wrath's wrist over to the skull. "My lord."

As the king brought up the blade, the ritualistic tattoos that delineated his lineage caught the glowing light—and then the razor-sharp edge as he scored his skin.

Red blood welled and fell into a silver cup that had been inset into the crown of the skull. "*My flesh,*" the king proclaimed.

After a moment, Wrath licked the wound closed. And then the huge male, with his waist-length black hair and his widow's peak and those wraparounds, was led over to Qhuinn.

Even without the benefit of sight, Wrath somehow knew exactly how their bodies were positioned, how tall Qhuinn was, where Qhuinn's face was. . . .

Because the king snapped out a hold right on Qhuinn's jaw. Then with brutal force, he shoved Qhuinn's head back and to the side, exposing his throat.

Now he knew what the fucking pegs were for.

Wrath's cruel smile exposed tremendous fangs, the likes of which Qhuinn had never seen before. "*Your flesh.*"

With a lightning-fast strike, the king latched on without mercy, piercing Qhuinn's vein in a brutal bite and then drawing in a series of ripping pulls that were swallowed one after another. When finally he retracted those canines, he drew his tongue over his lips and smiled like a warlord.

And then it was time.

Qhuinn didn't need to be told to brace the ever-loving shit out of himself. Bearing down on his hands, he locked his shoulders and his legs, ready to receive.

"*Our flesh,*" Wrath growled.

The king didn't hold back. With the same unerring accuracy, he curled up a fist inside that ancient glove and slammed the thing into Qhuinn's pec, the impact of those barbed knuckles so great, Qhuinn's lips flapped in the gale that blew up and out of his lungs. Vision went bye-bye-birdie for a little bit, but when it came back, he got a crystal-clear of Wrath's face.

The king's expression was one of respect—and a total lack of surprise, as if Wrath had expected Qhuinn to take it like a male.

And on it went. Tohr was next in line, accepting the glove and the dagger, saying the same words, scoring his forearm, bleeding into the skull, striking at Qhuinn's throat, then hitting as hard as a truck. And then Rhage. Vishous. Butch. Phury. Zsadist.

By the end of it, Qhuinn was bleeding from the wounds at his throat and his chest, his body was covered from sweat, and the only reason he wasn't on the floor was the bitch grip he had on those pegs.

But he didn't care what else they did to him; he was going to stay on his feet no matter what. He had no clue about the history of the Brotherhood, but he was willing to bet none of these guys had gone down like a bag of sand during their inductions—and he didn't mind being the first in some senses, but not in a sacless one.

Besides, so far so good, he guessed: The other Brothers were standing around and grinning from ear to ear at him, like they totally approved of how he was handling shit—and didn't that only make him even more determined.

With a nod, as if he'd been given an order, Tohr led the king back over to the altar and handed him the skull. Raising the collected blood high, Wrath said, "*This is the first of us. Hail to him, the warrior who birthed the Brotherhood.*"

A war cry burst forth from the Brothers, their combined voices thundering in the cave; and then Wrath approached Qhuinn. "Drink and join us."

Roger. That.

With a sudden surge of strength, he grabbed that skull and looked right into the eye sockets as he brought the silver cup to his mouth. Opening the way to his gut, he poured the blood down his throat, accepting the males into him, absorbing their strength . . . joining them.

All around, the Brothers growled their approval.

When he was finished, he put the skull back in Wrath's palms and wiped his mouth.

The king laughed deep in his massive chest. "You're going to want to hang on to those pegs again, son. . . ."

Annnnnnnnd that was the last thing he heard for a while.

Like a lightning bolt coming out of the sky and drilling him right in the head, a sudden burst of energy hit him, overtaking all of his senses. He jumped backward, finding the grips and locking on just as his body started to go into a seizure. . . .

He had every intention of staying conscious.

But alas . . . sorry, Charlie. The maelstrom was too great.

As his body shook, and his heart flickered, and his mind fizzled like a firecracker, *Boom!* it was lights-out.

SEVENTY-ONE

"Sola, why you no tell me we have visitors?"

Sola paused as she put her backpack down on the countertop in the kitchen. Even though her grandmother was clearly waiting for an answer, she was not going to turn around until she was sure her expression showed none of the surprise she was feeling.

When she was ready, she pivoted on one boot.

Her grandmother was sitting at their little table, her pink-and-blue housecoat coordinating with the curlers in her hair and the flowered curtains behind her. At the age of eighty, she had the gracefully lined face of a woman who had lived through thirteen presidents, a World War, and innumerable personal struggles. Her eyes, however, burned with the strength of an immortal.

"Who came to the door, vovó?" she asked.

"The man with the"—her grandmother lifted her heavily knuckled hand and encircled her curlers—"dark hair."

Crap. "When did he stop by?"

"He was very nice."

"Did he leave his name?"

"So you did no expect him."

Sola took a deep breath, and prayed that her neutral affect stayed in place in spite of the grilling. Hell, after having lived with her grand-mother for how many years, you'd think she'd be used to the fact that the woman was a one-way street when it came to questions.

"I wasn't expecting anyone, no." And the idea that someone had come a-knocking made her put her hand on her bag. There was a nine in there with a laser sight and a silencer—and that was a very good thing. "What did he look like?"

"Very big. And the dark hair. Deep-set eyes."

"What color were they?" Her grandmother didn't see all that well, but surely she would remember that. "Was he—"

"Like us. He spoke with me in the Spanish."

Maybe that erotic man she'd been tracking was bilingual—make that trilingual, given his strange accent.

"So did he leave his name?" Not that that would help. She didn't know what the man she'd been tracking called himself.

"He said you knew him, and that he would be back with you."

Sola glanced at the digital readout on the microwave. It was just before ten p.m. "When did he come by?"

"Not that long ago." Her grandmother's eyes narrowed. "You been seeing him, Marisol? Why you no tell me?"

At that point, everything flipped into Portuguese, their staccato speech overlapping, all kinds of I'm-not-dating-anyone interlacing with why-can't-you-just-get-married. They'd had the argument so many times, they basically just reassumed their well-practiced parts in this overdone play.

"Well, I liked him," her grandmother announced as she got up from the table and banged the surface with her open palms. As the napkin caddy with its payload of *Vanity Fair* jumped, Sola wanted to curse. "And I think you should bring him here for a proper dinner."

I would, Grandmother, but I don't know the guy—and would you feel this way if you knew he was a criminal? And a playboy?

"Is he Catholic?" her grandmother asked on the way out.

He's a drug dealer—so if he is religious, he's got incredible powers of reconciliation.

"He looks like a good boy," her vovó said over her shoulder. "A Catholic good boy." And that was that—for now.

As those slippers scuffed their way across to the stairs, undoubt-

edly there were all kinds of making the sign of the cross going on. She could just picture it.

With a curse, Sola dropped her head and closed her eyes. On some level, she couldn't imagine that man being all warm and fuzzy just because a little old Brazilian woman opened the damn door. Catholic, her ass.

"Damn it."

Then again, who was she to be sanctimonious? She was a criminal, too. Had been for years—and the fact that she'd had to provide for herself and her grandmother didn't justify all the breaking and entering.

Who did her mystery man support, she wondered as the next-door neighbor's dog began to bark. Those twins? They'd looked *really* self-sufficient. Did he have kids? A wife?

For some reason, that made her shudder.

Crossing her arms over her chest, she stared at the you-could-eat-off-of-it floor that her grandmother cleaned every day.

He had no right to come here, she thought.

Then again, she had visited his place uninvited, hadn't she—

Sola frowned and lifted her eyes. The window that was framed by those ruffled pink half drapes was jet-black because she hadn't turned any exterior lights on yet. But she knew someone was there.

And she knew who it was.

Breath going short, heart starting to beat fast, she put her hand up to the front of her throat for some reason.

Turn away, she told herself. Run away.

But . . . she did not.

Assail had not meant to go to his burglar's home. But the tracking device was still on her Audi, and when it had informed him that she'd returned to the address, he was incapable of not materializing there.

He did not want to be seen, however, so he chose the backyard, and how fortuitous: When his burglar walked into the kitchen, he got a full view of her—as well as her housemate.

The older human female was rather enchanting in an elderly kind of way, her hair in curlers, her robe bright as a spring day, her face beautiful in spite of her age. She was not happy, however, as she sat at the table and glared across at what Assail surmised had to be her grandaughter.

Words were exchanged, and he smiled a little in the darkness. Much love between the pair of them—much annoyance, too. And wasn't that the way with older relatives, whether you were human or vampire.

Oh, how he was eased by knowing she did not live with a male.

Unless, of course, that one she had met at the restaurant also stayed in the little house.

As he growled softly in the dark, the dog in the house next door began to bark, warning his human owners of that of which they were unaware.

A moment later, his burglar was left alone in the kitchen, her expression one of both resignation and frustration.

As she stood there, crossing her arms, shaking her head, he told himself he should go. Instead, he did what he should not: He reached through the glass with his mind and let his need unleash.

Instantly, she responded, that lithe body straightening from its lean against the counter, her eyes flipping to his through the window.

"Come to me," he said into the cold.

And she did.

The back door creaked as she opened it with her hip, forcing the bottom corner to carve a pie slice in the snow of the deck.

Her scent was ambrosia to him. And as he closed the distance between them, his body surged with a predatory lust.

Assail didn't stop until he was mere inches from her. Up close, chest-to-breast, she was so much smaller than he; yet the effect she had on him was mountainous: His hands curled up; his thighs tightened; his heart beat with hot blood.

"I didn't think I was going to see you again," she whispered.

His cock hardened even further, just from the sound of her voice. "It appears that we have unfinished business."

And it did not involve money, drugs, or information.

"I meant what I said to you." She brushed her hair back, as if she were having difficulty standing still. "No more spying on my part. I promise."

"Indeed, you have given me your word. But it seems that I miss having your eyes upon me." Her little hiss carried across the chilly air between their mouths. "Among other things."

She looked away quickly. Looked back. "This isn't a good idea."

"Why? Because of that human you were having dinner with last night?"

His burglar frowned—probably at the use of the word *human*. "No. Not because of him."

"So he does not live here."

"No, it's just my grandmother and me."

"I approve."

"Why would you have any opinion at all?"

"I ask myself that daily," he muttered. "But explain, if it's not because of that man, why shall we not meet?"

His burglar pushed her hair over her shoulder again and shook her head. "You're . . . trouble."

"Says the woman who is almost always armed."

She tilted up her chin. "You think I didn't see that bloody blade in your back hall?"

"Oh, that." He dismissed the comment with a flick of the hand. "Just taking care of business."

"I thought you'd killed him."

"Who?"

"Mark—my friend."

"Friend," he heard himself growl. "Is that what he is."

"So who did you kill?"

Assail took out a cigar to light, but she stopped him. "My grandmother will smell it."

He glanced up at the closed windows of the second floor. "How?"

"Just please don't. Not here."

With an incline of his head, he acquiesced—even though he couldn't remember ever declining one for anybody.

"Who did you kill?"

This was asked factually, without the hysteria one might expect from a female. "It is nothing that concerns you."

"Better I don't know, huh."

Given that he was a different species than her? Yes. Indeed.

" 'Twas nobody you would ever know. I will tell you, however, that I had grounds. He betrayed me."

"So he deserved it." Not a question; more a statement of approval.

He couldn't help but favor her take on things. "Yes, he did."

There was a period of silence, and then he had to ask, "What is your name?"

She laughed. "You mean you don't know?"

"How would I have found out?"

"Good point—and I'll tell you, if you explain what you said to my vovó." She hugged her torso, as if cold. "You know, she liked you."

"Who likes me?"

"My grandmother."

"How ever does she know me?"

His burglar frowned. "When you came before now. She said she thought you were a good man, and she wants to invite you back for dinner." Those astonishing dark eyes returned to his. "Not that I'm advocating—what? Hey, ow."

Assail forced his hold to loosen, unaware of having gripped her arm. "I did not come by earlier. At no time have I spoken to your grandmother."

His burglar opened her mouth. Shut it. Opened it again. "You weren't here tonight?"

"No."

"So who the hell is looking for me?"

As a vast protective urge came over him, his fangs elongated and his upper lip began to curl back—but he caught himself, tamping down the outer show of his inner emotions.

Abruptly, he nodded in the direction of the kitchen. "We go inside. Now. And you will tell me more."

"I don't need your help."

Assail stared at her from his superior height. "You shall have it anyway."

SEVENTY-TWO

rez was not used to being chauffeured around. He liked driving himself. Being in control. Choosing the left or the right. That kind of self-determination was not on the menu tonight, however.

At the moment, he was riding phat in the back of a Mercedes that was the size of a house. Up in front, Fritz, as his name was, was driving like a bat out of hell—not exactly something you expected from a butler who looked like he was seven thousand years old.

Now, given that Trez was still a little off after the previous night's headache, he supposed he was okay with being a passenger in this instance. But if he and iAm were going to live here, they were going to have to know where the damn property was—

What. The. Fuck.

For some reason, his senses were picking up on a change in the atmosphere, something tingling on the edges of his consciousness—a warning. And what do you know, outside the window, the moonlit landscape grew wavy, a vital distortion tweaking his vision.

His eyes checked out the inside of the Mercedes. Everything was fine: the grain of the black leather, the burled walnut trim, the partition that had been raised into place all exactly as they should appear. So it wasn't his optical nerves going bad.

Shifting his eyes back to the great outdoors, he knew the distortion wasn't because a fog had rolled in. Not some weird-ass sleet thing, either. No, this shit was not the weather—it was something else entirely . . . as if dread had crystallized in the very particles of the air, and was causing the landscape to morph out of shape.

Niiiiiiiiiice protective cover, he thought.

And here he'd assumed he and his brother were the only ones with tricks up their sleeves.

"We're close," he said.

"What is this stuff?" iAm murmured as he too looked out his window.

"I don't know. But we need to get some of it."

Abruptly, the car went into an ascent, which, given the speed of Old Man Lead Foot, resembled the launch of a roller coaster. They didn't crest and free-fall at the top, though: From out of nowhere, a massive stone mansion materialized, making such a quick appearance, Trez grabbed for the hand rest and braced himself.

But their chauffeur knew exactly where they were, and how much distance was required to bring the Benz to a halt. With the expertise of a Hollywood stunt driver, the butler wrenched the wheel and nailed the brakes, bringing them to a park between a GTO Trez had an immediate hard-on for . . . and a Hummer that looked like an abstract sculpture rather than anything that was drivable.

"Maybe he made his mistakes on that one," Trez said dryly.

As the locks were released, he and iAm got out at the same time.

Man. Get a loada the house, Trez thought as he tilted back his head and looked up, up, way up. In comparison to the giant pile of rock, he felt about the size of a thumb.

Like, a two-year-old's thumb.

Looming high into the cold night, with gargoyles that watched from eaves, and a pair of sinister-looking, four-story wings that extended off on either side, the place appeared to be exactly like what you'd expect the king of the vampires to live in: spooky, creepy, threatening.

It was all that Halloween shit, except this was for real. The people in there did bite, and not just when they were asked to.

"Cool," Trez said, feeling instantly at home.

"Sires, why do you not proceed inside," the butler said cheerfully. "And I shall endeavor to get your bags."

"Nah," Trez countered as he headed over to the trunk. "We got a lot of shit—er, crap."

It was kind of hard to curse in front of a guy in tails.

iAm nodded. "We'll take care of this for you."

The butler looked back and forth between them, smile still firmly in place. "Please do go in for the festivities, sires. We shall handle these mundane things."

"Oh, no, we can—"

"Yeah, I mean, it won't take—"

Fritz looked confused, and then slightly panicked. "But please, sires, you must join the others. I shall take care of this. This is my position within the household."

The distress seemed so out of place, but it wasn't as if it could be argued with without causing more upset: Clearly, the guy was going to throw a clot if they took their own luggage through that front door.

When in Rome . . . Trez thought. "Okay, yeah, thanks."

"Yes, thank you very much."

That endearing, wide-open grin immediately returned. "Very well, sires! Very well indeed."

As the butler indicated the way to the door, as if the purpose of that grand, cathedral-like entrance was a mystery, Trez shrugged and headed up the steps.

"Do you think he'll let us wipe our own asses?" he said under his breath.

"Only if he doesn't see us go to the loo."

Trez barked out a laugh and looked over. "Was that a joke, iAm? Huh? I think it was."

After elbowing his brother, and getting a growl in response, he reached out and grabbed the heavy portal's handle. He was a little surprised to find that it wasn't locked, but then again, with that . . . whatever it was . . . all around, why would you need the likes of anything Schlage-ish? No squeak when he opened the way in, and that wasn't a surprise. The place was landscaped to within an inch of its life, everything fully shoveled, thoroughly salted, absolutely ordered.

Then again, with that butler in charge? One dust bunny was probably a national emergency.

Stepping out of the cold, he found himself in a small anteroom with a mosaic floor and a tall ceiling, facing a check-in station that included a camera lens. He knew what that was for—and he shoved his mug right into its field of vision.

Instantly, the inner door, which could have lapped a bank vault when it came to heft, was opened wide.

"Hello!" a female said. "You're here."

Trez barely even noticed Ehlena as he took note of what was behind her. "Hey . . . how are you . . ."

He didn't hear her response.

Oh . . . wow. Oh . . . what beautiful color.

Trez was unaware of walking forward, but he did . . . into the most incredible architectural wonder he had ever seen. Great columns of malachite and marble rose to a ceiling higher than the heavens. Crystal chandeliers and golden sconces twinkled. A bloodred staircase as big as a city park rose up from a mosaic floor that seemed to depict . . . an apple tree in full bloom.

As dour as the exterior was, the interior was absolutely resplendent.

"It rivals the palace," iAm said with wonder. "Oh, Ehlena, hey, girl."

Trez was dimly aware of his brother hugging Rehvenge's *shellan*. And there were other people milling around, females, mostly, but he recognized Blay and a blond male, along with John Matthew, and, of course, Rehv, who was coming across the floor with the help of his cane.

"The party's not for you two, but you can pretend it is."

iAm and Rehv embraced, but again Trez wasn't paying any attention to them.

Matter of fact, the rainbow-colored oh-my-God had completely disappeared, too.

Standing in the archway of what appeared to be a formal dining room, the Chosen that he'd seen up at Rehv's Great Camp was talking to someone else who was also in a white robe.

Trez's vision went tunnel and then some, his eyes latching onto her, and staying put.

Look at me, he willed. *Look at me.*

At that moment, as if she felt the command, the Chosen glanced over.

Trez instantly hardened, his body swelling with the need to go over to the female, pick her up, and carry her to somewhere private.

Where he could mark her.

iAm's voice was exactly, precisely, what he did not need to hear in his ear: "Still not for you, brother."

Fuck that for a laugh, Trez thought as his Chosen refocused on the female she had been talking with.

He was going to have her, even if it killed him.

And if it came down to that? Well, his life wasn't really a party right now, was it.

When Qhuinn came back around, he was lying on top of the altar. The skull was right next to his head, as if the first Brother was looking after him as he recouped from the drinking. Blinking his eyes clear, he realized he was staring at a wall of names: Every square inch of the vast marble slab he'd stood against had been etched with names in the Old Language.

Well, except for where the twin pegs were.

As he sat up and swung his legs free, his back cracked loudly and his head swam. Rubbing his face, he jumped off and walked forward . . . until he could touch the carvings.

"You're down at the far end," Zsadist said from behind him.

Qhuinn wheeled around. The Brotherhood was once again standing down below, each of them smiling like a motherfucker.

Butch's Bostonian accent rang out: "It's a rush to see your name up there. You gotta check it out."

Qhuinn turned back around. Sure enough, after heading down to the right, he found the cop's name . . . and then his own.

His legs went loose and he lowered himself, going down on his knees before the precise lineup of symbols. Then he looked across the wall, the distinct names disappearing into nothing but a single, cohesive pattern across the marble. Just like the Brotherhood. No individuals in it; the group was the thing.

And he was part of it.

Goddamn it . . . he was there.

Qhuinn got ready for a transformative experience—like something along the lines of a great ringing bell of "You Belong" getting struck in his chest, or maybe a light-headed joy thing . . . or shit, a big-ass load of "You th' Man" singing in his brain.

Didn't happen. He was glad, yeah. He was proud, fuck, yeah. He was ready to get out there and fight like a mack bastard.

But as he got to his feet, he realized that in spite of that newfound wholeness, part of him remained separate and checked out. Then again, it had been a helluva couple of days—as if Fate had put his life in the pulse blender, and was busy making salsa out of his ass.

Maybe it was more because he'd never been good at the emotion thing? And nothing was going to change that.

At least he wasn't running, though.

Going down to the Brothers, he got so many slaps on the back and chest bumps, he knew what a lineman felt like after practice.

And then it dawned on him . . . he was going home to Blay.

Holy Mary Mother of God, to borrow a saying from the cop, he was *so* ready to lock eyes on that guy. Maybe sneak off and tell him what it was like, even though he probably wasn't supposed to do that. Maybe go up to his room after the party was over and . . . um, yeah . . . for a while.

Okay, now he was pumped.

Rhage threw his black robe at him. "So, welcome to the insane asylum, you sorry son of a bitch. You're stuck with us for life."

Qhuinn frowned and thought of John. "What about my *ahstrux nohtrum* position?"

"Gone," V said as he robed up as well. "You're a free man."

"So John knew?"

"Not that you were getting this kind of promotion, no. But he was told that you couldn't be his private soldier anymore." As Qhuinn touched the tattoo under his eyes, V nodded. "Yeah, we're going to change that—it's an honorable-discharge thing, though, not a death or firing."

Oh, cool. Better than a pink slip in the center of the chest and a shallow grave.

As they filed out, Qhuinn spared one last look at the cave. It was so weird; yeah, he was history happening, but this also felt like the culmination of all those nights fighting with the Brothers, an internal logic making this extraordinary event seem . . . inevitable.

Retracing the trip they'd taken in, Qhuinn soon found himself in a hallway that was lined with shelves from floor to superhigh ceiling.

"Jesus . . . Christ," he breathed as he took in all the *lesser* jars.

Everyone stopped.

"The jars?" Wrath asked.

"Yeah," Tohr said with a chuckle. "Our boy looks impressed."

"Should be," Rhage muttered as he jacked the belt on his robe. "We are awesome."

Multiple groans at that point. Rolled eyes.

"At least he didn't pull out the 'totes amazeballs,'" somebody muttered.

"That's Lassiter," came an answer.

"Man, that son of a bitch has got to stop watching Nickel-fucking-odeon."

"Among other things."

"Focus, people," Rhage cut in. "Can we just have a moment here?"

Growls of approval replaced the bitching, the throaty sound rising up and threading through the mementos of their dead enemies.

"Just think," Tohr said as he put an arm around Qhuinn's shoulders, "now you get to put your own in here."

"Good deal," Qhuinn murmured as he checked out all the different kinds of containers. "Good deal."

They exited through gates that were both old, and the kind of thing a blowtorch would have needed a couple of hours to get through. Then there was another obstruction that was pushed aside, one that sure as hell looked like a cave wall—and what do you know, they walked out of a shallow nook in the earth, and were back at the Escalade. It took a while to drive back through the forest, and the second the mansion's lights came into view, he started to get excited, his body jerking forward in his seat, his hand searching for the door latch.

The SUV had barely slowed down when he was popping shit free and leaping out. Laughter erupted from the Brotherhood as they took a more reasonable exit from things, following in his wake as he jumped up the steps. At the grand front entrance, he yanked the door open and shot into the vestibule, throwing his face into the security camera.

Behind him, he heard the voices of the Brothers—

His brothers, now, though. Weren't they.

His *brothers* were yukking it up as they joined him, and the interior door was opened by Fritz.

Qhuinn nearly knocked the butler over as he jumped inside. Lot of smiling faces, the *shellans* of the house, the queen, *doggen* everywhere . . . iAm, Trez, and Rehv with Ehlena . . .

He looked for red hair, searching the dining room, then going back across to the billiards room. Where was—

Qhuinn stopped.

On the far side of the pool table, on the couch that faced the TV that was mounted over the fireplace, Blay and Saxton were sitting side by side. Their faces were turned to each other, a pair of gin and tonics in their hands, the two of them looking like they were in a deep discussion.

Abruptly, Blay started to laugh, his head tilting back. . . .

At that moment, he looked over at Qhuinn.

Instantly, his expression tightened up.

"Congratulations!"

The sound of Layla's voice scrambled him, and he turned to her blindly, his mind reeling even though it shouldn't have: he'd known all along that Saxton was returning after his vacation.

"I'm so happy for you!" As Layla hugged him, he put his arms around her automatically.

"Thanks." He pulled back and rubbed his hair. "So, ah, how are you feeling?"

"Nauseous and terrific!"

Qhuinn sagged in his own skin, trying to find joy in the pregnancy. "I'm so glad. I'm really . . . glad."

SEVENTY-THREE

ola banged into the stove as she brought the man into her house. And then as part of her course correction, she knocked into the chair her grandmother had been in—but at least she was able to cover that one up by pulling the thing out and sitting down.

"You haven't told me your name, either," she murmured, even though proper nouns were the last thing on her mind.

The man joined her across the little table. Between his expensive clothes and the sheer size of him, he made everything look flimsy, from the stretch of laminate that seperated them, to the seats, to the kitchen.

The whole house.

He extended his hand across the table top. In that deep, heavenly accented voice, he said, "I am Assail."

"Assail?" She cautiously extended her own palm, prepared to meet him in the middle. "Odd name—"

The instant contact was made, a lightning bolt licked up her arm and landed in her heart, speeding it up, making her flush.

"Do you not like it?" he whispered knowingly, as if he were fully aware of her reaction.

Except he was talking about his name, wasn't he? Yes, that was it. "It's . . . unexpected."

"Give me yours." He issued the command without letting go. "Please."

As he waited, as he held her hand, as they breathed together, she realized that sometimes there were things even more intimate than sex.

"Marisol. But people call me Sola."

He purred. *Purred.* "I shall call you Marisol."

And didn't that fit. God, in that accent . . . he turned what she had been called all her life into a poem.

Sola pulled her hand out of his and put it in her lap. But her eyes stayed right on him: His expression was one of arrogance, and she got the impression that that was an unconscious default, not anything to do with her. His hair seemed impossibly thick, and undoubtedly styled with product—nothing merely human could keep that perfect wave off his forehead like that. And his cologne? Forget about it. Whatever the hell it was, she was nearly getting high off the incredible scent.

Between those good looks, that body, and all his brains? She was willing to bet the house on the fact that his life was one big world-is-my-oyster sport.

"So tell me about this visitor of yours," he said.

As he waited, his chin lowered, and he stared at her from under his lids.

So not a surprise he had killed someone.

She shrugged. "I have no idea. My grandmother just said the man had dark hair and deep-set eyes. . . ." She frowned, noticing that his irises were as always that moonlight color—the kind of thing that just didn't seem possible in nature. Contacts? she wondered. "She—ah, she didn't mention a name, but he must have been polite—if he hadn't been, I would have heard about it and then some. Oh—and he spoke to her in Spanish."

"Is there anyone who would be looking for you?"

Sola shook her head. "I don't talk about this house—ever. Most people don't even know my real name. That's why I thought it was you—who else . . . I mean, nobody else has ever come here but you."

"There is no one in your past?"

Exhaling, she glanced around the kitchen; then scooped the napkins out of the caddy and rearranged them. "I don't know. . . ."

With the life she led? It could be any number of people.

"Do you have a security alarm here?" he asked.

"Yes."

"You should assume he is dangerous until proven otherwise."

"I agree." As the man—Assail, that was, reached into his coat, she shook her head. "No cigars. I told you—"

He made an exaggerated show of extracting a gold pen and holding it up. Then he took one of the napkins she'd just fiddled with and wrote down a seven-digit phone number.

"You will call me if he comes again." He slid the flat square across the table, but kept his forefinger right by the numerals. "And I shall take care of it."

Sola got up too fast, her chair squeaking. Instantly, she froze and looked to the ceiling. When there were no sounds from above, she reminded herself to keep it down.

She paced over to the stove quietly. Came back again. Paid a visit to the back door onto the porch. Came back again. "Look, I don't need your help. I appreciate it—"

As she turned around to take the route to the stove again, he was right in front of her. Gasping, she jumped—she hadn't even heard him move—

His chair was in the same position it had been when he'd sat in it.

Not like hers, pushed aside.

"What . . ." She fell silent, her mind spinning. Surely, she was not about to ask him *what* he was—

As he reached out and cupped her face, she knew she would have had trouble saying no to anything he suggested.

"You will call me," he commanded, "and I shall come to you."

The words were so low they nearly warped, his voice deep . . . so very deep.

Pride formed a protest in her brain, but her mouth refused to speak it. "All right," she said.

Now he smiled, his lips curling upward. God, his canines were sharp, and longer than she remembered.

"Marisol," he purred. "A beautiful name."

As he started to lean in to her, subtle pressure on her jaw lifted her chin. Oh, no, hell, no, she should not be doing this. Not in this house. Not with a man like him . . .

Screw it. With a sigh of surrender, she closed her eyes and lifted her mouth to accept his—

"Sola! Sola, what you doing down there!"

They both froze—and instantly, Sola regressed to the age of thirteen.

"Nothing!" she called out.

"Who is with you?"

"No one—it's the television!"

Three . . . two . . . one . . . "That does not sound like no TV!"

"Go," she whispered as she pushed against his broad chest. "You have to leave now."

Assail's lids dropped low. "I think I want to meet her."

"You don't."

"I do—"

"Sola! I'm coming down!"

"Go," she hissed. "*Please.*"

Assail drew his thumb across her lower lip and leaned into her, speaking directly into her ear. "I have plans to pick this up where we've been interrupted. Just so that you know."

Turning away, he moved with frustrating leisure to the door. And even as her grandmother's slippers closed in down the stairs, he took the time to glance across his shoulder while he opened the way out.

His glowing eyes raked over her body. "This is not over between you and me."

And then he was gone, thank the good Lord.

Her grandmother rounded the corner a split second after the exterior screen door clicked into place. "Well?" she said.

Sola glanced over to the window by the table, reassuring herself that it was still dark as the inside of a hat out there. Yup. Good.

"See?" she said, sweeping her arms around the otherwise empty kitchen. "No one's here."

"The television is not on."

Why, oh, why couldn't her grandmother have the grace to get soft in the head like so many other geriatrics?

"I turned it off because it was disturbing you."

"Oh." Suspicious eyes roamed about. . . .

Shit. There was melting snow on the linoleum from where they'd tracked it in.

"Come on," Sola said as she steered the woman into an about-face. "Enough upset for tonight. We go to bed now."

"I'm watching you, Sola."

"I know, vovó."

As they headed up the stairs together, part of her was wondering exactly who the hell had come looking for her here and why. And the other half? Well, that part was still in the kitchen, on the verge of kissing that man.

Probably better that they had been interrupted.

She had the unmistakable impression that her protector . . . was also a predator.

The phone call Xcor had been waiting for came at a most opportune time. He had just finished stalking and killing a lone slayer under the bridges downtown, and was cleaning his lady love, the black blood on the blade of the scythe coming off easily as he ran a chamois cloth up and down.

He put his female away on his back first, and only then took out his phone. As he answered, he looked over at his fighters as they gathered together and talked of the night's fighting in the cold wind.

"Is this Xcor, son of the Bloodletter?"

Xcor gritted his teeth, but didn't bother to correct the inaccuracy. The Bloodletter's name was of use to his reputation. "Yes. Who is this?"

There was a long pause. "I do not know whether I should be speaking to you."

The tones were aristocratic, and informed him of the caller's identity well enough. "You are the associate of Elan."

Another long pause—and, Fates, that tried his patience. But that was another thing he kept to himself.

"Yes. I am. Have you heard the news?"

"About."

When a third stretch of silence came along, he knew this was going to take a while. Whistling to his soldiers, he indicated they were all to proceed to their skyscraper, a number of blocks to the east.

A moment later he was up on its roof, the gusts so much stronger at his preferred elevation. As such a gale precluded discourse, he took cover in the lee of some mechanicals.

"News about what," he prompted.

"Elan is dead."

Xcor bared his teeth as he smiled. "Indeed."

"You do not sound surprised."

"I am not." Xcor rolled his eyes. "Although naturally, I am bereft."

Which was somewhat true: It was rather like losing a handy gun. Or, more accurately, a screwdriver. But those things could be replaced.

"Do you know who did it?" the caller demanded.

"Well, I believe you do, am I right?"

"It was the Brotherhood, of course."

Another misconception, but again, Xcor was prepared to let it stand. "Tell me, are you expecting me to *ahvenge* him?"

"That is not my concern." The stilted tones suggested the male was in fact worried about facing the same fate himself. "His family shall go after redress."

"As is their right." When there was nothing further coming, Xcor knew what was awaited and required. "I can assure you of two things: my confidentiality, and my protection. I can guess that you were at the gathering at Elan's house in the fall. My position vis-à-vis the king has not changed, and I am surmising that this call places you in a sympathetic orientation to mine own views. Am I correct."

"I am not one who seeks political or social power."

Bullshit. "Of course not."

"I am . . . worried about the future of the race—in this, Elan and I were aligned. I did not agree with the tactics he proposed, however. Assassination carries too many risks, and ultimately, it will not accomplish what is warranted."

Au contraire, Xcor thought. A bullet through the brain fixed many things—

"The law is the way to bring down the king."

Xcor frowned. "I do not follow."

"With all due respect, the law is mightier than the sword. To paraphrase a human saying."

"Your oblique references are a waste of words to me. Be specific, if you do not mind."

"The Old Laws provide the power that Wrath wields. They spell out his unilateral dominion over all manner of our lives and our society, giving him free rein to act as he chooses, with a complete lack of accountability."

Which was why Xcor wanted the job, thank you very much. "Go on."

"There are no restrictions on what he may do, what courses he may take—in fact, he can also change the Old Laws if he so chooses, and alter the very fabric of our traditions and foundations."

"I am well aware of this." He checked his watch. Assuming he didn't get stuck on this damn phone for the next two hours, there was still plenty of time left to fight. "Mayhap you and I should get together in person tomorrow evening—"

"There is but one caveat."

Xcor frowned. "Caveat?"

"He must needs be capable of producing, and I quote, 'a full-blooded heir.'"

"And this is relevant how? He is mated already, and no doubt in the future—"

"His *shellan* is a half-breed."

Now Xcor was the one who fell silent—and Elan's solicitor took advantage of the quiet: "Let us be clear with each other. There is human blood in the species. From time to time, there have been matings outside the race. One could argue nobody is truly 'full-blooded.' There is, however, a vital difference between a civilian straying into the human mating pool, and the king producing an offspring whose very mother is a half-breed—said offspring to inherit the throne upon his death."

Throe leaned around the corner of the HVAC blower. "All is well?" he mouthed.

Xcor cupped the phone. "Take the others down to the streets. I shall join you apace."

"As you wish," Throe said with a brief bow.

As his fighter ducked away, the aristocrat on the other end continued. "There is disquiet among many members of the ruling class, as you are well aware. And I believe if someone comes forth with this, it will be far more effective at displacing Wrath, son of Wrath, than any attempt on his life. Especially after he made such a show of strength at the Council meeting the other evening. Indeed, many were frightened into a kind of submission thereafter, their wills conscripted unto his physical bearing, which was rather fierce."

Xcor's mind began to turn over the possibilities. "So tell me, gentlemale, in your mind, you would succeed him, no?"

"No," came the strident response. "I am a solicitor, and as such, I value logic above all else. In this climate of unrest and war, only a soldier could lead the race—and should. Elan was a fool for his ambitions, and you have been taking advantage of this. I know because I saw you at his house that night in the fall—you were positioning him where you wanted him, even as he thought it was the other way around. I want change, yes. And I am prepared to make it happen. But I have no illusions as to my utility, and no interest in Elan's outcome becoming my own."

Xcor found himself turning in the direction of that mountaintop. "No king has been dethroned in this manner."

"No king has e'er been dethroned."

Good point.

As he stared to the northeast, where that strange disturbance in the landscape was located, he thought of the king there with his queen . . . and Xcor's pregnant Chosen.

There was a time when he would have much preferred the bloodier path, the one that was marked with the satisfaction of ripping the throne away from Wrath's dying hand. But this war of letters was . . . safer. For his female.

The last thing he wanted to do was raid where she ate, where she slept . . . where her condition was treated.

Closing his eyes, he shook his head at himself. Oh, how the mighty had fallen . . . and yet they would rise up nonetheless, he vowed.

"How would you suggest proceeding?" he said roughly.

"Quietly, at first. I must needs gather precedents for the manner in which 'full-blooded' has been construed in cases brought forth for decision. The advantage is that there has been a long-standing dis-crimination against humans, and it was even more pronounced in the past—when Wrath's father was actually issuing proclamations and in-terpreting the law. That will be the key. The stronger the precedent, the more successful this will be all around."

How ironic. Wrath's own sire's reading of the wording was going to be what brought the son down.

"The issue for us will be the king himself. He needs to remain breathing—and he needs to not recognize the weakness inherent in his reign and fix it before we can get things in order."

"You will e-mail my associate the relevant passages, and then you will meet with me."

"This will take a number of days."

"Understood. But I expect your call promptly."

As names were exchanged, and Xcor gave over Throe's e-mail ad-dress, he began to feel a certain buoyancy. If this male was correct? Wrath's kingship was going to be over without any more bloodshed.

And then Xcor would be free to determine the future of the race: As far as he knew, Wrath had no direct family, so if he were removed, there was no one with a strong claim to the throne. Although that didn't mean there wouldn't be relations coming out of the woodwork.

Interlopers he could deal with, however. And with the support of the Council? He was willing to bet he could become a populist leader—provided everyone got in line.

Wrath wasn't the only one who could change the laws.

"Do not waste time with this," Xcor said. "You have a week. No longer."

The answer that came back at him was gratifying: "I shall proceed with all haste."

And wasn't that a lovely way to end a phone call.

SEVENTY-FOUR

The tunnel that connected the mansion with the training center was cool, dim, and quiet.

As Qhuinn walked through it, he was by himself and glad of it. Nothing worse than being surrounded by happy people when you felt like death.

When he got to the door that led into the back of the office's closet, he put in the code, waited for the lock to pop, and pushed his way inside. A quick trip past the stationery and pens, and through another door, and he was going around the desk. Next thing he knew, he was in the corridor in front of the weight room, but exercise wasn't what he was looking for. After what the Brotherhood had done to him, he was stiff and achy—especially in the arms, thanks to having held himself upright on those pegs.

Man, his hands were still numb, and as he flexed his fingers, he knew what arthritis felt like for the first time in his life.

Moving along, he stopped again when he got to the clinic area. As he went to straighten his clothes, he realized he was still wearing only the robe.

He wasn't going back to change; that was for sure.

Knocking on the recovery room's door, he said, "Luchas? You up?"

"Come in," was the hoarse reply.

He had to brace himself before he entered. And he was glad he did.

Lying on the bed with his head propped up, Luchas still looked as if he were on the verge of extinction. The face that Qhuinn had remembered as intelligent and young was lined and grim. The body was painfully thin. And those hands . . .

Jesus Christ, the hands.

And he thought his ached a little bit?

He cleared his throat. "Hey."

"Hello."

"So . . . yeah. How you been?"

Fucking duh on that one. The guy was staring at weeks of bed rest, and then months of PT—and was going to be lucky if he could ever hold a pen again.

Luchas winced as he tried to lift his shoulders in a shrug. "I'm surprised you came."

"Well, you're my—" Qhuinn stopped himself. Actually, the guy was not, in fact, any relation of his. "I mean . . . yeah."

Luchas closed his eyes. "I have always, and will always, be your blood. No piece of paper can change that."

Qhuinn's eyes went to that mangled right hand, and its signet ring. "I think Father would very much disagree with you."

"He's dead. So his opinion is no longer relevant."

Qhuinn blinked.

When he didn't say anything, Luchas popped his lids open. "You seem surprised."

"No offense, but I never expected to hear that come out of your mouth."

The male indicated his broken body. "I have changed."

Qhuinn reached over and pulled a chair out for himself; as he sat down, he rubbed his face. He had come here because seeing your previously dead estranged brother was the only remotely acceptable reason for skipping a party thrown in your honor.

And spending the night watching Blay and Saxton together? Not going to happen.

Except now that he was here, he didn't think he was up to any kind of conversation.

"What happened with the house?" Luchas asked.

"Ah . . . nothing. I mean, after . . . what happened went down, no one claimed it, and I had no rights to it. When it reverted to Wrath, he gave it back to me—but listen, it's yours. I haven't been inside of it since I got kicked out."

"I don't want it."

Okaaaaaaaaaaay, another big surprise. Growing up, his brother had talked nonstop of everything he'd wanted to accomplish when he was older: the schooling, the social prominence, taking over where their father left off.

Him saying no was like someone turning down a throne—unfathomable.

"Have you ever been tortured?" Luchas murmured.

His childhood came to mind. Then the Honor Guard. But he sure as shit wasn't going to bust the guy's balls. "I been knocked around some."

"I'll bet. What happened afterward?"

"What do you mean?"

"How did you get used to normal again?"

Qhuinn flexed his sore hands, looking at his own fingers that were all perfectly functional and intact in spite of the aches. His brother wasn't going to be able to count to ten anymore: Healing was one thing, regeneration another entirely.

"There is no normal anymore," he heard himself say. "You kind of . . . just keep going, because that's all you got. The hardest thing is being with other people—it's like they're on a different wavelength, but only you know it. They talk about their lives and what's wrong with them, and you kind of, like, just let them go. It's a whole different language, and you've got to remember that you can only respond in their mother tongue. It's really hard to relate."

"Yes, that's exactly right," Luchas said slowly. "That's right."

Qhuinn scrubbed his face again. "I never expected to have anything in common with you."

But they did. As Luchas looked over, those perfectly matched eyes met Qhuinn's fucked-up ones, and the connection was there: They had both been through hell, and that lockstep was more powerful than the common DNA they shared.

It was so weird.

And funny, he guessed tonight was the night for him to find family everywhere.

Except the one place he wanted it.

As silence prevailed, with nothing but the steady beeping of the machinery by the bedside to break up the quiet, Qhuinn stayed for a long while. He and his brother didn't talk much, and that was okay. That was what he wanted. He wasn't ready to open up to the guy about Layla or the young, and he supposed it was telling that Luchas didn't ask if he was mated. And he sure as hell wasn't bringing up the Blay thing.

It was good to sit with his brother, though. There was something about the people you grew up around, the ones you'd seen throughout your childhood, the folks you couldn't remember not knowing. Even if the past was a complicated mess, as you aged, you were just glad the sons of bitches were still on the planet.

It gave you the illusion that life wasn't as fragile as it actually was— and on occasion, that was the only thing that got you through the night.

"I'd better go so you can rest," he said, rubbing his knees, waking up his legs.

Luchas turned his head on that hospital pillow. "Odd dress for you, isn't it?"

Qhuinn glanced down at the black robe. "Oh, this old thing? I just threw it on."

"Looks ceremonial."

"You need anything?" Qhuinn stood up. "Food?"

"I'm doing well enough. But thank you."

"Well, you let me know, okay."

"You are a very decent fellow, Qhuinn, you know that?"

Qhuinn's heart stopped, and then beat hard. That was the phrase that their father had always used to describe gentlemales . . . it was the A-plus of compliments, the top of the pile, the equivalent of a bear hug and a high five from a normal guy.

"Thanks, man," he said roughly. "You, too."

"How can you say that?" Luchas cleared his throat. "How in the name of the Virgin Scribe can you say that?"

Qhuinn exhaled hard. "You want the bottom line? Well, I'll give you it. You were the favorite. I was the curse—we were on opposite ends of the scale in that household. But neither one of us had a chance. You were no more free than I was. You had no choice about your future—it was predetermined at birth, and in a way, my eyes? They were my get-out-of-jail, because it meant he didn't care about me. Did he fuck me over? Yeah, but at least I got to decide what I wanted to do and where I wanted to go. You . . . never had a fucking chance. You were nothing but a math equation already solved when you were conceived, all the answers predetermined."

Luchas closed those lids again and shuddered. "I keep running it through my head. All those years growing up, from my first memory . . . to the last thing I saw that night when . . ." He coughed a little, like his chest hurt, or maybe his heart rhythm went wonky. "I hated him. Did you know that?"

"No. But I can't say it surprises me."

"I don't want to go back in that house again."

"Then you don't have to. But if you do . . . I'll go with you."

Luchas looked over once again. "Really?"

Qhuinn nodded his head. Even though he was in no hurry to walk through those rooms and dance with the ghosts of the past, he would go there if Luchas did.

Two survivors, back to the scene of crimes that had defined them.

"Yeah. Really."

Luchas smiled a little, the expression nothing close to what he'd used to sport. And that was okay. Qhuinn liked it much better. It was honest. Fragile, but honest.

"I'll see you soon," Qhuinn said.

"That would be . . . very nice."

Turning away, Qhuinn pushed open the door, and—

Blay was waiting for him out in the corridor, smoking a cigarette as he sat on the floor.

As Qhuinn came out of his brother's room, Blay got to his feet and stabbed his Dunhill out on the lip of the drink he'd been nursing. He wasn't sure what he expected the fighter to look like, but it hadn't been this: So tense and unhappy, in spite of the incredible honor he'd been paid. Then again, spending time at your brother's bedside was hardly a joyous occasion.

And Blay wasn't stupid. Saxton was back in the house.

"I thought I'd find you here," he said, when the other male didn't even offer a hello.

In fact, Qhuinn's blue and green stare went around the corridor, hitting pretty much everything except him.

"So, ah, how's your brother?" he prompted.

"Alive."

Guess that was the best they could hope for right now.

And guess that was all Qhuinn intended to say. Maybe he shouldn't have come down here. "I, ah, I wanted to say congratulations."

"Thanks."

Okay, Qhuinn still wasn't looking at him. Instead, the guy was focused in the direction of the office, like in his mind he'd already walked down to the damn thing and put that closet full of paper supplies to good use—

The sound of Qhuinn cracking his knuckles was loud as gunshots. Then he flexed his hands, spreading the fingers as if they hurt.

"So it's historic." Blay went to take another cigarette out of his pack, and stopped himself. "A real first."

"Been a lot firsts around here lately," Qhuinn said with an edge.

"What's that supposed to mean?"

"Nothing. It really isn't relevant."

Christ, Blay thought, he shouldn't have done this. "Can you look at me? I mean, would it fucking kill you to look at me?"

Those mismatched eyes shot around. "Oh, I saw you, all right. Guess your man's home. You gonna tell him you fucked me while he was gone? Or you gonna keep that a dirty little secret. Yeah, shhhhhhh, don't tell my cousin."

Blay gritted his teeth. "You sanctimonious son of a bitch."

"Excuse me, I'm not the one with a boyfriend—"

"You are actually going to stand here and pretend you were all out in the open about us? Like when Vishous came out of that room"—he jabbed his forefinger across the hall—"you didn't jump up like your ass was on fire? You want to pretend that you were all proud that you were fucking a guy?"

Qhuinn seemed momentarily stunned. "You think that was why? And not, oh, lemme think, trying to respect the fact that you were *cheating* on the love of your life!"

By this point, they were both jacked forward on their hips, their voices careening up and down the corridor.

"Oh, bull*shit*." Blay slashed his hand through the air. "That is such total bullshit! See, this has *always* been your problem. You've never wanted to come out—"

"Come out? Like I'm gay?!"

"You fuck men! What the good goddamn do you think it means!"

"That is *you*—*you* fuck guys. You don't like women and females—"

"You have *never* been able to accept who you are," Blay bellowed, "because you're afraid of what people think! The great iconoclast, Mr. Pierced, crippled by his fucking family! The truth is, you're a pussy and you always have been!"

Qhuinn's expression was one of absolute fury, to the point that Blay was ready to get hit—and hell, he wanted to have a punch thrown at him just so he could have the pleasure of corking the guy back.

"Let's get this straight," Qhuinn barked. "You keep your shit on *your* side of the aisle. And that includes my cousin and the fact that you fucked around on him."

Blay threw up his hands and had to pace before he jumped out of his own skin. "I just can't stand this anymore. I can't take this with you again. I feel like I've spent a lifetime dealing with your shit—"

"If I'm gay, why are you the only male I've ever been with!"

Blay stopped dead and just stared over at the guy, images of all those men in bathrooms filtering through his brain. For the love of all that was holy, he remembered each and every one of them, even though Qhuinn no doubt didn't. Their faces. Their bodies. Their orgasms.

All getting what he'd been desperate for, and denied.

"How dare you," he said. "How fucking *dare* you. Or do you think I don't know your sexual history? I had to watch it for far longer than I cared for. Frankly, it wasn't that interesting—and neither are you."

As Qhuinn blanched, Blay started to shake his head. "I'm so done. I'm *so* over this—the fact that you can't accept yourself is going to fuck up what's left of your life, but that's your issue, not mine."

Qhuinn cursed long and low. "I never thought I'd say this . . . but you don't know me."

"I don't know you? I think the shoe's on the other foot, asshole. You don't know *yourself*."

At that, he expected some kind of explosion, some theatrical, over-the-top, light-up-the-world emotion to roll out of the guy.

He didn't get it.

Qhuinn just set his shoulders, leveled his chin, and spoke with control. "I've spent the last year trying to figure out who I am, dropping the act, getting clean—"

"Then I say you've wasted three hundred and sixty-five nights. But like everything about this, that's on you."

With a vicious curse, Blay turned and strode away—and he didn't

look back. No reason to. There wasn't anyone in the corridor he wanted
to see.

Man, if the definition of insanity was doing the same thing over
and over again and expecting a different result, then he'd lost his mar-
bles years ago. For his mental health, his emotional well-being, and his
very life, he needed to put this all—

Qhuinn hauled him around by the arm, the guy's furious face
shoving into his own. "Don't you walk away from me like that."

Blay felt a wave of exhaustion tackle him. "Why. Because you have
something else to say? Some insight into yourself that's supposed to
put the puzzle pieces together in a way that fits? Some big confession
that's going to right the ship and make everything sunset-on-the-beach
perfect? You don't have that kind of vocabulary, and I'm not that naive
anymore."

"I want you to remember something," Qhuinn growled. "I tried
to make this work between us. I gave us a shot."

Blay's mouth dropped open. "You gave us a *shot*? Are you fucking
kidding me? You think having sex with me as a way to get back at your
cousin is a relationship? You think a couple of sessions in secret is some
kind of love affair?"

"It was all I had to work with." Those mismatched eyes raked
around Blay's face. "I'm not saying it was a grand romance, but I
showed up because I wanted to be with you any way I could."

"Well, congratulations. And now that we've both sampled the
goods, I can solidly say that you and I are not meant to be together."
As Qhuinn started cursing up a storm, Blay shoved a hand into his hair
and wanted to rip the shit out of his head. "Listen, if it helps you sleep
during the day—and I can't believe this is really going to bother you
for longer than a night—tell yourself you did what you could, but it
didn't work out. Myself? I prefer reality. What happened between you
and me is exactly what you've done with all the other randoms you've
been with. Sex—just sex. And now we're done."

Qhuinn's eyes burned. "You've got me wrong on this."

"Then you're delusional as well as in denial."

"People can change. I'm not like that anymore, and certainly not
with you."

God . . . it was a sad relief to feel nothing as those words were
spoken to him. "You know . . . there was a time when I would have
fallen to your feet to hear something like that," he murmured. "But

now . . . all I see is you jumping up from the floor the second someone came out a door and saw us together. You say that reaction is because of Saxton's and my relationship? Fine. But I'm really sure . . . no, I'm *totally* sure . . . that if you scratch the surface on that, you're going to discover it had much more to do with you rather than your cousin. You've hated yourself for so many years, I don't think it's possible for you to really love anybody or have any sense of who you are. I hope you figure it out sometime, but I'm not going to be part of that Lewis and Clark—I promise you."

Qhuinn shook his head, his frown so deep it looked like a gully had grown between his brows. "Guess you've got me sewn up tight."

"It's really not that hard."

"Just so you know, I was in love with you."

"For three days, Qhuinn. Three days. During which there was enough drama going on to make *War and Peace* looked like a comic book. That's not love. That's good sex as a distraction from life being a shithole."

"I'm not gay."

"Fine. You're bi. You're bi-curious. You're experimenting. Whatever. I don't care. I really don't. I know who I am and that's how I get through my life. You've got another drill going entirely—and good luck with that. It's clearly working *so* fucking well for you."

With that, he walked away again.

And this time . . . Qhuinn let him go.

SEVENTY-FIVE

ONE WEEK LATER . . .

Wherein life resumed its normal course, Qhuinn thought as he pulled his leathers up his thighs, yanked a muscle shirt on over his head, and grabbed his weapons and his leather jacket.

God, he couldn't believe just seven nights ago he was inducted into the Brotherhood.

Seemed liked forever.

Leaving his room, he stalked down past the marble statuary, went by Wrath's study, and knocked on Layla's door.

"Come in?"

"Hey," he said he went inside. "How you doing?"

"I'm great." Layla shoved herself up higher on her stack of pillows and then rubbed her belly. "Make that, *we're* great—Doc Jane was just here. Levels look perfect, and I'm sticking with ginger ale and saltines, so I'm good."

"You should have some protein, no?" Shit, he didn't want that to sound like a demand. "Not that I'm telling you what to eat."

"Oh, no, it's okay. As a matter of fact, Fritz poached some chicken breasts for me and it stayed down, so I'll be trying to do that every day, too. As long as food doesn't taste like much, I can stomach it."

"Do you need anything?"

Layla's eyes narrowed. "As a matter of fact, I do."

"Name it and it's yours."

"Talk to me."

Qhuinn jacked his brows up. "About?"

"You." She let out an exasperated curse, tossing the magazine she'd been reading to the side. "What is going on? You're dragging around, you aren't talking to anybody, and everyone is worried."

Everyone. Fantastic. Why the hell didn't he live alone?

"I'm fine—"

"You're fine. Right. Uh-huh."

Qhuinn held his hands out in quasi-submission. "Hey, come on, what do you want me to say? I get up, I go to work, I come home— you're doing well and so is the young. Luchas is slowly recovering. I'm in the Brotherhood. Life is great."

"Then why do you look like you're in mourning, Qhuinn."

He had to glance away. "I'm not. Listen, I've got to go grab something to eat before I—"

"Doyoustillwanttheyoung."

Layla's words came out so fast, his brain had to work to decipher what she'd said. And then he— *What?*

As her hands started to tangle in that way they did when she was nervous, he went over to the bed and sat beside her. Putting his jacket and his holsters full of weapons down, he stilled those twining fingers of hers.

"I am *thrilled* about the young." Matter of fact, that baby inside of her was the only thing keeping him going at the moment. "I am already in love with him or her."

Yup. Young were the only safe place to put your heart, as far as he was concerned.

"You've got to believe that," he said stridently. "You really have to."

"All right. Okay, I do." Layla reached up and brushed the side of his face, making him jerk. "But then what has broken you, my dear friend. What has happened?"

"Just life." He smiled over at her. "No big deal. But no matter what mood I'm in, you need to know I'm right with you in this."

Her eyes closed in relief. "I am grateful for that. And for what Payne did."

"As well as Blaylock," he muttered. "Don't forget him."

How fucking ironic. The guy had stabbed him in the chest, but also given him a new heart.

"I'm sorry?" she said.

"Blaylock went to Payne. It was his idea."

"In truth?" Layla whispered. "He did that?"

"Yup. Stand-up guy. Blaylock's a real gentlemale."

"Why are you calling him that?"

"It's his name, isn't it." He patted her arm and got to his feet, picking up his gear. "I'm going out for the night. As always, I have my phone with me, and you call if you need anything."

The Chosen frowned. "But Beth said you were off rotation."

Great. So he really was a topic of conversation. "I'm going out." As she looked like she was about to argue, he leaned down and put a chaste kiss on her forehead, hoping to reassure her. "Don't worry about me, 'kay?"

He left before she could marshal another attack on his boundaries. Out in the hall, he closed the door and—

He stopped dead. "Tohr. Ah, what's doing?"

The brother was leaning against Wrath's doorway like he'd been waiting. "I thought you and I talked about the schedule last night."

"We did."

"So what's up with all the weapons?"

Qhuinn rolled his eyes. "Look, I'm not staying in this house until dawn traps me in for a grand total of twenty-four hours straight. Not going to happen."

"No one said you had to hang here. What I *am* telling you, brother-to-brother, is that you will *not* be out in the field with us tonight."

"Oh, come on—"

"Go see a fucking movie if you want. Hit a CVS, but remember to take your car keys in with you this time. Go to a late-night mall and give Santa your list, I don't care. But you're *not* fighting—and before you keep arguing, this is a rule for all of us. You're not special. You're not the only one not going out in the field. Clear?"

Qhuinn muttered under his breath, but when the Brother extended his palm, he clapped his own against it and nodded.

As Tohr took off, jogging down the grand staircase, Qhuinn wanted to go on a cursing spree: a whole evening to himself. Yay.

Nothing like having a date night with a depressive.

Hell, maybe what he should do is go up to the movie theater, throw on some hormone-replacement-therapy patches, and cheer himself up by watching *The Sound of Music* and painting his toenails.

Maybe *Steel Magnolias* . . . *Like Water for Coconuts*.

Or was that *Chocolate*, he wondered.

Then again, maybe he could just shoot himself in the head.

Either would work.

Blay's family's safe house was out in the countryside, surrounded by snow-covered fields that undulated gently to forested boundaries. Made of cream-colored river stone, the manor wasn't grand, but rather cozy, with low-beamed ceilings, plenty of fireplaces that were always lit in the cold weather, and a state-of-the-art kitchen that was the only modern thing on the property.

In which his mom cooked positive ambrosia.

As he and his father emerged from the study, his mother looked over from her eight-burner stove. Her eyes were wide and worried as she stirred the cheese she was melting in a copper double boiler.

Not wanting to make a big deal out of the huge deal that had just gone down in that book-lined room, Blay flashed a discreet thumbs-up at her and took a seat at the rough oak table in the alcove.

His mother put her hand over her mouth and closed her lids, still stirring even as the emotions welled.

"Hey, hey," his father said as he came up to his *shellan*. "Shh-hhh . . ."

Turning her to him, he wrapped his arms around his mate and held her close. Even as she kept up with that stirring.

"It's okay." He kissed her head. "Hey, it's all right."

His father's stare drifted over, and Blay had to blink repeatedly as their eyes met. Then he had to shield his watery eyes.

"People! For the Virgin Scribe's sake!" The older male sniffled himself. "My beautiful, healthy, smart, priceless son is gay—this is nothing to mourn!"

Someone started laughing. Blay joined in.

"It's not like somebody died." His father tilted his mother's chin up and smiled into her face. "Right?"

"I'm just so glad it's out and everyone's together," his mother said.

The male recoiled as if any other outcome was unfathomable to him. "Our family is strong—don't you know this, my love? But more to the point, this is no challenge. This is no tragedy."

God, his parents were the best.

"Come here." His dad beckoned. "Blay, come over here."

Blay got up and went across. As his parents wrapped their arms around him, he took a deep breath and became the child he had once been a lifetime ago: His father's aftershave smelled the same, and his mother's shampoo still reminded him of a summer night, and the scent of the baking lasagna in the oven teed off his hungry stomach.

Just as it always had.

Time truly was relative, he thought. Even though he was taller and broader, and so many things had happened, this unit—these two people—were his foundation, his steady rock, his never perfect but never failing standard. And as he stood in the lee of their familiar, loving arms, he was able to breathe away every bit of the tension he'd felt.

It had been hard to tell his father, to find the words, to break through the "safety" that came with not running the risk of having to recast his opinion of the male who had raised him and loved him as no other had. If the guy had not supported him, if he'd chosen the *glymera's* value system over the authentic him? Blay would have been forced to view someone he loved in a totally different light.

But that hadn't happened. And now? He felt like he'd jumped off a building . . . and landed on Wonder Bread, safe and sound: The biggest test yet of their family structure had not just been passed, but completely triumphed over.

When they pulled apart from the huddle, his father put his hand on Blay's face. "Always my son. And I am *always* proud to call you my son."

As the guy dropped his arm, the signet ring on his hand caught the glow from the overhead lighting, the gold flashing yellow. The pattern that had been stamped into the precious metal was exactly what was on Blay's ring—and as he traced the familiar lines, he recognized that the *glymera* had it so wrong. All those crests were supposed to be the symbols of this space now, of the bonds that strengthened and bettered people's intertwined lives, of the commitments that ran from mother to father, father to son, mother to young.

But as was so often the case with the aristocracy, the value was misplaced, being based on the gold and the etchings, not the people. The *glymera* cared what things looked like, over what was: As long as shit appeared pretty on the outside, you could have half-dead or wholly depraved going on underneath and they'd still be cool with it.

As far as Blay was concerned? The communion was the thing.

"I think the lasagna's ready," his mother said as she kissed them both. "Why don't you two set the table?"

Nice and normal. Blissfully so.

As Blay and his dad moved around the kitchen, pulling out silverware and plates and cloth napkins in shades of red and green, Blay felt a little trippy. In fact, there was a total high associated with having laid it all on the line and finding out, on the far side, that everything you had hoped for was in fact what you had.

And yet, when he sat down a little later, he felt the emptiness that had been riding him return, sure as if he had stepped briefly into a warm house, but had had to leave and go back out into the cold.

"Blay?"

He shook himself and reached forward to accept the plate full of home-cooked loveliness that his mother was extending to him. "Oh, this looks amazing."

"Best lasagna on the planet," his father said, as he unfolded his napkin and pushed his glasses up higher on his nose. "Outside piece for me, please."

"As if I don't know you like the crunchy parts." Blay smiled at his parents as his mom used a spatula to get out one of the corner pieces. "Two?"

"Yes, please." His father's eyes were riveted on the crockery pan. "Oh, that's perfect."

For a while, there were no sounds except for polite eating.

"So tell us, how are things at the mansion?" his mother asked, after she sipped her water. "Anything exciting happening?"

Blay exhaled. "Qhuinn was inducted into the Brotherhood."

Cue the dropped jaws.

"What an honor," his father breathed.

"He deserves it, doesn't he?" Blay's mother shook her head, her red hair catching the light. "You've always said he's a great fighter. And I know things have been so hard for him—like I told you the other night, that boy has been breaking my heart since the first moment I met him."

Makes two of us, Blay thought. "He's having a young, too."

Okay, his father actually dropped his fork and had to cough it out.

His mother reached over and clapped the guy on the back. "With whom?"

"A Chosen."

Total silence. Until his mother whispered, "Well, that's a lot."

And to think he'd kept the real drama to himself.

God, that fight they'd had down in the training center. He'd replayed it over and over again, going over every word that had been thrown out, every accusation, every denial. He hated some of the things he'd said, but he stood by the point he'd been trying to make.

Man, his delivery could have used work, though. He truly regretted that part.

No chance to apologize, however. Qhuinn had all but disappeared. The fighter was never down at the public meals anymore, and if he was working out, it was not during the day at the training center's gym. Maybe he was consoling himself up in Layla's room. Who knew.

As Blay took seconds, he thought of how much this time with his family, and their acceptance of him, meant—and felt like an asshole all over again.

God, he'd lost his temper so badly, the break finally coming after all the years of back-and-forth drama.

And there was no going back, he thought.

Although the truth was, there never had been.

SEVENTY-SIX

"Hello?"

As Sola waited for her grandmother to answer from upstairs, she put one foot on the lower step and leaned into the bannister. "Are you up? I'm finally home."

She glanced at her watch. Ten p.m.

What a week. She had accepted a PI job for one of Manhattan's big divorce attorneys—who suspected his own wife was cheating on him. Turned out the woman was, with two different people as a matter fact.

It had taken her nights and nights of work, and when she'd finally gotten the ins and outs settled—natch—she'd been gone for six days.

The time away had been good. And her grandmother, with whom she'd spoken every day, had reported no more visitors.

"You asleep?" she called up, even though that was stupid. The woman would have answered her if she were awake.

As she backed off and went into the kitchen, her eyes shot immediately to the window over the table. Assail had been on her mind nonstop—and she knew on some level that her little project in the Big Apple had been more about putting some distance between them than

any pressing need to make money or further her side career as a gum-shoe.

After so many years of her taking care of herself and her grand-mother, the out-of-control she felt when she was around him was not her friend: She had nothing but herself to go on in this world. She hadn't gone to college; she had no parents; unless she worked she had no money. And she was responsible for an eighty-year-old with medical bills and declining mobility.

When you were young and you came from a regular family, you could afford to lose your head in some fucked-up romance, because you had a safety net.

In her case, Sola *was* the safety net.

And she was just praying that after a week of no contact—

The blow came from behind, clipping her on the back of the head, the impact going right to her knees and taking them out. As she hit the lineoleum, she got a good look at the shoes of the guy who'd struck her: loafers, but not fancy.

"Pick her up," a man said in a hushed voice.

"First I gotta search her."

Sola closed her eyes and stayed still as rough hands rolled her over and felt around, her parka rustling softly, the waistband of her pants jerking against her hips. Her gun was taken from her, along with her iPhone and her knife—

"Sola?"

The men working on her froze, and she fought her instinct to take advantage of the distraction and try to assume control of the situation. The issue was her grandmother. The best case was getting these men out of the house before they hurt the older woman. Sola could deal with them wherever they took her. If her vovó got involved?

Someone she cared about could die.

"Let's get her out of here," the one on the left whispered.

As they picked her up, she stayed limp, but cracked one lid. Both were wearing ski masks that had eye and mouth holes.

"Sola! What are you doing?"

Come on, assholes, she thought as they struggled with her arms and her legs. Move it. . . .

They bumped her into the wall. Nearly knocked over a lamp. Cursed loud enough to carry as they humped her deadweight through the living room.

Just as she was about to come to life and help them the hell out, they made it to the front door.

"Sola? I coming down—"

Prayers formed in her head and rolled out, the old, familiar words ones she'd known her whole life. The difference with these recitations was that in this case they weren't rote—she desperately needed her grandmother to be slow on the dime for once. To not make it down those stairs before they were out of the house.

Please, God . . .

The bitterly cold air that hit her was good news. So was the sudden speed the men gained as they carried her over to a car. So was the fact that as they put her in the trunk, they failed to tie her hands or feet. They just tossed her in and took off, the tires spinning on the ice until traction was acquired and forward momentum accomplished.

She could see nothing, but she felt the turns that were made. Left. Right. As she rolled around, she used her hands to search out anything she could use as a weapon.

No luck.

And it was cold. Which would limit her physical reactions and strength if this was a long trip. Thank the good Lord she hadn't taken her parka off yet.

Gritting her teeth, she reminded herself that she had been in worse situations.

Really.

Shit.

"I promise I'm not going to wreck it."

As Layla stood in the mansion's kitchen and waited for Fritz to argue, she finished pulling on the wool coat that Qhuinn had gotten her earlier in the month. "And I won't be gone long."

"I shall take you then, ma'am." The old *doggen* perked up, his bushy white eyebrows rising in optimism. "I shall drive you wherever you wish—"

"Thank you, Fritz, but I'm just going to sightsee. I have no desti-nation."

In truth, she was stir-crazy from being holed up in the house, and after the further good news from Doc Jane's most recent blood test, she'd decided she needed to get out. Dematerializing wasn't an option,

but Qhuinn had taught her to drive—and the idea of sitting in a toasty car, going nowhere in particular . . . being free and by herself . . . sounded like absolute heaven.

"Mayhap I shall just call—"

She cut him off. "The keys. Thank you."

As she put out her hand, she leveled her eyes on the butler's and kept her stare in place, making the demand as graciously but as firmly as she could. Funny, there was a time, before the pregnancy, when she would have caved and given in to the *doggen's* discomfort. No longer. She was getting quite used to standing up for herself, her young, and her young's sire, thank you very much.

Going through the hell of nearly losing that which she wanted so badly had redefined her in ways she was still getting in touch with.

"The keys," she repeated.

"Yes, of course. Right away." Fritz scurried over to the built-in desk in the rear of the kitchen. "Here they are."

As he came back and presented them with a tense smile, she put her hand on his shoulder, even though no doubt that would fluster him more—and, in fact, did. "Worry not. I shan't go far."

"Have you your phone?"

"Yes, indeed." She took it out of the central pocket of her pullover fleece. "See?"

After waving a good-bye, she went out into the dining room and nodded at the staff who were already setting up for Last Meal. Crossing through the foyer, she found herself walking faster as she approached the vestibule.

And then she was free of the house entirely.

Outside, standing on the front steps, her deep breath of frosty air was a benediction, and as she looked up at the starry night sky, she felt a burst of energy.

Much as she wanted to leap off the front steps, however, she was cautious going down them, and also careful striding across the courtyard. As she rounded the fountain, she hit the button on the key fob, and the lights of that gigantic black car winked at her.

Dearest Virgin Scribe, let her please not wreck the thing.

Getting in behind the wheel, she had to move the seat back, because clearly the butler had been the last one to drive the vehicle. And then, as she put the key fob in the cup holder and hit the start button, she had a moment's pause.

Especially as the engine flared and settled into a purr.

Was she really doing this? What if . . .

Stopping that spiral, she flicked the right-hand toggle upward and looked to the screen on the dashboard, making sure there was nothing close behind her.

"This is going to be fine," she told herself.

She eased off the brake, and the car smoothly moved back, which was good. Unfortunately, it went in the opposite direction than she wanted and she had to wrench the wheel over.

"Shoot."

Some to'ing and fro'ing happened next, with her piloting the car into a series of stop-and-gos that eventually had the circular hood ornament pointed at the road that went down the mountain.

One last glance at the mansion and she was off at a snail's pace, descending the hill, keeping to the right as she'd been taught. All around, the landscape was blurry, thanks to the *mhis*, and she was ready to get rid of that. Visibility was something she was desperate for.

When she got to the main road, she went left, coordinating the turn of the wheel and the acceleration so that she pulled out with some semblance of order. And then, surprise, surprise, it was smooth sailing: The Mercedes, she believed it was called, was so steady and sure that it was nearly like sitting in a chair, and watching a movie of the landscape going by.

Of course, she was going only five miles an hour.

The dial went up to one hundred and sixty.

Silly humans and their speed. Then again, if that was the only way one could travel, she could see the value of haste.

With every mile she went, she gathered confidence. Using the dashboard screen's map to orient herself, she stayed very far from downtown and the highways, and even the suburban parts of the city. Farmland was good—lots of room to pull over and not a lot of people, although from time to time a car would come out of the night, its headlights flaring and passing on her left.

It was a while before she realized where she was going. And when she did, she told herself to turn around.

She did not.

In fact, she was surprised to discover that she knew where she was going at all: Her memory should have dimmed since the fall, the passage of the intervening days, but even more so, events, obscuring the

location she was seeking. There was no such buffering. Even the awkwardness of being in a car and having to be restricted to roads didn't mitigate what she saw in her mind's eye . . . or where her recollections were taking her.

She found the meadow she sought many miles away from the compound.

Pulling over at the field's base, she stared up at the gradual ascent. The great maple was precisely where it had been, its stout main trunk and smaller arterial branches bare of the leaves that had once offered a colorful canopy.

Between one blink and the next, she pictured the fallen soldier who had been stretched out on the ground at its roots, recalling everything about him, from his heavy limbs to his navy blue eyes to the way he had wanted to refuse her.

Bending forward, she put her head on the steering wheel. Banged it once. Did that a second time.

It was not simply unwise to find any gallantry in that denial, but downright dangerous.

Besides, sympathizing with a traitor was a violation of every standard she'd ever had for herself.

And yet . . . alone in the car, with naught but her inner thoughts to contend with, she found her heart was still with a male who by all rights and morals, she should have hated with a passion.

It was a sad state of affairs, it truly was.

SEVENTY-SEVEN

Trez won the lottery at around ten-thirty that night.

He and iAm had been given front-facing rooms on the third floor of the mansion, opposite the restricted-access suite that housed the First Family. The digs were super-sweet, with en suite baths and huge soft beds, and enough antiques and royalty-worthy accoutrements to give a museum a case of the oh-mans.

But what made the accommodations truly outstanding was the roof they were under.

And not because there was a quarry's worth of slate keeping the elements out overhead.

Leaning into the mirror over the sink, Trez checked his black silk shirt. Smoothed his cheeks to make sure his careful shave job had been meticulous enough. Jacked up his black slacks.

Relatively satisfied, he resumed the dressing ritual. His holster was next. Black, so it wouldn't show. And the pair of forties he wore under both arms were well hidden.

Usually he was a leather-jacket kind of guy, but for the last week he'd been breaking out the wool double-breasted overcoat iAm had given him years ago. Slipping it onto his shoulders, he tugged the

sleeves sharply, and shook his shoulders back and forth so the folds of black settled correctly.

Stepping back, he regarded himself. No signs of the weapons. And in his fancy-ass dress, there were no clues that his business was booze and prostitutes, either.

Meeting his own eyes in the mirror, he wished he was in a better field. Something classier, like . . . political analyst or college professor or . . . nuclear physicist.

Of course, that was all human shit he didn't give a crap about. But it sure beat what he actually did for a living.

Checking his Piaget watch—which was not the one he usually wore—he knew he couldn't wait any longer. He walked out into his bloodred room, with its heavy velvet drapery and its damask silk walls, his footfalls making no sound across the Bukhara that covered the floor.

Yup, given his most recent . . . predilection . . . he liked the way he felt in the decor, in these clothes, with this mind-set.

Of course, the illusion was going to be shattered as soon as he reached his club, but here was where the up-and-up mattered.

Or . . . might matter.

For fuck's sake, he hoped to goddamn hell it would finally matter.

His Chosen, the one he'd met up north at Rehv's Great Camp, and had seen that first night he'd arrived, hadn't been around. So in a way, he thought as he walked out, all this wardrobe nonsense and appearances stuff had been for nothing much.

He was optimistic, though. Through a series of carefully orchestrated conversations with various household members, he'd learned that the Chosen Layla had been servicing the blood needs of folks who'd had them—but could no longer do so, thanks to her pregnancy.

Blessed event, indeed.

So the Chosen Selena . . .

Selena. What a great name that was. . . .

Anywho, the Chosen Selena had been coming to take care of these things, and that meant, sooner or later, she had to be back. Vishous, Rhage, Blay, Qhuinn, and Saxton all had to feed regularly, and given the way those boys had been fighting for the past couple of nights, they were going to need a vein.

Which meant she *had* to come.

Although . . . damn. He couldn't say he really appreciated the reason why. The idea of someone else at her vein kind of made him want to go Ginsu on whoever it was.

All things considered, his obsession was a little sad, particularly in its manifestations: Every night for the past week, he'd hung around after First Meal, waiting, looking casual, talking to the godforsaken Lassiter—who was actually not that bad a guy when you got to know him. Matter of fact, that angel was a font of information about the house, and so into his crap TV that he didn't seem to notice how many questions were clustered around the subject of the females. The Primale. Whether there was any hooking up going on anywhere, with anybody outside of mated couples.

Pausing by his computer, he turned off *The Howard Stern Show*, cutting short another round of Baba Booey bashing; then he left his room, stalking past the vaulted wall that retracted whenever Wrath or Beth wanted to come or go from their quarters. Hitting the carpeted stairs, he emerged at the head of the hall of statues.

Or hall of buck-ass naked dudes, as he thought of it.

Rounding to the right, he went by the king's study, which was closed, and descended the grand staircase into that incredible foyer. On the way down, he bitched about the time, wishing he didn't have to go. Business was business, however, and—

He was halfway to the mosaic floor below when the female he had wanted to see emerged from the billiards room and headed in the direction of the library.

"Selena," he called out, going across to the balcony and leaning on all that gold leaf.

As he looked over the drop, her head lifted, and her eyes rose to his own.

Pound. Pound. Pound.

His heart got loud as a war chant in his chest, and his hands automatically went to his coat, making sure that the front stayed closed. She was a female of worth, after all—and he didn't want to frighten her with his weapons.

Oh, man, she was beautiful.

With her dark hair twisted high off her nape, and her diaphanous robe draping her body, she was far too precious and gentle to be around anything violent.

Or anything like him.

"Hello," she said with a slight smile.

That voice. Sweet Jesus, that voice . . .

Trez went on full high-tail, doing a down-and-around at a dead run. "How are you?" he said as he all but skidded to a halt in front of her.

She bowed a little. "Very well."

"That's good. That's real good. So . . ." Fuck. "Do you come here often?"

He wanted to smack himself in the head. What, like this was a bar? Shit—

"When I am called, yes." Her head tilted to one side, her eyes narrowing. "You're different, aren't you?"

As he glanced at the dark skin of his hands, he knew she wasn't talking about chromatics. "Not that different."

He had fangs, for instance—that wanted to bite. And . . . other things. That happened to be getting aroused just being in her presence.

"What are you?" Her stare was steady and strong, as if she were assessing him on some level deeper than sight or hearing or scent. "I cannot . . . place it."

That is not for you.

As his brother's voice checked in, Trez pushed it aside. "I'm a friend of the Brotherhood's."

"And the king's, or you would not be here."

"That's right."

"Do you fight with them?"

"If they call on me."

Now her eyes shone with respect. "That is right and proper." She bowed again. "Your service is laudable."

Silence cropped up between them, and as he racked his brain for something, anything, he was reminded of all that fucking he'd been doing. Now, that shit he was able to tee up at a moment's notice. Polite conversation, on the other hand? Talk about your foreign languages.

God, he hated thinking of any of that around her.

"Are you all right?" the Chosen asked.

And that was when she touched him. Reaching out, she put her hand on his forearm—and even though there was no skin-to-skin contact, his body felt the connection all over, his arms and legs stilling, his mind going into a kind of blankness, as if he were in a trance.

"You are . . . incredibly beautiful," he heard himself say.

The Chosen's eyebrows shot up.

"Just being honest," he murmured. "And I've got to tell you . . . I've been waiting to see you all week."

Her hand, the one that touched him, retracted and rose to the collar of her robing, closing the lapels. "I . . ."

That is not for you.

As her awkwardness tore through him, Trez dropped his lids, a sense of what-the-hell-was-he-thinking hitting him hard: From what he understood about the Scribe Virgin's Chosen, they were the purest and most virtuous variety of female on the planet. The polar opposite of his "partners" of late.

What did he think was going to happen if he started laying lines on her? She was going to hop up and throw her legs around his hips?

"I'm sorry," she said.

"No, listen, you don't have to apologize." He took a step away, because although she was tall, she was a quarter of his size, and the last thing he wanted was for her to feel crowded. "I just wanted you to know."

"I . . ."

Great. Anytime a female had to search her mind for appropriate words? You knew you'd really put your foot in it.

"I'm sorry," she said again.

"No, it's okay. It's cool." He lifted his hand. "Don't worry about it."

"It's just that I—"

I'm in love with someone else. I'm taken. I'm not interested in you on any level.

"No." He cut her off, not wanting to hear the specifics. They were just vocabulary for the inevitable. "It's all right. I understand—"

"Selena?" came a voice from over on the left.

It was Rhage's. Shit.

As her head turned in that direction, the light hit her cheeks and lips from a different angle, and they looked every bit as good, of course. He could so stare at her forever. . . .

Hollywood leaned out from the arches of the library. "We're ready for you—oh, hey, man."

"Hey," Trez shot back. "How you been?"

"Good. Little business to take care of."

Fucker. Cocksucker. Bas—

Trez rubbed his face. Right. Okay. There was no room in this five-bajillion-square-foot house for that kind of aggression, particularly when it was about a female who he'd met twice. Who didn't want to know him. While she was doing her job.

"I'm heading out," he said to the Brother. "I'll catch you before dawn."

"Roger that, big guy."

Trez nodded at Selena and strode off, proceding through the vestibule and dematerializing off to downtown—where the hell he belonged.

He couldn't believe he'd waited a week for that; and he should have guessed how it was going to go.

Feeling like a fool, he reassumed form behind the Iron Mask, in the shadows of the parking lot. Even out in the back, he could hear the bass beat of the music, and as he approached the rear door, with its scraped paint and well-worn handle, he knew his foul mood was a complication that was going to have to be managed carefully for the next six or eight hours.

Humans + alcohol x urge to kill = body count.

Not what he or his business interests needed.

Inside, he went directly to his office and ditched his dumb-ass Halloween costume of legitimacy, removing his fancy coat, as well as the silk shirt, so that all he had on was his black wifebeater and those fine slacks.

Xhex wasn't in her office, so he waved a greeting at the working girls who were getting ready for their shifts in the locker room and went out into the land of the great unwashed.

The club already had a critical mass of people, all of whom were wearing dark, stringy clothes and cultivated expressions of boredom—both of which would be lost for many of them as time wore on and their livers broke down the chemical makeup of the booze they were drinking and the drugs they were taking.

"Hi, Daddy," someone said to him.

Looking over, he found a short, curvy something-or-other staring up at him. With eyes lined with so much black she might as well have had sunglasses on, and a bustier cinched up tight as a fist, she was like an anime character come to life.

Snooze.

"I'm *blah-blah-blah*. Do you come here often?" She took a sip from the red straw in her drink. "*Blah-blah-blah* college student *blah-blah* psychology. Blah-blah-blah?*"

In the corner of his eye, he saw the crowd part, as if they were getting out of the way of a bouncer or maybe a wrecking ball.

It was Qhuinn.

Looking as grim as Trez felt.

Trez nodded to the guy, and the fighter nodded back as he kept going toward the bar.

"Wow, do you know him?" College Student asked. "Who is he? *Blah-blah* threesome maybe *blah-blah*?"

As she tee-hee-hee'd like she was a Very Naughty Girl, Trez swung his eyes back and downward.

On so many levels, the plate of hors d'oeuvres being offered was totally unappetizing.

"*Blah-blah-blahblahblah.*" Giggle. Hip shake. "*Blah?*"

Dimly, Trez was aware of his head nodding, and then they were moving into a dark corner. With every step he took, another part of him shut down, turned off, went into hibernation. But he couldn't stop himself. He was the junkie hoping that his next hit would be as good as the first had been—and finally bring that relief he was fucking desperate for.

Even though he knew that wasn't going to happen.

Not tonight. Not with her.

Not anywhere in his life.

Probably never, ever.

But sometimes you just had to do something . . . or go insane.

"Tell me that you love me?" the chick said to him, as she pressed herself against his body. "Pleeeeeeeeease."

"Yeah," he said numbly. "Sure. Whatever you want."

Whatever.

SEVENTY-EIGHT

Xcor linked his hands and placed them on the glossy tabletop. Beside him, Throe was speaking in low tones; he himself had remained quiet since they had taken the weight off their feet in these matching oxblood armchairs.

"This certainly seems persuasive." His soldier flipped over another page in the set of documents that had been proffered. "Very persuasive, indeed."

Xcor looked across at their host. The *glymera* solicitor was built like a pamphlet, so thin that one wondered when he lay out flat whether he presented any verticality a'tall. He also spoke with an exhausting thoroughness, his verbal paragraphs of small font and crowded, complicated wording.

"Tell me, how comprehensive is this brief?" Throe asked.

Xcor's eyes went to the bookshelves. They were crammed with leather volumes, and he quite believed that the gentlemale had read each and every one. Mayhap twice.

The solicitor launched another well thought-out, well-articulated cruise through the English language. "I would not have turned it over to you both without ensuring that all efforts were made to . . ."

In other words, yes, Xcor filled in in his head.

"What I do not see here"—Throe turned more pages—"is any notation of counter-opinion."

"That is because I was unable to find any. The term 'full-blooded' has been used in only two contexts—that of lineage, as in a full-blooded offspring of a given sire or a dam, and that of racial identity. Over time, there has been some minor dilution of the wider gene pool, some contamination from humans—and yet individuals with distant Homo sapiens blood ties have as yet been construed by law as being full-blooded provided they go through their transitions. Now, of course, that is not the case of the direct offspring of a human and a vampire. That is a true half-breed. And those individuals, even if they survive the change, have historically been held to a different standard by the law, with lesser rights and privileges than other civilians. The concern is thus—if the king's *shellan* is a half-breed, there is a chance that any male offspring of theirs may not go through the transition."

Throe frowned as if considering the implications. "But within twenty-five years, we shall know one way or the other—and the royal couple could always attempt to have multiple young."

Xcor interjected dryly, "You assume we will still be on the planet in two and a half decades. At this rate, we are nearing extinction as it is."

"Precisely." The solicitor inclined his head in Xcor's direction. "From a practical standpoint, being a quarter human could be enough to prevent the transition from occurring—there have been documented incidences of this, and I'm sure Havers could give even more examples. Further, there is among many people of my generation a fear that an offspring with that close a nexus to the human race could in fact prefer a human mate—i.e., go out and seek one unaffiliated with our kind. In which case, we could have a human queen, and that is"—the male shook his head with distaste—"absolutely untenable."

"So there are two issues," Xcor said as he sat back, the chair creaking under his weight. "The legal precedent and the social implications."

"Indeed." The solicitor once again pulled a head bob. "And I believe that the social fears could be properly leveraged to fill in the gray areas around the relevant portion of the law concerning the king's offspring."

"I concur," Throe murmured as he closed the papers. "The question is how to proceed."

As Xcor opened his mouth to speak, a strange vibration went through him, cutting off his thought process, his body becoming a tuning fork struck by some unseen hand.

"Would you care to review the documentation?" the solicitor asked him.

As if he could, Xcor thought grimly. Indeed, one had to wonder what this learned male would think if he knew the decision maker in all this was an illiterate.

"I am persuaded." He got up, thinking mayhap a stretch would cure whate'er ailed him. "And I believe this information should be shared with members of the Council."

"I have sufficient contacts to call the *princeps* together."

Xcor went over to a window and looked out, letting his instincts roam. Was it the Brotherhood?

"Do that," he said with distraction as that hum in his gut increased, creating an urgency he found impossible to ignore. . . .

His Chosen.

His Chosen had breached the compound and was close by—

"I must needs go," he said in a rush as he headed for the door. "Throe, you wrap up here."

There was a certain commotion behind him, conversation sprouting up from the pair of males in his wake—about which he cared naught. Breaking out through the front entrance, he regarded the farmland around him. . . .

And located her signal.

Between one heartbeat and the next, he was gone, his body and will drawn to his female sure as a dying thief to redemption.

At the Iron Mask downtown, Qhuinn went over to the bar and parked it on one of the leather-topped stools. All around, the music was pounding, and sweat and sex were already curling into the hot air, making him feel claustrophobic.

Or maybe that was just his headspace.

"Haven't seen you in a while." The bartender, a nice-looking female with a rack and a half, slid a napkin in front of him. "Same as usual?"

"Double."

"You got it."

As he waited for his Herradura Selección Suprema to arrive, he could feel the eyes of the humans in the club lingering on him.

Come out? Like I'm gay . . .

You fuck men! What the good goddamn do you think it means!

Shaking his head, he really could have used a break: That happy little exchange had been banging around his head, just underneath the surface of his consciousness, ever since shit had gone down a week ago. On the whole, he'd done an outstanding job of sublimation . . . unfortunately, that winning streak appeared to be over. As his tequila arrived and he downed one shot glass, and then the other, he knew that there were no other distractions he could bring into play, no more putting the introspection off.

Oddly—or maybe not so oddly—he thought of his brother. He still hadn't shared anything with Luchas about the young. It all felt too tenuous: Even though the pregnancy was hanging in and continuing to look good, it just seemed like an extra layer of drama the guy didn't need at this point.

And he most certainly hadn't mentioned anything about his sex life or Blay. For one thing, his brother was still a virgin—or at least, that had been Qhuinn's understanding: The *glymera* were far more restrictive about what females could do before mating, and certainly if Luchas had banged a female casually, it would have been tolerated as long as he didn't hook up with her long-term. But all of Luchas's feedings after his transition had been witnessed, so there had been no opportunity there, and the guy's nights had been heavily scheduled with learning and studying and chaperoned social events. No chance there.

Somehow going into all the shit Qhuinn had done didn't seem appropriate. It also, in Blay's words, wasn't that interesting.

Qhuinn scrubbed his face. "Two more?" he called out.

As the bartender hopped right on that, he thought, damn it, he'd assumed the sex he'd had with Blay had been *really* interesting. And Blay hadn't seemed bored when it was happening. . . .

Whatever. Back to Luchas. In all those bedside chats he'd been having with his brother, females hadn't come up—and males certainly weren't on the menu. Back before the raids, Luchas had been hetero like their father—which was to say strictly the female you were mated to in the missionary position on your birthday and maybe once a year after a festival.

Males, females, men, women, in various combinations, sometimes

in public, rarely in a bed at home? Not something Luchas had any frame of reference for.

When Herraduras three and four were slid in front of him, he nodded a thank-you.

Reaching down deep, even though he hated that expression as well as what it meant, he tried to see if there was anything else in and among his reticence to talk to the remaining member of his family about his life. Any shame. Embarrassment. Hell, maybe a little rebellious gotcha that he didn't want to inflict on his crippled brother . . .

Qhuinn squirmed in his own clothes.

Well. What do you know.

If he was brutally honest? Yeah, he was a bit tetchy. But it was on the level of not wanting to be looked at funny for yet another reason . . . as his conservative, probably-virgin of a brother would no doubt do if he was told about the males and the men.

That was it.

Yup. That was all.

I don't know how to explain it. I just see myself with a female long-term.

He'd said that to Blay a while ago, and had meant every word—

Some kind of emotion curled up inside his gut, twisting things down there, rearranging his bowel and his liver.

He told himself it was the hooch.

The sudden fear he felt suggested otherwise.

Qhuinn swallowed his third shot in hopes of getting rid of the sensation. And the fourth. And meanwhile, the faces and breasts and sexes of the many females and women he'd fucked flashed through his mind—

"No," he said out loud. "Nope. No."

Oh, God . . .

"No."

As the guy next to him gave him a weird look, he shut up.

Wiping his face, he was tempted to order more to drink, but held off. Something seismic was trying desperately to break through; he could feel it trembling around the foundation of his psyche.

You don't know who you are, and that's always been your problem.

Fuck. If he got more tequila, if he kept swallowing, if he stayed his avoidance course, what Blay had said about him was always going to be true. The trouble was, he didn't want to know. He just really fucking didn't want . . . to . . . know. . . .

Jesus, not here. Not now. Not . . . ever.

Cursing under his breath, he felt the geyser of realization start to really bubble, a loud-and-clear from the middle of his chest threatening to break out—and he knew that once it was free, he was never going to get it back underground again.

Damn it. The only person he wanted to talk to about this wasn't speaking to him.

He guessed he was going to have to man up and deal with it on his own.

On some level, the idea that he was . . . well, you know, as his mother would have said . . . shouldn't have affected him. He was stronger than the *glymera's* condescension, and, shit, he lived in an environment where whether you were gay or straight, it didn't matter: Long as you could handle yourself in the field and you weren't a total asshole, the Brotherhood was down with you. Look at V's sexual history, for fuck's sake. Black candles used as something other than a light source in the dark? Hell, just being into males was a cakewalk compared to that stuff.

Plus, he did not live in his parents' house anymore. That was not his life.

That was *not* his life.

That was not *his life.*

And yet even as he told himself that over and over again, the past that no longer existed was right behind him, staring over his shoulder . . . judging and finding him not just wanting, not simply inferior, but utterly and completely unworthy.

It was like phantom limb pain: The gangrene was gone, the infection cut out, the amputation complete . . . but the horrible sensations remained. Still hurt like a bitch. Still crippled him sure as a limp.

All those women . . . all those females . . . what was the true nature of sexuality, he wondered suddenly. What counted as attraction? Because he'd wanted to fuck them, and he had. He'd picked them up in clubs and bars, hell, even that store in the mall where they'd gone to get John Matthew some real clothes after his transition.

He'd chosen the women, singled them from the crowd, applied some kind of data screen that had weeded out some and highlighted others. He'd had them blow him. He'd sucked them off. He'd ridden them from behind, from the side, from in front. He'd grabbed their breasts.

He'd done all of that by choice.

Had it been different with the guys? And even if it had been, did he have to label himself at all?

And if he didn't slap a definition on himself, did that mean he wasn't something that his parents, who were goddamn *dead* and who had hated him anyway, hadn't approved of?

As the questions fired through his brain, pelting him with precisely the kind of self-analysis he had always stabbed out of his thought processes, he came to an even more shocking realization.

As important as all that shit was, as Christopher Columbus as he was getting, none of it came close to the most critical issue.

Not in the fucking slightest.

The real problem that he discovered made all that crap look like a walk in the park.

SEVENTY-NINE

Assail did not condone swearing. In his mind, it was common and unnecessary. That being said, he'd had a shitty fucking week.

Down in the cellar of his house, in the vault, he and the twins had just finished organizing the haul for the last few days: Bills were stacked in bundles that had been through the counter, banded, and then sorted according to denomination—and the total was impressive, even by his standards.

All told, they had about two hundred thousand dollars.

The *Fore-lesser* and his merry band of slayers had been doing excellent work.

You'd think he'd be happy.

Not so.

In fact, he'd been a miserable fucking son of a bitch—and the reason for the bad humor just made him crankier.

"Go to Benloise," he told the twins. "Get the next batch of cocaine and come back here to separate it."

The twins were masters at cutting the stuff with additives and

parceling it out into Baggies, and that was a good thing. The slayers were moving three times what had been sold before.

"Then make the delivery." Assail checked his watch. "It's set for three a.m., so you should have enough time."

Getting up from the table, he stretched his arms over his head and arched his back. His body had been stiff lately, and he knew why: Being in a constant state of low-level arousal had tightened up the muscles in his thighs and his shoulders, among other physical aspects . . . which had been utterly resistant to self-regulation.

After years of not particularly caring for tending to his own erections, he'd fallen into a rut of pleasuring himself.

And all it seemed to do was underscore what he was not getting.

For the last week, he'd waited for Marisol to get in touch with him, expecting the phone to ring, and not because some unknown had shown up at her door again. The woman had wanted him as much as he had her, and surely that would lead to a reunion. It had not, however. And the fact that she had exhibited the kind of restraint he was struggling with, made him question not only his self-control, but his very sanity.

Indeed, he feared he was going to crack before she did.

Taking his leave, he went up the stairs and into the kitchen. The first thing he did was go over to his phone, in case she had called or in the event that Audi of hers had finally moved after seven nights of going nowhere fast: The damn thing had been parked in front of that house since he'd paid his visit, as if she mayhap knew he'd put a tracer on it.

Checking the screen, he saw that someone had called him, but it was a number that was not in his contact list.

And there was a voice mail.

He was not interested in fielding some human's mis-dials, but as there was a chance it was a *lesser* breaking protocol, he knew he had to listen to the message.

As he accessed it, he walked in the direction of his humidor. He'd been smoking a lot lately, and probably doing too much coke. Which was painfully counter-intuitive—if one was already twitchy and frustrated, adding stimulants to that internal chemistry was gasoline to a fire—

"*Hola.* This is Sola's grandmother. I am trying to reach . . . an Assail . . . please?" Assail stopped dead in the middle of his living room. "Please call me back now? Thank you—"

With a feeling of dread, he cut the message off and hit *Call Back*.

One ring. Two rings—

"*¿Hola?*"

Indeed, he didn't know her name. "This is Assail, madam. Are you all right?"

"No, no—I am not. I found your number on her bedside table so I call. There is something wrong."

He gripped his iPhone hard. "Tell me."

"She is gone. She came home, but then she leave out the door right after she arrived—I hear her go? Except all of her things, her backpack, her car, it is all here. I was sleeping and I hear downstairs, someone is moving. I call out her name and no one answered—then I hear this hard noise—loud sound—and so I come down. The front door is open, and I fear she has been taken—I do no know what to do. She always told me, we do not call the police. I do not know—"

"Shh, it is all right. You did the correct thing. I'm coming directly."

Assail ran to the front door without bothering to communicate with the twins; nothing was on his mind except getting over to that little house as fast as he could.

A second was all it took to dematerialize, and as he resumed form in the front yard, he thought that of all the scenarios he'd run through in his mind for coming back, this was not it.

As the grandmother reported, the Audi was parked on the street at the end of the walkway. Just where it had been. But what was of note? There was a scramble of messy footfalls disturbing the snow, the trail crossing the lawn to the street in a diagonal pattern.

She's been kidnapped, Assail thought.

Goddamn it.

Jogging up the squat steps, he hit the doorbell and stamped his feet. The idea that someone had taken his female—

The door opened and the woman on the other side was visibly shaken. And then she seemed further taken aback as she took him in with her eyes. "You are . . . Assail?"

"Yes. Please let me in, madam, and I shall be of aid to you."

"You are not the man who came before."

"Not that you saw, madam. Now, please, let me in."

As Marisol's grandmother stepped aside, she lamented, "Oh, I do not know where she is. *Mãe de Deus*, she is gone, gone. . . ."

He glanced around the tidy little living room, and then stalked out

into the kitchen to look at the back door. Intact. Opening it wide, he leaned out. No footprints other than those he'd left a week ago. Closing things back up and locking the dead bolt, he returned to her grandmother.

"You were upstairs?"

"*Sí*. In the bed. As I said, I was asleep. I hear her come in, but I was half-awake. Then I hear . . . that sound, of someone falling. I say I come down, then the front door opens."

"Did you see a car drive off?"

"*Sí*. But it was very far away, and the license plate—nothing."

"How long ago?"

"I called you fifteen, maybe twenty minutes after. I went to her room and looked around—that is where I found the napkin with your number on it."

"Has anyone called?"

"No one."

He checked his watch, and then grew concerned about how pale the elderly woman was. "Here, madam, sit down."

As he settled her onto the floral couch in the living room, she took out a dainty handkerchief and pressed it to her eyes. "She is my life."

Assail tried to remember how humans addressed their superiors. "Mrs.—ah, Mrs. . . ."

"Carvalho. My husband was Brazilian. I am Yesenia Carvalho."

"Mrs. Carvalho, I need to ask you some questions."

"Can you help me? My granddaughter is—"

"Look into my eyes." When the woman did, he said in a low voice, "There is nothing I will not do to bring her back. Do you understand what I'm saying."

As he sent his intention out into the air between him, Mrs. Carvalho's eyes narrowed. Then, after a moment, she calmed and nodded once—as if she approved of his means, though there was a good chance they were going to be violent. "What do you need to know?"

"Is there anyone you can think of who would want to hurt her?"

"She is a good girl. She works at an office nights. She keeps to herself."

So Marisol hadn't told her grandmother anything about what she really did. This was good. "Does she have any assets?"

"Money, you mean?"

"Yes."

"We are simple people." She eyed his handmade, tailored clothes. "We have nothing but this house."

Somehow he doubted that, even though he knew little of his woman's life: He found it hard to believe she hadn't made some cash doing what she did—and she certainly didn't have to pay taxes on the kind of income she'd been bringing in from the likes of Benloise.

But he feared that a ransom call was not going to be forthcoming.

"I do not know what to do."

"Mrs. Carvalho, I do not want you to worry." He got to his feet. "I shall handle this promptly."

Her eyes narrowed again, belying an intelligence that made him think of her granddaughter. "You know who did this, do you?"

Assail bowed low as a measure of respect. "I shall bring her back to you."

The question was how many people he was going to have to kill to get that done—and whether Marisol herself was going to be alive at the end of it.

The mere thought of bodily harm to that woman had him growling in his throat, his fangs descending, the civilized part of him shedding as the skin from a cobra.

Whilst Assail left the modest house, he had a feeling what this was all about, and if he was right? Even just twenty minutes into the kidnapping, he might well be too late.

In which case, a certain business associate of his was going to learn new lessons in pain.

And Assail was going to be the man's teacher.

EIGHTY

Layla stayed in the Mercedes. It was warm in the interior, and the seat was comfortable, and she felt safe within the confines of the great steel cage around her. And she had a landscape of sorts to ponder: The headlights shone brightly in front of the car, the beams reaching out into the night quite some distance before fading.

After a while, flurries began to float downward through the illumination, their lazy, circuitous routes suggesting that they didn't want their descent from the clouds above to end.

As she sat in silence, cycling the engine on and off as Qhuinn had taught her to do during cold weather, her mind was not blank. No, her mind was not empty at all. Although she stared straight ahead and took note of the silent snowfall, and the straightaway of the road, and the peaceful farmland . . . what she saw was that fighter. That traitor.

That male who seemed always with her, especially when she was by herself.

Even as she sat alone in this car out in the middle of nowhere, his presence was tangible, her memories of him so strong, she could swear he was within reach. And the yearning . . . dearest Virgin Scribe, the yearning she felt was nothing she could share with any of those whom she loved.

It was such a cruel fate to have a reaction like this to one who was—

Layla jerked back in the seat, a shout breaching her lips and resonating through the interior of the car.

At first, she was unsure whether what had materialized in the beams was in fact real: Xcor appeared to be standing with his boots planted on the road ahead, his huge, leather-clad body seeming to absorb the twin beams of light as a black hole would.

"No," she barked. "No!"

She wasn't sure who she was talking to, or what she was denying. But one thing was clear—as he took a step forward, and then another, she knew that the soldier was not a figment of her mind or her terrible desires, but very much real.

Put the car in gear, she told herself. Put it in gear, and hit the gas pedal hard.

Flesh and blood, even as terrifyingly fierce as his, was no match for an impact like that.

"No," she hissed, as he came ever closer.

His face was exactly as she had remembered: perfectly symmetrical, with high cheekbones, narrowed eyes, and a permanent frown between his straight brows. His upper lip was twisted up, such that he appeared to be snarling, and his body . . . his body moved like a great animal's, his shoulders shifting with barely restrained power, his heavy thighs carrying him forward with the promise of brutal strength.

And yet . . . she was not afraid.

"No," she moaned.

He stopped when he was but a foot from the car's grille, his leather coat blowing out to the side of him, his weapons gleaming. His arms were down at his sides, but they did not stay that way. He reached up, moving slowly. . . .

To remove something from his back.

A weapon of some kind. Which he laid upon the vehicle.

And then his hands, those black leather-clad hands, went to the front of his chest . . . and he took two guns out from under that coat. And daggers from the holster that crossed his pectorals. And a length of chain. And something that flashed but which she didn't recognize.

He put it all on the hood of the car.

Then he stepped back. Held his arms aloft. And turned in a slow circle.

Layla breathed hard.

She was not of a warring nature. Never had been. But she knew instinctively that within the code of the warrior, to disarm yourself before another was a kind of vulnerability not easily taken. He remained deadly, of course—a male of his build and training was capable of killing simply with bare hands.

He was offering himself to her, however.

Proving in the most visible way possible that he meant her no harm.

Layla's hand went to the row of buttons on the side panel beside her and froze there. She was not still, however—she breathed heavily, as if she were in flight, her heart pounding, sweat dotting her upper lip. . . .

She unlocked the doors.

The Scribe Virgin help her . . . but she unlocked the doors.

As the punching sound reverberated around the interior, Xcor's eyes closed briefly, his expression loosening, as if he had been given a gift he had not expected. Then he came around. . . .

When he opened the far side, cold air rushed in, and then his big body folded itself into the seat beside her own. The door shut solidly, and they turned to each other.

With the interior lights glowing, she was able to get an even better look at him. He was breathing heavily, too, his broad chest pumping up and down, his mouth slightly open. He looked harsh, the thin veil of civility stripped from his features—or more aptly, it had likely never been there. And yet though others would have called him ugly because of his deformity, to her . . . he was beautiful.

And that was a sin.

"You are real," she said to herself.

"Aye." His voice was deep and resonant, a caress in her ears. But then it cracked, as if he were in pain. "And you are with young."

"I am."

He closed his eyes again, but now it was as if he'd been struck by a body blow. "I saw you."

"When?"

"At the clinic. Nights and nights ago. I thought they had beaten you."

"The Brotherhood? Why ever—"

"Because of me." His eyes opened, and there was such anguish in them, she wanted to comfort him in some way. "I would never have chosen for you to be in this position. You are not of the war, and my lieutenant should never, ever have brought you into it." His voice grew deeper and deeper. "You are an innocent. Even I, who have no honor, recognized that instantly."

If he had no honor, why had he disarmed himself just now, she thought.

"Are you mated?" he said roughly.

"No."

Abruptly, his upper lip peeled back from tremendous fangs. "If you were raped—"

"No. No, no—I chose this for myself. For the male." Her hand went to her abdomen. "I wanted a young. My needing came, and all I could think of was how much I wanted to be a *mahmen* to something that was mine."

Those narrowed eyes closed again, and he brought up a callused hand to his face. Hiding his irregular mouth, he said, "I wish that I . . ."

"What?"

". . . I were worthy to have given you what you desired."

Layla again felt an unholy need to reach out and touch him, to ease him in some way. His reaction was so raw and honest, and his suffering seemed rather like her own whenever she thought of him.

"Tell me that they are treating you well in spite of your having aided me?"

"Yes," she whispered. "Very well indeed."

He dropped his hand and let his head fall back as if in relief. "That is good. That is . . . good. And you must forgive me for coming here. I sensed you, and found I was unable to deny myself."

As if he were attracted to her. As if he . . . wanted her.

Oh, dearest Virgin Scribe, she thought, as her body warmed from the inside out.

His eyes appeared to latch onto the tree out in the field beyond. "Do you think of that night?" he said in a soft voice.

Layla looked down at her hands. "Yes."

"And it pains you, does it not."

"Yes."

"Myself as well. You are e'er on my mind, but for a different reason, I venture to guess."

Layla took a deep breath as her heart pounded anew in her ears. "I'm not certain . . . it is so different from your own."

She heard his head snap around.

"What did you say?" he breathed.

"I believe . . . you heard me quite well."

Instantly, a vital tension sprang up between them, shrinking the space they inhabited, bringing them closer even though neither of them moved.

"Must you be their enemy," she thought aloud.

There was a long silence. "It is too late now. Actions have been taken that cannae be undone through words nor vows."

"I wish it were not so."

"On this night, in this moment . . . I wish that as well."

Now her own head turned quickly. "Mayhap there is a way—"

He reached out and silenced her with his fingertip, laying it ever so gently upon her mouth.

As his eyes focused on her lips, a nearly imperceptible growl vibrated out of him . . . but he didn't allow it to continue for long, shutting the sound off as if he didn't want to burden her, or mayhap frighten her.

"You are in my dreams," he murmured. "Every day, you haunt me. Your scent, your voice, your eyes . . . this mouth."

He shifted his hand around and brushed her lower lip with his callused thumb.

Closing her lids, Layla leaned into the touch, knowing that this was all she would ever get from him. They were on opposite sides of the war, and though she knew not the particulars, she had heard enough in the household to know that he was right.

He could not undo what he had done.

And that meant they were going to kill him.

"I cannae believe you let me touch you." His voice grew hoarse. "I shall remember this for all my nights."

Tears speared into her eyes. Dearest Virgin Scribe, for all her life, she had waited for a moment like this. . . .

"Do not cry." His thumb went to her cheeks. "Beautiful female of worth, do not cry."

If any had told her someone as harsh as he was capable of such compassion, she would not have believed them. But he was. With her, he was.

"I shall go," he said abruptly.

Her instinct was to beg him to be careful . . . but that would mean she was wishing Wrath's dethroner well.

"Lovely Chosen, know this. If e'er you need me, I shall be there."

He took something out of his pocket—a phone. Facing it toward her, he lit up the screen with the touch of a button. "Can you read this number?"

Layla blinked hard and forced her eyes to focus. "Yes. I can."

"That is me. You know how to find me. And if your conscience demands you give this information to the Brotherhood, I will understand."

He couldn't read the numbers, she realized—and not for lack of visual acuity.

Whatever kind of life had he led, she wondered sadly.

"Be well, my beautiful Chosen," he said, as he stared at her with the eyes of not just a lover, but a *hellren*.

And then he was gone without another word, leaving the car, picking up his weapons and arming himself . . .

. . . before dematerializing into the night.

Layla immediately covered her face with her hands, her shoulders beginning to quake, her head sagging, her emotions overflowing.

Caught in the middle, between her mind and her soul, she was torn asunder even as she remained whole.

EIGHTY-ONE

"Come in."

As Blay spoke up, he glanced over the top of *A Confederacy of Dunces*—and was surprised to find Beth walking into his room.

One look at the queen's face and he sat up from the chaise, putting the book down. "Hey, what's wrong?"

"Have you seen Layla?"

"No, but I've just been here since I got back from my parents'." He glanced at the clock. After midnight. "She's not in her room?"

Beth shook her head, her dark hair shining as it slipped around her shoulders. "She and I were going to hang out, but I can't find her. She's not in the clinic, or the kitchen—and I looked for Qhuinn down in the training center as well as up here. He's gone as well."

Maybe they were having a romantic dinner, like, sharing a plate of pasta and meeting in the middle thanks to a strand of frickin' linguine.

"Have you tried their phones?" he asked.

"Qhuinn's is in his room. And Layla isn't answering hers if it's with her."

As he got to his feet and started to get a little hyped, he thought, calm down—this was not a national emergency. In fact, this was a big house with a lot of rooms, and more to the point, they were grown adults. Two people should be allowed to go off together and have it not be a crisis.

Especially if they were having a young together . . .

The sound of a vacuum off in the distance drew his attention.

"Come with me," he told the queen. "If there's one person in this place who'll know? He's down the hall with a Dyson."

Sure enough, Fritz was working in the second-floor sitting room, and as Blay walked in, he got slapped in the face with all the memories of him and Qhuinn doing it up but good on the rug by the couch.

Great. Just fabulous.

"Fritz?" the queen called out.

The *doggen* stopped the back-and-forth and killed the machine. "Well, hello, Your Majesty. Sire."

Lots of bowing.

"Listen, Fritz," Blay said, "have you seen Layla?"

Instantly, the butler's face became downcast. "Oh. Yes. Indeed."

When he didn't fill anything else in, Blay prompted him with an, "Annnnnd?"

"She took the car. The Mercedes. It was about two hours ago."

What the hell, Blay thought. Unless . . . "So Qhuinn was with her."

"No, she was alone." As a boatload of uh-oh hit Blay's stomach, the butler shook his head. "I tried to insist that I take her, but she would not let me."

"Where was she going?" Beth asked.

"She said she had no destination. I knew that Master Qhuinn had taught her to drive, and when she ordered me to tender upon her palm the keys, I knew not what to do."

The queen spoke up. "You are not at fault here, Fritz. Not at all. We're just worried about her."

Blay took out his phone. "And there's GPS on the vehicle, so this is going to be fine. I'll just hit up V and he'll be able to locate her for us."

After he sent the text, the queen reassured the butler some more, and Blay hung around, waiting for a response.

Ten minutes later? Nada. Which meant the Brother with the IT skills was in the middle of some business downtown.

Fifteen minutes.

Twenty.

He even called, and didn't get an answer. So he could only assume that someone was bleeding—or that V's phone had gotten shanked during fighting.

"Qhuinn's not in the gym?" he said, even though that question had already been answered.

Beth shrugged. "Not when I checked."

Blay put in a quick call, got Ehlena, and a moment later was informed that the workout room was empty, Luchas was asleep, and there was no one in the pool or on the basketball court.

The guy wasn't in the house. And not in the field, because he was off rotation. That left only one other conceivable place.

"I know where he is," Blay said gruffly. "I'll go get him while we wait for V to check in."

After all, that female was carrying his young—so if she went AWOL into the big world by herself, he had a right to be involved in locating her. And sure, maybe Qhuinn knew where she was, but Blay had a feeling he didn't: hard to believe he would have left his phone in his room if he was aware that she was going out in the car. He'd want some way for her to get in touch with him.

On that note, why had he left his cell behind at all? Not like him.

Unless he thought Layla was doing okay . . . and he didn't want to be interrupted.

Great.

Looping back to his room, Blay picked up a gun—because you never knew when you might need one—and a coat that was only to cover his hardware. Then he jogged down the stairs and went out the vestibule . . . and dematerialized into the night.

He resumed form in the back parking lot of the Iron Mask, and when he got to the club's rear door, he hit the bell and showed his face to the security camera. Xhex opened the way in.

"Hey," she said, giving him a quick hug. "How you been? Long time no see around here."

"I'm looking for—"

"Yeah, he's at the bar."

Of course he was. "Thanks."

Blay nodded to the bouncers, Big Rob and Silent Tom, and pushed out of the staff area into the club proper. As he emerged on the far side, the bass drum of the music went right into his sternum—or maybe that was his heartbeat.

Annnnd there he was: Even though there were a hundred people crowded around the bar, Qhuinn was a neon sign to him, standing out from the rest. The fighter was sitting at the far end, his back to Blay, his elbows splayed on the black varnished wood, his head hanging low.

Blay exhaled a curse as he thought, here they were, back at the beginning. And yup, before he could even make it over, a woman closed in, her body sliding up to Qhuinn, her hand lingering on his arm, his head turning so he could get a good look at her.

Blay knew what was next. A quick up-and-down with that mismatched stare, a slow smile, a couple of drawled words—and the pair would go off to the bathrooms—

Qhuinn shook his head, and put his palm out in a stop. And though she was inclined to make a second appeal, it just got her a another round of talk-to-the-hand.

Before Blay could get moving again, a guy with hair down to his ass and a pair of sprayed-on velvet pants made an approach. His smile was brilliant white, and his lean body seemed made for acrobatics.

A sudden nausea blendered Blay's gut—even as he reminded himself that after their last run-in, Qhuinn would not be looking for sex from him ever again—so why should he care who the fighter fucked. And God knew the male had a sex drive—

Mr. Lounge Suit with the extensions was given the heave-ho as well.

After which, Qhuinn just refocused ahead of himself.

An abrupt vibration went off in Blay's pocket, his phone letting him know there was a text. Taking the thing out, he saw that it was from Beth: *All good—Layla home safe. Just went for a joyride, and is going to watch some tube with me.*

Blay texted back a thanks, and returned his cell to his inner pocket. No reason to stay and bother the fighter with what had been a nonevent . . . although this was a chance to do a little damage control on his H-bomb delivery from a week ago.

Blay walked over, wending in and out of the bodies. When he got within range, he cleared his throat and spoke up over the din. "Hey—"

That hand shot up above Qhuinn's shoulder. "For the love of fucking God, I'm not interested, okay?"

At that moment, the person on the left decided to vacate with whatever drink he'd ordered.

Blay took the human's place.

"I told you to get the fuck—" Qhuinn froze in mid-blow-off. "What . . . are you doing here?"

Okay, where to start with that.

"Is there something wrong?" Qhuinn said.

"No, no. Really, not anything . . . you know, wrong." Blay frowned as he realized there was no alcohol in front of the guy. "Did you just get here?"

"No, I've been hanging around for . . . couple of hours, I guess."

"You're not drinking?"

"I did when I first sat down. But then . . . yeah, no."

Blay studied that face he knew so well. It was so grim, with hollows under the cheekbones and a perma-frown that suggested the guy hadn't slept in seven days, either.

"Listen, Qhuinn—"

"Did you come to apologize?"

Blay cleared his throat again. "Yeah. I did. I'm—"

"Right."

"What?"

Qhuinn put his hands up and scrubbed his eyes . . . then stayed put with his palms covering himself from forehead to chin. He said something that didn't carry, and that was when Blay knew something momentous had happened.

Then again, the poor bastard had probably come to the realization that Blay was in fact not a saint.

Blay leaned in closer. "Talk to me. Whatever it is, you can tell me."

Fair, after all, was fair. He'd sure as hell unloaded everything on his mind when they'd last seen each other.

"You were right," Qhuinn said. "I didn't know . . . I was . . ."

When nothing else came, Blay's ribs tightened up hard, his brows shooting sky-high as the gist hit him. Oh . . . my God.

As shock went through his whole body, he realized he'd never expected the guy to come around. Even as he'd yelled those hard-core words, it had been more a function of finally snapping, rather than out of any expectation that they would sink in.

Qhuinn shook his head, those hands staying in place. "I just . . . all those years, all that shit with them . . . I couldn't face another strike against me."

Blay was more than aware of who the "them" was.

"I did a lot of things to make it go away, to cover crap up—

because even after they kicked me out, they were still in my head. Even after they died . . . still in there, you know. Always in there with the . . ." One hand made a fist and started banging his brain. "Always in there . . ."

Blay caught that thick wrist and guided the male's arm down. "It's okay. . . ."

Qhuinn didn't look at him. "I didn't even know I was bending everything. I wasn't, like, aware of the shit in my mind—" That deep voice caught. "I just didn't want to give them another reason to hate me, even though they didn't fucking matter. What the fuck is that, you know? What the fuck have I been thinking?"

The pain that wafted out of Qhuinn's body was so great, it changed the air temperature around him, lowering things until the hair on Blay's forearms pricked from the chill.

And at that moment, faced with the abject misery in front of him, Blay wished he could have taken what he'd said back—not because it wasn't true, but because he wasn't the one who should have ripped off that Band-Aid. Mary, Rhage's *shellan,* should have done it as part of a therapy session or something. Or maybe Qhuinn should have gradually become aware of it.

But not like this . . .

The devastation that was written in every line of Qhuinn's body, in the hoarseness of his voice, in the barely restrained scream that seemed to be just under the surface, was terrifying.

"I never knew how much they got to me, especially my father. That male . . . he contaminated everything about me, and I didn't even know it was happening. And it ruined . . . everything."

Blay frowned, not following that part. But what he was clear on was the juxtaposition between his parents and Qhuinn's—not that he needed yet another reminder: All he could think of was that hug in front of the stove, his mom and dad wrapping their arms around him, their acceptance openhanded, honest, and without reservation.

And here Qhuinn was going through this alone. In a club. With no one there to support him as he struggled with the legacy of discrimination he had been condemned to . . . and the identity he couldn't change, and could no longer, seemingly, ignore.

"It ruined *everything.*"

Blay put his hand on that bunched-up biceps. "No, nothing's ruined. Don't say that. You are where you are, and it's okay—"

Qhuinn's head cranked around, leaving its cage of the hand that had remained, his blue and green eyes red rimmed and watery. "I have loved you for years. I have been in love with you for years and years and years . . . throughout school and training . . . before transitions and afterward . . . when you approached me and yes, even now that you're with Saxton and you hate me. And that . . . *shit* . . . in my fucking head locked me down, locked everything down . . . and it cost me you."

As the sound of screeching tires roared between Blay's ears, and the world started to spin, Qhuinn just kept going. "So you'll excuse me if I have to disagree with you. It is not okay—it will not ever be okay—and whereas I'm more than willing to live with the fact that I was a walking, talking lie for decades, the idea that it sacrificed what could have been between us . . . is absolutely, positively *not* okay to me."

Blay swallowed hard as Qhuinn went back to staring at the wall of liquor bottles behind the bar.

Opening his mouth, Blay intended to say something, but instead he just ran that monologue through again from start to finish. Jesus Christ . . .

And then something dawned on him.

If I'm gay, why are you the only male I've ever been with.

Suddenly, all of the blood drained out of Blay's head as he deciphered the truth in the words he'd so grossly misconstrued. That meant . . . that that night when he'd . . .

"Oh, God," he said in a low voice.

"So that's where I am," the fighter said gruffly. "You want a drink—"

The words jumped out of his mouth: "I'm not with Saxton anymore."

EIGHTY-TWO

huinn wrenched his head around a second time. Surely he couldn't have heard that. . . . "What . . . ?"

"I broke up with him, like, two weeks ago."

Qhuinn felt his lids blink a number of times. "Why . . . wait, I don't understand."

"It wasn't working. It hadn't been working for a long time. When he came back that night after having been with someone else? We weren't together, so he didn't cheat on me."

For some insane reason, all Qhuinn could think of was Mike Myers saying, *Ex-squeeze me? Baking powder?*

"But I thought . . . wait, you two looked really happy. It used to kill me every night to . . . yeah."

Blay winced. "I'm sorry I lied."

"Shiiiiiiit. I nearly killed him."

"Well, arguably you were being gallant. He knew that."

Qhuinn frowned and shook his head. "I had no idea you two weren't . . . well, I already said that."

"Qhuinn, I have to ask you something."

"G'head." Assuming he could focus at all.

"When you and I were together . . . that night . . . and then you said you had never . . . you know . . ."

Qhuinn waited for the guy to continue. When he didn't, he had no idea what Blay was alluding—

Oh, that.

Qhuinn couldn't believe it, but he felt his cheeks redden and warm. "Yeah, that night."

"Well, had you never . . ."

Considering everything he'd just thrown out there, that little ditty seemed like a minor detail. Besides, the truth was the truth. "You are the first and only male I've ever been with like that."

Silence from the other guy. And then, "Oh, my God, I'm so sorry I—"

Qhuinn jumped in, cutting off the unnecessary apology. "I'm not sorry. There is no one I'd rather have had taking my virginity. The first one you always remember."

Congratulations, Saxton, you lucky fucking cocksucker.

Another long silence. And just as Qhuinn was about to check his watch and suggest they take a break from the awkwardness, Blay spoke up.

"Aren't you going to ask me why Saxton and I were never going to work?"

Qhuinn rolled his eyes. "I know it wasn't problems in the bedroom. You're the best lover I've ever been with, and I can't imagine my cousin felt any differently."

Fucking cocksucking son of a bitch Saxton.

As he realized the other guy wasn't saying anything, Qhuinn glanced over. Blay's blue eyes had an odd light in them.

"What." Oh, for God's sake. "Fine. Why wouldn't it ever work out?"

"Because I was, and I remain, utterly and completely and totally . . . in love with you."

Qhuinn's mouth dropped open. As his ears began to hum, he wondered if he had heard that right. He leaned in closer. "I'm sorry, what did you—"

"Hey, baby," a female voice cut in.

On the right side of him, a woman with enough cleavage to fill a pair of salad bowls pressed into his body. "How would you like a partner in crime—"

"Back off," Blay barked. "He's with me."

Abruptly, Qhuinn's spine straightened: It was amply clear from the cold blue fire spitting out of Blay's eyes that the guy was prepared to tear the throat of that woman wide-open if she didn't disappear quick.

And that was . . .

Awesome.

"Okay, okay." She put her hands up in submission. "I didn't know that you were together."

"We are," Blay hissed.

As the woman with the formerly bright idea skulked off, Qhuinn turned to Blay, well aware that his shock was showing.

"Are we?" he breathed to his former best friend.

With the club music pounding, and a stadium full of strangers milling around them, with the bartender delivering drinks and the working girls working, with a thousand other lives rolling onward . . . time stopped for both of them.

Blay reached forward and took Qhuinn's face in his hands, that blue stare warming as it roamed around. "Yes. Yes, we are—"

Qhuinn nearly jumped on the guy, closing the distance between their mouths and kissing the love of his life once, twice . . . three times—even though he had no fucking idea what was happening, or whether it was real or if his alarm was about to go off.

After all the suffering, he was parched for the relief, even if it was just temporary.

When he pulled back, Blay frowned. "You're shaking."

Was it possible he wasn't imagining this? "Am I?"

"Yes."

"I don't care. I love you. I love you so damned much, and I'm sorry that I wasn't male enough to admit—"

Blay stopped him with a kiss. "You're plenty male enough now— the rest of it's in the past."

"I just . . . God, I really am shaking, aren't I?"

"Yeah. But it's okay—I've got you."

Qhuinn turned his face into one of the male's palms. "You always have. You've always had me . . . and my heart. My soul. Everything. I just wish it hadn't taken this long for me to man up. That family of mine . . . nearly killed me. And not just thanks to that Honor Guard of theirs."

Blay's eyes drifted. And then his hands dropped.

"What," Qhuinn blurted. "Did I say something wrong?"

Oh, God, he knew this was too good to be true. . . .

There was a long moment when Blay just stared at him. But then the male held out his palm. "Give me your hand."

Qhuinn obeyed instantaneously, as if Blay's command ran his body more than his own brain did.

When something slid onto his finger, he jumped and looked down.

It was a signet ring.

Blay's signet ring. The one the male's father had given him immediately after his transition.

"You are perfect the way you are." Blay's voice was strong. "There is nothing wrong with who and what you have always been. I'm proud of you. And I love you. Now . . . and always."

Qhuinn's vision got wavy. Hard-core.

"I'm proud of you. And I love you," Blay repeated. "Always. Forget about your old family . . . you have me now. I am your family."

All he could do was stare at the ring, seeing the crest, feeling the weight on his finger, watching how the light reflected off the precious metal.

He had wanted one of these all of his life, it had seemed.

And what do you know . . . as usual, as always, Blay was the one who had come through for him.

As a sob ripped up Qhuinn's windpipe, he felt himself get pulled in close to a big, powerful chest, strong arms wrapping around him and holding him. And then, from out of nowhere, a dark spice wafted up, the scent—Blay's bonding scent—the single most beautiful thing that had ever been in his nose.

"I'm proud of you, and I love you," Blay said yet again, that old, familiar voice cutting through all of those years of rejection and judgment, giving him not just a rope of acceptance to hang onto, but a flesh-and-blood hand to lead him out of the darkness of his past. . . .

And into a future that didn't require lies or excuses, because what he was, and what they were, was both extraordinary—and nothing out of the ordinary.

Love, after all, was universal.

Qhuinn closed his fist up tight, and knew he would never, ever take that ring off.

"Always," Blay murmured. "Because family is an always kind of thing."

Sweet Jesus, Qhuinn was sobbing like a pussy. But Blay didn't seem to mind in the slightest—or judge.

And that was the point, wasn't it.

"Always," Qhuinn echoed hoarsely. "Always . . ."

EPILOGUE

Whereupon life was pretty frickin' awesome.

"So did you like last night?"

As Qhuinn spoke into Blay's ear, Blay rolled his eyes in the near darkness. "What do you think."

With their naked bodies under warm, weighty covers, Qhuinn was pressed in behind him, their arms linked, their legs entwined.

Turned out Qhuinn was a snuggler. Who knew—and how fabulous.

"I think you liked it." Qhuinn licked his way up the side of Blay's throat. "Tell me you liked it."

By way of reply, Blay flexed his spine and drove his ass right into the other male's erection. The resulting groan made Blay beam.

"Sounds like *you* were into it," Blay murmured.

"Fuck, yeah, I was."

The night before they'd both been off rotation, and after a workout in the gym and a pool game against Lassiter and Beth—which they'd lost—Blay had suggested they hit the Iron Mask for a very specific reason.

As Blay remembered what had transpired after they'd gone back

there, Qhuinn's cock got into places where it was very much welcome . . . and Blay once again gave himself up to the delicious penetration and the slow, riding rhythm his mate established.

The things that he recalled from the club just made everything
hotter: The pair of them had gone over and sat at the bar and had a
couple of drinks, Herradura for Qhuinn, and a couple of G&Ts for
Blay. And then Qhuinn had gotten that look in his eye.

And Blay had gotten down to business.

He'd led the male back to one of the bathrooms, and as they'd
gone inside together, it had been a fantasy come to life, the kissing, the
hands in the pants, the frantic get-naked from the waist down. . . .

A moan came out of Blay's mouth as what was happening, and
what had happened, mixed, the erotic cocktail taking him to the brink
of an orgasm—and then, thanks to Qhuinn's grip pumping him off,
right over the edge, his cock coming hard into his lover's hand, his
body jerking and sending Qhuinn into a release as well. . . .

After a period of recovery, and a very satisfying round two, Qhuinn
drawled, "Any chance you were thinking about that bathroom?"

"Maybe."

"We can do that any night, if you like."

Blay chuckled. "Well, I guess we're free again this evening, so . . ."

The Brotherhood had been ordered to stay in, and as there had
been no explanation in Tohr's text, Blay figured it had to be a meeting
with the king. The Band of Bastards and the *glymera* had been quiet
for two weeks—no e-mails, no troop movements downtown, no phone
calls. Never a good sign.

Probably an update or a strategy session about that Council member's death and its implications. Although Blay really couldn't see any
downside to Assail's having killed the dumb son of a bitch.

Bye-bye, Elan. P.S., Next time you implicate someone falsely, try
to pick a pacifist.

The prospect of a meeting made him think about Qhuinn's inte-
gration into the Brotherhood—which had been seamless, as it turned
out. The fighter's behavior was no different, his attitude just the same.
And that was one more reason to love the guy. Even with the elevated
status he'd been given, he hadn't let shit go to his head.

And that teardrop tattoo that had been changed to purple on his
face? Totally hot. Just like that new star-shaped scar on his pectoral.

"We're defo going to be doing that again," Qhuinn said as he

slowly retracted himself and rolled over on his back. Putting his arms above his head, he smiled and stretched, the far-off light from the bathroom illuminating things just enough so that Blay could make out the lift to those incredible lips. "That was fucking hot. You are totally fucking hot."

"What can I say, it's been a fantasy of mine for a long time." As Qhuinn got serious, Blay touched the male's frown. "Hey. Stop that. Fresh slate, remember?"

After the night of the big reveal at the Mask, they'd had a number of long talks, and decided that they were going to take the relationship thing step by step, without making assumptions. They had been friends, then sort of enemies, then lovers of a kind . . . before they'd finally gotten their shit together. And just because they'd hung out for years, and they knew each other in a lot of ways, boyfriends was a different thing.

"Yeah. Fresh slate." As Qhuinn leaned in for a kiss, Blay's phone went off with a text.

Naturally, Qhuinn wasn't interested in communications from the outside world, and continued to lick his way into Blay's mouth, even as Blay reached out for the cell.

Blay had to hold it over Qhuinn's heavy shoulders as the guy maneuvered on top, rubbing his still-hard cock on Blay's—

"What the hell?" Blay said, breaking the lip contact.

"Have we been interrupted?"

"Yeah . . . Butch says he needs me in the Pit for a wardrobe consult?"

"Well, you do have perfect style."

For some reason, the comment made him think of Saxton. As soon as Qhuinn and he had decided to make things legit, Blay had told the lawyer what was going on—and the gentlemale had been gracious beyond measure . . . and not at all surprised. He'd even said it was a kind of relief in a strange way, a sign that all was right in the world, even though it had sucked for him.

At least Blay had gotten his true love, he'd said.

Now, if only Saxton could find his.

"I'd better head over there," he muttered. "Maybe it's date night."

As he went to get out of bed, Qhuinn's hands locked on his hips and pulled him in for another long, lingering kiss.

When Qhuinn eased back, his eyes were half-closed. "Date night's a great idea. You wanna go dancing with me sometime?"

"Dancing?" Blay laughed. "You would go dancing. With me."

It was everything Qhuinn hated: kind of schmaltzy, lot of eyes on them, and, assuming they did it in public, they had to be fully clothed.

"If you wanted me to, I would in a heartbeat."

Blay put his hand on the male's face. Qhuinn was trying really hard, and Blay was more than willing to wait for the day when the guy was ready to be into the PDA. The Brotherhood and the household knew that they were together—it was kind of obvious after Qhuinn had moved his stuff into this room. But you didn't spend a lifetime in denial and automatically feel comfy sucking face with your boyfriend in front of God and everyone else.

But he was trying. And he was talking—a lot—about his family and his brother, who was slowly, painfully trying to recover down in the clinic.

Behind closed doors, though? It was magic, without any barriers at all.

Exactly what Blay had always wanted.

"Are you going down to First Meal?" Blay asked as the shutters began to rise from the windows.

"Maybe I'll just stay here and wait to eat you when you come back."

Ah, yes, that naughty growl was in Qhuinn's voice again, and didn't that make Blay want to hop back in between the sheets.

"You are—" As a groan echoed up, Blay stopped in the process of heading into the bathroom. "Where is your hand?"

"Where do you think it is." Qhuinn arched, one fang biting down on his lower lip.

Blay thought of the text that he didn't intend to ignore. "You suck."

"Yes, I do, don't I." Qhuinn licked his lips. "And you like me to."

Blay cursed and marched into the bath. At this rate, he was never going to get out of their room. . . .

And sure enough, one hot shower and a shave later, Qhuinn was still in bed, lounging like a lion, his black hair tousled from Blay's hands, his half-lidded, mismatched eyes promising all kinds of pneumatics when Blay returned.

Horny motherfucker.

"You're just going to lie there?" Blay chided from over at the exit.

"Oh, I don't know . . . might get some exercise in while you're

gone." A hiss was followed by another one of those groans—and what do you know, under the sheets and duvet, the up-and-down motion of his arm made Blay remember all kinds of messy, sweaty, marvelous things. "Working out is so important, you know."

Blay gritted his molars and wrenched the door open. "I'll be back."

"Take your time. Anticipation just makes me harder."

"Yeah, like you need help with that."

Shutting things firmly, he rearranged himself in his loose nylon track pants and cursed again. Butch had better have a good fucking reason for needing Blay's opinion.

And a problem that could be solved quickly.

The second Blay was out of Dodge, Qhuinn threw back the covers and leaped out of bed. Grabbing his phone off his bedside table, he hit *send* on the text that he'd pretyped and then beelined for the shower. Fortunately, the water was already warm.

Soap at a dead run. Shampoo in a New York minute. Shave—

"Ow!" he barked as he cut himself on the chin.

Closing his eyes, he forced himself to slow the fuck down before he sliced off his nose: razor on the cheek, moving carefully, going around the jawline, down the neck. Repeat. Repeat.

Why the hell did he insist on doing this in the shower? On a night like tonight, he should be in front of a mirror. . . .

"Yo, beauty queen, you ready?" Rhage's voice cut through into the bathroom. "Or do you want to wax your eyebrows."

Qhuinn did a quick whisker check with his hand. Clear. "Fuck off, Hollywood," he yelled over the spray.

Cutting the water, he stepped out, and dried off on his way into the bedroom.

Standing next to a smiling Tohr, Rhage had his arms behind his back. "That's a helluva way to talk to your frickin' stylist."

Qhuinn leveled a glare at the Brothers. "If that shit is a Hawaiian print, I'm going to kill you."

Rhage looked over at Tohr and grinned. When the other Brother nodded, Hollywood brought forward what he was hiding behind his big body.

Qhuinn stopped dead. "Wait a minute . . . that's a . . ."

"Tuxedo, I believe is the name," Rhage cut in. "T-U-X-E-D-O."

"It's in your size," Tohr said. "And Butch says the designer is the best there is."

"Named after a car," Rhage muttered. "You'd think a high-falutin—"

"Hey, have you been watching Honey Boo Boo, too?" Lassiter demanded as he barged in. "Woooow, nice tux—"

"Only because you insist on putting that godforsaken traffic accident of a show on in the billiards room." Hollywood glanced over as V came in behind the angel. "He didn't even know what it was, Vishous."

"The tux?" V lit a hand-rolled. "Of course he didn't. He's a real male."

"That makes Butch a girl, then," Rhage pointed out. "Because he bought it."

"Hey, it's a party already," Trez called out as he and iAm arrived. "Oh, nice tux. Isn't that Tom Ford?"

"Or was it Dick Chrysler," Rhage interjected. "Harry GM—wait, that sounds dirty. . . ."

"Better get dressed, Rapunzel." V checked his watch. "We don't have a lot of time."

"That is a *beautiful* tuxedo," Phury announced as he and Z pushed the door wide. "I have one just like it."

"Fritz has the candles lit," Rehv said from behind the twins. "Hey, nice tux. I have one just like it."

"Me, too," Phury agreed. "The fit is fantastic, isn't it."

"The shoulders, right? Tom Ford is the best—"

Total. Fucking. Pandemonium.

And as Qhuinn took it in, all of the males talking over one another, slapping hands, slapping asses, he had a moment of breathlessness. Then he looked down at the ring Blay had given him.

Having a family was . . . really, incredibly wonderful.

"Thank you," he said softly.

Everyone froze, all those faces turning and locking on him, those bodies stilling, the din settling.

Z was the one who spoke up, his yellow eyes shining. "Put the zoot suit on. We'll meet you downstairs, lover boy."

Lot of shoulder claps as all the fighters checked in on their way out the door. And then he was alone with the tux.

"Let's do this," he said to the thing.

The shirt went on fine, but the buttons weren't regular ones. They

were cuff link–like, and took forever. Then he faced off with the slacks . . . and decided to keep it real and go commando. Finally, a pair of shiny shoes had been dropped on the messy bed by one of that cast of thousands—as well as a set of black silk socks that were just this side of being panty frickin' hose.

But he was going to do this right.

When he finally put the jacket on, he braced himself for feeling constricted, but Phury and Rehv were right—the material went over his bulk like a dream. Heading into the bathroom, he took the strip of black silk off the top of the hanger and confronted himself in the mirror.

Man . . . he looked pretty hot, actually.

Popping the starched collar, he wound the bow tie around the back of his neck and pulled it left and right a couple of times to make sure that it was in the right place. And then he did what he'd seen his father and his brother do when they hadn't been aware he was watching . . . he tied a perfect knot at the front of his throat.

Probably would have been easier if he'd taken the suit jacket off.

And if his hands weren't shaking so badly.

But whatever, he got the job done.

Stepping back, he checked himself from the left and the right. From behind.

Yeah, he was totally spank. The trouble was, he just didn't look like himself. At all.

That was a problem for him. Authentic had recently become *totally* important to him.

Thanks to a lack of attention, his hair had settled flat and smooth, and on impulse, he went for the product Blay and he shared, slicking up his palms and running them through the nap, spiking things up.

Better. Made him feel less like a tool.

But something still wasn't right. . . .

As he tried to figure out what was so off, he thought about how things had been rolling: After he and Blay had had their big talk at the Iron Mask, he'd been amazed at how light he felt, the burden he'd been unaware of carrying freed from his shoulders. It was so weird . . . but he'd caught himself taking these random deep breaths from time to time, his chest rising slowly and sinking back into place on an easy fall.

On some level, he continued to expect that he'd wake up and find out that it was all a dream. But every night, he came to with his arms around Blay, the guy's bonding scent in his nose, that warm body right beside his own.

I love you. You're perfect, just the way you are.

Always.

As Blay's voice rebounded in his head, he closed his eyes and swayed. . . .

Abruptly, he popped his lids and looked at the cupboard under the sinks.

Yes, he thought. That was what he needed.

A couple minutes later, he left their bedroom feeling exactly as he should, tux and all.

When he came to the head of the grand staircase, the votives that had been lined up on either side all the way down glowed and flickered. There were more below in the foyer: on the mantelpieces, on the floor, mounted up and around the archways that led into the other rooms.

"You look good, son."

Qhuinn turned and glanced over his shoulder. "Hey, m'lord."

Wrath came out of the study with his queen on one arm, and his dog on the other side. "I don't need my eyes to tell me you do the penguin duds justice."

"Thanks for letting me do this."

Wrath smiled, flashing those huge white fangs. Tugging his female in for a quick kiss, he laughed. "I'm a fucking romantic at heart, don't you know that."

Beth laughed and reached out to squeeze Qhuinn's arm. "Good luck—but you don't need it."

He wasn't so sure about that. In fact, as he let the First Family go down alone, he struggled to pull his shit together. Rubbing his face, he wondered why in the hell he'd thought this was a good idea—

Do *not* be a pussy, he told himself.

Starting on the descent, he pulled the two halves of the jacket together and buttoned them. Just like a gentlemale should.

He was halfway down when the vestibule's inner door opened wide, the draft causing all the votives to shimmer.

Qhuinn stopped as Fritz escorted two figures in, the pair of them stamping their feet to warm up. On cue, both looked over at him.

Blay's parents were dressed formally, his father in a tuxedo, his mother in the most beautiful blue velvet gown Qhuinn had ever seen.

"Qhuinn!" she called out, picking up her skirting and rushing across the mosaic floor. "Look at you!"

Feeling his cheeks burn, he ducked his head and shuffled down to her. Even though she was a whole foot shorter, even in her heels, he felt about twelve as she took his hands and held them out wide.

"Oh, you are the most handsome thing I've ever seen!"

"Thanks." He cleared his throat. "I, ah, wanted to look nice."

"You do! Doesn't he, my *hellren*?"

Blay's father came over and stuck out his hand. "Well done, son."

"It's a Ford. Thingy." God, way to sound stupid. "Or something."

As he and Blay's father shook, and then embraced, Blay's dad said, "I couldn't be happier for you both."

Blay's mom started sniffling and took out a white handkerchief. "This is so wonderful. I have another son—two sons! Come here, I have to hug you. Two sons!"

Qhuinn gave in immediately, as he was categorically incapable of denying the female anything—most certainly not one of her hugs. They were even better than her lasagna.

God, he loved Blay's parents. He and Blay had gone to see them a couple of nights after they'd decided to make a go of it, and although Qhuinn had been pants-shitting terrified, the pair of them had been nothing but gracious, relaxed, and . . . normal.

But Blay hadn't been aware of the visit Qhuinn had paid the night before, just after nightfall, before they'd hit the club. . . .

As Qhuinn eased back, he caught sight of Layla standing just outside the dining room. Motioning her over, he put his arm around her shoulders, because he could tell she was feeling awkward.

"This is the Chosen Layla."

"Just Layla," she murmured as she extended her hand.

In response, Blay's father bowed deeply, and his mother curtsied.

"Please, that's not necessary," the Chosen started, only to relax when the couple immediately dropped the formality.

"My dear, Qhuinn has told us the blessed news." Blay's *mahmen* beamed. "How ever are you feeling?"

Score number two for Blay's 'rents. Qhuinn couldn't believe how cool they'd been when he'd shared the news of the pregnancy—and they were just as easygoing as ever as they put Layla at ease.

Man, they had been like this for as long as Qhuinn had known them, uncontaminated by all the *glymera's* bullshit, unconcerned by the judgment of the aristocracy, ready to do the right thing at the drop of a hat.

No wonder Blay had come out so well. . . .

"He's heading over," V yelled from the pitch-black of the billiards room. "We've got to scatter, people—right now."

"Come with us," Blay's *mahmen* said as she tucked Layla's arm into her own. "You need to make sure we don't hit any furniture."

As they headed off, Layla glanced over her shoulder and beamed. "I'm so excited for you!"

Qhuinn smiled back. "Thanks."

Cue a moment of nausea, he thought, as he turned and faced the entrance into the mansion.

With the house quiet and the candles still, he waited, feeling numb all over.

Showtime.

Okay, this made no sense, Blay thought as he hotfooted it across the courtyard.

"You look great!" Butch called out from the Pit's front door.

He still didn't understand how he'd ended up in a tuxedo. Butch had laid out some kind of story about needing Blay to model the damn thing for Vishous in hopes of getting the guy to buy one. But that was crazy. Butch could have just thrown on one of the four he owned and paraded around himself.

Besides, nobody talked V into anything. The Brother was as unpersuadable as a rock.

Whatever—he just wanted to get this over with so he could head back upstairs—and hopefully find Qhuinn still in bed.

As he bounded up the stairs to the grand entrance of the mansion, his slick shoes made the salt crackle like a fire, and as soon as he got inside the vestibule, he stamped his feet so the glossy leather didn't get ruined. Putting his face into the security camera, he—

The door opened, and at first he didn't know what he was looking at. Everything was dark—no, that wasn't true. There was candlelight glowing in every corner of the foyer, reflecting off the gold of the balustrade, and the chandeliers, and the mirrors. . . .

Qhuinn was standing in the middle of the great space. Alone.

Blay walked through the threshold on feet that he couldn't feel.

His lover and his best friend was dressed in the most beautiful tuxedo Blay had ever seen—then again, that was less about the garment, more about the male who was wearing it: The black jacket set off his spiked hair, the white of the shirt made the male's tanned skin look luminous, and the cut . . . was a reminder of how perfect that warrior body was.

But that wasn't what really got to him.

It was those mismatched eyes, the blue and the green, that glowed so beautifully they put the votives to shame. Qhuinn seemed nervous, though, his hands fidgeting, his weight going back and forth in a pair of shiny shoes.

Blay walked forward, stopping when he was in front of the fighter. And even as his brain started to churn over what all this meant, and began to come to some crazy conclusions, he had to grin like crazy. "You put your piercings back in."

"Yeah. I just . . . I wanted to make sure you knew this was me, you know."

As Qhuinn fingered the neat row of gunmetal gray hoops that ran up his ear, Blay leaned in and kissed those lips—and the hoop that was once again in the lower one. "Oh, I know it's you. It's all you—but I'm glad they're back. I love them."

"Then they're never getting taken out."

In the beat of silence that followed, Blay thought, Oh, God . . . was this really . . . maybe he'd misconstrued—

Qhuinn got down on one knee. Just dropped right onto the depiction of an apple tree in full bloom.

"I don't have a ring. I don't have anything fancy in my mind or on my tongue." Qhuinn swallowed hard. "I know this is too early, and that it's out of the blue, but I love you and I want us to—"

For once in his life, Blay had to agree with the guy—enough with the fucking talking.

With a decisive shift of his body, he leaned down and kissed all that conversation right into silence. Then he pulled back and nodded. "Yes. Yes, absolutely, yes . . ."

With an explosive curse, Qhuinn came up off the floor and they wrapped their arms around each other. "Thank fuck. Oh, man, I've been having a heart attack for days—"

All at once, the sound of clapping erupted, filling the foyer's three-story space, echoing around.